The Sum Of All Men

DAVID FARLAND

BCA

LONDON   NEW YORK   SYDNEY   TORONTO

Thanks are due to the many people who helped shape this book. Perhaps foremost among them is Jonathan and Laurel Langford, who not only read the book once, but twice, and made detailed notes. Beyond this, certainly I must thank my editors at Tor for their care and consideration – David Hartwell, Tad Dembenski, and Tom Doherty. Others who gave valuable input include my writing group, Pilgrimage – Lee Allred, Russell Asplund, Virginia Baker, Scott Bronson, Michael Carr, Grant Avery Morgan, Scott Parkin, Ken Rand, and Bruce Thatcher. Thanks are also due to Les Pardew, Paul Brown III, Sandy Stratton, John Myler, and Dave Hewitt.

I'm particularly grateful to my wife, Mary, and to my children, who had to live without a dad while I wrote.

MAPS

Internook

Ashoven

Eyremoth

Alnick

Eyremoth

...nook

Seward

Lonnock

Toom

Havesind

Caroll Sea

Mystarria

Alcair Mountains

Inkarra

Kingdoms of Inkarra

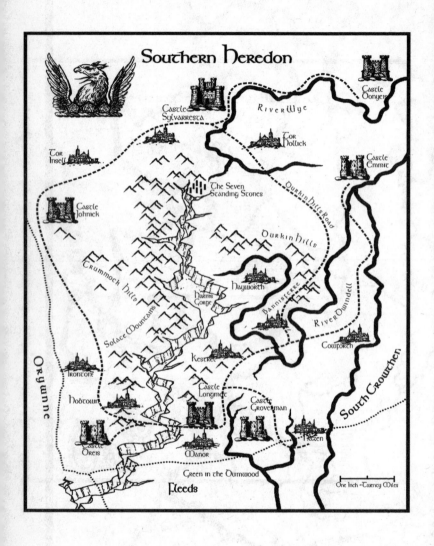

Southern Heredon

Castle Donyers

River Wye

Castle
Sylvarresta

Tor
Hollick

Tor
Insell

Castle
Emmit

The Seven
Standing Stones

Castle
Johnick

Durkin Hills Road

Durkin Hills

Crummock Hills

Hayworth

Bannisferre

River Dunnell

Harm's
Gorge

Solace Mountains

Kestrel

Cowforth

Ironton

Castle
Longmot

Castle
Groverman

Hodtown

South Crowthen

Castle
Dreis

Bredsfor
Manor

Fazen

Green in the Dunwood

Fleeds

Orywnne

One Inch = Twenty Miles

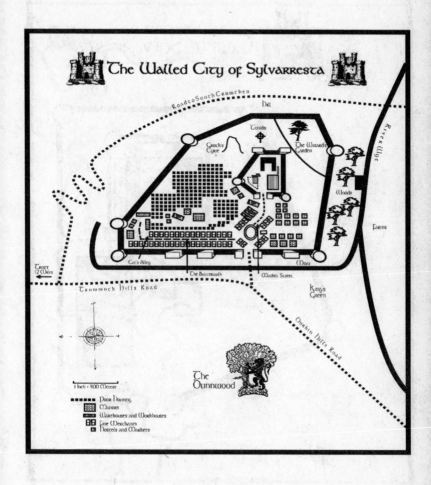

The Walled City of Sylvarresta

Road to South Crowthen

Dill

River Wye

Groch's Eyrie

Tombs

The Wizard's Garden

Woods

Farms

Cat's Alley

The Butterwalk

Moat

Market Street

King's Green

Trott 12 Miles

Tamnock Hills Road

Durkin Hills Road

1 Inch · 900 Merces

The Dunnwood

- - - - - Poor Housing
- Manors
- Warehouses and Workhouses
- Fine Merchants
- Hostels and Markets

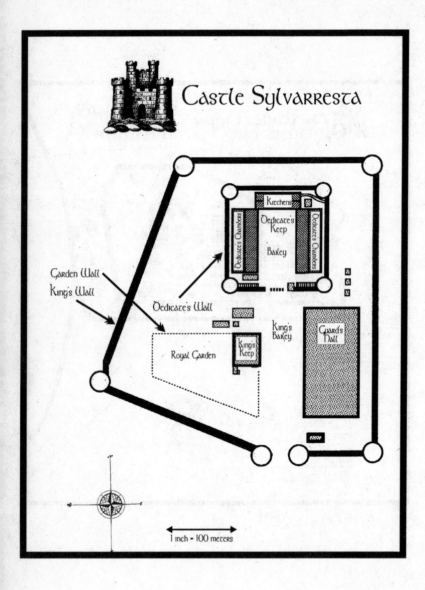

Castle Sylvarresta

Garden Wall
King's Wall

Dedicate's Wall

Kitchens
Dedicate's Keep
Dedicate's Chambers
Dedicate's Chambers
Bailey

King's Bailey
Guard's Hall

Royal Garden
King's Keep

1 inch = 100 meters

Book 1:
Day 19 in the Month of Harvest, A Glorious Day for an Ambush

ONE: IT BEGINS IN DARKNESS

Effigies of the Earth King festooned the city around Castle Sylvarresta. Everywhere the effigies could be seen – hanging beneath shopwindows, standing upright against the walls of the city gates, or nailed beside doorways – stationed any place where the Earth King might find ingress into a home.

Many of the figures were crude things crafted by children – a few reeds twisted into the form of a man, often with a crown of oak leaves in its hair. But outside the doors of shops and taverns were more ornate figures of wood, the full size of a man, often elaborately painted and coiffed in fine green wool traveling robes.

In those days, it was said that on Hostenfest Eve the spirit of the earth would fill the effigies and the Earth King would waken. At his wakening, he would protect the family for another season and help bear the harvest home.

It was a festive season, a season of joy. On Hostenfest Eve, the father in a home would play the role of Earth King, by setting gifts before the hearth. Thus, at dawn on the first day of Hostenfest, adults received flasks of new wine or kegs of stout ale. For the young girls the Earth King brought toy dolls woven of straw and wildflowers, while boys might get swords or oxcarts carved from ash.

All these bounties delivered by the Earth King represented but a token of the Earth King's wealth – the vast hoards of the "fruits of the forest and of the field" which legend said he bestowed on those who loved the land.

So the homes and shops around the castle were well adorned that night, on the nineteenth day of the Month of Harvest, four days before Hostenfest. All the shops were clean and well stocked for the autumn fair that would shortly come.

The streets lay barren, for dawn was approaching. Aside from the city guards and a few nursing mothers, the only ones who had reason to be up so late of the night were the King's bakers, who at that very moment were drawing the foam off the King's ale and mixing it with their dough so that the loaves would rise by dawn. True, the eels were running on their annual migration in the River Wye, so one might imagine a few fishermen to be out by night, but the fishermen had emptied their wicker eel traps an hour past midnight and had delivered kegs of live eels to the butcher for skinning and salting well before the second watch.

Outside the city walls, the greens south of Castle Sylvarresta were dotted with dark pavilions, for caravans from Indhopal had come north to sell the harvest of summer spices. The camps outside the castle were quiet but for the occasional braying of a donkey.

The walls of the city were shut, and all foreigners had been escorted from the merchants' quarter hours ago. No men moved on the streets at that time of night – only a few ferrin.

Thus there was no one to see what transpired in a dark alley. Even the King's far-seer, who had endowments of sight from seven people and stood guard on the old graak's aerie above the Dedicates' Keep, could not have spotted movement down in the narrow streets of the merchants' quarter.

But in Cat's Alley, just off the Butterwalk, two men struggled in the shadows for control of a knife.

Could you have seen them, you might have been

reminded of tarantulas in battle: arms and legs twisting in frenzy as the knife flashed upward, scuffling as feet groped for purchase on the worn cobblestones, both men grunting and straining with deadly intent.

Both men were dressed in black. Sergeant Dreys of the King's Guard wore black livery embroidered with the silver boar of House Sylvarresta. Dreys' assailant wore a baggy black cotton burnoose in a style favoured by assassins out of Muyyatin.

Though Sergeant Dreys outweighed the assassin by fifty pounds, and though Dreys had endowments of brawn from three men and could easily lift six hundred pounds over his head, he feared he could not win this battle.

Only starlight lit the street, and precious little of that made its way here into Cat's Alley. The alley was barely seven feet wide, and homes here stood three stories tall, leaning on sagging foundations till the awnings of their roofs nearly met a few yards above Dreys' head.

Dreys could hardly see a damned thing back here. All he could make out of his assailant was the gleam of the man's eyes and teeth, a pearl ring in his left nostril, the flash of the knife. The smell of woodlands clung to his cotton tunic as fiercely as the scents of anise and curry held to his breath.

No, Dreys was not prepared to fight here in Cat's Alley. He had no weapons and wore only the linen surcoat that normally fit over his ring mail, along with pants and boots. One does not go armed and armored to meet his lover.

He'd only stepped into the alley a moment ago, to make certain the road ahead was clear of city guards, when he heard a small scuffling behind a stack of yellow gourds by one of the market stalls. Dreys had thought he'd disturbed a ferrin as it hunted for mice or for some bit of cloth to wear. He'd turned, expecting to see a pudgy rat-shaped creature run for cover, when the assassin sprang from the shadows.

Now the assassin moved swiftly, grasping the knife

tight, shifting his weight, twisting the blade. It flashed dangerously close to Dreys' ear, but the sergeant fought it off – till the man's arm snaked around, stabbing at Dreys' throat. Dreys managed to hold the smaller man's wrist back for a moment. "Murder. Bloody murder!" Dreys shouted.

A spy! he thought. I've caught a spy! He could only imagine that he'd disturbed the fellow in mapping out the castle grounds.

He thrust a knee into the assassin's groin, lifting the man in the air. Pulled the man's knife arm full length and tried to twist it.

The assassin let go of the knife with one hand and rabbit-punched Dreys in the chest.

Dreys' ribs snapped. Obviously the little man had also been branded with runes of power. Dreys guessed that the assassin had the brawn of five men, maybe more. Though both men were incredibly strong, endowments of brawn increased strength only to the muscles and tendons. They did not invest one's bones with any superior hardness. So this match was quickly degenerating into what Dreys would call "a bone-bash."

He struggled to hold the assassin's wrists. For a long moment they wrestled.

Dreys heard deep-voiced shouts: "That way, I think! Over there!" They came from the left. A street over was Cheap Street – where the bunched houses did not press so close, and where Sir Guilliam had built his new four-story manor. The voices had to be from the City Guard – the same guards Dreys had been avoiding – whom Sir Guilliam bribed to rest beneath the lantern post at the manor gate.

"Cat's Alley!" Dreys screamed. He only had to hold the assassin a moment more – make sure the fellow didn't stab him, or escape.

The Southerner broke free in desperation, punched him again, high in the chest. More ribs snapped. Dreys felt little pain. One tends to ignore such distractions when struggling to stay alive.

In desperation the assassin ripped the knife free. Dreys felt a tremendous rush of fear and kicked the assassin's right ankle. He felt more than heard a leg shatter.

The assassin lunged, knife flashing. Dreys twisted away, shoved the fellow. The blade struck wide of its mark, slashed Dreys' ribs, a grazing blow.

Now Dreys grabbed the fellow's elbow, had the man half-turned around. The assassin stumbled, unable to support himself on his broken leg. Dreys kicked the leg again for good measure, and pushed the fellow back.

Dreys glanced frantically into the shadows for sign of some cobblestone that might have come loose from its mortar. He wanted a weapon. Behind Dreys was an inn called the Churn. Beside the flowering vines and the effigy of the Earth King at its front window sat a small butter churn. Dreys tried to rush to the churn, thinking to grab its iron plunger and use it to bludgeon the assassin.

He pushed the assassin, thinking the smaller man would go flying. Instead the fellow spun, one hand clutching Dreys' surcoat. Dreys saw the knife blade plunge.

He raised an arm to block.

The blade veered low and struck deep, slid up through his belly, past shattered ribs. Tremendous pain blossomed in Dreys' gut, shot through his shoulders and arms, a pain so wide Dreys thought the whole world would feel it with him.

For an eternity, Dreys stood, looking down. Sweat dribbled into his wide eyes. The damned assassin had slit him open like a fish. Yet the assassin still held him – had thrust his knife arm up to the wrist into Dreys' chest, working the blade toward Dreys' heart, while his left hand clutched Dreys' pocket, groping for something.

His hand clutched at the book in Dreys' pocket, feeling it through the material of the surcoat. The assassin smiled.

Dreys wondered, Is that what you want? A book?

Last night, as the City Guard had been escorting foreigners from the merchants' quarter, Dreys had been approached by a man from Tuulistan, a trader whose tent was pitched near the woods. The fellow spoke little Rofehavanish, had seemed apprehensive. He had only said, "A gift – for king. You give? Give to king?"

With much ceremonial nodding, Dreys had agreed, had looked at the book absently. *The Chronicles of Owatt, Emir of Tuulistan*. A thin volume bound in lambskin. Dreys had pocketed it, thinking to pass it along at dawn.

Dreys hurt so terribly now that he could not shout, could not move. The world spun; he pulled free of the assassin, tried to turn and run. His legs felt as weak as a kitten's. He stumbled. The assassin grabbed Dreys' hair from behind, yanking his chin up to expose his throat.

Damn you, Dreys thought, haven't you killed me enough? In one final desperate act, he yanked the book from his pocket, hurled it across the Butterwalk.

There on the far side of the street a rosebush struggled up an arbor near a pile of barrels. Dreys knew this place well, could barely see the yellow roses on dark vines. The book skidded toward them.

The assassin cursed in his own tongue, tossing Dreys aside, and limped after the book.

Dreys could hear nothing but a dull buzz as he struggled to his knees. He glimpsed movement at the edge of the street – the assassin groping among the roses. Three larger shadows came rushing down the road from the left. The flash of drawn swords, starlight glinting off iron caps. The City Guard.

Dreys pitched forward on to the cobblestones.

In the predawn, a flock of geese honked as it made its way south through the silvery starlight, their voices sounding to him for all the world like the barking of a distant pack of dogs.

TWO: THOSE WHO LOVE THE LAND

That morning a few hours after the attack on Dreys and a hundred or so miles south of Castle Sylvarresta, Prince Gaborn Val Orden faced troubles that were not so harrowing. Yet none of his lessons in the House of Understanding could have prepared the eighteen-year-old prince for his encounter with a mysterious young woman in the grand marketplace at Bannisferre.

He'd been lost in thought at a vendor's stall in the south market, studying wine chillers of polished silver. The vendor had many fine iron brewing pots, but his prize was the three wine chillers – large bowls for ice with complementing smaller pitchers that fit inside. The bowls were of such high quality that they looked to be of ancient duskin workmanship. But no duskin had walked the earth in a thousand years, and these bowls could not have been that old. Each bowl had the clawed feet of a reaver and featured scenes of hounds running in a leafy wood; the pitchers were adorned with images of a young lord on a horse, his lance at the ready, bearing down on a reaver mage. Once the pitchers were set into their silver bowls, the images complemented one another – the young lord battling the reaver mage while the hunting dogs surrounded them.

The ornaments on the wine chiller were all cast using some method that Gaborn could not fathom. The silversmith's detailed workmanship was breathtaking.

Such were the wonders of Bannisferre's goods that Gaborn hadn't even noticed the young woman sidle up to him until he smelled the scent of rose petals. (The woman who stands next to me wears a dress that is kept in a drawer filled with rose petals, he'd realized, on some subconscious level.) Even then, he'd been so absorbed in studying the wine chillers that he imagined she was only a stranger, awed by the same marvelous bowls and pitchers. He didn't glance her way until she took his hand, seizing his attention.

She grasped his left hand in her right, lightly clasping his fingers, then squeezed.

Her soft touch electrified him. He did not pull away.

Perhaps, he thought, she mistakes me for another. He glanced sidelong at her. She was tall and beautiful, perhaps nineteen, her dark-brown hair adorned with mother-of-pearl combs. Her eyes were black, and even the whites of her eyes were so dark as to be a pale blue. She wore a simple, cloud-colored silk gown with flowing sleeves – an elegant style lately making its way among the wealthy ladies of Lysle. The young lady wore a belt of ermine, clasped with a silver flower, high above the navel, just beneath her firm breasts. The neckline was high, modest. Over her shoulders hung a silk scarf of deepest crimson, so long that its fringes swept the ground.

She was not merely beautiful, he decided. She was astonishing.

She smiled at him secretively, shyly, and Gaborn grinned back, tight-lipped – hopeful and troubled all at once. This felt like one of the endless tests that any of his hearthmasters might have devised for him in the House of Understanding – yet this was no test.

Gaborn did not know the young woman. He knew no one in all the vast city of Bannisferre – which seemed odd – that he should not have one acquaintance from a city this large, with its towering gray stone songhouses with their exotic arches, the white pigeons wheeling through the blue sunlit sky above the chestnut trees. Yet it was true. He was that far from home.

He stood near the edge of a market, not far from the docks on the broad banks of the south fork of River Dwindell – a stone's throw from Smiths' Row, where the open-air hearths gave rise to the rhythmic ring of hammers, the creaking of bellows, and plumes of smoke.

He felt troubled that he'd been so lulled by the peacefulness of Bannisferre. He'd not even bothered to glance at this woman when she had stood next to him for a moment. Twice in his life, he'd been the target of assassins. They'd taken his mother, his grandmother, his brother and two sisters. Yet Gaborn stood here now as carefree as a peasant with a stomach full of ale.

No, Gaborn decided quickly, I've never seen her; she knows I'm a stranger, yet holds my hand. Most bewildering.

In the House of Understanding, in the Room of Faces, Gaborn had studied the subtleties of bodily communication – the way secrets revealed themselves in an enemy's eyes, how to differentiate traces of worry from consternation or fatigue in the lines around a lover's mouth.

Gaborn's hearthmaster, Jorlis, had been a wise teacher, and over the past few long winters Gaborn had distinguished himself in his studies.

He'd learned that princes, highwaymen, merchants, and beggars all wore their expressions and stances as if part of some agreed-upon costume, and so Gaborn had mastered the art of putting on any costume at will. He could take command of a roomful of young men simply by standing with head high, cause a merchant to lower his prices with a balking smile. Concealed by nothing more than a fine traveling cloak, Gaborn learned to lower his eyes in a busy marketplace and play the pauper, slinking through the crowd so that those who saw him did not recognize a prince, but wondered, Ah, where did that beggar boy steal such a nice cloak?

So Gaborn could read the human body, and yet he remained a perpetual mystery to others. With two endowments of wit, he could memorize a large tome in an hour. He'd learned more in his eight years in the House of Understanding than most commoners could learn in a life of concerted study.

As a Runelord, he had three endowments of brawn and two of stamina, and in battle practice he could easily cross weapons with men twice his size. If ever a highwayman dared attack him, Gaborn would prove just how deadly a Runelord could be.

Yet in the eyes of the world, because of his few endowments of glamour, he seemed to be little more than a startlingly handsome young man. And in a city like Bannisferre, with its singers and actors from across the realm, even beauty such as his was common.

He studied the woman who held him, considered her stance. Chin high, confident – yet slightly tilted. A question. She poses a question of me.

The touch of her hand – weak enough to indicate hesitancy, strong enough to suggest . . . ownership. She was claiming him?

Is this an attempt at seduction? he wondered. But no – the body stance felt wrong. If she had wanted to seduce, she'd have touched the small of his back, a shoulder, even his buttock or chest. Yet as she held him she stood slightly away, hesitating to claim his body space.

Then he understood: a marriage proposal. Very uncustomary, even in Heredon. For a woman of her quality, the family should have easily arranged a marriage.

Gaborn surmised, ah, she is orphaned. She hopes to arrange her own match!

Yet even that answer did not satisfy him. Why did not a wealthy lord arrange a match for her?

Gaborn considered how she must see him now. A merchant's son. He'd been playing the merchant; and though he was eighteen, his growth had not come in fully. Gaborn had dark hair and blue eyes, traits common in North Crowthen. So he'd dressed like a fop from that kingdom, one with more wealth than taste, out wandering the town while his father conducted more important business. He wore green hose and pants that gathered above the knee, along with a fine white cotton shirt with ballooning sleeves and silver buttons. Over the shirt, he wore a jerkin of dark green cotton trimmed in finely tooled leather, decorated with freshwater pearls. Completing the disguise was a broad-brimmed hat, on which an amber clasp held a single ostrich plume.

Gaborn had dressed this way because he did not want to travel openly on his mission to spy out Heredon's defenses, to gauge the true extent of the wealth of its lands, the hardiness of its people.

Gaborn glanced back toward his bodyguard Borenson. The streets here were crowded, made narrow by the vendors' stalls. A beefy, bronze-skinned young man with no shirt and red pants was herding a dozen goats through the throng, whipping them with a willow switch. Across the road, beneath a stone arch beside the door to the inn, Borenson stood grinning broadly at Gaborn's predicament. He was tall and broad-shouldered, with a balding head of red hair, a thick beard, and laughing blue eyes.

Beside Borenson stood a skeletal fellow with blond hair cropped short. To match his chestnut eyes he wore a historian's austere brownish robes and a disapproving scowl. The man, simply called by his vocation, Days, was a chronicler of sorts – a devotee of the Time Lords – who had been following Gaborn now since Gaborn was an infant, recording his every word and deed. He took his name from the order of "the Days." Like every man of his sect, Days had given up his own name, his own identity, when he'd twinned his mind with that of another of his order. Days watched Gaborn now, keenly. Alert, eyes flickering about. Memorizing everything.

The woman who held Gaborn's hand followed his

glance, noting the bodyguard and Days. A young merchant lord with a guard was common. One shadowed by a Days was rare. It marked Gaborn as someone of wealth and import, perhaps the son of a guildmaster, yet this woman could not possibly have known Gaborn's true identity.

She pulled his hand, invited him to stroll. He hesitated.

"Do you see anything in market that interests you?" she asked, smiling. Her sweet voice was as inviting as the cardamom-flavored pastries sold here in the market, yet slightly mocking. Clearly, she wanted to know if she interested him. Yet those around her would mistakenly believe she spoke of the wine chillers.

"The silver shows some decent handiwork," Gaborn said. Using the powers of his Voice, he put a slight emphasis on *hand*. Without ever recognizing why, she would believe that in Understanding's House, he had studied in the Room of Hands, as rich merchants did. *Let her believe me to be a merchant.*

The vendor of the stall, who had patiently ignored Gaborn until now, lurched from under the shade of his rectangular umbrella, calling, "The sir would like a fine chiller for the madam?"

Until a moment ago Gaborn had seemed only a merchant boy, one who might have reported to his father any interesting wares. Now perhaps the merchant thought him a newlywed, with a wife far more handsome than himself. Merchant lords often married their children off young, seeking monetary alliances.

So the vendor thinks I must buy the silver to humor my wife. Of course such a lovely woman would rule her household. Since the merchant did not know her, Gaborn imagined that she would also have to be a stranger to Bannisferre. *A traveler from the north?*

The young woman smiled kindly at the vendor. "I think not today," she teased. "You have some fine chillers, but we have better at home." She turned her back, playing her role as wife exquisitely. *This is how it would be if we married*, her actions seemed to say. *I'd make no costly demands.*

The vendor's face fell in dismay. It was unlikely that more than one or two merchants in all the Kingdoms of Rofehavan had such a fine wine cooler.

She pulled Gaborn along. Suddenly, Gaborn felt uneasy. In the far south, ladies of Indhopal sometimes wore rings or brooches with poisoned needles in them. They would try to lure wealthy travelers to an inn, then murder and rob them. It could be that this beauty had nefarious designs.

Yet he doubted it. A quick glance showed that Borenson was certainly more amused than concerned. He laughed and blushed, as if to ask, *And where do you think you're going?*

Borenson, too, was a student of body language – particularly that of women. He never took risks with his lord's safety.

The woman squeezed Gaborn's hand, readjusting her grip, holding him more firmly. Was she seeking a greater claim to his attentions?

"Pardon me if I seem overfamiliar, good sir," she said. "Have you ever noticed someone from a distance, and felt a tug of your heart?"

Her touch thrilled him, and Gaborn wanted to believe that, indeed, she'd seen him from afar and fallen in love.

"No, not like this," he said. Yet he felt it a lie. He'd once fallen in love from afar.

The sun shone on them; the skies were brilliant. The air blowing off the river smelled warm and sweet, carrying the scent of hay fields from across the shore. On such a fine day, how could anyone feel anything but invigorated, alive?

The cobbles on the street here were smooth with age. Half a dozen flower girls strolled barefoot through the crowd, calling for patrons in clear voices. They blew past, a breeze rippling a wheat field. They all wore faded dresses and white aprons. They held the centers of their aprons up with one hand, making their aprons into a kind of sack, sacks filled with riotous colors – brilliant burgundy cornflowers and white daisies, long-stemmed roses in deepest reds and peaches. Poppies and bundles of sweet-scented lavender.

Gaborn watched the girls drift by, feeling that their beauty was as stunning as that of larks in flight, knowing he would never forget their smiles. Six girls, all with blond or light-brown hair.

His father was camped with his retinue not more than a few hours' ride off. Seldom did his father let Gaborn wander without heavy guard, but this time his father had implored him to take a little side excursion, saying, "You must study Heredon. A land is more than its castles and soldiers. In Bannisferre you will fall in love with this land, and its people, as I have."

The young woman squeezed his hand tighter.

Pain showed in her brow as she watched the flower girls. Gaborn suddenly realized what she was, how desperately this young woman needed him. Gaborn nearly laughed, for he saw how easily she could have bewitched him.

He squeezed her hand, warmly, as a friend. He felt certain that he could have nothing to do with her, yet he wished her well.

"My name is Myrrima . . ." she said, leaving a silence for him in which to offer his own name.

"A beautiful name, for a beautiful girl."

"And you are?"

"Thrilled by intrigue," he said. "Aren't you?"

"Not always." She smiled, a demand for his name.

Twenty paces behind, Borenson tapped the scabbard of his saber against a passing goat cart, a sign that he'd left his post at the hostel's doorway and was now following. The Days would be at his side.

Myrrima glanced back. "He's a fine-looking guardsman."

"A fine man," Gaborn agreed.

"You are traveling on business? You like Bannisferre?"

"Yes, and yes."

She abruptly pulled her hand away. "You don't make commitments easily," she said, turning to face him, her smile faltering just a bit. Perhaps she sensed now that the chase was up, that he would not marry her.

"No. Never. Perhaps it is a weakness in my character," Gaborn said.

"Why not?" Myrrima asked, still playful. She stopped by a fountain where a statue of Edmon Tillerman stood holding a pot with three spigots that poured water down over the faces of three bears.

"Because lives are at stake," Gaborn answered. He sat at the edge of the fountain, glanced into the pool. Startled by his presence, huge polliwogs wriggled down into the green water. "When I commit to someone, I accept responsibility for them. I offer my life, or at least a portion of it. When I accept someone's commitment, I expect nothing less than total commitment – their lives – in return. This reciprocal relationship is . . . it must define me."

Myrrima frowned, made uneasy by his serious tone. "You are not a merchant. You . . . you talk like a lord!"

He could see her considering. She would know he was not of Sylvarresta's line, not a lord from Heredon. So he would have to be a foreign dignitary, merely traveling – in Heredon, an out-of-the-way country, one of the farthest north in all the Kingdoms of Rofehavan.

"I should have known – you are so handsome," she said. "So you're a Runelord, come to study our land. Tell me, do you like it enough to seek betrothal to Princess Iome Sylvarresta?"

Gaborn admired the way that she drew the proper conclusion. "I'm surprised at how green your land is, and how strong your people are," Gaborn said. "It is richer than I'd imagined."

"Will Princess Sylvarresta accept you?" Still she was searching for answers. She wondered which poor castle he hailed from. She sat beside him on the edge of the fountain.

Gaborn shrugged, feigning less concern than he felt. "I know her only be reputation," he admitted. "Perhaps you know her better than I. How do you think she will look on me?"

"You are handsome enough," Myrrima said, frankly studying his broad shoulders, the long dark-brown hair that fell from under his plumed cap. By now she must have realized he was not dark enough of hair to be from Muyyatin, or any of the Indhopalese nations.

Then she gasped, eyes going wide.

She stood up quickly and stepped back, unsure whether to remain standing, curtsy, or fall down and prostrate herself at his feet. "Forgive me, Prince Orden – I, uh – did not see your resemblance to your father!"

Myrrima lurched back three paces, as if wishing she could run blindly away, for she now knew that he was not the son of some poor baron who called a pile of rocks his fortress, but that he came from Mystarria itself.

"You know my father?" Gaborn asked, rising and stepping forward. He took her hand once again, trying to reassure her that no offense had been taken.

"I – once he rode through town, on his way to the hunt," Myrrima said. "I was but a girl. I can't forget his face."

"He has always liked Heredon," Gaborn said.

"Yes . . . yes, he comes often enough," Myrrima said, clearly discomfited. "I – pardon me if I troubled you, my lord. I did not mean to be presumptuous. Oh . . ."

Myrrima turned and began to run.

"Stop," Gaborn said, letting just a little of the power of his Voice take her.

She stopped as if she'd been struck by a fist, turned to face him. As did several other people nearby.

Unprepared for the command, they obeyed as if it had come from their own minds. When they saw that they were not the object of his attention, some stared at him curiously while a few started away, unnerved by the appearance of a Runelord in their midst.

Suddenly, Borenson hovered at Gaborn's back, with the Days.

"Thank you for stopping, Myrrima," Gaborn said.

"You – may someday be my king," she answered, as if she'd reasoned out her response.

"Do you think so?" Gaborn said. "Do you think Iome will have me?" The question startled her. Gaborn continued. "Please tell me. You are a perceptive woman, and beautiful. You would do well at court. I value your opinion."

Gaborn held his breath, waiting for her frank assessment. She couldn't know how important her answer was to him. Gaborn *needed* this alliance. He needed Heredon's strong people, its impregnable fortresses, its wide-open lands, ready to till. True, his own Mystarria was a rich land – ripe, its markets sprawling and crowded – but after years of struggle the Wolf Lord Raj Ahten had finally conquered the Indhopalese Kingdoms, and Gaborn knew that Raj Ahten would not stop there. By spring, he would either invade the barbarian realms of Inkarra or he would turn north to the kingdoms in Rofehavan.

In reality, it didn't matter where the Wolf Lord attacked next. In the wars to come, Gaborn knew he'd never be able to adequately defend his people in Mystarria. He needed this land.

Even though Heredon had not seen a major war in four hundred years, the realm's great battlements remained intact. Even the fortress at lowly Tor Ingel, set among the cliffs, could be defended better than most of Gaborn's estates in Mystarria. Gaborn needed Heredon. He needed Iome's hand in marriage.

More important, though he dared not admit it to anyone, something deep inside told him that he needed Iome herself. An odd compulsion drew him here, against all common sense. As if invisible fiery threads were connected to his heart and mind. Sometimes at night he'd lie awake, feeling the tug, an odd glowing sensation that spread outward from the center of his chest, as if a warm stone lay there. Those threads seemed to pull him toward Iome. He'd fought the urge to seek her hand for a year now, until he could fight no more.

Myrrima studied Gaborn once again with her marvelous frankness. Then laughed easily. "No," she said. "Iome will not have you."

There had been no hesitancy in her answer. She had said it simply, as if she'd seen the truth of it. Then she smiled at him seductively. *But I want you*, her smile said.

"You sound certain." Gaborn tried to seem casual. "Is it merely my clothes? I did bring more suitable attire."

"You may be from the most powerful kingdom in Rofehavan, but . . . how shall I put this? Your politics are suspect."

It was a kind way to accuse him of being immoral. Gaborn had feared such an accusation.

"Because my father is a pragmatist?" Gaborn asked.

"Some think him pragmatic, some think him . . . too acquisitive."

Gaborn grinned. "King Sylvarresta thinks him pragmatic . . . but his daughter thinks my father is greedy? She said this?"

Myrrima smiled and nodded secretively. "I've heard rumors that she said as much at the midwinter feast."

Gaborn was often amazed at how much the commoners knew or surmised about the comings and goings and doings of lords. Things that he'd often thought were court secrets would be openly discussed at some inn a hundred leagues distant. Myrrima seemed sure of her sources.

"So she will reject my petition, because of my father."

"It has been said in Heredon that Prince Orden is 'much like his father.'"

"Too much like his father?" Gaborn asked. A quote from Princess Sylvarresta? Probably spoken to quell any rumors of a possible match. It was true that Gaborn had his father's look about him. But Gaborn was not his father. Nor was his father, Gaborn believed, as "acquisitive" as Iome accused him of being.

Myrrima had the good taste to say no more. She pulled her hand free of his.

"She *will* marry me," Gaborn said. He felt confident he could sway the princess.

Myrrima raised a brow. "How could you imagine so? Because it would be pragmatic to ally herself with the wealthiest kingdom in Rofehavan?" She laughed musically, amused. Under normal circumstances, if a peasant had laughed him to scorn, Gaborn would have bristled. He found himself laughing with her.

Myrrima flashed a fetching smile. "Perhaps, milord, when you leave Heredon, you will not leave empty-handed."

One last invitation. *Princess Sylvarresta will not have you, but I would.*

"It would be foolish to give up the chase before the hunt has begun, don't you think?" Gaborn said. "In Understanding's House, in the Room of the Heart, Hearthmaster Ibirmarle used to say 'Fools define themselves by what they are. Wise men define themselves by what they shall be.'"

Myrrima rejoined, "Then I fear, my pragmatic prince, that you shall die old and lonely, deluded into believing you will someday marry Iome Sylvarresta. Good day."

She turned to leave, but Gaborn could not quite let her go. In the Room of the Heart, he'd also learned that sometimes it is best to act on impulse, that the part of the mind which dreams will often speak to us, commanding us to act in ways that we do not understand. When Gaborn had told her that he thought she would do well in court, he had meant it. He wanted her in his court – not as his wife, not even as a mistress. But intuitively he felt her to be an ally. Had she not called him "milord"? She could as easily have called him "Your Lordship." No, she felt a bond to him, too.

"Wait, milady," Gaborn said. Once again Myrrima turned. She had caught his tone. With the word "milady," he sought to make his claim on her. She knew what he expected: total devotion. Her life. As a Runelord, Gaborn had been raised to demand as much from his own vassals, yet he felt hesitant to ask as much from this foreign woman.

"Yes, *milord*?"

"At home," Prince Orden said, "you have two ugly sisters to care for? And a witless brother?"

"You are perceptive, milord," Myrrima said. "But the witless one is my mother, not a brother." Lines of pain showed in her face. It was a terrible burden she held. A terrible price for magic. It was hard enough to take an endowment of brawn or wit or glamour from another, to assume the financial responsibilities for that person. But it became more painful still when that person was a beloved friend or relative. Myrrima's family must have lived in horrible poverty, hopeless poverty, in order for them to have felt compelled to try such a thing – to gift one woman with the beauty of three, the cleverness of two, and then to seek to marry her to some rich man who could save them all from despair.

"However did you get the money for the forcibles?" Gaborn asked. The magical irons that could drain the attributes of one person and endow them on another were tremendously expensive.

"My mother had a small inheritance – and we labored, the four of us," Myrrima said. He heard tightness in her voice. Perhaps once, a week or two ago, when she'd newly become beautiful, she'd have sobbed when speaking of this.

"You sold flowers as a child?" Gaborn asked.

Myrrima smiled. "The meadow behind our house provided little else to sustain us."

Gaborn reached to his money pouch, pulled out a gold coin. One side showed the head of King Sylvarresta; the other showed the Seven Standing Stones of the Dunnwood, which legend said held up the earth. He was unfamiliar with the local currency, but knew the coin was large enough to take care of her small family for a few months. He took her hand, slipping it into her palm.

"I . . . have done nothing for this," she said, searching his eyes. Perhaps she feared an indecent proposal. Some lords took mistresses. Gaborn would never do so.

"Certainly you have," Gaborn said. "You smiled, and thus lightened my heart. Accept this gift, please. You will find your merchant prince someday," Gaborn said, "and of all the prizes he may ever discover here in the markets of Bannisferre, I suspect that you will be the most treasured."

She held the coin in awe. People never expected one as young as Gaborn to speak with such grace, yet it came easily after years of training in Voice. She looked into his eyes with new respect, as if really seeing him for the first time. "Thank you, Prince Orden. Perhaps . . . I tell you now that if Iome does accept you, I will praise her decision."

She turned and sauntered off through the thickening crowd, circled the fountain. Gaborn watched the graceful lines of her neck, the clouds of her dress, the burning flames of her scarf.

Borenson came up and clapped Gaborn on the shoulder, chuckling. "Ah, milord, there is a tempting sweet."

"Yes, she's altogether lovely," Gaborn whispered.

"It was fun to watch. She just stood back, eyeing you like a cutlet on the butcher's block. She waited for five minutes" – Borenson held up his hand, fingers splayed – "waiting for you to notice her! But you – you day-blind ferrin! You were too busy adoring some vendor's handsome chamber pots! How could you not see her? How could you ignore her? Ah!" Borenson shrugged in exaggeration.

"I meant no offense," Gaborn said, looking up into Borenson's face. Though Borenson was his bodyguard and should thus always be on the watch for assassins, the truth was that the big fellow was a lusty man. He could not walk through a street without making little crooning noises at every shapely woman he passed. And if he didn't go wenching at least once a week, he'd croon even at the woman who had no more shape than a bag of parsnips. His fellow guards sometimes joked that no assassin hiding in between a woman's cleavage would ever escape his notice.

"Oh, I'm not offended," Borenson said. "Mystified, maybe. Perplexed. How could you not see her? You must have at least smelled her?"

"Yes, she smells very nice. She keeps her gown in a drawer layered in rose petals."

Borenson rolled his eyes back dramatically and groaned. His face was flushed, and there was a peculiar excitement, an intensity in his eyes. Though he pretended to be jesting, Gaborn could see that Borenson had indeed been smitten by this northern beauty more than he cared to admit. If Borenson could have had his way, he'd have been off chasing the girl. "At least you could have let her cure you of that vexing case of virginity you suffer from, milord!"

"It is a common enough malady for young men," Gaborn said, feeling offended. Borenson sometimes spoke to Gaborn as if he were a drinking partner.

Borenson reddened even more. "As well it should be, milord!"

"Besides," Gaborn said, considering the toll a bastard child sometimes took on a kingdom, "the cure is often more costly than the malady."

"I suspect that *that* cure is worth any price," Borenson said longingly, with a nod in the direction Myrrima had gone.

Suddenly, a plan blossomed in Gaborn's mind. A great geometer had once told him that when he discovered the answer to a difficult calculation, he knew that his answer was right because he felt it all the way down to his toes. At this moment, as Gaborn considered taking this young woman home to Mystarria, that same feeling of *rightness* struck him. Indeed, he felt that same burning compulsion that had drawn him to this land in the first place. He yearned once again to take Myrrima back to Mystarria, and suddenly saw the way.

He glanced at Borenson, to verify his hunch. The guardsman stood at his side, more than a head taller than Gaborn, and his cheeks were red, as if his own thoughts embarrassed him. The soldier's laughing blue eyes seemed to shine with their own light. His legs shook, though Gaborn had never seen him tremble in battle.

Down the lane, Myrrima turned a corner on a narrow market street, breaking into a run. Borenson shook his head ruefully, as if to ask, *How could you let her go?*

"Borenson," Gaborn whispered, "hurry after her. Introduce yourself graciously, then bring her back to me, but take a few minutes to talk as you walk. Stroll back. Do not hurry. Tell her I request an audience for only a moment."

"As you wish, milord," Borenson said. He began running in the swift way that only those who had taken an endowment of metabolism could; many in the crowd parted before the big warrior, who wound his way gracefully between those who were too slow or clumsy to move for him.

Gaborn did not know how long it might take Borenson to fetch the woman, so he wandered back to the shadows thrown by the inn. His Days followed. Together they stood, annoyed by a cloud of honeybees. The front of the inn here had an "aromatic garden" in the northern style. Blue morning-glory seeds were sewn in the thatch of the roof, and a riot of window boxes and flowerpots held creeping flowers of all kinds: palest honeysuckle dripped golden tears along the walls; mallow, like delicate bits of pearl, fluttered in the gentle breeze above the snow-in-summer; giant mandevilla, pink as the sunrise, was nearly strangled by the jasmine. And interspersed with all of these were rose vines, climbing every wall, splotches of peach. Along the ground were planted spearmint, chamomile, lemon verbena, and other spices.

Most northern inns were decorated with such flowers. It helped mask the obnoxious scents of the market, while herbs grown in these gardens could be used for teas and spices.

Gaborn stepped back into the sunlight, away from the heavy perfume of the flowers. His nose was too keen to let him stay.

Borenson returned in a few moments with his big right hand resting gently on Myrrima's elbow, as if to catch her should she trip on a cobblestone. It was an endearing sight.

When the two of them stood before him, Myrrima bowed slightly. "Milord wished to speak to me?"

"Yes," Gaborn said. "Actually, I was more interested in having you meet Borenson, my body." He left off the word *guard*, as was the custom in Mystarria. "He has been my body for six years now, and is captain of my personal guard. He is a good man. In my estimation, one of the finest in Mystarria. Certainly the finest soldier."

Borenson's cheeks reddened, and Myrrima glanced up at the big guard, smiling discreetly, gauging him. She could not have failed to notice by now that Borenson had an endowment of metabolism to his credit. The hastiness of his speeded reactions, the apparent inability to rest, were sure sign of it.

"Recently, Borenson was promoted to the rank of Baron of the Realm, and given title to a land and manor in . . . the Drewverry March." Immediately Gaborn recognized his mistake. To give such a large holding was impetuous. Yet now that the words had been spoken . . .

"Milord, I've never heard -" Borenson began to say, but Gaborn waved him to silence.

"As I say, it was a recent promotion." The Drewverry estate was a major holding, more land than Gaborn would normally give to a distinguished soldier for a life of service, if he'd had time to consider. But now, Gaborn reasoned, this sudden act of generosity would only make Borenson that much more loyal – as if Borenson's loyalty would ever waver. "In any event, Myrrima, as you can see, Borenson spends a great deal of time in my service. He needs a wife to help him manage his holdings."

The look of surprise on Borenson's face was a joy to behold. The big man was obviously taken by this northern beauty, and Gaborn had all but ordered them to marry.

Myrrima studied the guard's face without reserve, as if noticing for the first time the strength of his jaw, the imposing bulge of muscle beneath his jerkin. She did not love him, not yet. Perhaps she never would. This was an arranged marriage, and marrying a man who lived his life twice as fast as you, one who would grow old and die while you floundered toward middle age, could not be an overwhelmingly attractive proposition. Thoughtfully, she considered the virtues of the match.

Borenson stood dumbfounded, like a boy caught stealing apples. His face told that he'd considered the match, hoped for it.

"I told you I thought you'd do well in court," Gaborn said to Myrrima. "I'd like you to be in my court."

Certainly the woman would take his meaning. No

Runelord could marry her. The best she could hope for would be some merchant prince, burdened by adolescent lust.

Gaborn offered her a position of power – more than she could normally hope for – with an honorable and decent man whose life doomed him to a strange and lonely existence. It was no promise of love, but then Myrrima was a pragmatic woman who had taken the beauty of her sisters, the wisdom of her mother. Having taken these endowments, she would now have to assume responsibility for her impoverished kin. She knew the burden of power. She'd be a perfect woman to hold a place in Mystarria.

She looked up into Borenson's eyes for a long moment, face and mouth suddenly hard, as she considered the offer. Gaborn could see that now that the proposal was made, she realized what a momentous decision this was.

Almost imperceptibly, she nodded, sealing the bargain.

Borenson offered none of the hesitancy that Myrrima had found with Gaborn. He reached out and took her slender hand in both fists.

He said, "You must understand, fair lady, that no matter how sturdy my love for you grows, my first loyalty will always be to my lord."

"As it should be," Myrrima said softly, with a slight nod.

Gaborn's heart leapt. *I have won her love as surely as Borenson shall*, he thought.

At this moment, he felt strange – as if gripped by some great power. It seemed he could feel that power, like a buffeting wind, encircling – invisible, potent, overawing.

Gaborn's pulse raced. He glanced around, certain the source of this emotion must have a cause – a shifting in the earth in preparation for a quake, an approaching thunderstorm. But he saw nothing out of the normal. Those around him did not seem troubled.

Yet he could feel . . . the earth preparing to move beneath his feet – the rocks to twist or breathe or shout.

It was a distinctly odd sensation.

As suddenly as the rush of power had come, it dissipated. Like a gust of wind passing over a meadow, unseen, but subtly disturbing all in its wake.

Gaborn wiped perspiration from his brow, worried. I've come a thousand miles to heed a distant, unheard call. And now I feel this?

It seemed madness. He asked the others, "Do you – do you feel anything?"

THREE: OF KNIGHTS
AND PAWNS

When Chemoise got news that her betrothed was attacked while on guard duty, gutted by some spice merchant, it was as if the dawn sun went black, losing power to warm her. Or it was as if she'd turned to pale clay, her flesh losing all color, no longer able to hold her spirit.

Princess Iome Sylvarresta watched Chemoise, her Maid of Honor, her dearest friend, desperately wishing for a way to know what to do. If Lady Jollenne had been here, she'd have known what to do. But the matron had been called away for a few weeks to care for her grandmother, who'd had a bad fall.

Iome, her Days, and Chemoise had been up at dawn, sitting near the huge, U-shaped storyteller's stone in the Queen's topiary garden, reading the latest romance poems by Adallé, when Corporal Clewes broke in on their reverie.

He told the news: A scuffle with a drunken merchant. An hour or more past. Cat's Alley. Sergeant Dreys. Fought nobly. Near death. Slit from crotch to heart. Called for Chemoise as he fell.

Chemoise took the news stoically, if statues can be said to be stoic. She sat stiffly on the stone bench, her hazel eyes unfocused, her long, wheat-colored hair stirring in the wind. She'd been weaving a chain of daisies as Iome read. Now she laid them in her lap, on a skirt of coral-colored chiffon. Sixteen and heartbroken. She was to have been married in ten days.

Yet she dared not show her emotions. A proper lady should be able to bear such news lightly. She waited for Iome's permission to go to her fiancé.

"Thank you, Clewes," Iome said when the corporal continued standing at attention. "Where is Dreys now?"

"We laid him out on the common, outside the King's Tower. I didn't want to move him any farther. The others are laid out down by the river."

"The others?" Iome asked. She was sitting beside Chemoise; now she took the girl's hand. It had gone cold, so cold.

Clewes was an old soldier to have such a low station. His trim beard was stiff as oat stubble. It poked out from under the broken strap of his iron pikeman's cap.

"Aye, Princess," he said, remembering to address Iome properly for the first time since he'd intruded into the garden. "Two of the City Guard died in the fight. Poll the Squire and Sir Beauman."

Iome turned to Chemoise. "Go to him," she said.

The girl needed no further urging. She leapt up and ran down the path through the topiaries to the little wooden Bailey Gate, opened it and disappeared round the stone wall.

Iome dared not stay long in the corporal's presence alone, with no one other than the Days, who stood quietly a few paces off. It would not be proper. But she had questions to ask him.

Iome stood.

"You're not going to look at the sergeant, are you, Princess?" Clewes asked. He must have caught the anger in her eye. "I mean – it's a messy sight."

"I've seen injured men before," she said stoically. She looked out of the garden, over the city. The garden, a small patch of grass with trimmed hedges and a few shaped shrubs, sat within the King's Wall, the second of the three walls within the city. From here, she could see four of the King's guards on the wall-walk, behind the parapet. Beyond that, to the east, lay the city market, just within the castle's Outer Wall. The streets in the market below were a jumble – roofs of slate, some covered with a layer of sand and lead, forming narrow chasms above the rocky streets. Smoke rose from cooking fires here and there. Fourteen minor lords had estates within the city walls.

Iome studied the area where Cat's Alley could be found, a narrow market street just off the Butterwalk. The merchants' wattle houses there were painted in shades of cardinal, canary, and forest green, as if such bright colors could deny the general decrepitude of buildings that had been settling on their crooked foundations for five hundred years.

The city looked no different today than it had yesterday. She could see only rooftops; no sign of murderers.

Yet beyond the castle walls, beyond the farms and haycrofts, in the ruddy hills of the Dunnwood to the south and west, dust rose in small clouds along the roads for miles. People were traveling to the fair from distant kingdoms. Already, dozens of colorful silk pavilions had been set out before the castle gates. In the next few days, the population of the city would soar from ten thousand to four or five times that number.

Iome looked back at the corporal. Clewes seemed like a cold man to have been sent to carry such ill news. Blood had been everywhere after the fight. That much Iome could see. Crimson smeared the corporal's boots, stained the silver board embroidered into the black of his livery. The corporal himself must have carried Sergeant Dreys up to the common.

"So the fellow killed two men and wounded a third," Iome said. "A heavy loss, for a mere brawl. Did you dispatch the spice merchant yourself?" If he had, she decided, the corporal would get a reward. Perhaps a jeweled pin.

"No, milady. Uh, we busted him up a bit, but he's still alive. He's from Muyyatin. A fellow named Hariz al Jwabala. We didn't dare kill him. We wanted to question him." The corporal scratched the side of his nose, displeased at having left the trader alive.

Iome began to stroll toward the Bailey Gate, wanting to be with Chemoise. With a nod, she indicated that the corporal should follow, as did her Days.

"I see . . ." Iome mused, unsettled. A rich merchant then, from a suspect nation. Come to the city for next week's fair. "And what was a spice trader from Muyyatin doing in Cat's Alley before dawn?"

Corporal Clewes bit his lip, as if unwilling to answer, then said coldly, "Spying, if you ask me." His voice choked with rage, and now he took his eyes from the stone gargoyle up on the keep's wall, where he'd been staring, and briefly glanced at Iome, to see her reaction.

"I do ask you," Iome said. Clewes fumbled to unlatch the gate, let Iome and her Days through.

"We've checked the inns," Corporal Clewes said. "The merchant didn't drink at any of them last night, or else he'd have been escorted from the merchants' quarter at ten bells. So he couldn't have gotten drunk in the city walls, and I doubt he was drunk at all. He's got rum on his breath, but precious little of it. Besides, there was no reason for him to be creeping through the streets at night, unless he's spying out the castle walls, trying to count the guard! So when he gets caught, what does he do? He feigns drunk, and waits for the guards to close – then, out with the knife!" Clewes slammed the gate shut.

Just around the rock wall, Iome could see into the bailey. A dozen of the King's Guard stood there in a knot around the bodies of the dead and the dying. A physic knelt over Sergeant Dreys, and Chemoise stood over them, shoulders hunched, arms crossed tightly across her chest. An early-morning mist was rising from the green.

"I see," Iome whispered, heart pounding. "Then you

are interrogating the man?" Now that they were in the public eye, Iome stopped by the wall.

"I wish we could!" Corporal Clewes said. "I'd put a coal to his tongue myself! But right now, all the traders from Muyyatin and Indhopal are in an uproar. They're calling for Jwabala's release. Already they're threatening to post a ban on the fair. And now it's got the Master of the Fair in a fright: Guildmaster Hollicks has gone to the King himself, demanding the merchant's release! Can you believe it? A spy! He wants us to release a murdering spy!"

Iome took the news in, surprised. It was extraordinary that Hollicks would seek audience with the King just after dawn, extraordinary that the Southern merchants would threaten a ban. All of this spoke of large matters spinning wildly out of control.

She glanced over her shoulder. Her Days, a tiny woman with dark hair and a perpetually clenched jaw, was listening. Standing quietly just outside the gate, petting a lanky yellow kitten that she held. Iome could read no reaction on the Days' face. Perhaps the Days would understand who this spy was, knew who sent him. Yet the Days always claimed to remain completely neutral of political affairs. They would answer no questions.

Iome considered. Corporal Clewes was probably right. The merchant was a spy. Her father had his own spies in the Indhopalese Kingdoms.

But if the killer was a spy, it might be impossible to prove. Still, he'd killed two of the City Guard, and wounded Dreys, a sergeant of the King's Guard – and for that, by all rights, the merchant should die.

But in Muyyatin a man who committed a crime in a drunken stupor, even the crime of murder, could not be executed.

Which meant that if her father gave the death sentence, the Muyyatin – and all their Indhopalese kinsmen – would bridle at the injustice of the execution.

So they threatened a ban.

Iome considered the implications of such a ban. The Southern traders primarily sold spices – pepper, mace, and salt for curing meats; curry, saffron, cinnamon, and others for use in foods; medicinal herbs. But the traders brought much more: alum for use in dyeing and tanning hides, along with indigo and various other dyes needed for Heredon's wool. And they carried other precious goods – ivory, silks, sugar, platinum, blood metal.

If these traders called a ban on the fair, they'd deal a fearsome blow to at least a dozen industries. Even worse, without the spices to preserve food, Heredon's poor would not fare well through the winter.

So this year's Master of the Fair, Guildmaster Hollicks – who, as Master of the Dyers' Guild, stood to lose a fortune if a ban succeeded – was suing for a reconciliation. Iome didn't like Hollicks. Too often he'd asked the King to raise the import taxes on foreign cloth, hoping thus to bolster his own sales. But even Hollicks needed the merchandise the Indhopalese brought to trade.

Just as desperately, the merchants here in Heredon needed to sell their own wool and linen and fine steel to the foreigners. Most of the bourgeois traders had large amounts of money that they both borrowed and loaned. If a ban were enforced, hundreds of wealthy families would go bankrupt. And it was the wealthy families of Heredon who paid taxes to support King Sylvarresta's knights.

Indeed, Sylvarresta had his hand in dozens of trading deals himself. Even he could not afford a ban.

Iome's blood felt as if it would boil. She tried to resign herself to the inevitable. Her father would be forced to release the spy, make a reconciliation. But she would not like it.

For in the long run, Iome knew full well, her family could not afford such reconciliations: it was only a matter of time before Raj Ahten, the Wolf Lord of Indhopal,

made war against the combined kingdoms of Rofehavan.
Though traders from Indhopal crossed the deserts and
mountains now, next year – or the year after – the trading
would have to stop.

Why not stop the trading now? Iome wondered. Her
father could seize the merchandise brought by the
foreign caravans – starting the war he'd long hoped to
avert.

But she knew he would not do it. King Jas Laren
Sylvarresta would not start a war. He was too decent a
man.

Poor Chemoise! Her betrothed lay near death, and
would not be avenged.

The girl had no one. Chemoise's mother had died
young; her father, a Knight Equitable, had been taken
captive six years ago while on a quest to Aven.

"Thank you for the news," Iome told Corporal Clewes.
"I will discuss this matter with my father."

Iome hurried up now to the knot of soldiers. Sergeant
Dreys lay on a pallet in the green grass. An ivory-colored
sheet lay over Dreys, pulled up almost to his throat. Blood
looked as if it had been poured liberally over the sheet,
and it frothed from the corner of Dreys' mouth. His pale
face was covered in sweat. The slant of the morning sunlight left him in shadows.

Corporal Clewes had been right. Iome should not have
seen this. All the blood, the smell of punctured guts, the
impending death – all nauseated her.

A few children from the castle were up early and had
gathered to witness the sight. They looked up at Iome,
shock and pain in their eyes, as if hoping that she could
somehow smile and set this whole tragic thing aright.

Iome rushed to one small girl of nine, Jenessee, and put
an arm around the girl, then whispered, "Please, take the
children away from here."

Shaking, Jenessee hugged Iome briefly, then did as
told.

A physic knelt over Dreys. Yet the physic seemed in no hurry. He merely studied the soldier. When he saw Iome, saw her questioning look, the physic just shook his head. He could do nothing.

"Where is the herbalist, Binnesman?" Iome asked, for the wizard was this physic's superior in every way.

"He's gone – to the meadows, gathering costmary. He won't be back until tonight."

Iome shook her head in dismay. It was a terrible time for her master physic to be out hunting for herbs to drive spiders from the castle. Yet she should have known. The nights were growing colder, and she herself had complained to Binnesman yesterday about spiders seeking warmth in her rooms.

"I fear there is nothing I can do," the physic said. "I dare not move him more, for he bleeds too badly. I cannot sew the wounds, but dare not leave them open."

"I could give him an endowment," Chemoise whispered. "I could give him my stamina." It was an offer made in pure love. As such, Iome would have wanted to honor it.

"And if you did, would he thank you for it?" the physic asked. "Should you die next time the fever season comes around, he'd rue the bargain."

It was true. Chemoise was a sweet girl, but she showed no sign of having more stamina than anyone else. She got fevers in winter, bruised easily. If she gave her stamina to Sergeant Dreys, she'd be weak thereafter, more susceptible to plagues and ills. She'd never be able to bear him a child, carry it full-term.

"It's only his endowments of stamina that have kept him alive this long," Chemoise mused. "A little more – and he might live."

The physic shook his head. "Taking an endowment, even an endowment of stamina, gives some shock to the system. I wouldn't dare try. We can only wait and see if he strengthens. . . ."

Chemoise nodded. She knelt, cleaned the blood bubbling from the corner of Dreys' lips with the corner of her gray skirt. Dreys breathed hard, filling his lungs with air as if each breath would be his last.

Iome marveled. "Has he been gasping like this long?"

The physic shook his head, almost imperceptibly, so that Chemoise would not see him answer. Dreys was dying.

They watched over him thus for a long hour, with Dreys gasping more fiercely for each failing breath, until, finally, he opened his eyes. He looked up as if waking from a troubled sleep.

"Where?" he gasped, gazing into Chemoise's face.

"Where is the book?" one of the Castle Guard asked. "We got it – gave it to the King."

Iome wondered what the guard was speaking about. Then blood gurgled from Dreys' mouth, and he arched his back, reaching toward Chemoise, grasping her hand.

His breathing stopped altogether.

Chemoise grabbed the sergeant's head roughly, bent low and whispered fiercely, "I wanted to come. I wanted to see you this morning. . . ."

Then Chemoise burst into tears. The guards and physic all moved away, leaving her a few moments to speak some final words of love, in case his spirit had not yet fled the dying body. When she finished, she stood.

Only Corporal Clewes still waited at her back. He drew his battle-axe, saluted smartly, touching the cross formed by the blades to the bill of his iron cap. He did not salute to Iome, but to Chemoise.

He sheathed his axe and said softly, repeating his earlier tale, "He called for you as he fell, Chemoise."

Chemoise startled at a thought, looked up at Corporal Clewes and said, "A small miracle – that. Most men, when so struck, only manage to gasp once before they piddle on themselves."

She wielded the truth like an open palm, striking back

at the man who had brought her the bad news. Then she added more mildly, "But thank you, Corporal Clewes, for a kind fantasy to ease a lady's pain."

The corporal blinked twice, turned away, heading toward the Guards' Keep.

Iome put her hand on Chemoise's back. "We'll get some rags, clean him for burial."

Chemoise stared up at her, eyes going wide, as if she'd just remembered something important. "No!" she said. "Let someone else clean him. It doesn't matter. He's – his spirit isn't in there. Come on, I know where it is!"

Chemoise raced down the street toward the King's Gate.

She led Iome and her Days downhill through the markets, then past the Outer Gate to the moat. The fields beyond the moat were already filling with traders come for the fair, Southerners in their bright silk tents of cardinal, emerald, and saffron. The pavilions sat arrayed on the south hill, up against the edge of the forest, where thousands of mules and horses from the caravans were tethered.

Past the moat, Chemoise turned left and followed an overgrown trail beside the water to a copse on the east side of the castle. A channel had been dug from the River Wye to fill the moat; this copse sat between the channel and river.

From this little rise, one could see upstream the four remaining arches of the old stone bridge, spanning a river that glinted like beaten silver. Beyond the old bridge stood the new bridge – one whose stonework was in far better shape, but which lacked the beautiful statuary that adorned the older bridge, images of Heredon's Runelords of old, fighting great battles.

Iome had often wondered why her father did not destroy the old bridge, have the statues placed on the new bridge. But looking at it now, she understood. The old statues were rotting, the stone pitted by years of exposure

to ice and sun, eaten by the lichens that stained the
statues in vermilion and canary and dull green. There was
something picturesque, something venerable about those
ancient stones.

The place where Chemoise led Iome to look for
Sergeant Dreys' spirit was very quiet. The waters in the
channel flowed as slowly as honey, as was the custom in
late summer.

The high castle walls loomed some eighty feet above
the copse, casting blue shadows, bruising the waters of
the moat. There was no burbling or tinkle. Pink water
lilies bloomed placidly in the shadows. No wind stirred
this air.

The grass here grew lush. A hoary oak had once spread
its branches over the river, but lightning had blasted it,
and the sun had bleached it white as bone. Beneath the
oak, an ancient autumn rose made its bower, its trunk as
thick as a blacksmith's wrist, its old thorns as sharp as
nails.

The rose climbed the oak some thirty feet, creating a
natural bower. Roses of purest white hung above
Chemoise, like enormous stars in a dark-green sky.

Chemoise took a place on the grass beneath the rose
bower. The lush grass here was bent. Iome imagined that
it had been used as a bed for lovers.

Iome glanced over her shoulder at her Days. The thin
woman stood atop the copse, some forty feet back, arms
folded, head bowed. Listening.

Then Chemoise did an odd thing in the privacy
afforded by the rosebush: she lay on the grass and hiked
her skirts up a little higher on her hips, and just lay, with
legs spread. It was a shocking pose, and Iome felt embarrassed to see such a thing. Chemoise looked for all the
world as if she waited for a lover to take her.

On the banks of the river, frogs chirped. A dragonfly as
blue as if it had been dipped in indigo flew near
Chemoise's knee, hovered, flew away.

The air was so still, so silent. It was so beautiful, Iome imagined that Sergeant Dreys' spirit really might come.

All through the walk here, Chemoise had remained calm, but suddenly tears spilled over her long lashes, ran in rivulets down her face.

Iome lay beside the girl, put an arm over her chest, held her, the way that *he* must have.

"You've been here before, with him?" Iome asked.

Chemoise nodded. "Many times. We were supposed to meet here this morning." At first, Iome wondered how – how did they get outside the city gates at night? But, of course Dreys was a sergeant, in the King's Guard.

The notion was scandalous. As Iome's Maid of Honor, it was Chemoise's duty to see that her mistress remained pure and undefiled. When Iome became betrothed, Chemoise would have to swear to Iome's virtue.

Chemoise's lip began trembling. She whispered low so that the Days could not hear: "He filled me with child, I think, six weeks ago." At the confession, Chemoise reached up and bit her own knuckle, punishing herself. By carrying this child, Chemoise brought dishonor to Iome.

Who would believe any oath that Chemoise swore, if one could see that she herself had been defiled?

Iome's Days might know that Iome was virtuous, but the Days was sworn to silence by her own vows. She would never reveal any detail so long as Iome lived. Only when Iome died would the Days publish the chronicles of her life.

Iome shook her head in dismay. Ten days. In ten days Chemoise was to have been married, and then no one would have been able to prove that she'd been unchaste. But with her betrothed dead, the whole city would soon find out.

"We can send you away," Iome said. "We can send you to my uncle's estate in Welkshire. We'll tell everyone that you're a newlywed, newly widowed. No one will know."

"No!" Chemoise blurted. "It's not *my* reputation I worry about. It's yours! Who will swear for you, when you become betrothed? I won't be able to!"

"Plenty of women at court can serve in that capacity," Iome lied. If she sent Chemoise away, it could still tarnish Iome's reputation. Some people might think that Iome had disposed of her Maid of Honor in order to hide her own indiscretion.

But Iome couldn't worry about such things now, couldn't consider her own reputation when her friend hurt so.

"Maybe, maybe you could marry soon?" Chemoise said. At nearly seventeen, Iome was certainly old enough. "The Prince of Internook wants you. And then – I've heard – King Orden is bringing his son for Hostenfest. . . ."

Iome drew a sharp breath. King Sylvarresta had spoken to Iome several times during the past winter, hinting that the time would soon come for her to marry. Now her father's oldest friend was finally bringing his son to Heredon. Iome knew full well what that meant – and she felt shocked that she'd not been forewarned. "When did you hear this?"

"Two days ago," Chemoise said. "King Orden sent word. Your father didn't want you to know. He . . . didn't want you to be in an excitable humor."

Iome bit her lip. She had no desire to become allied with King Orden's spawn – would never have considered it for a moment.

But if Iome accepted Prince Orden's proposal, then Chemoise could still fulfill her obligation as Maid of Honor. So long as no one knew that Chemoise carried a child, then her sworn statement of Iome's fidelity would not be challenged.

Iome bristled at the thought. It seemed unfair. She wouldn't consent to a hasty marriage just to save her reputation.

As the anger flared in her, Iome stood. "Come on," she

said. "We're going to see my father."

"Why?" Chemoise asked.

"We'll make this Inhopalese assassin pay for his murder!" Iome hadn't realized what she intended to do. But she was angry now, angry with her father for not telling her about the impending proposal, angry with Chemoise for her embarrassing lack of scruples, angry that Raj Ahten's assassins could murder Heredon's guards – and that the city's merchants would then beg their king for clemency.

Well, Iome could do something about this mess.

Chemoise looked up. "Please, I need to stay here."

Then Iome understood. An old wives' tale said that if a man died while his lover carried his child, the woman could capture her lover's spirit in the unformed child, so that he would be born again. Chemoise only needed to be present at sunset in the place where she'd first conceived, so that the father's ghost might find her.

Iome couldn't believe Chemoise would put credence in that old fable, yet she dared not deny the girl such a boon. Letting her sleep under the rose bower could do no harm, would only cause Chemoise to love her babe more fiercely.

"I'll see that you come back before sunset," Iome said. "And you can stay an hour after. If Dreys can come to you, he'll do so then. But for now, I must speak to the King."

Before speaking to the King, Iome took her Maid of Honor to look upon Dreys' murderer, while the silent but omnipresent Days followed at Iome's heel.

They found the spice merchant chained in the dungeon beneath the Soldiers' Keep, the sole occupant of that dreadful place. Iron shackles and cages hung from the stone walls, and the whole dungeon carried the scent of ancient death. Huge beetles scurried about. In one far corner of the dungeon was a great hole, the oubliette, where prisoners could be kept. The sides of the hole were stained from urine and feces, for those condemned to that awful hole lived in the muck that guards threw down from above.

Dreys' murderer was chained hand and foot to a post. He was a young man, perhaps twenty-two.

His eyes were dark, as dark as Iome's, but his skin was more brown. He smelled strongly of anise, curry, garlic and olive oil, as did the rest of his countrymen. The murderer had been stripped to nothing but a breech-cloth. Both his legs were broken. A ring had been ripped from his nose. His jaw was swollen. Fresh welts covered his face and ribs. Someone had bitten a chunk out of his shoulder. He'd live.

On his thin ribs, one could see runes of power branded into the flesh, white scars each about an inch to the side. Five runes of brawn, three of grace, one of stamina, one of wit, one of metabolism, one of hearing, two of sight.

No merchant in Heredon wore so many runes of power. This man was a soldier, an assassin. Iome felt certain.

But mere feelings were not proof. In the South, where blood metal was mined, merchants could purchase the precious metals more easily, then purchase endowments from the poor.

Though Iome doubted that this man was a merchant, his overabundance of endowments alone could not convict him.

Chemoise stared deep into the prisoner's eyes, then slapped his face, just once.

Afterward, the two young women went to the King's Keep.

King Sylvarresta was in the informal audience chamber on the first story. He sat on a bench in the corner, talking softly with Iome's mother, a rather somber Chancellor Rodderman, and a terrified Guildmaster Hollicks.

Fresh rushes had been strewn over the floorboards, mixed with balm and pennyroyal. Three hounds sat before the empty hearth. A cleaning girl was polishing the unused tongs and pokers. Iome's Days immediately crossed the room, went to stand out of the way with the King's Days, and the Queen's.

As Iome entered the hall, her father glanced up expectantly. Sylvarresta was not a vain man. He wore no crown, and his only ring was a signet, which he kept chained to his neck. He preferred to be called "Lord" rather than King. But one could see he was a king when one looked into his gray eyes.

Guildmaster Hollicks, though, was another matter. He wore gaudy clothes – a shirt with false sleeves, particolored pants, a vest and half cape with cowl – in a rainbow of complementary colors. He was Master of the Dyers' Guild; his clothes advertised his wares. Beyond this penchant for gaudy attire, Hollicks was not a bad man. He showed uncommonly good sense, and would have been likable, if not for the way his unsightly black nose hairs formed half his mustache.

"Ah," King Sylvarresta said on seeing Iome, "I'd thought you might be someone else. Have you seen any of the foresters this morning? Were they in the bailey?"

"No, milord," Iome answered.

The King nodded thoughtfully at this news, then said softly to Chemoise, "My condolences. It is a sad day for us all. Your betrothed was admired – a promising soldier."

Chemoise nodded, her face suddenly pale again. She curtsied. "Thank you, milord."

"You won't let this assassin get away with murder, will you?" Iome asked. "You should have killed him by now!"

"You see," Hollicks blurted in his high voice, "you're all leaping to conclusions. You have no proof that this was anything other than an unfortunate, drunken brawl!"

King Sylvarresta strode to the door to the hall, looked into the courtyard a moment, then closed the door, shutting them all in.

The room suddenly became dark, shadowed, for only

two small windows with wooden shutters stood open.

King Sylvarresta strode across the room, head bent in thought. "Despite your pleas for leniency, Master Hollicks, I know this man is a spy."

Hollicks feigned an expression of incredulity. "You have proof?" he asked, as if he held serious doubt.

"While you were off entertaining your whining cronies," King Sylvarresta said, "I had Captain Derrow track the man's scent. One of my far-seers spotted this same man yesterday just after dawn. He'd been on a roof in town, and we feared he'd been counting guards to the Dedicates' Keep. We tried to catch him then, but lost him in the market.

"Now he shows up again today. It is no coincidence. Derrow said the man had not been within a hostel all night. Instead, he followed Dreys from outside the gates by climbing the Outer Wall. He killed Dreys because he was searching for this. . . ." Sylvarresta pulled out a slim tome bound in tan-colored lambskin. "It's a book, a very strange book."

Hollicks frowned at that news. It was bad enough to have the trader accused of spying. He didn't wish to see any damning evidence mount against the man.

"So," Hollicks said, "is that your proof? A drunken man is wont to do strange things, you know. Why, my stable-master, Wallis, climbs our apple trees every time the liquor has him. The fact that Dreys had a book means nothing."

King Sylvarresta shook his head woefully. "No, the book has a note in it, addressed to me, from the Emir of Tuulistan. He is blind, you know. His castle was taken by Raj Ahten, and the Wolf Lord forced the Emir to give an endowment of sight. Yet the Emir wrote the story of his life, and sent it to me."

"He wrote his own chronicles?" Iome asked, wondering why anyone, much less a blind man, would bother when the Days watched their every move, and wrote their chronicles after their deaths.

"Is there news of battles in it?" Hollicks asked. "Does it describe anything of import?"

"Many battles," the King said. "The Emir tells how Raj Ahten broke his defenses and took neighboring castles. I've only had time to glance at the book, but it may prove important. Important enough that Raj Ahten's spy felt he needed to kill Dreys to retrieve the book."

"But – the Southerner's papers are in order!" Hollicks objected. "He has a dozen letters of commends from various merchants in his pouch. He has loans to repay! He is a merchant, I tell you! You still have no proof against him!"

"And he has more endowments than any merchant you've ever seen," King Sylvarresta said, "and they are a warrior's mix in proportion."

Hollicks seemed deflated by this.

Iome's father mused, "You know, twenty years ago, when I went south to court Lady Sylvarresta in Jomateel, I once played chess with Raj Ahten himself." Sylvarresta glanced at his wife, put a comforting hand on Hollicks' shoulder.

Iome's mother stirred uncomfortably. She did not like being reminded that she was the Wolf Lord's cousin.

"Do you know how he opened?" King Sylvarresta asked.

"King's pawn to king four?" Hollicks guessed, choosing the most common opening.

"No. King's knight to king's wizard three. An unusual opening."

"Is this significant?" Hollicks asked.

"It is how he played the game. He left his pawns at home, and attacked with his knights, wizards, castles, queens – even brought out his king. Rather than seeking to control the center of the board, he attacked with pieces he felt could seize control even at the far corners."

King Sylvarresta waited for the merchant to grasp the

import of what he was saying, but Hollicks seemed oblivious. The King put it more simply: "That spice merchant
in the dungeon – he is one of Raj Ahten's knights. The
calluses inside his thumb come from years of sword
practice."

Hollicks considered this. "Surely you don't believe Raj
Ahten will come here?"

"Oh, he's coming," Sylvarresta said. "That's why we've
sent a thousand knights, plus squires and archers, to
fortify Castle Dreis." Iome's father failed to mention that
seventeen kings of Rofehavan planned to meet in two
months, to discuss strategies should Raj Ahten invade.
Apparently her father felt it was not the merchant's
business.

Iome's mother, Queen Venetta Sylvarresta, could have
told some tales to frighten Master Hollicks.

Iome's mother once told Iome how her cousin "Young
Ahten," at the age of eight, had visited her father's keep.
Venetta's father had thrown the boy a feast, inviting all the
captains of the King's Guard, various counselors, and
important merchants to the extravaganza. When the
tables were laid out, piled with roast peacocks and puddings and wine, Venetta's father invited young Raj Ahten
to speak. The boy then stood, turned and addressed
Venetta's father, asking, "Is this feast not in my honor, a
gift to me?"

Venetta's father had answered, "Indeed, it is all in your
honor."

The boy then indicated the hundred guests with a
sweep of his hand, and said, "If this is my feast, then send
these people away. I will not have them eating my dinner."

Appalled, the guests departed in outrage, leaving the
boy with more food than he could consume in a year.

Iome's mother used to say that if her father had been
wiser, he'd have slit the rapacious child's throat then.

For years, Venetta had tried to convince King
Sylvarresta of the necessity of striking the first blow, of

crushing Raj Ahten when he was young. Somehow, Iome's father never believed the boy would conquer all twenty-two kingdoms in Indhopal.

Iome urged her father now, "So you will put this spy to death? You must insist on justice."

King Sylvarresta answered, "I will have justice. Raj Ahten will pay dearly. But I won't kill the knight."

At this news, Hollicks sighed in relief.

Iome must have appeared crestfallen, for her father quickly added. "Your idealistic solution to this matter is laudable, but hardly practical. We can't execute the spy.

"So, I'll hold him ransom."

"Ransom?" Hollicks asked. "Raj Ahten will never admit that this spy is his man!"

Iome smiled to hear Hollicks finally admit that the man was a spy.

"Of course not," King Sylvarresta said. "But the Indhopal merchants claim him as their own. They'll pay the ransom to save the fair. It's a common practice in Indhopal. They say a farmer can hardly go to market without coming home to find the neighbors holding his pigs hostage."

"And how can you be sure they'll pay?" Iome asked.

"Because the merchants want to save the fair. And because, I believe, Raj Ahten has soldiers hiding in the Dunnwood, waiting for the information this man will give. At least some of these merchants must know this – which is why they are so hasty to demand the fellow's release – so they will be eager to ransom the spy lest we manage to torture a confession from him."

"And why do you suspect that warriors are hiding in the Dunnwood?" Hollicks asked.

"Because days ago I sent five foresters into the woods to find out where the largest boars are laying up before next week's hunt. They were to report to me yesterday morning. None have returned. Five men. Had it been one, I'd suspect an accident. But these were trustworthy men. Nothing would keep them from obeying my command. They've either been captured, or killed. I've sent scouts to confirm my fears, but I think we already know what they'll find."

Hollicks' face paled at this news.

"So, Raj Ahten's soldiers hide in the Dunnwood, and they need to attack within the next three days – before the hunts begin, lest they be discovered." King Sylvarresta folded his hands behind his back, paced over to the hearth.

"Will it be a large battle, milord?" Hollicks asked.

Sylvarresta shook his head. "I doubt it. Only some pre-war maneuvering is likely, so late of the year. I think we have a band of assassins out there. They'll either strike the Dedicates' Keep, seeking to weaken me, or they'll strike at the royal family itself."

"But, what of us merchants?" Hollicks asked. "Couldn't they as easily strike our manors? Why, why, no one is safe!"

The idea that Raj Ahten would strike at the bourgeois seemed ludicrous.

Sylvarresta laughed. "Come, old friend, bolt your doors tonight, and you'll have nothing to fear. But now, I need your counsel. We must set a price for this 'merchant's' ransom. How much damage shall we say he caused the King?"

"I would say a thousand silver hawks," Hollicks answered cautiously.

Iome had listened to her father, followed his reasoning and found it both flawless and infuriating. "I don't like the idea of ransoming this spy. It's . . . a form of surrender. Certainly, you aren't considering Chemoise's feelings! Her betrothed was murdered!"

King Sylvarresta looked up at Chemoise, a certain sadness, a certain pleading in the troubled creases around his eyes. Chemoise's tears had dried, yet Iome's father looked as if he could see the sadness still burning there. "I am sorry, Chemoise. You trust me, don't you? You trust I am doing the right thing? If I am right, you'll have that murderer's head on a stick by the end of the week – plus a thousand silver hawks of the ransom money."

"Of course, as you please, milord," Chemoise said. She could hardly debate the matter.

"Good," Sylvarresta said, taking Chemoise's words at face value. "Now, Master Hollicks, let's consider that ransom. A thousand pieces of silver, you say? Then it's good you're not king. We'll start by demanding twenty times that – along with fifty pounds of mace, fifty of pepper, and two thousand of salt. And I'll want blood metal. How much have the traders weighed in this year?"

"Why, I don't know for certain!" Hollicks said, all a bluster at the King's outrageous demands.

King Sylvarresta raised a brow in question. Hollicks knew how much blood metal was available – to the ounce. Ten years before, in recognition of Hollicks' service to the King, Sylvarresta had granted the merchant a petition to take out an endowment of wit. Though an endowment of wit did not make the merchant any wiser or more creative or let him think more clearly, that endowment did let Hollicks remember trivial details almost faultlessly.

Taking an endowment of wit was like opening a door into another man's mind. A man who got an endowment of wit suddenly had the capacity to enter a mind and store whatever he liked, while the man who gave the wit had the doors of memory barred and was forbidden to even peek at the contents hidden within his own skull. Now Hollicks stored his tallies in the mind of his Dedicate.

Indeed, it was said that the guildmaster could quote every contract he'd ever written, word for word; Hollicks always knew to the moment when his loans came due.

Certainly, he knew how much blood metal the Southern traders had weighed out in the past week. As Master of the Fair, he was in charge of assuring that all goods were properly weighed, that products sold were of highest quality.

"I . . . uh, so far, the Southern merchants have weighed in only thirteen pounds of blood metal. They . . . say the mines in Kartish have not produced well this year. . . ." Enough to make less than a hundred forcibles. Hollicks cringed, as if Sylvarresta might fly into rage at the news.

Iome's father nodded thoughtfully. "I doubt Raj Ahten knows that so much made it across his borders. We won't see any more, next year. Then to our tally of damages, add a ransom of thirty pounds of blood metal."

"They don't have that much!" Master Hollicks complained.

"They'll find it," Sylvarresta said. "If they're smuggling it in, they'll have some secreted away.

"Now, go, send word to our foreign friends. Tell them that the King is beside himself with rage. Urge them to act quickly, for Sylvarresta can hardly be restrained from taking vengeance. Tell them that even now, I'm in my buttery, getting blind drunk on brandy, vacillating about whether I should torture secrets from the man first, or if I should just slit his belly and strangle him with his own guts."

"Aye, milord," Hollicks said, flustered. The particolored merchant bowed and took his leave, sweating profusely at the thought of the negotiations about to begin.

During this whole discussion, the somber Chancellor Rodderman had kept silent, sitting on a bench by the Queen, narrowly studying the exchange between the King and the Master of the Fair. Sometimes he stroked his long white sideburns. When Hollicks left, the Chancellor said, "Your Grace, do you think you'll get that much ransom?"

King Sylvarresta said simply, "Let us hope."

Iome knew her father needed money. The costs of armor and endowments and supplies associated with waging the upcoming war would be onerous.

Sylvarresta glanced about. "Now, Chancellor, fetch me Captain Derrow. If I am not mistaken, we shall be visited by assassins tonight. We must arrange a proper greeting."

The chancellor got up stiffly, rubbed the small of his back and then left.

Iome's father looked deep in thought. As she prepared to leave, a nagging question took her. "Father, when you played chess with Raj Ahten, who came off victor?"

King Sylvarresta smiled appreciatively. "He did."

Iome began to leave, but another perplexing question came to mind. "Father, now that we've seen Raj Ahten's knight, should we prepare for him to bring out his wizards?"

Her father's frown was answer enough.

FOUR: ADDLEBERRY WINE

Borenson studied Gaborn's eyes. "Do I feel anything, milord? What do you mean? Like hunger, excitement? I feel many things."

Gaborn couldn't quite express the odd sensation that assailed him in the market at Bannisferre. "No, nothing so ordinary. It's like . . . the earth . . . trembling in anticipation? Or . . ." He suddenly caught an image in his mind. "It's like that moment when you put your hand to the plow, and you thrill to see dark soil fold over, knowing that the seeds will soon be in the ground, and fruit will come of it. Endless trees and fields spreading across the horizon."

It was odd, but the image came to mind with such force that Gaborn could not think to say anything else. Words did not suffice for what he felt, for he could literally feel his hand wrapping around the worn wooden handles of the plow, feel the strain of the lines from the ox cutting into his back, feel the keen edge of the plow biting into the soil, turning over dark dirt, discovering worms. He could taste the metallic tang of soil in his mouth, see fields and forests streaming out before him. His pockets were heavy with seeds, ready to plant.

He felt as if he were experiencing all these things at once, and he wondered if any gardener had really ever felt such a keen thrill of anticipation as the one that assailed him at this moment. Oddest of all, Gaborn had never done these things – had never hitched himself to a plow or stooped to plant the earth.

Yet he wished at this moment that he had. He wished that at this very second, he stood in the earth.

Myrrima looked at him strangely. Gaborn's Days gave no reply, playing the invisible observer.

But Borenson's eyes shone with laughter. "Milord, I think you have had too much air today. Your face is pale and sweaty. Do you feel well?"

"I feel . . . very . . . healthy," Gaborn said, wondering if he was ill. Wondering if he was mad. Few weaknesses ever impaired a Runelord. An endowment of wit could repair a lord with poor memory, an endowment of stamina could bolster a sickly king. But madness . . .

"Well then," Gaborn said, suddenly wanting to be alone with his thoughts, to consider what could cause these profound feelings of . . . planting, "I think you two should spend some time getting acquainted – the afternoon."

"My lord, I am your body -" Borenson said, not willing to leave his side. Gaborn could count the times on his fingers when Borenson had been away for more than a night.

"And I will be lounging in a hostel, with nothing more dangerous than a joint of pork before me." Borenson could hardly refuse. Custom dictated that he go privately to the woman's house to beg her hand in marriage. With a witless mother and no father, custom might be somewhat circumvented in this case, but it could not be put aside entirely.

"Are you certain? I don't think this is wise," Borenson said, his manner becoming deadly earnest. Gaborn was in a strange country, after all, and he was heir apparent to the wealthiest nation in Rofehavan.

"Just go, will you?" Gaborn urged them, smiling. "If it makes you feel better, I promise that as soon as I lunch, I will go to my room and bolt the door."

"We'll be back well before dark," Myrrima said.

Gaborn said, "No, I'll seek out your home. I'd like to meet your kind sisters, and your mother."

Myrrima urged, breathlessly, "Across the Himmeroft Bridge – four miles down the Bluebell Way, a gray cabin in the meadow."

Borenson shook his head adamantly. "No, I'll come back for you. I won't have you riding alone."

"Farewell, then, until this afternoon," Gaborn said. He watched them scurry off through the crowd, hand-in-hand, a certain lightness to their steps.

For a few moments, Gaborn stayed in the market, watching an entertainer who had trained albino doves to do all manner of aerial acrobatics; then he wandered the cobbled streets of Bannisferre, every step dogged by his Days.

In the City's center towered a dozen graystone song-houses, six and seven stories tall, with elaborate friezes and statuary about them.

On the steps of one songhouse, a handsome young woman sang a delicate aria, accompanied by woodwinds and harp. A group of peasants crowded round. Her voice drifted hauntingly, echoing from the tall stone buildings, mesmerizing. She merely advertised, of course. She hoped to attract an audience for her performance later tonight.

Gaborn decided he would attend, bring Borenson and Myrrima.

Sturdy bathhouses and gymnasiums squatted farther down the street. On the broad avenues, several carriages could maneuver with ease. Fine shops displayed bone china, silver goods, and gentlemen's weaponry.

Bannisferre was a young city, less than four hundred years old. It had started simply as a meeting ground for local farmers to exchange wares, until iron was dis-covered along the Durkin Hills. The ironsmiths opened a foundry, where the quality of the goods soon attracted a wealthy clientele who demanded fine accommodations and entertainment.

So Bannisferre had grown to be a center for the arts, attracting smiths who worked iron, silver, and gold; ceramists famed for their cloisonné and bone china; glassblowers who constructed bewitching mugs and vases in magnificent colors – until finally, the city became crowded with craftsmen and performers from all walks of life.

Bannisferre was a fine place, a city free of grime. Now everywhere it was festooned with images of the Earth King – elaborate wooden images, painted and dressed with loving care. The streets had no urchins running about underfoot. And the reeves hereabout were dressed in fine leather coats with gold brocade, as if they were just another adornment to Bannisferre, not working lawmen.

Somehow, the loveliness of this place saddened Gaborn. The city's defenses seemed woefully inadequate. It was built beside a river, without benefit of a fortress. A low wall of rocks around the city would barely repel a cavalry charge – and then only if the cavalry was not riding force horses. Perhaps a few soldiers could hold out for a bit in the songhouse, skirmishing among the statuary.

No, in a war, Bannisferre would be overrun, its beauty defiled. The graceful songhouses and bathhouses were made of stone, but the stonework was wrought for ornament, not with defense in mind. The doorways were too wide, the windows too expansive. Even the bridges across River Dwindell were wide enough so carriages could drive across four abreast. They could not be easily defended.

Gaborn returned to the South Market, ambled back through the cloud of honeybees into the shade of his hostel.

He intended to keep his promise to Borenson, keep safe. He found a corner table, ordered a dinner suitable to a refined palate, then rested his feet on the table.

His Days sat across from him. Gaborn felt like celebrating Borenson's good fortune. He tossed a silver coin to a towheaded servant boy perhaps five years younger than himself. "Bring us wine. Something sweet for the Days. Addleberry for me."

"Yes, sir," the boy answered. Gaborn looked around. The room was fairly empty. Three dozen chairs, but only a few of them filled. At the far end of the room, two gentlemen of dark complexion sat talking softly about the relative virtues of different inns in town. A few green-bottle flies wheeled in slow circles. Outside, a pig squealed in the market.

Toward evening, the inn would fill.

The serving boy returned with two brown clay mugs and two genuine bottles of yellow glass, not the hide flasks used in the south. Each bottle had a red wax seal over the cap, with the initial B inscribed. It seemed a fine vintage, the bottles well aged and covered with grime. Gaborn was not used to such nice drink. Wine laid up in bags turned vinegary after six months.

The boy poured a draught for each man, then left the bottles on the table. Moisture began to condense on the bottles. They were that cold.

Gaborn studied the bottles absently, reached out with an index finger and touched the dust on a bottle, tasted the soil. Good, sweet earth. Good for planting.

The Days took a swallow of wine, regarded it carefully. "Hmmm . . ." he said. "I've never tasted anything so fine." In seconds he downed the whole mug, thought for a moment, then poured himself a second.

Gaborn simply stared at the Days. He'd never seen the like. The Days was such a sober man – he never drank to excess. Neither did he womanize or waste time with any other form of diversion. He was singularly committed to his discipline, to chronicling the lives of kings on behalf of the Time Lords. Since he was twinned with another – each man having given the other an endowment of wit –

the two completed a circle. Both men shared a single mind, knowing the same things. Such sharing usually led to madness, both members of the pair struggling for control of the joint minds. But somewhere, in a monastery in the isles beyond Orwynne, Days' partner transcribed all that the Days learned. It was only because the two Days had given complete control of their own identities to their order that they both survived.

So it was odd to watch a Days guzzle wine. It was an extraordinarily selfish act.

Gaborn tasted his own wine. Addleberry wine was not truly made with any kind of berry, only with sweet grapes that were treated with herbs – such as vervain, evening primrose, and elderflower – that stimulated thought and reduced the detrimental effects of alcohol. It tasted spicier, less sweet than common wine, and the cost tended to be prohibitive. Its name was a jest: ironically, addleberry wine did not dull the wits, but instead stimulated them. If one were to be intoxicated, Gaborn reasoned, it was best to be intoxicated on insight.

Here in the inn, with the pleasant smells of cooking bread and pork, Gaborn felt a little more at ease. He took a couple of sips of wine, found it surprisingly good, but not as addictive as the vintage Days guzzled.

Yet Gaborn still worried. Outside, an hour earlier, he'd felt an odd rush of power. Outside, he'd just married off his bodyguard, and he'd congratulated himself on doing so. But inside the hostel, it seemed . . . so peculiar. An impulsive, childish thing to do.

Though he'd someday be sovereign over one of the world's great realms, under normal circumstances he'd never have dared use his position to act as a matchmaker.

Gaborn wondered. He was shouldered with the responsibility of becoming a king. But what kind of king would he make, if he did such foolish things?

In the House of Understanding, in the Room of the Heart, Hearthmaster Ibirmarle had once said, "Not even a Runelord can rule affairs of the heart. Only a fool would try."

Yet Gaborn had convinced Borenson to take a wife.

What if he ends up hating her? Gaborn wondered. *Will he resent what I've done?*

It was such a muddling thought. And what of Myrrima? Would she love Borenson?

The Days began drinking his second mug of wine, downed it in a few gulps despite his attempts at restraint.

"I did a good thing, didn't I?" Gaborn said. "I mean, Borenson is a good man, isn't he? He'll love her."

The Days smiled a tight-lipped smile, watching Gaborn from slitted eyes. "There is a saying among our kind: Good deeds portend good fortune."

Gaborn considered the words "our kind." Though the Days were human, they considered themselves as creatures apart. Perhaps they were right. Their service to the Time Lords required great sacrifices. They forsook home and family, loyalties to any king. Instead, these mysterious men and women simply studied the great lords, wrote the chronicles, published the deeds of a man's life when he died, and in all other ways remained aloof from common politics.

Yet Gaborn did not entirely trust these watchers, with their secretive smiles. They only feigned aloofness in the affairs of men, of that Gaborn felt certain. Every Runelord was followed by a Days who recorded his words and deeds. Sometimes, when two Days met, they reported to one another in coded phrases. Gaborn's ancestors had been studying the Days for generations, trying to break their codes.

But how aloof were they really? Gaborn suspected that the Days had sometimes betrayed secrets to enemy kings. Certain battles could only have been won on the advice of informers – informers who were probably Days.

Yet if as a group the Days took sides in wars between nations, neither Gaborn nor anyone else had ever been able to determine where the Days placed their allegiance.

No discernible battle lines were drawn. Evil kings prospered from Days' spying as often as did good. And no king could escape them. Some kings tried ridding themselves of the Days, either through assassination or banishment. But such kings never reigned for another season. As a group, the Days were too powerful. Any king who dared strike down one Days would discover just how much information a Days' partner could divulge. Distressing information would be revealed to enemy kings, fortunes would be ruined, peasants would revolt.

No one could defy the Days. Nor did Gaborn feel certain that any man should want to do so. An old adage went, "A man who will not bear scrutiny cannot bear a crown." It was said that those words were given by the Glories themselves, when the Days were first partnered to the kings. "A Runelord should be a servant to man," the Glories had said.

So Gaborn's title came with a price. He would never be free of this man, never be alone. Though he might rule a kingdom, some things were rightfully denied even to Gaborn.

Lost in thought, Gaborn wondered once again about Borenson. The man was a soldier, and soldiers did not necessarily make good lords, for they were trained to solve every problem through use of force. Gaborn's father preferred to sell titles to merchants, who were trained to barter for what they wanted. Gaborn suddenly realized that the Days had never fully answered him, had avoided the question.

"I said, 'Borenson is a good man, isn't he?'"

The Days looked up, his head nodding just a bit. The disciple was well on his way to being solidly drunk. He poured more wine. "Not nearly so good as you, Your Lordship. But he'll make her happy enough, I'd wager."

Your Lordship. Not *my lord.*

"But he's a good man, isn't he?" Gaborn asked a third

time, suddenly angry at the Days' evasion.

The Days looked away, started to mumble something.

Gaborn struck the table hard enough so the wine bottles jumped and the mugs clanked. He shouted, "Answer me!"

The Days gaped in surprise. He knew to take warning. Fists would soon fly. Gaborn had endowments of brawn from three men. His blow could kill a commoner.

"Hah – what does it matter, Your Lordship?" the Days averred, struggling to clear his muddled thoughts. "You've never worried about his goodness before. You've never questioned his moral fiber."

The Days took another swig of wine, seemed to want more, but thought better of it and carefully set the mug aside.

Why am I questioning Borenson's moral character? Gaborn wondered, and the answers flowed to him: Because you were drinking addleberry wine and noticed how Days tried to evade the question. Because Myrrima said that Princess Iome doubts your own goodness, and now you are worrying at what others think. Because . . . because you know that any lout can win a parcel of land, but it takes a special kind of king to win the hearts of his people.

Gaborn hoped to win the hearts of Iome and her people. But he dared not reveal details of his plan to Days – or to anyone. If Gaborn's father, King Orden, learned what Gaborn planned, the King might try to stop him.

The wine was having its way with Gaborn now, bringing the world into focus. But Gaborn would not be sidetracked from his questioning by other observations. "Answer my question, Days! What do you think of Borenson?"

The Days put both hands on the table, screwed up his courage. "As you wish, Your Lordship: I once asked Borenson what his favorite animal is, and he told me he 'admires dogs.' I asked him why, and he answered: 'I love to hear them snarl. I love the way they greet strangers with senseless aggression."'

Gaborn laughed. It was the kind of perfect thing Borenson would say. The man was a terror in battle.

The Days seemed relieved by Gaborn's good humor. He leaned forward conspiratorially. "To tell you the truth, Your Lordship, I think Borenson admires another attribute in dogs. One he did not name."

"Which is?"

"Loyalty."

Gaborn laughed harder. "So, Borenson is a dog?"

"No. He only aspires to be one. If I may be so bold, I fear he has all of dog's finest virtues *but* loyalty."

"So you don't believe he is a good man?"

"He's an assassin. A butcher, Your Lordship. That is why he is captain of your guard."

This angered Gaborn. The Days was wrong. The historian smiled drunkenly, took another swig to fortify his courage.

The Days continued, "In fact, none of your friends are very good people, Your Lordship. You don't value virtue in your friends."

"What do you mean?" Gaborn asked. He'd always thought his friends had an acceptable level of virtue.

"It is simple, Your Lordship," the Days said. "Some men pick their friends based on looks, others on wealth or political station, others on common interests. Some choose friends based on their virtue. But you do not value any of these traits, highly."

It was true, Gaborn had friends among the ugly, the powerless. His friend Eldon Parris sold roasted rabbits in a public market. And Gaborn also enjoyed the company of more than one person who might best be described as a scoundrel.

"Then how do I pick my friends?" Gaborn asked.

"Because you are young, you value men based upon their insights into the human heart, Your Lordship."

This statement struck Gaborn like a blast of air off a frozen lake. It was stunning, refreshingly honest, and, of course, obviously true.

"I had never noticed . . ."

The Days laughed. "It's one of the seven keys to understanding motives. I fear, young master Gaborn, you are lousy at picking friends. Hah! I sometimes imagine how it will be when you are a king: You'll surround yourselves with eccentrics, and scholars. In no time they'll have you taking garlic enemas and wearing pointy shoes! Hah!"

"Seven keys? Where did you learn such lore?" Gaborn asked.

"In the Room of Dreams," the Days said. Then he suddenly sat up straight, recognizing his mistake.

In the House of Understanding, the Room of Dreams was forbidden to Runelords. The secrets one learned there, of human motivation and desires, were considered by scholars to be too powerful to put in the hands of a king.

Gaborn smiled triumphantly at this little tidbit, raised his glass in toast. "To dreams."

But the Days would not toast with him. The man would most likely never drink in Gaborn's presence again.

From a far corner of the room, a small ratlike ferrin woman came out of the shadows, bearing one of her pups in hand. The pup squealed in its small way, but the Days did not hear it, didn't have Gaborn's keen ears. All six of the ferrin woman's nipples were red and swollen, and she wore a yellow rag tied round her shoulders. She stood only a foot tall, and her pudgy face was accented by thick jowls. She waddled up behind the Days, nearly blinded by daylight, and stuffed the pup in the Days' coat pocket.

The ferrin were not an intelligent people. They had a language of sorts, used some crude tools. Most folk considered them vermin, since the ferrin constantly tunneled into houses to steal food.

Gaborn had heard it was common for a ferrin woman

to wean her pups this way, by finding an inn, then sending the pup off in the pocket of a stranger. But he'd never seen it happen.

Many a man would have tossed a dagger into the ferrin. Gaborn smiled blandly, averted his eyes.

Good, he thought, let the pup eat the lining of the damned historian's coat.

He waited until the ferrin finished.

"And what of me?" Gaborn asked the drunken Days. "Am I a good man?"

"You, Your Lordship, are the soul of virtue!"

Gaborn smiled. He could expect no other answer. In the back of the common room, an Inkarran singer struck up the mandolin, began to practice for the crowd that would gather later. Gaborn had seldom seen an Inkarran play, since his own father would not let them cross the borders, and he enjoyed the diversion now.

The Inkarran had skin as light as cream and hair that fell like liquid silver; his eyes were as green as ice. His body was tattooed in the manner of his tribe – blue symbols of vines twining up his legs, with images that brought to mind the names of his ancestors and his home village. On his knees and arms were images of knots and other magic symbols.

The man sang with a throaty crooning, a very powerful voice. It was beautiful in its own way, and hinted that this singer wore the "hidden runes of talent." The art of creating hidden runes was mastered only by a few Inkarrans. Yet, despite these runes, the singer's voice could not duplicate the ethereal tones sung by the virtuoso outside the songhouse an hour ago. His voice was more generous, Gaborn decided. The woman at the songhouse had sung for wealth and prestige, but this man sung now merely to entertain. A generous gesture.

The Days stared down at his mug, knowing he'd said too much, needing to say one thing more. "Your Lordship, perhaps it is well that you do not value virtue in your friends. You will know not to trust them. And if you are wise, you will not trust yourself."

"How so?" Gaborn asked, wondering. With each Days twinned to another, they were never alone, never had the luxury of trusting themselves. Gaborn wondered if this pairing was really an advantage.

"Men who believe themselves to be good, who do not search their own souls, most often commit the worst atrocities. A man who sees himself as evil will restrain himself. It is only when we do evil in the belief that we do good that we pursue it wholeheartedly."

Gaborn grunted, considering.

"If I may be so bold, Your Lordship, I'm glad you question yourself. Men don't become good by performing an occasional kindly deed. You must constantly reexamine your thoughts and acts, question your virtue."

Gaborn stared at the thin scholar. The man's eyes were getting glassy, and he could barely hold his head up. His thinking seemed somewhat clearer than a common drunk's, and he offered his advice in a kind tone. No Days had ever offered Gaborn advice before. It was a singular experience.

At that moment, the inn door opened. Two more men entered, both with dark complexion, both with brown eyes. They were dressed as merchants fresh off the road, but both wore rapiers at their side, and both had long knives strapped at their knees.

One man smiled, one frowned.

Gaborn remembered something his father had taught him as a child. "In the land of Muyyatin, assassins always travel in pairs. They talk with gestures." Then Gaborn's father had taught him the assassins' codes. One man smiling, one man frowning – *No news, either good or bad*.

Gaborn's eyes flicked across the room, to the two dark men in the far corner. Like himself, they had chosen a secure position, had put their backs to the wall.

One man in the corner scratched his left ear: *We have*

heard nothing.

The newcomers sat at a table on the far side of the room from their compatriots. One man put his hands on the table, palms down. *We wait.*

Yet this man moved with a casual quickness that could only be associated with someone who had an endowment of metabolism. Few men had such an endowment – only highly trusted warriors.

Gaborn almost could not believe what he was seeing. The gestures were so common, so casual. The speakers did not stare at one another. Indeed, what Gaborn thought was a discussion could have been nothing.

Gaborn glanced around the room. No one in the room could be a target for assassins – no one but him. Yet he felt certain he was not their target. He'd traveled in disguise all day. Bannisferre was full of wealthy merchants and petty lords – the assassins could be hunting one of them, or could even be tracking one of their kinsmen from the South.

Gaborn was not properly armed to fight such men.

He rose without explanation and left the inn to search for Borenson. Just as he stood, the serving boy brought a passable dinner of roast pork and fresh bread with plums.

Gaborn left it, made his way into the streets, his Days rising drunkenly to follow after.

Whereas in the morning the city had seemed cool, invigorating, alive, now the heat of the day had intensified the odor. The smell of evaporating urine from pack animals filled the market, along with the scents of dirt and human sweat. The closeness of the buildings in the market held the stench in.

Gaborn hurried down the streets to the stables, where an old horseman from Fleeds brought Gaborn his dun-colored stallion. The horse neighed on seeing Gaborn, held its head high, and raised its blond tail. It seemed as eager to be off as Gaborn did.

Reaching out a hand to stroke his horse's muzzle,

Gaborn inspected the stallion. It had been well tended. Its coat was brushed, tail and mane plaited. Even the teeth were clean. Its belly was fat, and it was still chewing hay.

A few moments later, the stablemaster brought out the Days' white mule. Though it was no force stallion with runes of power branded into its neck, the mule looked as if it had been well groomed, too.

Gaborn kept glancing over his shoulder, looking for signs of more assassins, but spotted nothing out of the ordinary here by the stables.

Gaborn asked the stablemaster, "Have you noticed any men ride into town – men of dark complexion, traveling in pairs?"

The stablemaster nodded thoughtfully, as if just struck by the answer, "Aye, now that you mention it, four like men 'ave their horses stabled wit' me, and I seen four more ride through town late last night, too."

Gaborn frowned. Assassins all along the road, heading north. To where? Castle Sylvarresta, a hundred miles away?

As he left town, Gaborn became more concerned. He took his dun stallion over the Himmeroft Bridge, a picturesque bridge of stone that spanned the broad river. From its top, Gaborn could see large brown trout sunning in the deeper pools, rising up to leap at flies in the shallows, in the shade of the willows. The river here was broad, with deep cold pools. Peaceful.

He saw no sign of assassins here at the bridge.

On the far side of the river, the cobbles gave way to a dirt road that wound off through the country west. A side road went north. The roads met in the woods, and bluebells grew in the woods to the north. So late in the season, none were in bloom. Only a couple of dead flowers stood, ragged and faded to violet. Gaborn turned on to Bluebell Way, let the horse run. It was a force stallion, and had runes of metabolism, brawn, grace, and wit branded on its neck, giving it the speed of three, the strength and grace of two, the wit of four. The stallion was a field hunter by body type – a spirited animal bred for running and jumping through woodland trails. Such a beast was not made to rest in Bannisferre's stables, growing fat on grain.

The Days struggled to keep up on his own white mule, a vile creature that bit at Gaborn's stallion at every opportunity. It soon fell far behind.

Then a bizarre thing happened: Gaborn had been riding through fields, where the newly stacked haycocks hunched beside the river. And the fields were fairly empty, now that the heat of the day was on.

But as Gaborn topped one small hill, three miles out of Bannisferre, he suddenly found himself confronted by a low wispy fog that clung to the ground, shrouding the haycocks ahead in mist.

It was a strange sight, fog rolling in on a sunny day, in the early afternoon. Oak trees and haycocks rose from the mist. The fog seemed off in color, too blue. He'd never seen the like.

Gaborn halted. His horse whinnied, nervous at the sight. Gaborn entered the wall of fog slowly, sniffing.

There was an odd scent in the air, something hard to define. Gaborn had but two endowments of smell, wished he had more. Sulfur, he thought. Perhaps there were hot pools around, and the fog rose from those.

Gaborn spurred his horse forward, along the fields for another half-mile, and the fog grew steadily thicker, until the sun in the sky was only a single yellow eye peering through the haze. Crows cawed in the lonely oak trees.

A mile farther, Gaborn saw a gray house through the mist. A young woman with hair that hung out like straw was chopping wood in front of it. She looked up. From a distance, her skin looked as rough as burlap, her features plain and skeletal, her eyes yellow and sickly. This was one of the sisters who had given Myrrima her beauty.

He spurred his stallion, called out to the young woman.

She gasped, put one arm up to hide her face.

Gaborn rode to her, looked down with pity. "No need to hide. One who diminishes herself to enlarge another is worthy of honor. A foul face often hides a fair heart."

"Myrrima is inside," the girl mumbled. She fled into the house. Borenson quickly came out, Myrrima on his arm.

"It is a beautiful autumn day." Gaborn smiled at Borenson. "I smell sunbaked wheat fields on the wind, and autumn leaves, and . . . treachery."

Borenson gaped at the fog, perplexed. "I thought it was getting cloudy," he said, "I had no idea . . ." He would not have been able to see the fog through the house's parchment windows. He sniffed. Borenson had four endowments of scent. His nose was far keener than Gaborn's. "Giants. Frowth giants." He asked Myrrima, "Do you have many giants around here?"

"No," she said, surprised. "I've never seen one."

"Well, I smell them. A lot of them," Borenson said.

He looked into Gaborn's eyes. They both knew something odd was afoot. Gaborn had come hours ahead of schedule.

Gaborn whispered, "Assassins rode into town. Muyyatin. At least ten are on the road north to Castle Sylvarresta, but I saw none on my way here."

"I'll scout this out," Borenson said. "It could well be that someone is laying a trap for your father. His retinue will pass through town tomorrow."

"Wouldn't I be safer with you?" Gaborn asked.

Borenson considered, nodded. He retrieved his own horse from behind the house, just as the Days rode up through the mist.

"We'll be back in a bit," Gaborn told Myrrima, then spurred his stallion out into the meadow behind her cottage. He felt uneasy leaving her, with giants about. Yet he and Borenson were certainly riding into danger.

A slight breeze sighed from the north, carrying the

haze. They rode toward it, over green meadows. The river twisted west, and they soon found themselves riding along the banks of River Dwindell, on a hay trail.

Along the river, the unnatural fog deepened, rising in a great cloud, making it dark, dark enough so swallows quit dipping in the water, and instead a few bats began diving for insects. Fireflies rose like green sparks out of the bushes. The grass along the river was deep, lush, but cropped short.

All along here, in the floodplain, the farmers had harvested hay. The haycocks stood out along the river, like great rocks in a sea, and each time Gaborn saw one rising from the mist, he wondered if it was a giant, wondered if a giant might be hiding behind it.

Gaborn could smell giants now, too. Their greasy hair smelled bitter, the musk and dung on their skins overwhelming. Mold and lichens grew on their aging bodies.

Until a hundred and twenty years ago, no one in all Rofehavan had heard of frowth giants. Then, a tribe of four hundred of the huge creatures had come over the northern ice one winter, battle-scarred, fearful. Many of them wounded.

The frowth could not speak well in any human tongue, had never quite been able to communicate what fearful enemies chased them over the ice. Yet with a few gestures and the odd spoken command, the giants had learned to work beside men to some extent – lugging huge boulders in quarries, or trees for foresters. The rich lords of Indhopal in particular had taken to hiring frowth giants, so that, in time, most of them migrated south.

But the frowth excelled in only one thing – making war.

Gaborn and Borenson came to a small croft on a hill beneath some trees, beside the river. The cottage's windows were dark. No smoke roiled from its chimney. A dead farmer lay half in the doorway, hand outstretched. His head lay as if he'd died trying to reach for it as it rolled away. The coppery scent of blood hung heavy in the air.

Borenson swore, rode forward. The mist ahead grew thicker. Heavier.

In the green grass, they found steaming human footprints. The grass beneath the footprints was blackened, dead. Gaborn had never seen the like.

"Flameweavers," Borenson said. "Powerful ones – powerful enough to transmute to flame. Five of them."

There were flameweavers in Mystarria, of course, sorcerers who could warm a room or cause a log to burst into flame, but none so powerful that they blackened the ground they trod upon. Not like this.

These were creatures of legend, wizards of such power that they could pry secrets from men's souls, or summon beings of terror from the netherworld.

Gaborn's heart pounded; he looked at Borenson, who was suddenly wary. There were no flameweavers like this in the northern kingdoms, nor so many frowth giants. They could only have come from the south. Gaborn tasted the air again. That fog, that strange fog, a thinly disguised smoke? Raised by the flameweavers? How big an army did it hide?

So our spies were wrong, Gaborn realized. *Raj Ahten's invasion won't wait for spring.*

The flameweavers' footsteps led north, along the banks of the River Dwindell. Raj Ahten's troops must be marching through the woods, to hide their numbers. But they would not go far into the wood, for this was the Dunnwood. Wild, old, and powerful. Few men dared enter its heart. Even Raj Ahten would not do so.

If Gaborn took the road north, he could reach Sylvarresta in half a day.

But of course that was why the assassins watched the road, looking to waylay anyone who sought to warn King Sylvarresta. Gaborn reasoned that given the nature of his horse, a good solid hunter, he might be safer riding through the woods. He knew the dangers. He'd been in the Dunnwood before, hunting the great black boars.

The giant boars in the wood often grew almost as tall as Gaborn's stallion, and over the centuries they had learned to attack riders. But there were more dangerous things in these woods, it was said – ancient duskin ruins still guarded by magic, and the spirits of those who'd died here. Gaborn had once seen such a spirit.

Raj Ahten's men would be on warhorses, heavy creatures bred for battle in the desert, not for speed in the woods.

But even riding fast through the woods, it would take Gaborn a day to reach King Sylvarresta. Such a journey would be hard on his stallion.

Meanwhile, Gaborn's own father was not far south. King Orden was coming north for the autumn hunt, as was his custom, and this time he had a company of over two thousand soldiers. Gaborn was to have formally proposed betrothal to Iome Sylvarresta in a week, and King Orden had brought an impressive retinue for his son.

Now those troops might well be needed in battle.

Gaborn raised his hand, manipulated his fingers quickly in battle sign. *Retreat. Warn King Orden.*

Borenson looked wary, signed, *Where are you going?* *To warn Sylvarresta.*

No! Dangerous! Borenson signed. *Let me go!*

Gaborn shook his head, pointed south.

Borenson glared, signed, *I'll go north. Too dangerous for you!*

But Gaborn could not let him. He'd intended to take a dangerous road to power, to try to become the kind of lord who would win men's hearts. How better to win the hearts of the people of Heredon, than to come to their aid now?

I must go, Gaborn signed forcefully.

Borenson began to argue again. Gaborn whipped out his own saber, aiming just so, slashing Borenson's cheek. The cut was so shallow, the soldier could have got it shaving.

Gaborn fought down his rage. Almost immediately he regretted this impetuous act. Yet Borenson knew better than to argue with his prince in a dangerous situation. Arguments were poison. A man who believes he is doomed to fail tends to fail. Gaborn would listen to no poison arguments.

Gaborn pointed south with his sword, looked at both the Days and Borenson meaningfully. With his free hand, he signed, *Check on Myrrima*. If Raj Ahten's troops slaughtered peasants just to make certain their force wasn't discovered, Myrrima would be in danger.

It seemed a long moment as Borenson considered. Gaborn was no commoner. With his endowments of wit and brawn, he acted more like a man than he did a child, and in the past year, Borenson had begun treating him as an equal, rather than as a charge.

Perhaps more to the point, Borenson himself had to be torn. Both King Orden and King Sylvarresta needed to be warned as soon as possible. He couldn't ride two directions at once.

There are assassins on the road, Gaborn reminded him. *The woods are safer. I will be safe.*

To Gaborn's surprise, the Days turned his mule, headed back. Gaborn had seldom been free of the historian's scrutiny. But the Days' mule couldn't keep up with a force stallion. If he tried to follow, the historian would only get killed.

Borenson reached behind his saddle, pulled his bow and quiver, backed his horse, and handed the weapons to Gaborn. He whispered, "May the Glories guide you safely."

Gaborn would need the bow. He nodded, grateful.

When the men had disappeared through the mist, Gaborn licked his lips, his mouth dry with fear. Preparedness is the father of courage, he reminded himself. A teaching from the Room of the Heart. Yet suddenly all that he'd learned in the House of Understanding seemed . . . inadequate.

He prepared to fight. First he dismounted, removed his fancy feathered hat, tossed it to the ground. It wouldn't do to ride ahead looking like a wealthy merchant. He needed to seem a humble peasant, without benefit of endowments.

He reached into his saddlebags, drew out a stained cloak of gray, threw it over his shoulders. He strung the bow. He had no battle-axe to cut through armor – only his dueling saber, and the dirk strapped at his knee.

Gaborn stretched his arms and shoulders, limbering them. He slid his saber from its sheath, as familiar with its balance as if it were part of his own body, then slid it back carefully.

He couldn't disguise his horse. The beast stood too proudly, like a being of stone or iron come to life. Its eyes glowed with fierce intelligence.

Gaborn whispered in his horse's ear. "We must hurry, my friend, but travel quietly."

The horse nodded. Gaborn couldn't be certain how much it understood. It couldn't follow a conversation. But with endowments of wit from other horses in its herd, it followed several simple verbal commands – which was more than could be said of some men.

Gaborn dared not ride the beast at first. Instead, he led it. There would be outriders, he knew, both behind and before Raj Ahten's army. Gaborn didn't want to be a silhouette in the fog for some archer to practice on.

He began running lightly at a pace he could keep up for days. In the unnatural fog, the fields were strangely quiet.

Field mice scurried from his approach; a lone crow cawed from an oak. Sparrows flew up in a cloud. Somewhere, in the forest, he could hear a cow lowing, wanting to be milked.

For a long time as he ran, there was only the dry rattle of bending grass, the muted thump of his horse's hooves.

As he sprinted north through the close-cropped fields,

he made a personal inventory. As far as Runelords were concerned, he was not powerful. He'd never wanted to be so. He could not bear the guilt he'd have borne to become powerful, the cost in human suffering.

But shortly after birth, his father had begun purchasing endowments for him: two endowments of wit, two of brawn, three of stamina, and three of grace. He had the eyes of two, the ears of three. Five endowments of voice, two of glamour.

Not a powerful man. A weakling compared to Raj Ahten's "Invincibles." He had no endowment of metabolism. Gaborn wore no armor. None to protect him, none to slow him down.

No, Gaborn could rely only on cunning, courage, and the speed of his stallion.

Gaborn passed two more houses, both with dead occupants. At the first, he stopped at a garden, let the horse eat apples from a tree, pocketed a few for himself.

A little beyond the last house, the fields ended at a forest of ash, oak, and maple. The border to the Dunnwood. The leaves on the trees were dull, as they will get in late summer, but so low in the valleys the colors had yet turned.

Following the edge of the field, Gaborn smelled the scent of leather now, of horses hard-ridden, of oiled armor. Still he'd seen no one.

Gaborn found a track for woodcutters' carts leading into the forest. He stopped at the edge of the trees to tighten the cinch on his saddle, preparing to ride hard, when he suddenly heard the creaking of branches.

Just inside the line of trees, not forty feet away, stood a frowth giant. The huge creature, its fur a tawny yellow, stared at him from wide silver eyes, peering into the mist, perhaps unsure whether Gaborn was friend or foe. The sun slanted over the woods, sending shafts of golden light into the giant's face.

The giant stood twenty feet tall, eight feet wide at the

shoulder. Ring mail covered its thick hide; for a weapon it carried a large oak pole bound with iron rings. Its snout was much longer than that of a horse, its mouth full of sharp teeth. The frowth giants looked like nothing human.

The giant flicked one small, round ear, ridding itself of some stinging fly, then pushed a tree aside as it leaned forward, peering.

Gaborn knew enough not to make a quick move. If he did, the giant would know he was an enemy. The fact that the giant hadn't attacked already told Gaborn something: the outriders would be dressed like him, wearing dark robes, riding force horses.

The giant merely wanted to smell Gaborn, to learn whether he was friend or foe. Gaborn would not smell of curry, olive oil, and cotton, as did the soldiers in Raj Ahten's forces.

One way or another, the frowth giant would be after Gaborn in a moment.

Gaborn wanted to strike, but he couldn't drive a sword through such thick ring mail. He couldn't engage the monster in a drawn battle. Couldn't let it cry out in warning. An arrow wouldn't kill the beast quickly.

No, Gaborn's best chance was to let the giant draw close, bend near enough to sniff him, so that Gaborn could pull his saber and slice the monster's throat. Quickly, quietly.

"Friend," Gaborn said softly, reassuringly. He dropped the horse's reins as the giant approached, dropped his bow. The giant warily leaned on his pole, hunched forward, sniffed from ten feet away. Far, too far.

It drew a foot closer, sniffed again. Frowth giants do not have keen noses. The monster must have been two feet between the eyes. Its broad nose wrinkled as it sniffed.

Gaborn smelled rotting meat on its breath, saw dried blood matted into its fur. It had fed on carrion recently.

It drew half a step closer. Gaborn ambled forward, making soft noises as if he were a friendly soldier trying to prove himself.

The size of the beast overwhelmed him. I am nothing beside it. Nothing. It could lift me like a pup. The beast's huge paws were each almost as long as Gaborn's body. It did not matter that Gaborn was a Runelord. Those enormous paws could smash his bones, rake through his muscles.

The silver eyes drew near, each as large as a plate. Not the throat, Gaborn realized. It was too far for a lunge. Don't stab the throat. The eye. The huge silver eyes were not protected by thick pelt.

The creature was old, its face scarred beneath the fur. One of the ancients, then, that had come over the northern ice. A venerable creature. Gaborn wished he knew some of its tongue, had some way to bribe it.

The frowth giant knelt forward, sniffed, and its eyes drew wide in surprise.

Gaborn pulled his saber and lunged, ramming the blade deep. The blade twisted when it hit the giant's eye, slid behind the socket, far into the monster's brain. Gaborn wrenched his saber and danced aside, slicing as he pulled free. He was unprepared for the volume of blood that gushed from the wound.

The giant lurched back, grabbing its eye. Its lower jaw went slack in that moment. It pulled upright, staggered a pace to the left, and raised its muzzle to the sky.

Even as it died, the giant bellowed in warning. A thunderous howl shook the forest.

And all around Gaborn, to the north, south, and west, giants howled in answer.

FIVE: IN THE DEDICATES' TOWER

Below Castle Sylvarresta that evening, the city lay quiet, hushed. Traders from the South had come in unusually large numbers throughout the day – caravans bringing valuable spices and dyes, ivory and cloth from Indhopal.

Bright silk pavilions decorated the greens before the castle, the lanterns within the tents making them glow like multicolored gems – jade, emerald, topaz, and sapphire.

From the dark, forbidding stone of the castle walls, it seemed a beautiful yet discomfiting sight.

The guards on the wall all knew that the "spice merchant" had been ransomed too quickly that day, the King's outrageous price accepted without argument. But the Southerners could not be happy about the ransom. Tempers were short. Everyone feared the Indhopalese might riot.

But with caravans of pack mules and horses came something new and marvelous, something never seen in all the centuries merchants had traveled from Indhopal:

Elephants. Fourteen white elephants, one branded with runes of power. The elephants wore colorful mats made of silk and beads and gold and pearls on their heads, and bore decorative reins and silk pavilions on their backs.

Their owner, a one-eyed man with grizzled beard, said he'd brought them as a curiosity. But in Castle Sylvarresta it was known that in Indhopal force elephants were often dressed in armor, then sent to ram castle gates.

And the merchants had too many "guards" hired to protect the caravans. "Ah, yes," the merchants would say, clasping their hands beneath their chins and bowing. "The hill bandits are very bad this year. Almost as bad as the reavers in the mountains!"

Indeed it seemed a record year for reavers. Troops of them had harried the mountain borders to the south in Fleeds, and to the west in Orwynne. Sylvarresta's soldiers had even discovered tracks in the Dunnwood last spring – the first such tracks seen in thirty years.

So the people of Heredon were willing to overlook the hordes of guards in the caravans, and few but King Sylvarresta and his troops worried about elephants in their midst.

A cool wind blew in after sunset, and fog began roiling off the river. A fog that wreathed the city in mist, crept to the parapets of the Outer Wall.

No moon burned in the sky. Only stars. Bright eternal diadems shining in the fields of night.

It is no surprise that the assassins made it over the Outer Wall unobserved. Perhaps the men came into the city during the day, acting the part of traders, then hid in some dovecote or manor-house stable. Or perhaps in their escalade the men took advantage of the way wisps of fog seemed to play between the merlons like tendrils.

Nor was it a surprise when a lone sentry in the King's Keep spotted shadowy figures, like black spiders, scrambling over the King's Wall, down by the Butterwalk.

The King had set extra eyes to watch that direction. Indeed, eyes watched from every arrow slit along each tower.

No, it was no surprise that the assassins attempted an escalade that night. But even the guards felt amazed at how swiftly the assassins came, how silent and deadly.

Only men with endowments of metabolism could move

so fast, so swiftly that if you blinked, you almost believed you hadn't seen them. To take such endowments was suicide: an endowment of metabolism let you move nearly twice as fast as a normal man, but also caused you to age at twice the speed.

Yet as the King's far-seer, Sir Millman, watched the escalade, he suspected that some of those assassins were moving at three times the normal human rate. Men so endowed would be decrepit in ten years, dead in fifteen.

And only men with inhuman strength could climb those walls, prying with toes and fingers to grip at cracks in the stone. Sir Millman couldn't even guess how many endowments of brawn each assassin had.

Millman had been watching from inside the King's Tower. With endowments of sight from seven men, he was well qualified for this post. Now he called softly at the door to the King's chamber, "Milord, our guests have arrived."

King Sylvarresta had been sitting in his father's favorite old reading chair, his back to the wall, studying the tome of Emir Owatt of Tuulistan, trying to decipher which of Raj Ahten's battle tactics were so original that he'd kill to keep them secret.

Now Sylvarresta blew out his lantern, went to the oriel, and gazed out a clear pane in the stained-glass window. The window was so old that the glass was all wavy and distorted, had flowed down like lumps of melted butter.

The assassins had just reached the final defensive wall in Castle Sylvarresta, the wall of the Dedicates' Keep, which houses those people who had granted endowments to House Sylvarresta, for the use of the King's family and soldiers.

So, Raj Ahten's assassins came to destroy Sylvarresta's Dedicates, murder those whose minds and strength and vitality fed the King's forces.

It was a vile deed. The Dedicates could not protect themselves. The brilliant young men who'd given endowments of wit no longer knew their right hands from their left. Those who had granted brawn now lay like babes, too weak to climb from their beds. It was craven to kill Dedicates.

Yet, sadly, too often it was the easiest way to assail a Runelord. By murdering those who constantly fed a Runelord strength and support, one deprived the lord of his powers, making him into a common man.

As the attack progressed, Sylvarresta barely had time to marshal his defenders. Boiling oil had been lugged up to the wall-walk shortly after dark. Though the normal complement of three guards marched along the parapet, a dozen more crouched behind the battlements out of sight.

Still, defenders needed to be warned. Archers manned the towers; soldiers hiding in the city needed to be notified so that they could cut off the assassins' escape.

From behind his stained-glass window, Sylvarresta watched the assassins reach the halfway point on the stone wall of the keep; then the King opened the window and blew a soft, shrill, whistle.

As one, his soldiers leapt up and poured oil down the keep's walls, tossing great iron cauldrons over as they emptied. The oil did not have the desired effect. It had cooled too much since sunset, and though the assassins cried in dismay at their burns and some plummeted when swept from the walls by falling cauldrons, more than twenty still scrambled up the walls, swift as lizards.

The guards atop the Dedicates' Keep drew swords and pikes. From the King's Keep, some hundred yards distant, archers let arrows fly. A few more assassins plummeted, but Raj Ahten's knights were frighteningly swift, terrifyingly determined.

King Sylvarresta had imagined the assassins would run when they met resistance. Instead they scurried faster, reaching the tops of the parapet, where razor wire hindered them. Sylvarresta's soldiers hacked at the assassins, so that a dozen more plummeted from the keep's tower.

Still, seven assassins won the top of the tower, where their incredible skills as fighters came into play. The assassins moved so swiftly, Sylvarresta's men could not well defend themselves. Yet four more assassins got cut down, while a dozen defenders were slaughtered.

The three remaining assassins hurtled down the steps into the Dedicates' Keep – just as the King's pikemen rushed from the guardroom beneath the portcullis.

The assassins ignored the guards, instead leapt to the iron gate that covered one low door to the Dedicates' Hall. Though the door was barred with heavy iron, two assassins grabbed a bar and pulled, ripping it from the wall, dislodging two-hundred-pound stones set with mortar.

The third assassin faced the pikemen, ready to defend.

But these pikemen were no common soldiers.

Captain Derrow and Captain Ault came, side by side, holding back nothing. Captain Ault stabbed at the assassin's head, a lightning thrust.

The assassin dodged, his own short sword snaking out, biting Ault's gloved hand. The assassin was a dark monster, draped in robes of black, a man whose speed astonished. He shifted on his feet, weaving from side to side so quickly that no commoner could have landed a blow. He drew a second knife, his hands whirling in the deadly Dancing Arms style.

In that second, the door to the Dedicates' Keep screamed as if in agony. The two assassins pulled the door wide. One assassin bolted through the door.

Captain Derrow swung his pike as if it were an axe. An assassin by the door took a firm knock to the head.

The assassin guard ducked. As Ault had anticipated his move and lunged. Ault slammed the pike into the man's chest, then lifted, flinging the assassin up and aside.

Ault tossed away the pike, drew a long dagger, and bolted into the Dedicates' Keep.

*

Inside, Ault found that the last assassin had already slaughtered two guards posted by the door, then had run into the hall, felling some five or six Dedicates who should have been abed. Even now, the assassin knelt over a victim, scimitar in hand.

Ault threw his short sword, caught the assassin solidly in the back. Had the assassin been a commoner, he'd have collapsed. Had he been an angered man with great stamina, he'd have turned and gone berserk.

What the assassin did next chilled Ault to the bone.

The assassin turned, all dressed in a black caftan and black cotton pants, a black kerchief hiding his face. A gold ring glittered in his ear.

He studied Ault thoughtfully, eyes filled with deadly intent. Ault's heart pounded, for he wondered how many endowments of stamina it took for a man to ignore a sword in his back.

A dozen soldiers rushed through the broken door, filling the Dedicates' Keep. Ault took a hammer from a dead guard.

The assassin looked Captain Ault in the eye, then raised his hands. He said in a thick accent, "Barbarian: As you see this tide of men sweep over me, so shall my lord's Invincibles sweep over you!"

Raj Ahten's Invincibles were elite troops – men with great stamina, each of whom had at least one endowment of metabolism. The assassin made as if to charge. Yet Ault knew it would be a feint. Having won through to the Dedicates' Keep, the assassin would now continue with his duty, to slay as many Dedicates as possible.

Ault lunged, swinging his hammer, just as the assassin spun toward the beds of the sleeping. The warhammer bit into the assassin's neck.

"Don't bet on it," Ault said.

In his keep, King Sylvarresta felt the deaths of his Dedicates as he began to lose his magical connection to them. It was a nauseating sensation, like a cold snake writhing through his innards. Men who had endowed him with wit died, and Sylvarresta was assailed by a sudden emptiness as rooms of memory closed off forever.

He'd never know what he'd lost – memories of friends from childhood or a picnic in the forest, memories of important sword strokes practiced time and again with his father, or a perfect sunset, or a wife's kiss.

He only became aware that he was sundered. The doors to the rooms of memory slammed shut. The shutters to the windows fell. And in his mind there was a great moment of darkness, a keen sense of loss.

As he rushed downstairs to guard his Dedicates himself if need be, he felt as if he wallowed through the darkness.

A minute later, Sylvarresta reached the Dedicates' Bailey, counted his losses. Ten guards dead, five wounded. And five Dedicates lost.

In studying the corpses of the Muyyatin assassins, he found that each had been formidable. Their leader, whom Ault had slain had over seventy runes burned into his flesh. With so many endowments, he had to have been a captain among the Invincibles. Many others had twenty runes or more, making them equal to Captain Derrow.

Five of Sylvarresta's Dedicates lay dead. Two gentlemen who had granted Sylvarresta wit, two who had granted sight to the King, and one who had granted sight to the King's far-seer. Sylvarresta imagined that the blind men must have been telling stories by the hearth, and the sound of their voices had brought the idiots.

When the body count was taken, Sylvarresta considered himself lucky. It could have been worse. If the assassins had made it farther into the Dedicates' Keep, the result would have been devastating.

Yet King Sylvarresta could not help but wonder at what he'd lost. He'd had endowments of wit from five men. Now he'd lost forty percent of all his memories, of years of studies. What had he known five minutes ago that he might need to remember in days to come . . .?

He considered the dead, wondering. Was this attack a precursor to next year's war?

Had Raj Ahten sent assassins to attack all the kings of the North, in an attempt to weaken them? Or was this a part of some more daring scheme?

Sylvarresta's readings in the Emir's book made him worry. Raj Ahten seldom bothered with feints. Instead he singled out castles, striking with ferocity, overwhelming his opponents, then consolidated his position before moving on.

It seemed odd to Sylvarresta that Raj Ahten would target Heredon. It was not the closest neighbor to Raj Ahten. Nor was it the least defensible of the northern realms.

Yet he recalled his chess game from so many years ago. The way Raj Ahten struggled to control even far corners of the board. Though Heredon was at the edge of Raj Ahten's board, the consequences of its loss would be devastating: Raj Ahten would take a Northern country, forcing Fleeds and Mystarria to defend on fronts both to their north and south. Heredon was not a poor country. Sylvarresta's smiths were the finest makers of arms and armor in Rofehavan, and the land was rich in cattle for food, sheep for wool, in timber to build fortifications and engines of war, and in vassals to give endowments.

Raj Ahten would need all of these to take the North.

My wife is his cousin, Sylvarresta reminded himself. Perhaps he imagines she is a danger to him. Heaven knows, Venetta Sylvarresta would have stabbed Raj Ahten in his sleep years ago, if she'd had the chance.

Is this part of a grander scheme? Sylvarresta worried. Attacks like this could be taking place in every castle in Rofehavan. If all the assassins struck simultaneously, Sylvarresta would not have time to warn his fellow kings.

He rubbed his eyes, lost in speculation.

Book 2:
Day 20 in the Month of Harvest,
A Day of Sacrifice

SIX: MEMORIES OF SMILES

In the forests of the Dunnwood, Prince Gaborn rode in silence through the starlight, avoiding the narrow gullies and darker woods where wights might congregate.

The trees above him were twisted things, with limbs half-bare, the yellow birch leaves waggling in the night wind like fingers. The carpet of leaves beneath his horse's hooves was deep and lush, making for a quiet ride.

Shortly after dusk the sorcerous mists had begun to fail. Raj Ahten no longer needed such mists to hide him. Instead, now the stars overhead shone with unnatural clarity, perhaps because of some spell cast by Raj Ahten's flameweavers, gathering light so that they might let the Wolf Lord's army pick their way through the woods.

For hours Gaborn had been circumventing Raj Ahten's army, evading pursuers. He'd managed to kill two more frowth giants, and he shot an outrider from his saddle. But Gaborn had seen no sign of pursuit for three hours.

As he rode, he wondered. The Dunnwood was an old wood, and a queer place by any standard. There were the ghosts and magic pools, of course. The headwaters of the River Wye were said to be magical places, where three-hundred-year-old sturgeons as wise as any sage lived in the deep pools.

But it was not these that Gaborn wondered at. It was the woods' legendary affinity for "right" and "law." The Sky Lords, it was said, avoided flying their ships of cloud above these woods. Few outlaws had ever penetrated the forest. There was Edmon Tillerman, of course, who came into the woods as an outlaw, a madman who took endowments of brawn and wit from bears until he became a creature of the wood himself. According to the folktales, he left off his stealing, and in time became a hero – avenging poor farmers wronged by other outlaws, protecting the woodland creatures.

But there were stranger stories still: the old woman centuries ago who was murdered and hidden in a pile of leaves in the Dunnwood, who then became a creature of wood and sticks that hunted down her killers.

Or what of the giant "stone men" that some said walked these woods? Creatures that sometimes came to the edge of the forest and stood gazing thoughtfully to the south?

And why had the ancient duskins split these woods, creating Harm's Gorge, that great tear in the fabric of the earth? And why did they erect the legendary Seven Standing Stones of the Dunnwood, which "upheld" the world?

There was a time – centuries ago, it was said – when these woods loved man more than they did now. A time when men could travel them freely. Now, a stillness, a heaviness, had come under the trees, as if the wood itself were outraged and considering retaliation against so many uninvited men. Certainly the heat of the flameweavers, the iron-shod hooves of horses, the mass of men and giants would all cause some damage to the forest.

Raj Ahten's march was nothing like the more gentle hunts that King Sylvarresta arranged, where men asked permission of the wood before the hunt, and offered plantings of trees and heaps of dung as gifts. During last year's hunt, Sylvarresta's men had brought in their own wood to burn, had asked the blessings of Binnesman the Earth Warden before entering.

This march of Raj Ahten's was much like a rape. But what could the forest do?

The owls had fallen silent this night, and twice Gaborn had seen huge harts bounding through the trees, shaking their great antlers from side to side as if prepared to fight.

Off to his right, the armies marched. A feeling pervaded the forest, like the electric thrill of a brewing storm. Perhaps the forest would let tree branches drop on the men, Gaborn wondered, or the leaves of the trees would draw tight, blanketing the army's path with darkness; or maybe roots would grasp at horses' hooves, felling riders – though Gaborn had only heard of such things in fairy tales.

He doubted that the forest could stop the men. Not with the flameweavers ready to offer reprisals. No, the forest would have to suffer the ill use.

For long hours, Gaborn rode through the trees, a heaviness growing in his heart, a drowsiness fogging his mind. It was a sweet, organic tiredness – like that brought on by mulled wine while one sits beside a fire, or like the drugged sleep induced by an herbalist's concoction of poppy petals.

Gaborn's eyelids began to feel weighty. He half-dozed as he rode up a ridge, around a peak, and back down into a valley, where brambles and limbs blocked his every path.

He became angry, drew his saber, and considered hacking his way through the trees, but stopped when he heard curses just ahead of him, and the sound of someone else, a man in armor, hacking through the same copse.

Almost too late he recognized the source of this danger. Somehow he'd turned around in his ride.

The trees. He wondered if *they* had led him to danger.

In the shadowed woods, Gaborn stopped. Among the trees, he glimpsed one of Raj Ahten's patrols. A dozen scouts hacked a path through the brush, while Gaborn held perfectly still.

They passed in the darkness. Gaborn feared even to breathe.

He reined in his horse, hard, and inhaled deeply. For long moments he tried to focus his thoughts. *No harm*, he wanted to say to the woods. *I mean you no harm*.

It required all his will to merely sit ahorse, to keep from riding headlong toward destruction. Sweat broke out on Gaborn's forehead, his hands trembled, and his breathing came ragged.

I am your friend, he wanted to say. *Feel me. Test me*. For long moments, he tried to open himself, his mind and heart, to communicate to the wood.

He felt the tendrils of thought move slowly, seeking him, grasping him as a root might grasp a stone. He could feel their ponderous power.

The trees seized him, infiltrated every portion of his mind. Memories and childhood fears began to flash before Gaborn's eyes – unwanted bits of dreams and adolescent fantasies. Every hope and deed and desire.

Then, just as slowly, the seeking tendrils began to withdraw.

"Bear me no malice," Gaborn whispered to the trees when at last he could speak. "Your enemies are my enemies. Let me pass safely, that I may defeat them."

After many long heartbeats, the heaviness around him seemed to ease. Gaborn let his mind drift and dream, though with his stamina he needed no sleep.

He thought upon the thing that had brought him north, his desire to see Iome Sylvarresta.

On a mad impulse last year, he had come secretly to Heredon for the autumn hunt, so that he could take the measure of her. His father came annually for Hostenfest, the autumn celebration of the great day, some sixteen hundred years past, when Heredon Sylvarresta had speared a reaver mage here. Now, each year in the Month of Harvest, the lords of Heredon rode through the Dunnwood, hunting the great boars, practicing the same skills with lance that had been used to defeat the reavers.

So Gaborn had come to the hunt hidden in his father's

retinue as if he were a mere squire. His father's soldiers all knew he'd come, of course, but none dared openly speak his name or break his cover. Even King Sylvarresta had noted Gaborn's presence during the hunt, but because of his fine manners dared not speak of it, until Gaborn chose to reveal himself.

Oh, Gaborn had played his part as squire well for the casual observer, helping soldiers don their armor for the tournament games, sleeping in Sylvarresta's stables at night, caring for horses and gear through the week's hunt. But he'd also been able to sit at table in the Great Hall during the feast marking the end of Hostenfest, though as a mere squire he sat at the far end, away from the kings and nobles and knights. There he'd gawked openly, as if he'd never eaten in the presence of a foreign king.

All the better to view Iome at a distance, her dark smoldering eyes and dark hair, her flawless skin. His father had said she was beautiful of face, and by recounting the tales of things she'd said over the years, Gaborn felt convinced she was beautiful of heart.

He'd been well schooled in etiquette, but he learned a bit about Northern manners at that dinner. In Mystarria, it was customary to wash one's hands in a bowl of cool water before the feast, but here in the North one washed both hands and face in bowls that were steaming hot. While in the South one dried one's hands by wiping them on one's tunic, here in the North thick towels were provided, then draped over one's knee afterward, where they could be used for wiping grease or for blowing one's nose.

In the South, small dull knives and tiny forks were provided for feasts, so that if a fight broke out, no one would be properly armed. But here in the North, one ate with one's own knife and fork.

The most disgusting difference in custom came in the matter of dogs. In the South, a gentleman always threw his bones over the right shoulder to feed the dogs. But

here in the Great Hall, all the dogs had been taken outside, so bones were left cluttering the place – in a most
beastly and uncivilized pile – until the serving children
removed them.

Yet one more thing came to Gaborn's attention. At first
he'd thought it a custom of the North, but soon realized
it was only a custom of Iome.

In all realms that Gaborn knew of, table servants were
not allowed to eat until the King and his guests finished
dining. Since the feast lasted from noon until long in the
night – with entertainment provided between courses by
minstrels and jesters and games of skill – the servants, of
course, wouldn't eat until near midnight.

So as the King and his guests dined, the serving
children stared longingly at the puddings and capons.

Gaborn had eaten greedily, clearing his plate – a show
of respect for the lord's fare. But soon he saw that Iome
left a bite or two of food on each plate, and Gaborn wondered if he'd erred in his manners. He studied Iome: as
her serving girl, a child of perhaps nine, would bring each
plate, one would see the longing on the girl's face.

Iome would smile and thank the girl, as if she were
some lord or lady bestowing a favor instead of a mere servant. Then Iome would gaze at the serving girl's face,
gauging how savory the child thought the dish. If the girl
liked the food well, Iome would leave a few bites, and the
girl would snatch them from the plate as she headed for
the kitchens.

So Gaborn felt surprised when Iome hardly touched a
stuffed partridge in orange sauce, but ate a plate of cold
spiced cabbage as if it were a delicacy.

It was not until the fourth curse that Gaborn noticed
that his own serving boy, a lad of four, had been steadily
growing more pale at the thought that he might not get a
bite to eat till midnight.

When the boy brought a trencher of rich beef stewed
in wine, shallots, and walnuts, Gaborn waved it away, let-

ting the child rush off and nibble while the food was yet warm.

To Gaborn's surprise, King Sylvarresta noted his action and stared hard at Gaborn, as if Gaborn had given insult. Gaborn marked the look well.

However, when Iome did the same thing not five seconds later, completely unaware of Gaborn's faux pas or her father's reaction to it, Sylvarresta sat chewing his beef thoughtfully, then addressed his daughter in a loud voice, "Is the food not to your liking, precious? Perhaps the cooks could be brought in and beaten, if they have offended you?"

Iome blushed at the jest. "I . . . no – the food is too good, milord. I fear I am a bit full. The cooks should be commended, rather than reprimanded."

King Sylvarresta laughed, gave Gaborn a sly wink. Though Gaborn had not yet declared himself, the King's wink had said, *You two are alike. I would welcome the match.*

But, in fact, from his few glimpses, Gaborn had decided that perhaps he was not worthy of Iome. Her serving girl's eyes had shone with too much love for Iome, and when those around her spoke, they held a tone of mingled affection and respect that bordered on reverence. Though Iome was herself only a girl of sixteen at the time, those who knew her best did not merely love her: they treasured her.

When Gaborn had prepared to leave Heredon, his father had taken him to speak privately with King Sylvarresta.

"So," King Sylvarresta had said. "You've come to visit my realm at last."

"I'd have come before," Gaborn said, "but my schooling prevented it."

"You will come again next year," King Sylvarresta had said. "More openly, I hope."

"Indeed, milord," Gaborn had said. His heart had

pounded as he added, "I look forward to it. There is a matter between us, milord, that we must discuss."

Gaborn's father had reached out and touched Gaborn's elbow, warning him to be silent, but Sylvarresta had merely laughed, his gray eyes wise and knowing. "Next year," he'd said.

"But it is an important matter," Gaborn had said.

With a look of warning, King Sylvarresta had said. "You are overeager, young man. You come seeking my greatest treasure. Perhaps it shall be yours. But I will not command my daughter in this matter. You must win her. Next year."

The winter had seemed long and cold, gray and lonely.

It felt odd now for Gaborn to be coming north, seeking to win the love of a woman he'd never spoken to.

As he reflected, the twang of a bowstring roused him, followed immediately by a brilliant burning in the flesh of his right arm as an arrow scraped his skin.

Gaborn gouged his heels into the flanks of his mount. It leapt forward so swiftly that Gaborn fell back and barely was able to cling on as the horse raced under the trees.

The world went dark. Gaborn's mind blanketed from pain. He couldn't imagine where the bowshot had come from. He'd smelled no one, heard no warning.

Almost immediately he passed a thick knot of trees. A darkly cowled rider there was tossing down his horse bow, drawing a curved scimitar from the sheath at his back. As Gaborn passed, he saw only the frantic, killing gleam in the man's eyes, the taper of his grizzled goatee.

Then Gaborn's horse raced past, leapt a fallen tree, and became a blur in the starlight. Gaborn pulled himself upright in the saddle, dizzy with pain, feeling blood flow liberally from the gash on his arm. Three inches to the left, and the arrow would have punched into a lung.

Behind him, his attacker howled like a wolf and began his pursuit. The answering howls of dogs came from off to

Gaborn's right – war dogs that would catch his scent.

For a long hour he rode over hills, not stopping to stanch his wound. He'd been at the rear of the army, trying to circle behind their scouts. Now he sought to evade pursuit by rushing ahead of the hosts to the west, striking deep into the heart of the wood. As he got farther away, the stars dimmed, as if high clouds obscured their light, and he found it hard to keep to any trail.

So, hoping his pursuers would think he'd fled, Gaborn veered back toward the main force of the army, directly into danger. For he still had not been able to learn the number and types of their forces.

When the starlight suddenly came bright, he heard the sounds of the army in the woods below – branches snapping, iron-shod feet tramping in the night. His horse rested near the crest of a ridge, in a sheltered grotto that let him look down over a long bed of ferns.

Dogs began baying in the distance behind him. They'd discovered his ruse.

Gaborn sat tall in his saddle, looking down into the dark. He'd veered in front of the army. A mile ahead he could see a break in the woods – a wide swale that would have been a frozen lake in the winter. But the waters had receded over the summer, leaving only tall grasses.

There, in the grasses, Gaborn saw a sudden light as Raj Ahten's flameweavers stepped from beneath the shelter of the pines – five people, naked but for the red flames that licked their hairless skins, strode boldly across the swale. Behind and around them Gaborn saw something else – creatures that loped over the grass, black shadows darker than those thrown by the pines. They were roughly man-shaped, but often seemed to fall to all fours, running on their knuckles.

Apes? Gaborn wondered. He'd seen such creatures brought north as curiosities. Raj Ahten had frowth giants and flameweavers in his retinue, along with Invincibles and war dogs. Gaborn thought it might be possible to grant endowments to apes, turn them into warriors.

But instinctively Gaborn knew that these creatures were nothing he'd ever seen. Larger than apes. Nomen, perhaps – creatures recalled only in ancient tales. Or maybe some new horror in the earth. Thousands of them issued from the woods, a dark tide of bodies.

Frowth giants waded among them, and Raj Ahten's Invincibles rode behind in armor that flashed in the starlight.

Far below to the west, war dogs howled and snarled, following Gaborn's blood scent. Gaborn glimpsed a dog on the trail in the starlight – a huge mastiff with an iron collar and a leather mask to protect its face and eyes. The pack leader. It would be branded with runes of power, to let it run faster and farther than its brothers, smell Gaborn more easily, and plot with the supernatural cunning of its kind.

Gaborn couldn't escape the pack, not with that dog alive.

He nocked an arrow, the last in his quiver. The grizzled mastiff raced up the path at incredible speed, it's back and head showing from time to time as it leapt through low ferns. With endowments of strength and metabolism, such dogs could cover miles in minutes.

Gaborn watched its progress, gauged where it would exit the ferns below him. The mastiff burst from the ferns a hundred yards down, snarling in rage, its mask making it look skeletal in the starlight.

The beast was only fifty yards away when Gaborn loosed his arrow. It flew to its mark, striking the dog's leather mask, then ricocheted over its head.

The mastiff raced forward.

Gaborn didn't have time to clear his saber from its scabbard.

The mastiff leapt. Gaborn saw its jaws gaping, the huge nick in its forehead where the arrow had pierced the leather, scraped away flesh.

Gaborn threw himself back in the saddle. The mastiff jumped and brushed past Gaborn's chest, the spikes on its collar slashing Gaborn's robe, drawing blood on his chest.

The stallion whinnied in terror and leapt over the crest of the hill, raced through the pines as Gaborn struggled to dodge low branches and remain ahorse.

Then his steed was racing down a steep, rocky hill. Gaborn managed to draw his sword clear, though his bow had been swept away in the branches.

I don't need it, Gaborn tried to reassure himself. I'm ahead of Raj Ahten's army now. I only need to race him.

He put heels to horse flesh, let the beast run its heart out, and raised his sword flashing in the night.

Here in the mountains, the trees had begun to thin, so that for the first time in hours he could test this horse's speed.

It leapt an outcropping of rocks, and Gaborn heard a snarl at his left elbow.

"Clear!" Gaborn shouted. His steed leapt and kicked – a maneuver all his father's hunting horses were taught. It was meant to clear wolves or charging boars from beneath the horse's hooves.

Now the war dog took an iron shoe full in the muzzle, yelped as its neck snapped.

But on the ridge above him, Gaborn heard yammers and growls of another dozen dogs. He looked up. Riders in dark mantles thundered behind the dogs, and one man raised a horn to his lips and blew, calling his fellows to the hunt.

Too close, I'm too close to the army, he realized.

But Raj Ahten was only skirting the edge of the Dunnwood, afraid to get too far under the older trees. For good reason.

Last fall, when Gaborn had hunted here with his father and King Sylvarresta, a hundred men had ringed themselves with campfires, feasting on roasted chestnuts, fresh venison, mushrooms, and mulled wine.

Sir Borenson and Captain Derrow had practiced their swordplay, each man mesmerizing the crowd with his tactics. Borenson was a master of the Dancing Arms style of battle, could swing a sword or axe in dizzying patterns so quickly that one seldom saw when he would deal his deadly blow. Captain Derrow was a more thoughtful fighter, who would choose his moment, then lunge in with a spear and slash a man into morsels with fascinating precision.

Gaborn's father and King Sylvarresta had been playing chess on the ground, beside a lamp, ignoring the mock combats, when a moaning floated through the trees, a sound so distinctly odd and eerie that goose pimples rose, cold as ice, on Gaborn's back.

Borenson, Derrow, and a hundred retainers had all stopped instantly at that sound, and someone called, "Hold! Hold! No one move!" for everyone knew it was deadly dangerous to attract a wight's attention.

Gaborn recalled clearly how Borenson had smiled, his teeth flashing in that deadly way of his, as he stood sweating, looking up at the hillside of the narrow gully outside camp.

A pale figure rode there, a lone man on a horse, moaning like some strange wind that whipped through lonely crags. A gray light shone from him.

Gaborn only glimpsed the wight, yet his heart had pounded in terror at the sight. His mouth went dry, and he could not catch his breath.

He'd looked over at his father to see his reaction. Both his father and King Sylvarresta remained playing at their board, neither bothering to glance up toward the wight.

Yet Gaborn's father moved his wizard on the board, taking a pawn, then caught Gaborn's eye. Gaborn's face must have been pale as death, for his father smiled wryly and said, "Gaborn, calm yourself. No prince of Mystarria need fear the wights of the Dunnwood. We are permitted here."

King Sylvarresta had laughed mirthlessly and turned to

give Gaborn a sly, secretive look, as if the men shared a private joke.

Yet Gaborn had felt it was true, felt he was somehow protected from the wights. It was said that in days of old, the King of Heredon had commanded this forest, and all the creatures in the wood had obeyed him. The kings of Heredon had fallen in stature. Still, Gaborn wondered if Sylvarresta really did command the wights of Dunnwood.

Now, as the war dogs and the hunters trailed him, Gaborn gambled that it was true. He spurred his horse west, deeper into the forest, shouting, "Spirits of the wood, I am Gaborn Val Orden, Prince of Mystarria. I beg you, protect me!"

Even as he called for aid, he knew it would do no good. The spirits of the dead care nothing for the concerns of mortal men. If Gaborn attracted their attention, they'd only seek to make sure he joined them in the afterlife.

His horse thundered down a long ridge, under the boughs of some huge oaks and into a swamp, where it had to swim through brackish water to reach the brush on the far bank.

Gaborn heard no haunting moans as his horse climbed the far shore, only the grunts and squeals of hundreds of huge pigs that raced from him as if they were hunted. He'd inadvertently wandered into a sounder of wild boar. One of the great black shaggy beasts, as tall as his horse, stood its ground for a moment, ivory tusks curling out like sabers, and Gaborn thought it would skewer his horse. At the last second the boar turned and rushed away with the herd.

Gaborn took the opportunity to ride his horse under the oaks in a few quick circles, then drove his horse harder than ever – jumped a screen of rushes over a steep embankment and landed sixty feet out into the deep water before swimming to the far shore.

*

Just past noon the next day, Gaborn raced out of the Dunnwood. Bedraggled and smeared with blood, he shouted to the guards at the city gates a warning of the impending attack. Upon showing the guards his signet ring, which identified him as the Prince of Mystarria, he was immediately escorted to King Sylvarresta.

The King met Gaborn in the Great Hall, where he was already closeted with all his counselors. Gaborn rushed forward to grasp hands, but the King stopped him with a look. Though Gaborn had met him before, Sylvarresta seemed distant.

"Milord," Gaborn said, bowing only slightly, as befitting his rank. "I've come to warn you of an attack, Raj Ahten's armies are south – in the Dunnwood, coming fast. They should arrive by nightfall."

A look of concern and uncertainty flashed over the King's face, and he glanced at Captain Ault, saying, "Prepare for the siege – quickly." Many another king would have trusted his captains to see to the details, but now Sylvarresta spoke . . . uncertainly, it seemed to Gaborn, listing odd commands as if for Ault's approval. "Send a detail through the city to make sure our roofs are fire-proofed. As for the Southern traders camped outside – I fear we must do them the discourtesy of seizing their goods. But don't engage in unnecessary butchery. Leave them mounts to ride home, and enough stores so that they don't starve on the trek. Oh, and kill the elephants outside the castle. I won't have them battering down our gates."

"Yes, milord," Ault said, his face clouded with concern. Then he saluted and rushed out.

The preparations were begun hastily enough, and in that moment, several counselors took leave of the room. Gaborn felt that something was terribly amiss.

As the counselors filed out, during an uncomfortable silence, King Sylvarresta studied Gaborn from worried gray eyes. "I owe you a great debt, Prince Orden. We suspected something like this, but hoped it would not come until spring. We already suffered an attack by Raj Ahten last night. Assassins struck at our Dedicates. We were ready for them, though, so the damage is not too great."

Suddenly, Gaborn understood, Sylvarresta's coldness, his uncertainty. The King did not remember him.

Sylvarresta said, "Well met, Prince Orden!"

He shouted over Gaborn's shoulders, "Collin, get food and a bath for Prince Orden – and clean clothes. We can't have our friends wandering about in bloody rags."

Gaborn felt thankful for the embrace, for just then an overwhelming fear struck him and Gaborn needed support. If Sylvarresta has forgotten my face, Gaborn realized, what else has he forgotten? What of tactics in battle? What of self-defense.

Of course, that was why the King's advisors had gathered, to pool their knowledge. But against a monster like Raj Ahten, would their resources be enough?

SEVEN: PREPARATIONS

That afternoon Sylvarresta's people were still preparing for battle. The initial hysteria of the impending attack – the screaming of children and peasants, the mad rush as the elderly and infirm fled the city – had all passed. Now uneasy farmers and soldiers alike manned the Outer Wall, and had thrown up hasty barriers to serve as battlements in the streets. Not in four hundred years had so many people gathered on the walls – for many who would not fight stood watch out of sheer curiosity.

Pigs, cattle, sheep, and chickens scurried through the alleys and greens, frightened, disoriented. All the animals in the countryside had been herded within the walls – to feed the city's inhabitants during siege, while at the same time denying a similar succor to Raj Ahten's troops.

In the brown fields outside the castle, the Southern merchants had disbanded, driven off with their bright pavilions and little else.

Throughout the afternoon, Raj Ahten's troops began massing on the southern hilltop at the edge of the forest, consolidating their forces. At first, only the Invincibles showed themselves, knights in dark splint mail or plate, wearing tunics of gold and red. Yet they kept to the edge of the forest, hiding their numbers. As the day lengthened, giants and war dogs also joined their ranks.

By then, the city was effectively under siege. No one would dare come in or go out, though Raj Ahten's siege engines had not yet made it through the woods. Instead, the Southern soldiers began to busy themselves by cutting trees to build fortifications.

Defenders on the castle walls stood ready – archers and pikemen, spearmen and artillery. King Sylvarresta had sent messengers to neighboring castles, calling for aid.

But while the rest of Castle Sylvarresta stood poised for battle, in the Dedicates' Keep, the deepest and most protected heart of the fortress, preparations for battle were still afoot.

The walls of the Dedicates' Keep rang with pain as men and women offered up endowments to their lord.

Two hundred of Sylvarresta's servants and vassals had gathered to offer endowments. While Sylvarresta's chief facilitator, Erin Hyde, worked the forcibles, two of his apprentices walked among the volunteers, prodding and testing, seeking those who had enough brawn, wit, grace, or stamina to justify the rigor and cost involved in taking endowments. For if a lord sought strength, he got it best from those who had it in abundance.

A counselor worked as an advisor with those who were fortunate enough to have adequate attributes. He helped illiterate peasants fill out contracts which promised, in return for the endowments, Sylvarresta's lifelong protection and succor.

Among those who gathered to grant endowments lingered the well-wishers, those who had come to offer comfort to friends or kin who would soon be horribly maimed.

Last of all, throughout the courtyard, were those who had long ago given endowments to their lord. The Dedicates' Keep harbored some fifteen hundred Dedicates, most of them ambulatory enough to come watch the dedicatory ceremonies.

Iome knew many of them well, for she often helped care for the old Dedicates – blind Carrock, one of her servants who had given his eyes; the drooler Mordin, once a bright young man, who had given his wit. The deaf, the sickly, the ugly, those nearly bedridden from weakness. Hundreds and hundreds of others – an army of shambling people.

In the very center of this throng, in the keep's bailey, looking as fierce as the sun, as regal as the night sky with all its stars, King Sylvarresta himself sat on a gray rock among the sea of grass, his weapons handy, half in battle armor, his chest naked.

Those still waiting to give endowments lay on low cots, waiting for Erin Hyde to come among them with his spells and his forcibles.

Among those who had just given endowments wandered King Sylvarresta's own chief physic and herbalist, Binnesman. He was short, with a stooped back, green robes, and hands dirt-stained from his labors. He wore a perpetual smile as he spoke to the new Dedicates, offering comfort here, a whiff of medicinal aromas there.

Binnesman's skill was much wanted along the castle walls. The powers of his herbs were legendary: his blended teas of borage, hyssop, basil, and other spices could give a warrior courage before a battle, lend energy during the conflict, and aid in healing wounds after.

But despite the fact that he was needed on the walls, the need here was more pressing, for the granting of major endowments could be deadly. A great brute who gave strength to King Sylvarresta would fall down afterward, perhaps so weakened that for a moment or two his heart could not beat. One who had offered an endowment of grace, who'd always been limber, would suddenly convulse into spasms, become rigid as a board, his lungs unable to relax enough to let him draw another breath.

For the moment, Binnesman could not go to the walls. He needed to help keep alive those who'd offered endowments. Sylvarresta could only benefit from the endowments so long as the giver still lived.

Iome herself lent a hand in the preparations, her Days watching impassively from the shadows by the keep's kitchens. At the moment, Iome knelt in the dusty court-yard, above a cot where lay the matron who had cared for her since childhood. The matron, a husky woman named Dewynne, sweated profusely from nervousness, despite the cool evening. The high walls of the fortress kept everyone in shade.

Iome's father spoke, the power of his voice cutting across the courtyard: "Dewynne, are you sure you can do this?"

Dewynne smiled at him weakly, her face rigid from fear. "We all fight as we can," she whispered. Iome could hear love in her voice, love for King Sylvarresta.

The chief facilitator, Erin Hyde, stepped between Dewynne and the King, inspecting a forcible. The rod looked like a branding iron of reddish blood metal. It was a foot long, with a rune forged in a one-inch circle at one end. Hyde gently pressed the rune to Dewynne's fleshy arm.

Hyde began his incantation, chanting in a high voice, his words more a piping birdlike song rather than any-thing a human would utter. The words came so quickly that Iome could hardly distinguish one from another. The facilitators called it a song of power. In conjunction with the runes carved on the forcible, the song drew out a Dedicate's attribute.

The symbol on this forcible reminded Iome of an eagle flying with a giant spider dripping from its mouth. Yet the sinuous lines on the rune varied greatly in thickness, curled at odd yet seeming natural angles. The symbol for stamina. Dewynne had always been healthy – never sick a day of her life. Now King Sylvarresta would need her stamina in battle, need it desperately if he took a serious wound.

The facilitator kept chirping in his high voice, then suddenly cried with a throaty growl, making earthy sounds – like lava bubbling, like lions roaring in the wilderness.

The end of the forcible began to glow. Its blood metal blossomed from a dull rusty rose to a fierce titanium white.

Dewynne screamed "Ah, by the Powers, it hurts!" and struggled away from the burning rune. Sweat poured from her as if she had a raging fever. Her face contorted in pain.

Her jaw quivered, and her back arched off the cot. She began panting, sweat streaming from her face.

Iome held the woman, forcing her down, forcing her still. A strong soldier took Dewynne's right arm so that she couldn't break contact with the forcible, spoil the spell.

"Look at my father," Iome said, trying to distract Dewynne from the pain. "Look to your lord! He'll protect you. He loves you. My father has always loved you, just as you love him. He'll protect you. Just keep looking at your lord."

Iome shot a fierce glare at the facilitator, so he moved a bit, opening Dewynne's view.

"Ah, and I thought having a child hurt!" Dewynne sobbed, yet she turned and looked fondly at King Sylvarresta. It was necessary. It was necessary for her to remember why she had to pass through this pain. It was necessary for her to want this, to want to give up her stamina more than anything else in the world. And the only way to keep her focused on this desire was to put the object of her devotion before her eyes.

King Sylvarresta, a strong man in his mid-thirties, was stripped to the waist, and sat on a stone in the courtyard. His long auburn hair fell down round his shoulders, and his wavy beard was neatly trimmed. At the moment, his armorer was trying to get him to put on a leather under-jerkin in preparation for the full mail, but Sylvarresta needed to keep his upper torso bare so that the facilitator could apply the runes of power.

The King's chancellor, Rodderman, was demanding

that King Sylvarresta go out to the walls now, to bolster the courage of his people, while the King's old sage, Chamberlain Inglorians, urged him to stay, to get as many endowments as possible.

King Sylvarresta elected to stay. He glanced Iome's way, caught Dewynne's eyes, and just held the suffering woman with his gaze.

For that moment, nothing else mattered. The King ignored his counselors, his armorer, the resounding tumult of an impending war. There was infinite love in the King's eye, infinite sadness. His look told Dewynne that he knew what she was giving him, that she mattered. Iome knew that her father hated this, hated having to suck others dry in order to protect his vassals.

In that second, something must have changed in Dewynne; she must have reached that necessary moment of yearning, that moment when the transfer of attributes could take place. The facilitator's growls turned to demanding shouts as the full force of his spell came unleashed.

The white-hot blood metal of the forcibles trembled and twisted, like a snake in the facilitator's hands.

Dewynne shrieked from a pain unimaginable. Something within her seemed to collapse – as if a great crushing weight pressed down on her, or as if she had become diminished, had grown smaller.

The smell of burning hair and seared skin rose on wisps of smoke.

Dewynne writhed, tried to squirm away. The sergeant held her, a man of inhuman strength.

Dewynne turned from King Sylvarresta, teeth clenched. She was biting off the tip of her tongue, blood and spittle flowing from her chin.

In that moment, Iome thought she could see all the pain in the world in that good woman's eyes.

Dewynne collapsed into unconsciousness. The stamina had gone from her, so much so that she could no longer keep her eyes open, could not resist the fatigue of the day.

Instead, the blood-metal runes glowed white hot and throbbed. The facilitator, a narrow-faced man with a crooked nose and a long gray goatee, studied the molten rune of power for a moment, its light reflecting in his black eyes; then his shouting turned to a song of joy, of triumph.

He held the forcible over his head with both hands, waving it, so that a trail of white light held in the air, like a meteor's trail, but did not fade. The ribbon of light hung in the air, tangible. The facilitator inspected it carefully, as if judging its width, its heft.

He broke into a piping song and ran to Sylvarresta, trailing the ribbon of light. Everyone stopped, no one daring to come near that light, to risk breaking the connection about to be forged between lord and Dedicate.

At his lord's side, the facilitator bowed, placed the white-hot blood metal beneath the King's breast. The facilitator's song softened now, coaxing, and slowly the small forcible in his hand began to disintegrate, to crumble and blow away like white ash, even as the white umbilical of light faded.

Iome had not taken a vassal's endowment since childhood. She had no way to remember how it had felt. But just as giving an endowment caused unspeakable pain to the giver, so the receiver felt an inexpressible euphoria.

King Sylvarresta's eyes widened, and sweat poured from him. But it was a sheen of excitement, an almost demented thrill. His eyes glowed with joy, and every line in his face, every muscle, relaxed.

He had the decency not to sigh, not to make a great show of his pleasure.

Binnesman rushed up beside Iome, leaned near. His breath smelled of anise. His robe was a garment of darkest green, woven of some strange fabric that looked like mashed roots. It had the rich, clean scent of herbs and spices, which he kept in his pockets. His hair had grasses woven into it. Though he was not a handsome man, with fat cheeks as red as apples, there was a certain sexual quality to him. Iome could not have him so near without feeling aroused, a distinctly annoying sensation. But Binnesman was an Earth Warden, a magician of great skill; as such, his creative powers tended to affect those around him, whether he willed it or not.

He knelt down, and with dirt-stained hands felt the pulse in Dewynne's neck, his face looking grave, worried.

"Damn that worthless facilitator," Binnesman muttered softly, fumbling for something in the pocket of his mud-stained robe.

"What's wrong?" Iome breathed, not daring to speak loud enough for others to hear.

"Hyde's using the Scorrel version of chants, draining these people too much, hoping I can mend them. Dewynne would not live another hour if I weren't here, and he knows it!"

Binnesman was a kind man, a compassionate man. The kind who took pity on fledgling sparrows when they fell from a nest, or who would nurse a grass snake back to health after it got crushed by a passing oxcart. His sky-blue eyes studied Dewynne from under bushy brows.

"Can you save her?" Iome asked.

"Perhaps, perhaps. But I doubt I'll save them all." He nodded to the other Dedicates, who lay on their cots, some fighting for their lives after giving up an endowment. "I wish your father had hired that facilitator from the Weymooth school last year."

Iome understood little of the various schools of facilitators. The competing philosophies and masters could be quite vociferous in proclaiming the superiority of their schools, and only someone well versed in the various breakthroughs and ongoing experiments in each school could really judge which was best on a given day. Some master facilitators excelled at processing certain kinds of endowments. Hyde was an excellent man for taking endowments of hearing and smell – endowments her father considered most valuable in a forest kingdom. But his work on major endowments – on taking stamina and metabolism in particular – suffered in comparison. At least, unlike some facilitators, he did not spend a fortune in blood metal to do research on dogs or horses.

Finally Binnesman found something in his pocket. He pulled out a fresh camphor leaf, bruised it between his fingers, and set each half beneath Dewynne's nostrils. The sweat on her upper lip held the leaf in place.

Reaching in the same pocket, he pulled out petals of lavender, several brown seeds, and other herbs, applying them to Dewynne's sweaty body, placing some under her lips. It was a marvel to behold. The old magician had only two pockets, each filled with a tangled glut of his loose herbs, yet he didn't bother even looking in those pockets, just seemed to recognize by touch the herbs he wanted.

Iome glanced over to another cot. The butcher's apprentice, a husky boy named Orrin, lay ready to offer his lord an endowment of brawn. The sight of him, so full of courage and love and youthful strength, nearly broke her heart. If he gave an endowment now, he might spend the rest of his days unable to rise from his cot. It did not seem fair to take his life when it had hardly begun.

Yet the boy faced no greater dangers than she. If Raj Ahten conquered Heredon, this boy's fate could be better than hers, she imagined. If her father were killed, the boy's endowment of brawn would return to him. Unable to ever give another endowment, the boy would be free to practice his craft in peace. Meanwhile, if Raj Ahten defeated House Sylvarresta, what would await Iome? Torture? Death?

No, the butcher's boy knows what he's doing, Iome told herself. He makes a wise choice, perhaps the best choice available to him. By giving endowments to his king now, he might only have to lose a day in such dear service.

Binnesman muttered, "So little time," began smearing Dewynne with healing soils, touching them to her lips.

The woman began panting, as if every breath were a great labor, and Binnesman helped her by pushing down on her chest.

"What can I do?" Iome begged, frightened that the matron would die here, accomplishing nothing.

"Just . . . please, stay out of my way," Binnesman said in a tone seldom spoken to Runelords. "Ah, I almost forgot. A young man wants to see you – up there. The Prince of Mystarria."

Iome glanced up the keep's wall. A stone staircase led to the south tower, where siege engines were poised to strike over the town.

Up there, at the top of the tower, she could see her Maid of Honor, Chemoise, waving to her urgently. A watchman in black livery paced behind her.

"I've no time for such foolishness," Iome said.

"Go to him," her father commanded from fifty feet away. He'd used his Voice, speaking so that it sounded as if he confided in her ear. Even here in the courtyard, with all the noise and commotion, he'd heard her whispered comment. "You know how long I've wanted to unite our two families."

So, he'd come to offer a betrothal. Iome was of the proper age, though she'd had no worthy suitors. The sons of a couple of minor lords wanted her, but none had holdings to equal her father's.

But would Prince Orden propose now? Now, when the kingdom was under attack? No, he'll offer no proposal, only extend apologies, Iome realized.

A waste of precious time. "I'm too busy," Iome said. "There's too much to do."

Her father stared at her, his gray eyes full of sadness. How handsome he was. "You've been working for hours. You need rest. Take it now. Go speak to him, for an hour."

She wanted to argue, but looked in her father's eyes, which said, *Speak to him now. Nothing you do can make a difference in the fight to come.*

EIGHT: LESS THAN AN HOUR

An hour is not enough time to fall in love, but an hour is all they had that cool autumn afternoon.

In better times, Iome would have felt grateful even for that slight allotment of time in which to meet a suitor alone. Over the past winter her father had told her much about Gaborn, praised him highly, hoping that when this day came, she'd accept him willingly.

Under normal circumstances, Iome would have hoped for love. She would have prepared her heart for it, nurtured it.

But on this day, when her father's kingdom was about to topple, meeting the son of King Orden served no purpose other than to satisfy a morbid curiosity.

Would she have loved him? If so, then this meeting would accomplish nothing more than to chain her with a painful reminder of what might have been.

More likely she'd have despised him. He was, after all, an Orden. Still, being wed to a man she despised would have seemed a minor inconvenience compared with what she feared lay ahead. Right now, she was acutely aware that her people owed Gaborn a debt for his service, and though she wanted nothing to do with him, she decided to treat him cordially, make the best of it.

As Iome climbed the stone stairway to meet Gaborn, her Days close behind, feet whispering across the ancient stone, Chemoise descended, met her halfway.

"He's been waiting for you," Chemoise said, smiling stiffly. Yet there was a certain excitement shining in the girl's eyes. Perhaps Chemoise hoped that Iome would find love, was reminded too much of the lover she herself had lost a day past. Chemoise had been Iome's playmate. Iome knew the girl's every slightest gesture. As Iome glanced up, Chemoise's features softened and her eyes shone. She obviously approved of the prince.

Iome forced a smile. Of all the times to see such excitement in the girl's eyes, today seemed most inappropriate. Chemoise had walked in a fog for the past day. Shocked by her lover's death, planning for her unborn child, forgetting to eat if Iome did not beg her to do so.

Right now it seemed as if Chemoise didn't recognize that a war brewed. Part of her mind seemed to sleep. Perhaps she really doesn't see, Iome realized. Chemoise could be so innocent. Once, Sergeant Dreys had teased her, saying, "Chemoise believes sword fighting is much like carving a duck, the only difference being that you don't eat your foe after you slice him up."

Chemoise took Iome's hands, urged her up the steps, until they stood in the sunlight. After the coolness of the shadowed keep, the warmth of the sunlight felt good.

When she reached the top, Chemoise waved toward the prince in introduction. "Princess Iome Sylvarresta, may I have the honor to present Prince Gaborn Val Orden."

Iome did not look at the Prince. Instead she looked out over the battlements. Chemoise scurried to the far side of the tower, some forty paces off, to give Iome and the Prince some privacy.

To Iome's surprise, the young soldiers who manned the catapults followed Chemoise, affording even more privacy. Iome glanced down at the catapults, noted the metal shot in the weapons' baskets. These catapults had never fired on invaders before. The only time she'd seen them used was on feast days, when her father fired loaves of bread, sausages, and tangerines out over the castle walls to the peasants.

Iome's Days stayed only a dozen paces away. She said, "Prince Sylvarresta, your Days is currently in your father's company. I will act as recorder in his stead, for this portion of your chronicles."

The Prince said nothing to the Days, though Iome heard his cloak rustle, as if he nodded.

Iome still did not look in the Prince's direction. Instead she hurried to the far side of the tower, sat on a merlon, and gazed out over the autumn fields at her father's kingdom.

Iome found herself trembling slightly. She did not want appearances to spoil her perceptions of him. So she looked away, beyond the castle walls.

Still, when Gaborn gave a sigh of appreciation for her beauty it drew a tight smile from Iome's lips. She felt certain he had seen finer women in the South.

A slight wind stirred, a breeze that carried the scent of cooking fires up from the Great Hall. Iome shifted from her perch on the merlon, sending flakes of rock to plunge eighty feet below. Cocks crowed in the evening light, and just within the outer fortress walls, cows bawled, calling their milkers.

Thatch-roofed stone houses dotted the brown fields outside the castle. And from here she could see several villages north and east along the River Wye. But the fields and villages were utterly empty.

The farmers, merchants, and servants had all gathered with the soldiers in their black-and-silver livery on the city walls. Boys and old men alike stood poised with bows and spears. A few local merchants, creeping along the wall-walk, hawked pastries and chicken as if this were the fair, and they were all watching the tournaments.

Down at the Outer Wall, carts, barrels, and crates lay piled against the city gates. If Raj Ahten broke down the gate, the trash would trap his men there in the inner court, where her father's bowmen could do some damage.

It was nearing dusk. Crows and pigeons circled over the oak and ash forests to the south. Raj Ahten's armies disturbed the birds, kept them from roosting.

Lowering campfires burned out there under the woods, so that the hills below her seemed to seethe with smoke, the trees glowing with flame. Iome could not guess how large Raj Ahten's army might be, hidden among the trees.

But signs of the invaders were everywhere: A spy balloon in the shape of a graak had launched from the forest, manned by two of Raj Ahten's men. It had been tethered four hundred feet in the air for nearly two hours. Along the wide banks of the River Wye, which wound through this realm in a broad ribbon, two thousand warhorses were tethered in a dark line, kept by a hundred or so knights and squires who seemed unconcerned about the possibility of an attack. Spearmen and shaggy frowth giants stood watch. Deeper in the forest, Iome could hear the sound of axes falling as Raj Ahten's men cut trees for scaling ladders and siege engines. Indeed, every moment or two, a tree would shiver and topple, leaving a hole in the forest's canopy.

So many men, so huge an army coming from the south. Iome still marveled that they'd heard no advance word. The Duke of Longmot should have sent warning. He should have known of the army's movements. One could only hope that Raj Ahten had found a way to move without Longmot's notice. If that were true, Longmot could send his knights to aid their king, once they discovered the siege. But Iome smelled treachery in the air, and feared that Longmot would send no aid.

Prince Orden cleared his throat, politely begging Iome's attention. "This should have been a fairer meeting between us," he said. His voice was gentle. "I'd hoped to bring joyful news to your kingdom, not tales of invasion."

As if his proposal would have been joyful! She

suspected that her wiser vassals would have mourned the match, even though they'd see the necessity of tying Heredon to Mystarria, the richest kingdom in Rofehavan.

"I thank you for your hasty ride," Iome said. "It was good of you to risk it."

Prince Orden stepped to her side and looked out over the edge of the tower. "How long, do you think, before they mount an attack?" He sounded detached, too tired to think. A curious boy fascinated by the prospect of battle.

"By dawn," she said. "They won't want anyone slipping from the castle, so they'll strike soon." Considering the renowned strength of Raj Ahten's troops – the giants and mages and his legendary swordsmen – tomorrow, her father's kingdom would likely fall.

Iome glanced at Gaborn's back profile from the corner of her eye, a young man who would have broad shoulders when he got his full growth. He had long dark hair. He wore a clean blue traveling cloak, a narrow saber.

She averted her gaze, not desiring to see more. Broad-shouldered, like his father. Of course he will be stunning. After all, he draws glamour from his subjects.

Not like Iome. While some Runelords drew glamour heavily from their subjects, appropriating great resplendence to mask an imperfect countenance, Iome had been blessed with some natural beauty. When she was but a mere infant, two fair maids had stepped forward, offering to endow the princess with their own glamour, and her parents had accepted in Iome's behalf. But once Iome was old enough to understood what the endowments cost her subjects, she had refused further gifts.

"I would not stand so close to the wall," Iome said to Gaborn. "You don't want to be seen."

"By Raj Ahten?" Gaborn asked. "What would he see from here? A young man talking to a maid on the tower wall?"

"Raj Ahten has dozens of far-seers in his band. Surely

they will know a princess when they see her – and a prince."

"Such a fair princess would not be hard to spot," Gaborn agreed, "but I doubt that any of Raj Ahten's men would give me a second glance."

"You wear the device of Orden, do you not?" Iome asked. If Gaborn believed that Raj Ahten's men would not recognize a prince by his countenance alone, she would not gainsay him. Still, she imagined the green knight embroidered on his cloak. "Better not to have it spotted within these walls."

Gaborn chuckled mirthlessly. "I'm wearing one of your soldiers' cloaks. I won't give my presence away. Not before my father arrives. If history is any guide, this could be a long siege. Castle Sylvarresta has not fallen in eight hundred years. But you need only hold out three days – at the most. Only three days!"

Prince Orden sounded confident. She wanted to believe him, to believe that the combined forces of her father's men with King Orden's soldiers could turn back the giants and sorcerers of Raj Ahten. Orden would raise a cry, call for help from Heredon's lords as he came.

Despite the eighty-foot height of the castle's outer walls, despite the depth of Castle Sylvarresta's moat, despite the archers and ballisteers on the walls and the caltrops hidden in the grassy fields, beating Raj Ahten seemed too much to hope. His reputation was that terrifying. "King Orden is a pragmatic man. Will he even come? Surely he would not throw his life away to protect Castle Sylvarresta?"

Gaborn took offense at her tone. "He may be pragmatic about some things, but not where friendship is concerned. Besides, fighting here is the right thing to do."

Iome considered. "I see. . . . Of course, why should your father fight at home, watch his own people bleed and die, watch his castle walls crumble, when he could make as good a defense here?"

Gaborn nearly growled in answer, "For twenty years my father has traveled here for Hostenfest. Do you know how much envy that has aroused elsewhere? He could have celebrated at home – or elsewhere – but he comes here! My father may visit other kings for political reasons, but only one does he name 'friend.'"

Iome had only a vague idea what other kings thought of her father. None of it seemed good. "A softhearted fool," they called him. As an Oath-Bound Lord, he'd sworn never to take endowments from his own people unless they were freely given. Her father could have bought endowments – many a man might sell the use of his eyes or voice. But Sylvarresta would not lower himself to purchasing another's attributes. Of course, her father would never consider strongarming or blackmailing men for endowments. He was not a Wolf Lord, not Raj Ahten.

But Gaborn's father was another matter. Orden was a self-proclaimed "pragmatist" when it came to taking endowments – a man who took endowments freely offered but who, as a younger man, had also engaged in the dubious act of purchasing endowments. He seemed to Iome to verge on being more than pragmatic. He seemed morally suspect. He was too successful at winning the trust of lesser men; he purchased endowments far too cheaply and too often, both for himself and his troops. Indeed, Gaborn's father was said to personally hold over a hundred endowments.

Yet, even then, Iome knew that Gaborn's father, King Orden, was no Raj Ahten. He'd never "forced a peasant's gift," collecting some poor farmer's brawn in lieu of back taxes. He'd never won a maiden's love and then asked her to give him an endowment as well as her heart.

"Forgive me," Iome said, "I spoke Orden an injustice. I'm overwrought. He has been a good friend, and a decent king to his people. Yet I have a nagging fear that your father will use Heredon as a shield. And when we buckle under Raj Ahten's blow, he will toss us aside and flee the battlefield. That would be the wise thing to do."

"Then you don't know my father," Gaborn said. "He is a true friend." He was still hurt, yet his tone carried such liquid notes of sincerity that Iome wondered briefly how many endowments of Voice Gaborn owned. How many mutes do you have in your service? she almost asked, sure it must be a dozen.

"Your father won't throw his life away in our defense. Surely you know better."

Gaborn said coldly, "He'll do what he must."

"I wish it were not so," Iome whispered. Almost unwillingly she glanced down into the Dedicates' Keep. Against the far wall stood one of her father's smelly idiots, a woman whose mind was so drained of wit that she could no longer control her own bowels; she was being led to the dining hall by a blind man. Together, they weaved around an old fellow whose metabolism was so slowed that he could only shuffle from one room to another in the course of a day – and he was lucky to move at all, for many who were drained of metabolism would simply fall into an enchanted sleep, waking only when the lord who held their endowment died. The sight repulsed her.

As Runelords, Iome and her family were heirs to great boons from their subjects, but at a horrifying cost.

"Your compassion does you credit, Princess Sylvarresta, but my father has not earned your disrespect. Little more than his pragmatism has shielded our kingdoms from Raj Ahten this past dozen years."

"That's not entirely true," Iome objected. "My father has sent assassins south over the years. Many of our most cunning warriors have given their lives. Others are held captive. Whatever time we've bought, we bought it in part with the lifeblood of our best men."

"Of course," Gaborn said in a flippant tone that hinted that he dismissed her father's efforts. She knew that Gaborn's father had been preparing for this war for decades, had struggled harder than any other to bring down Raj Ahten. She also realized she'd been trying to goad Gaborn into arguing, but he didn't have his father's temper. Iome wanted to dislike Gaborn, to tell herself that under no circumstances would she have been able to love him.

She felt tempted to look at him, but dared not. What if his face shone like the sun? What if he was handsome beyond all telling? Would her heart flutter within her ribs like a moth beating its wings against a glass?

Beyond the castle walls, it was growing dark. The blush of firelight under the deep woods reminded Iome of glowing embers – red flame flickering under leaves of gold and scarlet. Frowth giants moved at the edge of the trees. In the gloaming, one could almost mistake them for haycocks – their golden heads and backs were that shaggy.

"Forgive me for arguing," Iome said. "I'm in a foul mood. You don't deserve harsh treatment. I suppose that if we want to fight, we could always go down to the battle-field and carve up a few of Raj Ahten's troops."

"Surely you would not go into battle?" Gaborn asked. "Promise me that! Raj Ahten's swordsmen are not commoners."

Iome felt tempted to laugh at the idea of going into battle. She kept a small poniard strapped to her leg, under her skirt, as many a proper lady did, and she knew how to use it. But she was no swordswoman. She decided to bait the Prince one more time.

"Why not?" she demanded, only half in jest. "Farmers and merchants man the castle walls! Their lives mean as much to them as ours do to us! They are endowed with only the gifts their mothers gave them at birth. Meanwhile, I have endowments of wit and glamour and stamina to defend me. I may not have a strong sword arm, but why should I not fight?"

She expected Gaborn to warn her how dangerous the battle would be. The frowth giants would have muscles of iron. Raj Ahten's men each had endowments of brawn, grace, metabolism, and stamina. Moreover, they were trained to war.

Yet now Iome realized she would not concede to common sense, for her argument was just. Her vassals valued their lives as much as she valued her own. She might be able to save one of them, or two or three. She would help defend the castle walls. Just as her father would.

Yet Gaborn's answer surprised her: "I don't want you to fight, because it would be a shame to mar such beauty."

Iome laughed, clear and sweet, like the call of a whippoorwill in a glade. "I have refused to look at you," she said, "for fear my heart would overwhelm my common sense. Perhaps you should have done the same."

"Truly, you are beautiful," Gaborn said, "but I'm no boy to be made dizzy by a pretty face." That use of Voice again, so sensible. "No, it is your decency that I find beautiful."

Then, perhaps sensing the darkness about to descend, Gaborn said, "I must be honest, Princess Sylvarresta. There are other princesses I could ally with, in other kingdoms. Haversind-by-the-Sea, or Internook." He gave her a moment to think. Both kingdoms were as large as Heredon, as wealthy, and perhaps even more defensible – unless, of course, you feared invasion from the sea. And the beauty of Princess Arrooley of Internook was legendary, even here, twelve hundred miles away. "But you intrigued me."

"I? How so?"

Gaborn said honestly, "A few years ago, I had an argument with my father. He'd arranged to purchase grace for me from a young fisherman. I objected. You've seen how those who give up grace often cling to life tenuously. The muscles of their guts cannot stretch, and so they cannot digest food. They can seldom walk. Even to attempt speech or to close their eyes can cause pain. I've seen how they waste away, until they die after a year or so. To me it seems that of all the traits one might endow to another, grace would be hardest to lose.

"So I refused the endowment, and my father grew angry. I said it was wrong to persist in this 'shameful economy,' accepting endowments from those vassals poor enough in intellect and worldly goods to count themselves fortunate to give up the best parts of themselves for our benefit.

"My father laughed and said, 'You sound like Iome Sylvarresta. She called me a glutton when last I ate at her table -- not a glutton for food, but a glutton who fed on the misery of others! Hah! Imagine!'" When Gaborn quoted his father, he sounded exactly like the King. He was using his Voice again.

Iome remembered that comment well. For her impertinence, her father had administered a firm spanking in the presence of King Orden, then locked her in her room for a day without food or water. Iome had never regretted the remark.

Her face burned with embarrassment. She'd often felt torn between admiration and loathing for King Orden. In ways, he cut a heroic figure. Mendellas Draken Orden was powerful, a stubborn king, and it was rumored that he fought well in battle. For two decades he'd kept the Northern kingdoms united. A glance from him would cow many a would-be tyrant, and with a curt word he could insure that a prince would fall out of favor with his own father.

Some called him the Kingmaker. Others called him the Puppet Master. The truth was, Orden had been making himself into a man of heroic proportions for a reason. Like the Runelords of old, he had to become more than human because his enemies were more than human.

"Forgive me those words," Iome said. "Your father did not deserve such chastisement from a self-righteous nine-year-old girl."

"Forgive it?" Prince Gaborn answered. "What is to forgive? I agreed with you. Perhaps a thousand years ago, there was reason for our ancestors to put one another to the indignity of the forcibles. But the reaver invasions are long past. The only reason you and I are Runelords is because we were born into this 'shameful economy'! I was so intrigued by your words that I asked my father to repeat every word you had ever uttered in his presence, and the conditions under which they were spoken.

"So he began recalling things you'd said since the time you were three, and recited anything he found pertinent."

He gave Iome only a split second to consider the implications. King Orden, like any who had such heavy endowments of wit, would naturally recall everything he'd ever seen, every word he'd ever heard, every innocent phrase. With his endowments of hearing, Orden could listen to a whisper three rooms away through the thick stone walls of the castle. As a child, Iome hadn't quite understood the breadth of powers a mature Runelord held. No doubt, she'd spoken many things that she'd never have wanted King Orden to hear. And he remembered it all faultlessly.

"I see . . ." Iome said.

"Don't be offended," Gaborn said. "You didn't embarrass yourself. My father reported every jest you made to Lady Chemoise." He nodded toward the maid. Iome felt the gesture more than saw it. "Even as a child, my father found you to be amusing, generous. I wanted to meet you, but I had to wait for the proper time. Last year I came to Hostenfest in my father's retinue so I could look on you. . . . I sat in the Great Hall and watched you through dinner, and elsewhere. I dare say, I feared my stare would bore a hole through you.

"You impressed me, Iome. You laid siege to my heart. I watched those who sat around you, the serving children and guards and Maids of Honor, and saw how they craved your affection. I watched the next morning as we left, how a flock of children gathered round you as our caravan made to depart, and you kept the young ones out from under the horses' hooves. You are well loved by your people, and you give love freely in return. In all the Kingdoms of Rofehavan, you have no equal. That is why I've come. I'd hoped that like all those around you, I too might have the hope of someday sharing your affection."

Fair words. Iome wondered furiously. King Orden always brought a dozen or two retainers to the Great Hall for dinner. It was only right that those who participated in the hunt share in the prize boar, served at the height of the feast. Iome tried to recall the faces of those men: several wore the scars of the forcibles, and were therefore lesser lords in their own right. Prince Gaborn would have been one of them. And he would be young.

Yet, to a man, Orden's guards and retainers were older, more trusted men. Orden was wise enough to know that the best swordsmen were seldom spry youths bursting with enthusiasm at the thought of swinging a battle-axe or sword. No, the best were old, masters of technique and strategy who often stood their ground in a battle, seeming to hardly move, slashing and thrusting with deadly economy.

Orden had had no young men in his retinue. Except . . . for one she recalled: a shy boy who'd sat at the far end of the tables – a handsome boy with straight hair and piercing blue eyes that twinkled with intelligence, though he gaped at his surroundings like some commoner. Iome had thought him merely a trusted body servant, perhaps a squire in training.

Surely that common youth could not have been a prince of the Runelords! The very thought left her unsettled, made her heart pound. Iome turned to look at Prince Orden, to verify her suspicions.

And laughed. He stood, a plain young man with a straight back, dark hair, and those clear blue eyes. He'd filled out in a year. Iome could hardly contain her surprise. He was . . . nothing much to look at. He had no more than one or two endowments of glamour.

Gaborn smiled, charmed at her mirth. "Having seen me now, and knowing my reasons for coming," he said, "had I asked your hand in marriage, would you have given it?"

From the core of her heart, Iome answered sincerely, "No."

Gaborn stepped back as if she'd slapped him, as if her rejection were the last thing he'd expected. "How so?"

"You're a stranger. What do I know of you? How could I love someone I don't know?"

"You would learn my heart," Gaborn answered. "Our fathers desire a political union, but I desired a union of like minds and like hearts. You will find, Lady Sylvarresta, that you and I are . . . one in many matters."

Iome laughed lightly. "Honestly, Prince Orden, if you had come seeking only the realm of Heredon, perhaps I could have given it to you. But you would have asked for my heart, and that I could not promise to a stranger."

"As I feared," Gaborn said honestly. "Yet you and I are strangers only by accident. Had we lived nearer one another, I think we could have forged a love. Could I not persuade you, give you a gift that might change your mind?"

"There's nothing I desire," Iome said; then her heart pounded. Raj Ahten's armies stood at her gate. She wanted him gone. She realized she'd spoken too quickly.

"There is something you desire, though you don't know it," Gaborn said. "You live here, tucked away in your castle near the woods, and you say there is nothing you want. Yet certainly you must be afraid. There was a time when all Runelords were like your father, men bound by oath to serve their fellows, men who took no endowment but that which was freely given.

"Now, here we are, cornered. Raj Ahten is at your gates. All around you, the kings of the North call themselves 'pragmatists,' and have given themselves to the pursuit of gain, telling themselves that in the end they will not become like Raj Ahten.

"You see the fallacy of their arguments. You saw my father's weakness when you were little more than a child. He is a great man, but he has vices, as do we all. Perhaps he has been able to remain good in part because people like you sometimes spoke up, sometimes warned him to beware of greed.

"And so I have a gift for you, Princess Sylvarresta, a gift I give freely, asking nothing in return."

He strode forward, took her hand. Iome imagined that he would place something in her palm, a precious stone or a love poem.

Instead, Gaborn took her hand in his, and she felt the calluses on his palm, felt the warmth of his hand.

He knelt before her and whispered an oath, an oath so ancient that few now understood the language of it, an oath so crippling that almost no Runelord ever dared speak it:

"This oath I take in your presence, and my life will bear witness in every point:

"I, a Runelord, swear to serve as your protector. I your Runelord, am your servant above all. I promise now that I will never take an endowment by force, nor by deception. Nor will I purchase such from those in need of wealth. Instead, if any man stands in need of gold, I will give it freely. Only those who would join me as I battle evil may serve as my Dedicates.

"As the mist rises from the sea, so does it return."

He had sworn the vow of the Oath-Bound Runelords, an oath normally spoken to vassals, but given also to underlords or to friendly monarchs that one intended to defend. It was not an oath spoken lightly to one person. Rather, it was a covenant, declaring a way of life. The very thought made Iome feel faint.

With Raj Ahten battling the North, the House of

Orden would need all its strength. For Gaborn to speak that oath now, in her hearing, was – suicidal.

Iome had never expected such greatness of heart from House Orden. To live the oath would prove hard beyond bearing.

She'd not have done the same. She was too . . . pragmatic.

Iome stood gaping for just a moment, realizing that if he had sworn that oath to her under fairer skies, she would have thought well of him. But to speak the oath now, under these conditions . . . was irresponsible.

She looked to her Days, to see the girl's reaction. The young woman's eyes were wide, the thinnest show of surprise.

Iome looked back to Gaborn's face, found herself wanting to memorize it, to hold this moment in her memory.

An hour is not enough time to fall in love, but an hour is all they had that day. Gaborn had won her heart in far less time, and shown Iome her own heart more clearly in the process. He had seen that she loved her people, and it was true. Yet she had to wonder: Even if Gaborn takes this oath as an act of love for mankind, is it not sheer folly? Does Gaborn love his honor more than the lives of his people?

"I hate you for that," was all that Iome could answer.

At that instant, a heavy beating of drums rose from the valley floor. The sun was dipping below the horizon. Two Frowth giants at the wood's edge pounded on heavy copper drums, and a dozen dappled gray horses spurred out from the gloom under the trees. Their riders all wore black chain mail beneath yellow surcoats, with the red wolves of Raj Ahten upon their chests. The foremost rider carried a green triangular pennant on a longspear, a request for a parlay.

The others in the guard all bore axes and shields the color of copper – an honor guard, with the emblem of the sword beneath the star of Indhopal upon their shields.

That is, all bore the same uniform but one –

Upon the last horse in the group, in his black chain armor, his high helm with white snow owl's wings sweeping wide, Lord Raj Ahten rode himself, shield on one arm, a horseman's long-handled warhammer in the other.

Where he rode, it was as if light shone from him, as if he were one star in a black and empty night, or one lowly signal boat with its pyres lit upon the water.

Iome could not take her eyes from him. Even at this distance, his glamour struck her breathless. She could not distinguish his features – for at such a distance, he was nothing more than a tiny stick figure. Yet she had the impression of great beauty, even from here. And she knew that to look upon his face would be dangerous.

Iome admired his helm, with its sweeping white wings. In her bedroom she kept two ancient helms of the type. *What a fine addition it would make to my collection,* she thought, *with Raj Ahten's skull smiling out at me.*

Behind Raj Ahten's forces came a more common brown mare, the Wolf Lord's Days, struggling to catch up. Iome wondered what secrets he could tell. . . .

Down by the gates, her father's soldiers began shouting at one another in warning: "Beware the face! Beware the face!"

She looked at her own men on the walls, saw many of them fumbling with their arms. Captain Derrow, who had great endowments of strength, ran along the parapet with a steel great bow that no other man in the kingdom could draw, hoping to send a few darts into Raj Ahten.

As if in answer to her soldiers' warnings, a swirling cloud of golden light formed above Raj Ahten, a whirlwind of embers that descended, drawing the eyes of many to his features.

It was some flameweavers' trick, Iome realized. Raj Ahten wanted her people to look at him.

Iome did not fear Raj Ahten's visage from so far away. She doubted that from here his glamour could muddy her judgment.

Raj Ahten hurried toward the city gates. His warriors' horses issued forth in formation, rippling over the fields like a gale, for these were no common beasts. They were force stallions. Herd leaders, like that their masters were transformed by the Runelords' art. The sight of them, shooting over the darkening fields like cormorants skimming the sea, filled Iome's heart with wonder. She'd never seen such fine force horses gallop in unison. She'd never seen anything so magnificent.

Prince Orden ran tot he top of the stairs, shouted down into the Dedicates' Keep, "King Sylvarresta, you are needed. Raj Ahten seeks a parlay."

Iome's father cursed, began pulling on his armor. It clattered as he dressed.

Behind Raj Ahten, beside the deserted farms that dotted the edge of the woods, Raj Ahten's troops began to emerge from the gloom. Five flameweavers, so close to becoming one with the elements that they could no longer wear clothes, shone like blazing beacons, clad in twisting tongues of green fire. The dry grasses at their feet burst aflame.

As warriors moved out of the shadowed woods, the light blazing from the flameweavers suddenly reflected on polished armor, glinted from swords.

Among the thousands of warriors who began to advance, stranger things than flameweavers could be seen.

The shaggy frowth giants, twenty feet tall at the brow, lumbered forward clumsily in their chain mail, clutching huge ironbound staves. They struggled to keep from crushing Raj Ahten's swordsmen in their advance.

War dogs kept pace with the giants, huge beasts, mastiffs with runes branded into them.

Bowmen by the score.

And at the edge of the forest, black shadows flickered. Furred creatures with dark manes hissed and growled, loping forward in a crouched gate on clawed knuckles, each bearing an enormous spear. "Nomen!" someone shouted. "Nomen from beyond Inkarra!"

Nomen to scale the walls, scampering up the stone like monkeys. Nomen with their sharp teeth and red eyes.

Iome had never seen one – alive. Only once had she seen an ancient, shedding pelt. They were the stuff of legend.

Nomen. No wonder Raj Ahten's army traveled by day only through the woods, attacked only at night.

It was all show of course. Raj Ahten appearing in his glory with all his entourage. The power of his army was astonishing, his wealth enormous.

You see me? he was saying. *You Northerners squat here in your barren kingdom, never knowing how impoverished you are. Behold the Wolf Lord of the South. Behold my wealth.*

But Iome's people were ready for battle. She saw boys and old men shifting on the castle walls, gripping the hafts of their spears tighter, reaching over to make sure that the arrows placed beside them lay just so. Her people would put up a battle. Perhaps a battle that would be sung about in years to come.

Just then, Iome's father finished dressing, grabbed his weapons, and came bounding up the steps of the tower behind her. His Days, an elderly scholar with white hair, hobbled behind as fast as possible.

Iome was not prepared for the change in her father. In the past few hours, he'd taken sixty endowments from his people, had grown much in power. He leapt up six stairs at a time, even while bearing his arms, wearing full armor. He moved like a panther.

When he reached the top of the tower, the frowth giants quit drumming, and Raj Ahten's army halted. The untrained nomen growled and hissed in the distance, as if eager to do battle.

Lord Raj Ahten himself gave a shout, reining in his

stallion, and such was the power of his call – for he bore endowments of voice from hundreds and hundreds of people – that his words carried clearly even this high on the citadel, even blowing on the wind. He sounded kindly and pleasant, belying the threat inherent in his deeds.

"King Sylvarresta, people of Heredon," Raj Ahten called, his voice as fair as the tinkling of a bell, as resonant as a woodwind. "Let us be friends – not combatants. I bear you no malice. Look at my army–" He spread his arms wide. "You cannot defeat it. Look at me. I am not your enemy. Surely you will not force me to squat here in the cold tonight, while you dine beside your hearths? Throw open your gates. I will be your lord, and you will be my people."

His voice sounded so pleasant, so brimming with reason and gentleness, that had she been on the walls, Iome would have found it hard to resist.

Indeed, in that moment, she heard the gears to the main portcullis grind, and the drawbridge began to lower.

Iome's heart pounded. She leaned forward, shouting "No!," astonished that some of her fool subjects, over-whelmed by a monster's glamour and Voice, were doing his bidding.

Beside her, King Sylvarresta also shouted, ordering his men to raise the bridge. But they were far from the gates, so high up. The sound of Orden's shout was muffled by the visor on his helm. He pulled it up to call more clearly.

In keeping with her own feelings of anger, down at the gates, Captain Derrow let a bolt loose at the Wolf Lord. Derrow's bolt flew with incredible speed, a blur of black iron that would have driven through any other man's armor.

But the speed and strength of Raj Ahten outmatched him. The Runelord simply reached up and caught the bolt in midair.

Such speed. Raj Ahten had done the unthinkable, taking so many endowments of metabolism. Even from here, she saw that he must move five or six times as fast as a common man. Living at such speed, he'd age and die in a matter of years. But before then, he might well conquer the world.

"Here now," he called, sounding reasonable. "We'll have no more of that." Then with great force, with a sound of gentleness that slid past all of Iome's defenses, Raj Ahten commanded, "Throw down your weapons and your armor. Give yourselves to me."

Iome leapt to her feet, found herself grasping for her poniard, ready to toss it over the walls. Only Gaborn's hand, which reached to stop her, kept her from dropping the weapon over the wall.

Immediately she regretted it, saw how foolish it had been, and she glanced at her father, afraid at how angry he might be. She saw him struggling, struggling, to keep from tossing his own warhammer over the tower wall.

For half a heartbeat she stood, terrified of how her people might respond to Raj Ahten's voice and glamour, fearing that those closer to the monster would be fooled.

With a shout, as if in celebration, her people began tossing bows and weapons over castle walls. Swords and fouchards clattered on the stones beside the moat, along with helms and shields. The ballistas on the south wall crashed to the water, raising a plume of spray. From here, the sound of her people cheering was almost deafening, as if Raj Ahten had come as their savior, not their destroyer, and in that moment, the city gates opened wide.

Several of House Sylvarresta's most loyal soldiers began to struggle, hoping to close the gates. Captain Derrow swung his steel bow as a weapon, fending off townsmen. A few warriors with great heart but lesser gifts never made it from their posts at the walls. As soon as they shouted in defiance, those standing nearby grabbed them. Brawls broke out. Iome saw several of the city guards get tossed over the walls to their deaths.

From here, Iome could not see the beauty of Raj Ahten's face. From here, surely the wind diminished the sweetness of his voice.

From here on the castle wall, even though Iome could comprehend how her city was lost, she could not quite believe what she saw with her own eyes.

She was stunned. She found herself shaken more than she could have imagined.

The drawbridge came down. The portcullis lifted. The inner gate opened.

Without one enemy loss, Castle Sylvarresta fell.

Amid cheers, Raj Ahten rode into the inner court, just inside the great wall, while Iome's people tossed aside the carts and barrels that littered the area, and chickens flew up out of the Wolf Lord's path.

How could I have been so blind? Iome wondered. How could I have not seen the danger?

Only moments before, Iome had hoped that her father and King Orden would be able to withstand Raj Ahten.

How simpleminded I am.

From beside her, Iome's father shouted, calling across the distance, calling for his men to surrender. He did not want to watch them die.

The stiff evening wind carried away his words.

In shock, Iome glanced at her father's face, saw him pale and shaken, beaten, beaten, and utterly hopeless.

My father's voice is as dry and insubstantial as ash blowing in the wind, Iome thought. He is nothing before Raj Ahten. We are all nothing.

She'd never imagined this.

Raj Ahten leaned forward in his saddle, moving ever so lightly. From so far away, his face was no larger in her field of vision than a sparkling bit of quartz sand glittering on a beach; she imagined him beautiful. He seemed young. He seemed fair. He wore his armor more lightly than another man might wear his clothes, and Iome watched him in wonder. It was rumored that he had endowments of brawn from thousands of men. If not for fear of breaking his bones, he could leap the walls, slice through an armored man as if slicing through a peach.

In battle he would be nearly invincible. With his endowments of wit – drained from hundreds of sages and generals – no swordsman could take him by surprise. His endowments of metabolism would let him move through the courtyard, dodging between startled guards, an unstoppable blur. With enough endowments of stamina, he could withstand almost any blow in battle.

For all intents and purposes, Raj Ahten was no longer even a human. He'd become a force of nature.

One intent on subduing the world.

He needed no army to back him, no force elephants or shaggy frowth giants to batter down the palace gates. No nomen to scale the walls. No flameweavers to set the city's roofs aflame.

They were all minor terrors, distractions. Like the ticks that infested a giant's fur.

"We can't fight," her father whispered. "Sweet mercy, we can't fight."

Beside her, Gaborn's breath came ragged, and he moved so close that Iome could feel the warmth of him beside her face.

Iome felt disconnected from her body as she simply watched the events unfold below. People were running to the courtyard, trying to press close to the new lord, their Lord, who would destroy them all.

Iome feared Raj Ahten as she feared death; yet she also found that she welcomed him. The power of his Voice made her welcome him.

Prince Gaborn Val Orden said softly, "Your people don't have the will to resist. My regrets to House Sylvarresta – to your father, and to you – for the loss of your kingdom."

"Thank you," Iome said, her voice weak, far away.

Gaborn turned to King Sylvarresta. "My lord, is there

anything I can do?" Gaborn was looking at Iome. Perhaps he hoped to take her from here, to take her away.

Iome's father turned to the Prince, still in shock. "Do? You are but a boy? What could you possibly do?"

Iome's mind raced. She wondered if Gaborn could help her escape. But, no, she couldn't imagine it. Raj Ahten would know she was in the castle. The royals were marked. If Gaborn tried to free her, Raj Ahten would hunt them down. The most Gaborn might accomplish would be to save himself. Raj Ahten did not know that Prince Orden was on the grounds.

Apparently, King Sylvarresta reached the same conclusion. "If you can make it from the castle, give my regards to your father. Tell him I regret that we won't hunt together again. Perhaps he can avenge my people."

Her father reached under his breastplate, pulled out a leather pouch that held a small book. "One of my men was murdered while trying to bring this to me. It contains writings from the Emir of Tuulistan. Much of the end of it is only philosophical ramblings and poetry – but it contains some accounts of Raj Ahten's battles.

"I believe the Emir wanted me to learn something from it, but I have yet to figure out what. Will you see that it gets to your father?"

Gaborn took the leather pouch, pocketed it.

"Now, Prince Orden, you had better leave, before Raj Ahten learns you're here. Considering the present state of my loyal subjects, it won't be long till he finds out."

"Then with regrets, I take my leave." Gaborn bowed to the King.

To Iome's surprise, Gaborn stepped forward, kissed her cheek. She was astonished to find how hard her heart beat in response to his touch. Gaborn stared keenly at her, whispered in a fierce tone, "Keep heart. Raj Ahten uses people. He does not destroy them. I am your protector. I will return for you."

He turned smartly and hurried to the stairs, running so

softly she did not hear his feet scuff the stone. If not for the racing of her heart and the warmth on her cheek where he'd kissed her, she almost would have thought she'd imagined him.

Captain Ault stepped in behind Gaborn and followed him down into the bailey.

How will he escape, she wondered, with Raj Ahten's guards watching the city?

She glanced down at his retreating back, at his blue cloak flapping, as Gaborn made his way through the throng of the blind, the deaf, the idiots and other crippled Dedicates of House Sylvarresta. He was not tall. Perhaps a young man could escape the castle without regard.

How odd, she considered, her thoughts still disjointed, to think I love him. She almost dared hope that they really might wed.

But of course, Prince Orden had to save himself, and she had nothing to offer him. Dully, she realized that this day could not have turned out any other way.

Perhaps we are both more pragmatic than we want to believe, she wondered.

"Goodbye, my lord," she whispered to Gaborn's retreating form, and added an old blessing for wayfarers. "May the Glories guide your every step."

She turned back to look down on Lord Raj Ahten, grinning and waving to his new subjects. His dappled gray stallion strode proudly through the cobbled streets, and the peasants parted for him easily, their cheers becoming steadily more deafening. He'd already made it into the second tier of the city, past the Market Gate. He spurred his way up through the streets, and for a moment was hidden from Iome's view.

Suddenly Chemoise stood at Iome's elbow. Iome swallowed hard, wondering what Raj Ahten would do to her. Would she be put to death? Be tortured? Disgraced?

Or would he leave her some position, let her father reign as a regent? It seemed possible.

One could only hope.

Down below, Raj Ahten suddenly rounded a corner and was now only two hundred yards away.

She could see his face beneath the sweeping white wings of his helm – the clear skin, glossy black hair, the impassive dark eyes. Handsome, handsome. As perfectly formed as if he were sculpted by love or goodness.

He looked up at Iome. Because she was beautiful as only a princess of the Runelords could be, Iome was growing accustomed to the occasional rapacious stares of men. She knew how sorely her appearance could arouse a man.

Yet of all the predatory gazes she'd ever been granted, nothing compared to what she saw laid bare in Raj Ahten's eyes.

NINE: THE WIZARD'S GARDEN

Gaborn nearly flew down the stairs of the Dedicates' Tower, making his way through the crowded courtyard, past the smelly idiots, the cripples.

Captain Ault was at his side, and he said, "Young sir, please go into the Dedicates' kitchens, and wait until I send someone for you. The sun will be down in moments. We can find a way to get you over a wall after nightfall."

Gaborn nodded. "Thank you, Sir Ault."

He'd known for hours that he'd have to make his escape from Castle Sylvarresta, but hadn't believed it would happen so soon. He'd imagined that the castle's defenders would have put up a great battle. The castle walls were certainly thick enough, high enough to hold Raj Ahten's army at bay.

He'd wanted some sleep. He'd had almost none over the past three days. In truth, he needed almost no sleep. As an infant, he'd been given three endowments of stamina, and fortunately two of those who'd granted the endowments still lived. So, in the way of those who had great stamina, Gaborn was able to get his rest on horseback, to let his mind rest, as he moved about as if through a waking dream. Still, he sometimes wanted a nap.

Food was another matter. Even a Runelord with great stamina needed food. Right now Gaborn's stomach was cramping. Yet he had almost no time to eat.

Worse than that, he'd taken a wound – nothing major,

but an arrow had pierced his right bicep. His sword arm. He'd washed and bandaged it, but the thing throbbed, burned.

And Gaborn had no time to take care of any of these needs. Right now, he needed a disguise.

He'd killed one of Raj Ahten's outriders, three of his frowth giants. His arrows had taken half a dozen war dogs.

Raj Ahten's outriders would want vengeance on Gaborn. He was cornered. He didn't feel certain that he could escape, even if he waited an hour for full darkness. Gaborn had two endowments of scent, but his keen sense of smell was nothing compared to that of some of Raj Ahten's troops: men with noses more keen than a hound's. They would track him.

Despite his show of confidence to Iome, Gaborn felt terrified.

Still, he took one thing at a time. He smelled food cooking in the Dedicates' kitchens, hurried through a broad plank door. Its brass handle felt loose in his hand.

He found himself not in the kitchen, but in the wide entrance to the dining chamber. To the right of the door, he could see past several heavy beams into kitchens where the cooking fires burned like a blast furnace. Several plucked geese hung from the rafters, along with cheeses, strings of garlic, smoked eels, and sausages. He could hear soup boiling in one of the big kettles next to the fire. The smell of tarragon, basil, and rosemary lay heavy in the air. A worktable lay between him and the kitchens, and a young blind girl was there, stacking boiled eggs, turnips, and onions on a huge metal tray.

Down at her feet, a tawny cat toyed with a chewed and frightened mouse.

Ahead, the room opened wide to the thick plank dining tables, black from age and grime, benches running down each side. Small oil lamps sat burning atop each table.

The bakers and chefs of Castle Sylvarresta were hard at

work, piling the tables with loaves of bread, bowls of fruit, filling plates with meat. While the rest of Sylvarresta's followers had run to the walls to gawk at the battle, the cooks here knew where their duty lay: in caring for the wretches who had given up endowments to House Sylvarresta.

As in most Dedicates' kitchens, the staff was composed mostly of those who had given up endowments themselves: the ugly people who had given up glamour served the tables and ruled the kitchens. The mutes and the deaf worked the bakery. The blind and those who had no sense of smell or touch swept the plank floors and scoured the burnt kettles.

Gaborn immediately noticed the silence here in the kitchens. Though a dozen people bustled about, no one spoke, aside from a curt order here and there. These people were terrified.

The kitchens offered a mixed palate of smells: the scents of butchered animals and baked bread struggled to overpower the odors of moldering cheese, spilled wine, rancid grease. It was a ghastly combination, yet Gaborn found himself salivating.

He hurried into the dining hall. A narrow corridor behind it led to the bakers' ovens. Gaborn smelled fresh, yeasty bread still steaming.

He grabbed a hot loaf from the table, earning a scowl from a pretty serving girl. Yet he took the food as if it were his, and gave her a glance that said, *I own this*.

The wench could not withstand the unspoken rebuke, hurried away. She held her arms in close, in the careful way of those who've given up an endowment of touch. Gaborn took a good knife, cut a thigh off a goose that lay on another plate. He thrust the dagger into the belt of his tunic, and stuffed as much meat as he could in his mouth; he uncorked a bottle of wine from the table, washed down the goose meat as fast as he could, surprised at the quality of the wine.

One of the King's own red hunting hounds had been

lounging under the table. It saw Gaborn eating, came up and sat at Gaborn's feet, eyes expectant, casually sweeping the floor with its tail.

Gaborn tossed it the meaty goose bone, then grabbed another loaf of bread, began eating.

All this time, his mind raced. Though someone would come to help guide him from the castle, he knew that it would not be easy, and he could not safely rely on others. He considered various plans. Castle Sylvarresta had a moat, a river flowing along its eastern wall, with a water mill for the grain mill.

There would be a boathouse by the mill, where the royals could go out for a casual row. Often, an underground passage led down to the boathouse from the castle.

But the boathouse would be well watched by Raj Ahten's troops. The Wolf Lord had nomen with him, nomen who could see in the dark. It wasn't likely that Gaborn could make it out of the boathouse.

The kitchen staff might have some sort of a sewer that would connect to the river. But that was unlikely. Nothing ever went to waste in the kitchens. Bones were fed to the King's dogs. Vegetable peels and animal guts went to the swine. Hides went to tanners. Anything that was left went to the gardens.

Gaborn had to escape through the river. He couldn't risk trying to go out by land. The war dogs would find him.

And he couldn't stay, couldn't hide in the castle for the night. He had to leave before nightfall. Once darkness fell, and the city quieted, Raj Ahten's hunters would begin searching for him, out for vengeance.

The pretty serving wench returned with another bottle of wine, more bread and meat to replace what Gaborn had taken.

Gaborn spoke to the back of her neck. "Pardon me. I am Prince Orden. I need to reach the river. Do you know of a passage I can take?" Almost immediately he felt stupid. I should not have given my name, he thought. Yet he'd felt the need to impress upon her the nature of his predicament, and revealing his name was the swiftest way to do so.

The girl looked at him, lamplight reflecting in her brown eyes. Gaborn wondered why she'd divested herself of feeling. A love affair gone awry, the desire to never touch or be touched again? Life could not be easy for her. Those who gave endowments of touch could not feel heat or cold, pain or pleasure. All their senses dulled somewhat – hearing, sight, and smell.

Because of this, life for them was as empty as if they were opium addicts. They would often burn or cut themselves, never knowing. In the cold of winter, they could get frostbite and bear it without tears.

Gaborn didn't know who she'd given her endowment of touch to – whether it had gone to the King, to the Queen, or to Iome. Yet he felt certain that King Sylvarresta would be put to death. Possibly within hours, before dawn. Unless Raj Ahten wanted to torture the man first.

Would this wench sit before a fire tonight, waiting for the first touch of warmth to her skin? Or would she stand out in the cold mists, feeling the play of it over her face? Certainly life could not be easy for her.

"There's a trail out back," she said, her voice surprisingly husky, sweet. "The baker's path leads down to the mill. There are some low birches that sweep out over the water. You might make it."

"Thank you," Gaborn said.

He turned, thinking to go out to the courtyard. He wanted to leave Castle Sylvarresta, but he needed to strike a blow against Raj Ahten. He'd seen dozens of forcibles lying on the green, where the facilitators had recently worked.

The forcibles, forged from valuable blood metal from the hills of Kartish, were a mixture of metals believed to be derived from human blood. Only blood metal could be used to make forcibles. Gaborn couldn't let Raj Ahten have them.

But as he turned to go, the maid tapped Gaborn's shoulder and asked, "Will you take me with you?"

Gaborn saw fear in her eyes. "I would," he answered softly, "if I thought it would help. But you may be safer here." In Gaborn's experience, Dedicates were seldom very courageous. They were not the type of people to seize life, to grasp. They served their lords, but served passively. He did not know if this girl would have the emotional fortitude necessary to make her escape.

"If they kill the Queen . . ." she said. "The soldiers – they'll use me. You know how they take vengeance on captured Dedicates."

Then Gaborn understood why she had given up feeling, why she feared to be touched, to be hurt again. She feared rape.

She was right. Raj Ahten's soldiers might hurt her. These people who were too weak to stand, or whose metabolisms were so slow they could not blink more than five times an hour – all were a part of their Runelord. They were his invisible appendages, the source of his power. By upholding their lord, they opposed their lord's enemies.

If King Sylvarresta were put to death, these wretches wouldn't escape retribution.

Gaborn wanted to tell the maid to stay, that he couldn't take her. Wanted to tell her how dangerous the trip would be. But for her, perhaps the greater danger lay in remaining here in the Dedicates' Keep.

"I plan to try to swim out through the river," Gaborn answered. "Can you swim?"

The wench nodded. "A little." She shook at the thought of what she planned to do. Her jaw trembled. Tears filled her eyes. Swimming would not be a valuable skill here in Heredon, but in Mystarria Gaborn had learned the finer points of the arts from water wizards. He still had protective spells cast over him to help keep him from drowning.

Gaborn leaned closed, squeezed her hand. "Be brave, now. You'll be all right."

He turned to leave, and she shouldered past, taking a loaf of bread for herself as she scurried out. In the doorway she grabbed a walking stick and an old shawl, wrapped her head, and hurried out.

On a peg near where the walking stick had been, Gaborn spotted a baker's tunic, an article of clothing too warm to be worn near the ovens. The bakers typically would strip down to a loincloth while baking.

Gaborn put on the tunic, a grimy thing that smelled of yeast and another man's sweat. He hung Sylvarresta's fine blue robe in its place.

He looked now like a menial servant, but for his sword and poniard. He couldn't help those. He'd need them.

He hurried into the courtyard to gather the forcibles. The clear evening sky had darkened. In the courtyard, the shadows had grown surprisingly deep. Guards were carrying torches out of the guardroom to light the bailey.

As he got out the door, Gaborn saw his mistake. The great wooden gates to the Dedicates' Keep lay open, and Raj Ahten's battle guard had just ridden in, men who even to the most casual observer could be seen to move with heightened speed, warriors with so many endowments that Gaborn was but a pale shadow in comparison. All around the courtyard, King Sylvarresta's Dedicates had gathered, staring in dismay at Raj Ahten's troops.

Raj Ahten himself, just outside the gates, was leaving the keep with Lord Sylvarresta and Iome.

Gaborn glanced at the ground in the yard. The forcibles he'd wanted to collect were gone. Taken.

A warrior in the guard pinned Gaborn with his eyes. Gaborn's heart beat fiercely. He shrank back, tried to remember his training in the House of Understanding.

A wretch. *I'm a wretch*, he wanted to say with his whole

body. *Another miserable cripple, in service to Lord Sylvarresta.* But the sword he wore told another story.

A mute? A deaf man, one who still hoped to fight?

He shrank back a pace, farther into the shadows, hunched his right shoulder and let his arm hang down, stared at the ground, mouth dropping open stupidly.

"You!" the guard said, spurring his stallion forward. "What is your name?"

Gaborn glanced at the Dedicates around him, as if unsure whether he was being addressed. The Dedicates weren't armed. He could not hope to blend in.

Gaborn put on an idiot's grin, let his eyes go unfocused. There was a class of person who could be found in a Dedicates' Keep that he might play, a servant who had no attributes worth taking, yet who loved his lord and therefore performed what service he could.

Squinting, Gaborn grinned up at the soldier, pointed a finger at his force stallion. "Ah! Nice horse!"

"I said, what is you name?" the soldier demanded. He sported a slight Taifan accent.

"Aleson," Gaborn answered. "Aleson the Devotee." He said "devotee" as if it were a lord's title. In fact, it was a name given to one rejected as a Dedicate, one found worthless. He fumbled at his sword as if trying to draw it. "I . . . I'm going to be a knight."

Gaborn managed to draw the sword halfway, as if to show it off, then shoved it back into the scabbard. The soldier would recognize fine steel if he saw it.

There, he had his disguise. A mentally deficient boy who wore a sword as an affectation.

At that moment, a heavy wain pulled through the portcullis, an open wagon filled with men in hooded robes – men slack-jawed, with vacant eyes, their wits drained. Men so weak from granting brawn they could not rise, but only lay exhausted, arms hanging over the edge of the wagon. Men so cramped from granting grace that every muscle seemed clenched – backs curved, fingers and toes curled into useless claws.

Raj Ahten was bringing Dedicates of his own to the keep. Four huge draft horses pulled the wain. The honor guards' own stallions danced and kicked. There was little room for so many beasts here in the square, not with Dedicates standing around, gawking.

"That's a fine sword, boy," the guard grumbled at Gaborn as his horse shied from the wagon. "Be careful you don't cut yourself." His words were a dismissal; he fought to move away from the wagon without crushing the nearest bystander.

Gaborn shuffled forward, knowing the surest way to get rid of someone was to hang on for dear life. "Oh, it's not sharp. Do you want to see?"

The wagon halted, and Gaborn saw Iome's Maid of Honor, Chemoise, in its very back, holding the head of one of the Dedicates there. "Father, father . . ." she cried, and then Gaborn knew that these were not just any Dedicates to Raj Ahten, but captured knights, brought back to their homeland as trophies. The man Chemoise held was in his mid-thirties, hair of palest brown. Gaborn watched the maid and her father, wished that he could save them. Wished he could save this whole kingdom. You too, he vowed silently, dazed. If I have my way, I will save you, too.

From out of the shadows at Gaborn's side, a heavy man in a dirty robe approached. He growled, "Aleson, you stinking fool! Don't just stand in the way. You didn't empty the Dedicates' chamber pots, like I told you! Come along now and do your job. Leave the good men alone."

To Gaborn's surprise, the fellow thrust two buckets full of feces and urine into Gaborn's hand, then cuffed him on the head. The buckets reeked. For one who had endowments of scent, the odor was unbearable. Gaborn choked back his desire to vomit, twisted his neck, gave the man a wounded glare. The fellow was stout, with bushy brows, a short brown beard going gray. In the shadows he looked like just another Dedicate in dirty robes, but Gaborn recognized him: Sylvarresta's herbalist, a powerful magician, the Earth Warden Binnesman.

"Carry these off to the gardens for me, before it gets too dark," the herbalist whispered viciously, "or you'll get another beating worse than the last."

Gaborn saw what was happening. The herbalist knew that Raj Ahten's scouts had his scent. But no man with endowments of scent would come too near these buckets.

Gaborn held his breath, hefted the buckets.

"Don't stub your toes in the shadows. Must I watch your every moment?" Binnesman hissed. He kept his voice low, as if to keep from being overheard, knowing well that each soldier in Raj Ahten's guard had enough endowments of hearing to discern the very sound of Gaborn's heart at this distance.

Binnesman led him round to the back of the kitchens. There they met the kitchen maid. "Good, you found him!" she whispered to Binnesman.

The herbalist just nodded, held a finger up, warning her not to speak, then led theme both through a small iron gate out the back of the Dedicates' Keep, along a worn trail, into a garden. The cook's herb garden.

Along the south wall of the garden grew some dark green vines, climbing the stone wall. Binnesman stopped, began picking leaves. In the failing light, even Gaborn recognized the narrow, spade-shaped leaves of dogbane.

As soon as he'd picked a handful, Binnesman rolled them in his palm, bruising them. To a common man the dogbane had only a slightly malodorous scent, but it was poison to dogs. They avoided it. And Binnesman was a master magician capable of strengthening the effects of his herbs.

What Gaborn smelled in that moment was indescribable – a gut-wrenching oily reek from a nightmare, like evil incarnate. Indeed, an image filled Gaborn's mind – as if suddenly a giant spider had strung webs of murder here across the path. Deadly. Deadly. Gaborn could imagine how the stuff would affect a hound.

Binnesman sprinkled these leaves on the ground, rubbed some on Gaborn's heel.

When he'd finished, he led Gaborn through the cook's garden, ignoring other herbs as he went. They jumped a low wall, came to the King's Wall – the second tier of the city's defenses.

Binnesman led Gaborn along a narrow road with the King's Wall on one side, the backs of merchants' shops on the other, till he reached a small gate with iron bars, small enough so a man would have to duck to pass through. Two guards stood at the gate in the stone wall. At a gesture from Binnesman, one guard produced a key, unlocked the iron gate.

Gaborn set down the stinking buckets of feces, wanting to be rid of the burden, but Binnesman hissed, "Keep them."

The guards let the three through. Outside the wall was a kingly garden, a garden more lush, more magnificent than any Gaborn had ever seen. In the sudden openness, the last failing light of day still let Gaborn see better than he had in the shadows of the narrow streets.

Yet the term "garden" did not feel entirely correct. The plants that grew here were not pampered and set in rows. Instead they grew in wild profusion and in great variety all about, as if the soil were so alive that it could not help but produce them all in such great abundance.

Strange bushes with flowers like white stars joined in an arch over their heads. Creepers trailed up all along the garden's stone walls, as if seeking to escape.

The garden rolled away for a half mile in each direction. A meadow full of flowers spread before them, and beyond it lay a hillock overgrown with pines and strange trees from the south and east.

In this place, odd things had happened: orange and

lemon trees grew beside a warm pool, trees that should never have survived these winters. And there were other trees beyond, with strange hairlike leaves and long fronds, and twisting red branches that seemed to rake the sky.

A stream tinkled through the meadow. A family of deer there drank at a small pool. The pale forms of flowers and herbs sprouted everywhere, blossoming in profusion.

Exotic forests rose to both the east and the west.

Even this late in the evening, with the sun having fallen, the drone of honeybees filled the air.

Gaborn inhaled deeply, and it seemed that the scents of all the world's forests and flower gardens and spices rushed into his lungs at once. He felt he could hold that scent forever, that it invigorated every fiber of his being.

All the weariness, all the pain of the past few days seemed to wash out of him. The scent of the garden was rich. Intoxicating.

Until this moment, he thought, he'd never truly been alive. He felt no desire to leave, no hurry to leave. It was not as if time ceased here. No, it was a feeling of . . . security. As if the land here would protect him from his enemies, just as it protected Binnesman's plants from the ravages of winter.

Binnesman bent low, pulled off his shoes. He motioned for Gaborn and the serving wench to do the same.

This had to be the wizard's garden, the legendary garden that some said Binnesman would never leave.

Four years earlier, when the old wizard Yarrow had died, some scholars at the House of Understanding had wanted Binnesman to come, to assume the role of hearthmaster in the Room of Earth Powers. It was a post of such prestige that few wizards had ever rejected it. But then there had been a huge uproar. Binnesman had published an herbal several years earlier, describing herbs that would benefit mankind. An Earth Warden named Hoewell had attacked the herbal, claiming that it con-

tained numerous errors, that Binnesman had misidenti-
fied several rare herbs, had drawn pictures of plantains
hanging upside down, had claimed that saffron – a
mysterious and valuable spice brought from islands far to
the south – came from a specific type of flower when, in
fact, everyone knew that it was a mixture of pollens collected from the beaks of nesting hummingbirds.

Some sided with Binnesman, but Hoewell was both a
master scholar and a ruthless politician. Somehow he had
succeeded in humiliating and disaffecting a number of
minor herbalists, even though, as an Earth Warden by
training, his own magical powers dealt with the creation
of magical artifacts – a field apart from herbalism. Still,
his political maneuvering swayed a number of prominent
scholars.

So Binnesman never got the post as hearthmaster in
the Room of Earth Powers. Now some people said that
Binnesman had refused the post in shame, others that his
appointment would never have been ratified. As Gaborn
saw it, such were the lies and rumors that Hoewell
promulgated to aggrandize himself.

Yet a rumor more persistent than any other arose, and
this one Gaborn believed: In the House of Understanding, some good men whispered that despite the
pleas of many scholars, Binnesman simply would not go
to Mystarria, not for any prestigious post. He would not
leave his beloved garden.

On seeing the exotic trees, tasting the scents of rare
spices and honeyed flowers on the wind, Gaborn understood. Of course the herbalist could not leave his garden.
This was Binnesman's life's work. This was his master-
piece.

Binnesman tapped Gaborn's boot with his foot again.
The serving wench already had her shoes off. "Forgive
me, Your Lordship," Binnesman said, "but you must
remove your shoes. This is not common ground."

In a daze, Gaborn did as ordered, pulling off his boots.

He got up, wanting nothing more than to stroll through these grounds for a day, to taste the exotic scents.

Binnesman nodded meaningfully toward the buckets of feces. Gaborn hefted his unsavory burden, and they were off, strolling across a carpet of rosemary and mint that emitted a gentle, cleansing scent as their feet bruised the leaves.

Binnesman led Gaborn through the meadow, past the deer that only looked at the old Earth Warden longingly. He reached a particular rowan tree, a tree that was phenomenally tall, a perfect cone. He studied it for a moment, then said. "This is the place."

He dug a small hole in the detritus beneath the tree, motioned for Gaborn to bring the dung.

When Gaborn brought the buckets, Binnesman emptied them into the pit. Something clanked. Among the feces Gaborn saw objects dark and metallic.

With a start he recognized Sylvarresta's forcibles.

"Come," Binnesman said, "we can't let Raj Ahten have these." He picked up the forcibles, placed them back into the bucket, ignoring the dung on his hands. He walked fifty paces to the brook, where trout snapped at mosquitoes, slapping the water.

Binnesman stepped into the stream and rinsed the forcibles one by one. Then he placed them together on the bank. Fifty-six forcibles. The sun had set nearly half an hour ago, and the forcibles now seemed but dark shadows on the ground.

When Binnesman finished, Gaborn tore a strip of cloth from his tunic and wrapped the forcibles into a bundle.

Gaborn looked up, caught Binnesman appraising him, squinting in the half-light. The herbalist seemed lost in thought. His beefy jowls sagged. He was not a tall man, but he was broad of shoulder, stocky.

"Thank you," Gaborn said, "for saving the forcibles."

Binnesman did not acknowledge his words, merely studied him, as if peering behind Gaborn's eyes, or as if he sought to memorize Gaborn's every feature.

"So," Binnesman said after a long moment. "Who are you?"

Gaborn chuckled. "Don't you know?"

"King Orden's son," Binnesman muttered. "But who else are you? What commitments have you made? A man is defined by his commitments."

A cold dread filled Gaborn at the way the Earth Warden said "commitments." He felt certain that Binnesman was speaking of the oath he'd made this night to Princess Sylvarresta. An oath he'd rather have kept secret. Or perhaps he spoke of the promise Gaborn had made to the kitchen wench, the promise to save her, or even the silent vow he'd made to Chemoise and her father. And, somehow, he felt, these commitments might offend the herbalist. He glanced at the kitchen wench, who stood with hands folded, as if afraid to touch anything.

"I'm a Runelord. An Oath-Bound Lord."

"Hmmm . . ." Binnesman muttered. "Good enough, I suppose. You serve something greater than yourself. And why are you here? Why are you in Castle Sylvarresta now, instead of next week, when your father was scheduled to arrive?"

Gaborn answered simply. "He sent me ahead. He wanted me to see the kingdom, to fall in love with its land, with its people, as he had."

Binnesman nodded thoughtfully, stroking his beard. "And how do you like it? How do you like this *land*?"

Gaborn wanted to say that he admired it, that he found the kingdom beautiful, strong and almost flawless, but Binnesman spoke with a tone in his voice, a tone of such respect for the word "land," that Gaborn sensed they were not speaking of the same thing. Yet perhaps they were. Was this garden not also part of Heredon? Were not the exotic trees, gathered from far corners of the earth, part of Heredon?

"I have found it altogether admirable."

"Humph," Binnesman grunted, glancing around at the bushes, the trees. "This won't last the night. The flameweavers, you see. Theirs is a magic of destruction, mine a magic of preservation. They serve fire, and their master will not let them resume human form unless they feed the flame. What better food than this garden?"

"What of you? Will they kill you?" Gaborn asked.

"That . . . is not in their power," Binnesman said. "We have reached a turning of the seasons. Soon, my robes will turn red."

Gaborn wondered if he meant that literally. The old man's robes were a deep green, the color of leaves in high summer. Could they change color of themselves? "You could come with me," Gaborn offered. "I could help you escape."

Binnesman shook his head. "I've no need to run. I have some skill as a physic. Raj Ahten will want me to serve him."

"Will you?"

Binnesman whispered, "I've made other commitments." He said the word "commitments" with that same odd inflection he used when speaking of the land. "But you, Gaborn Val Orden, must flee."

At that moment, Gaborn caught the sound of a distant barking, the snarling and raucous baying of war dogs.

Binnesman's eyes flickered. "Do not fear them. The dogs cannot pass my barrier. Those that try will die."

Binnesman had a certain sadness in his voice. It pained him to kill the mastiffs. He grunted, climbed up out of the stream, his shoulders sagging as if worried. To Gaborn's surprise, the wizard stooped in the near total darkness, plucked a vine at the water's edge, and told Gaborn, "Roll up your right sleeve, I sense a festering wound."

Gaborn did as asked, and Binnesman set the leaves on the wound, held them in place with his hand. Immediately the leaves began drawing out the heat and pain. Gaborn carefully unrolled his sleeve, letting his shirt help hold the poultice in place.

As if making small talk, Binnesman asked both Gaborn and the kitchen maid, "How do you feel? Tired? Anxious? Are you hungry?"

Binnesman began strolling through the meadow, and as he walked, he would stoop in the shadows and pluck a leaf here, a flower there. Gaborn wondered how he could find them at all in the darkness, but it was as if the wizard had memorized their positions, knew exactly where each grew. He rubbed Gaborn's feet with lemon thyme one moment, something spicier the next. He stopped to pick three borage flowers, their blue leaves glowing faintly in the darkness, and gently took each five-petaled flower between his fingers, then pulled so that the black stamens remained with the petals. He told Gaborn to eat the honeyed flower petals, and Gaborn did, feeling a sudden rush of calmness take him, a perfect fearlessness he'd never thought he could experience under such duress.

The herbalist fed several more borage flowers to the kitchen wench, gave her some rosemary to help fight fatigue.

Binnesman then strolled to a grassy slope, reached down and broke the stem of a flowering bush. "Eyebright," he whispered, taking the stem. A fragrant oily sap was dripping from it, and Binnesman drew a line over Gaborn's brows, another high up on his cheek.

Suddenly, the night shadows did not seem so deep, and Gaborn marveled. He had endowments of sight to his credit, and could see fairly well in the dark, but he'd never imagined anything like this: it was as if the herbalist had added another half-dozen endowments in the matter of a moment. Yet Gaborn recognized that he was not actually seeing more light. Instead, it was as if, when he glanced at something that he might have been able to recognize after minutes of study and squinting in the darkness, he felt no strain, yet instantly discerned shapes and colors.

He looked off to the woods, saw a dark shape there – a man hiding among the trees. A tall man, in full armor. Powerful. If not for the eyebright, he'd never have seen the man at all. He wondered what the fellow might be doing, and yet . . . knew the fellow belonged.

When Binnesman finished administering the herb to the kitchen maid, he said softly to her. "Keep this stem in your pocket. You may need to break it and apply fresh sap again before dawn."

Gaborn realized now that the herbalist was not just chatting about idle matters when asking how they felt, that perhaps this wizard never chatted about idle matters. He was preparing Gaborn and the maid to flee in the darkness. The ministrations of leaves rubbed over his skin would change his scent, throw off his trackers. Other herbs would magnify his abilities.

This took less than three minutes, then the herbalist began asking more penetrating questions. To the maid he asked, "Now how tired are you? Did the borage make your heart race too fast? I could give you skullcap, but I don't want to overtax you."

And sometimes he spoke quickly, gave Gaborn commands. "Keep this poppy seed in your pocket; chew it if you are wounded. It will dull the pain."

He took them next to the edge of the wood, where three dark trees with twisted branches reared up like great beasts with twiggy fingers and mossy limbs, forming a dark hollow that enclosed a small glade. Here, Gaborn felt smothered, constricted. Something about the closeness of the trees gave a sense that he was being watched and judged and would shortly be dismissed. The earth was all around him here, he felt – in the soil beneath his feet, in the trees that surrounded him and nearly covered him. He could smell it in the soil, in leaf mold, in the living trees.

Among many small shrubs that huddled on a hummock near the glade's center, Binnesman stopped. "Here we

have rue," he said. "Harvested at dawn, it has some
medicinal and culinary value, but if you harvest just after
the heat of the day, it is a powerful irritant. Gaborn, if the
hunters come at you from downwind, toss this into their
eyes, or into a fire – the smoke from such a fire is most
dangerous."

Gaborn dared not touch it. Even going near the bushes
made his lungs feel constricted, his eyes water. But
Binnesman walked up to a low bush that held a few wilt-
ing, yellow flowers. He pulled off some leaves, taking no
harm.

The kitchen maid would not draw close, either. Though
she could feel nothing, she had grown careful.

The herbalist looked back at Gaborn, and whispered,
"You do not need to fear it."

But Gaborn knew better.

Binnesman reached down to his feet. "Here." He
picked a handful of rich, loamy soil, placed it in Gaborn's
palm.

"I want you to make a commitment," Binnesman said,
in that special way that let Gaborn know this was serious,
that much depended on how he answered. He spoke each
word with gravity and ceremony, almost chanting.

Gaborn felt dazed by all that had happened, frightened. As he took the soil in his hand, he felt almost as if
the ground wrenched beneath his feet. He was suddenly
so weary. The soil seemed tremendously heavy in his
palm, as if it contained hidden stones of enormous
weight.

The wizard is right, Gaborn thought. This is not common ground.

"Repeat after me: I, Gaborn Val Orden, swear to the
earth, that I will never harm the earth, that I dedicate
myself to the preservation of a seed of humanity in the
dark season to come."

Binnesman stared into Gaborn's eyes, unblinking, and
waited, with bated breath, for Gaborn to speak the vow.

Something inside Gaborn trembled. He felt the soil in his hand, felt . . . a tickling at the back of his consciousness, a presence, a powerful presence.

It was the same great presence he'd recognized yesterday, in Bannisferre, when he'd felt the impulse to ask his bodyguard Borenson to marry the beautiful Myrrima.

Only now that presence came immensely stronger. It was the feeling of rocks in motion, of trees breathing. An odd power pulsed beneath his feet, as if the earth trembled in anticipation. Yes, he could feel it – through his bare feet, the power of the earth rising beneath him.

And Gaborn saw that he'd been traveling here toward this destination for days. Had his father not told him to come here, to learn to love the land? Had some Power inspired his father to say those words?

And in the inn at Bannisferre, when Gaborn drank the addleberry wine, the best wine he had ever tasted, the wine with the initial B on its wax seal, he had felt this power. Gaborn knew now, knew without asking, that Binnesman had put up that bottle of wine. How else could it have had such a marvelous effect? The wine had quickened his wits, led him here.

Gaborn feared to take the wizard's vow, to become a servant of the earth. What would it require? Was he to become an Earth Warden like Binnesman? Gaborn had already taken other vows, vows he considered sacred. As Myrrima had said, he did not take vows lightly.

Yet somehow he also feared *not* to take this vow. Even now, Raj Ahten's hunters would be coming after him. He needed help to escape, wanted Binnesman's aid.

"I swear," Gaborn told Binnesman.

Binnesman chuckled. "No, you fool. Don't swear to me, swear to the earth, to that which is in your hand, and that beneath your feet. Say the whole oath."

Gaborn opened his mouth, painfully aware of how the herbalist clung to his words, painfully aware that this vow was more significant than he could imagine. Wondering

how he could maintain a balance, keep his vows to both
the earth and to Iome.

"I–" Gaborn began to speak, but the earth quivered at
his feet. All around, through the fields and woods and garden, the earth went still. No wind stirred, no animal
called. The dark trees surrounding him seemed to loom
larger, shutting out all light.

Darkness, darkness. I am beneath the earth, Gaborn
thought.

Gaborn glanced round in astonishment, for he had
thought the evening quiet until that moment. Now,
absolute stillness reigned over the face of the land, and
Gaborn sensed a strange and powerful presence rushing
toward him.

In reaction to this, Binnesman backed away from the
rue plant, stood with an astonished demeanor, gazing
about. The soil twisted near his feet, grass parting as if
some great veil of cloth ripped.

And from the bushes at the forest's edge, a man
emerged, a black form stepping from the shadows.
Gaborn had discerned his shape moments before, had
seen his shadow once the eyebright was administered,
but had never guessed at the creature's true appearance.

For this was no mortal man. Rather it was a creature of
dust, formed from rich black soil. Minuscule specks of
dirt and pebbles clung together, molding his features.

Gaborn recognized the form. Raj Ahten trod toward
him. Or, more accurately, a being of dust in the form of
Raj Ahten marched from the woods, complete in armor,
scowling imperiously, his high helm spreading wide with
owl's wings, black as onyx.

Immediately, Gaborn froze in terror, wondering what
this manifestation might mean. He looked at Binnesman;
the wizard had fallen back in astonishment.

The creature of dust stared down at Gaborn, a slight
mocking disdain on its face. In the gathering shadows of
the wood, it might have seemed human to a casual

observer, but for its lack of color. Every eyelash, every fingernail, every feature and fiber of its clothing seemed perfectly formed.

Then the earth spoke.

The creature of dust did not move its mouth. Instead the words seemed to come from all around. Its voice was the sound of wind sighing through a meadow or hissing through lonely peaks. The groan of rocks moving through a stream, or tumbling downhill.

Gaborn understood none of it, though he recognized it as speech. Beside Gaborn, Binnesman listened intently, and interpreted, "He says to you, Gaborn, 'You would speak an oath to me, O son of a man?'"

The strange sounds continued, and Binnesman thought a moment before he added. "'You say you love the land. But would you honor your vows to me, even if I wore the face of an enemy?'"

Gaborn looked to Binnesman for answer, and the wizard nodded, urging Gaborn to speak to the earth directly.

Gaborn had never seen anything like this creature, had never heard tales of it. Earth had come to him, choosing a form that Gaborn could see and comprehend. Some men claimed to look into fire and see the face of the Power behind it, but it often seemed to Gaborn that fire was the most approachable of elements, while air was the least. Gaborn had never heard of the earth manifesting itself in this way.

"I do love the land," Gaborn said at last.

The strange clamor of faraway noises rose again. "'How can you love what you cannot comprehend?'" Binnesman interpreted.

"I love what I do comprehend, and suppose I would love the rest," Gaborn tried to answer truthfully.

Earth smiled, mocking. Boulders rumbled. Binnesman said, "'Someday you shall comprehend me, when your body mingles with mine. Do you fear that day?'"

Death. Earth wanted to know if he feared death.

"Yes." Gaborn dared not lie.

"Then you cannot love me fully," Earth whispered. "Will you aid my cause despite this?"

Raj Ahten. The thing looked so much like Raj Ahten. Gaborn knew what Earth desired of him. Something more than embracing life. Something more than serving man. To embrace death and decay and the totality that was Earth.

A strangeness showed in Earth's dark face, emotions not human. Gaborn looked into those eyes, and images came to mind: a pasture far south of Bannisferre where white stones protruded from the green grass like teeth; the scenic purple mountains of Alcair as seen in the distance south of home. But there was more – vast crevasses and caverns and canyons deep beneath the ground, places he had never seen. Many-colored soils and dark rock by the shapeless ton, so deep within the earth that no man could hold it all, no man could begin to comprehend it. Gems and mud and leaves rotting on the forest floor among the bones of men. Smells of sulfur and ash and grass and blood. Rivers thrumming and tumbling in the dark places of the world, and endless seas lying over the face of the earth like sweet tears.

You cannot know me, the earth was saying. *You cannot comprehend me. You see only surfaces. Though you want me as an ally, I must also be your enemy.*

Painfully, Gaborn considered each word of the vow, wondering if he could keep it.

"Why would you want me to take this vow?" Gaborn asked. "What does it mean, to never harm the earth? What does it mean, to preserve a seed of humanity?"

This time, Binnesman did not hesitate when he translated Earth's answer, which came more as a sighing of wind than a grumble. "You will not seek to thwart me," Earth said, leaning back casually against the bole of one dark tree that seemed to cup him like a hand. "You will seek to learn my will, discern how best to serve the earth."

"In what capacity?" Gaborn asked, seeking to know more precisely what the earth wanted.

Clamorous noises. Binnesman frowned thoughtfully as he sought for words. . . . "As you cannot comprehend me," Earth said, "I cannot comprehend you. Yet this much I know: You love your people, seek their welfare. You seek to save men.

"There was a time when Fire loved the earth, and the sun drew nearer to me. That time is no more. So in this dark season, I must call others to champion my cause. I ask you to save a remnant of mankind."

Gaborn's heart pounded. "Save them from what?"

Hissing rose through the woods. "Fire. All of nature is out of balance. That which you call 'the First Power' has long been withdrawn, but now it will waken and sweep over the world, bringing death. It is in Fire's nature to seek constantly to consume and grow. It shall destroy much."

Gaborn knew enough wizardry to know that while all Powers combined to create life, the alliance of Powers was uneasy, and different Powers favored different kinds of life. Air loved birds, while Water loved fishes, and Earth loved plants and the things that crept upon its face. Fire seemed to love only serpents, and creatures of the netherworld. Earth and Water were powers of stability. Air and Fire were unstable. Earth itself was a protector, and combined with Water to protect nature.

Immediately, Gaborn reasoned, I am a Runelord, Prince of Mystarria – a nation strong in water magics – who loves the land. So Earth seeks to make an ally of me.

"You seek my service," Gaborn said, "and only a fool would refuse to consider your offer. You want me to save someone, and this I would do gladly. But what do you offer in return?"

Boulders rumbled, and nearby the ground vented steam as Earth laughed. Yet Binnesman did not smile as he translated, "'I ask but one thing of you, to save a seed of humanity. If you succeed, the deed itself shall be your reward. You shall save those you deem worthy to live.'"

"*If* I succeed?" Gaborn asked.

Lonely wind hissing through trees. "Once there were toth upon the land. Once there were duskins. . . . At the end of this dark time, mankind, too, may become only a memory."

Gaborn felt his heart nearly freeze. He'd imagined that the earth wanted him to help save the people of Heredon from Raj Ahten. But something more dangerous than a war between two nations was at hand – something more devastating.

"What is going to happen?" Gaborn asked.

The wind hissed as Earth spoke softly. Binnesman merely frowned for a long time, then answered for himself, "Gaborn, I can't tell you what the earth is saying. It is too complex to interpret. The earth does not itself know the full answer. Only the Time Lords see the future, but even for the earth, the answer is unclear. Earth senses wide destruction. The skies will be black with smoke, and everything will burn. The sun at high noon will shine dimly, as red as blood. Seas will be choked with ash. . . . I – it's too much for me to untangle, too much to answer."

The wizard fell silent then, and Gaborn saw that his face was ashen, as if trying to make sense of Earth's words was a great labor, even for him. Or perhaps the things he'd learned terrified Binnesman to the core, so that he could speak no longer.

Gaborn did not understand how to keep the vow, yet no matter what it required, he had to take it. He fell to his knees and vowed, "I, Gaborn Val Orden, swear to you that I will never harm the Earth, that I dedicate myself to the preservation of a seed of humanity in the dark season to come."

Gaborn's whole body trembled. The man of dust leaned over until its helm almost touched Gaborn's forehead. The sound of wind whispered in Gaborn's ears, and the earth rumbled ominously. Binnesman croaked the words: "'I shall hold you to your word, though in time you curse me.'"

Earth raised two fingers of dust, the first and second fingers of its left hand, to Gaborn's forehead, and there traced a rune.

When it had finished, Earth stuck the two fingers to Gaborn's lips.

Gaborn opened his mouth. Earth placed its fingers inside. Gaborn bit, tasting clean soil on his tongue.

In that moment, the fine filaments of hair on the creature of dust fell away, and its muscles slackened, until a pile of dust sloughed to the ground.

Immediately, the suffocating presence of earth power diminished. Light shone thinly still through the trees, and Gaborn breathed deep.

When Binnesman next moved, his face was pale, and the wizard stared at the mound of dust in awe. Reaching down, he respectfully prodded it with a finger, then tasted the dirt.

He took another pinch and sprinkled it over Gaborn's left shoulder, then his right, and then his head, chanting. "The earth heal, the earth hide you, the earth make you its own!"

"Now," Binnesman whispered, placing his hands on Gaborn's shoulders, "Gaborn Val Orden, I name you Earthborn indeed. As you serve the land, it serves you in return."

Gaborn still smelled rue here in the glade, but now its powerful scent only made his nose itch. He went to the bush, caressed a faded yellow flower, pulled a few leaves from branches.

Gaborn glanced over, saw Binnesman staring at him with something like awe etched into his features.

When Gaborn had taken a dozen more leaves, Binnesman grumbled, "You don't need enough to wipe out a whole village. Come now, time is short."

The wizard rolled the rue leaves between his hands, and when he held out his palm, the leaves had crumbled to powder. Binnesman took a pouch from around his own neck, put the crumbled leaves into the pouch, and placed it around Gaborn's throat.

Gaborn took it stiffly, wanting to ask a hundred questions. But when he'd first come into this wild, tangled garden, he'd felt a sense of safety, of being protected. Now he recognized time was drawing short, and he felt a sense of urgency. He had no time to question now.

The kitchen maid had been standing this whole while at the edge of the glade, a terrified expression on her face. Now Binnesman led her and Gaborn downhill, to the south wall of the garden, and they hurried along a narrow trail, Gaborn clutching the forcibles in one hand, the hilt of his saber in the other.

He felt so odd. So numb. He wanted to rest, to have time to sort things out.

When they'd reached the far side of the meadow, beneath the shade of the exotic trees, Gaborn heard shouting behind. He glanced back up the trail.

Night had almost completely fallen. Gaborn could see lights shining now from the watchtowers of the Dedicates' Keep, and from down below at the Soldier's Keep, and from the King's own chambers. A few lonely stars had begun to glow in the sky. This surprised him, for the eyebright so aided his vision that it did not seem night.

But uphill, on the trail behind them, far brighter than any other lights, a fiery man strode into view, the green flames flickering across his shoulders like the tongues of snakes, licking the clean skin of his hairless skull.

The flameweaver was behind the gate still, the same gate Gaborn had entered only minutes before. The guards had fallen back from this sorcerer, and the flameweaver reached out a hand. A bolt of sunlight seemed to burst hungrily from his palm, and the iron gate melted and twisted. The flameweaver pushed past the ruined gate, entered the garden.

Behind him came Raj Ahten's scouts. Men in dark robes, searching for Gaborn's scent.

"Hurry!" Binnesman whispered. If these had been normal men, Gaborn would not have feared. But he sensed now that this was no fight between mere mortals that he engaged in. This was Fire, seeking him.

Then they were running through the woods, over marshy ground beside the stream. Just downhill a few hundred yards, the stream would meet with the River Wye, and there Gaborn hoped to find a means of escape. The maid and the wizard could not match Gaborn's speed. He jumped some low bushes, and in a few moments they reached a small cottage with whitewashed wattle and a thatch roof.

"I must go and save my seeds," Binnesman hissed. "Rowan, you know the way to the mill. Take Gaborn. May the Earth be with you both!"

"Come," the maid, Rowan, said. "This way."

She reached back for his sleeve, pulled him down a brick road. Gaborn did as he was told, rushing with a renewed sense of urgency. He could hear shouting in the meadows behind him. He still had his boots in hand, was painfully aware with each step that he needed to put them on, yet Rowan ran over the uneven stones recklessly, feeling nothing.

Yet even as he ran, he felt . . . astonished, full of wonder, incapable of comprehending all that had just happened. He wanted to stop, to take time to ponder. But at the moment, he knew it was too dangerous to do so.

At the edge of the garden, Gaborn told Rowan, "Stop, stop. Put on your shoes, before you break every bone in your foot!"

Rowan stopped, put on her own shoes while Gaborn pulled on his boots; then they ran with greater speed.

She raced out the garden gate, along a street to the King's stables, an enormous building of new wood. She pulled one of the doors open.

A stableboy sleeping in the hay just inside the door shouted in alarm, but Gaborn and Rowan rushed past him, past the long stalls. Here, slung from the ceiling in belly harnesses, were dozens of the King's Dedicate horses – horses robbed of wit or brawn, stamina, or metabolism so that the King's own force horses could have greater power. Rowan ran past the long row of stalls, then fled out the back door. Here a stream, the same stream that had flowed through the wizard's garden, wound through a muddy corral, where the horses stamped and neighed in fear. The stream passed under a great stone wall, the Outer Wall to the city's defenses.

Gaborn could not climb that wall, some fifty feet in height. Instead, Rowan squirmed under the wall, where the stone had eroded over the ages. The passage was narrow, too narrow to admit a warrior in armor, but the thin girl and Gaborn squeezed through, getting wet in the icy water.

Now the stream tumbled downhill, down a steep green. All around the stream grew tall pussy willows.

Gaborn looked up. An archer on the walls was posted just above them. He looked down, saw them escape, and pointedly looked the other way.

The ground here was kept open near the walls, so that archers could shoot from above. Gaborn could never have sneaked into the castle from here, not unobserved.

The hillside became steep just below the pussy willows, where it led into some deep birch and alder woods that were so dark that Gaborn could hardly see. Yet it was only a small grove, a triangle of trees barely two hundred yards long and a hundred wide.

Through the trees Gaborn spotted the river now, broad and black, He could hear its soft voice burbling.

He halted, grabbed Rowan's ankle to stop her from

crawling farther. On the far side of the river he saw movement: nomen and frowth giants setting camps in the darkness. The nomen were black shadows in the fields of grain, hunched and clawing. Gaborn knew that the nomen, who preferred to leap on their prey from trees in the starlight, would be able to see well in the night, but he did not know how well.

Though the nomen had invaded from the sea a thousand years before, the Runelords had decimated their numbers, had even gone so far as to sail to their own dark lands beyond the Caroll Sea to wipe them out. Long had their war cries been silenced. They had not been fierce warriors, but were cunning fighters in the darkness. The nomen were now little more than legend. Still, rumor said that nomen inhabited the Hest Mountains, beyond Inkarra, and that they sometimes stole children to eat. The Inkarrans seemed never quite able to wipe the last of the creatures from the rain forests. Gaborn didn't know how much of the tales to believe. Perhaps the nomen could see him even now.

But the woods grew thicker off to the left – and Gaborn spotted a wide diversion dam made of stones. The mill. Its huge water wheel made a great racket, with its grinding and the water splashing.

"Let me lead," he whispered. He moved slowly now through the pussy willows, eeling on his belly, not wanting to attract the attention of the nomen on the far side of the river till he reached the shelter of the woods.

They were outside the city wall now, on a steep bank that overlooked the River Wye to the east, the moat to the south. He hoped Raj Ahten didn't have soldiers posted in these woods.

He took his time as he led Rowan deeper into the grove, careful not to snap a twig.

Up on the hills behind him, in the heart of Castle Sylvarresta, he could hear distant cries of dismay, shouts. Perhaps a battle had broken out.

Other shouts nearby mingled with the noise, cries of
hunters, shouting in Taifan, "Go that way! Look over
there! After him!" Raj Ahten's trackers were searching on
the other side of the city wall.

Gaborn crept down a steep ridge, keeping to the trees,
till he and Rowan nearly reached the river.

There he studied the far banks from the deep shadows.

On the hill behind, a fire had begun raging. He smelled
smoke. Binnesman's garden was ablaze. The flames
looked like the lights thrown by a fiery sunrise.

Gaborn spotted giants on the far bank of the river,
hoary things with shaggy manes. The blaze reflected in
their silver eyes. Nomen prowled among them, naked.
Shades, who shielded their eyes from the conflagration.

The river looked shallow. Though autumn was on its
way, little rain had fallen in the past few weeks. Gaborn
feared that no matter how far he dove beneath the water,
the nomen would see him. But it looked as if the whole
city might burst into flame, for the nomen were somewhat blinded.

Gaborn hugged the shadows. He pointed out twigs for
Rowan to avoid with each step.

He heard a branch snap. He spun, drew his saber. One
of Raj Ahten's hunters stood on the ridge above, half-
hidden by trees, framed by firelight from the wizard's
burning garden.

The man didn't rush Gaborn and Rowan, only stood
silently, trusting to the night to hide him. Rowan stopped
at the sound, looked uphill. She apparently couldn't see
the fellow.

He wore a dark robe, and held a naked sword with a
lacquered leather vest for armor. Only the eyebright
Binnesman had given Gaborn let him spot the hunter.

Gaborn didn't know what endowments the man might
have, how strong or swift he might be. But the hunter
would be equally wary of Gaborn's attributes.

Gaborn let his gaze flicker past the hunter, searched

the woods to the man's right, as if he hadn't spotted him. After a long moment, Gaborn turned his back, watched the far bank.

He set his bundle of forcibles on the ground, then pretended to scratch himself and drew the dagger from his belt with his left hand. He held the haft in his grip, the blade flat against his wrist, so that it remained concealed.

Then he just listened. The mill wheel made a noise like the rumble of rocks sliding down a slope, and Gaborn could hear distant shouts, perhaps the sound of folks fighting a fire in the city. "Let's wait here," Gaborn told Rowan.

He stilled his breathing as the hunter drew closer.

Stealthy, a stealthy man, but quick. The man had an endowment of metabolism. Gaborn had no endowments of metabolism. He moved with the speed of youth, but he was no match for a force warrior.

Gaborn couldn't risk letting the man cry an alarm, attract the attention of the nomen across the river.

He waited till the hunter drew close, twenty feet. A twig crunched softly. Gaborn pretended not to hear. Waited half a second.

He waited until he judged that the hunter would be gazing at his feet, concentrating on not making another sound; then Gaborn spun and leapt past Rowan silently.

The hunter raised his sword so fast it blurred. He took a ready stance – knees bent, swordpoint forward. Gaborn was outmatched in speed. But not in cunning.

He flicked his dagger from ten feet, and its pommel hit the man's nose. In that split second, when the hunter was distracted, Gaborn lunged, aimed a devastating blow at the hunter's knee, slicing his patella.

The hunter countered by dropping the tip of his sword, trying too late to parry. On the backstroke Gaborn whipped his blade up, slashing the warrior's throat.

The hunter lunged, not yet realizing he was dead. Gaborn twisted away from the blade, felt it graze the left side of his rib cage. Fire blossomed there, and Gaborn swept aside the warrior's sword with his own, danced back.

Gurgling escaped the hunter's throat, and he staggered forward a step. Blood spurted from his neck, a fountain that gushed in time with the warrior's heartbeat.

Gaborn knew the man couldn't live much longer, tried to back away, afraid of taking another wound. He tripped over a root, and fell on the ground, his sword tip still held high to parry any attacks.

As the hunter's brain drained of blood, he began to lose his sight, looked around dumbly for half a second. He grasped at a sapling and missed, dropped his sword and fell forward.

Gaborn watched the ridge above. He could see no more of Raj Ahten's hunters. Silently he thanked Binnesman for the spices that masked his scent.

Gaborn felt his ribs. They bled, but not badly, not as bad as he had feared. He stanched the blood, then retrieved his forcibles.

Rowan was panting in fear. She studied him in the darkness as he climbed back down toward her, as if terrified that his wound would kill him.

He stood a little straighter, trying to calm her, then led her down the steep bank to the river's edge, and they hid among the pussy willows. The fires burned brighter.

The nomen were poised high on the far bank, looking anxiously in his direction. They had heard the ringing swords, but so long as the fire blinded them, so long as Gaborn and Rowan hid in the shadows, the nomen searched in vain. Perhaps the sound of the mill wheel upriver confused them; perhaps they were not sure if a fight had been fought in the woods. None seemed desirous to brave the river, to fight half-blind. Gaborn recalled vaguely that nomen feared the water.

Wading among pussy willows into water up to his waist, Gaborn looked downstream. Rowan gulped in fear.

Three frowth giants stood knee-deep in the water at

the river's bend. One held a fiery brand aloft, while the other two held their huge oak rods poised like spears. They peered into the water like fishermen waiting for someone to try to escape.

The firelight that blinded the nomen would only help the giants to see better. For a moment, Gaborn studied them. The water downstream could not be more than three feet deep. There was no way that he and Rowan could make it past the giants.

Rowan suddenly gasped in pain and doubled over, clutching her stomach.

TEN: THE FACE OF PURE EVIL

Iome stood atop the south tower of the Dedicates' Keep as Raj Ahten and his guard rode up to the gates. Out in the fields, night was falling, and the flameweavers had begun heading for town, walking across the dry grasses. A small range fire burned in their passage, but to Iome's surprise, it did not rage uncontrollably. Instead, a hundred yards behind them, the fire extinguished, so that the flameweavers looked like comets, with trails of dying fire in their wake.

Behind them came a great wain from the forest, filled with men in robes, bouncing over the rutted mud road that led from the castle into the Dunnwood.

Raj Ahten's legendary Invincibles also began marching into the city, forming up in twenty ranks of a hundred each.

But others stayed behind, out on the plains. The shaggy frowth giants kept to the tree lines and stalked along the rivers, while the dark nomen, their naked bodies blacker than night, circled the castle, squatting on the fields. There would be no escaping them this night.

To the credit of the guards at the wooden gates of the Dedicates' Keep, they did not open to Raj Ahten immediately. When the Wolf Lord made his way up to the city streets to this, the most protected keep within the castle, the guards held fast.

They waited for King Sylvarresta to descend from the

tower, with Iome walking at his side, hand-in-hand. Two Days followed immediately behind, and Chemoise trailed.

Good, Iome thought. Let the Wolf Lord sit outside the gates for a moment longer, waiting on the true lord of Castle Sylvarresta. It was a small retribution for what she knew would come.

Though Iome saw no outward sign of fear in her father's face, he held her hand too tightly, clenching it in a death grip.

In a moment they descended from the tower to the gates of the Dedicates' Keep. The guards here were the best warriors in the kingdom, for this was the sanctum, the heart of Sylvarresta's power. If a Dedicate were killed, Sylvarresta's power would be diminished.

The guards looked smart in their black-and-silver livery over their hauberks.

As King Sylvarresta strode to them, both men pulled their swords, tips pointed to the ground. On the far side of the keep wall, Raj Ahten could be seen through the portcullis gates.

"My lord?" Captain Ault asked. He was ready to fight to the death, if Iome's father so desired. Or to slay both the King and Iome, save them from the torturous end Iome feared.

"Put them away," Sylvarresta said, his voice shaken with uncertainty.

"Do you have any orders?" Ault asked.

Iome's heart pounded. She feared that her father would ask him to slay them now, rather than let them fall into enemy hands.

A debate had long raged among the lords in Rofehavan as to what one should do in such circumstances. Often a conquering king would try to take endowments from those he defeated. In doing so, he became stronger. And Raj Ahten was far too powerful already. Some thought it more noble to kill themselves than to submit to domination.

Others said that one had a duty to live in the hope of serving one's people another day. Iome's father vacillated on this point. Since two days past, when he'd lost two endowments of wit, the King had become suddenly cautious, fearful of what he'd forgotten, afraid to make mistakes.

King Sylvarresta looked down at Iome, tenderly. "Life," he whispered, "is so sweet. Don't you think?"

Iome nodded.

The King said softly, "Life . . . Iome, is strange and beautiful, full of wonders, even in the darkest hours. I have always believed that. One must choose life, if one can. Let us live, in the hope of serving our people."

Iome trembled, fearing that he'd made the wrong choice, fearing that the death of herself and her father would better serve her people.

King Sylvarresta whispered to Ault, "Open the gate. And bring us some lanterns. We'll need some light."

The burly captain nodded grimly. From his eyes, Iome knew Ault would rather die than watch Sylvarresta lose his kingdom. He did not agree with the King's decision.

Ault saluted, touching the flat of his sword to the peak of his iron cap. *You will always be my lord*, the gesture said.

King Sylvarresta gave him a curt nod. The guards unbarred the gates; each took a handle, pushing them outward.

Raj Ahten sat on his gray stallion with white speckles on its rump. His guards surrounded him. His Days, a tall, imperious man with graying temples, waited at his back. The Wolf Lord's horses were large, noble beasts. Iome had heard of the breed but had never seen one before. They were called imperial horses, brought from the almost legendary realm of the Toth, across the Caroll Sea.

Raj Ahten himself looked regal, his black mail covering his body like glistening scales, the wide owl wings on his helm drawing the eye to his face. He stared impassively at the King, at Iome.

His face was neither old nor young, neither quite male nor female, as was the case with those who'd taken many endowments of glamour from persons of both sexes. Yet he was beautiful, so cruelly beautiful that Iome's heart ached to look into his black eyes. His was a face to worship, a face to die for. His head weaved from side to side, minutely, as will happen with those who have many endowments of metabolism.

"Sylvarresta," he said from his horse, omitting any title, "is it not customary to bow to your lord?"

The power of Raj Ahten's Voice was so great that Iome felt almost as if her legs had been kicked out from under her. She could not control herself, and fell down to give her oblations, though a voice in the back of her head whispered, Kill him, before he kills you.

Iome's father fell to one knee, too, and cried out. "Pardon me, my lord. Welcome, to Castle Sylvarresta."

"It is now called Castle Raj," Raj Ahten corrected.

Behind Iome, there was a clanking of metal as the keep's guards brought a gleaming lantern from the guard-room.

Raj Ahten stared at them a moment, firelight reflecting from his eyes, then dismounted his horse, jumping lightly to the ground. He walked up to Sylvarresta.

He was a tall man, this Wolf Lord, half a head taller than Iome's father, and she had always thought her father to be a big man.

In that moment, Iome felt terrified. She didn't know what to expect. Raj Ahten could sweep out his short sword in a blur, decapitate them both. She wouldn't even have time to flinch.

One could not anticipate this man. He'd conquered all the Southern kingdoms around Indhopal in the past few years, growing in power at a tremendous speed. He could be magnanimous in his kindness, inhuman in his cruelty.

It was said that when the Sultan of Aven got cornered

in his winter palace at Shemnarvalla, that Raj Ahten responded by capturing his wives and children at their summer home, and threatened to catapult the Sultan's sons over the palace walls. The Sultan responded by standing on the castle walls, grasping his groin, and calling out, "Go ahead, I have a hammer and anvils to make better sons!" The Sultan had many sons, and it was said that on that night, as each was set aflame, the cries were horrifying, for Raj Ahten waited until the child's cries died before he sent the flaming body over the castle walls. Though the Sultan would not surrender, his own guards could not bear to hear the cries, and so his men opened the gates. When Raj Ahten entered, he took the Sultan, determined to make an example of him. What happened next, Iome could not say. Such things were never discussed in civilized countries.

But it was known that Raj Ahten sat in judgment on the kings he conquered before his wars were ever begun. He knew which he would butcher, which he would enslave, which he would make regents.

Iome's heart pounded. Her father was an Oath-Bound Lord, a man of decency and honor. In her opinion, he was the most compassionate ruler in all the realms of Rofehavan.

And Raj Ahten was the blackest usurper to walk the earth in eight hundred years. He dealt with no king as an equal, considered the world his vassals. The two could not share the throne to Heredon.

Raj Ahten pulled the horseman's warhammer from the sheath at his back. It was a long-handled thing, almost as tall as he.

He planted its crossbars in the cobblestones at his feet, then clasped his hands on its hilt, leaned his chin on one knuckle, and smiled playfully.

"We have things between us, you and I, Sylvarresta," Raj Ahten said. "Differences of opinion."

He nodded toward the street behind him. "Are these

your men?"

The huge wain Iome had seen clanking across the fields now pulled up between the graystone shops. In the wagon were men – soldiers all, one could tell by their grim faces. As they neared the lantern, in horror Iome recognized some of them – Corporal Deliphon, Swordmaster Skallery. Faces she'd not seen in years.

Behind Iome, Chemoise gasped, cried out and ran forward. Her own father, Eremon Vottania Solette, lay in the very front of the wagon, a ruined man who did not blink. His back arched cruelly, and his ruined hands clutched in useless fists. His face grimaced in pain; all his muscles were stiff and unyielding as rigor mortis. Iome followed Chemoise a few steps, but dared not go nearer to Raj Ahten.

Yet even from thirty feet, she could smell the stink and dirt on the men. Many had eyes that stared vacantly, stupid. Some had jaws slack, from weariness. Each soldier had been drained of one of the "greater" endowments – wit, brawn, grace, metabolism, or stamina – and thus made harmless.

As Chemoise clutched her father to her breast and cried, Ault drew close with a flickering torch. In the wavering light, the faces in the wagon seemed pale and horrible.

"Most of those were once my men," King Sylvarresta admitted warily. "But I released them from service. They are free soldiers, Knights Equitable. I am not their lord."

It was a dubious denial. Though all the men in the wagon were Knights Equitable, knights who were sworn by oath to destroy all Wolf Lords like Raj Ahten, and though such an oath was considered to override any other oath of fealty to a single lord, the truth was that Iome's father served as patron to these knights – he'd supplied them with money and arms needed to fulfill their quest to destroy Raj Ahten. For him to deny responsibility for their actions was like an archer refusing to take the blame for damage done by an arrow once it had left his bow.

Raj Ahten did not accept the King's excuse. A grimace of pain crossed Raj Ahten's face, and he looked away for a moment. Iome felt her heart lurch as she saw tears glisten in Raj Ahten's eyes. "You have done me a great wrong," Raj Ahten said. "Your assassins killed my Dedicates, slaughtered my own nephew, and executed some I considered to be dear friends, good servants."

The tone of his voice filled Iome with guilt, overwhelming guilt. She felt like a child caught tormenting a kitten.

It pained her all the more because Iome saw that Raj Ahten's pain seemed to be genuine. Raj Ahten had loved his Dedicates.

No, something in the back of her mind said, you must not believe that. He wants you to believe that. It is only a trick, a practiced use of Voice. He loves only the power his people give. Yet she found it difficult to cling to her skepticism.

"Let us go to your throne room," Raj Ahten said. "You've given me no choice in the matter but to come settle our differences. It grieves me that we must discuss . . . terms of surrender."

King Sylvarresta nodded, kept his head bent. Perspiration dotted his brow. Iome's breathing came easier. They would talk. Only talk. She dared hope for leniency.

With a glance from Raj Ahten, his guards rode into the Dedicates' Keep, leading his horse into the courtyard, while Raj Ahten headed down the road toward the King's Keep.

Iome followed behind her father, numb. Her slippered feet did not like the rough paving stones. Chemoise stayed behind, following the wagon into bailey of the Dedicates' Keep, holding her father's hand, whispering words of reassurance to Eremon Vottania Solette.

Iome, her father, and the three Days all followed Raj

Ahten through the walled market, the richest street of Heredon, past the fine shops where silver and gems, china and fine cloth were sold, down to the King's Tower.

The lanterns in the tower had already been lit. It was, Iome had to admit, an ugly tower. A huge square block, six stories tall, with nothing in the way of adornment but the granite statues of past kings that circled its base. The statues themselves were enormous things, each sixteen feet tall. Along the gutters atop the tower were carved minstrels and dancing gargoyles, but the figures were so small that one could not see them well from the ground.

Iome wanted to run, to dart into an alley and try to hide behind one of the cows that had bedded there for the night. Her heart hammered so badly.

When she crossed the threshold into the King's Keep, she nearly fainted. Her father held her hand, helped her keep standing. Iome wanted to vomit, but found herself following her father up the broad staircases, five stories, until they reached the King's chambers.

Raj Ahten led them through the audience room, into the huge throne room. The King's and Queen's thrones were made of lacquered wood, with cushions covered in scarlet silk. Gold filigree adorned the leaves carved into the thrones' arms and feet, and adorned the headboards. They were unimposing ornaments. Sylvarresta had better thrones stored in the attic. But the room itself was enormous, with two sets of full-length oriel windows that looked north, south, and west over the kingdom. Two lanterns burned at each side of the throne, and a small fire danced in the huge hearth.

The Wolf Lord took a seat on the King's throne, seeming comfortable in his armor.

He nodded at King Sylvarresta. "I trust my cousin Venetta is well? Go and fetch her. Take a moment to freshen up. We will hold audience when you are more comfortable." He waved at Sylvarresta's armor, an order for him to remove it.

King Sylvarresta nodded, not a sign of acknowledgement, more a bending of the neck in submission, then went to the royal apartments. Iome was so frightened, she followed him rather than go to her own room.

Neither the King's Days nor Iome's followed. The Days chronicled every public movement of their lords, but even they did not dare defile the sanctity of the Runelords' bedchamber.

Instead, Raj Ahten's Days held a convocation with the Days of the royal family in an ancient alcove outside the bedchamber, where guards and servants often waited for their lord. There, the Days stood speaking briefly in code. It was often thus when Days from opposing kingdoms met. Iome understood none of their code, and simply closed the bedroom door on their chatter.

In the King's bedchamber, Queen Venetta Sylvarresta sat in a chair, dressed in her finest robes and regalia, staring out the windows to the south. Her back was to the door. She'd been painting her nails with a clear lacquer.

She was vain, with ten endowments of glamour – much more beautiful than Iome. Venetta had black hair and an olive complexion, like Raj Ahten's – both darker than Iome's. The diadems in Venetta's crown could not match the casual loveliness of her face. Her scepter lay across her lap, a gold column with pearls embedded in a ball at one end.

"So," she sighed without turning, "you've lost our kingdom." She sounded more hurt than Iome had ever heard her.

Iome's father pulled off his armored gauntlets, tossed them on the huge, four-poster bed.

"I told you you'd lose it," Queen Sylvarresta said. "You were too soft to hold it. It was only a matter of time." More painful words, unlike anything Iome had ever heard her mother say before. Unlike, Iome felt sure, anything she'd ever said.

King Sylvarresta unstrapped his helm, threw it next to

the gauntlets, then worried at the pins on his vambraces. "I'll not regret what I've done," he said. "Our people grew up in relative peace."

"Without allies, without a strong king to protect them," Iome's mother said. "How much peace could you have really given them?"

The bitterness in the words stunned Iome. Her mother had always seemed calm, austere, a quiet support to her husband.

"We gave them the best I could," her father answered.

"And they love us little enough in return. If you were more of a lord, they would rise up in your defense. Your people would fight beside you, beyond all hope."

Iome helped her father remove his pauldrons, then the rerebrace from his upper arms. Within a moment, he had his breastplate on the bed. Only then did Iome notice how her father was laying out the armor, like a man of steel, lying facedown, suffocating in the deep feather mattress.

Venetta was right. King Sylvarresta never got the respect, the admiration he deserved. An Oath-Bound Runelord should have drawn followers, should have had the respect of his people.

Instead, those people who gave endowments went to foreign kings, like King Orden, where they could sell their attributes at a higher price.

A king like Sylvarresta seldom got the support he needed, unless a Wolf Lord like Raj Ahten came along. Only when confronted with a usurper who won his endowments through blackmail would good people flock to the banner of a king like Sylvarresta.

Of course, that is why Raj Ahten attacks here first, Iome realized, when he could have laid waste other kingdoms closer by.

"Did you hear me, milord?" Venetta said. "I'm belittling you."

"I hear you," King Sylvarresta said, "and I love you still."

Iome's mother turned then, her face full of tears of love, her mouth tight in pain. She looked to be a young woman. Just as a faithful dog in great pain will snap at the master who tries to save it, Iome's mother had snapped at her father, and now Iome saw the regret there.

"I love you, forever," Venetta said. "You're a thousand times more the king than my wicked cousin could ever be."

King Sylvarresta pulled off his chain, stood in his leather jerkin. He glanced pointedly at Iome, and she left the room, gave her parents their privacy.

She dared not go out through the hall, into the throne room. Not with Raj Ahten there. So she waited in the alcove outside her father's door, and listened to the Days talk excitedly. In ancient times, guards and servants would have been stationed here during the night, but King Sylvarresta had never wanted either. Still, the small room with its benches was large enough to hold Iome and the Days.

Several long minutes later, Iome's mother and father exited their room. Her mother still in her regalia, her father wearing a lordly robe and a determined expression.

As her mother passed, she said to Iome, "Remember who you are."

Her mother intended to play the role of queen to the very end.

Iome followed them, back into the audience chamber.

To her surprise, two of the Raj Ahten's Invincibles had joined him. They stood to either side of the throne. The three of them made an imposing sight.

King Sylvarresta came forward, to the end of the crimson carpet before the throne. He knelt on one knee, bowed his head. "Jas Laren Sylvarresta, at your service, Lord. And I present my wife, your dear cousin Venetta Moshan Sylvarresta, as requested."

Queen Sylvarresta watched her husband bow, stood uncertainly for a moment, then bowed slightly, eyes wary, watching the Wolf Lord.

When her head was nearest the floor, Raj Ahten leapt forward, his body a blur, and drew the short sword from his sheath.

Venetta's crown, snatched from her head by Raj Ahten's blade, went flying, rang off the stone ceiling.

"You are presumptuous!" Raj Ahten warned.

Iome's mother watched the Wolf Lord, eyes wary.

"I am a queen, still," she said in her own defense.

"That will be for me to decide," Raj Ahten said. He drove the sword through the cushion of the Queen's throne, left it as he sat back down. He pulled off his gauntlets, tossed them beside him on the Queen's throne. He clutched the arms of his chair, betraying to Iome just the slightest nervousness. He wanted something from them. Needed something. She could tell.

"I've been more than patient with you. You, Jas Laren Sylvarresta, financed knights who attacked me without provocation. I've come to insure that such attacks cease. I require . . . an acceptable tribute."

Iome's father said nothing for a moment. Her mother knelt near the throne. "What would you have of us?" King Sylvarresta asked at last.

"Assurance, that you will never fight me again."

"You have my word," Sylvarresta said. He looked up now, focused all his attention on the Wolf Lord.

Raj Ahten said heavily. "I thank you. Your oath is not a thing I take lightly. You have been an honorable lord to your people, Sylvarresta. An evenhanded lord. Your realm is clean, prosperous. Your people have many endowments to give me. If times were not so dark, I would like to think you and I could have been allies. But . . .

"We have great enemies massing, south of our borders."

"Inkarrans?" Sylvarresta asked.

Raj Ahten waved his hands in dismissal. "Worse. Reavers. They have been breeding like rabbits for thirty years. They've laid the forests of Denham bare. They've driven the nomen from their sanctuaries in the mountains. In another season, the reavers will come against us. I intend to stop them. I'll need your help, the help of all the Northern kingdoms. I intend to take control."

Iome felt confused by this. Apparently, her father was just as confused.

"We could beat them!" Sylvarresta said. "The Northern kingdoms would unite in such a cause. You don't need to prosecute this war alone!"

"And who would lead our armies?" Raj Ahten asked. "You? King Orden? Me? You know better than that."

The heart seemed to go out of Iome's father. Raj Ahten was right. No one could lead the Northern kings. There were too many political divisions, too many moral strifes, too many petty jealousies and ancient rivalries. If Orden led an army south, someone would stay to attack his weakened cities.

Least of all would anyone trust Raj Ahten, the Wolf Lord. For hundreds of years, the Runelords had attacked any leader who sought too much power, who grasped too far. In ancient times, certain robbers, greedy for any power they could get, would use the forcibles to take endowments from wolves, and thus became known as Wolf Lords.

Men who desired an uncanny sense of smell or hearing often took endowments from pups, for dogs gave them willingly and required little in the way of support thereafter. Even stamina or brawn were taken from mastiffs, bred for just that purpose.

Yet men who took endowments from dogs became subhuman, part animal themselves. Thus the euphemism *Wolf Lord* became a term of derision used for any man of low morals, including men like Raj Ahten, who might never have taken an endowment from a dog.

No king of the North would follow Raj Ahten. Men who earned the title Wolf Lord became outcasts. Honorable lords were duty bound to fund the Knights

Equitable in their wars and assassinations. Like wolves caught in the sheep fold, Wolf Lords were accorded no mercy.

"It doesn't have to be this way," Sylvarresta said. "There are other ways to prosecute this war. A tithe of knights from each kingdom . . ."

"It does have to be this way," Raj Ahten corrected. "Would you dare dispute me on this point? I have a thousand endowments of wit, to your . . ." He gazed into King Sylvarresta's eyes a flickering second, studying the intelligence there. ". . . two."

It could have been a guess, Iome thought, but she knew better. There was a saying: "A wise king does not garner all wit, instead he also allows his counselors to be wise." In the North, it was considered wasteful to take more than four endowments of wit. A lord who did so remembered everything he ever heard, all he ever saw or thought or felt. Sylvarresta would not have taken more than four. Yet how had Raj Ahten recognized that Iome's father had but two endowments active?

Raj Ahten's declaration that he'd taken wit from a thousand took the breath from Iome. She could not comprehend such a thing. Some lords swore that a few more endowments of wit granted a Runelord some benefit – extra creativity, deeper wisdom.

Raj Ahten folded his hands. "I've studied the reavers – how they are spreading into our kingdoms in tiny pockets, each with a new queen. The infestation is wide.

"Now, Sylvarresta, despite your peaceable assurances, I require more from you. Lay bare your flesh."

Clumsy from nervousness, with all the grace of a trained bear, King Sylvarresta untied the sash of his robe, shrugged off the midnight blue silk, till his hairy chest lay bare. The red scars of forcibles showed beneath his right nipple, like the mark of a lover's teeth. Raj Ahten read Sylvarresta's strengths in a glance.

"Your wit, Sylvarresta. I will have your wit."

Iome's father seemed to cave in on himself, dropped to both knees. He knew what it would be like, to pee his own pants, not knowing his name, not recognizing his wife or children, his dearest friends. In the past days he'd already felt keen loss as memories were lost to him. He shook his head.

"Do you mean you will not give it, or cannot?" Raj Ahten asked.

King Sylvarresta spread both hands wide, shaking his head, unable to speak.

"Will not? But you must—" Raj Ahten said.

"I can't!" Iome's father cried. "Take my life instead."

"I don't want your death," Raj Ahten said. "What value is that to me? But your wit!"

"I can't!" Sylvarresta said.

To give an enemy an endowment was one thing, but Raj Ahten would take more than just Sylvarresta's wit. Because Sylvarresta was already endowed, Raj Ahten would make King Sylvarresta his *vector*.

A man could only grant one endowment in his life, and when that endowment was granted, it created a magical channel, a bond between lord and vassal that could only be broken by death. If the lord died, the endowment returned to its give. If the vassal died, the lord lost the attributes he had gained.

But if a man like Sylvarresta granted his wit to Raj Ahten, he would give not only his own wit, but also all the wit he'd ever received from his living Dedicates, plus all the wit he might receive in the future. As a vector, Sylvarresta became a living conduit. He would give Raj Ahten the wit he had taken, and might even be used to channel the wit of hundreds to Raj Ahten.

"You can give it me, with the proper incentive," Raj Ahten assured him. "What of your people? You care for them, don't you. You have trusted friends, servants, among your Dedicates? Your sacrifice could save them. If I have to kill you, I won't leave your Dedicates alive – men and women who can no longer offer endowments, men and women who might seek vengeance against me."

"I can't!" Sylvarresta said.

"Not even to buy the lives of a hundred vassals, a thousand?"

Iome hated this, hated the pregnant silence that followed. Raj Ahten had to get the endowment willingly. Some lords sought to assure the necessary degree of longing through love, others by offering lucre. Raj Ahten used blackmail.

"What of your beautiful wife – my cousin?" Raj Ahten asked. "What of her life? Would you give the endowment to buy her life? To buy her sanity. You would not want to see such a lovely thing ill-used."

"Don't do it!" Iome's mother said. "He can't break me!"

"You could save her life. Not only would she keep it, but she would remain on the throne, ruling as regent in my stead. The throne she loves so much."

King Sylvarresta turned to his queen, jaw quivering. He nodded, hesitantly.

"No!" Venetta Sylvarresta cried. In that moment, she spun and ran. Iome thought she would hit the wall, but realized too late that she'd not headed for the wall, but for the full-length windows behind the Days.

Suddenly, faster than sight could account, Raj Ahten was at her side, holding her right wrist. Venetta struggled in his grasp.

She turned to him, grimacing. "Please!" she said, grasping Raj Ahten's own wrist.

Then, suddenly, she squeezed, digging her nails into the Wolf Lord's wrist until blood flowed. With a victorious cry, she looked Raj Ahten in the eyes.

Venetta shouted to her husband, "Now you see how to kill a Wolf Lord, my sweet!"

Iome suddenly remembered the clear lacquer on the nails, and she understood – the Queen's distress had been a ruse, a plot to get Raj Ahten near so that she could plunge her poisoned fingernails into his flesh.

Venetta stepped back, holding her bloodied nails high, as if to display them for Raj Ahten before he collapsed.

Raj Ahten raised his right arm, stared at the wrist in dismay. The blood in it blackened, and the wrist began to swell horribly.

He held it up, as if in defiance, and gazed into Venetta's eyes for a long moment, several heartbeats, until Venetta paled with fear.

Iome glanced at the arm. The bloody cuts in Raj Ahten's wrist had healed seamlessly in a matter of seconds, and now the blackened arm began to regain its natural color.

How many endowments of stamina did the Wolf Lord have? How many of metabolism? Iome had never seen such healing power, had heard of it only in legend.

Raj Ahten smiled, a terrifying, predatory smile.

"Ah, so I cannot trust you, Venetta," he whispered. "I am a sentimental man. I had hoped family could be spared."

He slapped her with the back of his fist, the slap of Runelord. The side of Venetta's face caved in under the force of the blow, splattering blood through the air, and her neck snapped. The blow knocked her back a dozen feet, so that she hit the glass of the oriel.

She crashed through, the weight of her dead body pulling at the long red drapes as she did, and for half a second she seemed to stand still in the night air, before she plummeted the five stories.

Her body splattered against the broad paving stones in the courtyard below.

Iome stood in shock.

Her father cried out, and Raj Ahten stared at the splintered panes of colored glass, the red drapes waving in the stiffening breeze, annoyed.

Raj Ahten said, "My condolences, Sylvarresta. You see that I had no other choice. Of course, there are always those who think it easier to kill or die, than to live in service. And they are correct. Death requires no effort."

Iome felt as if a hole had ripped in her heart. Her father only sat on bended knees, shaking. "Now," Raj Ahten continued, "we were about to conclude a bargain. I want your wit. A few more endowments of it benefits me little. But it gains much for you. Give me your wit, and your daughter, Iome, will rule in your stead, as regent. Agreed?"

Iome's father sobbed, nodded dumbly, "Bring your forcibles then. Let me forget this day, my loss, and become as a child."

He would give the endowment to keep his daughter alive.

In that moment, Iome knelt again, terrified. She could not think, could not think what to do. "Remember who you are," her mother had said. But what did that mean? I am a princess, a servant of my people, she thought. Should I strike at Raj Ahten, follow my mother through the window? What does that buy?

As regent she would have some power. She could still fight Raj Ahten subtly, as long as she lived. She could give her people some measure of happiness, of freedom.

Certainly, that was why her father still lived, why he didn't choose to fight to the death, as her mother had.

Iome's heart hammered, and she could think of nothing to do, could formulate no plan of hope, but remembered Gaborn's face earlier in the day. The promise on his lips. "I am your Protector. I will return for you."

But what could Gaborn do? He couldn't fight Raj Ahten, couldn't hope to beat the Wolf of the South.

Yet Iome had to hope.

Raj Ahten nodded to a guard. "Call the facilitators."

In moments, Raj Ahten's facilitators entered the room, cruel little men in saffron robes. One bore a forcible on a satin pillow.

Raj Ahten's facilitators were well practiced, masters of

their craft. One began the incantation, and the other held King Sylvarresta, coached him through it. "Watch your daughter, sirrah," he said in a thick Kartish accent. "This you do for her. Do for her. She everything. She the one you love. You do for her."

Iome stood before him, dazed, listened to her father's cries as the forcible heated. She daubed the sweat from his brow as the metal suddenly twisted like something alive. She gazed into his clear gray eyes as the forcible drew away the endowment, sucked the intelligence from him, until she could tell that he no longer remembered her name, but only cried in stupid agony.

She sobbed herself when he gave his final scream of pain, and collapsed at her feet.

Then the facilitators went to Raj Ahten, bearing the white-hot forcible trailing a ribbon of light, and Raj Ahten pulled off his helm, so that his long dark hair fell around his shoulders, then pulled off his scale mail, opened his leather jerkin to expose his muscular chest. It was a mass of scars, so marked by forcibles that Iome could see only a few faint traces of unmarked flesh.

As he took the endowment, Raj Ahten sat back on the throne, eyes glazed in satisfaction, watching Iome narrowly.

She wanted to rage against him, to pummel him with her fists, but dared do nothing but sit at her father's head, smoothing back his hair, trying to comfort him.

The King opened his eyes, regaining consciousness for half a second, and he stared up at Iome, his mouth open, as if wondering what strange and beautiful creature he beheld. "Gaaagh," he bawled; then a pool of urine began to spread on the red carpets beneath him.

"Father, Father," Iome whispered softly, kissing him, hoping that in time he would at least learn that she loved him.

Finished with their incantations, the facilitators left. Raj Ahten reached over to his sword, pulled it from the

Queen's throne.

"Come, take your place beside me," he said. Once again, she saw that undisguised lust in his face, and did not know if he lusted for her body or for her endowments.

Iome found herself halfway to the throne before she realized that he'd used his Voice to order her. To be manipulated this way angered her.

She sat on the throne, tried not to look at Raj Ahten's face, at his incredibly handsome face.

"You understand why I must do this, don't you?" he asked.

Iome didn't answer.

"Someday you will thank me." Raj Ahten studied her frankly. "Have you studied in the House of Understanding, or have you read the chronicles?"

Iome nodded. She'd read the chronicles – at least selected passages.

"Have you heard the name of Daylan Hammer?"

Iome had. "The warrior?"

"The chroniclers called him 'the Sum of All Men.' Sixteen hundred and eighty-eight years ago, he defeated the Toth invaders and their magicians, here on Rofehavan's own shores. He defeated them almost single-handedly. He had so many endowments of stamina that when a sword passed through his heart, it would heal up again as the blade exited. Do you know how many endowments that takes?"

Iome shook her head.

"I do," Raj Ahten said, pulling back his shirt. "Try it, if you like."

Iome had her poniard strapped under her skirts. She hesitated just a moment. It seemed ghoulish, yet she might never have another chance to stab the man.

She pulled it, looked into his eyes. Raj Ahten watched her, confident. Iome plunged the dagger up between his ribs, saw the pain in his eyes, heard him give a startled gasp. She twisted the blade, yet no blood flowed down the runnel. Only a slight red film oozed where the blade met flesh. She pulled the blade free.

The wound closed as the bloody blade exited.

"You see?" Raj Ahten asked. "Neither your mother's poison nor your own dagger can hurt me. Among Runelords, there has never been another of Daylan's equal. Until now.

"It is said in my country that when he'd received enough endowments, he no longer needed to take them. The love of his people supported him, it flowed to him. When his Dedicates died, his powers remained, undiminished."

She'd never read that. It defied her understanding of the art of the Runelords. Yet she hoped it was true. She hoped that such a thing could be, that Raj Ahten would someday quit draining people like her father.

"I think," Raj Ahten said softly, "that I am nearly there. I think I shall be his equal, and that I shall defeat the reavers without the loss of fifty million human lives, as would happen under any other plan."

Iome looked into his eyes, wanting to hate him for what he'd done. Her father lay in his own urine on the floor at her feet. Her mother was dead on the paving stones outside the keep. Yet Iome looked into Raj Ahten's face, and she could not hate him. He seemed . . . so sincere. So beautiful.

He reached out, stroked her hand, and she dared not pull away. She wondered if he would try to seduce her. She wondered if she'd have the strength to fight him if he did.

"So sweet. If you were not my kin, I'd take you as a wife. But I'm afraid propriety forbids it. Now, Iome, you too must do your part to help me defeat the reavers. You will give me your glamour."

Iome's heart pounded. She imagined how it would be, with skin as rough as leather, the cobwebs of her hair falling from her head, the way the veins would stick out on her legs. The dry smell of her breath. To look, to smell, to be repulsive.

Yet that was not half the horror of it. Glamour was more than beauty, more than physical loveliness. It could be recognized partly as form, but just as much was manifest in the color of one's skin, the glossiness of one's hair, the light that shone in one's eyes. It could be seen in posture, in poise, in determination. The heart of it often lay somewhere in a person's confidence in and love of self.

So, depending on the ruthlessness of the facilitator involved, all these could be drawn away, leaving the new Dedicate both ugly and filled with self-loathing.

Iome shook her head. She had to fight him, had to fight Raj Ahten any way she could. Yet she could think of nothing, no way to strike back.

"Come, child," Raj Ahten said smoothly. "What would you do with all your beauty, if I left it to you? Lure some prince to your bed? What a petty desire. You could do it. But afterward you would only spend your life in regret. You've seen how men look at you with lust in their eyes. You've seen how they stare, always wanting you. Certainly you must tire of it."

When he put it that way, in such a silky voice, Iome felt wretched. It seemed vile and selfish to want to be beautiful.

"In the desert near where I was born," Raj Ahten said, "a great monument, a statue, stands three hundred feet tall, half tilted in the sand. It is the statue of a king, long forgotten, his face scoured away by wind. A banner at his feet, written in an ancient language, says, 'All bow to the Great Ozyvarius, who rules the earth, whose kingdom shall never fail!'

"Yet all the scribes in the world cannot tell me who that king is, or how long ago he reigned.

"We have always been such fleeting creatures," Raj Ahten whispered. "We have always been so temporary. But together, Iome, we can become something more."

The craving in his voice, the hunger, almost drove all reason from Iome's mind. almost she felt willing to give him her beauty. But a wiser voice in the back of her mind nagged. "No, I would die, I would be nothing."

"You would not die," Raj Ahten said. "If I become the Sum of All Men, your beauty would live on in me. Some part of you would always remain, to be loved, to be admired."

"No," Iome said in horror.

Raj Ahten glanced at the floor, where King Sylvarresta still lay in a foul heap. "Not even to save *his* life?"

Then Iome knew, she knew, that her father would tell her not to make this bargain. "No," Iome shuddered.

"It is a horrible thing, to put an idiot among the torturers. All that pain your father would have to endure, never understanding why, never knowing that there is such a thing as death that could bring him release, with the torturers repeating your name each time they put the hot irons to him, so that in time, even at the mention of your name, he would cry out in pain. It would be truly horrible."

The cruelty inherent in such an idea left Iome numb. She looked at Raj Ahten, her heart breaking. She could not say yes.

The Wolf Lord nodded to one of his men. "Bring in the girl."

The guard left the chamber, returned quickly with Chemoise. Chemoise, who should have been in the Dedicates' Keep, comforting her father. Chemoise, who had already suffered so much this week, lost so much to Raj Ahten.

How had Raj Ahten known what Iome felt for her dear friend? Had Iome betrayed the girl with a glance?

Chemoise had wide, frightened eyes. She began weeping in terror when she saw the King lying on the floor. Shrieked when Raj Ahten's guard took her to the broken window, poised to throw her over the edge.

Iome's heart hammered, as she watched her childhood friend begin to gibber in fear. Two lives. Raj Ahten would be killing two – Chemoise and her unborn child.

Chemoise, forgive me for this betrayal, Iome wanted to say. For she knew, she knew with her whole soul, that surrender was wrong. If no one had ever surrendered, Raj Ahten would be dead by now. Yet she also knew that to give her glamour to Raj Ahten would benefit him little, while it saved the lives of Iome's friends.

"I cannot give *you* an endowment," Iome said, unable to disguise the loathing in her words. She could not give it to him. Not to him personally.

"If not me, a vector, then," Raj Ahten offered.

Something in Iome's heart tripped. A balance was found. She could give her beauty – give it for her father, for Chemoise. So long as she did not have to give it to Raj Ahten. Her voice broke as she said, "Bring your forcible, then."

Moments later the forcibles were fetched, along with a wretched woman who had given her glamour. So Iome looked upon the hag in dirty gray robes and saw what she would become, and struggled to see what beauty had ever been hidden inside the woman.

Then the chants began. Iome watched Chemoise, still poised on the ledge, and silently willed her beauty away, willed herself to buy something lovely and eternally precious with it. The life of a friend, and the baby she carried.

There was a rustling in the darkness, and a tiny glowing streamer of phosphorous fire as the facilitator approached, put the forcible low on her neck, almost against her bosom.

For half a moment, nothing happened, and someone whispered, "For your friend. Do it for your friend."

Iome nodded, sweat pouring down her brow. She held the image of Chemoise in her mind, Chemoise holding a child in her arms, nuzzling it.

Iome felt the unspeakable pain of the forcible, opened her eyes, saw the skin of her hands dry and crack as if they burned in the infernal heat. The veins rose on her wrists like roots, and her nails became brittle as chalk.

Her firm young breasts sank, and she grabbed at them, feeling the loss keenly. She regretted the trade now, but it was too late. She felt . . . as if she stood in the river, and the sand at her feet flowed out from under her, undermining her. Everything that was hers, all her beauty, her allure, flowed out and away, into the forcible.

Her lustrous hair withered and twisted on her head like worms.

Iome cried in pain and horror, and more flowed out from her still. For a moment, it was as if she gazed into oblivion and saw herself, and loathed what she saw. She understood for the first time in her life that she was nothing, had always been nothing, a no one, a cipher. She feared to cry out, lest others take offense at the sound of her wretched voice.

That is a lie. I am not so ugly as that, she cried out to Raj Ahten in her soul. *My beauty you can have, but not my soul*.

And then she moved away from the precipice, and felt only . . . alone. Utterly alone, and in unspeakable pain.

Somehow, she managed a rare feat: she did not faint from the rigors of the forcible, though she imagined that her whole body would be consumed in the fires.

ELEVEN: COMMITMENTS

Cold black river water swirled around Gaborn's thighs, like a dead hand trying to pull him downstream. Rowan, in the darkness on the bank just above him, groaned fiercely in pain, doubled over.

"What's wrong?" Gaborn whispered, hardly daring to part his lips.

"The Queen – she's dead," Rowan whispered.

Then he understood. After years of loss of feeling, years of numbness, now the whole world of sensation rushed upon Rowan – the cold of the water and of the night, the pain of her bruised feet, her fatigue after a hard day's work, and countless other minor injuries.

Those who gave an endowment of touch, once all their senses returned, felt all the world anew, as if for the first time. The shock of it could be phenomenal, even deadly, for the sensations came twenty times stronger than before. Gaborn worried for the young woman, worried that she might not be able to travel. The water here was bracing cold. Certainly he could not hope to bring Rowan through it.

Yet, even worse, if the Queen was dead, Gaborn feared that Raj Ahten was slaughtering the other members of the royal family – King Sylvarresta and Iome.

Commitments. Gaborn had made too many commitments. He felt overwhelmed. He'd accepted responsibility for Rowan, dared not move her, dared not try to take her through the river. Yet he'd also promised to save Iome, to go to her.

Gaborn wanted to kneel in the river, let it cool the burning wound in his ribs. Overhead, a slight breeze made the branches of the alders and birches sway. Here in the deep shadows, he could see the water downstream, reflecting the orange of firelight up above.

Binnesman's garden was aflame. On the far bank of the river, the nomen were grunting, shadows moving in a greater darkness, trying to spot Gaborn. Yet he was well hidden here in this thicket, so long as he didn't move. The frowth giants hunted in the shallows downstream. He suspected that he could swim out of here alone, flee Castle Sylvarresta and bear the news of its fall to his father. He was a fast swimmer. In spite of the fact that the water was shallow, he thought he might make it. But he couldn't hope to do so with Rowan.

Gaborn could not possibly leave Castle Sylvarresta.

I swore to Iome, he realized. *I took an oath. She is under my protection, both as a Runelord, and now as a part of my vow to the earth.* Both were vows he could not lightly break.

A day earlier, in the market at Bannisferre, Myrrima had chided Gaborn for not making commitments easily. It was true. He dared not make them.

"What is a Runelord," his mother had taught him as a child, "but a man who keeps an oath? Your vassals give you endowments, and you grant them protection in return. They give you wit, and you lead wisely. They grant you brawn, and you fight like a reaver. They bestow stamina, and you work long hours in their behalf. You live for them. And if you love them as you should, you die for them. No vassal will waste an endowment on a Runelord who lives only for himself."

These were the words Queen Orden had taught her son. She had been a strong woman, one who taught Gaborn that beneath his father's callous exterior, there lived a man of firm principle. It was true that in years past, King Orden had purchased endowments from the poor, and while some considered this behavior morally suspect, a way of taking advantage of the poor, King Orden had seen it differently. He'd said, "Some people love money more than they love their fellow men. Why not turn such people's weakness into your strength?"

Why not indeed? It was a good argument, from a man who sought only the betterment of his kingdom. Yet in the past three years, his father had given up the practice, had quit taking endowments from the poor. He'd told Gaborn, "I was wrong. I'd buy endowments still, if only I had the wisdom to judge others' motives." But the poor who sought to sell endowments usually had many reasons for doing so: even the most craven of them had some ennobling love of family and kin and could therefore imagine that by selling an endowment, they were performing an act of self-sacrifice. But then there were the desperate poor, those who saw no other way to escape poverty than to sell themselves. "Purchase my hearing," one farmer had once begged Gaborn's father after the great floods four years past. "What need have I of ears, when all I hear are the cries of hungry children?"

The world was full of despairing creatures, people who for one reason or another had given up on life. Gaborn's father had not purchased the farmer's hearing. Instead, he'd given the man food to last the winter, timber and workers to rebuild his home, seed to plant for the coming spring.

Hope. He'd given the man hope. Gaborn wondered what Iome would think of his father if she knew this tale. Perhaps she'd think better of him. He hoped that she would live to hear it.

Gaborn glanced up through the tree trunks, slashes of black against a dark background. To look toward the city, to look toward the castle walls, filled him with despair.

I can do little to fight Raj Ahten, he considered. It was

true that he might be able to hide in the city, perhaps ambush a soldier here and there. But how long could he last? How long could he keep it up before he was caught?

Not long.

Yet of what help am I to my charges, if I flee now? Gaborn wondered. He should have done more. He should have tried to save Iome, and Binnesman . . . and all the rest.

True, his father needed to know that Castle Sylvarresta had fallen, and he needed to know the manner of its capture.

And the lure of home drew Gaborn. No matter how much he admired the strength of people in Heredon, the stately stone buildings with their ceilings so high, so cool and breezy, the pleasure gardens at every turn, it was not a familiar place.

Gaborn had not been to the palace much for eight years, had spent nearly all his time some fifty miles from home, in the House of Understanding, with its resolute scholars and stark dormitories. He'd looked forward to going home after this trip. For years now he'd longed to sleep in the big, cotton-filled bed he'd enjoyed as a child, to wake to the feel of the morning wind blowing from the wheat fields through his lace curtains.

He'd imagined that he'd spend his winter eating decent food, studying battle tactics with his father, dueling with the soldiers in the guard. Borenson had promised to introduce Gaborn to some of the finer alehouses in Mystarria. And there was Iome, whose gentleness among her people had seduced him as no other could. He'd hoped to take her home.

So many pleasures he'd imagined.

Gaborn wanted to go home. It was silly, this wish to be taken care of, to live without cares, as if he were a child.

Gaborn remembered being a child, hunting rabbits in the hazelnut orchard with his old red hound. He remembered days when his father had taken him to fish for trout in Dewflood Stream, where the weeping willows bent low over the water and green inchworms hung from the willow branches on silken threads, taunting the trout. In those days, life, it seemed, was an endless summer.

But Gaborn could not return.

He despaired at the thought of even getting away from Castle Sylvarresta alive.

For the moment, he could see no convincing reason to leave here. Gaborn's father would hear of the castle's fall soon enough. Peasants would noise the tale abroad. King Orden was on his way. Perhaps three days. He'd hear of this by tomorrow.

No, Gaborn did not need to warn his father, could not leave the castle. He needed to get Rowan to safety, someplace warm, where she could heal. He needed to help Iome. And he'd made a greater commitment.

He had made a vow never to harm the earth. It should be an easy vow to keep, he thought, for he wished the earth no harm. Yet as he considered, he wondered at the intent of the oath. Right now, the flameweavers were burning Binnesman's garden. Was Gaborn bound by oath to fight the flameweavers, to stop them?

He listened deep in his heart, wondering, seeking to feel the earth's will in this matter.

The fire on the hill suddenly grew brighter, or perhaps the firelight was now also reflecting from clouds of smoke above. The smell of sweet smoke was cloying. Across the river, a noman barked. Gaborn could hear others growling. It was said that nomen feared water. Gaborn hoped they feared it enough that they would not swim the river to search for him.

In the matter of the garden, Gaborn felt nothing. No urge to either stop the burning or to accept it. Certainly, if Binnesman had wanted to fight for it, he'd have done so.

Gaborn silently slogged up from the river, went to Rowan, who still crouched among the willows.

He put his arm around her, held her, wondering what to do, where to hide. He wished the earth would hide him now, wished for some deep hole to crawl into. And he felt . . . a rightness on wishing that, felt that the earth would protect him that way.

"Rowan, do you know a place here in the city where we can hide? A cellar, a pit?"

"Hide? Aren't we going to swim?"

"The water's too shallow and too cold. You can't swim it." Gaborn licked his lips. "So I'm going to stay and fight Raj Ahten as best I can. He has soldiers and Dedicates here. I can best strike a blow against him if I stay."

Rowan leaned close, seeking to warm herself. Her teeth chattered. He felt the tantalizing softness of her breasts against his chest, her hair blowing against his cheek. She was trembling, perhaps more from the cold than from fear. She'd gotten wet crawling through the stream, and she did not have Gaborn's stamina to help her weather the cold.

"You're staying because you're afraid for me," she whispered, teeth chattering. "But I can't stay. Raj Ahten will demand an accounting . . ."

It was common for a new king to take an accounting of all his people, to find out who owed money to the kingdom. Of course, Raj Ahten's facilitators would be there, looking for potential Dedicates. When Raj Ahten's men learned that Rowan had been a Dedicate for the dead queen, they would probably torment her.

"Perhaps," Gaborn said. "We can worry about that later. But now we need to hide. So tell me of such a place: a hole. A place where the scent is strong."

"The spice cellars?" Rowan whispered. "Up by the King's stables."

"Cellars?" Gaborn said, sensing that this was the place. This was where the earth would lead him.

"In the summer, Binnesman lays up herbs for sale, and at the festival the King buys others. The cellar is full now, with many boxes. It's up the hill, above the stables."

Gaborn wondered. They wouldn't have to go far into the city, and would merely be doubling back on their own trail, confusing the scent. "What about guards? Spices are valuable."

Rowan shook her head. "The cook's boy sleeps in a room above the cellars. But he – well, he's been known to nap through a thunderstorm."

Gaborn picked up the little bundle of forcibles, struggled to put them in the wide pocket of his robe. The cellars seemed to be the kind of place he needed. Someplace secretive, someplace where his scent would be covered.

"Let's go," he said, but he didn't head directly back uphill. Instead, he picked up Rowan in his arms, carried her down to the river, and began creeping upstream in the shallows, hunching low, trying to cover his scent.

He headed upriver, hugging the reeds. Ahead of him, the waters grew fast. A millrace split off from the river, fed into the moat. The banks along the race had been built high, so that when Gaborn reached it, he was able to wade through the shallows with good cover, until he came right up under the thundering waterwheel, splashing and grinding. To his right was a stone wall, dividing the millrace from the main course of the river and its broad diversion dam. To his left was the mill house and a steep trail up to the castle.

Gaborn stopped. He could go forward no farther, needed now to climb the banks of the millrace, then take the trail up through the trees, to the castle walls again.

He turned, began climbing the bank of the millrace. The grass here was brown and dying, tall rye stubble.

Ahead, he spotted a ferrin, a fierce little rat-faced man with a sharp stick to use as a spear, outside the mill house. He stood guard over a hole in the foundation, his back to Gaborn.

As Gaborn watched, a second ferrin scooted out from

the hole, carrying a small cloth by its ends. They'd stolen flour from the floor of the mill, probably nothing more than sweepings. Yet it was dangerous business for a ferrin. Many had been killed for less.

Before standing in plain view and frightening the creatures, Gaborn searched downstream for signs of pursuit, his eyes just level with the tops of the grass.

Sure enough, six shadows moved at the edge of the water, under the trees. Men with swords and bows. One wore splint mail. So Raj Ahten's scouts had found his trail again.

Gaborn clung to the side of the slope of the millrace, hidden in tall grass. He watched the soldiers for two long minutes. They'd discovered their dead comrade, followed Gaborn's and Rowan's scent to the river's edge.

Several men were looking downstream. Of course they expected him to go downstream, to swim past the giants, into the relative safety of the Dunnwood. It seemed the only sane thing for Gaborn to do. Now that he'd fled the castle, they wouldn't expect him to sneak back in.

If they pursued him into the Dunnwood, they'd find his scent aplenty, for Gaborn had ridden through this morning.

But the fellow in splint mail was staring toward the mill, squinting. Gaborn was downwind from them. He didn't think the man could smell him. Yet perhaps the man was just cautious.

Or perhaps he'd seen the ferrin above Gaborn, spotted movement. The ferrin was dark brown in color, standing before gray stone. Gaborn wanted it to move, so that the scout below would see the creature more clearly.

In his years in the House of Understanding, Gaborn had not bothered to study in the Room of Tongues. Beyond his own Rofehavanish he could speak only a smattering of Indhopalese. When he had a few more endowments of wit and could grasp such things more easily, he planned to make languages a further study.

Yet on cold nights during the winter, he'd frequented an alehouse with certain unsavory friends. One of them, a minor cutpurse, had trained a pair of ferrin to hunt for coins, which he exchanged for food. The ferrin could have gotten coins anywhere – lost coins dropped in the street, stolen from shop floors, taken from dead men's eyes in the tombs.

This friend had spoken a few words of ferrin, a very crude language composed of shrill whistles and growls. Gaborn had enough endowments of Voice that he could duplicate it.

He whistled now. "Food. Food. I give."

Up above him, the ferrin turned, startled. "What? What?" the ferrin guard growled. "I hear you." The word *I-hear-you* was often a request for the speaker to repeat himself. The ferrin tended to locate others of their kind by their whistling calls.

"Food. I give," Gaborn whistled in a friendly tone. It was a full tenth of all the ferrin vocabulary that Gaborn could command.

From the woods above the mill, a dozen answering voices whistled. "I hear you. I hear you," followed by phrases Gaborn didn't understand. It might have been that these ferrin spoke another dialect, for many of their shrieks and growls sounded familiar. He thought he heard the word "Come!" repeated several times.

Then, suddenly, half a dozen ferrin were running around the paving stones of the mill house, coming down from the trees. More ferrin had been hiding up there than Gaborn had seen.

They stuck their small snouts in the air and approached Gaborn cautiously, growling, "What? Food?"

Gaborn glanced downriver, wondering at the scouts' reaction. The man in splint mail could see the ferrin now, a dozen of them, sauntering around the foundations of the mill. Reason dictated that if Gaborn were near, the ferrin would have scattered.

After a moment's hesitation, the scout in splint mail waved his broadsword toward both banks, while he shouted orders to his men. With the thundering of the waterwheel in his ears, Gaborn could not hear the orders. But presently, all six hunters hurried back uphill into the trees, angling south. They would search the woods, downstream.

When Gaborn felt sure they were gone, and that no prying eyes watched his direction, he carried Rowan uphill.

TWELVE: OFFERS

Chemoise Solette felt dazed. Watching her best friend, Iome, lose her glamour horrified Chemoise to the core of her soul.

When Raj Ahten finished with the Princess, he turned and gazed into Chemoise's eyes. His nostrils flared as he judged her.

"You are a beautiful young creature," Raj Ahten whispered. "Serve me."

Chemoise could not hide the revulsion she felt at those words. Iome still lay on the floor, dazed, barely conscious. Chemoise's father still lay in the wagon down in the Dedicates' Keep.

She said nothing in response. Raj Ahten smiled weakly.

Raj Ahten could take no endowment from a woman who hated him so intensely, and his Voice would not sway Chemoise. But he could take other things. He let his gaze drift down to her waist, as if she stood naked before him. "Put this one in the Dedicates' Keep, for now. Let her care for her king and her princess."

A chill of horror crept over Chemoise, and she dared hope that while she was in the keep Raj Ahten would forget her.

So a guard took Iome's elbow, pulled her down the narrow stairs out of the Great Hall and up the street to the Dedicates' Keep, and thrust her through the portcullis. There he spoke a few words in Indhopalese to the guards who'd just been posted. The guards smiled with knowing grins.

Chemoise ran back to her father, who had been dragged into the Dedicates' Hall, and now lay on a clean pallet.

The sight of him felt painful, for this wound ran deep and had festered so many years.

Chemoise's father, Eremon Vottania Solette, was a Knight Equitable, sworn to bring down the Wolf Lord Raj Ahten. It was an oath he had not taken lightly seven years ago, the day he disavowed himself from Sylvarresta's service to ride through the spring-green fields for the far kingdom of Aven.

It was an oath that had cost him everything. Chemoise remembered how tall he'd sat in the saddle, how proud she'd been. He'd been a great warrior, had seemed invincible to a nine-year-old girl.

Now his clothing smelled of moldy straw and sour sweat. His muscles clenched uselessly, his chin shoved against his chest. She got a rag and some water, began to clean him. He cried out in pain as she rubbed his ankle. She studied it, found both legs horribly scarred. The skin around his ankles was red, hair rubbed away.

Raj Ahten had kept her father in chains these past six years. Such treatment for Dedicates was unheard of. After years of such abuse, she felt amazed that he even remained alive. Here in the North, Dedicates were pampered, honored, treated with affection. It was rumored that Raj Ahten had begun taking slaves to feed his need for Dedicates.

While Chemoise waited for the cooks to bring broth from the kitchens, she merely held his hand, kissing it over and over. He stared up at her with haunted eyes, unable to blink.

Chemoise heard a scream from the King's Keep, someone giving endowments. To take her mind from the noise, she began whispering. "Oh, Father, I'm so glad you're here. I've waited so long for this."

His eyes crinkled in a sad smile, and he breathed heavily.

She didn't know how to tell him she was carrying a child. She wanted him to be happy, to believe that all was well in her life. She did not want to admit how she'd dishonored the Princess. She hoped her father would never need to know the truth, that grand illusions might give him some peace.

"Father, I'm married now," she whispered, "to Sergeant Dreys, of the palace guard. He was only a boy when you left. Do you remember him?"

Her father twisted his head to the side, half of a shake. "He's a good man, very kind. The King has granted him lands here near town." Chemoise wondered if she was spreading it on too heavily. Sergeants seldom got landed. "We live there with his mother and sisters. We're going to have a child, he and I. It's growing inside me."

She could not tell him the truth, tell how the father had died at the hands of Raj Ahten, tell how she'd gone to call his ghost to the place where she'd made love to him so many nights, bringing dishonor to her family and to her princess. She dared not tell how Dreys' wight had come to her that evening, a cold shade that now lodged within her.

Yet that night, when she had felt the first fluttering movements of the babe within her, it had seemed a miracle.

Chemoise took her father's hand, which seemed clenched in a permanent fist, and smoothed out his fingers, opened it, after years of its having lain useless. Her father squeezed her hand, a sign of affection and thanksgiving, but he squeezed so hard. With several endowments of strength, he had a grip like a vise.

At first, Chemoise tried to ignore it. But it grew too strong. She whispered, "Father, don't squeeze so hard."

His hand tightened in fear, and he tried to pull his arm away, to loosen his grip. But those who gave endowments of grace could not relax, could not easily let their muscles stretch. He clenched her hand more painfully, so that

Chemoise bit her lip. "Please . . ." she begged, wondering if somehow her father knew that she'd lied, was trying to punish her.

Eremon Solette grimaced in apology, struggled with all his might to relax, to stretch his muscles, release Chemoise. For a minute, he only managed to hold her tighter; then Chemoise felt his grip soften.

The cooks had still not brought the broth around for those who'd given endowments of metabolism. Chemoise's father would not be able to eat anything more solid. The smooth muscles of his stomach would not contract properly.

"Father," Chemoise cried. "I've waited so long. I wanted you so long. . . . I wish you could speak, I wish you could tell me what happened."

Eremon Vottania Solette had been captured at Aven, at Raj Ahten's winter palace by the sea. He'd scaled the white tower where gauzy lavender curtains fluttered in the wind, and found himself in a room thick with jasmine incense, where many dark-haired women slept on cushions, naked but for thin veils to cover their flesh. Raj Ahten's harem.

A brass water pipe lay on a sandalwood table, with eight mouthpieces wriggling from it like the tentacles of an octopus. The balls of rolled greenish-black opium in the pipe's bowl had all burned to ash. For one moment, he permitted himself to stand, admiring the beauties at his feet.

Coals glowed in golden braziers around the beds, keeping the room pleasantly warm. The sweet musk of the women would have made this room smell of paradise, if not for the bitter tang of opium.

In an adjoining room, he had heard a woman's deranged squealing laughter, the sounds of cavorting. He suddenly had the wild hope he might take Raj Ahten while the Runelord lay naked, his attention diverted.

But as he stood, quietly unsheathing his long dagger, all dressed in black, his back against the wall, a maiden woke, saw him behind the gauzy curtains, hiding.

Eremon had tried to silence her, had leapt to plunge the knife into her throat, but not before she screamed.

A eunuch guard of little note leapt from an alcove, suddenly wakened, and clubbed Eremon with a staff.

The eunuch's name was Salim al Daub, a heavy man with the roundness and womanly voice common to eunuchs, and the soft brown eyes of a doe.

As a reward for capturing an assassin, Raj Ahten presented Salim with a great gift. He offered Salim an endowment of grace, from Eremon himself.

Eremon had thought he would rather die than grant an endowment to Raj Ahten's guard, but Eremon held two secret hopes. The first great hope was that someday he would return to Heredon and see his daughter once more.

He gazed at her, saw how she'd grown beautiful like her mother, and he could not help but weep at seeing his greatest dream fulfilled.

Chemoise watched her father's eyes fill with tears. He gasped for breath, struggling from moment to moment to stay alive, unable to relax enough to let his lungs fill. She wondered how he could have kept this up for six long years.

"Are you all right?" she asked. "What can I do for you?"

For a long moment he struggled to speak two words: "Kill . . . us."

Book 3:

Day 21 in the Month of Harvest,
A Day of Deception

THIRTEEN: PRAGMATIC KING ORDEN

Thirty miles to the south of Castle Sylvarresta, a high rock called Tor Hollick rose four hundred feet above the Dunnwood, and from its crags one could gaze far.

Once, long in the past, a fortress had stood here, but few of the stones remained one atop another. Many had been carried away to build walls for peasants' homes.

King Mendellas Draken Orden sat uncomfortably on a broken, lichen-crusted pillar, staring away over the rolling hills, the tops of trees that stirred in the night wind. His cape of green samite fluttered on the small breeze. A cup of too-sweet tea warmed his hands. In the air above him, a pair of nesting graaks circled on leather wings, calling out softly in the darkness, their batlike shapes huge against the stars.

King Orden ignored them, his attention focused elsewhere. A fire burned on a distant hill. Castle Sylvarresta aflame?

Orden found the very thought to be harrowing. It was more than a pain of the heart, it was a pain of the mind and of the soul. Over the years, he'd learned to love this realm and its king dearly. Perhaps, he loved it too dearly. He was riding now into danger.

According to Orden's scouts, Raj Ahten had reached the castle by midday. The Wolf Lord could have mounted a quick attack, burned the castle.

On seeing the glowing sky, Orden feared the worst.

Two thousand troops camped in the woods below his perch. His men were exhausted after a day of riding at an incredible pace. Borenson had raced to his king after leaving Gaborn. A hard flight it had been – Borenson had left four assassins dead in his trail.

King Orden found his heart hammering at the thought of his son, there in that burning castle. He wanted to send a spy in and learn where Gaborn was, how he'd fared. He wanted to charge the castle and save his son. Such useless thoughts preyed on him. He would have stood and paced, if his rocky perch had given him the room.

No, he could do nothing except grow angry at Gaborn. So foolhardy, such a strong-willed boy. And yet so hopelessly stupid. Did the boy really believe Raj Ahten sought to take only the castle? Surely Raj Ahten knew that Orden journeyed each year to Castle Sylvarresta for the hunt. And the key to destroying the North was to destroy House Orden.

No, this entire escapade was little more than a trap. A lion hunt, in the manner of the South, with beaters in the bushes and the spearmen somewhere in the rear. Clever of Raj Ahten to beat the bushes, to take Castle Sylvarresta as a distraction. Orden had already sent scouts to the south and to the east, hoping to discover what spearmen blocked his road home. Surely every path was guarded. If Raj Ahten played his part well, he might yet destroy House Orden and take Heredon in the bargain. King Orden expected to hear nothing from his scouts for a day or more.

It was foolhardy of Gaborn to go to Sylvarresta. Foolhardy and great of heart.

Yet King Orden had long been Sylvarresta's friend, and he knew that had the tables been turned, had he been the first to hear that Jas Laren Sylvarresta stood in need, he'd have ridden hard to fight beside his old comrade.

Now Orden had to satisfy himself by watching the city burn from afar, awaiting reports from the scouts who rode ahead. He had six scouts on good force horses. It would not be a long wait. Though his soldiers and their horses needed rest, Mendellas would not sleep this night, perhaps not for many nights to come. With some forty endowments of stamina, he need never sleep again, if he did not so desire.

Certainly, Raj Ahten would not sleep tonight.

On the rock above him sat Orden's Days, and his son's. King Orden looked up at the men, wondering. Why did Gaborn's Days not go to him? If Gaborn was at Castle Sylvarresta, then the Days should follow. He'd know if another Days spotted Gaborn. Or perhaps Gaborn's whereabouts did not matter. Perhaps his son was captured, or dead?

As he kept his slow watch over the next hour, letting his mind drift and dream, he considered his own defences at home. King Orden sometimes had . . . impressions . . . of danger, felt the presence of reavers on his southern border. As a child, his father had told him that these impressions were the heritage of kings, a birthright. He considered now, but felt nothing.

He wondered about the fortresses on his borders. Were they secure?

A scout soon reached King Orden with news. Sylvarresta had indeed fallen – captured at sunset without a fight.

Worse than Orden had feared. At that news, King Orden took a lacquered oak message case that had been tucked inside his belt. It was a message to King Sylvarresta, sealed with the signet of the Duke of Longmot.

King Orden's scouts had intercepted Longmot's messenger at dawn, if "intercepted" was the proper word. More particularly, Orden's scout had found the man dead, his corpse concealed in the brush beside the road, killed by an assassin's arrow. Orden's scouts would not have recovered the message box if not for the stink of the body.

The countryside was crawling with assassins, set along the road in pairs.

Under normal circumstances, Orden would have respected the privacy of the parties involved, would have delivered the message case to Sylvarresta himself. But Sylvarresta had fallen, and Orden worried that Longmot had sent word of evil tidings. Perhaps it, too, was besieged. It was, next to Castle Sylvarresta, the largest fortress in all Heredon. Though nineteen other fortifications dotted the kingdom, they guarded smaller cities and villages. Five of the fortresses were only minor keeps.

So King Orden broke the wax seal on the message case, pulled out the fine yellow parchment scroll, unrolled it, and read by starlight. The flowing script was obviously written by a feminine hand, but had been written hastily, with words crossed out:

To His Most Rightful Sovereign King, Jas Laren Sylvarresta: All Honor and Good ~~Cheer~~ Wishes, from His Most Devoted Subject, The Duchess Emmadine Ot Laren

Dearest Uncle: You are betrayed. ~~My hus~~ Unbeknown to me, my husband has sold you, permitting Raj Ahten's forces to move through the Dunnwood. Apparently, my husband hoped to rule as regent in your stead, should Heredon fall.

But Raj Ahten himself was here two nights ago, with a powerful army. My husband ordered the drawbridge lowered for him, kept our soldiers at bay.

In one long night, Raj Ahten came and took endowments from many. He repaid my husband's treachery with treachery of his own, hanging him by his guts from the iron grates outside the window of his own bedroom.

Raj Ahten knows better than to trust a traitor.

As for me, he treated me badly, using me as only a husband should use his wife. Then he forced me to grant him an endowment of glamour, and he left a regent, some scholars, and a small army to ~~manage~~ cow the city in his absence.

For two days his regent has tried to suck this land dry, taking endowments by the hundreds. He cares little whether those who give the endowments live or die. So many Dedicates lie heaped in the bailey, no one will be able to care for them. I myself he used as a vector, taking glamour from hundreds of women, while my sons, Wren and Dru, though they are mere children, now vector stamina and grace to the Wolf Lord.

It was not till an hour ago that our own servants and a few guards managed to revolt, overthrowing our tormentors. It was a bloody struggle.

But all was not for nothing. We have captured forty thousand forcibles!

Here, King Orden halted, for his breath suddenly left him. He stood up, began pacing. He felt faint.

Forty thousand forcibles! It was unheard of! In all the Northern Kingdoms, not so many endowments had been given in twenty years. Orden glanced up at the pair of Days sitting on the rock above. These men knew that those forcibles were hidden there. By the Powers, Orden wished he knew a hundredth of what the Days must know.

Raj Ahten was a fool to hold such great wealth in one place. Someone would steal those forcibles.

By the Powers, I'll steal them! Orden thought.

Unless it was a trap! Had Raj Ahten really believed he could hold Longmot?

Orden pondered. If one went into a foreign castle, took major endowments from all the royalty, all the finest soldiers, one could supplant one's enemies in a single night, steal their strength and leave them gasping in defeat.

The Duchess had said it was the house servants who managed the revolt – few soldiers. So her soldiers were dead – or drained of endowments. Perhaps it was not a trap.

Raj Ahten had trusted his own men to hold his treasure for him in Longmot – a fine castle, with stunning defenses. What better place to keep so many forcibles? And from there, he would have taken forcibles to Castle Sylvarresta, to drain his enemies. Indeed, he probably already had some in his possession.

King Orden read on:

I trust that these forcibles shall be of great use to you in prosecuting this war. Meanwhile, an occupying army approaches from the south. According to communiqués, it should be here in four days.

I've sent to Groverman and Dreis, requesting aid. I believe we can withstand a siege, with their help.

The Wolf Lord left me no palace guard, no soldiers. Those who have given endowments are vectored to Raj Ahten through my sons.

Raj Ahten is on his way to you in Castle Sylvarresta. I do not believe he can reach you until the night before Hostenfest.

He is dangerous. He has so many endowments of glamour, he shines like the sun. For decades now, Longmot has been home to many vain women, each hoping to be more beautiful than her neighbor. Their beauty is all vectored through me.

I will not uphold your enemies.

In two days, all those who have granted endowments in Longmot shall die by my hand. It grieves me that I must kill my own sons, but only by doing so can I revive enough troops to defend the city.

I've hidden the forcibles. They are buried beneath the turnip field at Bredsfor Manor.

I suspect you will not see me again, not alive. I'm placing Captain Cedrick Tempest, of the palace guard, in temporary command of Longmot.

My husband hangs from his window still, his own intestines serving as a rope for his neck. I will not cut the vil-

*lain down. If I had known beforehand of his treachery, I'd
not have dealt with him so kindly.*

*I go now, to sharpen a knife. Should I fail, you know
what to do.*

Your Devoted Niece,
The Duchess Emmadine Ot Laren

Mendellas Orden finished reading the letter, heart
hammering, then laid it aside. "You know what to do."
The age-old cry of those forced to serve as vectors: Kill
me, if I can't kill myself.

King Orden had often met the Duchess. She'd always
struck him as a mousy little lady, too timid for grand
deeds.

It took a strong woman to kill herself, her children. Yet
King Orden knew that there was a time when one could
follow no other course. So, Raj Ahten had vectored the
soldiery through the royal family, forced them to grant
major endowments, so the soldiers would never be able
to fight again – unless the royal family was slaughtered.

The Duchess would have to do her duty, butcher her
own children to save the kingdom. It was an evil trade.
King Orden only hoped his own son did not fall into Raj
Ahten's clutches. Orden imagined that he had the
strength to kill his own son, if the need arose.

But he dreaded the deed.

King Orden turned over the letter, read the date.
Harvest 19. Written almost two days past, over a hundred
miles away.

The Duchess hadn't expected Raj Ahten to reach
Castle Sylvarresta until tomorrow. So she planned to kill
herself at dawn, before the occupying army arrived.

A pity she hadn't killed herself this morning. Her sacrifice might have done Lord Sylvarresta some good.

Orden quickly scrawled letters to the Duke of
Groverman and the Earl of Dreis – the lords with castles
closest to Longmot – begging them both to send aid while

at the same time requesting it from neighbors. Though the Duchess had already sought aid from those lords, Orden feared that her messengers might have met the same fate as the man he'd found on the road. To be certain that Dreis and Groverman came, he said bluntly that Raj Ahten had left a hoard of treasure at Longmot.

"Borenson?" King Orden called when he finished. The captain was sitting on the rocks above him, just a few feet below the tangled limbs of the graaks' nest.

"What is it, milord?" he asked, scrambling down to Mendellas' side.

"I have a job for you, a dangerous job."

"Good!" Borenson said, his voice full of cheer. Borenson dropped beside the King in the starlight. He was a full head taller than the King, his red hair spilling down from under his helm, over his shoulders. It wasn't right for vassals to be so large. He watched the King expectantly.

"I'm taking five hundred men south, to Castle Longmot – right now. A thousand more will follow at dawn. I want you to take five hundred men with you now. Our scouts tell us that a few thousand nomen are in the woods at Castle Sylvarresta. If you ride hard, you can meet them at dawn, outside the castle, and let the men practice their archery.

"Keep your forces in the woods. The Wolf Lord won't dare send reinforcements from the castle if he can't guess your number. If he should attack, retreat gracefully, heading for Longmot. At noon, your men will retreat to Longmot in any case.

"It seems that the Duchess of Longmot has her hands full. Raj Ahten took her castle, stole endowments from hundreds of her people. At dawn she plans to kill herself, and anyone else who is a Dedicate to Raj Ahten. And it seems that she's captured a great treasure. So I must go to relieve her of it. I'll want you to keep the Wolf Lord off my back."

King Orden considered his next move. He knew these woods well, had hunted the Dunnwood many times over the past twenty years. He needed to use that knowledge to his advantage.

"I will be destroying the bridge at Hayworth, for all the good it will do. So you will send your men to Boar's Ford – to that narrow canyon below the ford. There they will sit in ambush. When Raj Ahten's troops come through, your men will attack – push boulders on them from above, loose arrows, set the east end of the canyon ablaze. But don't let your men draw sword unless you have to. Your troops will then race for Longmot. You understand? Your only purpose is to harry the Wolf Lord, to cause damage, to nibble at the edge of his defenses, to slow his journey."

Borenson was smiling even wider, grinning like a maniac by now. It was practically a suicide mission. Orden wondered why that proposition delighted him. Did the man wish for death, or was it merely the deadly challenge that thrilled him?

"Unfortunately, you may not be with your troops."

"I won't?" Borenson's smile faltered.

"No, I have something more reckless in mind for you. Tomorrow at noon, while your troops retreat toward the ambush, I want you, personally – and you alone – to ride into Castle Sylvarresta, to deliver a message to Raj Ahten."

Borenson began grinning again, but it was not the crazed, reckless grin he'd had before. Instead, he seemed more determined. Beads of sweat began to form on his brow.

"Be surly, abuse Raj Ahten as best you know how. Tell him that I've captured Longmot. Crow about it. As proof of my deed, tell him that I killed his Dedicates there at dawn–"

Borenson swallowed hard.

"Make him believe that I have taken forty thousand of his forcibles into my possession, and that I've put them to good use. Tell him that I will sell . . . five thousand of them back to him. Tell him that he knows the price."

"Which is?" Borenson asked.

"Don't name it," Orden answered. "If he has my son, then he will offer my son. If he does not have my son, then he will think you speak of King Sylvarresta's family, and he will offer the King.

"No matter what hostage is offered, check on the condition of the hostage before you leave. See if Raj Ahten has forced Gaborn – or King Sylvarresta – into giving an endowment. I suspect he will use the royal family as vectors for major endowments. In fifteen hours, he could easily take hundreds of such endowments. If so, then you know what to do."

"Pardon me?" Borenson asked.

"You heard right. You know what to do."

Borenson laughed, almost a coughing sound, but there was no longer a smile on his face, no longer a gleam of delight in his eye. His face had gone all hard, impassive, and his voice carried a tone of disbelief. "You would have me kill King Sylvarresta, or your son?"

Overhead, one of the huge graaks called out, swept low. There was a time in Orden's life when he had been small enough to ride one of the huge reptiles. When he'd weighed fifty pounds, at the age of six, his father had let him take long journeys on the backs of tamed graaks with the other skyriders, over the mountains to the far kingdom of Dzerlas in Inkarra. Only boys with endowments of strength and wit and stamina and grace could take such journeys.

But when King Orden's son, Gaborn, became a skyrider in his turn, Mendellas never let Gaborn take a far journey. He'd tried hard to protect his son. He'd loved the boy too much. He'd hoped the lad would have time to grow, gain some maturity – a commodity all too rare among Runelords, who were often forced of necessity to take endowments of metabolism, grow old far before their time. There were things that King Orden still needed to teach his son, arts of diplomacy and strategy and intrigue that could not be learned in the House of Understanding.

Moreover, Orden's own father had been captured when he was but a boy, and then had been forced to give endowments to a Wolf Lord in the Southern Wastes. His father's friends had rescued him from his fate – with a sword.

Borenson could never know how much giving this order hurt. King Orden felt determined that his men would never know: Gaborn's great heart might well have earned him a death sentence.

King Orden clapped the big warrior on the shoulder in sympathy. Borenson was trembling. It would be a hard thing to go from being Gaborn's sworn protector to his assassin. "You heard me right. When Raj Ahten gets your message, he will race to Longmot, to meet me in battle. He will have hundreds of Dedicates in Castle Sylvarresta by dawn – Dedicates that he won't be able to carry south in such a hurry, Dedicates that he won't be able to properly guard.

"I want you to go into the Dedicates' Keep at Castle Sylvarresta, once Raj Ahten leaves, and slaughter everyone left within."

The big warrior's grin had now faded completely.

"You understand that this must be done. My life, your life, the lives of everyone in Mystarria – everyone you've ever known and loved – might well depend on it.

"We can show no weakness. We can show no mercy."

From a pouch at his hip, King Orden withdrew a small ivory flask. Captured inside were mists from the fields of Mystarria. Orden's water wizards had said that the flask contained enough mist to hide an army should the need arise. Borenson's army might need such a mist. He handed the artifact to Borenson, and wondered if he should also give the man his golden shield. It had a powerful spell of water warding in it. Orden had brought it as a betrothal gift to Sylvarresta. Now, he considered that he might need that shield himself.

Orden wondered. He did not want to kill Sylvarresta. Yet if Sylvarresta succumbed to Raj Ahten, then it became Orden's duty. The Kings of Rofehavan needed to know that no one could give endowments to the Wolf Lord. No one would be permitted to do so and live. Not even Orden's best friend.

"We will do what we must to our friends, our kin," King Orden said to himself as much as to Borenson, "if they serve the enemy. That is our duty. This is war."

FOURTEEN: A WIZARD IN CHAINS.

Shortly before dawn, the sounds of many clanking chains preceded Binnesman into the King's audience hall; then the guards dragged the herbalist in to face Raj Ahten, as Iome watched.

She shuddered and hid in a darkened corner, afraid somehow that Binnesman would spot her, would loathe her very existence. In the past few hours, she'd had time to inspect the rune of power branded into the skin of her breast. It was a complex thing, a horrid thing that tried to draw far more than mere beauty from her. It tried to draw her pride, her hope. Though she fought the influence of the rune, though she denied this boon to Raj Ahten, still she felt less than human. A mere rag in the corner, something that cringed and watched.

Legend said that long ago, the facilitator Phedrosh had created a rune of will, a symbol that sapped the strength of mind from its victims. Had Raj Ahten had such a magic symbol built into the rune that had branded Iome, she'd not have been able to deny him.

Now she felt grateful that Phedrosh had destroyed that rune of power and the secret of its making, before he fled to Inkarra.

As Binnesman was dragged to the room, his shackles rattled. Strong irons bound Binnesman neck to foot, hand to hand. Two guards merely lugged him across the plank floor, threw him at Raj Ahten's feet.

Four of the Wolf Lord's flameweavers walked beside the herbalist, all hairless, dark of skin. Three young-looking men and a single woman, all with that peculiar dancing light in their eyes that only flameweavers have. The male flameweavers had donned saffron silk robes, the woman a crimson mantle.

Yet as the woman drew near, in the lead, Iome could feel the heat of her skin, a dry heat, as if her flesh were a warming stone to put in a bed on a cold night.

Iome felt the woman's powers in another way: a feverish lust came with her, mingled with a curious intellectual arousal. This lust was nothing like the earthy sensuality that Iome felt in Binnesman's presence – a desire to bear children, to feel small lips suckling at her breast. No, the flameweavers carried a consuming need to rape, to take, an undirected rage all finely controlled by keen intellect.

Poor Binnesman looked a dirty wreck. He was covered from head to foot in grimy ash, yet his sky-blue eyes showed no fear as he looked up.

You should fear, Iome thought. You should. No one could withstand Raj Ahten, the light in his face, the power of his voice. In the past few hours, she'd seen things she could not have imagined: Two hundred of her father's guard had granted endowments. Most needed little persuasion. A look at Raj Ahten's face, an encouraging word, and they gave themselves.

Few even thought of resisting. Captain Derrow, of the palace guard, asked to forbear swearing fealty to Raj Ahten, saying he was oath-bound to serve House Sylvarresta. He therefore begged to serve as a guard in the Dedicates' Keep, pointing out that other great houses would now send assassins to dispatch Sylvarresta. Raj Ahten agreed, but only on the condition that Derrow give a lesser endowment, one of hearing.

Another who begged no boon faced rougher treatment. Captain Ault refused the Wolf Lord entirely, had cursed him and wished him death.

Raj Ahten had borne the reviling with patience and a smile, but afterward, the woman in crimson had taken the captain's hand, tenderly. Then her eyes flashed in laughter as the captain burst into flames from toe to head and just stood, screaming and writhing as the fires consumed his flesh, melted his armor. The room had echoed with his shrieks. The odor of charred flesh and hair clung to the walls of the room even now.

Ault's blackened corpse was placed downstairs at the entry to the King's Keep.

So humbly now the people of Castle Sylvarresta came to stand before their new lord and give obeisance. Raj Ahten spoke calmly to them, his face shining like the sun, his voice as unperturbable as the sea.

All night long, Raj Ahten's troops had been marshaling the richest of the local merchants into the keep, seeking tributes of gold and endowments. The people gave to him whatever he asked, would give all that they had.

Thus, Raj Ahten had finally heard the name of the young man who had killed his giants, his outriders, and a dozen mastiffs on his errand to warn King Sylvarresta of the impending invasion. Even now, Raj Ahten's trackers scoured the Dunnwood, searching for young Prince Orden.

King Sylvarresta sat on the floor at Raj Ahten's feet. His neck had been tied to the foot of the throne, and King Sylvarresta, with all the naïveté of a kitten, kept pulling at the rope, trying to chew it in half. The idea of untying himself did not occur to the King. Iome watched her father at Raj Ahten's feet, and even to her, Raj Ahten seemed great. His glamour so affected her that somehow she felt it fitting that her father should be there. Other kings kept dogs or great cats at their feet as pets. But Raj Ahten was more than a common leader. He deserved to have kings at his feet.

At Raj Ahten's side stood his personal guard, two counselors, and the fifth of his flameweavers, a woman whose very presence made Iome tremble, for she could sense the flameweaver's power. She wore a midnight-blue robe, loosely tied over her naked body. And she stood now before a silver brazier, like a large platter on a pedestal, on which she had placed twigs and knots of fiery wood. The green flames rose some three or four feet above the brazier.

Once that night, the woman had looked up from her brazier, her eyes shining with fierce delight, and said to Raj Ahten, "Good news, O Shining One, your assassins seem to have slaughtered King Gareth Arrooley of Internook. His light no longer shines in the earth."

On hearing this, Iome felt awed. So Raj Ahten was attacking more than one king of the North. She wondered at the depth of his plans. *Perhaps we are all fools compared with him,* she wondered, *as ignorant as my father tied at Raj Ahten's feet.*

Now Raj Ahten gazed down at Binnesman in the light thrown from the pyromancer's brazier, and thoughtfully scratched at his beard.

"What is your name?" Raj Ahten asked the wizard.

Binnesman looked up, "My name is Binnesman."

"Ah, Binnesman. I know your work well. I've read your herbals." Raj Ahten smiled at him, patiently, glanced up at the pyromancer. "You bring him in chains? I would not have it so. He seems harmless."

The flameweaver beside the Wolf Lord gazed at Binnesman as if in a trance, eyes unfocused, staring past him, as if she sought to work up the nerve to kill him.

"Harmless enough, Your Lordship," Binnesman answered in a strong voice. Though he still crouched on all fours, he watched the Wolf Lord casually.

"You may rise," Raj Ahten said.

Binnesman nodded, struggled to his feet, though his chains kept him bowed so he could not raise his neck. Now Iome could see more clearly that he wore manacles at his feet, that his hands were cuffed, and that a short, heavy iron chain led from manacles to cuffs to neck. Though Binnesman could not stand upright, the bowed stance did not bother him. He'd hunched over plants for so many years, his back had become stooped.

"Beware of him, my lord," the pyromancer at Raj Ahten's side whispered. "He has great power."

"Hardly," Binnesman chided. "You've destroyed my garden, the work of master gardeners for over five hundred years. The herbs and spices I'd have harvested are all lost. You are known as a pragmatic man, Raj Ahten. Surely you know these were things of no small benefit!"

Raj Ahten smiled somewhat playfully. "I'm sorry my sorcerers destroyed your garden. But we haven't destroyed you, have we? You can grow another garden. I have some fine gardens, near my villas and palaces in the South. Trees from the far corners of the world, rich soil, plentiful water."

Binnesman shook his head. "Never. I can never have another garden like the one you burned. It was my heart. You see . . ." He clutched at his robes.

Raj Ahten leaned forward. "I'm sorry. It was necessary to clip your wings, Earth Warden." He spoke this title with solemnity, with more respect than he'd shown anyone else this night. "And yet, Master Binnesman, I truly did not want to harm you. There are few notable Earth Wardens in the world, and I've tested the efficacy of the herbs that each of your kind grows, studied the ointments and infusions you provide. You, Binnesman, are the master of your craft, of that I am sure. You deserve greater honor than you have been accorded. You should be serving as hearthmaster in the Room of Earth Powers in the House of Understanding – not that fraud Hoewell."

Iome marveled. Even in far Indhopal, Raj Ahten knew of Binnesman's work. The Wolf Lord seemed almost omniscient to her.

Binnesman watched him from beneath bushy brows. The wrinkled lines of Binnesman's face were wise, and after years of smiling, made him look kind and soft. But there was no kindness behind his eyes. Iome had seen him smash bugs in his garden with that calculating gaze. "The honors of men do not interest me."

"Then what does interest you?" Raj Ahten asked. When Binnesman did not answer, he said softly, "Will you serve me?"

The tone of voice, the subtle inflections, were all such that many another man would have prostrated themselves.

"I serve no king," Binnesman answered.

"You served Sylvarresta," Raj Ahten gently reminded him, "just as he serves me now!"

"Sylvarresta was my friend, never my master."

"You served his people. You served him as a friend."

"I serve the earth, and all people on it, Lord Raj."

"Then will you give yourself to me?"

Binnesman gave him a scolding look, as if Raj Ahten were a child caught doing wrong when he knew better. "Do you desire my service as a man, or as a wizard?"

"As a wizard."

"Then, alas, Lord Raj, I cannot take a vow to serve you, for it would diminish my powers."

"How so?" Raj Ahten asked.

"I've vowed to serve the Earth, and no other," Binnesman said. "I serve the trees in their hour of need, as well as the fox and the hare. I serve men with no greater and no less devotion than I serve other creatures. But if I break my vow to serve the Earth, if I seek instead to serve you, my powers would perish.

"You have many men who will serve you, or who will serve themselves in your interest, Raj Ahten. Content yourself with them."

Iome wondered at Binnesman's words. He lied now, she knew. He did serve men more than animals. He'd once told her it was his weakness, this peculiar devotion to mankind. In his eyes, it made him unworthy of his master. Iome feared that Raj Ahten would see through the lies, punish Binnesman.

Raj Ahten stared down at Binnesman. The Wolf Lord's beautiful face was untroubled, and it seemed to Iome to be full of kindness.

Binnesman said softly to Raj Ahten, "You understand, as a Runelord, you must care for your Dedicates, or else in time they would starve or sicken. If they died, you would lose the powers you draw from them.

"The same principles apply to me . . . or to your flameweavers. See how they feed the fire, knowing they will gain strength from it in return?"

"Milord," the flameweaver at Raj Ahten's side whispered, "let me kill him. The flames show that he is a danger. He helped Prince Orden escape from his garden. He supports your enemies. The light within him is against you."

Raj Ahten touched the flameweaver's hand, calming her, asking, "Is it so? Did you help the Prince escape?"

Don't answer him, Iome wanted to shout. *Don't answer.*

But Binnesman merely shrugged. "He had a wound. I tended it, as I would if he were a rabbit or a crow. Then I pointed his way into the Dunnwood, so he could hide."

"Because?" Raj Ahten asked.

"Because your soldiers want him dead," the herbalist answered. "I serve life. Your life, your enemy's life. I serve life, as surely as you serve death."

"I do not serve death. I serve mankind," Raj Ahten said calmly. His eyes hardly narrowed, but his face suddenly seemed harder, more passionless.

"Fire consumes," Binnesman said. "Certainly, when you surround yourself with so many flameweavers, you too must feel their tug, their desire to consume. It has you in its sway."

Raj Ahten casually leaned back on the throne. "Fire also enlightens and reveals," he said. "It warms us in the cold night. In the right hands, it can be a tool for good, even for healing. The Bright Ones and the Glories are creatures of the flame. Life comes from fire, as well as from the earth."

"Yes, it can be a tool for good. But not now. Not in the age to come. Certainly no beings of the greater light will come do your bidding," Binnesman said. "I think that you would do better to rid yourself of these . . . forces." He waved casually at the flameweavers. "Other wizards would serve you better."

"So you will serve me?" Raj Ahten asked. "You will supply my armies with your herbs and ointments?" He smiled, and that smile seemed to light the room. Certainly Binnesman will help him, Iome thought.

"Herbs for the sick and the wounded?" Binnesman asked. "I can do this in good conscience. But I do not serve you."

Raj Ahten nodded, clearly disappointed. Binnesman's devotion would have been a great boon.

"Milord," the flameweaver hissed, glancing from brazier to Raj Ahten, "he is not truthful. He does serve a king! I see a man in my flames, a faceless man with a crown! A king is coming, a king who can destroy you!"

Raj Ahten studied the herbalist, leaning even closer in his chair, the green flames from the brazier licking the side of his face. "My pyromancer sees a vision in the flames," he whispered. "Tell me, Binnesman, has the earth granted you such visions? Is there a king who can destroy me?"

Binnesman stood straighter, folded his arms. His fists were clenched. "I am no friend of the Time Lords, to know the future. I don't gaze into polished stones. But you have made many enemies."

"But is there a king whom you serve?"

Binnesman stood for a long moment, deep in thought, his brows furrowed. Iome almost believed that the old herbalist would not answer, but then he began to mutter,

"Wood and stone, wood and stone, these are but my flesh and bone. Metal, blood, wood and stone, these I own, these I own."

"What?" Raj Ahten asked, though surely he could not have failed to hear the old man.

"I serve no man. But, Your Lordship, a king is coming, a king of whom the earth approves. Fourteen days ago, he set foot in Heredon. I know this only because I heard the stones whisper it in the night, as I slept in the fields. A voice called to me, plain as a lark, 'The new King of the Earth is coming. He is in the land.'"

"Kill him!" the flameweavers all began shouting at this revelation. "He serves your enemy."

Raj Ahten tried to silence their yammering with an upraised hand, and asked, "Who is this Earth King?" His eyes blazed. The flameweavers kept calling for Binnesman's death; Iome feared that Raj Ahten would grant their boon. The light in their eyes increased, and the woman at the brazier raised her fist, let it burst into flame. In a moment, Raj Ahten's desires would not matter. The flameweavers would kill Binnesman.

In an effort to save the herbalist, Iome shouted, "It's Orden. King Orden crossed our border two weeks ago!"

At that very moment, the chains holding Binnesman dropped away, both hand and foot, and Binnesman unclenched his fists, tossed something into the air –

Yellow flower petals, withered roots, and dry leaves that fluttered in the green light.

The flameweavers shrieked in dismay and fell back, as if blasted by the weight of the flowers.

The brazier snuffed out. Indeed, all the lanterns in the audience chamber winked out at once, so that the only light in the room was early-morning starlight, shining in from the oriels.

When her eyes adjusted, Iome looked around, mystified. The flameweavers had all fallen backward from Binnesman as if struck by lightning. They lay stunned, gazing without seeing, whimpering in pain.

The room had suddenly filled with a clean, pungent scent, as if a wind had carried with it the air of a distant meadow. Binnesman stood tall and straight, glaring at Raj Ahten from under bushy brows. The cuffs and manacles he'd worn now lay at his feet, still firmly locked. It was as if his limbs had merely melted through them.

Though flameweavers lay dazed and wounded at Binnesman's feet, Iome had felt nothing during the attack. A flower had touched her face, then dropped to the floor, nothing more.

Raj Ahten stared at the herbalist, slightly annoyed, gripped the arms of the throne. "What have you done?" Raj Ahten asked softly, evenly, in the starlight.

"I will not suffer your flameweavers to kill me," Binnesman said. "I've diminished them for a moment, nothing more. Now, you will excuse me, Your Lordship. I've much work to do. You wanted herbs for your armies?" Binnesman turned to leave.

"Is it true that you back King Orden? Will you fight beside him?"

Binnesman gave the Wolf Lord a sidelong glance, shook his head as if appalled. "I do not wish to fight you," Binnesman intoned softly. "I have never taken a man's life. You are asleep to the powers of the earth, Raj Ahten. The great tree of life arches over you, and the leaves of it whisper to you, but you do not hear them rustle. Instead, you merely sleep among its roots, dreaming of conquest.

"Turn your thoughts to preservation. Your people need you. I have great hope for you, Raj Ahten. I would call you friend."

Raj Ahten studied the old wizard a moment. "What would it take for you and I to become friends?"

Binnesman said, "Swear an oath to the earth, that you will not harm it. Swear that you will seek to preserve a seed of humanity in the dark season to come."

"And what do you mean by these oaths?" Raj Ahten

asked.

"Divest yourself of the flameweavers who desire to consume the earth. Value life – all life, plant and animal. Eat from plants without destroying them, harvest only the animals you need. Waste no creatures, either animal or man. Turn your armies back from this war you have initiated. There are reavers on your southern borders. Your struggle should be with them."

For a long time, Raj Ahten sat on the throne, simply staring at Binnesman. During that moment, a servant rushed in with a fresh lantern from the anteroom, so that it illuminated the Wolf Lord's face. He appeared thoughtful.

Iome could see the longing in Raj Ahten's eyes, and almost she believed he would take the oath.

But as the servant drew near with the lantern, it seemed to Iome that Raj Ahten's resolve flickered like the tongues of the fire. "I swear, to protect mankind from the reavers – for their own good," Raj Ahten said. "I . . . do only what I know I must–"

"You do nothing of the sort!" Binnesman shouted. "Listen to you: You've taken so many endowments of Voice that when you talk, you convince yourself of your own mad arguments. You are deluded!"

Iome's heart pounded, for she suddenly realized that Binnesman was right. Raj Ahten was swayed by the sound of his own mad Voice. It had never occurred to her that such a thing might happen.

Binnesman shouted, "Yet – there is time to change your mind – barely! Divest yourself of these mad notions. Don't dare rob these people and call yourself good!"

He turned and ambled from the room, looking every bit the bent old man. Yet he walked without fear, as if, Iome thought, he had conducted the interview, as if he had dragged Raj Ahten to this room in chains.

Then he was gone.

Iome watched in astonishment, for no one else that

night had merely chosen to leave Raj Ahten's presence. Iome feared that Raj Ahten might try to imprison the old man, or drag him back and bully him into service.

But the Wolf Lord remained thoughtful, watched the dark corridor through which Binnesman had exited.

Moments later, as the flameweavers began to regain consciousness, a guard hurried to the King's chamber to announce that the herbalist had just been spotted outside the city gates, hobbling across the fields to the Dunnwood. "Our bowmen on the wall could have shot him," the guard said, "but we did not know your will in this matter. The nomen are camped in the fields, but none detained him. Shall I send scouts to fetch him back?"

Raj Ahten frowned. It seemed far too short a time for a man to have left these halls and escaped the castle. And it was equally as bizarre that none of Raj Ahten's highly trained soldiers had stopped the old man.

"Did he reach the edge of the forest?" Raj Ahten asked.

"Aye, milord."

"What is he planning?" Raj Ahten wondered aloud. He stood swiftly, pondering. Then added, "Send a party of hunters to find him – if they can."

But Iome knew it was too late. Binnesman had gained the woods, the Dunnwood, the ancient forest, a focus for the earth powers. Even Raj Ahten's most accomplished hunters could not track an Earth Warden through the Dunnwood.

FIFTEEN: POETICS

Once the trackers left, Gaborn made his way alongside the mill, carrying Rowan. For a young man with three endowments of brawn, she did not pose much of a burden, and Gaborn realized that carrying her now offered an added benefit: she would not leave her scent on the ground.

It is hard to track a man who has just left a river. His body oils get washed away, so that when he steps on dry land, he is harder to smell. Gaborn wanted to leave only his small traces of scent.

As he struggled up the incline, out of the millrace, the ferrin saw him coming, growled in fear, and scurried for cover.

"Food, food," he whistled, for these creatures had performed him a service. How great a service, they would never know. Gaborn had little food to give, but as he reached the mill, he lifted the wooden latch on the front door, went in. A hopper above the grindstones was filled with wheat. Gaborn opened the hopper, turned to look behind him. The ferrin stood just outside the door, eyes wide in the darkness. One little gray-brown ferrin woman was wringing her paws nervously, sniffing the air.

"Food. I give," he whistled softly.

"I hear you," she chirped in return.

Gaborn slowly walked past them, left the ferrin just outside the door. They waited, blinking at him nervously, afraid to enter the mill with him watching.

Gaborn hurried up the trail to the castle, under the trees, then crept along the tree line until he reached the small stream that wound through the pussy willows.

Here, he slogged through the marshes quietly. The sky was red on the hill now, and the archer on the city wall stood out bright against the sky. He was watching the fire, Binnesman's garden burning. Ashes drifted slowly through the air.

Gaborn crept through the willows, up to the city wall, unseen. At the wall, he set Rowan down and squirmed under first, through the cold water, then waited for Rowan. She wriggled beneath the wall, teeth gritted in pain at the touch of the icy water. She staggered up to her knees, inside the castle gate, then pitched forward in a faint.

He caught her, laid her in the grass beside the stream. He took off his dirty cloak, wrapped it around her for what little warmth it could give, then began making his way through the streets.

It was an odd sensation, walking that street. Binnesman's garden was afire, the flames shooting now eighty feet into the air. The castle was alive with people shouting, running to and fro, afraid the fire would spread.

On the street leading to the stables, dozens of people raced past Gaborn, many of them carrying buckets to the stream so that they could douse the thatch roofs of cottages, protecting them from falling cinders.

Yet of all the people who passed Gaborn, none asked his name or sought to learn why he carried an unconscious woman. Is Earth protecting me, he wondered, or is this such a common sight this night that no one notices?

Gaborn found the spice cellars from Rowan's description. It was a fair-sized building, something of a warehouse whose back was dug into the hill. A loading dock by the wide front doors was just the height of a wagon.

Gaborn cautiously opened the front door into an antechamber. The scents of spices assailed him – drying garlic and onions, parsley and basil, lemon balm and mint, geranium, witch hazel, and a hundred others. The cook's son was supposed to be sleeping here. A pallet lay in a corner with a blanket over it, but Gaborn saw no sign of the boy. On a night like tonight, with soldiers in town and a huge fire burning, the boy was probably with friends.

A wall of stone and mortar stood on the far side of the antechamber. Gaborn carried Rowan to it, opened it wide. A huge chamber was behind the door. A lantern hung by the wall, burning low, next to a flask of oil and a couple of spare lanterns. Gaborn poured oil into a lantern and lit the wick so that it burned brightly, then gaped.

Gaborn had known that the King dealt in spices, but hadn't guessed how much. The chamber was filled to the brim with crates and sacks. Off to the left were common culinary spices in huge bins, enough to supply the castle through the year. Ahead were smaller casks of Binnesman's medicinal herbs and oils, ready for shipment. To the far right lay thousands of bottles of wine, along with casks of ale, whiskey, and rum. The chamber must have reached back a hundred feet into the side of the hill.

The place held a miasma of scents – spices rotting, spices fresh, dust and mold. Gaborn knew he'd found safety. Here beneath the earth, in the far chambers under the hill, no hunter would be able to track him.

He closed the great door, made his way with the lantern to a corner of the cellar, stacked some crates to form a little hiding place, then laid Rowan behind them.

He lay down with her, warmed her with his body, and for a time he slept, curled against her back.

When he woke, Rowan had turned, was gazing into his eyes. He felt a pressure on his lips, realized that she'd just kissed him awake. She breathed softly.

Rowan had dark skin, with thick, lustrous black hair and a gentle, caring face. She was not beautiful, he decided, merely pretty. Not like Iome, or even Myrrima. Both of those women were blessed with endowments that made them more than human. Both of them had faces that could make a man forget his name or haunt a man for years after a mere glimpse of them.

She kissed him again, softly, and whispered, "Thank you."

"For what?" Gaborn asked.

"For keeping me warm. For bringing me with you." She cuddled closer, spread his robe over them both. "I've never felt so . . . alive . . . as I do right now." She took his hand, placed it on her cheek, wanting him to stroke her.

Gaborn dared not do it. He knew what she wanted. She'd just reawakened to the world of sensation. She craved his caress – the warmth of his body, his touch.

"I . . . don't think I should do this," Gaborn said, and he rolled away, put his back to her. He felt her stiffen, hurt and embarrassed.

He lay for a moment, ignoring her, then reached into the pocket of his tunic, pulled out the book that King Sylvarresta had given him earlier in the day. *The Chronicles of Owatt, Emir of Tuulistan*.

The lambskin cover on it was soft and new. The ink smelled fresh. Gaborn opened it, fearing he wouldn't be able to read the language. But the Emir had already translated it.

On the cover leaf, in a broad, strong hand, he'd written,

> *To my Beloved Brother in Righteousness, King Jas Laren Sylvarresta, greetings:*
>
> *It has been eighteen years now since we dined together at the oasis near Binya, yet I think fondly on you often. They have been hard years, full of trouble. I give you one last gift: this book.*
>
> *I beg of you, show it only to those you trust.*

Gaborn wondered at the warning. After running out of space at the bottom of the page, the Emir had not bothered to sign his name.

Gaborn calmed himself, prepared to memorize everything in the book. With two endowments of wit, it was a daunting task, but not impossible.

He read swiftly. The first ten chapters told of the Emir's life – his youth, his marriage and family connections, details of laws he had authored, deeds he had done. The next ten told of ten battles fought by Raj Ahten, campaigns against entire royal families.

The Wolf Lord began destroying the smaller families of Indhopal first, those most despised. He worked not to take a castle or to bankrupt a city, but to decimate entire family lines. In the South, the code of honor made it obligatory to avenge one's relatives.

Among the horsemen of Deyazz, he'd attack a palace in one city, then slay Dedicate horses of those who might come to the city's aid, while also taking children for ransom on another front. With multiprong attacks, he overwhelmed his foes.

Gaborn quickly saw that Raj Ahten was a master of illusion. Always one could see the knife flashing in his right hand, while his left hand kept busy elsewhere. A small army might lay siege to a king's palace in one land while five others quietly ripped at the underbelly of some lord two kingdoms away.

Gaborn studied that pattern of the assaults. He grew terrified.

Raj Ahten had taken Castle Sylvarresta with nothing more than his glamour and fewer than seven thousand knights and men-at-arms. True, he brought Invincibles, the heart of his army. But it left many questions unanswered. Raj Ahten had millions of men who could march at his command.

Where were they?

Gaborn wondered as he read. The tales of Raj Ahten's battles contained no hidden knowledge. The Emir had laid bare Raj Ahten's tactics, but a good spy could have gleaned as much information.

Gaborn skimmed the Emir's poetry, found it dull, mere doggerel, each line ending in a full rhyme, each line perfectly metered.

Some poems were sonnets that enjoined the reader to seek for some virtue, in the way of poems given to young children who are learning to read. Yet in the sonnets, the Emir did not always rhyme flawlessly. Sometimes he ended in near rhyme, and on a swift reading, Gaborn found that the near rhymes leapt out at him.

It was not until reading ten pages that Gaborn stumbled on the first of these near rhymes, in an odd poem, a form called a *sonnette menor*.

Now Gaborn focused on that poem, for it held Sylvarresta's name in the title.

> *A Sonnette for Sylvarresta*
> *When the wind strokes the desert in the night,*
> *so that veils of sand obscure the starlight,*
> *we lie on pillows by the fire to read*
> *In books of puissant philosophy.*
>
> *Ah, how they clear the mind, focus the eye,*
> *Of mortal men who linger, love and die!*

Gaborn rearranged words in each line, seeing if he could form sentences that might convey some hidden meaning. He found nothing.

He wondered at the words, longed for the days when men from the North could have traveled openly in Indhopal. He'd recently heard a trader bemoan those times by saying, "Once there were many good men in Indhopal. Now it seems they are all dead – or perhaps just frightened into evil."

Five poems later, Gaborn came upon another poem in the same form, yet its near rhymes came in the first two lines.

Warriors Take Heart
Woe to the warrior who walks behind,
men of greater courage and surer spine.
For a coward's shame will hold him fast
when he longs to escape his errant past.

Be a man upon whom others may depend –
quick to attack, yet quicker to defend.

Gaborn thought back to the near rhymes in the previous poem: "Read, philosophy." Now the near rhymes here: "Behind, spine."

He thumbed through the next five pages quickly, found another near rhyme, with the words, "Room, of dream."

"Read philosophy behind spine. Room of Dreams," he muttered. His heart pounded. The teachings that the Days learned in the Room of Dreams were forbidden to Gaborn's kind. Surely, the Days would destroy this chronicle if they found the Emir disseminating such knowledge among Runelords.

Thus the Emir's warning: "Show it only to those whom you trust."

Gaborn glanced at the remainder of the book. The last section was dedicated to philosophical musings – treatises on the "Nature of a Goodly Prince," exhorting would-be kings to mind their manners and avoid slashing their father's throats while waiting for the old men to die off.

The cover, back, and spine of the book were made of stiff leather, sewn to a softer covering of lambskin.

He glanced over his back. He'd been reading for hours. Rowan lay quiet, breathing in the slow way of those who sleep.

Gaborn unsheathed his knife, cut the threads that bound the cover to the book. As he did so, he kept fumbling; his hands shook badly.

His forefathers had wondered at the teachings in the House of Dreams for generations. A man had died to bring this to Sylvarresta. Probably without reason. A spy knew that a book came from Tuulistan, and figured that it warned of Raj Ahten's invasion plans. So the spy had struck down an innocent man.

Yet Gaborn worried – even though he suspected that it was irrational – that he, too, would be killed, if the Days ever learned he'd read these teachings.

From inside the back cover dropped five thin sheets of paper with a small diagram and the following note:

My Dear Sylvarresta:

You remember at Binya, when we discussed those men who revolted against me, for they said I stole their wells to water my cattle? I had been taught that as prince, all the land in my realm belonged to me, as did the people on it. These things were my birthright, granted by the Powers. So I planned to punish the men for their theft.

But you enjoined me to slaughter my cattle instead, for you said that every man is lord of his own land, and that the lives of my cattle should serve my people, not my people the cattle. You said that Runelords could rule only if our people loved and served us. We rule at their whim.

Your views seemed wonderfully exotic, but I bowed to your wisdom. I have spent years since considering the nature of what is just and what is unjust.

We both have heard forbidden fragments of doctrine from the Room of Dreams, but recently I learned something most secret from that place. I give you this diagram for your instruction:

In the Room of Dreams, the Days are taught that even the ugliest sparrow knows itself to be a lord of the skies, and knows in its heart that it owns all it surveys.

They teach in the room that every man is the same. Every man defines himself as a lord unto himself, and inherits a birthright of three Domains: the Visible Domain of things we can see and touch; the Communal Domain made up of our relationships with others; and the Invisible Domain –

The Three Domains of Man

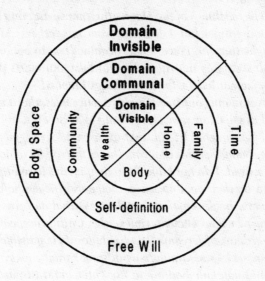

territories we cannot see, but which we actively protect nonetheless.

While some men teach that good and evil are defined by the Powers or by wise kings in authority, or change according to time and circumstance, the Days say that the knowledge of good and evil is born into us, and that the just laws of mankind are written on our hearts. They teach that the three domains are the sole medium by which mankind defines good and evil.

If any man violates our domain, if he seeks to deprive us of our birthright, we call him "evil." If any man seeks to take our property or life, if he attacks our family or honor or community, if he strives to rob us of free will, we can justly protect ourselves.

On the other hand, the Days define goodness as the voluntary enlarging of another's domain. If you give me money or property, if you bestow upon me honor or invite me to be *your friend, if you give time in my service, then I define you as good.*

The teachings of the Days – they are so different in implication from what I learned from my fathers. My father taught that the Powers had ordained me to be lord of my realm. As was my right, I could take any man's property, any woman's love, for these things I owned.

Now I am confused. I hold to what my father taught, yet feel in my heart that I am wrong to do so.

I fear, my old friend, that we are under judgment by the Days, and that this diagram shows the rod by which we are measured. I do not know how they intend to manipulate us – for by their own measure, they would be evil to slay us.

Some books say that the Glories paired the lords with the Days, but in ancient times, the Days were called "the Guardians of Dreams." So I wonder: Is it possible that the Days seek to manipulate us in some strange way? Do they manipulate our hopes and aspirations? Most particularly, they write the chronicles of our lives, but are the chronicles true? Did the heroes we aspire to emulate even exist? Were such men heroes even by their own standards? Or do the Days seek to manipulate truth for purposes we cannot guess?

So, I have secretly written this chronicle and sent it to you. I am growing old. I will not live long. When I die and the Days write the tale of my life, I wish you to compare the two chronicles, to see what you can find. What part of my life story will the Days omit? What part will they embellish?

Farewell, My Brother in Righteousness

Gaborn read the document several times. The teachings of the Days did not seem particularly profound. Indeed, they seemed rather obvious and straightforward, though Gaborn had never encountered their like. Gaborn could see no reason why they should be kept secret, particularly from the Runelords.

Still, the Emir had guarded these writings, had feared some unnamable retribution.

Yet Gaborn knew that, sometimes, small things could be powerful. As a child of five, he'd often tried to lift the huge halberds that his father's guards bore in the portcullis. At that age, he'd been given his first endowment of brawn, and immediately had gone out and discovered that he could lift the halberd and swing it with ease. A single endowment of strength had seemed a great thing. Now, as a Runelord, he knew that it was nothing.

Yet he wondered at these teachings. They seemed simple, yet he knew that the Days were anything but simple. An odd devotion, taken to an extreme, could have profound effects on a person – in just the same way that a simple love of food led to obesity and death.

Gaborn had seldom wondered if he was good. In reading these teachings from the Room of Dreams, he wondered if it was possible to be a "good" Runelord by the Days' standards. Those who gave endowments usually regretted it, in time. Yet once the gift was given, it could not be returned. At that point, any endowment that the Runelord held would be considered a violation by the Days.

Gaborn wondered if there might be some acceptable circumstances when it was all right for a person to grant an endowment. Perhaps if two men desired to combine their strength to fight a great evil. But this could only happen if he and his Dedicate were one in heart.

Yet at the center of the Days' teachings lay a concept he could barely apprehend: Every man is a lord. Every man is equal.

Gaborn was descended from Erden Geboren himself, who gave and took life, whom the earth itself had ordained king. If the Powers favored one man above another, then men could not be considered equal. Gaborn wondered where the balance lay, felt as if he stood poised at the edge of receiving a revelation.

He had always thought himself a rightful lord over his people. Yet, he was also their servant. It was the Runelord's duty to protect his vassals, to shield them with his own life.

The Days thought all men were lords? Did this mean that no man was a commoner? Did Gaborn really have no rights to lordship?

For the past few days he'd wondered if he was a good prince. He'd floundered at the question, but he'd had no clear definition for good. So Gaborn began to test the Days' teachings, to consider their implications.

As Gaborn lay on the cellar floor, the Days' teachings began to alter the way he would think forever after.

Gaborn wondered how he could protect himself without violating another's Domains. He saw from the diagram that the outer ring, the ring of Invisible Domains, detailed realms that were often fuzzy. Where does my body space end and another man's begin?

Perhaps, Gaborn wondered, there was an approved list of reactions. If someone violated your Invisible Domain, you should warn him about it. Simply speak to him. But if he violated your Communal Domains, if, say, he sought to ruin your reputation, you would take your case to others, publicly confront that person.

Yet if a person sought to violate your Visible Domains, if they sought to kill you or steal your property, Gaborn could see no other recourse but to take up arms.

Perhaps that was the answer. Inevitably, it seemed to him, each type of Domain became more intimate as you moved from the outer circle toward the center. Thus, protecting that more intimate Domain required a more forceful response.

But would it be good to do so? Where did goodness fit in here? A measured response seemed appropriate, just, but the diagram suggested to Gaborn that justice and virtue were not the same. A good man would enlarge the domain of others, not merely protect his own Domains.

Thus, when administering justice, one had to choose: Is it better to be a just man at this moment, or a good one?

Do I give to the man who robs me? Praise the man who belittles me?

If Gaborn sought to be good, he could do little else. But if he sought to be a protector for his people, was that not also good? And if he sought to protect his people, he could not afford to be virtuous.

The Days' teachings seemed muddling. Perhaps, he thought, the Days hide these teachings from the Runelords out of compassion. By the Days' standards, it is a hard thing for a man to be virtuous. Raj Ahten seeks my realm. By their standards, if I were good, perhaps I would give it to him.

Yet that seemed wrong. Perhaps it is a greater virtue for a Runelord to be just and equitable?

He began to wonder if even the Days understood the implications of their diagram. Perhaps it was not three circles of Domains, but more. Perhaps if he rearranged the individual types within the Domains, forming nine circles, he could better gauge how to react to an attempt at invasion for each.

He considered Raj Ahten. The Wolf Lord violated men's Domains at every level. He took their wealth and their homes, destroyed families, murdered, raped, and enslaved.

Gaborn needed to protect himself, his people, from this beast who would ravage the world. But he could not simply frighten Raj Ahten away, could not bully the man or reason with him or cow him by denouncing him to the people.

The only thing Gaborn could do to save his people would be to find a way to kill Raj Ahten.

Gaborn listened closely, asking the earth if that was its will, but felt no response – no shaking of the earth, no burning in his heart.

At the moment, Gaborn could not touch the Wolf

Lord. Raj Ahten was too powerful. Still, Gaborn thought he might spy on Raj Ahten, maybe discover best how to wound him. Perhaps Raj Ahten had prized Dedicates he carried with him, or perhaps a certain counselor drove the Wolf Lord relentlessly in pursuit of conquest. Staying a counselor could accomplish much.

Gaborn might discover such things. But he'd have to get close, first. He'd need to find a way into the inner circles of the castle.

Gaborn wondered if the earth would approve. Should I fight Raj Ahten? By doing this, would I violate my oath?

It seemed a good plan, daring, to spy on the Wolf Lord and learn his weakness. Gaborn had already established some cover in the Dedicates' Keep, as Aleson the Devotee.

Gaborn judged that if he and Rowan went to the gate of the Dedicates' Keep just after dawn, after Raj Ahten's night guard changed, and took some odd item of spice with them, perhaps they could gain entry.

All that night, he lay awake, considering. . . .

The sun rose pink in the east, stirring a dawn chill as Gaborn and Rowan left the spice house, carrying small bales of parsley and peppermint. A low mist was creeping up from the river, over the walls, making a blanket on the fields. The rising sun dyed the blanket gold.

Gaborn stopped outside the door, tasted the mist. It had an odd scent, the tang of sea salt where there should be none. Almost he could imagine the cries of gulls in that mist, and ships sailing from harbor. It made him long for home, but Gaborn thought he just imagined the odd scent.

The sounds of morning were like any other morning. The cattle and sheep were still wandering about the city, and their bawling and baaing filled the air. Jackdaws chatted noisily from their nests among the chimneys of houses. The blacksmith's hammer rang, and from the cooking chamber in the Soldiers' Keep one could smell fresh loaves baking. But overwhelming the sumptuous scent of food, even the sea mist, was the acrid stench of burned grasses.

Gaborn did not fear being spotted. He and Rowan were dressed like commoners, anonymous inhabitants of the castle.

Rowan led Gaborn up a fog-shrouded street, until they reached an old shack, a sort of hermitage on the steep side of the hill, near where the wizard's garden had stood. Grapevines climbed the back wall of the shack. It would take only a minor freeze to bring out the sweetness in the grapes.

Gaborn and Rowan filled their stomachs, unsure what other food they might get that day. At the sound of coughing within the hermitage, Gaborn got up, prepared to leave. Someone began thumping inside the cottage, hobbling on a cane. It was but a matter of time before the occupant came outside and discovered them.

Gaborn pulled Rowan to her feet just as hunting horns sounded over the fields south of the castle.

This blare of horns was followed immediately by grunts and shrieks. Gaborn climbed a little higher up the hill to look over the Outer Wall, to the mist-shrouded fields. The river lay to the east, with fields beyond it. The trees of the Dunnwood sat on a hill across the valley to the south.

At the edge of the wood on the south hill, Gaborn suddenly spotted movement in the fog: the glint of steel armor, peaked helms – lances raised in the air. Horsemen rode at the edge of the woods, cantering through the fog.

Before them raced a thousand nomen, black shadows who lumbered over the ground on all fours, shrieking and howling in terror. The nomen fled toward the castle, half-blinded by daylight.

There, Gaborn saw a rider wearing the midnight-blue livery of House Orden, with the emblem of the green knight.

He could not fathom it – his father attacking the castle. No! he wanted to shout.

It was a suicide charge. His father had brought a few men as a retinue. They had come as a light escort – mere decoration – not prepared for war! They had no siege engines, no wizards or ballistas.

As Gaborn realized all this, he knew it hardly mattered. His father believed that Gaborn was in Castle Sylvarresta and that the castle had fallen. His father would do whatever he thought necessary to win back his son.

That recognition filled Gaborn with guilt and horror, the thought that his stubbornness, his stupidity, had suddenly put so many people's lives in jeopardy.

Though his father's soldiers had come as "mere decoration," they did not fight like decorations. The horses plunged downhill, churning the fog; their horsemen's axes were raised high overhead. Gaborn saw nomen running, naked, fleeing the knights' axes. They shrieked in horror, their yellow fangs gaping wide. Some nomen turned, set their spear butts in the mud.

His father's knights surged forward on armored horses, lances shattering, axes falling, blood and mud and fur filling the air, along with the howls of nomen, the screams of the dying.

Hoofbeats thundered from the south. Hundreds of voices rose in a shout, the battle cry of "Orden! Brave Orden!"

In answer, a tremendous roar came from the east. A contingent of frowth giants rushed over the fields on the far side of the river, making toward the Dunnwood from the eastern fields – eighty giants lumbering like moving hills in the fog.

Shouts arose from guards on the castle walls, the blare of horns as Raj Ahten's soldiers were called to battle, roused from their beds. Gaborn feared Raj Ahten would send his own knights riding on to the battlefield. House Orden had at most a contingent of two thousand men, unless his father had managed to summon reinforcements from one of Sylvarresta's minor keeps.

Almost as quickly as that fear of Raj Ahten's counterattack arose, it was assuaged. Gaborn heard shouts at the southern gates, the clanking of gears as Raj Ahten's troops hurried to raise the drawbridge. The fog in the valley was so thick, Gaborn could not see if any nomen made it over the bridge.

Raj Ahten could not counterattack now. He could not be certain what size force House Orden had brought. If he attacked, he might find himself ambushed by a force so large he could never withstand it. It was, after all, a common tactic to try to lure a castle's defenders out by feigning an inadequate force.

A contrary wind blew from the east, and the fog suddenly thickened. Gaborn could see nothing more of the battle. Even the giants disappeared in the mist.

Yet he heard horses neigh in terror, the battle cries of House Orden. On the hill across the valley, horns sounded – two short blasts, one long. An order to regroup.

"Come on!" Gaborn told Rowan, and he took her hand. Together they raced up the streets, uphill toward the King's Keep.

The city was in chaos. Raj Ahten's troops were throwing on armor, rushing to man the city walls.

As Gaborn and Rowan ran to the King's Gate, the soldiers were lowering the portcullis leading into the business district. They ordered Gaborn back.

Five hundred of Raj Ahten's troops rushed down from the King's Keep, trying to reach the Outer Walls. A small herd of startled cattle dashed this way and that before them, seeking escape.

In the confusion, Gaborn and Rowan shouldered their bales of spices, raced through the portcullis into the market.

The market district was undefended. Raj Ahten's men

had not yet formed a plan for resisting attack. None of his soldiers had been posted to specific turrets. Watching the walls, Gaborn saw dozens of soldiers rush to the catapults, others manning the towers at each corner of the castle – but Raj Ahten's troops spread themselves thin. Some rushed for the Outer Wall; others tried to nail down defenses in the Dedicates' Keep.

Practically no one manned the second wall of the city's defenses, the King's Wall.

From the plain below – mingled with the screams of nomen, the neighing of horses as they died, the roars of giants – the knights of House Orden broke into song, their deep voices celebrating the glory of war.

Gaborn's father had always insisted that each of his personal guard have three endowments of Voice, so that orders could be easily shouted across the battlefields. Their death song erupted from the fog, shook the very stones of Castle Sylvarresta, reverberated from hill to hill. It was a song to strike terror in the hearts of foe:

> "Bring your honor, swing your sword,
>   You mighty men of Orden.
> Reap your foes in fields of gore,
>   You bloody men of Orden!"

There were the sounds of horses neighing and dying – so many horses. Gaborn did not understand why the horses screamed, until he realized that Raj Ahten's horses were still tethered on the far hill. His father's troops were slaughtering the Wolf Lord's mounts.

Gaborn and Rowan stopped on the cobbled street, a hundred yards beneath the King's Keep, and stood gazing over the fog-covered greens, trying to see the battle. Gaborn was suddenly aware of several men rushing past.

He turned just as a burly soldier pushed him aside, shouting, "Out of the way!"

And there, racing past in black scale mail, the white

owl's wings sweeping wide from his black helm, came Raj Ahten with his personal guard, counselors, and Days. Three weary flameweavers ran at his side.

Gaborn almost reached to draw his sword, to strike at the Wolf Lord, but knew it would be foolish. He turned away, the blood in his face rising in anger.

Raj Ahten ran past Gaborn at arm's length, issuing orders to his guard in Indhopalese: "Ready your men and horses! You flameweavers – to the walls. Send lines of fire from here to the woods, so that we can see into that fog. I'll lead the counterattack! Damn that insolent Orden!"

"It is an unnatural fog," his flameweaver worried. "A water wizard's fog."

"Rahjim, don't tell me you fear some young water wizard who hasn't even grown his gills yet?" Raj Ahten scoffed. "I expect more from you. This fog will work against Orden as much as work for him."

The wizard shook his head woefully. "Some Power fights us! I feel it!"

Gaborn could have reached out and touched the Wolf Lord, could have lopped off his head, yet had done nothing.

The enormity of the lost opportunity weighed on Gaborn. As Raj Ahten and his troops hurried down Market Street, Gaborn fumbled to draw his sword.

"No!" Rowan hissed, grabbing his wrist, pressing the blade back into its sheath.

She was right. Yet as he surveyed the street, he saw that it was a perfect spot for an ambush. The shops would not normally open for another two hours – and this day was far from normal. Perhaps they would not open at all.

Market Street twisted southwest, so that even though one was not far from the King's Keep and the inner tier of defenses for the city, one could not be seen from the Keep's walls above, nor from the outer walls below. The three-story stone buildings along Market Street blocked such a view.

Gaborn halted. The morning shadows were still deep, the street deserted. Gaborn wondered if he should wait for Raj Ahten to return up the cobbled road.

He glanced up toward the King's Keep.

A woman ran toward him, a woman dressed in a midnight-blue silk robe that was tied indecently, half revealing her pert breasts. She bore in her right hand a silver chain that held a small metal ball in which to burn incense, but the incense in the ball was aflame. Lights danced madly in her dark eyes, and her head was bald. She carried herself with such authority, Gaborn knew she must be someone important.

It was not until she was nearly upon him that he felt the heat of her – the dry burning under her skin – and knew she was a flameweaver.

The woman lurched to a stop, gazed at him as if in recognition. "You!" the flameweaver cried.

He did not think. He knew with every fiber of his being that she was his enemy. In one smooth stroke he drew his blade, swung it up, and lopped off the woman's head.

Rowan gasped, put her hand to her mouth and stepped backward.

For a split second the flameweaver stood, her head flying back, the incense burner still in hand.

Then her entire body turned into a green pillar of flame that sprouted high into the air. The heat of it made the rocks at her feet scream in protest, cremated her own body in a portion of a second, and Gaborn felt his own eyebrows curl and singe. The blade of his sword burst into flames as if stricken with a curse, and the fire raced down the bloodstained metal toward the hilt so that Gaborn had to thrust the thing to the ground.

For good measure, he somehow felt compelled to pull off his scabbard, throw it down too – as if it might burst into flame from its long association with the blade.

Too late he realized his mistake in killing the flameweaver.

A powerful flameweaver cannot be killed. She can be disembodied, and in time she will dissipate, become one with her element. But there is a space of time, a moment of consciousness between death and dissipation, where the full power of the flameweaver is unleashed, where the flameweaver combines with the element she served.

Gaborn staggered backward as quickly as he could, pulling Rowan with him. Even in death, the flameweaver sought to remain human, sought to retain her form, so that one moment a great fountain of green fire rose skyward, and the next a huge woman of flame, some eighty feet tall, began to take shape.

The inferno assumed bodily form – a marvelously compact assortment of topaz and emerald flames, her sculpted cheeks and eyes perfect, the small breasts and firm muscles of her legs all reproduced with marvelous accuracy. She stood as if confused, looking blindly to the south and to the east, from whence came the noise and clamor of battle.

The flameweaver's elemental reached out, curious, touched the rooftop of an ancient shop on Market Street. As she steadied herself with one fiery hand, the lead on the roof melted, began running molten from the gutters.

This was a wealthy district, and many of the shops had large glass windows, which shattered from the searing heat. Wooden posterns and signs burst into flame.

Yet the elemental was not fully conscious. The flameweaver perhaps did not realize yet that she'd been murdered. For a few moments, Gaborn suspected, he would be safe.

Then she would come for him.

"Run!" Gaborn hissed, and pulled Rowan.

But she stood in shock, for the fierce heat burned her more than it could him. Rowan screamed in pain, her fresh nerves suffering from the close proximity of the elemental.

A china shop was to his left, and Gaborn hoped only

that it had a back entrance as he raised his arm, ran headlong through its glass windows.

Shards of glass rained down on him, cutting his forehead, but he dared not slow to assess the damage. He pulled Rowan through the mess as he ran for the back of the shop, toward an open door that led to a workshop. He glanced back in time to see a fiery green hand snake through the shopwindow behind them.

A green finger touched Rowan's back. The young woman screamed a bloodcurdling cry as fire pierced her like a sword. A long tongue of flame exited through her belly.

Gaborn let go her hand, astonished by the pain in her eyes, by her horrible dying scream. He felt as if the fabric of his mind suddenly ripped. He could do nothing for her.

He ran through the workshop door, slammed it behind him. The chisels and awls of a wood sculptor lay all about. Wood shavings cluttered the floor.

Why her? Gaborn wondered. Why did the elemental take her and not me?

A back door stood here, bolted from inside. He threw open the bolt, felt a wall of heat rushing up behind him. He fled into an alley.

Began to dodge left, up a blind run, but went right. He shot into a narrow boulevard, some twelve feet from doorstep to doorstep.

Gaborn felt desolate, hurt, remembering Rowan's face, how she'd died. He'd sought only to protect her, but his impetuousness had killed her. He almost could not believe it, wanted to turn back for her.

He rounded another corner.

Two of Raj Ahten's swordsmen stood not twenty feet from Gaborn, eyes wide with fear. Both of them scrabbled backward, seeking escape, oblivious of Gaborn.

Gaborn turned to see what they stared at.

The flameweaver's elemental had climbed a rooftop, now straddled it like a lover, and the whole roof was sprouting in flames, a terrible inferno of choking smoke that roiled black as night.

The elemental was losing her womanly form – the flames of it licking out greedily, stretching in every direction to wreak havoc. As a flame touched a building, the elemental grew in size and power, became less human.

The fiery whites of her eyes gazed about, searching all directions. Here was a marketplace to burn – below lay the wooden buildings of the poorer market. To the east stood the stables, and to the south the mist-shrouded Dunnwood with its cries of death and shouts of horror.

Her eyes swept past Gaborn and seemed to focus on the two soldiers, an arm's length away. The soldiers turned and ran. Gaborn merely stood, afraid the elemental, like a wight, would be attracted by movement.

Then the elemental gazed back toward the vast rolling hills of the Dunnwood, the tree limbs reaching above the fog. It was too tasty a feast for the elemental to ignore. The flameweaver became a hungry monster now, a devourer. The stone buildings of the market offered little sustenance.

She stretched her hand, grasped a bell tower, and pulled herself upright, then began racing toward the woods, legs of flame spreading over rooftops.

There were shouts of dismay down below as she reached the portcullis at the King's Gate. Soldiers manning the towers at either side of the gate burst into fire at her approach, dropped in flaming gobbets like chunks of meat burning on the spittle of a campfire.

Friend, enemy, tree or house – the flameweaver's elemental cared not what she consumed. To get a better view, Gaborn climbed an external stairway behind an inn. There he crouched just beneath the eaves of a roof.

The stone towers at either side of the portcullis cracked and blackened from the heat as the elemental passed. The iron bars of the portcullis melted.

And as she hurried down toward the lower bailey,

toward the city gates, hundreds of voices broke out in unison, screaming in fear and terror.

By the time she reached the outer gates, the flameweaver had begun to lose her human form entirely, and instead was a creeping pillar of fire. She climbed the city wall, just above the drawbridge, and stood for a moment atop the towers, perhaps fearing the moat. A face flickered in the flames, so much like a woman's face, which gazed back longingly toward the wooden shacks in the lower part of the city, down toward the Butterwalk.

Then the flames leapt the wall, over the moat, and raced through the fields toward the Dunnwood.

Distantly, Gaborn became aware again of the sounds of war, the battle horns of his father's soldiers as they sounded retreat upon those mist-shrouded fields. His heart had been pounding so hard that he had not heard any other sounds for half a minute.

The light of the elemental's fire blazed, cutting through that blanket of fog. In that light, Gaborn could see – as if lit by a flash of lightning – three mounted soldiers battling among the nomen, swinging their great horseman's axes wide over their heads, locked in furious combat.

Then the soldiers were gone, consumed in fire. The elemental began sweeping over the plain, so greedy for dry grass and timber and human life that she seemed to dissipate altogether, to lose consciousness, and become nothing but a great river of flame gushing across the fields.

Gaborn felt sick of heart. When the elemental had touched Rowan, he'd almost felt as if it pierced him, too. Now he heard shouts of despair in the fields, mingled with screams from the injured and dying here in Castle Sylvarresta. He could not block out that last horrid look of pain on Rowan's face. Almost a look of betrayal.

He did not know if he had done well or ill in slaying the flameweaver. Killing the flameweaver had been impetuous – almost a reflex that felt somehow right, yet carried dire consequences.

For the moment, the walls of fire rising up from the field kept Raj Ahten from exiting Castle Sylvarresta, from sending his men into battle.

That might be a saving stroke for my men, Gaborn thought.

But perhaps not. Gaborn had no idea how many of his troops died in that river of flames. He only hoped that in that fog, the men had seen the fiery elemental crouching on the castle walls, had been able to flee.

Men were dead and dying in the castle. Dozens, maybe hundreds of Raj Ahten's troops had burned in the flames. The portcullis of the King's Gate had been incinerated.

Even as Gaborn watched, the huge oak drawbridge to the Outer Gate was aflame; the towers beside it crumbled in ruin. The gears to raise and lower the bridge had melted in the wreckage.

With one fell swipe of his blade, Gaborn had just compromised Castle Sylvarresta's defenses.

If his father sought to attack now, today, he'd have an entrance into the castle.

Gaborn became aware of a tiny figure atop the Outer Wall, gazing over the walls of flames – the figure of a man in black armor, the white owl's wings of his helm sweeping back.

He clutched a long-handled horseman's warhammer in one hand, and shouted with the voice of a thousand men, so his words rang clear from the hills, made the castle walls reverberate. "Mendellas Draken Orden: I will kill you and your spawn!"

From his perch at the top of the stairs, Gaborn fled to hide in the nearest alley.

SIXTEEN: THE FEINT

During his ride from Tor Hollick, Borenson had been lost in thought. The impending battle did not occupy his mind. It was Myrrima, the woman he'd betrothed in Bannisferre. Two days past, he'd escorted her, her sisters, and her mother into the city, to keep them from harm as Raj Ahten's troops wreaked havoc through the country-side.

Myrrima had borne the attack well, kept a stout lip about it. She'd make a fitting soldier's wife.

Yet in his few tender hours with the woman, Borenson had fallen deeply, irrevocably in love. It wasn't just her beauty, though he prized that well. It was everything about her – her sly, calculating manners; her grasping nature; the unabashed lust that flashed in her eyes when she rode with him alone to her mother's farm.

She'd actually turned and smiled up into his face, her dark eyes all innocence as she asked, "Sir Borenson, I assume you are a man who has endowments of stamina?"

"Ten of them," he'd said, bragging.

Myrrima had raised a dark brow. "That should be inter-esting. I've heard that on her wedding night, a maid often discovers in bed that a soldier's great stamina is good for something more than insuring that he doesn't die from battle wounds. Is it true?"

Borenson had tried to stammer some answer. He'd never dreamed that a woman so lovely would ask him so frankly about his skill in bed. Before he could manage a reply, she stopped him by saying, "I love the color red on you. It looks so good when you wear it on your face." He'd blushed more fiercely, felt grateful when she looked away.

Borenson had fancied himself lost to love more than once. But this felt different. He was no moon-sick calf, bawling in the night for some heifer. This felt . . . right. Loving her felt right, all the way down to the bone.

He'd realized he was in love as he rode to warn King Orden of the invasion. He'd been racing full-speed along a road, horse galloping, and had passed three lovely maids picking berries at the edge of the road. One had smiled at him seductively, and he'd been so lost in thought about Myrrima, it wasn't until he was ten miles down the road that he realized he hadn't smiled back.

That was how mad he'd gone.

On riding to Castle Sylvarresta, he'd driven Myrrima from his mind with this thought: The sooner I finish this battle, the sooner I can ride back to her.

Yet well before he reached the castle, Borenson's troops began to run into Raj Ahten's scouts, hunting parties in fives and tens along the road. His fastest knights hunted and slaughtered the scouts gleefully as Borenson plotted his attack on the nomen.

Near the castle he stooped at the banks of the River Wye and opened the flask of mist King Orden had given him. He struggled to hold it as fierce winds howled from the bottle's neck.

By opening the flask over water, he'd doubled the amount of mist it normally would give. So he stoppered the bottle when it was still half-full.

Yet as the smell of sea fog swept across the little valleys around Castle Sylvarresta, Borenson tasted the salt in the air and thought of home. He dreamt how it would be to take Myrrima back to his new manor at Drewverry March. He knew the estate – a fine manor, with a hearth in the master bedroom.

He quickly drove such thoughts from his mind, ordered his archers to string their bows and charge through the dawn woods. Five minutes later, his men surprised the nomen, sleeping in trees. Arrows flew; nomen dropped like black fruit from the oaks of the Dunnwood — some of them dead, some seeking the safety of the castle.

His men thundered and screamed across the downs, herding nomen before them, a great mass of dark fur, snarling fangs, red eyes blazing with fear and rage.

Borenson always laughed in battle, he was told, though he seldom noticed it. It was an affectation he'd learned young, when Poll the squire used to beat him. The older boy had always laughed when he dished out punishment, and as Borenson grew old enough to mete out some retribution, he'd taken to laughing, too. It terrified some foes, angered others. Either way, it caused his opponents to make mistakes while his comrades took heart.

Thus he found himself in the midst of the plain, in a thick fog, surrounded by a dozen nomen. The creatures hissed and roared.

He put his warhammer to work, parried blows with his shield, called on his horse to kick and paw the air, clearing away attackers.

Lost in the rhythmic rise and fall of the warhammer, he was surprised when a great wall of flames shot through the fog to his left.

He shouted for his horse to retreat, to run for its life. It was a force stallion, after all, able to outrace the wind.

But then the wall of flame veered, stretched out tendrils to grasp them all, like some living monster groping for them. The nomen saw their own deaths racing toward them, and one yanked Borenson's foot, trying to pull him from his mount, so that they might die in one another's embrace.

He hacked at the creature with his warhammer, realizing that he might die, that he might never deliver the message King Orden had asked him to bear to Raj Ahten. He planted his warhammer in the noman's face, kicked the creature away, and his horse lunged through the mist.

Borenson raced back over the plains, calling "Orden, Orden!" for his men to regroup. The fire raced after him, like slender fingers that would grasp and tear.

Then he raced under the dark trees.

When the fire reached the oaks, it hesitated, as if . . . uncertain. It prodded a large oak, exploding it into flame, and then seemed to forget Borenson.

Only half a dozen men managed to follow Borenson back into the woods, but he'd seen dozens of others scatter from the flames, into the mists.

He waited for several long minutes for his men to regroup, hoping they'd reached safety. Here in the trees, he felt safe, hidden. The leaves hung over him, closing him in. Surrounding him like a cloak. The branches were shields against arrow and claw, a wall to slow the flames.

Down in the valley, he heard a tremendous cry – Raj Ahten shouting threats of murder against House Orden. Borenson did not understand the reason, but the fact that Raj Ahten would be so outraged made him giddy.

Borenson blew his war horn, calling men to regroup. Minutes later, four hundred men had gathered from all around the valley near Castle Sylvarresta. Some bore alarming news of battling frowth giants east of the castle. Others said nomen were regrouping, trying to reach the castle gates. Other warriors had chased nomen deeper into the woods and hunted them to good effect. Some men had busied themselves slaughtering Raj Ahten's horses. This whole battle was getting crazy, losing focus, and Borenson almost wished now that he'd not covered the battlefield in fog.

He considered what to do, felt it would be safest to stay in the woods, hunting the last of the nomen. But more tempting game lay before the castle, in the fog.

"Right then," he ordered. "We'll do a sweep from east

to west before the castle. Lancers in front, to handle the giants. Bowmen to the sides to clear the nomen."

The air was filling with smoke from the fires in the fields and in the woods downhill.

The knights of Orden formed ranks, charged through the trees, down to the east field. Borenson had no lance, and so took the middle of the pack, near the front, so that he could direct.

As his horse thundered through the mist, Borenson saw a huge giant looming off to his left, a great shaggy mound in the dense fog. Two lancers veered, slammed into the beast.

The wounded monster bawled out, slashed with its enormous claws, sent a warhorse sprawling as if it were a pup, snapped a warrior in half with its tremendous jaws.

Then Borenson was charging past that battle. A few bowmen had spurred into that fray.

Two more giants came wading through the fog. Nomen had gathered in their wake, taking courage. Twenty of Borenson's knights veered toward them. Borenson's heart hammered. One giant roared in rage, calling others.

A vast horde of giants and nomen came rushing together, dark hills with a black tide of spearmen behind. A shout of triumph rose from the monsters' throats.

Borenson's heart nearly stopped. For in their midst rode hundreds of soldiers with brass shields. At their head, one huge warrior in black scale mail, with a helm of white owl's wings, raised a great warhammer and shouted a war cry with a voice of a thousand men: "Kuanzaya!"

The fellow struck terror into Borenson's heart, for he bore the armor and the weapons of kings.

Raj Ahten had his helm raised, and he was the most astonishingly handsome man Borenson had ever seen. The magnificent volume of the Runelord's voice made Borenson's horse stagger in its tracks. Witless with fear at the sound of the war cry, it could not decide whether retreat or turn aside. Borenson shouted for it to charge, but Raj Ahten's voice had been so deafening, perhaps it had damaged the mount's hearing.

The horse thundered to a halt, fighting its reins, trying to turn on Borenson. Borenson managed to pivot it toward the enemy. Then they were in thick battle. Borenson's lancers frantically charged the giants, spreading the cavalry dangerously thin, bowmen firing a hail of arrows, while Borenson himself struggled to charge Raj Ahten.

His mount would not go near that man, fought instead to flee. It raced to Borenson's left, and Borenson found himself charging into the thick of giants as Raj Ahten swept past, warhammer rising and falling with incredible speed as he blazed a bloody trail through the ranks of defenders.

A giant rushed at Borenson through the fog, swung a huge oaken staff. Borenson ducked the blow, fled past the giant, into a knot of nomen who hissed and snarled, happy to see a lone soldier in their midst. Several giants raced past Borenson, seeking the heart of the battle.

Somewhere behind him, one of Borenson's lieutenants began blowing his war horn, desperately sounding retreat.

Borenson raised his hammer and shield, began to chuckle as he fought for his life.

SEVENTEEN: IN THE QUEEN'S TOMB

Three hours after a perfect pink dawn, Iome stood atop the Dedicates' Keep and watched as Raj Ahten and a thousand of his Invincibles rode back into the castle, along with dozens of frowth giants and hundreds of war dogs – all amid cheers and shouts of celebration. The fog on the downs had burned away, but a few wisps still clung amid the shadows of the Dunnwood.

Apparently, the Wolf Lord had taken a great chance, had gone to skirmish with Orden's troops in the woods, and had succeeded in killing and scattering them.

Raj Ahten's men rode smartly, weapons raised in salute.

Chemoise had brought Iome here to the Dedicates' Keep at first sign of attack. "For your own protection," she'd said.

The remains of many a tent and farm still burned out on the fields, and a wildfire ran amok through the Dunnwood, blown now by the easterly winds, two miles from the castle.

For a while the flames had squirmed more like a living thing – tendrils shooting out in odd directions, plucking a tree here, exploding a haycock there, consuming a home with greed.

The blazes within the castle had extinguished, for Raj Ahten's flameweavers drew the power from them. And though Raj Ahten sent men among the streets to seek the murderer of his flameweaver, his beloved pyromancer, he did so to poor effect. The elemental had consumed most of Market Street, destroying any trace of the identify of her murderer.

In the charred and smoking ruins outside the gates of Castle Sylvarresta, one could see many signs of destruction. A thousand nomen had burned near the moat, where they'd sought to make their stand against Orden's mounted knights. One could count Orden's fallen knights among them, too – two hundred or so blackened lumps that had once been men in bright armor, clustered in smoking heaps along the battle lines.

Hundreds more nomen lay strewn at the edge of the woods, where the battle must first have raged fierce and heavy. The trees there were now nothing but blackened skeletons.

Three dozen frowth giants littered the battlefield, strange-looking creatures, with their hair burned off. Iome had never envisioned them thus – each with pink skin and a long snout like a camel's, the hugeness of their claws. From atop the Dedicates' Keep, they looked like misshapen, hairless mice, dotting the battlefield. Some dead giants still held knights and their horses in their paws.

Raj Ahten's horses were dead, cut down with many of the guards who'd been stationed at the edge of the wood.

Yet now his men celebrated a victory, a battle won.

Iome did not know if she should rejoice at Raj Ahten's victory, or weep for Orden.

She was a Dedicate now to Raj Ahten. Rather than fear Raj Ahten, Iome now had to fear assassination at the hands of other kings, or from the Knights Equitable who battled the Wolf Lord.

Chemoise stood at Iome's side, gazed over the blackened fields, weeping as Raj Ahten's troops rode to the castle. Smoke still crept over the ash, and stumps burned all the way to the hill and into the woods.

Why does Chemoise cry? Iome wondered. Then she

realized that she, too, had eyes filled with tears.

Iome understood. Chemoise cried because the world had gone black. Black fields. Black woods. Black days ahead. Iome drew her hooded robe more tightly around her hiding her face. The heavy wool seemed thin protection.

Some of Raj Ahten's troops waited down in the lower bailey. Raj Ahten rode from the battlefield toward the city gates, to meet with his flameweavers and counselors. Even the frowth giants ducked under the posterns of the gates and came into the lower bailey, seeking protection.

In the hills to the south, a hunting horn rang out, followed by another farther east, and another. A few last stragglers from Orden's army perhaps, calling to one another.

Iome waited for Raj Ahten's men to turn around, ride out, and mop up the survivors. Given the strength of his forces, she did not understand why so many of his men remained here in the castle.

Unless something had happened on the battlefield that she couldn't see. Perhaps Raj Ahten feared for his own men. Perhaps they were weaker than she believed. The Wolf Lord must have feared to chase Orden's men any farther, for he knew full well that he could get drawn into an ambush.

Raj Ahten's wisdom went far beyond Iome's. If he was frightened, perhaps he had good reason to fear. Yesterday, Gaborn had told Iome that King Orden could soon reach the castle with reinforcements.

Iome hadn't given it much thought. Orden often brought a couple of hundred men in his retinue. What could they do?

Yet Gaborn clearly believed the force was powerful enough to strike at Raj Ahten. Gaborn had never spoken the number of his father's troops, she now realized. Wisely so. House Sylvarresta could not divulge information it didn't have.

Iome glanced at her Days, who sat a few paces off, with her mother's Days, both of them watching the dark fields. They knew how many men Orden had brought, knew every move each king was making. Yet for good or ill, the Days only watched the armies move like pieces across a chessboard.

How many men had Orden brought to Hostenfest this year? A thousand? Five thousand?

Mystarria was a rich country, populous. King Orden had brought his son with a proposal of marriage. It was common with such proposals for a royal family to make some display of wealth, to marshal some soldiers, engage the knights in friendly competitions.

Orden would have many of his best men on hand. Five hundred of them, perhaps.

Yet Orden was also pompous, given to vain display. So double that number.

The warriors of Mystarria were fierce. Their bowmen trained from youth to fire from horseback. The prowess of their knights with their long-handled horseman's axes and warhammers was legendary.

Perhaps the legend of Mystarria's warriors would keep Raj Ahten at bay, so that he would not dare leave the castle again.

Iome watched for a long moment from the Dedicates' Tower. No one else returned to the castle – not one black-maned noman.

Defiantly now, in the wooded hills to the east and south and west, battle horns blared in a dozen directions, sounding charges, calling new formations.

Orden's knights were still fighting nomen in the woods. It would be a long, grueling day for those warriors.

Down at the city gate, Raj Ahten turned in his saddle to look back over the fields one last time, as if wondering if he should ride once more; then he entered the city, and his men closed the ruined drawbridge.

Life went on. From the tower, Iome could see much of

the city. Down by the Soldiers' Keep, women and children hunted for eggs left by the hens. The miller was grinding wheat by the river. The fragrance of cooking fires mingled with the smoke and ash of war. Iome's own stomach felt tight.

When Iome judged that she had watched from the wall long enough, she went down to the bailey in the Dedicates' Keep, her Days following. Her mother's Days stood on the tower, kept watching the fields.

Iome's father sat in a shaft of sunlight, playing with a pup that snarled and chewed at his hand. Her father had soiled his britches while Iome stood on the wall, so Iome went to work with bucket and rag, to clean her father. He did not fight her, simply stared at her ruined face, frightened by her ugliness, not knowing who she was.

He was handsome as ever, with his endowments of glamour intact. Stronger than ever. A superman with the mind of a child. While she washed the feces off him, King Sylvarresta lay watching her with wide eyes, and made gawping noises, blowing bubbles. He smiled innocently at this newfound pleasure.

Iome nearly broke into tears. Twelve hours. Her father had given his endowments nearly twelve hours ago. This was a critical time, this first day – the worst for him. Those who gave greater endowments went through a time when they were in grave danger. The facilitators called it "endowment shock." One who gave wit would sometimes forget to breathe, or his heart would forget how to beat. But if he survived through this first day, if he survived the shock of the endowment, he might regain a small bit of his wit. Somehow, his body would claim a tiny fraction, enough to survive. At the moment, Iome's father was at his weakest, his most helpless, but later today he could go through a "wakening," a moment when the endowment between lord and vassal became firm, when he regained some small part of his mind.

Thankfully, Iome's father had suffered none of the

worst effects of endowment shock. Now that twelve hours had passed, she hoped he might regain some wit. It was possible – if he had not wished to grant the endowment with all his heart, if the forcible had not been perfectly fashioned, if the facilitator had not chanted his spell with precision – it was possible that he might even remember her name.

So Iome sang to her father softly as she finished cleaning and dressing him. Though he showed no signs of recognizing her, he smiled at her songs.

Even if he never remembers who I am, Iome told herself, it will be worth it to sing. In time, he might learn to love my singing.

When she finished changing him, Iome dressed him with a cloth diaper beneath his tunic.

The bailey of the Dedicates' Keep was filled with ruined men and women, people who had given endowments the night before. The influx had overwhelmed the caretakers. As quickly as Iome and Chemoise finished caring for their own fathers, they began caring for other men – guards who'd faithfully served House Sylvarresta since childhood.

The cooks got breakfast ready, and Iome carried plates of blackberry-filled pastries among the Dedicates. She knelt to waken one young woman who slept in the sunlight beneath a green blanket, a guard named Cleas, who'd escorted her on many a trip into the hills.

Rarely did women serve as guards. Even more rarely did they serve as soldiers of the line. Yet Cleas had done both in her life. She had endowments of brawn from eight men, had been one of the strongest swordmasters in Sylvarresta's service. Raj Ahten had delighted in taking the strength from her. Now Cleas did not breathe. Sometime during the night, she'd become too weak to draw breath.

Iome hurt at the sight, did not know whether to feel angry or grateful. With Cleas' death, fifteen people who had given her endowments would have suddenly become whole, easing the overcrowding in the Dedicates' Keep. Yet Iome had lost someone she'd loved. Iome's throat felt tight. She knelt over Cleas, weeping, looked back. Her Days stood watching. Iome expected the woman to be cold and dispassionate as ever, her little V of a face tight-lipped and empty. Instead, she could see lines of sorrow in her expression.

"She was a good woman, a good warrior," Iome said.

"Yes, it is a terrible waste," the Days agreed.

"Will you help me get her to the tombs?" Iome asked. "I know a vault we can use, a place to honor the guards. We will place her with my mother."

The Days nodded weakly. On such a dark day, this small gesture struck Iome powerfully. She felt grateful.

So Iome finished feeding the Dedicates; then she and the Days got a litter, spread a blanket over Cleas to use as a pall, and carried her to the south wall of the keep, laid her on the ground next to five other shrouded litters. Four of those litters held Dedicates who had not lived out the night.

Iome's mother, Venetta, lay under the last black burlap shroud. A slim golden circlet, resting atop her chest, identified the body of the Queen. A black-and-white jumping spider had climbed on to the circlet, hunting a bluebottle fly that buzzed about.

Iome had not seen her mother's face since her demise, almost dared not pull back the shroud to look at it. Yet she had to see if her mother's body had been properly prepared.

All morning, Iome had avoided this duty.

Chancellor Rodderman had come in the night to tend to Venetta's funeral arrangements. Iome had not seen him since. Perhaps he had business outside the King's Keep, but Iome suspected that he had decided it was best to avoid Raj Ahten. He might even have dodged his responsibilities in preparing the body.

Raj Ahten's men had brought the corpse here, to the Dedicates' Keep. He would not have left it in the Great Hall, where custom dictated it to be placed for the mourning, to be viewed by vassals. The Queen lying dead on a pallet, for all to see, might engender discord in the city.

Instead, it had been secluded within the high and narrow halls of the most inner keep, where only the Dedicates might see.

Iome pulled back the black burlap covering.

Her mother's face was not what she'd imagined. Apart from the terrible wound, it was like gazing into the face of a stranger. Her mother had once had several endowments of glamour, had seemed a great beauty. But at death the beauty had gone out of her. Unexpected threads of gray hair were woven into her black tresses. The shadows under her eyes looked dark and sunken. The lines on her soft face had grown hard and old.

The woman on the pallet had been cleaned, but nothing could hide the gash on the left side of her face where Raj Ahten's signet ring had torn her skin, the indentation in her skull where her head had met the paving stones.

The woman beneath the shroud seemed a stranger.

No, Raj Ahten had no need to fear the vassals. They would not rise up in outrage at the death of this old thing.

Iome went to the portcullis, to the captain of the guard, a dark little mustached man in big armor, a helm embossed with silver. It seemed strange for Ault to be gone, or Derrow, where they had stood under this stone alcove for so many years.

"Sir, I'd like permission to take the dead to the King's tombs," Iome said, holding her breath.

"De castle is onder attack," the captain said gruffly, his Taifan accent thick. "Is no safe."

Iome fought the urge to slink away. She did not want to antagonize the captain, yet she felt that it was her sacred duty to bury her mother, show the woman that one last act of dignity. "The castle isn't under attack," Iome tried to sound reasonable, "only a few nomen trapped in the woods are under attack." She waved her hand out over the burned battlefield before the castle. "And if Orden should attack, you would see him coming from half a mile, and he would have to breach the Outer Wall. No one is likely to reach the Dedicates' Keep."

The little man listened intently, his head cocked to the side. Iome could not tell whether he understood her. Perhaps she'd spoken too fast. She could have spoken to him in Chaltic, but she doubted he'd understand.

"No," the little man said.

"Then let her spirit take vengeance upon you, for I am guiltless. I do not wish to be haunted by a Runelord."

The little man's eyes flashed in fear. The spirits of dead Runelords were said to cause more trouble than most – particularly if they suffered violent deaths. Though Iome did not fear her mother's shade, this little Taifan captain was from a land where such things were taken far more seriously.

"Hurry," the little captain answered. "Now. Go. But take nothing more than half an hour."

"Thank you," Iome said, reaching out to touch him in gratitude. The captain shrank back from her touch.

Iome called out to Chemoise, to her Days. "Quickly, we need bearers to carry these litters – and some charnel robes."

Chemoise ran into the kitchens, brought out some of the deaf and mute bakers, the butcher and his apprentice, kitchen helpers with no sense of smell. In a few moments, two dozen people came to help bear the litters.

The butcher trundled over to the Dedicates' Hall, came out with an armload of black cotton charnel robes, with their deep hoods and long sleeves.

Each pallbearer donned a charnel robe, so that the ghosts in the tombs would know they had not come as grave robbers, and at the hem of each robe was a silver bell whose tinkling would drive off any malicious spirits.

When they had finished, they went to the litters and began carrying the dead to the portcullis. Iome took the front right handle of her mother's litter, as was her place.

When they were ready, the Taifan captain and his sergeant put their backs to work, raising the portcullis quickly, and shooed them all from the keep with a warning. "Be back, twenty minutes. No more!"

It would not be enough time, Iome knew, to set the bodies in place, sing the soothing funerary lullabies to the dead, yet she nodded yes, just to put the captain's mind at ease.

Then she began lugging the bodies to the back of the Dedicates' Keep, to a wooded hollow, the King's tombs.

Iome had never done such heavy labor, so she had not gone two hundred feet past the gate, round the corner of Feet Street, when she found herself, heart pounding, moist with sweat, begging the others to stop.

It was nearly noon. As she waited in the bright sunlight, the smell of ash cloying the air, a dirty young hunchback in a deep-hooded robe darted out from shadows beneath a market's awning.

Immediately she knew it was Binnesman. She could feel the earth power emanating from him, and she wondered what had brought him back, wondered why the wizard sought her.

The hunchback sidled up to Iome, forcing her back a step. "Let ol' Aleson give you a hand with that, lass," he whispered, pulling back his hood a bit, and he reached for the right front pole to the litter.

It wasn't Binnesman at all. Iome felt astonished to recognize Gaborn's face beneath a liberal coat of grime. Her heart pounded. Something was afoot. For some reason, Gaborn had not made it outside the castle gates and needed her help. And, somehow, Gaborn had grown in the past few hours.

Iome pulled her hood closer to hide her face. For a

moment, she felt once again as if all her pride and
courage would drain from her. The spell woven into Raj
Ahten's forcibles still sought to drain her self-esteem.

Over and over again, she whispered in her mind a
litany: This, I deny you. This I deny you.

Yet she could not bear the thought that Gaborn might
recognize her. She let him take the litter; then Iome
walked beside him as the pallbearers cut through an alley,
down the narrow streets that led to the tombs.

The tombs of House Sylvarresta consisted of hundreds
of small stone mausoleums, all painted white as bone,
rising among a sheltered grove of cherry trees. Many of
the mausoleums were designed to look like miniature
palaces, with absurdly tall pinnacles, and statues of the
dead kings and queens standing at the gates of each tiny
palace. Others of the mausoleums, those reserved for
trusted retainers and guards, were simply stone buildings.

When they reached the shelter of the grove, Gaborn
and the others set down their burdens. Gaborn whispered to Iome, "I am Gaborn Val Orden, Prince of
Mystarria. I'm sorry to impose upon you, but I've been
hiding all night, and I need information. Can you tell me
how House Sylvarresta fares?"

With a start, Iome realized that Gaborn didn't recognize her – not with her beauty gone, her skin rough as
bark. Behind her, Iome's Days had her face and historian's
robes covered beneath the charnel robes, just another
anonymous pallbearer.

Iome did not want Gaborn to know who she was. She
could not stand the thought of being ugly in his sight. Yet
another fear also struck her heart, for she saw a more
compelling reason to keep her identity hidden: Gaborn
might feel the need to kill her. She was, after all, a
Dedicate to an enemy king.

Iome spoke with a low, frightened, voice; hoping to disguise it. "Do you not even know whose corpse you carry?
The Queen is dead. But the King lives. He has given his

wit to Raj Ahten."

Gaborn grasped Iome's arm. "What of the Princess?"

"She is well. She was given a choice – to die, or to live and serve her people as regent. She was forced to give an endowment, also."

Gaborn asked, "What has she given?" He held his breath, his face full of horror.

Iome considered speaking the truth, revealing her identity, but she could not. "She has given her sight."

Gaborn fell silent. Abruptly he lifted the litter, signaling an end to the break, and began walking between the tombs again, thoughtful. Iome led Gaborn and the pallbearers to her parents' tomb, which was of classic design. Nine marble spires rose from the tiny palace atop it; outside its door stood statues of King Sylvarresta and his wife, images carved in white marble shortly after their wedding eighteen years before. Iome signaled for the bearers to also bring Cleas into the tomb. As a faithful guard, it was only right that she be interred beside her queen.

As they entered the shadowy tomb, Iome smelled death and roses. Dozens of skeletons of faithful guards lay in the tomb, bones gray and moldering. But last night, someone had brought bright red rose petals and strewn them across the floor of the tomb, to alleviate the smell.

Gaborn bore Queen Sylvarresta to her sarcophagus, in the sanctum at the back of the tomb. It was a red sandstone box, with her image and name chiseled into its lid. The roof above the sanctum was a slab of sheer marble, so thin that light broke through it, shining down on to the sarcophagus beneath.

Here in this deep corner, air breathed into the tomb from tiny slits in the stonework, so that the smell of death did not reach.

It took a great deal of effort for Gaborn and two bakers to slide the lid of the sarcophagus back, exposing the empty casket. Then they lifted the queen into place, and were about to set the lid on the box when Iome begged them to stop, to let her look for a while.

Pallbearers carried Cleas to a stone shelf, pushed back the bones of some loyal guard from a decade past, and laid Cleas in his place.

They did not have Cleas' armor and weapons to bury with her, so a baker took a warhammer from a nearby corpse, laid it across Cleas' chest, wrapped her hands around its handle.

Gaborn stood a minute in the dim light, studying the moldy skeletons, many of them still in armor, bearing weapons on their chests. Though the room was small, only forty feet long and twenty wide, five tiers of stone shelves were cut into the walls. Some guards had been entombed here for over twenty years. Bones from knuckles and toes littered the floor, borne there by rats.

Gaborn looked as if he would ask a question.

"You may speak freely here," Iome told him, still kneeling beside her mother's casket. "These pallbearers are all deaf or mute, sworn to the service of House Sylvarresta. No one here will betray you."

"You bury your dead with their weapons here in House Sylvarresta?" Gaborn asked.

Iome nodded.

He seemed delighted, looked as if he would rob a corpse. "In Mystarria, we bequeath fine weapons and armor to the living, so it can be put to good use."

"Mystarria does not have so many smiths to keep employed," Iome said dryly.

Gaborn asked, "Then no one will mind if I borrow a weapon? Mine was destroyed."

"Who can say what offends the dead?"

Gaborn did not immediately take a weapon. Instead, he paced nervously. "So," he breathed at last, "she is in the Dedicates' Keep?"

Iome hesitated to answer. Gaborn had not said who "she" was. Apparently he was distraught. "The Princess

came to the keep this morning, and washed her father
and fed him. Raj Ahten's guard put her there for safe-
keeping during the attack. But she may leave at any time.
I think she still occupies her room in the King's Keep,
with servants to attend her."

Gaborn bit his lip, quickened his step, thinking furiously. "Can you get a message to her for me?"

"It should not be hard," Iome answered.

"Tell her that House Orden is sworn to protect her. Tell
her that I will kill Raj Ahten, that she will look upon my
face again someday, no longer a Dedicate."

"Don't . . . please don't try," Iome said, choking back a
sob. Her voice cracked, and she feared Gaborn would
hear it, see through her disguise.

"Try what?" Gaborn asked.

"To kill Raj Ahten," she said deeply. "Queen Sylvarresta
clawed him with poisoned fingernails, yet he withstood
the venom. It is said that the wound of a sword thrust
through his heart heals before the blade is withdrawn."

"There must be a way to kill him," Gaborn said.

"You will be forced to kill House Sylvarresta, for both
the King and his daughter are Dedicates to Raj Ahten.
Lord Sylvarresta himself received eighty endowments of
wit last night, all in Raj Ahten's behalf."

Gaborn turned at this news, went to the door of the
tomb, staring out up into the sunlight, considering.

"I will not kill my friends," Gaborn said, "or their
Dedicates. If they gave endowments, they did not do so
willingly. They are not my enemy."

Iome wondered at this. It was common practice to kill
another's Dedicates, a necessary evil. Few Runelords
would shirk this most hateful responsibility. Did Gaborn
hope to let men live, simply because they did not intend
evil? She said, "Even if you spare House Sylvarresta, even
if you turn instead to other houses, kill other kings, they
are also innocents. They, too, deserve to live. They have
no love for Raj Ahten."

"There must be a way to get Raj Ahten without killing others," Gaborn said. "A decapitation."

Iome had no advice to give. With powerful Runelords, a decapitation was the most certain way to insure a kill, but plotting the deed and doing it were two different matters. "And who will decapitate him? You?"

Gaborn turned to her. "I could try, if I can get close to him. Tell me, is the herbalist Binnesman well? I need to speak with him."

"He's gone," Iome said. "He vanished in the night. Raj Ahten's men saw him . . . at the edge of the woods."

Perhaps of anything she could have said, this news seemed to dismay him most.

"Well," Gaborn said, looking lost, "I must change my plans. If the wizard is in the woods, perhaps I can find him there. Thank you for the news, Lady . . .?"

"Prenta," Iome whispered. "Prenta Vass."

Gaborn took her hand, kissed it, as if she were a helpful lady-in-waiting. He held her hand, just a moment too long, lightly sniffed the scent of her perfumed wrist, and Iome's heart skipped. Her voice had not faltered, she felt sure; he had not recognized her voice. But did he recognize her perfume?

He gazed into her face, with his penetrating blue eyes, and though a small frown formed on his lips, he did not speak. Iome pulled away, turned her face, heart pounding, fearing that she had been discovered.

She knew she was hideous, that every scrap of beauty had been stripped from her. Her yellow eyes, her wrinkled skin, were gruesome enough. But her features were nothing compared to the horror she felt inside, the insidious draw toward self-loathing.

Surely he would condemn her. Surely he would pull away in contempt. Instead, he stepped around, to better see her face.

Iome suspected that Gaborn recognized her. He regarded her silently now, trying to discern any traces of the woman he had seen yesterday. But he refused to embarrass her by voicing his recognition. Iome could not withstand that gaze, felt forced to raise a hand, and with it hid herself from those eyes.

"Don't hide from me, Prenta Vass," Gaborn said softly, taking her hand again, pulling it down. He'd spoken her name hesitantly. He knew her. "You are beautiful, even now. If there is any way I may serve you?"

Behind Gaborn, Iome's Days shifted nervously, and the bakers suddenly left the tomb as if they'd just recalled urgent matters elsewhere. Iome wanted to break into tears, to fall into his arms. She only stood, trembling terribly. "No. Nothing."

Gaborn swallowed hard. "Can you bear another message to the Princess for me?"

"What?"

"Tell her . . . that she haunts my dreams. That her beauty is indelible in my memory. Tell her that I'd hoped to save her, hoped to give her some small aid, and maybe I did some good – I killed a powerful flameweaver. Because I'm here, my father has come, though perhaps too late. Tell her I stayed the night in Castle Sylvarresta, but now see that I must leave. My father's soldiers are hunting for me in the woods. I dare stay no longer. I'm going to try for the woods, before my father charges the city."

Iome nodded.

"Will you come with me?" Gaborn asked. He stared into her face, and now she knew without a doubt that he recognized her. His eyes were filled not with contempt, but with pain, and so much gentleness, she longed to fall into his arms. Yet she dared not move.

Iome's eyes filled with tears. "Come? And leave my father? No."

"Raj Ahten will not hurt him."

"I know," Iome said. "I – don't know what to think. Raj Ahten is not totally evil, not as I feared. Binnesman hopes for some good from him."

"'When you behold the face of pure evil, it will be beautiful.'" Gaborn quoted an old saying among Runelords.

"He says he wants to fight the reavers, that he wants to unite mankind for our own defense."

"And when the war is won, can the Wolf Lord give your endowments back to you? Will he give his own life so that all those who were robbed of endowments can regain them, as Good King Herron did? I think not. He will keep them."

"You don't know that," Iome said.

"I do," Gaborn insisted. "Raj Ahten has revealed his nature. He has no respect for you or any other. He will take all that you have, leave you with nothing."

"How can you be sure? Binnesman seemed to want him to change. He hoped to convince the Wolf Lord to rid himself of the flameweavers."

"You believe he will do it? You can stand here, over the body of your dead mother, and believe Raj Ahten has any degree of decency whatsoever?"

"When he speaks, when you look in his face–"

"Iome," Gaborn said, "how can you doubt that Raj Ahten is evil? What do you have that he has not yet tried to take? Your body? Your family? Your home? Your freedom? Your wealth? Your position? Your country? He has taken your life, as surely as if he'd slain you, for he desires to strip away all that you have and all you hope to be. What more must he do to you, before you know him to be evil? What more?"

Iome could not answer.

"I'm going to cut off the bastard's head," Gaborn said. "I'm going to find a way to do it, but first we need to get out of here alive. Now will you come with me, if I bring your father out of the city, too?"

He took her hand, and when he touched her, all darkness fled. Iome's heart pounded. She almost dared not to believe her fortune, for when she looked into Gaborn's eyes, all her fears, all her self-loathing and sense of ugliness vanished. It was as if he were some living talisman that wrought a change on her very heart. A stone fortress, she thought. A haven. "Please," he begged, using all the powers of his Voice.

She nodded yes, numb. "I'll come."

Gaborn squeezed her hand. "I don't know how, yet, but I'll come for you and your father – soon – in the Dedicates' Keep."

Iome felt again that sensual thrill, the longing she associated with the presence of Binnesman. Her heart pounded. He had just held her tenderly, as though she still had her endowments of glamour, as if she were beautiful.

He turned, took a short sword from a corpse and tucked it in the folds of his robe, then hurried from the tomb, his fleeting shadow blocking the cold sunlight a moment.

As he fled, she almost dared not believe he would return for her, that he would not save her. Yet a warm certainty filled her. He would be back.

When he was gone, Iome's Days said, "You should be careful of that one."

"How so?"

"He could break your heart." Iome could not fail to note something odd in the Days' voice, a tone of respect.

Iome felt terrified. If Raj Ahten caught her trying to escape, he'd show no mercy. Yet she knew that her heart was not pounding in fear, but for another reason. She held her hand over her heart, trying to still it.

I think he already has broken it, she told herself.

EIGHTEEN: DUELING WITH DECEPTION

Two hours after Gaborn fled Iome in the tombs, Borenson rode up to the ruined gates of Castle Sylvarresta, a green flag of truce flying from a dead noman's lance. He forced a smile.

His muscles ached, and his armor was covered in blood. He now rode a new horse, gleaned from a fellow soldier who would never ride again.

It would be a game to match wits with Raj Ahten, one he did not want to play. Luck had not favored him. Most of his warriors had been slaughtered. He'd paid for every small victory. His soldiers had slain more than two thousand nomen. He had unhorsed most of the Wolf Lord's army, and had managed to slay or drive off a number of frowth giants – while a dozen more of the creatures had perished in that insane fire. Dozens of Raj Ahten's legendary Invincibles had followed Borenson's men into the woods, and the Invincibles were now so full of arrows that their corpses looked as prickly as hedgehogs.

Yet Borenson had not won a clear victory, despite heavy enemy losses. Raj Ahten had quit hunting Borenson's men when they got deep into the woods, fearing an ambush. In part, Borenson had hoped that Raj Ahten would brave the woods, where his own men, he felt sure, would have the advantage.

But Borenson also wanted Raj Ahten to fear that ambush, needed Raj Ahten to believe that the woods were full of men. King Orden had often said that even a man with great endowments of wit could be outsmarted, for "Even the wisest man's plots are only as good as his information."

So it was that Borenson rode up to the gates of Castle Sylvarresta, reined his horse in at the moat. Smiling.

On the charred wall above the ruined gate towers, one of Raj Ahten's soldiers waved his own lance overhead three times, an acceptance of Borenson's request for truce, then waved at him, beckoning him to ride into the castle. The drawbridge was down, its gears and chains melted. One side of the drawbridge was so charred it had a hole in it large enough to let a man ride through.

Borenson stayed where he was, not wanting to deliver messages in private, and shouted, "I'm in no mood for a swim, not in this armor. Raj Ahten, I bear a message for you! Will you face me, or must you hide behind these walls?"

It seemed madness to accuse the Wolf Lord of cowardice, but Borenson had long ago decided that sanity was no virtue in an insane world.

In twenty seconds, when he heard no response, Borenson shouted again. "Raj Ahten, in the South they call you the Wolf Lord, but my lord says you are no wolf, that you are born of a common whippet, and that you have not the natural affections of a man, but instead are given to fondling bitches. What say you?"

Suddenly, atop the wall, stood Raj Ahten, shining like the sun, the white owl's wings sweeping wide from his black helm. He gazed down, imperious, unperturbed by the insults.

"Serve me," he said softly, so seductively that Borenson almost found himself leaping from his horse, to fall on one knee.

But he recognized the use of Voice immediately, was able to ignore it. A captain in Orden's guard could not be the kind of man easily swayed by Voice.

"Serve you, the one who's been baying from these walls all morning, breathing out threats to my lord? You must be mad!" Borenson said. He spat on the ground. "I fear there is no profit in serving you. You don't have long to live."

"You claim to have a message?" Raj Ahten asked.

Borenson thought that the Wolf Lord seemed too eager to stem the tide of insults.

Borenson made a show of taking a long gaze at the soldiers along the castle walls. Thousands of archers were there, other defenders with pike and sword. And on the wall-walks behind them were citizens of Castle Sylvarresta – curious boys, eager to hear his message. Some farmers, merchants, and tradesmen stood now to defend the walls for Raj Ahten as vigorously as they would have stood to defend Sylvarresta the night before. Borenson felt acutely aware that his message was for these soldiers and townsmen more than for Raj Ahten. A message foretelling doom that was delivered in private might demoralize a single leader. The same message delivered before an army could subvert an entire nation.

"Such a small army, to be trapped so far from home," Borenson said, as if musing to himself. Yet he threw his own voice, loud enough so the men on the far walls could hear.

"They are a fine army," Raj Ahten said. "Good enough for the likes of you."

"Indeed," Borenson countered. "I do commend them. Your men died well in the woods this morning. They fought almost as well as expected."

Raj Ahten's eyes blazed. Borenson had succeeded in angering him. This is maybe not the smartest thing I've ever done, Borenson told himself.

"Enough of this," Raj Ahten said. "Your own men died well, too. If you desire a contest to see whose men die best, then I must concede that your men will win, for I slaughtered enough of them today. Now, deliver your message. Or did you come merely to try my patience?"

Borenson raised a brow, shrugged. "My message is this. Two days ago King Mendellas Draken Orden took the castle at Longmot!"

He waited a moment for this news to sink in, then added, "And though you have sent occupying forces to hold that piece of rock, King Orden bids me to let you know that your reinforcements have been slaughtered to the man."

This news shook the defenders on the castle walls. Raj Ahten's men were gazing at one another, trying to consider how to react.

"You lie," Raj Ahten said evenly.

"You accuse me of lying?" Borenson said, using his own gift of Voice as best as he could, trying to sound righteous and indignant. "You know the truth of it. As proof, you may search your own feelings. This morning at dawn, King Orden put to death all in Longmot who had given you endowments. You felt the attack. You felt his retribution. You cannot deny it!

"And now I shall tell you how it was done: We began our march three and a half weeks ago," Borenson said honestly, naming the time since he'd left Mystarria, then calculated when Raj Ahten's own troops would have set march, "shortly after we received word of your departure from the South.

"At the time, my lord King Orden sent word to the far corners of Rofehavan, setting his snare for a pup of a Wolf Lord. Now, Raj Ahten, the noose has your neck, and shortly you shall find yourself choking, choking on your greed!"

The men on the walls began talking, looking about in dismay, and Borenson guessed at their question. "You wonder how my lord knew that you would attack Heredon?" Borenson shrugged. "My lord knows many things. He heard of your plans from the spies who serve at your side." Borenson glanced meaningfully at the counselors and magicians who stood beside Raj Ahten, barely suppressing his smile. He held his gaze on the imperious-looking Days at Raj Ahten's side. Perhaps Raj Ahten might still trust these men, but from now on, Borenson suspected none of them would trust each other.

Raj Ahten chuckled at Borenson's ploy, countered with words that struck terror in Borenson's heart. "So, King Orden has sent you to get word of his son. Don't worry, the young man is for ransom. What does Orden propose to offer?"

Borenson took a deep breath, glanced at the castle walls in desperation. He'd been told to offer a ransom for a nameless friend, so that Raj Ahten would betray the names of those he held captive. But Raj Ahten had guessed his ploy. Now, Borenson hoped the words he spoke next might dishearten the Wolf Lord even further. "I was told to offer nothing – until I have inspected the Prince."

Raj Ahten smiled playfully. "If King Orden cannot keep track of his own son, I shall not oblige him. Besides, you would not like what you saw."

Borenson wondered. This game was becoming complex, more complex than he liked. If Raj Ahten really had Gaborn prisoner, then he should not have hesitated to show the young man. Unless, indeed, he had killed the Prince.

Yet, if Raj Ahten had not captured the Prince, then by Borenson admitting that he needed to inspect the merchandise, Borenson had revealed to the Wolf Lord that he, too, did not know Gaborn's whereabouts.

Belatedly, Borenson realized that he had departed from the script King Orden had written for him. He was trying too hard to be clever, working too hard to go his lord one better. By doing so, he might well have jeopardized his whole mission.

His face burning with shame, Borenson turned his horse around, began to leave. He doubted that Raj Ahten would let him go. The Wolf Lord had to be terrified, had to wonder whether King Orden had captured the forcibles in Longmot. Had to wonder how many might be offered in ransom.

"Wait!" Raj Ahten called at Borenson's back.

Borenson glanced over his shoulder.

"What will you offer me, if I show you the Prince?"

Borenson said nothing, for at the moment he feared to speak, so he just urged his horse to walk slowly away.

Borenson rode his horse a hundred yards, fully conscious that this little encounter could still go astray. He was within bowshot of the castle, and Raj Ahten's wizards manned the walls. Raj Ahten would not let him escape without trying to wring some information from him.

Yet Borenson asked himself once again, If Raj Ahten has the Prince, why does he not show him?

Borenson turned his horse, gazed up into Raj Ahten's dark eyes. "Gaborn safely reached our camp last night," he lied bold-faced, "and I fear that I can no longer offer any ransom. I came only to bring that message."

Raj Ahten showed no emotion, but the frightened, self-consciously determined faces of his counselors spoke volumes. Borenson felt sure he had guessed correctly, that Raj Ahten did not have the Prince. He remembered a few scouts his men had killed last night, and another party of scouts his men had fought deep in the woods an hour ago. Why else would so many of Raj Ahten's troops have been scouring the forest?

"However," Borenson continued, "House Sylvarresta is an old and valued ally to my lord. I can offer something for the King's family, for their safe return."

"What?" Raj Ahten asked.

Borenson departed further from the script Lord Orden had composed for him. "A hundred forcibles for each member of the royal family."

Raj Ahten laughed now, laughed with relief and scorn. Here in the North, where blood metal had been so scarce the past ten years, three hundred forcibles might seem a princely sum. But to Raj Ahten, who had forty thousand forcibles hidden in Longmot, it was nothing. Raj Ahten no longer believed that Orden had taken Castle Longmot, just as Borenson had planned.

"Consider the offer well, before you laugh me to scorn," Borenson said. Now it was time to put the Wolf Lord on the rack. Borenson said confidently, "Lord Orden captured forty thousand forcibles in Longmot, and for the past two days, he has had half a dozen facilitators putting them to good use. Perhaps to a man as rich as you, the loss of forty thousand forcibles seems a small thing – but my lord will not up his offer of ransom for the King and the royal family. Of what use to him are such people, when they only serve you as Dedicates? A hundred forcibles for each, nothing more!"

Borenson watched Raj Ahten's counselors tremble at the news, felt deeply gratified, though Raj Ahten himself stood stoically, the blood slowly draining from his face.

"You lie," Raj Ahten said, betraying no fear. "You do not have the Prince. You have no forcibles. And there is no spy. I know what your game is, messenger, and I am not dismayed by your ruse. You . . . merely annoy me."

By use of the Voice, Raj Ahten sought to bolster his troops. But the damage had already been done. Compared to the harrowing message Borenson had delivered, Raj Ahten's denial sounded hollow, thrown up vainly as a last defense.

And yet, and yet Borenson feared that Raj Ahten did see through him. He felt a nagging worry.

Borenson spurred his horse forward, out over the burned grass before the castle. Here and there, small puffs of smoke still boiled up from the ground. When he felt safely out of bow range, he wheeled about.

"Raj Ahten," he cried, "my lord begs you to meet him at Longmot if you dare. Bring with you any fool who wishes to die – your five thousand against his fifty! There, he swears, he will grant no quarter, and he will whip you like the vicious cur that you are!"

He raised his arm in signal, and out across the hills, his men began to blow their war horns in the woods, the short staccato blasts that commanded each squadron to re-form.

King Orden had sent two hundred horns on this expedition, for he had planned to have his men sound them in the hills when his son had secured Iome's hand.

Yet in time of war, such horns were issued only to each captain of a hundred. Raj Ahten would know this, and Borenson only hoped that the Wolf Lord's ears were keen enough to discern the number of horns.

It would be well if Raj Ahten believed that Borenson's eighty surviving men were eight thousand.

NINETEEN: SIFTING

Raj Ahten's most devoted counselor Jureem watched through slitted eyes as his master stood atop the burned walls of Castle Sylvarresta while Borenson rode away. His master's face glowed with beauty, seemed almost translucent. A face so bright, it was the light of the world. Raj Ahten seemed unperturbed by this dire news.

Yet Jureem found himself trembling. Though his master denied it, he knew something was wrong. Jureem could only wonder, for his master seldom confided in Jureem anymore, or sought his advice.

For years, these Northerners had been a thorn in his master's side, sending their Knights Equitable to assassinate his Dedicates. Raj Ahten's own beloved sister had died in his arms from a wound administered by a Knight Equitable. Over the years he had grown to detest these pale-skinned Northerners, until now, as Raj Ahten took their endowments and plotted ways to use them, he seemed to feel nothing for them. No remorse, no pity, no human compassion.

Now this.

At the moment, Jureem felt painfully distressed. He wanted to run to Longmot and learn if Borenson spoke the truth. He wanted to shoot Borenson in the back. He wished that Borenson had never spoken. Furthermore, Raj Ahten's flameweavers had seen visions of a king in their fires, a king who could destroy him. King Orden.

Now the wizard Binnesman had gone to join Raj Ahten's enemy.

Jureem held his hands in fists, trying not to let others see how they shook. He'd thought that eliminating House Orden would be easy. Now the matter seemed more complex.

A book could not contain words enough to relay the schemes that his master, Raj Ahten, had laid. Jureem only understood them in part. By tradition, King Orden came for the hunt here at Castle Sylvarresta, bringing a couple of hundred men in his retinue.

This year, his son was of an age that, Raj Ahten decided, the Prince too would have come. And so he'd laid his trap, besieging Castle Sylvarresta with a few men, hoping to send Orden scurrying south, where Raj Ahten's troops, hidden along the roads leading to Mystarria, would slaughter King Orden and his son. If the King did not run south, Raj Ahten's scouts would hunt him down eventually.

It was but one of a hundred plots set in motion. This very day, dozens of parties of assassins would strike at targets. Armies marched against fortresses to the west and south. In other places, armies would simply show themselves, then disappear into some forest or mountain pass, either freezing vital forces in some stronghold or drawing them away from intended targets.

Jureem knew that the heart of his master's plan lay here. The heart of his plan was to strike down both Orden and Sylvarresta.

Yet dire portents now warned against it. The pyromancer had seen a king here, a king who could destroy the Great Light of Indhopal.

Raj Ahten had left himself open to attack. He'd brought fewer than a thousand forcibles to Castle Sylvarresta, and over half of those had been used up last night, consumed by the spells that bound Raj Ahten and his Dedicates. He'd left forty thousand forcibles at

Longmot, true, and he'd judged that those forcibles would be safe. Longmot was a great castle, with high walls bound with magic spells. And though Raj Ahten's forces in Longmot had been small, their numbers were to have been bolstered soon.

The window of opportunity for someone to strike at Longmot had been dreadfully narrow. Given Longmot's defenses, it should have been able to withstand any attack from the smaller keeps within striking distance. Castles Groverman and Dreis were both within a days' ride from Longmot. But Raj Ahten's advance scouts had assured him that the garrisons there were small. Jureem's spies had seen none of Orden's forces in either castle.

His spies only sent word that Orden had brought a "larger than anticipated retinue" to celebrate Hostenfest, and that they were camped outside the village of Hazen, on the southern borders of Heredon. The retinue contained at most three thousand men – including knights, squires, cooks, and camp followers. It was a large force, larger than Raj Ahten had planned to engage. Normally Orden brought fewer than three hundred men to the hunt.

But now the scouts said that last night, over two thousand knights had been riding toward Castle Sylvarresta. How could that be? Did Sylvarresta bring two forces, one to attack Longmot, another to ride north?

Two days. Jureem hadn't received a report from Longmot in two days. He should have had a status report. Jureem suspected that Longmot had fallen. King Orden had somehow taken the castle.

Fifty thousand men, the messenger had said. Fifty thousand? The number unnerved Jureem, for it seemed too close to the number of knights he'd estimated Orden would marshal against his master next spring – if Orden escaped the trap. Lord Orden could marshal a quarter million knights of decent prowess, but he'd not attack with anywhere close to that number. He wouldn't dare leave his castles defenseless.

Elaborate schemes, all on the verge of crumbling. Raj Ahten needed to take the North, and he needed to take it quickly. For years now the blood-metal mines of Kartish had been playing out. They'd be empty by midwinter.

Only in Inkarra could he get more blood metal. It was said that the mines there still yielded well.

Yet no lord of Rofehavan or Indhopal had ever succeeded in invading Inkarra. Wizards there were not powerful, but they were plentiful. The Inkarrans had adopted battle tactics well suited to their terrain – quick strikes in the hills on solid little ponies. And the Inkarrans could not be defeated unless one also defeated the high lords of the arr.

Worst of all, in long ages past, a certain Master Facilitator named Tovil had fled Rofehavan to Inkarra, and there he had launched a new school for the study of forcibles. In Inkarra, amazing discoveries had been made, discoveries no other wizards had ever been able to duplicate. In Inkarra, forcibles had been developed that left no scar, so that one could learn from a mark the shape of a rune of power. These forcibles transmitted talents and skills from one person to another.

In all the years of spying, the lords of Rofehavan and Indhopal had never been able to duplicate the Inkarrans' discoveries.

Each time a Northern lord had tried to invade the South, he quickly found that the southerners did not just fight him – they also provided forcibles to his enemies.

Thus, no lord had ever been able to take Inkarra, drain its riches, or penetrate its secrets.

Jureem knew that Raj Ahten had to act soon. He had to drain the Northern kings now, subjugate them, and then move on. It was quite possible that in days now lost to legend, Daylan Hammer had taken endowments of will and talent, that these were an integral piece that Raj Ahten needed before he could become the Sum of All Men.

Jureem prided himself on being a man who was not easily deceived. He strongly suspected that Borenson had told an intricate tale based on some truth, twisted together liberally with lies. Yet as Jureem considered the message Borenson had brought, it was damnably difficult to know where the truth ended and the lies began.

After only a few moments on the castle wall, Raj Ahten looked to his side, at Jureem. "My counselors, let us walk," he said. The Wolf Lord seldom sought advice from Jureem or Feykaald anymore. Certainly his master was worried.

They came down from the city wall, walking along the steps, and had not gone far before they were out of the crowd, heading up a small rise toward the stables.

"Feykaald," the Wolf Lord asked the oldest of his counselors. "What think you: Does King Orden have his son?"

"Of course not," Feykaald hissed. "The messenger was too startled, too frightened, when you first mentioned the ransom. That messenger was full of lies. He spoke not a word of truth."

"I agree that Orden does not yet have his son, but though the messenger's manner showed him to be a liar, he spoke some truth."

"He does not have his son," Jureem agreed, replaying every nuance of the messenger's voice, every expression.

"Granted," Raj Ahten said. "What of Longmot?"

"He could not have conquered it," Feykaald spat quickly.

"He has done so," Raj Ahten said, his voice not betraying the concern that this must have caused. Jureem's heart nearly froze at the thought.

"O Greatest of Lights," Jureem said, "I must argue with you. The messenger's demeanor clearly indicated that this, too, was a lie. Orden must be a fool, to send such a poor liar on such an errand!"

"It is not the messenger's demeanor that convinced me," Raj Ahten said. "I felt a dizziness at dawn. Virtue left me. Many hundreds of Dedicates died, and their endowments are lost. Of that I am sure."

To lose so many endowments was a deep blow, a fearsome cut. Yet it did not terrify Jureem. In distant lands to the south, Raj Ahten's facilitators worked assiduously to find new Dedicates for him. These were men with great glamour and powers of Voice, who could lure others into Raj Ahten's service, put the forcibles to them. Raj Ahten was in a constant state of flux, gaining in strength and wit and glamour and stamina at an astonishing rate. Jureem no longer knew how many thousands served as his lord's Dedicates. He knew only that his lord grew in power, day by day. Jureem could not yet see what his lord would become, when he became the Sum of All Men.

But this morning he had suffered a blow.

In a day or two, Raj Ahten's occupying armies would arrive, a hundred thousand strong, and lay siege. Orden could not have anticipated so large an occupying force.

At the same time, three armies would enter the kingdom of Orwynne to the west, and King Theros Val Orwynne, upon seeing that he was caught in a vise, would have little choice but to either surrender or dig in for a siege. He would not be able to send aid to Orden in Longmot.

Meanwhile, saboteurs in Fleeds had begun poisoning the grain stock to the stables of High King Connel, preventing the horse clans from mounting their fierce cavalry attacks.

No, Orden had to be terrified. So he was sending this little yapping messenger to bark at Raj Ahten.

"Perhaps," Jureem said, "Orden has taken Longmot, but he cannot hold it." Yet if Raj Ahten was right, if Longmot had fallen, and this messenger had managed to feign dishonesty through his whole speech, was it yet possible that in every matter he had spoken the truth?

Now Raj Ahten said the thing Jureem dreaded most. "Do we have a spy in our midst?"

Jureem considered, could see no other way to explain how Orden had known that Raj Ahten planned to attack Heredon. Nor could Orden have known about the forcibles hidden in Longmot, or known that the garrison was undermanned.

Immediately, Jureem worried that he himself might have been the problem. Had he spoken of these things to any of his lovers? Had he spoken before any servants or strangers? A careless word to the wrong person?

It could have been me, Jureem thought. He'd confided his fears about leaving Longmot undermanned to one of his lovers, a horseman who bred fine stallions. But had he mentioned that the forcibles would be there? No. He had not spoken of them.

Jureem looked to his side. Feykaald had been with Raj Ahten for many years. Jureem trusted the man. As for the flameweavers, they cared nothing for Raj Ahten. They served the elemental fires, and would follow Raj Ahten only so long as he promised them war, promised to feed their master.

So Jureem did not worry that these men were spies. True, it could be that one of the captains was a spy. But how? How could even a spy have notified Orden of the opportunity at Longmot on such short notice?

No, it was the Days, the tall man with graying hair and chiseled, imperious features who most worried Jureem. He could have aided Orden in this battle. Only he.

Jureem dreaded this moment, had long suspected it would come. The Days claimed they were neutral, that they never aided any lord against another. To do so would have been to interfere in the affairs of men, an action that the Days said the Lords of Time would not tolerate. So they merely recorded events – but Jureem had heard too many rumors, too many hints at unscrupulous dealings in the past. For years, Raj Ahten had grown in power until he reached the point where Jureem suspected that the Days would unite against him.

In their own way, Jureem believed the Days were far more of a threat than the irrepressible Knights Equitable.

The Days, of course, knew Raj Ahten's actions. The Days knew well in advance that Raj Ahten planned to attack Longmot, knew he'd left the castle without a sufficient garrison. The Days' twin, the man or woman who shared his mind in the monastery to the north, of course knew what had come to pass. And anything learned by one Days could swiftly be relayed to many.

It was all Jureem could do to keep from whirling now and gutting the Days.

"I think, we are betrayed, my lord," Jureem said, glancing at the Days. "Though I know not how." His master was watching, had seen the covert accusation.

Yet what could the master do? If Jureem accused the Days falsely, and slew him, he might make matters worse. All of the Days would then openly fight Raj Ahten, betray his secrets into every ear.

On the other hand, if Jureem did not slay the Days, then a spy would remain in the camp.

Raj Ahten stopped.

"What will we do now?" Feykaald asked, wringing his little hands. They stuck out from his turquoise silk robes like twisted knots from a tree limb.

"What do you think we could do?" Raj Ahten asked. "You are my counselor, Feykaald. So counsel me."

"We should send a message," Feykaald whispered, "to General Suh, and divert his armies to us for reinforcement, instead of having him attack Orwynne."

Feykaald was old, tough, and full of experience. He'd lived long by being careful. But Jureem knew that Raj Ahten often desired less-cautious counsel. The Wolf Lord had grown in power by listening to Jureem.

He leaned his ear to Jureem. "And what would you do?"

Jureem bowed his head. He spoke carefully as he thought aloud. "Forgive me, O Blessed Light, if in this matter, I do not seem so alarmed." He flashed a distrustful glance at Feykaald. "It may be true that King Orden has captured your forcibles, but who will he use them on? You have already stripped endowments from everyone who was worthy at Longmot. Orden cannot use the local populace. Which means he would have to take endowments only from his warriors – an unfortunate proposition, for with each endowment he took to himself, he would weaken his own army."

"So you propose?"

"Go to Longmot and take your forcibles back!" It was, of course, the only possible answer. Raj Ahten could ill afford to wait for reinforcements. It would only give Orden time to either slip away with the treasure or draw reinforcements himself.

Raj Ahten smiled at this answer. It was risky, Jureem knew. Perhaps Orden wanted to draw them out of Castle Sylvarresta for an ambush. But all life was a risk. And Raj Ahten could ill afford to do nothing.

The Master had taken six endowments of metabolism. In doing so, he was able to thwart the assassins who came after him time and again.

But taking such endowments carried a great danger, the promise of an early death. Metabolism could serve as a weapon against its owner. Indeed, in one case, according to legend, a Dedicate who gave a great king metabolism was kidnapped by the King's enemies. Then, the enemies gave hundreds of endowments of metabolism to the Dedicate, making him a vector, so that the King died of old age in a matter of weeks. For this reason, Raj Ahten had vectored all his metabolism through a single Dedicate, a man he always kept near to his side, in case he needed to slay the man and break his own link.

Few kings ever dared take more than one or two endowments of metabolism. With six, Raj Ahten could run six times the speed of another man. But he also aged six times faster. And though Jureem's master had many thousands of endowments of stamina, and would grow old with incredible grace, Jureem knew that the human body was meant to wear out over time. His master had lived for thirty-two years now, but because of his many endowments of metabolism, he had aged far more than that. Physically, he was in his early nineties.

Raj Ahten could not hope to live much beyond the biological age of a hundred and ten, nor could he survive without his endowments.

Only a few years back, Raj Ahten had made the unfortunate mistake of slaying some of his Dedicates, so that he could slow his own aging. But within a week, a Northern assassin had nearly slain the Wolf Lord. Since then, Raj Ahten had been forced to bear this lonely burden of high metabolism.

Three years. He needed to unite the world, to become the Sum of All Men within three years, or he'd die. One year to consolidate the North. Two to take the South. If Jureem's master died, it might well be that the hope of all mankind would die with him. The reavers were that powerful.

"So we go to Longmot," Raj Ahten said. "What of Orden's army in the Dunnwood?"

"What army?" Jureem asked, certain from many small cues that there was no great threat. "Have you seen an army? I heard war horns blowing in the wood, but did I hear a thousand horses neighing? No! Orden's mists were there only to hide his weakness."

Jureem squinted up at his master. Jureem's obesity, his bald head, made him look like an oaf, but Raj Ahten had long known that Jureem was every bit as dangerous as a cobra. Jureem found himself saying, "You have twenty legions approaching Longmot – an army Orden cannot withstand, not if you fight at our head. We must go and take Longmot."

Raj Ahten nodded solemnly. Those forty thousand forcibles represented the labor of thousands of miners and craftsmen over the past three years. A large pocket of blood ore – now tapped dry. They were irreplaceable.

"Prepare the men to march," Raj Ahten said. "We will empty Sylvarresta's treasury, take what food we need from villages we pass. We leave in an hour."

"My lord, what of the horses?" Feykaald said. "We will need mounts."

"Our soldiers have enough endowments; most need no mounts," Raj Ahten said. "And common horses require food and rest, more than a man. My warriors shall run to Longmot. We will use what horses we can. We'll empty Sylvarresta's stables."

A hundred and sixty miles by road. Jureem knew that Raj Ahten could walk that distance himself in a few hours, but most of his archers would not bear the burden of more than a single endowment of metabolism. Such soldiers could not run to Longmot in less than a day.

Raj Ahten would have to leave his nomen here. They would only slow the march. The giants and war dogs, though, could take such abuse.

"But–" Feykaald urged, "what of your Dedicates here? You have two thousand in the Dedicates' Keep. We don't have horses to move them, nor do we have enough guards to protect them." His attention, too, had turned to logistics.

Raj Ahten's answer was chilling. "We need leave no warriors to guard the Dedicates' Keep."

"What?" Feykaald asked. "You practically beg Orden to attack. You'll get your Dedicates killed!"

"Of course," Raj Ahten said. "But at least their deaths will serve some higher purpose."

"High purpose? What higher purpose can their deaths serve?" Feykaald asked, wringing his hands, mystified.

But Jureem suddenly saw the plan in all its cruelty and magnificence: "Their murders shall nurture factiousness," Jureem reasoned. "For years, the Northern nations have united against us. But if Orden murders

Sylvarresta's Dedicates, as he must, if he destroys his oldest and dearest friend, what will he win? He might weaken us for a few days, but he will weaken himself forever. Even if he should escape with the forcibles, the lords of the North will fear Orden. Some here in Heredon will revile him, perhaps even seek vengeance. All this shall work against House Orden, and destroying Orden is the key to taking the North."

"You are most wise," Feykaald, whispered, glancing first at Raj Ahten, and then at Jureem, his voice filled with awe.

Yet such a waste saddened Jureem. So many men go through their lives content to do nothing, to be nothing. It was wise to harvest endowments from such men, put them to use. But wasting the lives of Dedicates this way – was a great shame.

Jureem and Feykaald shouted a few curt orders, and in moments the castle walls became alive as the troops prepared for the march. Men rushed to and fro.

Raj Ahten began heading along the narrow cobbled streets, wanting to be alone with his thoughts, walking past the King's stables – some fine new wooden buildings that stood two stories tall. The upper story held hay and grain. The lower stabled the horses.

His men rushed everywhere, claiming the first steeds they found, shouting orders to stablehands.

As he passed, Raj Ahten peered into several open doors. A few Dedicate horses were kept in stalls, many of them hanging from slings where stablemasters groomed and pampered the unfortunate beasts. Barn swallows darted in and out through the open doors, peeping in alarm.

The stables became tremendously busy. Not only were Sylvarresta's horses stabled there, but some of Raj Ahten's finer beasts had been brought last night, to be cared for by Raj Ahten's own stablemasters.

He had enough good warhorses to mount a decent cavalry.

Raj Ahten ducked into the last stable. The odor of dung and horse sweat clung in the air. Such stench irritated Raj Ahten, with his overdeveloped sense of smell. Raj Ahten's stablemaster washed the master's horses twice daily in lavender water and parsley, to diminish such offensive odors.

In the front of the stable, a boy with dark hair stood by a stall. He'd bridled a force horse – a good one by the number of runes on it – and stood grooming it, preparing it for the saddle. Several horses of equal merit stood by. The lad was too pale of face to be one of Raj Ahten's own stablehands, had to have been inherited from Sylvarresta.

The young man turned at the sound of Raj Ahten's entry, glanced nervously over his shoulder.

"Leave," Raj Ahten told the boy. "Take the horses to the gates and hold them yourself. Reserve the best for Counselor Feykaald and Chancellor Jureem here – no other. Understand?" Raj Ahten pointed at Jureem, who stood just outside the door, and Jureem nodded curtly at the boy.

The young man nodded, threw a small hunting saddle over the horse's back, and hurried past Raj Ahten and his counselors, gawking, terrified.

Raj Ahten sometimes had that effect on people. It made him smile. From behind, the boy looked familiar. Yet Raj Ahten suddenly felt a certain muzziness, a cloudiness of thought as he tried to recall. Then he had it – he had seen the boy on the street, earlier this morning.

But no, he now remembered, it had not been the boy. Merely a statue that looked like him. The young man led the horse from the stable, began buckling and cinching the saddle, trying on saddlebags, just out of earshot.

Alone with his Days in the shadowed stable, Raj Ahten whirled and caught the Days by the throat. The man had been following two paces farther back than normal.

Perhaps a sign of guilt, perhaps in fear.

"What do you know of this attack at Longmot?" Raj Ahten asked, lifting the Days from the ground. "Who betrayed me?"

"Not, aagh, me!" the Days responded. The man grabbed Raj Ahten's wrist with both hands, clung for dear life, trying to keep from strangling. Fear lined his face. Sweat beaded on his forehead.

"I don't believe you," Raj Ahten hissed. "Only you could have betrayed me – you or your kind."

"No!" the Days gasped. "We, ugh, we take no sides in the affairs of state. This is . . . your affair."

Raj Ahten looked in his face. The Days seemed terrified.

Raj Ahten held him, muscles strong as Northern steel, and considered breaking the man's neck. Perhaps the Days was telling the truth, but he was still dangerous. Raj Ahten longed to crush the fellow, to rid himself of this pest. But if he did, every Days across the world would unite, would reveal Raj Ahten's secrets to his enemies – the numbers of his armies, the locations of his hidden Dedicates.

Setting the Days down, Raj Ahten growled, "I am watching you."

"Just as I watch you," the Days said, rubbing his sore neck.

Raj Ahten turned, left the stable. The captain of his guard had said that Gaborn Val Orden had slain one of the Wolf Lord's scouts near here. The Prince would have left his scent behind.

Raj Ahten had endowments of scent from over a thousand men. Most of his scouts had taken endowments of scent from dogs, and hence feared the dogbane that the Prince carried.

"My lord, where are you going?" Jureem asked.

"To hunt Prince Orden," Raj Ahten decided on impulse. His men would be long at work preparing for the march. With Raj Ahten's endowments of metabolism, he could spend time doing something of value, while others worked. "He may still be in the city. Some jobs you should not leave to lesser men."

TWENTY: A PRINCE UNMASKED

"Och, orders is orders! His Lor'ship tol' me to put the King and his girl on proper 'orses – even if I had to tie 'em in the saddle! The wagon's too slow on such a long march, thru them woods," Gaborn said, affecting a Fleeds accent.

The finest horsemen came from Fleeds, and he wanted to play the part of a trusted stableboy.

Gaborn sat atop his stallion, gazing down at the captain in the Dedicates' Keep. The guards had raised the portcullis, and busily filled a great covered wain with Dedicates gained here at Castle Sylvarresta – those who acted as vectors for Raj Ahten, including King Sylvarresta.

"He say to me none of thees!" the captain said in his thick Taifan accent, glancing about nervously. His men had abandoned their posts to raid the kitchens for provisions. Some officers looted Sylvarresta's treasury, and others down on Market Street were breaking shopwindows. Every moment the captain spent talking to Gaborn meant there would be less time to stuff his own pockets.

"Aye, what do I know?" Gaborn asked.

Gaborn turned to leave, nudging his mount with his heels, pulling around the four horses he had on his lines. It was a delicate moment. Gaborn's mount grew skittish, laid its ears back, rolled its eyes. Several soldiers hurried

313

into the Dedicates' Keep, to help loot the treasury. Gaborn's stallion flinched at each soldier who crowded past, ventured a small kick at one man. One of the tethered stallions responded to the sudden move by bucking. Gaborn whispered soothing words to keep the whole bunch from bolting.

In the last few minutes, the streets had suddenly come alive with people – a mob of Raj Ahten's men sprinted to the armory to grab supplies, weapons, horses; merchants rushed hither and thither to protect what they had from looters.

"Halt!" the captain of the guard said before Gaborn got the horses turned. "I put King on horse. Which one ees for him?"

Gaborn rolled his eyes, as if the answer were obvious. If he'd truly been a stablehand, he'd have known which mount would remain calmest, which horse would try to keep the idiot king from falling. As it was, he feared that all five horses might bolt at any second. His own horse, the stallion he'd ridden into town the day before, had been trained to recognize the Wolf Lord's soldiers by their coat of arms, and to lash out against them with hoof and tooth. Surrounded by the Wolf Lord's troops, his stallion tossed its head from side to side, shifting its weight uneasily. Unsure. His mood unnerved the other horses.

"Och, today, who knows?" Gaborn said. "I smell a likely storm. They're all a wee skittish."

He looked at the horses. In truth, two mounts seemed less concerned by the commotion.

"Prop the King on Uprising, and here's to hopin' he don't fall!" Gaborn patted a roan mount, inventing the horse's name on the spur of the moment. "The Princess, she sits on his sister 'ere, Retribution. Their Days can ride the skittish 'orses and plummet to their asses for all I care. Oh, and watch that girth strap on the King's saddle. It wiggles loose. Oh, and Death Knell there, put her last in your line. She kicks."

Gaborn handed the lines to the captain, giving him the reins to all four mounts, and turned to leave.

"Wait!" the captain said, as Gaborn suspected he would.

Gaborn craned his neck, sat with a bored expression.

"You geet king on horse! Everyone on horse. I want you personal to geet them down through gates."

"I'm busy!" Gaborn objected. Sometimes the best way to secure a job was to pretend you did not want it. "I'm wanting to watch the soldiers leave."

"Now!" the captain shouted.

Gaborn shrugged, urged the horses through the portcullis, into the bailey of the Dedicates' Keep, near the huge wain.

No one had yet managed to bring the draft horses to pull the wain, so the wagon merely sat, its axletree lying on the ground.

Gaborn looked into the wagon, tried not to stare too hard at Iome. He wiped sweat from his forehead with the back of a sleeve, then got off his horse, helped Iome mount. He had no idea whether she could ride, felt relieved when she sat lightly atop her mare, took the reins confidently.

The drooling king was another matter. His eyes grew frightened and he hooted and grasped the horse's neck with both hands as soon as Gaborn got him saddled, then tried to slide off. Though the King had once been a fine horseman, he gave no evidence of it now. Gaborn realized he would, quite literally, have to tie the man to the pommel.

So Gaborn used one of his lead ropes and did just that, wrapping the rope around the King's waist twice, then tying him to the pommel in front, and to the hitches for the saddlebags in the rear.

Gaborn's heart pounded. He was taking an insane risk: Iome could ride, but the King would pose a definite problem.

Gaborn planned to take the King and Iome through the

city gates, then gallop for the woods, where Orden's forces could protect him. Gaborn hoped that none of the enemy archers would dare shoot the King. As a vector, he was too valuable to Raj Ahten.

Gaborn most feared that Raj Ahten's forces might lead a mounted pursuit.

Fortunately, the King's horse seemed more intrigued by the King's whooping and grasping antics than frightened. After Gaborn tied the King securely into his saddle, Sylvarresta became more interested in petting the mount and kissing its neck than in trying to unhorse himself.

Raj Ahten bent over the bloodstained ground, sniffing Gaborn's scent in the birch grove. On the ridge above stood his counselors and two guards, illuminated by the noon sun.

But here in the shaded forest, Raj Ahten searched alone, as only he could.

"That's the spot," one of his captains called.

But the ground held only the odor of mold and humus, desiccated leaves. Ash had rained down from the fires that incinerated the wizard's garden, fouling the scent. Of course the tang of a soldier's blood filled the air.

The Prince had passed through the herbalist's garden, so that his natural scent lay masked under layers of rosemary, jasmine, grasses, and other rich fragrances. Raj Ahten's own men had tramped here by the dozens last night, further fouling the trail.

The more he tasted the air, the more elusive the scent seemed.

But none of his hunting dogs could track as well as Raj Ahten did. So the Wolf Lord knelt in the loam, sniffing tenderly, dismissing some scents, seeking for that which was Gaborn. He crawled forward, searching for a vestige of Gaborn among the trees. Perhaps the young man had brushed a vine maple, or touched the bole of an alder. If he had, his scent would cling to the spot.

Raj Ahten found no scent near the blood, but found something nearly as interesting: the earthy musk of a young woman, a maid who worked the kitchens. Odd that none of his hunters had mentioned the scent. It might be nothing, or it might be a woman who accompanied the Prince.

Raj Ahten suddenly stood upright, startled. A half-dozen finches in a nearby tree took flight at the movement. Raj Ahten listened to a soft wind blow through the trees. He recognized the girl's scent, had smelled it –

This morning.

He'd passed her on Market Street, just outside the King's Keep.

Raj Ahten had endowments of wit from over a thousand men. He recalled every beat of his heart, remembered every word ever uttered to him. He visualized the woman now, at least the back of her head. A shapely young thing, in a hooded robe. Her long hair a deep brunette. She'd been next to a statue of gray stone. Once again, he felt an odd sensation – a peculiar muzziness of thought.

But – no, he suddenly realized. It could not have been a statue. The thing had moved. Yet when he'd passed it, he'd had the impression of stone.

He tried to recall the statue's face, to imagine the thing he'd passed as living flesh. But he could not see it, could not visualize it. A statue of a boy – a faceless, plain-looking lad in a dirty robe.

They'd stood in the streets near where his pyromancer had been murdered.

But wait. Raj Ahten had it now – the scent. He recalled their smell. Held it in his mind. Yes, it was here in the woods. And he'd smelled it at the stable. The young man Raj Ahten had seen at the stable, minutes ago.

Raj Ahten could remember everything he'd seen in years. Now he tried to dredge up the lad's face, to see him there in the stables.

Instead, he saw the image of a tree: a great tree in the heart of the wood at dusk, so vast that its swaying branches seemed to reach up and capture the stars.

It was so peaceful under that tree, watching it, that Raj Ahten raised his hands, felt the warmth of the starlight touching his own hands, penetrating them.

He longed to be that tree, swaying in the wind. Unmoved, unmovable. Nothing more than trunk and roots, reaching deep into the soil, tendrils of root tickled by the passing of countless worms. Breathing deep. The birds soaring through his limbs, nesting in the crooks of branches, pecking at grubs and mites that hid in the folds of his bark.

Raj Ahten stood, breath suspended, among the trees of the forest, looking down on his smaller brothers, tasting the wind that meandered slowly above him and through him. All cares ceasing. All hopes and aspirations fading. A tree, so peaceful and still.

Ah, to stand thus forever!

Fire blossomed in his trunk.

Raj Ahten opened his eyes. One of his flameweavers stood glaring at him, had prodded him with a hot finger.

"Milord, what are you doing? You've been standing here for five minutes!"

Raj Ahten drew a deep breath of surprise, looked at the trees around him, suddenly uneasy. "I . . . Gaborn is still here in the city," Raj Ahten said. Yet he could not describe the boy, could not see his face. He concentrated, and saw in rapid succession a stone, a lonely mountain, a gorge.

Why can I not see his face? Raj Ahten wondered.

Then he looked up at the trees around him, and knew. A small band of trees, narrow along the river. A finger of the Dunnwood. But powerful, nonetheless. "Set fire to this wood," he told the flameweaver.

Raj Ahten raced for the city gates, hoping he was not too late.

❖

Sweat poured from Gaborn's face as he urged the horses through the lower bailey. Thousands of troops clogged the gates.

Five hundred knights milled outside the city wall. Their warhorses wore the finest armor Sylvarresta's smiths could forge, blackened and polished.

Another thousand archers stood ready near the walls with bows strung, should an army race out from the woods.

Yet the fact that so many men had already left the castle did not ease the congestion. Thousands of soldiers did not travel completely alone – squires, cooks, armorers, tailors, bearers, fletchers, prostitutes, washwomen all thronged the streets. Raj Ahten had seven thousand soldiers in his legion, but his camp contained another thousand followers. Armorers dressed the horses in the bailey. Children darted about underfoot. Two cows had run down the Butterwalk and now tramped through the crowd.

In the turmoil, Gaborn rode from the castle, trailing Iome's mount, her father's, and those of two Days, trying to keep his horse from kicking and biting every soldier who wore the red wolves of Raj Ahten on his shield or surcoat.

One dark-faced sergeant grabbed the reins of Gaborn's horse, shouting, "Give me horse, boy. I take that one!"

"Raj Ahten told me to keep the reins myself," Gaborn said. "It's for Jureem."

The sergeant drew back his hand as if the words burned him, eyed the horse longingly.

Gaborn rode through the press of bodies, toward the throng of soldiers gathering on the blackened grass outside Castle Sylvarresta. He held the line to the King's horse tightly, glanced back.

The idiot king smiled at everyone, waving, his mouth wide with joy. Gaborn's own mount, with its surly nature, waded through the masses, breaking a path for the horses that followed. Iome's and King Sylvarresta's Days trailed last.

Near the blackened gates, everyone sought to surge across the damaged drawbridge. One side had burned through from the elemental's fires, but had been hastily repaired.

"Make way for the King's mounts! 'Ware the King's mounts!" Gaborn shouted.

Gaborn eyed the city walls as he passed beneath the portal. Archers everywhere guarded the outer wall, but most foot soldiers had deserted their posts.

Then, suddenly, he passed under the main arch. Gaborn did not entirely trust the ruined bridge to hold the weight of both his people and their horses. A few planks had been thrown over the rent, but they looked flimsy, so he dismounted, had Iome do the same. As for the King, he left the man mounted and cautiously walked each horse across, then entered the throng of soldiers milling about in the charred grass.

Raj Ahten's soldiers nervously watched the hills, anxious to be on their way. The troops bunched together, as men do when fearful. The sounds of King Orden's hunting horns less than an hour before had put them in a grim mood.

Iome crossed the bridge, and Gaborn helped her back into the saddle, then led her mount over the dirt road, holding the reins to his own horse, as if he were but a stableman delivering the animals.

From behind him came a sudden commotion. A strong voice shouted, "You, Prince Orden!"

Gaborn leapt ahorse, with a kick spurred the beast, shouting, "Game ho!" His mount surged forward so hard that Gaborn nearly fell from the saddle.

He'd taken his mounts from Sylvarresta's hunting stables, trusting they were trained for the chase. At his command, the horses ran like the wind. These were horses bred for the woods, strong of leg, deep of chest.

Some quick-thinking soldier leapt in Gaborn's path, battle-axe half-drawn. "Strike!" Gaborn shouted, and his horse leapt and lashed out with a forehoof, dashing the warrior's head open with the rim of its iron shoe.

From atop the castle wall, Raj Ahten cried, "Stop them! Hold them! Before they reach the woods!" His voice echoed from the hills.

Then Gaborn reached the fields, with Iome shouting and racing beside, clutching the reins to her father's mount.

Behind them, the pair of Days had not spurred forward. One soldier grabbed the King's Days by the hem of his robe, dragged the man down as the horse bucked. Three others joined into the task. Iome's Days, a thin woman with a straight mouth, let her horse dance around the commotion, taking the rear.

Dozens of knights spurred their own mounts, heavy warhorses trained for combat. Gaborn did not fear them. Under the crushing weight of their own armor and that of their armored riders, the horses should fall behind. But they were still force horses, with supernatural strength and endurance.

Gaborn glanced back, shouted for Iome to go faster. He had only a short sword – not much to fight against such men.

On the castle walls, many archers had great bows made of steel that could shoot five hundred yards. Dozens of them nocked arrows. At such a distance, no one could fire accurately, but a lucky shot could kill as easily as a skillful one.

His horse galloped so fluidly, he felt as if it were a creature of wind, come to life beneath him, hooves pounding a four-beat. The stallion raised his ears forward, raised his tail in contentment, grateful to be free of the stable, grateful to race over the ground like a storm.

The woods seemed to rush toward Gaborn.

An arrow whipped past Gaborn's neck, grazed the ear of his mount.

Behind him, a horse screamed in pain, and Gaborn

glanced back to see it stumble, an arrow in its neck. Iome's Days rode the mount, her thin mouth an O of surprise. She somersaulted over the horse's head, a black arrow in her back as she fell headlong into the charred field.

Half a dozen bowmen had let fly, the arrows sailing toward Gaborn in a long arc. Gaborn shouted, "Right, ho!" As one, all three remaining stallions veered, dodging from beneath the arrows' trajectory.

"Bowmen, cease fire!" Raj Ahten raged. His fool archers were going to kill his Dedicates.

Five dozen knights raced over blackened fields, pocked with dead nomen and frowth, toward the near hills where burned trees raised twisted limbs. If the knights did not catch the Prince before he entered the woods, Raj Ahten suspected Gaborn would find safety among King Orden's troops. Or worse, the woods themselves would fight for the boy.

As if to confirm Raj Ahten's suspicions, a lone war horn sounded from the woods – a high, lonely cry – from the peak of the first hill. A signal for Orden's men to charge.

Who knew how many knights lurked there?

Beside Raj Ahten, two flameweavers ran to the top of the wall. The hairless men leapt beside him, the heat of their bodies rising fierce as an inferno.

Raj Ahten merely pointed. He could not see the boy's face. Even when Gaborn turned, for some reason he could not focus on the boy's face. But he knew the back, the form. "Rahjim, see the young man who is falling behind, preparing to fight? Burn him."

A satisfied light shone from the flameweaver's dark eyes. Rahjim exhaled nervously; smoke issued from his nostrils. "Yes, O Great One."

Rahjim drew a rune of fiery power in the air with his finger, then raised a hand high, grasped for half a second toward the sun shining high in the sky. The heavens suddenly darkened as he gathered sunlight into fibers, threads like molten silk, and brought them all twisting down in ropes of energy, to focus in his hand – until his palm filled with molten flames.

Rahjim held the fire for a portion of a second – long enough to gather a proper focus. He threw with his might.

Gaborn fell forward as a blast of wind and energy smashed his back, felt a sudden burning. He wondered if an arrow had hit him, realized that his surcoat was afire.

One of Raj Ahten's knights raced his horse beside Iome, trying to grab her reins.

Gaborn ripped the dirty, rotting cloth that covered him, tossing the blazing thing in the air just in time to watch the rag burst into flame. He fancied that only the mud on the cloak had kept him from burning in that precious half-second. The garment fell over the face of Iome's pursuer's warhorse, catching the horse's helm. It almost looked to be a magician's trick.

The horse whinnied in terror, stumbled, threw its rider.

Gaborn glanced over his back. He was now hundreds of yards from the flameweaver – out of range of his most dangerous spells.

Having missed in his first attack, the flameweaver would now show his power in fury.

Atop the hill, on the winding road ahead, a war horn sounded for a second time, calling King Orden's men to charge. The very thought terrified Gaborn. If King Orden charged, Raj Ahten would learn just how few soldiers Gaborn's father had.

The skies darkened a second time, but the darkness held longer. Gaborn turned, spotted the flameweaver, hands raised. A ball of flame, bright and molten as the sun, formed between his fingers.

Gaborn pressed his face close to his mount, smelled the horse's sweat, the sweet odor of its hair.

The road ahead twisted east, though soon it would lead south. The road was broad, full of dust in this season, kicked up by the animals of thousands of traders. But ahead it led past some blackened trees to the promising shelter of the woods beyond. That was where the war horn had sounded. But if Gaborn left the road here, kept straight, he'd reach the woods more quickly.

Once in the woods, out of the flameweaver's sight, he'd be safer.

"Right, ho!" he shouted, urging the horses from the road. Ahead, Iome's mount obeyed the command, and the King's followed its lead. At the sudden turn, King Sylvarresta howled in fear, clung to his steed's neck. Gaborn let his mount leap an embankment like a hare, sailing over blackened logs.

To Gaborn's left, the ball of flame hurtled past – having expanded to the size of a small wagon even as it lost power over the distance.

The rush of heat and light smashed into the blackened turf, exploded. Black ash and fire worried in the air.

Then Gaborn was racing through the black tree trunks, dancing between the trees, using them to shield his back. Even in death, they provided some protection.

Raj Ahten's troops surged after, men shouting curses in Southern tongues. Faces lined with rage.

Only the fact that he now had no cloak, nothing to protect him but his skin, reminded Gaborn of Binnesman's herbs in the pouch tied about his neck.

Rue.

He grasped the pouch, ripped it from his neck, and waved the thing in the air. The powdered leaves floated out like a cloud.

The effect was devastating.

The soldiers who hit that cloud of rue began hacking. Horses whinnied in pain, faltered and fell. Men shouted. Metal clanged on ground. Gaborn glanced back.

A dozen knights lay coughing on the blackened hillside.

Others had all veered from their inexplicably fallen comrades. Most of them had deemed it wise to retreat from the insistent blowing of the war horn, for they now raced full-tilt back to Castle Sylvarresta.

Gaborn topped a small rise, saw the dirt road from the castle winding through a narrow valley.

Among the blackened trees near the ridgetop sat one lone warrior atop an unarmored gray mare. He wore his shield on his left hand – a small round device not much larger than a platter.

Borenson, waiting. White teeth flashed beneath his red beard as the big guard smiled a welcome to his prince. Gaborn never had thought he'd be so happy to see the green knight of House Orden on any warrior's shield.

Borenson raised his war horn to his lips again, sounded a charge, and raced toward Gaborn. His steed leapt the corpse of a frowth giant, lunged downhill.

"Archers, draw!" Borenson shouted an obvious ruse. The valley beyond held nothing but blackened trees and stone. The guard drew a long-handled battle-axe from its sheath on his saddle, waved it above his head, thundered past Gaborn to cover the Prince's retreat.

Only one of Raj Ahten's warriors had dared cross the ridge, come rushing down.

A huge man on a black steed – his white war lance poised, like a spear of light. Yet even in the half-second as Gaborn reined his horse to wheel about, he glanced back.

The knight wore blackened chain beneath a gold surcoat, with the emblem of Raj Ahten's wolves emblazoned in red. His lance, the color of ivory, had been stained with blood.

The knight's high helm had white wings painted on it, signifying that he was no common soldier – but a captain of Raj Ahten's guard, an Invincible with no fewer than fifty endowments.

Borenson could not equal the man.

Yet Borenson spurred to meet the warrior head-on, his

steed throwing dirt with every pounding of its hooves.

Then Gaborn understood: his father's troops had fled, would not come to his rescue. Borenson had to kill this knight or die in the attempt, lest Raj Ahten learn the truth.

Gaborn drew the short sword from the belt at his waist.

The Invincible charged downhill, lanced poised, holding as steady as the sun in the sky.

Borenson raised his battle-axe high. The wise thing to do would be to time his swing, parry the lance before its tip speared his mail.

But these were force warriors, and Gaborn did not know what kinds of strength or talents the Invincible might have. Gaborn was not prepared for their tactics.

Just as it appeared Borenson would be hit, he called "Clear!" His horse leapt and kicked.

The Invincible buried his lance in the horse's neck. Only then did Gaborn see that this was a 'pinned lance' – a lance held to the warrior's gauntlets with a metal pin. The pins helped when battling armored opponents, for it insured that the knight would not lose his grip when the lance hit metal.

Unfortunately, one could not release the lance without removing the heavy steel cotter pins that held it to his gauntlet. Now as the lance buried itself in the horse's flesh and bone, such was the weight of the horse that the knight's arm wrenched up and back, then snapped, bones shattering even as his lance cracked under tremendous pressure.

The Invincible howled in rage. His worthless right arm remained pinned to a broken lance.

He grabbed for his mace with his left hand as Borenson launched from his own mount, swinging his wicked axe so hard that it pierced the Invincible's mail shirt, drove through his leather underjerkin, and buried its head in the hollow beneath the Invincible's throat.

Borenson followed his weapon, the full weight of his

shield slamming against the big knight. Both of them bowled over the back of the knight's horse, landed in the ash.

Such fierce blows would have killed a normal man, but Raj Ahten's blood-crazed Invincible shouted a war cry, and shoved Borenson back downhill a few yards.

The Invincible leapt to his feet, drew his mace. Gaborn wondered if the knight would live up to his name, for he seemed invincible. Some of these knights had over twenty endowments of stamina, could recover from nearly any blow.

The Invincible rushed forward, nearly a blur. Borenson lay on his back. He kicked, slamming an iron boot into the knight's ankle. A bone snapped like the cracking of an axle.

The Invincible swung his mace. Borenson tried to block the blow with the edge of his shield. The shield crumpled under the impact, and the lower edge of it drove into Borenson's gut.

Borenson groaned beneath the blow.

Gaborn had nearly reached the battle, his own horse flying back uphill.

Gaborn leapt from his horse's back. The Invincible whirled to meet him. The big man swung his mace high, ready to smash Gaborn under its iron spikes.

The Invincible's full helm allowed no peripheral vision, so he could not see Gaborn till he turned. As he spun, Gaborn aimed his sword at the eye slits in the man's visor.

The blade slid in with a sickening thud, and Gaborn let himself fall forward, knocking the knight backward, piercing his skull.

He landed atop the armored knight, lay a moment, the breath knocked from him. Gasping. He looked the Invincible in the face, to be sure he was dead.

The fine blade had driven through the eye slit up to the hilt, driven through the Invincible's skull, then punctured through the back of his helm. Even an Invincible could not survive such a devastating wound. This one had gone as limp as a jellyfish.

Gaborn got up in shock, conscious of how close he'd come to death.

He quickly assessed himself, checking for wounds, glanced uphill, afraid another knight might charge down.

He tried to yank his short sword free of the Invincible's helm. The blade would not come loose.

Gaborn climbed to his hands and knees, gazed at Borenson, panting. Borenson rolled to his stomach, began vomiting on to the charred earth.

"Well met, my friend," Gaborn said, smiling. He felt as if it were the first time he'd smiled in weeks, though he'd left Borenson only two days past.

Borenson spat on the ground, clearing his mouth, and smiled at Gaborn. "I really think you should get your butt out of here before Raj Ahten comes down the road."

"Good to see you, too," Gaborn said.

"I mean it," Borenson grumbled. "He'll not let you go so easily. Don't you realize that he came all this way just to destroy House Orden?"

TWENTY-ONE:
FAREWELL

In the Dedicates' Keep, Chemoise grunted as she struggled to help her father from his bed of straw and dried lavender, dragged him out on to the green grass of the bailey so he could board the great wain for his trip back south. It was hard to move such a big man.

No, it was not his weight that made dragging him difficult. Instead it was the way he clutched her, grasping fiercely at her shoulders, his powerful fingers digging into her skin like claws, his legs unable to relax enough to walk.

She felt she had failed him years before, when she'd let him go south to fight Raj Ahten. She'd feared he would never return, that he'd be killed. She'd hoped her fear had been only a child's concerns. But now, after his years as a prisoner, Chemoise imagined she'd had a premonition, perhaps a cold certainty sent from her ancestors beyond the grave.

So now she carried not only her father, but also the weight of her failure all those years before, a weight that somehow tangled with her feelings of inadequacy at having found herself pregnant. Her, the Princess's Maid of Honor.

The western Great Hall in the Dedicates' Keep was huge, three stories tall, where fifteen hundred men slept on any given night. Smooth walnut planks covered the floors, and each wall held a huge hearth so the room could be kept comfortably warm all winter.

The eastern Great Hall, on the far side of the bailey, held a third as many woman.

"Where . . .?" Chemoise's father asked as she dragged him past the rows of pallets where Dedicates lay.

"South, to Longmot, I think," Chemoise said. "Raj Ahten has ordered you to be brought."

"South," her father whispered a worried acknowledgement.

Chemoise struggled to drag her father past a man who'd soiled his bed. If she'd had time, she'd have cared for the fellow. But the wain would leave any moment, and she couldn't risk being separated from her father.

"You . . . come?" her father asked.

"Of course," Chemoise said. She could not really promise such a thing. She could only throw herself on the mercy of Raj Ahten's men, hope they'd let her care for her father. They'd allow it, she told herself. Dedicates needed caretakers.

"No!" her father grumbled. He quit trying to walk, suddenly let his feet drag, making her stagger to one side. She bore the weight, tried to carry him against his will.

"Let die!" he whispered fiercely. "Feed . . . feed poison. Make sick. We die."

It worried her how he pleaded. Killing himself was the only way he could strike back at Raj Ahten. Yet Chemoise could not bear the thought of killing any of these men, even though she knew that life for them would be horrible, chained to some dirty floor. She had to hope that her father would return someday, whole, undefiled.

Chemoise hugged her father, bore him through the big oak door, into the light. The fresh wind carried the smell of rain. Everywhere, Raj Ahten's troops rushed to and fro, seeking the King's treasury and armory above the kitchens. She heard glass break down the street, the cries of merchants.

She dragged her father to the huge, covered wain in

the bailey. The sides and roof of the wain were made of thick oak planks, with only a thin grate to provide any light or fresh air. One of Raj Ahten's soldiers grabbed her father by the scruff of the neck, lifted him into the wain with no more care than if he were a sack of grain.

"Ah, de last," the soldier said in a thick Muyyatin accent.

"Yes," she said. The Raj's vectors were all in the wagon. The guard turned.

Chemoise glanced down the road through the portcullis gate, startled. Iome, King Sylvarresta, two Days, and Prince Orden were riding fine horses down Market Street toward the city gates.

She wanted to ride with them, or to shout a blessing to help them on their way.

She waited while the guard wrestled her father through the door. The wagon shifted with the movement. At the front of the wagon, some horsemen expertly began to back four heavy horses into their traces, hitching them to the axletree.

Chemoise climbed up the wagon steps, looked in. Fourteen Dedicates lay on straw inside the shadowed wagon. The place smelled fetid, of old sweat and urine that had worked into the floorboards and walls. Chemoise looked for a place to sit among the defeated men – the blind, the deaf, the idiots. At that moment, the guard was laying her father on the hay. He glanced over his shoulder at Chemoise

"No! You no get!" the guard shouted, hurrying up to push her back from the wagon door.

"But – my father! My father is there!" Chemoise cried.

"No! You no come!" the guard said, pushing her.

Chemoise backed completely out the door of the great wagon, tried to find her footing on the ladder behind. The guard shoved her.

She fell hard to the packed dirt of the bailey.

"Ees military. For just military," the guard said, with a

chopping motion of his hand.

"Wait!" Chemoise cried. "My father is in there!"

The guard stared impassively, as if a daughter's love for her father was a foreign concept.

The guard rested his hand on the hilt of the curved dagger in his belt. Chemoise knew there would be no reasoning, no mercy.

With a shout and a whistle, the driver of the huge wain urged the horses from the Dedicates' Keep. Guards ran before and behind the wagon.

Chemoise couldn't follow the wagon to Longmot. She knew she'd never see her father again.

TWENTY-TWO:
A HARD CHOICE

As Borenson smiled at Gaborn, watched the Prince suddenly reach the realization that Raj Ahten had come primarily to slay him and his father, a blackness came over Borenson's mind – a cloud of despair.

He saw King Sylvarresta, told himself, I am not death. I am not the destroyer.

He'd always tried to be a good soldier. Though he lived by the sword, he did not enjoy killing. He fought because he sought to protect others – to spare the lives of his friends, not to take the lives of his foes. Even his comrades-in-arms did not understand this. Though he smiled in battle, he smiled not in glee or from bloodlust. He did so because he'd learned long ago that the fey smile struck terror into the hearts of his opponents.

He had an assignment from his king: to kill the Dedicates of Raj Ahten, even though those Dedicates might be his lord's oldest and dearest friends, even if the Dedicate was the King's own son.

Borenson saw at a glance that King Sylvarresta had given his endowment. The idiot king no longer knew how to seat a horse. He leaned forward, eyes wide with fright, moaning incoherently, tied to the pommel of his saddle.

There, Borenson assumed, beside the King rode Iome or the Queen – he could not tell which – all the glamour leached from her, skin as rough as cracked leather. Unrecognizable.

I am not death, Borenson told himself, though he knew he'd have to bring death to these two. The thought sickened him.

I have feasted at that king's table, Borenson told himself, remembering past years when Orden took Hostenfest with Sylvarresta. The smells of roast pork and new wine and turnips had always been strong at the table – fresh bread with honey, oranges from Mystarria. Sylvarresta had always been generous with his wine, free with his jokes.

Had Borenson not thought the King too high above Borenson's own station, he'd have been proud to call him friend.

On the Isle of Thwynn, where Borenson was born, the code of hospitality was clear: to rob or kill someone who fed you was dastardly. Those who did so were afforded no mercy when slain. Borenson had once seen a man stoned near to death for merely affronting his host.

Borenson had ridden here hoping that he would not have to carry out his King's orders, hoping that the Dedicates' Keep would be so well guarded he'd never have a chance to gain entry, hoping that King Sylvarresta would have refused to grant an endowment to Raj Ahten.

Iome. Borenson recognized the Princess now, not from her features but from her graceful build. He remembered one late night, seven years past, when he'd been sitting in the King's Keep beside a roaring fire, drinking mulled wine, while Orden and Sylvarresta traded humorous tales of hunts long past. On that occasion, young Iome, wakened by the loud laughter beneath her room, had come to listen.

To Borenson's surprise, the Princess had come into the room and sat on his lap, where her feet could be near the fire. She had not sought out the King's lap, or that of one of the King's own guards. She'd chosen him, and just sat by the fire, gazing dreamily at his red beard. She'd been beautiful even as a child, and he'd felt protective, imagining that someday he might have a daughter so fine.

Now Borenson smiled at Gaborn, tried to hide his rage, his own self-loathing, at the duty he must perform. I am not death.

The dead enemy's warhorse had run downhill, stood now, ears back, regarding the situation calmly. Iome rode to it, whispered softly, and took its reins. The warhorse tried to nip her; Iome slapped its armored face, letting it know she was in command. She brought the horse to Borenson.

She sat rigidly as she drew near; her yellowed eyes filled with fear. She said, "Here, Sir Borenson."

Borenson didn't take the reins immediately. She was within striking range as she leaned near. Borenson could slap her with a mailed fist, break her neck without drawing a weapon. Yet here she stood, offering him a service, his host once again. He stood, unable to strike.

"You've done my people a great service this day," she said, "dislodging Raj Ahten from Castle Sylvarresta."

A thin hope rose in Borenson. It seemed barely possible that she did not serve as a vector for Raj Ahten, that she'd given her endowment only, and therefore did not pose a major threat to Mystarria. This would give him some reason to spare her.

Borenson took the horse's reins, heart pounding. The stallion did not fight or shy from his foreign armor. It whipped its plaited tail, knocking flies from its rump.

"Thank you, Princess," Borenson said with a heavy heart. *I'm under orders to kill you*, he wanted to say. *I wish I'd never seen you*. But he had to wonder at Gaborn's plan. Perhaps the Prince had a reason for bringing out the King and Iome, some reason Borenson didn't fathom.

"I heard more horns in the woods," Iome said. "Where are your men? I would like to thank them."

Borenson turned away. "They rode ahead an hour ago. We're alone here." It was not time to talk. He retrieved his weapons from his dead horse, strapped them to the enemy's warhorse, mounted up.

They raced through the blackened woods down to the road, then followed it, thundering over one burned hill after another until they nearly reached some living trees, with their promise of shelter.

By a burbling brook at the edge of the woods, Gaborn called a stop. Even a force horse with runes of power branded on its neck and breast needed to catch its wind and get a drink.

Besides, in the green grass at the edge of the stream lay a soldier of House Orden. A black nomen's spear protruded through the soldier's bloody neck. A gruesome reminder that although the small group would soon enter the woods, they'd still be in danger.

True, Borenson and his men had hunted nomen all morning, had scattered this band. But nomen were crafty nocturnal hunters, and usually fought in small bands. So some bands would be here in the woods, hiding under the shadows, hunting.

Gaborn dismounted as the horses drank, checked the soldier's body. He flipped open the man's visor.

"Ah, poor Torin," Borenson grunted. He'd been a good soldier, had a fine talent with the morning star.

Torin wore the normal dress of a Mystarrian warrior, black ring mail over a sheepskin jerkin. A dark-blue surcoat over the mail bore the emblem of Mystarria, the green knight – a man's face with oak leaves in its hair and beard. Gaborn traced the outline of the green knight on Torin's surcoat.

"Beautiful colors," Gaborn whispered. "The most beautiful a man could wear." Gaborn began stripping Torin. "This is the second corpse I've had to rob today," Gaborn grumbled as if displeased at the prospect.

"So, milord, you'll bring a new dignity to the profession," Borenson said, not wanting to discuss the problem facing him. He eyed Iome, saw terror in her posture.

She knew what he had to do. Even she knew.

Yet Gaborn seemed oblivious. Was Gaborn mad? Or just immature? What made him think he could escape Raj Ahten with a woman and an idiot in his charge? Fine horses are nothing if you can't ride them – and obviously Sylvarresta could not ride.

"Where's my father?" Gaborn asked, stripping the corpse.

"Can't you guess?" Borenson said, unprepared for the question. "Right now, I'd say he's fifty miles from Longmot, hoping to reach it near dark. Raj Ahten has forty thousand forcibles there, buried among the turnips behind Bredsfor Manor. You know where the manor is?"

Gaborn shook his head no.

"On the road three miles south of the castle," Borenson said, "a gray building with a lead roof and two wings. We intercepted a message from the Duchess Laran that says Raj Ahten expects an army to reach Longmot within a day or two. Your father hopes to beat them to the treasure."

"Raj Ahten knows this?" Gaborn asked, just as he got the ring mail untied from the body. "That's why he's abandoning Castle Sylvarresta? To reclaim the forcibles?"

Gaborn obviously thought this foolhardy. He angrily unstrapped the dead man's jerkin. Borenson wondered what occupied the Prince's mind. Did he not see that Sylvarresta must be slain? What was the boy thinking?

"Your father hoped to convince the Wolf Lord that Longmot was conquered days ago," Borenson explained, "and that he's been taking endowments day and night ever since."

"A desperate bluff," Gaborn said, inspecting the sheepskin jerkin, looking close to see if it harbored fleas or lice. But if Torin had suffered from fleas in life, they'd all hopped away as soon as the body cooled.

Gaborn put on the jerkin, pulled on the ring mail and the surcoat – all just a bit too large for him. A small shield lay by Torin's right hand – a target of wood, covered with a thin layer of brass, then painted dark blue. The lower edge of the shield was filed, so that if one slashed with that edge, it could slice a man's throat like a knife. Usually only a man with an endowment of metabolism kept such a small shield. Thrust quickly, it doubled as a weapon. Gaborn took the shield.

"What of Raj Ahten?" Borenson asked. "I can see that he is on the move, but will he go to Longmot?"

Gaborn said, "As Father hoped, he'll march within the hour."

Borenson nodded. The sun shone in his blue eyes; he smiled. It was not a smile of relief. It was a hard smile, his battle smile. "Tell me," Borenson half-whispered, "where are you taking them?" He nodded at Iome, her idiot father.

Gaborn said. "Longmot. I took the best horses in the King's stables. We can reach the castle by nightfall."

Perhaps, if your charges knew how to ride, Borenson wanted to say. Borenson licked his lips, whispered, "It's a long journey, and hard. Perhaps you'd best leave Sylvarresta here, milord." He spoke as if it were a friendly suggestion, tried to hide the hard edge to his voice.

"After all the trouble I went through to get them from Raj Ahten?" Gaborn asked.

"Don't play the fool with me," Borenson spoke, voice rising in anger. His face felt hot; his whole body coiled. "Sylvarresta has long been our friend, but now he serves the Wolf Lord. How many endowments of wit does Sylvarresta vector to Raj Ahten? How many endowments of glamour does the Princess vector?"

"It doesn't matter," Gaborn said. "I'll not kill friends."

Borenson held a moment, trying to contain the rage building in him. Can even a prince afford such generosity? he wanted to shout. Yet he dared not give that insult. He reasoned instead. "They're friends no longer. They serve Raj Ahten."

Gaborn said, "They may serve as vectors, but they

chose to live, so that by living, they can serve their own people."

"By letting Raj Ahten destroy Mystarria? Don't delude yourself. They serve your enemy, milord. Your enemy, and your father's and Mystarria's – and my enemies! It is a passive service – true – but they serve him no less than if they were warriors."

Oh, how Borenson sometimes envied them – the Dedicates who lived like fat cattle on their lord's wealth, pampered.

Certainly Gaborn must see that Borenson served his lord no less fully, gave his all, night and day. Borenson sweated and bled and suffered. He'd taken an endowment of metabolism, so that he aged two years for every other man's one. Though he was but twenty years old chronologically, little older than Gaborn, the hair on his head was falling out, and streaks of gray bled into his beard. For him, life rushed past as if he were adrift on a boat, watching the shore forever slipping by, unable to grasp anything, unable to hold on to anything.

Meanwhile, people admired Dedicates for their "sacrifice." Borenson's own father had given an endowment of metabolism to one of the King's soldiers before Borenson was born, and had thus lain in an enchanted slumber these past twenty years. It seemed to Borenson a cheat, the way his father stayed young, the way he suffered nothing while the man he endowed grew old and faded. What did his father sacrifice?

No, it was men like Borenson who suffered most for their lords, not some damned Dedicate, afraid to live his life.

"You must kill them," Borenson urged.

"I cannot," Gaborn answered.

"Then, by all the awful Powers, you'll make me do it!" Borenson growled. He reached to pull his axe from its sheath, glanced toward King Sylvarresta. Iome had heard the scrape of the axe handle against leather, jerked at the sound, staring at Borenson.

"Hold," Gaborn said softly. "I order you. They are under my protection. My sworn protection."

A gust of wind sent ash skittering across the ground.

"And I'm under order to kill Raj Ahten's Dedicates."

"I countermand that order," Gaborn said firmly.

"You can't!" Borenson said, tensing. "They're your father's orders, and yours cannot supersede his! Your father has given an order – a hard one that no man could envy. But I must carry it out. I will serve King Orden, even if you will not!"

Borenson did not want to argue. He loved Gaborn as a brother. But Borenson could not see how he could ever be faithful to House Orden if the Prince and the King did not agree on this issue.

In the distance, toward Castle Sylvarresta, the high call of Southern battle trumpets sounded – Raj Ahten marshaling his troops. Borenson's heart pounded. His men were supposed to delay the army, and even now were racing to Boar's Ford, where they would do little good.

Borenson shoved his axe back into its sheath, drew his own horn, sounded two long blasts, two short. The call to prepare arms. Raj Ahten's troops would not hurry to Longmot if they had to watch for an ambush every moment. Almost, Borenson wished his troops were still here, that he had the men to fight.

Borenson felt exposed at the edge of the woods. Gaborn took the helm off dead Torin, put it on his own head.

Gaborn looked up. "Listen, Borenson: If we have forty thousand forcibles, my father has no need to kill his friends. He can slay Raj Ahten, then place Sylvarresta back on the throne where he belongs."

"That is a frightening *if*," Borenson said. "Can we risk it? What if Raj Ahten kills your father? By sparing Sylvarresta, you may consign your father to death."

Gaborn's face paled. Certainly the boy had seen this

danger. Certainly he knew the stakes in this battle. But no, Borenson realized, the boy was too innocent. Gaborn promised, "I wouldn't let that happen."

Borenson rolled his eyes, clenched his teeth.

"Nor would I," Iome answered from where her horse stood beside the stream. "I'd rather kill myself than see another come to harm on my account."

Borenson had tried to keep his voice down so she would not hear, but of course his voice had been rising in anger. He considered. At this moment, King Orden was racing to Longmot with fifteen hundred warriors. Messages had been sent to other castles, calling for aid. Perhaps three or four thousand might meet at Longmot before dawn.

But Raj Ahten would stand at the head of a massive army, once his reinforcements arrived from the South.

King Orden had to get those forcibles, and once he had them, he'd have to hole up in Castle Longmot. No castle in this realm could better withstand a siege.

Desperate times call for desperate measures. In all likelihood, Raj Ahten had so many endowments from his people in the South that if Borenson killed Sylvarresta and Iome, it would gain no benefit for King Orden. That is what Gaborn believed.

On the other hand, times were uncertain. Orden and other kings had sent assassins south. Perhaps even traitors in Raj Ahten's own lands would see his absence as a perfect time to bid for power. One could not discount the possibility that at any given moment, the endowments Raj Ahten had gained here in Heredon would become vital to him.

No, Borenson needed to kill these vectors. He sighed. With a heavy heart, he pulled his war axe. Urged his horse forward.

Gaborn caught the horse by the reins. "Stay away from them," he growled in a tone Borenson had never before heard from the Prince.

"I have a duty," Borenson said, regretfully. He did not want to do it, but he'd argued the point so convincingly that now he saw he must.

"And I'm obligated to protect Iome and her father," Gaborn said, "as one Oath-Bound Lord to another."

"Oath-Bound Lord?" Borenson gasped. "No! You fool!" Now he saw it. Gaborn had been distant these past two weeks as they journeyed into Heredon. For the first time in his life, he'd been secretive.

"It's true," Gaborn said. "I spoke the oath to Iome."

"Who witnessed?" Borenson asked the first question that came to mind.

"Iome, and her Maids of Honor." Borenson wondered if news of this oath could be covered. Perhaps by killing the witnesses, he could undo the damage. "And her Days."

Borenson set his axe across the pommel of his saddle, looked hard at King Sylvarresta. Who knew how far this news had spread? From Iome's maids to the King's counselor, to all Heredon. He couldn't hide what Gaborn had done.

Gaborn had a fierceness in his eyes. What pluck! The little ass! Borenson thought. He plans to fight me. He'd really fight me over this?

Yet he knew it was true. To give the Oath of Protection was a serious matter, a sacred matter.

Borenson didn't dare raise his hand against the Prince. It was treason. Even if he carried out Orden's commands in every other matter, he could be executed for striking the Prince.

Gaborn had been watching Borenson's eyes, and now he ventured, "If you will not allow me to rescind my father's order, then I command you thus: Wait to carry it out. Wait until we reach Longmot, and I've spoken to my father."

Gaborn might well reach the castle before Gaborn. There, the King would be able to settle this tangled matter.

Borenson closed his eyes and hung his head in sign of acquiescence. "As you command, milord," he said. Yet a horrible sense of guilt assailed. He'd been ordered to kill the Dedicates at Castle Sylvarresta, and if he slew the King and Iome now, he would thus spare other lives; he would spare all those who were vectored through these two.

Yet to kill Sylvarresta would be cruel. Borenson did not want to murder a friend, regardless of the cost. And he dared not raise a weapon against his own prince.

Bits of arguments rushed at Borenson, fragmented. He looked up at King Sylvarresta, who had stopped moaning in fear, just as a jay went flying over the King's head in a streak of blue.

But if I do not murder these two now, how many others must I kill in the Dedicates' Keep? How many endowments has Sylvarresta taken? Are the lives of these two worth more than the lives of their Dedicates?

What harm has any of them done? Not one man in the keep would willingly toss a rotten apple at one of our people. Yet by their very existence, they lend power to Raj Ahten.

Borenson clenched his teeth, lost in thought. Tears began to water his eyes.

You will make me kill everyone vectored through these two, Borenson realized. That was his only choice. He loved his prince, had always served faithfully.

I'll do it, Borenson thought, though I hate myself forever after. I'll do it for you.

No! some deep part of his mind shouted.

Borenson opened his eyes, stared hard at Gaborn.

Gaborn let go the reins of Borenson's horse, stood testily, as if he was still ready to try to pull Borenson from the saddle if the need arose.

"Take them in peace, milord," Borenson said, trying to hide the sadness in his voice. Immediately Gaborn relaxed.

"I'll need a weapon," Gaborn said. "Can I borrow one of yours?" Other than the black spear in Torin's throat, nothing was handy.

The warhorse Borenson rode had a horseman's hammer sheathed from its previous owner. It was an inelegant weapon. Borenson knew that Gaborn preferred a saber, for he liked to slash and thrust quickly. But the hammer had its strengths: against an armored opponent, one could easily chop through chain mail or pierce a helm. The saber was as likely to snap in such a battle as to pierce a man's armor.

Borenson pulled the hammer, tossed it to Gaborn. He did not rest easy with his decisions. Even now, he barely restrained himself from attacking Sylvarresta. *I am not death,* Borenson told himself. *I am not death. It is not my duty to fight my prince, to kill kings.*

"Hurry to Longmot," Borenson said at last with a sigh. "I smell a storm coming. It will hide your scent, make you harder to track. Take the main road south at first, but don't follow it all the way – the Hayworth Bridge is burned. Go instead through the forest until you reach Ardamom's Ridge, then cut straight south to the Boar's Ford. Do you know where it is?"

Gaborn shook his head. Of course he did not know.

"I know," Iome said. Borenson studied her. Cool, confident, despite her ugliness. The Princess now showed no fear. At least she knew how to sit a horse.

Borenson urged his warhorse forward a step, pulled the longspear from poor Torin's neck, snapped it off, and threw the bladed end to the princess. She caught it in one hand.

"Won't you escort us?" Gaborn asked.

Doesn't he understand what I must do? Borenson wondered. Borenson had not yet confided that he planned to slay every Dedicate in the castle.

No, Borenson decided. Gaborn didn't know what he planned. The lad was that innocent. Indeed, if the Prince had even the slightest notion what Borenson intended, Gaborn would try to stop him.

Yet Borenson couldn't allow that. I'll do this alone, he thought. I'll take this evil upon me, stain my hands with blood so that you don't have to.

"I've other duties," Borenson said, shaking his head. He soothed the Prince with a lie. "I'll shadow Raj Ahten's army, make certain he doesn't strike some unexpected target."

To tell the truth, part of him wanted to escort Gaborn, to see him safe through the woods. He knew the Prince would need help. But Borenson did not trust himself to lead Gaborn for even an hour. At any moment, he might feel the need to turn on Gaborn, to kill good King Sylvarresta.

"If it will make it easier for you," Gaborn said, "when I reach Longmot, I'll tell my father that I never saw you in the woods. He does not need to know."

Borenson nodded, numb.

TWENTY-THREE:
THE HUNT BEGINS

Raj Ahten stood above his dead Invincible, fists clenched. Downhill, his army marched for Longmot, archers running the winding road, their colored tunics making them look like a golden snake twisting through a black forest.

Chancellor Jureem knelt over the fallen soldier, robes smudged, studying tracks in the ashes. It took no skill to see what had happened: One man. One man slew his master's Invincible, then stole his horse, rode off with Gaborn, King Sylvarresta, and his daughter. Jureem recognized the dead stallion on the ground nearby. It had been ridden by Orden's surly messenger.

The sight sickened him. If a few more soldiers had kept up the chase, Gaborn would surely have fallen into their hands.

"There are but five of them," Feykaald said. "Heading cross-country, rather than over the road. We could send trackers – a dozen or so, but with Orden's soldiers in the wood, perhaps we should just let them go. . . ."

Raj Ahten licked his lips. Jureem saw that Feykaald couldn't even count. Only four people were heading over the trail. His master had lost two scouts to Gaborn already, along with war dogs, giants, a pyromancer – and now an Invincible. Prince Orden looked to be not much more than a boy, but Jureem began to wonder if he had secretly taken a great number of endowments.

Raj Ahten's men had misjudged King Orden's whelp far

too often. From the mounts he'd chosen, it appeared Gaborn would head into the woods, shun the highway.

But why? Because he wanted to lead Raj Ahten into a trap? Did the boy have soldiers hidden in the forest?

Or did he merely fear to travel by road? Raj Ahten had a few powerful force horses left in his retinue. Fine horses, bred for the plains and the desert, each with a lineage that went back a thousand years. Perhaps the lad knew his mounts could not outrun the Wolf Lord's horses over even ground.

But Gaborn's mountain hunters, running without armor, with their thick bones and strong hindquarters, would be almost impossible to catch in this terrain. Jureem suspected that Gaborn and Iome would know these woods far better than even the most informed spy.

Jureem drew a ragged breath, calculating how many men to send. Gaborn Val Orden would make a fine hostage, if the Wolf Lord found things at Longmot to be as he suspected.

Though the woods were silent, little more than an hour ago Jureem had heard Orden's war horns blow in the Dunnwood.

In all likelihood, Gaborn had already gained the company of Orden's soldiers, was surrounded by hundreds of guards. Yet . . . he could not just let Gaborn go. At the thought of Gaborn escaping, a rage burned in Jureem. Mindless, seething.

"We should send men to find the boy," Jureem counseled. "Perhaps a hundred of our best scouts?"

Raj Ahten straightened his back. "No. Get twenty of my best Invincibles, and strip their horses of armor. I'll also want twenty mastiffs to track the Prince."

"As you wish, milord," Jureem said, turning away, as if to shout the orders down to the army that marched below. But a thought hit him. "Which of your captains shall lead?"

"I'll be the captain," Raj Ahten said. "Hunting the

Prince should prove an interesting diversion."

Jureem glanced at him sideways, raising a single dark brow. He bowed slightly, in acquiescence. "Do you think it wise, milord? Others could hunt him. Even I will come." The thought of such a ride, of the pain his buttocks would have to endure, gave Jureem pause.

"Others might hunt him," Raj Ahten said, "but none as tenaciously as I."

TWENTY-FOUR: HOPE FOR A RAGGED PEOPLE

The road to Longmot turned muddy in the late morning as storms rolled across the sky. King Orden raced south all the way to the village of Hayworth, a distance of a ninety-eight miles. It was a peaceful town spread along the banks of the River Dwindell, a village with a small mill. Green hills rolled as far south as one could see, each hill covered in broad oaks.

People here led a quiet life. Most were coopers who made barrels for wine and grain. In the spring, when the river swelled in flood, one could often see men on rafts made from hundreds of barrels all tied together, floating their goods down to market.

It displeased Mendellas Orden to have to burn the bridge. He'd stopped here often in his journeys, savouring the fine ale brewed in the Dwindell Inn, which sat beside the bridge on a promontory, overlooking the river.

But by the time Orden reached town, rain had soaked the bridge. Great rolling drops pelted his troops, dripped between the cracks of the four-inch planks. His men tried to light a fire, where berry vines grew thick beneath the north end of the bridge. But the banks of the river were steep and the road sloped so that water draining down the street became a veritable creek.

Orden had supposed a couple of well-oiled torches would do the job, but even they proved to be of little use.

Orden was cursing his fortune when a couple of local

boys pulled the innkeeper, old Stevedore Hark, out of the inn. Orden had been blessed by this man's hospitality many times.

"Here, here, Your Highness, what are you and your men about?" the innkeeper said in a belligerent tone, waddling down the street. Orden's fifteen hundred troops seemed not to alarm the innkeeper in the least. He was a heavy man in baggy pants, an apron over his broad belly. His fat face showed red beneath his graying beard, and rain streamed over his cheeks.

"I fear we must burn your bridge," Orden answered. "Raj Ahten will come down the highway tonight. I can't have him on my tail. I'll gladly reimburse the town for the inconvenience."

"Oh, I don't think you'll burn that bridge any time soon," the innkeeper laughed. "Perhaps you'd better come in and have a drink. I can get you and some of your captains a nice stew, if you don't mind a thin broth."

"Why won't it burn?" King Orden asked.

"Magic," the innkeeper said. "Lightning struck it fifteen years back, burned it to the ground. So when we built it back again, we had a water wizard put a spell on it. Fire won't hold to that wood."

Orden stood in the pouring rain, and the innkeeper's words took the heart from him. If he had had his own water wizard, he could easily have countered the spell. But he had no water wizard here. The way the rain was falling, perhaps the bridge could not be burned anyway.

"We'll have to chop it through then," Orden said.

"Here now," the innkeeper grumbled, "no call for that. If you want the bridge down, pull it down, but leave the planks so we can build it back again, after tomorrow. We can store them over in the mill."

Orden considered his proposition. Stevedore Hark was more than the innkeeper, Orden recalled. He was also the mayor, a man with a keen eye for business. The bridge was made of huge planks, bored and doweled together.

Three stone pillars planted in River Dwindell held the bridge. Pulling the bridge down piece by piece would take a bit longer, but with fifteen hundred men to perform the labor, it would come down fast enough. The Powers knew that even his force horses needed to rest.

There was also a matter of friendship. Orden could not easily destroy the man's bridge. If he did, on the next trip through the town, he'd find that the ale had somehow all gone to vinegar. "I'd thank you to get me some dinner, then, my old friend," Orden said, "while we hide the bridge for you."

The bargain was struck.

While the rain poured and his men worked, Orden went into the Dwindell Inn, and sat brooding before a huge fire in the hearth.

He'd been promised a quick dinner of undercooked stew, but half an hour later, the master of the inn himself brought out some bread pudding and a warmed joint of pork – from one of the great boars that made hunting in the Dunnwood famous. The meat smelled delicious, sprinkled with pepper and rosemary, marinated in dark beer, then baked on a bed of carrots, wild mushrooms, and hazelnuts. It tasted as fine as it smelled.

And of course, it was strictly illegal. Commoners were not allowed to hunt the King's boars; Stevedore Hark could have been whipped for doing so.

The meat was a fine and fitting gift. Though Hark had obviously hoped to lift Orden's spirits, his kind gesture had the opposite effect, throwing Orden into a dire melancholy that made him sit beside the fire, stroking his beard with his fingers, wondering at his own plans.

How many times had he eaten at this inn on his trips to visit Sylvarresta? How often had he feasted on the bounty of these woods? How often had he thrilled to the baying of the hounds as they chased the great boars, taken joy in the toss of the javelin as he rode a pig down?

The innkeeper's hospitality, the fineness of the meal,

somehow made King Orden feel . . . desolate.

Five years past, while Orden hunted here, an assassin had broken into his keep, had slain his wife in her bed, with a newborn babe. It had been only six months since two daughters died in a previous attack. The murder of King Orden's wife and babe sparked outrage. Yet the killer was never apprehended. Trackers followed his trail, lost the assassin in the mountains south of Mystarria. He could have been escaping southeast into Inkarra, or he could have headed southwest to Indhopal.

Orden had guessed Indhopal or Muyyatin. But he could not have struck out blindly at his neighbors, without proof.

So he'd waited, and waited, for assassins to strike again, to come for him personally.

They never did.

Orden had lost a part of himself, he knew. He'd lost his wife, the one love of his life. He'd never remarried, planned never to remarry. If one cannot replace a lost hand or a leg, how can one hope to replace half of himself?

For years now, he'd acutely felt the pain. With so many endowments of wit, he could perfectly recall her tone of voice, her face. In his dreams Corette yet walked and spoke with him. Often when he woke on a cold winter's morning, he felt surprised to find that her soft flesh was not cupping him, trying to drink his warmth, the way she had when still alive.

He found it hard to describe the sense of loss he felt. King Orden had once tried to express it to himself.

He did not feel that he had lost his future, that his life was at an end. His son was his future. He would continue, go on without him, if the Powers so willed it.

Nor did he feel he had lost his past, for Orden could remember perfectly the taste of Corette's kisses on the night of their wedding, the way she cried in joy when she first suckled Gaborn.

No, it was the *present* he had lost. The opportunity to be with his wife, to love her, to spend each waking moment in her company.

Yet as King Orden sat in the Dwindell Inn, eating roast off a fine china platter, he became keenly aware that something new had been ripped from him.

His past was gone. All of his good memories would soon become unbearable. King Sylvarresta was not dead yet, so far as Orden knew, but sometime this evening, Borenson would try to carry out his orders. Orden would be forced to kill the man he most loved and admired.

It was a foul thing, a bitter seasoning to a fine meal.

Perhaps Stevedore Hark understood what he felt, for the innkeeper got a thin stew cooking for some of the men, then came to sit a few moments at Orden's feet, commiserating.

"We heard the news last night from Castle Sylvarresta," he whispered. "Bad news. The worst of my life."

"Aye, the worst in several lifetimes," Orden grunted, looking at the old innkeeper. Stevedore had gotten a few more white hairs in his sideburns this year. Indeed, his hair was more white now than grizzled.

It was said that each year, the Time Lords would ring a silver bell, and at the ringing of the bell, all who heard it would age a year. For those whom the Time Lords disliked, a bell might be rung more than once, while those whom the Time Lords favored might not have such a bell rung in their presence at all.

The Time Lords had not favored Stevedore Hark this year. His eyes looked puffy. From lack of sleep? No, the man would not have slept last night, after such tragic news.

"Do you think you can dislodge the monster?" Stevedore asked. "He has you outnumbered."

"I hope to dislodge him," Mendellas said.

"If you do, then you will be our king," the innkeeper said flatly.

King Orden had not considered the possibility. "No, your royal family is intact. If House Sylvarresta falls, the Countess of Arens is next in title."

"Not likely. People won't follow her. She's married in Seward, too far away to rule. If you win back Heredon, the people will want no one but you for their lord."

Orden's heart skipped at the thought. He'd always loved the woods, the hills of Heredon. He'd loved the clean, friendly people, the sparkling air.

"I'll drive Raj Ahten out," Orden said. He knew it wouldn't be enough to drive Raj Ahten from this land. He'd have to go further. A Wolf Lord cannot be whipped like a pup. He must be slaughtered, like a mad dog.

In his mind's eye, King Orden saw the war unfold before him, realized he'd have to prepare to head south, to strike Deyazz and Muyyatin and Indhopal come spring, from there sweep south into Khuram and Dharmad and the kingdoms beyond.

Until all Raj Ahten's Dedicates lay dead, and the Wolf Lord himself could be slain.

If he won this war, there would be lands to plunder. He cared nothing for most of the Southern kingdoms, but he would take one thing: the blood-metal mines of Kartish, south of Indhopal.

King Orden changed the conversation, talked with the innkeeper of days past, of hunts with Sylvarresta. Orden joked, "If the day should come that I'm king of Heredon, I suppose I'll have to invite you on my next hunt."

"Indeed, I fear it is the only way you will keep me from poaching, Your Highness," Stevedore Hark laughed, then slapped the King on the back, a touch so familiar that no one in Mystarria would have dared anything similar.

But Orden imagined that Sylvarresta had been slapped on the back by friends many times. He was that kind of man. The kind who did not have to be cold and distant to be kingly.

"It is agreed then, my friend," Orden said. "You will

come on my next hunt." Orden changed the subject. "Now, tonight, Raj Ahten's army should come here and find that the bridge is out. I ask a favor of you. Remind them that Boar's Ford is shallow enough to cross."

"Well, that's where they'd naturally go, isn't it?" Hark asked.

"They're strangers to this land," Orden said. "Their spies may only have marked bridges on their maps."

"You have a surprise in mind?" Hark asked. Orden nodded. "Then I'll tell them."

On that note the innkeeper went back to work. Soon after, the rain let up, and King Orden took his leave of the inn, ready to set back out on the march.

He checked to make certain that the bridge at Hayworth was down, its huge beams and planks all safely stored, then let his men and horses finish their own brief meal.

His captains had purchased grain for the horses, and kegs of ale were opened for his troops. Though his men lost an hour in their ride, they felt much invigorated afterward.

So they set out on the road, much renewed, racing all the faster for Longmot.

They proceeded through the Durkin Hills for the rest of the afternoon, marching near the mountains to reach Longmot before sunset.

Castle Longmot sat on a steep, narrow hill among some downs, and had a cheery little town to its south and west. It was not huge, as castles go, but the walls rose incredibly high. The machicolations atop the walls were sturdily wrought. Archers could shoot through them or drop oil or stones on attackers from any part of the wall with little fear of reprisal.

The stonework on the walls was phenomenal. Many stones weighed twelve to fourteen tons, yet the stones fit together so cleanly, a man was hard-pressed to find a fingerhold.

Many considered Longmot unscalable. No one had ever achieved a successful escalade of the outer walls. The castle had fallen once, five hundred years earlier, when sappers managed to dig beneath the west wall, so that it collapsed.

Other than that, the castle had never been taken.

So as the troops neared Longmot, King Orden found himself longing for its safety. He felt unprepared for the scene of destruction before him.

The village at the base of the castle had been destroyed – hundreds of homes, barns, and warehouses, all burned to their foundation stones. Smoke curled up from some of the houses. No cattle or sheep grazed the fields. Not an animal was in sight.

The gray banners of Longmot rose on pennants on the castle towers, and had been draped over the castle walls. But the banners were all ripped and torn. Some few dozen soldiers manned the outer walls.

Orden had expected to find the village as it had been when last he saw it. He wondered if some great battle had been fought here, unbeknownst to him.

Then he realized what had befallen this land. The soldiers of Longmot had burned the town to its foundations and had brought in all the herds, expecting a siege by Raj Ahten's occupying forces on the morrow. By burning the city, they robbed the occupying forces of decent shelter. Here in these hills, with winter coming on, shelter would be a valuable commodity.

As Orden's little army rode to the castle gates, he saw relief on the faces of the soldiers stationed on the walls. Someone sounded a war horn, a short riff played only when friendly reinforcements were spotted.

The drawbridge came down.

As King Orden rode through the gates, men cheered from the castle – but so few voices.

He was not prepared for the sight that befell him: all along the walls inside the keep lay dead bodies and

wounded townsfolk sitting in the open. Many wore armor
– shields and helms robbed from Raj Ahten's defeated
troops. Blood smeared the stonework along the outer
wall-walks. Windows were broken. Axes, arrows, and
spears sat stuck in the beams of buildings. A tower to a
lordly manor had burned.

There, outside the Duke's Keep, the duke himself hung
from a window by his own guts, just as Duchess
Emmadine Ot Laren had described.

Everywhere was a sign of battle, few signs of survivors.

Five thousand people had lived here. Five thousand
men, women, and children who fought with tooth and
dagger to dislodge Raj Ahten's men.

They'd had no soldiers with heavy endowments and
years of training. They'd had no great weapons. They had,
perhaps, only an element of surprise, and their great
hearts.

They'd won the day, barely. Then the families had fled,
fearing retribution from Raj Ahten.

King Orden had anticipated that four or five thousand
people would occupy this castle and town, people he
could use to aid his defense, people he could tap for
endowments.

Chickens and geese roosted on rooftops inside the
keep. Some swine rooted just inside the bailey.

Weak cheers greeted Orden, but they soon faded. One
man called down from atop the Dedicates' Keep.

"King Orden, what news have you of Sylvarresta?"

Orden looked up. The man was dressed in a captain's
smart attire. This would be Captain Cedrick Tempest, the
Duchess's aide-de-camp, in temporary charge of the
castle's defenses.

"Castle Sylvarresta has fallen, and Raj Ahten's men
hold it."

Cold horror showed in Captain Tempest's face.
Obviously the man hoped for better news. He could not
have had more than a hundred men. He could not really

defend this castle, merely hold down the fort in hope that Sylvarresta would send aid.

"Take heart, men of Sylvarresta," Orden called, his Voice making his words ring from the walls. "Sylvarresta has a kingdom still, and we shall win it back for him!"

The guards on the walls cheered, "Orden! Orden! Orden!"

Orden turned to the man riding next to him, Captain Stroecker, and whispered, "Captain, go alone, south to the Bredsfor Manor, and check the turnip garden. Look for sign of fresh digging. You should find some forcibles buried there. If you do, bring me twenty forcibles with the runes of metabolism, then cover the rest. Hide them well."

King Orden smiled and waved to the ragged defenders of Longmot. It would not do to bring all the forcibles back here in the castle – not when Raj Ahten might attack, tear the castle apart in his search for them.

Only three people alive knew where those forcibles lay hidden – himself, Borenson, and now Captain Stroecker.

King Orden wanted to make certain it stayed that way.

TWENTY-FIVE:
WHISPERS

Iome had been in the Dunnwood for only an hour when she first heard the war dogs bay, a haunting sound that floated up like mist from the valley floor behind them.

Wet splashes of rain had just begun to fall, and distant thunder shook the mountains. Contrary winds, blowing every which way, made it so that one moment the baying of the dogs came clear, then softened, then blew back to them.

Here, on a rocky, barren ridge, the sound seemed far away, miles distant. Yet Iome knew the distance was deceiving. War dogs with endowments of brawn and metabolism could run miles in a matter of moments. The horses were already growing tired.

"Do you hear them?" Iome shouted to Gaborn. "They're not far behind!"

Gaborn glanced back as his mount leapt through some tall heather and plunged now into the deep woods. Gaborn's face was pale; he frowned in concentration. "I hear," he said. "Hurry."

Hurry they did. Gaborn gripped his horseman's hammer, and instead of weaving among trees, he urged his mount forward and struck down branches so that Iome and her father did not have to dodge them.

Iome feared this was a fool's race. Her father didn't know where he was, didn't know he was in danger. He simply stared up, watching rain drop toward him. Oblivious.

Her father didn't recall how to sit a horse, yet the men chasing them would be master horsemen.

Gaborn responded to the danger by pushing them faster. When they cleared the large stand of pine, he raced his mount down a saddleback ridge, into deeper woods, heading west.

The sound of hooves pounding, the straining lungs of the horses' breathing, was all swallowed by great dark trees, trees taller than any Iome recalled ever seeing in the Dunnwood.

Here, the force horses ran with renewed speed. Gaborn gave them their heads, so that the beasts nearly flew down the canyon, into deepening gloom. Overhead, the skies boomed with the sound of thunder. The upper boughs of the pine trees swayed in the wind, and the trees creaked down to their roots, but no rain pounded in these woods. To be sure, fat droplets sometimes wove through the pine boughs, but not many.

Because the horses raced so fast through these woods, Iome did not mind that Gaborn followed the canyon, deeper and deeper, so that they twisted around the roots of a mountain and found themselves heading northwest, circling back, somewhat, toward Castle Sylvarresta.

But no, she decided after a bit – not toward the castle, deeper to the west, toward the Westwood. Toward the Seven Standing Stones in the heart of the wood.

The thought unsettled her. No one ever went to the Seven Stones and lived – at least no one had seen them in the past several generations. Her father had told Iome that she need not fear the spirits that haunted the woods there among the stones. "Erden Geboren gave us these woods while he yet lived, and made us rulers of this land," he said. "He was a friend to the duskins, and so we are their friends."

But even her father avoided the stones. Some said that the line of Sylvarresta had grown weak over generations. Others said the spirits of the duskins no longer remembered their oaths, and would not protect those who sought the stones.

Iome considered these things for an hour as Gaborn raced west, through woods growing more dark and hoary by the minute, until at last they reached a certain level hilltop, and under the dark oaks she could see small holes all around, down in the forest floor, and from the holes she could hear distant cries and armor clanking, the whinny of horses, and the sounds of ancient battles.

She knew this place: the Killing Field of Alnor. The holes were places where wights hid from the daylight. She shouted, "Gaborn, Gaborn: Turn south!"

He looked back at her; his eyes were unfocused, like one lost in a dream. She pointed south, shouted, "That way!"

To her relief, Gaborn turned south, spurred his horse up a long hill. In five minutes they reached the top of a mountain, came back out into a low wood of birch and oak, where the sun shone brightly. But with these trees, the limbs often came low to the ground, and gorse grew thick beneath them, so the horses slowed.

Suddenly they leapt over a small ridge, into a wallow where a sounder of great boars lay resting beneath the shade of oaks. The ground here looked as if it were plowed, the pigs had rooted for acorns and worms so much.

The boars squealed in rage to find the horses among them. A huge boar, its back coming even with the shoulder of Iome's mount, stood and grunted, swinging its great curved tusks menacingly.

One moment her horse charged the boar, then the horse turned nimbly, almost throwing Iome from her saddle as she raced past the swine, headed downhill.

Iome turned to see if the boar would give chase.

But the force horses ran so swiftly, the pigs only grunted in surprise, then watched Iome depart from dark, beady eyes.

Gaborn rode down a ridge through the birches, to a small river, perhaps forty feet wide. The river had a shallow, gravelly bottom.

On seeing this river, Iome knew she was totally lost. She'd often ridden in the Dunnwood, but had kept to the eastern edge of the woods. She'd never seen this river. Was it the headwaters of the River Wye, or Fro Creek? If it was Fro Creek, it should have been dry this time of year. If it was the Wye, then they had wandered farther west over the past hour than even she'd imagined.

Gaborn urged the mounts into the water, let them stand for a moment to drink. The horses sweated furiously, wheezing. The runes branded on their necks showed that each mount had four endowments of metabolism, and others of brawn and stamina. Iome did some quick mental calculations. She guessed they had been running the horses for nearly two hours without food or water, but that was the equivalent of running a common horse for eight. A common horse would have died three times over at such a furious pace. From the way these mounts gasped and sweated, she wasn't sure they'd live through the ordeal.

"We have to rest the horses," Iome whispered to Gaborn.

"Will our pursuers stop, do you think?" Gaborn asked.

Iome knew they wouldn't. "But our horses will die."

"They're strong mounts," Gaborn said, stating the obvious. "Those who hunt us will find that their horses will die first."

"Can you be so sure?"

Gaborn shook his head, uncertainly. "I only hope. I'm wearing light chain, the armor of my father's cavalry. But Raj Ahten's Invincibles have iron breastplates – with heavier gauntlets and greaves, and ring mail underneath. Each of their horses must carry a hundred pounds more than the most heavily laden of our beasts. Their mounts are fine animals for the desert, with wide hooves – but narrow shoes."

"So you think they will go lame?"

"I've chosen the rockiest ridges to jump our horses over. I can't imagine their mounts will stay shod long. Your horse has already lost a shoe. If I'm any judge, half their animals are lame already."

Iome stared at Gaborn in fascination. She hadn't noticed that her mount had lost a shoe, but now stared down into the water, saw that her mount favored its left front hoof.

"You have a devious mind, even for an Orden," she told Gaborn. She meant it as a compliment, but feared it came out sounding like an insult.

He seemed to take no offense. "Battles such as ours are seldom won with arms," he said. "They're won on a broken hoof or a rider's fall." He looked down at his warhammer, resting across the pommel of his saddle like a rider's crop. Then added huskily, "If our pursuers catch us, I'll turn to fight, try to let you escape. But I tell you, I don't have either the weapons or the endowments to beat Raj Ahten's men."

She understood. She desperately wanted to change the subject. "Where are you heading?"

"Heading?" he asked. "To Boar's Ford, then to Longmot."

She studied his eyes, half-hidden beneath his overlarge helm, to see if he lied or was merely mad. "Boar's Ford is southeast. You've been heading northwest most of the past two hours."

"I have?" he asked, startled.

"You have," she said. "I thought perhaps you were trying to deceive even Borenson. Are you afraid to take us to Longmot? Are you trying to protect me from your father?"

Iome felt frightened. She was suspicious of Borenson, had not trusted the way he looked at her. He'd wanted to kill her, felt it was his duty. She feared he would attack her

Dedicates, though Gaborn did not seem to worry about it. And when Borenson had said that he needed to watch Raj Ahten's troops, Iome had felt obligated to accept his explanation. Still, a worm of doubt burrowed in her skull.

"Protect you from my father?" Gaborn asked, sounding only half-surprised at the accusation. "No."

Iome did not know how to phrase her next question, but she spoke softly. "He will want us dead. He will see it as a necessity. He'll kill my father, and if he can't kill the woman that serves as my vector to Raj Ahten, he will want to kill me. Is that why you turn away from the path south?"

She wondered if he so feared that road south, that without thought, without even knowing, he turned from it. Certainly, if King Orden felt it necessary to kill Sylvarresta, Gaborn would not dissuade him. The Prince would not be able to save her.

"No," he said quite honestly, frowning, perplexed. Then he sat up straight, said, "Do you hear that?"

Iome listened, held her breath. She expected to hear the baying of war dogs, or cries of pursuit, but she could hear nothing. Only wind on the ridge above them, suddenly gusting through yellow birch leaves.

"I hear nothing," Iome admitted. "Your ears must be stronger than mine."

"No – listen, up there in the trees! Can you hear it?" He pointed to the ridge above them, to the north and west.

The wind suddenly stilled, the leaves quit twisting. Iome strained to hear something – the snap of a twig, the sound of stealthy steps. But she discerned nothing.

Gaborn suddenly stood up in his stirrups, taller in the saddle, gazing into the trees.

"What did you hear?" Iome whispered.

"A voice, in the trees," Gaborn said. "It whispered."

"What?" Iome urged her horse forward, studying the copse he spoke of, trying to see it from a different angle. But she could see nothing – only the white bark of trees, the green and golden leaves fluttering, and the shadows deeper within the grove. "What did it say?"

"I've heard it three times today. At first I thought it called my name, but this time I heard it clearly. It called 'Erden, Erden Geboren.'"

A chill ran down Iome's back.

"We're too far west," she hissed. "There are wights here. They're speaking to you. We should go south, now, before it gets dark." Darkness would not come for another three hours, but they had come too close to the Westwood.

"No!" Gaborn said, and he turned to Iome. He had a faraway look in his eyes, as one half-asleep. "If it is a spirit, it wishes us no harm!"

"Perhaps not," Iome whispered fiercely, "but it is not worth the risk!" She feared the wights, her father's assurances aside.

Gaborn gazed back at Iome, as if for a moment he'd forgotten she stood there. On the hill, the birch leaves shivered again. Iome looked toward the grove. The skies were drizzling, a slight gray rain that fell evenly, making it hard to see deeply into the grove.

"There, it comes again!" Gaborn shouted. "Do you not hear it?"

"I hear nothing," Iome admitted.

Gaborn's eyes suddenly blazed. "I see it! I see now!" he whispered urgently. "'Erden Geboren' – that is the old tongue for 'Earthborn.' The woods are angry with Raj Ahten. He had abused them. But I am Earthborn. They wish to protect me."

"How do you know?" Iome asked. By claiming to be Earthborn, Gaborn was perhaps saying more than he knew. Erden Geboren was the last great king of Rofehavan when it had all been one nation. He had gifted these woods to his warden, Heredon Sylvarresta, after his brilliant service in the great wars against the reavers and the wizards of Toth. In time Iome's own forefathers had become called kings – and they were kings in their own right, but lesser kings than those who came from the loins of Geboren. Over the sixteen centuries since those days, Geboren's blood had spread widely among the nobility of Rofehavan, until it would be difficult to say who was most closely linked to the last great king.

But with the union of the houses of Val and Orden, Gaborn could certainly contend for that honor – if he dared. By calling himself "Earthborn," was Gaborn suddenly claiming these woods, this kingdom, as his own?

"I am certain," Gaborn answered. "These spirits – if spirits they be – wish us no harm."

"No, that's not what I want to know," Iome said. "How can you be certain you are Earthborn?"

"Binnesman named me that," Gaborn said easily, "in his garden. The earth asked me to swear an oath to protect it, and then Binnesman sprinkled me with soil and pronounced me Earthborn."

Iome's jaw dropped. She'd known Binnesman all her life. The old herbalist had once told her that the Earth Wardens used to grant blessings upon new kings, anointing them with the dust of the earth they were sworn to protect. But this ceremony had not been performed for hundreds of years. According to Binnesman, the earth had "withdrawn such blessing" from current rulers.

She recalled now Binnesman's words in her father's keep, as Raj Ahten questioned the old wizard. "The new King of the Earth is coming." She'd thought Binnesman spoke of King Orden, for he'd been the one to enter her father's realm on the day the stones spoke. Now she saw that it was not the old king whom the earth proclaimed: it was Gaborn, who would become king. . . .

Yet Raj Ahten believed Mendellas Orden was the king his pyromancers envisioned in the flames. Mendellas Orden was the king he feared, the one he rode to Longmot to destroy.

Suddenly Iome felt so faint that she needed to dismount before she fell from her horse, for she had a premonition, a fear Mendellas Orden would meet Raj Ahten at Longmot, and that no power on earth could save King Orden in that battle.

She slid from her saddle, stood a moment in the stream, letting cold water wash her ankles. She tried to think. She feared going to Longmot, for she knew that King Orden would want her dead. Yet she feared not going, for if Binnesman was right, then the only way Orden might be saved was if Gaborn was there to save him.

By going to Longmot, she might well trade her life, and her father's, for King Orden's – a man whom she'd always disliked. Yet even if she did not like the man, did not trust him, she couldn't let him die.

Nor could she sacrifice her own father for Orden's sake.

Her father sat now on his horse, staring dumbly into the stream, oblivious of all that was said around him. Raindrops spattered him, and he glanced this way and that, trying to discern what had hit him. Hopeless, Hopelessly lost to her.

Gaborn gazed down at Iome, as if worried at her health, and she realized he was oblivious of her dilemma. Gaborn hailed from Mystarria, from a kingdom near the ocean, where water wizards congregated. He had no knowledge of the lore of Earth Wardens. He had no idea that he'd been anointed to be King of the Earth. He had no idea that Raj Ahten feared him, would kill him, if only Raj Ahten knew Gaborn's identity.

Wind gusted on the hill again; Gaborn listened as if to a distant voice. A few minutes ago, she'd wondered if Gaborn was mad. Now she realized that something marvelous was happening. The trees spoke to him, called him, for purposes neither he nor she understood.

"What should we do now, milord?" Iome asked. She had never called any man but her father by that title, never submitted to another king. If Gaborn recognized the sudden shift in their relationship, he did not signal it.

"We should go west," he whispered. "Toward the heart of the woods. Deeper."

"Not south?" Iome asked. "Your father could be in danger – more danger than he knows. We might help him."

Gaborn smiled at her words. "You worry for my father?" he said. "I love you for that, Princess Sylvarresta." Though he said the words lightly, she could not mistake the tone of his voice. He indeed felt grateful, and he loved her.

The thought made her shiver, made her want him more than she'd ever wanted a man. Iome had always been sensitive to magics, knew that her desire for Gaborn was born of the earth powers growing in him. He was not handsome, she had to tell herself. Not really more handsome than any other man.

Yet she felt drawn to him.

How could he love me? she wondered. How could he love this face? It was like a wall between them, this loss of glamour, her loss of self-respect and hope. Yet when he spoke to her, when Gaborn assured her that he loved her, she felt warm all over. She dared hope.

Gaborn frowned in thought, said softly. "No, we shouldn't go south. We need to follow our own track – west. I feel the spirits drawing me. My father is going to Longmot, where castle walls will enfold him. Bone of the earth. The earth powers can preserve him. He's safer there than we are here."

With that, he urged his horse forward, reached down a hand to life Iome to her saddle.

On the wind came the sound of war dogs baying in the far hills.

TWENTY-SIX: A GIFT

For long hours they raced, leaping over wind-fallen aspens, climbing up and down the hills. Iome let Gaborn lead the way, half in wonder at the trails he chose.

Time became a blur – all the trees losing definition, time losing focus.

At one point, Gaborn pointed out that Iome's father seemed to be riding better. As if some portion of his memories had opened, and he recognized once again how to sit light in a saddle.

Iome wasn't so sure. Gaborn stopped the horses in a stream, and her father watched a fly buzz around his head as Gaborn asked time and again, "Can you ride? If I cut your hands loose from the saddle, will you hold on?"

King Sylvarresta made no answer. Instead, he looked up into the sky and began squinting at the sun, making a noise like, "Gaaaagh. Gaaaaagh."

Gaborn turned to Iome. "He could be saying yes."

But when Iome looked into her father's eyes, she saw no light in them. He wasn't answering, just making sense-less noise.

Gaborn pulled out a knife, reached down, and slit the ropes that held King Sylvarresta's hands to the pommel of the saddle.

King Sylvarresta seemed mesmerized by the knife, tried to grab it.

"Don't touch the blade," Gaborn said. Her father

grabbed it anyway, cut himself, and just stared at his bleeding hand in wonder. It was a small cut.

"Hold on to the pommel of the saddle," Gaborn told King Sylvarresta, then wrapped the King's hand around the pommel of the saddle. "Keep holding on."

"Do you think it will work?" Iome asked.

"I don't know. He's holding it tight enough now. He might stay on the horse."

Iome felt torn between the desire to have her father safely tied to the saddle, and the desire to let him be free, unencumbered.

"I'll watch him," Iome said. They let the horses forage for sweet grass alongside a hill for a few moments. Distant thunder was snarling over the mountains, and Iome became lost in thought. A thin rain began to fall. A golden butterfly flew near her father's mount, and caught his eye. He watched after it a moment, held out a hand toward it as it flew off into the shadowed woods.

Moments later, they headed into the forest, into the deep gloom. The trees gave shelter from the brief rain showers. For another hour they rode, as the darkness deepened, until they reached some old trail in a burn.

There, as they rode, another monarch butterfly flew up out of some weeds. Iome's father reached for it, called out.

"Halt!" Iome shouted, leaping from her saddle. She ran to her father, who sat askew, listening to his force horse breathe, lamely reaching a hand out.

"Bu-er-fly!" he shouted, grasping at the golden monarch that flashed ahead, as if racing the horses. "Bu-er-fly! Bu-er-fly!" Tears streamed from her father's eyes, tears of joy. If there was any pain behind those tears, any recognition of what he'd lost, Iome could not see it. These were tears of discovery.

Iome's heart pounded. She grabbed her father's face, tried to pull him close. She'd hoped he would regain some wit, enough to talk. Now he had it. If he knew one word, he could learn more. He'd experienced his "wakening" – that moment when the connection between a new Dedicate and his lord became firm, when the bounds of an endowment solidified.

In time, her father might learn her name, might know she loved him desperately. In time he might learn to control his bowels, feed himself.

But for the moment, as she tried to pull him close, he saw her ruined face, cried out in terror, and drew away.

King Sylvarresta was strong, so much stronger than her. With his endowments, he easily tore from grasp, and pushed her so hard that she feared he'd broken her collarbone.

It did not matter. The pain did not diminish her joy.

Gaborn rode back to them, leaned over on his mount, and took King Sylvarresta's hand. "Here now, milord, don't be afraid," he soothed. He pulled the King's hand toward Iome, put the King's palm on the back of her hand, let him pet it. "See? She's nice. This is Iome, your beautiful daughter."

"Iome," Iome said. "Remember? Do you remember me?"

But if the King remembered her, he did not show it. His wide eyes were full of tears. He stroked her hand, but for the moment he could give her nothing more.

"Iome," Gaborn whispered, "you need to get back on your horse. I know you can't hear them, but mastiffs are howling in the woods behind us. We don't have time to waste."

Iome's heart pounded so hard she feared it would stop. Darkness could not be far away. The rain had momentarily halted.

"All right," she said, and leapt on her horse. In the distance, war dogs began to bay, and nearby some lone wolf raised its voice in answer.

TWENTY-SEVEN: THE UNFAVORED

In the shadows of the birches, Jureem gazed down as his master's Invincibles took a moment to rest, throwing themselves on the ground. Beyond this ridge, the mountains wrinkled and folded like crumpled metal, and trees grew huge. Gaborn was fleeing into the darkest heart of the Dunnwood.

Yet Jureem knew enough to fear this region, as did the Invincibles. Maps showed the Westwood only as a blank, and at its center was a crude sketch of the Seven Standing Stones of the Dunnwood. In Indhopal, it was said that the universe was a great tortoise. On the tortoise's back sat the Seven Stones, and on the stones rested the world. A silly legend, Jureem knew, but intriguing. For ancient tomes said that millennia ago, the duskins, the Lords of the Underworld, had erected the Seven Stones to "uphold the world."

The Invincibles searched the ground under the birches for sign of Gaborn. Somehow, the Prince's scent eluded them, and now the mastiffs stood yapping stupidly, noses high, trying to catch the scent.

It should not have happened. Young Prince Orden had three people ahorse. Their scent should have been thick in the air, the prints of the horses' hooves deep in the ground. Yet even Raj Ahten could not smell the boy, and the earth was so dry and stony that it could not hold a print.

372

Most of Raj Ahten's men were already unhorsed. Twelve horses dead, several dogs dead, too. The men who ran afoot should have been able to keep up with Gaborn, but complained. "This ground is too hard. We can't walk on it."

An Invincible sat on a log, pulled off a boot. Jureem saw the black bruises on his sole, horrible blisters on his heels and toes. These rough hills had killed most of the horses and dogs. They'd kill men, too. So far, Jureem was lucky enough to retain a mount, though his butt hurt so badly he dared not climb off his mount for fear he'd never get back on. Even worse, he feared that at any moment his own horse would die. Not able to run with these men, he would be abandoned here in the woods.

"How does he do it?" Raj Ahten wondered aloud. They'd followed Gaborn for six hours, astonished at how the Prince eluded them. Each time, it had been in a stand of birches. Each time, they'd lost Gaborn's scent completely, had to circle the trees until he reached the pine. Yet it was getting harder and harder to find the Prince's trail.

"Binnesman," Jureem said. "Binnesman has put some Earth Warden's spell on the Prince, hiding him." Gaborn was leading them all somewhere they did not want to go.

One of Raj Ahten's captains, Salim al Daub, spoke with a soft, womanly voice. "O Light of the Earth," he said solemnly, "perhaps we had better relinquish this fruitless chase. The horses are dying. Your horse will die."

Raj Ahten's magnificent horse did show signs of fatigue, but Jureem hardly imagined it would die.

"Besides," Salim said, "this is not natural. The ground everywhere we walk is harder than stone, yet the Prince's horse runs over it like the wind. Leaves fall in his path, hiding his trail. Even you cannot smell him anymore. We are too near the heart of the haunted wood. Can't you hear it?"

Raj Ahten fell silent, and his beautiful face went

impassive as he listened. He had endowments of hearing from hundreds of men; he turned his ear to the woods, closed his eyes.

Jureem imagined that his master could hear his men rustling about, the beats of their hearts, the drawing of their breaths, the strangling noises their stomachs made.

Beyond that . . . must be silence. A pure, profound silence all across the dark valleys below. Jureem listened. No birds called, no squirrels chattered. A silence so deep that it was as if the very trees held their breath in anticipation.

"I hear," Raj Ahten whispered.

Jureem could feel the power of these woods, and he wondered. His master feared to attack Inkarra because it, too, harbored ancient powers – the powers of the arr. Yet here in the north the people of Heredon lived beside this wood and apparently did not harvest the power, or did not commune with it. Their ancestors had been a part of these woods, but now the northerners were sundered from the land, and had forgotten what they once knew.

Or maybe not. Gaborn was aided by the wood. Raj Ahten had lost the boy's trail, lost it hopelessly.

Now Raj Ahten turned his head to the northwest, and looked out over the valleys. The sun shone briefly on Raj Ahten as he gazed at a deep valley, far below.

The heart of the silence seemed to lie there.

"Gaborn is heading down there," Raj Ahten said with certainty.

"O Great Brightness," Salim begged. "Haroun asks that you leave him here. He feels the presence of malevolent spirits. Your flameweavers attacked the forest, and the trees want retribution."

Jureem did not know why this annoyed his master so. Perhaps it was because Salim asked him. Salim had long been a fine guard, but a failed assassin. He'd fallen from Raj Ahten's favor.

Raj Ahten rode to Haroun, a trusted man who sat on a

log, his shoes off, rubbing his maimed feet. "You wish to stay behind?" Raj Ahten asked.

"If you please, Great One," the wounded man asked.

Before Haroun could move, Raj Ahten drew a dagger, leaned over and planted it through his eye. Haroun gasped and tried to stand, then tripped backward over a log, gagging.

Jureem and the Invincibles stared at their lord in fear.

Raj Ahten asked, "Now, who else among you would like to stay behind?"

TWENTY-EIGHT: AT THE SEVEN STANDING STONES

Gaborn rode full-tilt, and though his mount was one of the strongest hunters in Mystarria, in the afternoon he felt it giving way beneath him.

The stallion wheezed for breath. Its ears drooped, lying almost flat. Serious signs of fatigue. Now, when it leapt a tree or jumped some gorse, it did so recklessly, letting brambles scrape its hind legs, setting its feet loosely. If Gaborn did not stop soon, the horse would injure itself. In the past six hours, he'd traveled over a hundred miles, circling south, then heading back northwest.

Gaborn felt certain Raj Ahten's scouts must have begun to lose mounts by now. He could hear but two or three dogs baying. Even Raj Ahten's war dogs had grown weary of the chase. Weary enough, he hoped, to make mistakes.

He rode on, leading Iome through a narrow gorge. Night's shadows were falling.

He could see quite well here. As if the eyebright administered the night before had not yet worn off. This amazed him, for he'd expected it to lose its effect long ago.

He felt thoroughly lost, had no idea where he'd managed to end up, yet it was with a light heart that he raced down into a deep ravine, covered in pine.

Here he found something he'd never expected to encounter so far into the Dunnwood – an ancient stone road. Pine needles had fallen on it over the ages, and trees grew up through the middle of it. Yet all in all, as he headed deeper into the gorge, the path could be tracked.

It seemed a decidedly odd road, too narrow for even a narrow wagon, as if it were made to be trod by smaller feet.

Iome must not have expected this road, either, for she watched it with wide eyes, looking this way and that. In the darkness, her pupils dilated.

The woods grew silent as they rode for the next half-hour, and the trees grew immense. The trio descended from the pines into a grove of vast oaks, trees larger than Gaborn had ever seen or imagined, spreading wide over their heads, the oak boughs creaking softly in the night.

Even the lowest branches rose eighty feet overhead. Old man's beard clung to those boughs in vast curtains, thirty and forty feet long.

On the hill beside him, in the trees, Gaborn saw lights winking among the boles of trees. Tiny holes had been dug beneath a rock shelf. A ferrin warrior rushed before the light, his tail whipping.

Wild ferrin, living off acorns and mushrooms. Some inhabited caves up there; others lived in the hollows of great oaks. Gaborn saw lights from their lamps among the immense roots and boles. City ferrin seldom built fires, since those attracted men who would dig the ferrin out of their burrows. Somehow, the presence of wild ferrin comforted Gaborn.

He strained his ears, listening for sign of pursuit, but all he could hear was a river, somewhere off to his right, rushing down the ravine.

Still the trail descended.

The trees grew old and more vast. Few plants thrived beneath these trees – no gorse or winding vine maple. Instead the soft ground was covered in deep moss, unmarred by footprints.

Yet as they traveled, Iome cried out, pointed deeper into the woods. Far back under the shadows, a gray form squatted – a heavyset, beardless man, watching them from enormous eyes.

Gaborn called out to the old fellow, but he faded like a mist before the sun.

"A wight!" Iome cried. "The ghost of a duskin."

Gaborn had never seen a duskin. No human living ever had. But this looked nothing like the ghost of a man – it was too squat, too rounded.

"If it is the spirit of a duskin, then all is well," Gaborn said, trying to put a good face on it. "They served our ancestors."

Yet Gaborn did not believe for a moment that all was well. He spurred his horse onward a bit faster.

"Wait!" Iome called. "We can't go forward. I've heard of this place. There is an old duskin road leading down to the Seven Standing Stones."

Gaborn flinched at this news.

The Seven Standing Stones lay at the heart of the Dunnwood, formed the center of its power.

I should flee, he realized. Yet he wanted to reach those stones. The trees had called him.

He listened for a long moment for sounds of pursuit. Distantly, he heard trees bending in the wind, speaking something . . . he could not quite distinguish.

"It's not much farther," Gaborn told Iome, licking his lips. His heart hammered, and he knew it was true. Whatever lay ahead, it was not far distant.

He spurred his horse into a canter, wanting to take advantage of the failing light by covering as much distance as possible.

Ahead he heard a far-off rasping sound – like the buzz of rattlesnakes.

He froze in his saddle. He'd never heard the sound before, but he recognized it from other's descriptions. It was the rasping of a reaver as air filtered from its lungs.

"Halt!" he shouted, wanting to turn his horse and retreat.

Yet almost immediately he heard a cry ahead, Binnesman calling, "Hold! Hold I say!" He sounded terrified.

"Hurry!" Gaborn shouted and rode like a gale now, the horses' hooves drumming over the mossy road, beneath the black boughs.

He drew his warhammer, and pounded the ribs of his failing horse with his heels.

Sixteen hundred years ago, Heredon Sylvarresta had slain a reaver mage in the Dunnwood. The deed was legend. He'd put a lance through the roof of its mouth.

Gaborn had no lance, did not know if a man could even kill a reaver with a warhammer.

Iome shouted, "Wait! Stop!"

Deeper the road dropped, into the endless ravine, so that when Gaborn tried to look up above the dark branches, he had the impression of endless land all around and above him.

"The earth hide you . . ." the words rang in his mind. Iome and her father followed Gaborn down, until he felt as if at any moment he would be swallowed up into the belly of the earth.

He raced under the great oaks, which spread above him taller than any he'd ever imagined, so he wondered if these had grown here since the world was first born – then suddenly he saw an end to the trees, an end to the trail ahead. The rasping of the reaver came from there.

A ring of misshapen stones lay a couple of hundred yards off. Dark, mysterious, shaped somewhat like half-formed men. Gaborn raced to them in the starlight, hurtling under dark trees.

Something seemed very wrong. Only moments before, at the top of the hill, the sun had been setting. It was dusk. Yet here, with the steep mountains rising all around – here in the deep hollow, full night had fallen.

Glorious starlight shone all around.

Though legend had named this place the Seven

Standing Stones, it seemed the ring had not been named aptly. Only one stone stood now – the stone nearest to Gaborn, the stone facing him. Yet it was more than a stone. Once it might have seemed human. Its features were ragged and chipped with age, and the statue shone dimly with a greenish hue, as if foxfire played over its features. The other six stones, all of similar design, seemed to have fallen in dark ages past; all had toppled out from the center of the ring.

And though they were of similar design, yet they were not. For this one's head lay askew, and another's leg was raised in the air, while a third looked as if it were trying to crawl away.

A tremendous blast of light erupted from what Gaborn had taken to be a huge boulder – a beam of fire that struck the remaining statue at its feet. Gaborn saw movement as the boulder took a step, then another blast struck the statue, a blast of frost that froze the air, cracked the statue's edges, flaking them away.

Before that single statue, a reaver mage spun to meet Gaborn.

Binnesman shouted, "Gaborn! Beware!.," though Gaborn could not see the old wizard.

Gaborn first saw the reaver's head, row upon row of crystalline teeth flashing like ice in the starlight as its jaws gaped.

It bore no common ancestor to man, looked like no other creature to walk the face of the earth, for its kind had evolved in the underworld, descended from organisms that formed countless ages ago in deep volcanic pools.

Gaborn's first impression was of vastness. The reaver stood sixteen feet at the shoulder, so that its enormous leathery head, the width and length of a small wagon, towered over him, though Gaborn rode on horseback. It had no eyes or ears or nose, only a row of hairlike sensors that skirted the back of its head, and followed the line of its jaw like a great mane.

The reaver scrambled quick as a roach on four huge legs, each seemingly made only of blackened bone, that held its slimy abdomen well off the ground. As Gaborn drew near, it raised its massive arms threateningly, holding out a stalagmite as a weapon, a long rod of clear agate. Runes of fire burned in that rod. Dire symbols of the flameweavers.

Gaborn did not fear the icy rows of teeth, or the deadly claws on each long arm. Reavers are fell warriors, but reaver mages are even more fell sorcerers.

Indeed, the whole art of the Runelords had developed in mimicry of the reavers' magic. For when a reaver died, others of its kind would consume the body of the dead, absorb its knowledge, its strength, and its accumulated magic.

And of all reavers, the mages were most fearsome, for they had amassed powers from hundreds of their dead.

This one lunged sideways, and Gaborn heard the rasping of air exhaled from the vents on its back as his horse charged. He detected a whispering sound in that exhalation, the chanting of a spell.

Gaborn shouted, putting all the force of his Voice into his call. He'd heard of warriors with such powerful voices that they could stun men with a shout.

Gaborn had no such gift. But he knew that reavers sensed movement – whether it be sound or vibrations of something digging beneath their feet – and he hoped his shout would confuse the monster, blind it as he charged.

The reaver pointed its stalagmite at him, hissed vehemently, and a coldness pierced Gaborn, an invisible beam that stung like the deepest winter. The air all around that beam turned to frost, and Gaborn raised his small shield.

Legend said that the greatest of flameweavers' spells could draw heat from a man, just as flameweavers could draw heat from a fire or from the sun – suck the warmth from a man's lungs and heart, leave him frozen on a sunny day.

Yet the spell was so complex, required such concentration, that Gaborn had never heard of a flameweaver who'd mastered it.

He felt that spell's touch now, and threw himself sideways in his saddle, dropped in a running dismount as his horse raced ahead. The chill struck him to the bone, left him gasping as he rushed behind his charger, let its body shield his attack.

"No! Go back!" Binnesman cried from somewhere behind the ring of fallen statues.

Gaborn inhaled deeply as he advanced on the monster. The reaver carried no scent. Reavers never do, for they mimic the scent of the soil around them.

Yet the reaver mage rasped now, in terrible fury. The air hissed from the anterior of its long body.

Gaborn's horse staggered beneath the beam of cold, and Gaborn leapt over the falling beast, rushed the reaver at stomach level, swinging his warhammer with all his might.

The reaver mage tried to step back, tried to impale him with its staff. Gaborn dodged the blow and swung at its shoulder, buried the warhammer deep into the reaver's leathery gray hide. He quickly pulled the spike free, and swung a second time, hoping to plunge deeper into the wound, when suddenly the reaver smashed the agate rod down at him.

Gaborn's hammer hit its great paw, pierced a talon, and the iron T of his hammer smashed into the reaver's blazing rod. The agate staff shattered along its entire length, and flame leapt in the reaver's paw, a hot flash that erupted with explosive force, cracking the wooden haft of the warhammer.

Iome rode in behind Gaborn now, shouting at the monster, and King Sylvarresta's horse danced to its left. The tumult and the horses circling round distracted the beast, so that it swung its great maw one way, then the other.

What happened next, Gaborn did not see, for at that

second, the reaver chose to flee – running over the top of him so that its huge abdomen knocked him backward.

Gaborn hit the ground, the wind knocked from him as the reaver scrambled away. Gaborn wondered if he'd die from the blow. As a boy in tilting practice, he'd once fallen from his saddle, and a fully armored warhorse had trampled him. The reaver far outweighed the warhorse.

Gaborn heard ribs crack. Lights flashed before his eyes, and he had the sense of falling, of swirling like a leaf into some deep and infinite chasm.

When he regained consciousness, his teeth were chattering. He smelled some sweet leaves beneath his nose, and Binnesman had reached down beneath Gaborn's ring mail, was rubbing him with healing soils and whispering, "The earth heal you; the earth heal you."

When the soil touched him, Gaborn's flesh seemed to warm. He still felt terribly cold, frozen to the bone, but the soil worked like a warming compress, easing each wound.

"Will he live?" Iome asked.

Binnesman nodded. "Here, the healing earth is very powerful. See – he opens his eyes."

Gaborn's eyes fluttered. He stared, uncomprehending. His eyes could not focus. He tried to look at Binnesman, but it required so much effort.

The old wizard stood over Gaborn, leaning on a wooden staff. His clothing smelled charred, yet when his right hand brushed Gaborn, it felt deathly cold.

The reaver had tried to kill Binnesman, too.

There was a look about the wizard. He trembled, as if in pain and shock. Horror showed in every line of his face.

The single standing statue was throbbing with light. Great icy blasts had chipped away corners of it, cracked it. Gaborn lay for a moment. He felt a bitter chill in the air. The sorceries of the reaver mage.

Distant war dogs bayed. Binnesman whispered, "Gaborn?"

The statue seemed to waver, and the aged half-human face carved into it glanced down at him. Gaborn thought his eyes were failing. But at that moment, the light within the statue died, turning black, like a candle snuffed out.

A great splitting sound tore the air.

"No! Not yet!" Binnesman cried, looking up toward the standing stone.

As if in defiance of his plea, the great stone rent in two and tumbled, the head of it landing almost at Gaborn's feet. The ground groaned, as if the earth might shake apart.

Gaborn's thoughts came sluggishly. He gazed at the huge statue, but ten feet from him, listened to war dogs baying.

The Seven Stones have fallen, he realized. The stones that hold up the earth. "What? Happening?" Gaborn gasped.

Binnesman looked into Gaborn's eye, and said softly, "It may be the end of the world."

TWENTY-NINE: A WORLD
GONE WRONG

Binnesman leaned over Gaborn, peering at his wounds. "Light," he grumbled. A wan green light began emanating from his staff – not firelight, but the glow of hundreds of fireflies that had gathered on its knob. Some flew up, circled Binnesman's face.

Gaborn could see the old man clearly now. His nose was blooded, and mud plastered his cheek. He did not look severely wounded, but he was clearly distraught.

Binnesman smiled grimly at Gaborn and Iome, bent his ear, listening to the baying dogs in the woods. "Come, my friends. Get inside the circle, where we'll be safer."

Iome seemed to need no prodding. She grabbed the reins of hers and her father's horse, pulled both mounts round the fallen statues.

Gaborn rolled to his knees, felt his sore ribs. It pained him to breathe. Binnesman offered Gaborn his shoulder, and Gaborn hobbled into the circle of stones.

His horse had already gone in, stood nibbling at the short grass, favoring its right front leg. Gaborn was grateful that it had survived the reaver's spell.

Yet he felt reticent to enter that circle. He sensed earth power. It was old – a terrible place, he felt sure, to those who did not belong.

"Come, Earthborn," Binnesman said.

Iome walked rigidly, watching her feet, apparently unnerved by the power that emanated from below. Gaborn could feel it, palpable as the touch of sunlight on his skin, rising from beneath him, energized every fiber of his being. Gaborn knelt to remove his boots, to feel the sensation more fully. The earth in this circle had a strong mineral smell. Though enormous oaks grew all round, taller than any he'd ever seen, none stood near the center of the circle – only a few low bushes with white berries. The earth smelled too potent, too vigorous for anything else to take root. Gaborn pulled off his boots, sat on the grass.

Binnesman stood gazing about, like a warrior surveying his battleground. "Do not be afraid," he whispered. "This is a place of great power for Earth Wardens." Yet he did not sound fully confident. He'd been battling the reaver here, and had been losing.

Binnesman reached into the pocket of his robe, drew out some spade-shaped dogbane leaves, crushed and threw them.

Up the ancient road, the baying of war dogs came fervently, high yips echoing through the limbs of ancient oaks. The sound sent chills down Gaborn's spine.

He sat, head spinning, and said, "I heard trees calling me here."

Binnesman nodded. "I asked them to. And I placed protective spells on you, to keep Raj Ahten from following. Though at such a distance, they did little good."

"Why do the trees name me wrong?" Gaborn asked. "Why do they call me Erden Geboren?"

"The trees here are old and forgetful," Binnesman said. "But they remember their king still, for this wood held allegiance to Erden Geboren. You are much like him.

"Besides, your father was supposed to have named you Erden Geboren."

"What do you mean, 'supposed to have named' me?"

Binnesman said, "The Lords of Time once said that when the seventh stone falls, Erden Geboren would come again to the stones with his Earth Warden and a retinue of faithful princes and kings, there to be crowned, there to plan for the end of their age, in hope that mankind might survive."

"You would have anointed me king?" Gaborn asked.

"If the world had not gone wrong," Binnesman said.

"And Raj Ahten?"

"Would have been one of your most ardent supporters, in a more perfect world. The obalin drew him here tonight, just as they drew you and King Sylvarresta." Binnesman nodded toward the fallen creature that looked like a statue.

The obalin, these creatures had been called, though Gaborn had never heard the term.

"Gaborn, we are in terrible jeopardy. Nothing is as it should be – the kings of all Rofehavan and Indhopal should be here tonight. Men who should have been great heroes in the war to come have either been slain or now lie as Dedicates in Raj Ahten's keeps. All the Powers shall rage in this war, but the protectors of the earth are few and weak."

"I don't understand," Gaborn said.

"I will try to make it clearer, when Raj Ahten arrives," Binnesman said.

Of a sudden, the shadowy forms of the mastiffs burst from beneath the trees, their baying more fervent.

Men and a few horses rushed out behind the dogs. Only three men rode still. The other mounts had succumbed during the chase. Twelve soldiers raced beside the horses. The fact that these twelve men had run so long, in armor, across such unforgiving terrain, made Gaborn nervous. Such warriors would be terribly powerful.

The garish dogs with their red masks and fierce collars raced up to within a hundred feet of the fallen stones, then snarled and leapt as if they'd confronted a wall, like shadows thrown by a flickering flame. They would not come near Binnesman's dogbane. Some began racing around the fallen stones.

"Quiet!" Binnesman said to the dogs. The fierce

mastiffs cringed and tucked the stumps of their tails between their legs, daring not even to whimper.

Jureem followed his master to the circle of fallen stones. His stallion sweated, drenched, as if it had swum a river. The horse's lungs worked like bellows. It would not have survived another ten miles of this chase.

Jureem felt half-astonished to see Prince Orden's horses still alive, limping among the fallen statues.

A strange scent filled the air – smoke and ice and dust.

Raj Ahten stared hard at Gaborn, his glance askew, as if looking for something in particular.

Something odd was going on, Jureem realized. All of the Seven Standing Stones lay fallen, like half-formed men – misshapen, as if in their death throes. The scents of smoke and ice said that a battle had been fought here. Binnesman was wounded, dirt and blood on his face.

Overhead, a soft wind blew. The enormous oaks creaked in the slow wind, waving at the stars. Pale light glowed within the circle of fallen stones.

The Earth Warden stood scrutinizing Raj Ahten's men from beneath bushy brows, starlight glowing on his wispy beard. Confident. Dirty and bloodied. Still, the wizard seemed too confident. Jureem wished that his master's flameweavers were here. It had been a mistake to enter these woods without them.

Raj Ahten finally slipped from the back of his weary mount, stood holding the animal's reins. He smiled. "Prince Orden," Raj Ahten called in his most seductive Voice while his men finished circling their quarry. "Your running comes to an end. You need not fear me. You need not run any longer. Come, my friend."

Jureem felt the overawing draw of that Voice. Surely the Prince would come to the Great Light now.

But the Prince stood fast.

"Princess, you, at least, would not refuse me?" the Great One asked. Jureem felt gratified to see Iome sway on her feet, compelled to draw closer.

"No one will come with you," Binnesman said, stepping in front of her. "You cannot draw near, Raj Ahten – any more than can your dogs, or your warriors." Binnesman menacingly crushed leaves in his hand.

Dogbane. Even when it was not in the hands of an Earth Warden, dogbane was as potent at driving away dogs as Solomon's Seal was at frightening off cobras. Raj Ahten's men began backing from the statues. The dog-bane would not kill them. Yet their dogs' noses feared the scent.

"Why have you come here?" Raj Ahten demanded of Binnesman. "This is none of your affair. Leave now, and no one will harm you."

"More importantly," Binnesman said, "why have *you* come here? You are a king of men. Did you hear the trees calling?"

"I heard nothing," Raj Ahten said.

But Binnesman shook his head. "There are runes of concealment all about this place. Powerful runes. No man could have found it alone. Some greater Power drew you." He nodded knowingly, and his tone broached no argument.

"Perhaps . . . I did hear a whisper, Earth Warden," Raj Ahten said. "But it was very faint, like the voices of the dead."

"That is good. You are strong in the earth powers, and only they can preserve us. The end of an age is upon us. If our people are to survive, we must hold council. The earth called you, Raj Ahten, just as it calls to kings you have enslaved. Can you hear it now?" Binnesman stood at ease, gazing deep into Raj Ahten's eyes.

"I feel it," Raj Ahten said. "This place is strong in the Power that you serve."

Binnesman leaned on his staff. The light of fireflies shone on his face, which had an odd tint, a metallic sheen. Perhaps Binnesman had once been human, but his devotion to Earth had leached him of some of that humanity. Jureem realized that the wizard was perhaps as alien to mankind as any frowth or ferrin.

"And what of you?" Binnesman asked. "Could you serve this Power? Could you serve something greater than yourself?"

"Why should I?" Raj Ahten asked. "My flameweavers ask me time and again to give myself into greater service to their Fires. But why should I? The Powers do not serve man."

Binnesman cocked his head, as if listening deeply to Raj Ahten's words. "But they do – oft times, when our purposes agree. And they serve in return those who serve them."

"Grudgingly they return service, when they serve at all."

Binnesman nodded. "I am troubled by your lack of faith."

Raj Ahten responded, "As I am troubled by your abundance of faith."

Binnesman raised a bushy brow. "I never sought to trouble you. If I have offended, I beg forgiveness."

Raj Ahten cocked his head to the side, studied young Gaborn. "Tell me, Earth Warden, what spell is this, that I cannot see the Prince, but instead see rocks or trees when I look at him? Such a spell would serve me well."

Jureem wondered at such a strange question, for the Prince seemed . . . visible enough to him. He wore no mask or cloak.

"It is a small thing, this spell," Binnesman answered. "But you asked another question of me but a moment ago. You asked why I had led you here. And I confess that I did lead you. Now I have something I want of you."

"What do you want?" Raj Ahten asked.

Binnesman said, waving to the stones that lay about, "These are the Seven Standing Stones of the Dunnwood. Doubtless you know of them. Perhaps you even know what a dire portent it is that they have fallen." He spoke sadly, as if he felt great loss.

"I see them," Raj Ahten said. "In your tongue they are the obalin. In mine they are called the Coar Tangyasi – the Stones of Vigilance, or so the old scrolls name them. It is said that the duskins fashioned the watchers to protect mankind."

"That is right," Binnesman said. "So you are familiar with the old scrolls. Then you know that the duskins were great wizards. Beside such, my power is nothing. Theirs were the powers of deep earth – of the shaping of things, of preservation. Mine is the power of the shallow earth – of the use of herbs and growing things.

"Long ago, the reaver mages made war on the Underworld, slaughtering the duskins. The duskins could not adequately defend themselves. In time they knew they would be destroyed, and that the reavers would also seek to destroy mankind. So they sought to protect us, give us time to grow. They raised the obalin of the Dunnwood, channeled life into them.

"In time, they were called the Seven Standing Stones. With eyes of stone they have watched the deep places of the world for us.

"Often have the obalin whispered to our kings, warning of the presence of reavers. But the obalin's voices can only be heard by those attuned to the Earth. Thus, among men, those most sensitive to earth powers have been chosen as kings.

"Surely, you, Raj Ahten, have felt urges that warned you to send your warriors to battle the reavers. You have been adept at thwarting them. Until now! Now the childhood of mankind is past. The reaver mages of the Underworld are free!"

Raj Ahten stood thoughtfully through Binnesman's lesson. "I've fought reavers well enough in the past. But I fear that you put too much trust in your stones. The duskins never imagined the Runelords, nor guessed the power we would wield. It does not matter that a stone has fallen in the Dunnwood, any more than it matters that a leaf has fallen."

Binnesman said, "Do not speak lightly of them. The obalin were more than mere stone, more by far." He looked down reverently. "But you, Raj Ahten, must fear the reavers that infest your borders. Perhaps you do not guess the full extent of the threat. When the Obalin lived, one could learn much by touching them. Perhaps here is something you did not know: The reavers are in Kartish."

In Kartish were the blood-metal mines. If the reavers captured them . . .

Binnesman continued, "In your gullibility you've allied yourself with flameweavers, for they are strong in war. But it is no accident that reavers also serve fire. Nor was it an accident that a reaver came tonight and administered a deadly wound to the last of the obalin in an effort to hurry the end of man."

Binnesman turned his back to Raj Ahten, as if no longer concerned with him, and said, "Yet, there are greater powers than those wielded by flameweavers."

Raj Ahten stepped toward Gaborn cautiously, as if he considered moving in to attack. Of the warriors here, only Raj Ahten had never taken an endowment from a dog. Thus, only he could have withstood Binnesman's dogbane. Certainly, the wizard and his rabble were no match for Raj Ahten.

"Hold," Binnesman said, whirling. "Let no man even think of harming another on this ground. This place is strong in the earth power, and such power must be used to protect life, to save it. Not to take it."

To Jureem's surprise, Raj Ahten halted in his advance, sheathed his weapon. Yet as Binnesman considered, he realized that the wizard's words had held a compelling tone. "Let no man even think of harming another on this ground. . . ."

Binnesman held Raj Ahten with his eyes. "You say you

want my help in fighting the reavers. Very well. I will help you, if you will join me. Give up your forcibles. Join us in our quest to serve the earth, Raj Ahten. Let its powers sustain you."

Raj Ahten countered the offer: "Convince King Orden to give the forcibles back into my hands. Then we shall see...."

Sadly, Binnesman shook his head. "You would not join us even then, I believe. You do not want so much to fight the reavers as you want the glory that would come from defeating them."

Gaborn stepped forward and said earnestly. "Raj Ahten, please, listen to reason. The earth needs you. Serve the earth, as I do. I am sure that if I talk to my father, we can work out a plan. We can divide the forcibles among both nations, so that none need fear the other...."

Gaborn stood, trembling, as if afraid to offer even this much. Obviously the young man doubted his ability to carry off a scheme. Yet he seemed so earnest, every bit as earnest as the wizard.

Raj Ahten dismissed Gaborn's offer without a reply and said to Binnesman, "You are right. I will not join you, Earth Warden – not because I seek honor, but because you serve the snakes and field mice as much as you do mankind. I do not trust you. Our affairs matter nothing to you." When he spoke of snakes and field mice, Raj Ahten glanced contemptuously toward young Prince Orden.

"Ah, but the affairs of men matter very much to me," Binnesman said. "In my estimation, men may be no greater than field mice, but certainly men are no less."

Raj Ahten said in a seductive voice, "Then serve me."

Binnesman leapt up on a fallen obalin with all the energy of a young man. He stared down among the tiny white flowers that shone in the starlight, there among the circle of stones, and with a motion bade Prince Orden and the others to step back.

He said to Raj Ahten. "You seek to use me as a weapon,

but it is given to me only to protect. You lack faith in the power that I serve. Here then. Let me show you a weapon. . . ."

Jureem thought that the wizard would uncover some staff of power that lay hidden in the grass, or perhaps some ancient unbreakable sword.

Binnesman's manner suddenly became somber, and he swung his staff above his head in three slow arcs, then reached down and, with its tip, pointed a few feet ahead.

Suddenly a long swath of grass tore its roots away from the ground.

There, on the dark earth, Jureem could discern what looked like bones, as if something had died here in ages past, and had laid rotting under the ground.

But as he peered closer, Jureem saw that these were not bones – merely stones and sticks and roots that had been hidden. They appeared to be laid out in the form of a man. Jureem saw it first as Binnesman drew near a stone shaped like a head. Yellowed boars' tusks were arranged around the stone skull, like enormous teeth. There were dark holes in the stone, as if for eyes.

As Jureem studied, he saw that other stones made up the bones of hands; the horns of oxen splayed out from them like claws.

But if these stones and pieces of tree limb formed the skeleton of a man, then it was a strange man. Tendrils of roots lay among the stones and spars, forming odd networks, like veins running through the huge skeleton.

Binnesman raised his staff. The oaks along the hills suddenly seemed to hiss. Wind stirred the high branches, so that leaves seemed to give voice. Yet here in the glade, the air was perfectly still.

Terror filled Jureem, for he could feel earth power rising, as if at some unspoken request, from the stone beneath the ground, filling this little field.

Binnesman again waved his staff high in slow circles as he chanted,

"War is brooding. Peace is gone,
  here upon the glade.
Earth is breathing. Life is born,
  from covenants long made."

Binnesman stopped moving his staff about, and stared hard at the pile of stones and wood. He breathed heavily, as if speaking these few words had cost him dear.

The cadence of the chant was lost as Binnesman stared fixedly at the ground. He whispered to the dirt, "I've served the earth, and always shall. My life I give. Grant life to my creation. Grant a portion of the life I lost."

In that moment, a strange and horrifying transformation occurred. A light, the color of emerald, began glowing brightly in Binnesman's chest, became a brilliant ball that exploded from him and smote the ground before him like a meteorite.

In that moment, in an infinite moment, Binnesman screamed in pain and clutched his staff, suddenly leaning against it to hold him upright. The fireflies on the staff all flew up and buzzed about, so that Jureem could see the wizard easily.

Binnesman's hair, which had been a nutty brown with streaks of gray, suddenly turned silver in the starlight. He leaned on the staff like a bent old man. His green cloak in that moment became washed in red, the russet shades of leaves in autumn, as if the wizard were some color-changing chameleon on the wall of Raj Ahten's Southern palace.

Jureem gasped, realizing what had happened: The old wizard had given years of his life to that pile of sticks and bones at his feet.

The earth surged as if in gratitude for his gift, emitted a groaning sound, as of timbers moving.

If there were words in that noise, Jureem did not understand them. But Binnesman listened, as if the earth spoke to him. Then his manner became grave.

He struggled slowly to lift his staff, looking weary almost to death, then began to wave his staff in circles again, and sparks now flew up from it in a blazing cloud. Binnesman chanted,

> "Dark flows your blood.
>> Bright knit are your bones.
>> Your heart is beating within the stone.
> Day lights your eyes, and fills your mind
>> with thoughts of teeth and claws that rend."

On the ground, the stones and horns and roots began to shiver and tremble. The spars that formed the bones of an arm rolled backward a pace. Binnesman threw his staff to the ground and shouted, "Arise now from the dust, my champion! Clothe yourself in flesh. I call your true name: Foul Deliverer, Fair Destroyer!"

There was a clap of thunder as the dust of the earth rushed to obey his command, flowing toward the stones and wood, rushing like water or a low fog. Leaves and green grass, twigs and pebbles were all swirling into the mix.

In one moment, there was but a pile of refuse strewn on the ground in its strange pattern, and the next moment, bones and sinew formed. Muscles pulsed and stretched, lungs gasped for one huge breath. Leaves and twigs and grass were woven into the flesh, mottling its body with a strange patina of greens and browns, reds and yellows.

It all happened so quickly that Jureem could not really discern how the soil flowed up to give the being shape and life.

"Foul Deliverer, Fair Destroyer" raised a hand, incredibly long, as flesh formed. At first it seemed only a creature of dust, but rapidly the skin hardened, shining emerald along the neck and back, with the yellow mottling of faded leaves.

He makes a warrior, Jureem thought. Hues of grass and the white of pebbles blossomed on the warrior's face and throat.

The warrior struggled up to its knees, neck craning, starlight striking its eyes. The eyes were as flat and dead as pebbles from a river bottom, until the gleaming starlight caught them and reflected; then they began glowing brighter and brighter. Fierce intelligence filled those eyes – and peace, a sense of peace that made Jureem yearn to be somewhere else, something else.

Jureem knew the meaning of this . . . creature. Among magicians, many sought to control earth powers. The most accomplished of these were the Arrdun, the great artificers and creators of magical implements among the arr. Compared with them, human Earth Wardens were often considered weak, for few Earth Wardens meddled in the affairs of men, and those who did took centuries to mature.

But it was said that a mature Earth Warden was among the most fearsome creatures one could ever encounter.

And the sign that an Earth Warden had matured came when he called forth his wylde – a creature born of the blood and bones of the earth, a living talisman that fought for its master. Eldehar had formed a giant horse to ride into battle against the Toth. Eldehar had said his wylde could be "destroyed, but never defeated."

Jureem did not understand such oblique references to the Earth Wardens and their wyldes. Knowledge of them had faded over the millennia.

Now as the wylde formed, everywhere, a terrible wind began to rise, shrieking about the treetops high in the glade, whipping through Jureem's hair. It had come fast and furiously, a veritable storm.

Then the warrior began to grow hair – long green hair like seaweed that flowed down its back and over its shoulders, covering its breasts.

As the warrior took full form, Jureem stood astonished,

for he recognized the rounded breasts, the feminine curves assuming shape.

A woman. A woman was forming, a tall and beautiful woman, with graceful curves, long hair, and clean limbs.

Jureem gasped. The wylde shouted a cry that shook the earth as the wind struck, lifted her in the air – so that she became a streak of green climbing high above the trees toward the south. Then she was gone.

The glade became quiet. The wind stilled.

Jureem stood, dumbfounded. He did not know if this was what Binnesman had sought. Had his wylde leapt away on some errand? Had the wind carried her off?

Had it really even been a green woman?

Jureem's heart was pounding, and he stood breathless, overawed. Confused.

He looked to his left and to his right, to see the reactions of the soldiers. It had all happened so quickly.

Prince Orden's mount neighed in terror, reared back and pawed the air nervously. To the horse, it would have seemed that the green woman simply materialized at its feet.

"Peace," Binnesman said to the horse. It calmed at his admonition, and Binnesman gazed steadily upward, where his creation had disappeared into the sky.

He appeared . . . crestfallen.

Something was wrong. Binnesman had not expected the wylde to flee like this.

Now Binnesman was drained. Weakened. Old and hunched in his crimson robes. If he'd planned for the wylde to fight for him, then the plan seemed to have gone horribly awry. Binnesman hung his head and shook it in dismay.

"Faagh," Raj Ahten hissed. "What have you done, you old fool of a wizard? Where is the wylde? You promised me a weapon."

Binnesman shook his head.

"Are you so inept?" Raj Ahten demanded.

Binnesman glanced at Raj Ahten, gave him a wary look. "It is not an easy thing to draw a wylde from the earth. It has a mind of its own, and it knows the earth's enemies better than I. Perhaps urgent matters call it elsewhere."

Binnesman held out a hand toward Raj Ahten's horse. The three remaining horses all responded by moving toward him, and Jureem had to fight his mount a moment, to keep it from stepping forward.

"What are you doing?" Raj Ahten asked.

Binnesman answered, "It is growing late. It is time for the enemies of the earth to rest their eyes, and to dream of peace."

Jureem fought his horse and watched in wonder as, almost instantly, Raj Ahten and his soldiers fell asleep. Most of them fell to the earth, snoring deeply, but Raj Ahten himself stood in place as he slept.

The old wizard looked at the sleeping warriors and whispered, "Beware, Raj Ahten. Beware of Longmot."

Then he looked up, caught Jureem's eye. "You are still awake? What a wonder! You alone among them are not an enemy of earth."

Jureem fumbled for words, aghast to see his master thus subdued, astonished to see the old wizard and his charges still alive.

"I . . . serve my master, but I wish the earth no harm."

"You cannot serve both *him* and the earth," Binnesman said, climbing up on to Raj Ahten's mount. "I know his heart now. He would destroy the earth."

"I am a king's man," Jureem said, for he could think of nothing else to say. His father had been a slave, and his father's father. He knew how to serve a king, and how to serve well.

"The Earth King is coming," Binnesman said. "If you would serve a king, serve him."

With a nod, he indicated for Prince Orden and Iome to mount up. King Sylvarresta was still ahorse.

Binnesman gave Jureem a long look. Then the wizard

and his charges rode into the night, back up the road from which they'd come.

For a long time, Jureem sat ahorse, watching as Raj Ahten slept.

The night seemed darker than any that Jureem could recall, though the stars were shining fierce enough. "A king is coming," the pyromancer had warned before her death. "A king who can destroy you."

Not since Erden Geboren, two thousand years ago, had an Earth King risen in the land. Now King Orden had come. At Longmot, King Orden would be preparing for Raj Ahten's attack.

Jureem gazed down at the obalin. Where once the Seven Stones had stood, now the creature lay in ruin. He wondered at this portent. His heart pounded. He felt the warm night air, tasted the mineral tang of earth scent. Almost he turned to follow the wizard. But the sound of the horses' hooves was lost in the night.

He stared at his master.

For years Jureem had given his all to the Great One, had followed his every whim. He had struggled to be a good servant. Now, he looked into his own heart and began to wonder why.

There was a time, a decade ago, when Raj Ahten had talked often of consolidating forces, of uniting the kings of the South under a single banner to repel the attacks of reavers. Somehow, over the years, the dream had changed, become twisted.

The "Great Light," Jureem had called him, as if Raj Ahten were a Bright One or a Glory from the netherworld.

Jureem turned his own horse.

I am the weakest man here, he told himself. Yet perhaps Orden will accept my service.

I will be branded a traitor, Jureem thought. If I leave now, Raj Ahten will believe that I am the spy who warned Orden where to find the forcibles.

Jureem considered. So be it. If I am branded a traitor, I will become one. He had many secrets that he could divulge. And if he left Raj Ahten's service, then it meant that the Wolf Lord would still have a spy in his midst.

He will expect me to head south, to Longmot, Jureem thought. And in time I will head south, to seek out Orden. But for tonight, I will head north to find a barn or a shed to sleep in.

He felt weary to the bone, and had no strength for a long ride. He rode hard into the night.

Book 4:
Day 22 in the Month of Harvest,
A Day of Slaughter

CHAPTER THIRTY: DEATH COMES TO THE HOUSE OF A FRIEND

Wind gusted from the southeast, carrying the smell of rain; dark clouds rushed behind it, covering the forest. Borenson heard distant thunder, but he could also hear neighing on the wind that afternoon, smell horses. Raj Ahten's troops were marching over the blackened hills.

It had been but half an hour since Gaborn mounted his horse, and with a nod, Borenson wished them good speed. In a moment Gaborn, Iome, and King Sylvarresta spurred up the ash-covered hill, into the shelter of the woods. A few snaps of branches and the snort of a horse announced their departure, yet the horses moved so swiftly, in a moment even those sounds faded.

Borenson also rode his warhorse to the edge of the silent woods, taking a different track. Ahead lay a line of ancient oaks and ash – many of which had the tips of branches burned to nothing.

But as he neared the tree line, Borenson noticed something that only now struck him as incredibly odd: It looked as if there were an invisible wall before him, and the trees beyond it had not caught fire. Not a brown twig had kindled, not a spider's web burned.

As if . . . the flames had raged before the trees, incinerating everything, until the trees had said, "These woods are ours. You can come no farther."

Or perhaps, Borenson reasoned, the unnatural fire had turned aside for reasons of its own. An elemental had consciously directed the flames for a time, before it lost focus, faded.

Borenson halted just outside the line of trees, listening, afraid to go in. No birds sang under the trees. No mice or ferrin rustled through dead leaves under the boughs. Old man's beard hung from the hoary oaks in an odd way, like great curtains. This was an ancient forest, vast.

Borenson had hunted these haunted woods, but he'd never ridden through them alone. He knew the dangers of doing so.

No, it was not the fire that turned away, Borenson reasoned. The forest had confounded it. Old trees lived here, trees old enough to remember when the duskins first raised the Seven Stones. Ancient spirits walked here, powers that no man should face alone.

He thought he could feel them now, regarding him. A malevolent force that caused the air to weigh heavy. He looked up at the graying skies, the lowering clouds sailing in from the southeast. Wind buffeted him.

"I'm not your enemy," Borenson whispered to the trees. "If you seek enemies, you'll find them soon enough. They come."

Cautiously, reverently, Borenson urged his mount to walk under the dark boughs. Only a few yards, far enough so he could tie the big warhorse in a shallow ravine, then creep back to the wood's edge to watch Raj Ahten's army pass on the road below.

He did not have to wait long.

In a few moments, twenty men raced over the hills below, war dogs leaping to keep ahead. To Borenson's horror, Raj Ahten himself led them.

For a moment, Borenson feared the trackers would follow his trail, but down by the river they stopped for a long time, searching the ground at the spot where Gaborn had taken Torin's armor.

Borenson made out some muffled shouting, but did not understand the dialect of Indhopalese the men spoke.

They hailed from a Southern province, but Borenson knew only a few curse words in the Northern dialect.

Raj Ahten recognized that Gaborn's party had split.

They followed Gaborn. Borenson felt terrified, wondered why Raj Ahten himself would head a party to capture Gaborn. Perhaps the Wolf Lord valued Iome and Sylvarresta more than Borenson imagined. Or perhaps he wanted Gaborn as a hostage.

Silently, he willed Gaborn to hurry, to ride hard and fast and never slow till he reached Longmot.

The trackers had hardly raced over the hills to Borenson's left when the army of the Wolf Lord came marching down the road, their golden surcoats bright in the last rays of sunlight before the oncoming storm.

Archers came first, thousands strong, marching four abreast. Mounted knights followed, a thousand. Then came Raj Ahten's counselors and magicians.

Borenson cared little for the Wolf Lord's soldiers. Instead he watched what followed next. A huge wain, encased in wood. A wagon to hold Dedicates – probably fewer than three dozen of them. The wagon was guarded closely by hundreds of Invincibles.

An arrow could not pierce its wooden walls. Borenson could see that one man alone would find it impossible to assault the wagon's occupants.

No, he knew the truth.

Raj Ahten could haul only a few vectors with him, hoping no one would slaughter the hundreds of poor Dedicates in Sylvarresta's keep, or in other castles he might have taken here in the North.

When the Dedicates' wagon passed, when the cooks and armorers and camp followers and another thousand swordsmen hurried past, followed by the last thousand archers in the rear guard, Borenson grimly realized that killing Raj Ahten's vectors would be impossible.

He would have to concentrate on breaking into the Dedicates' Keep in Castle Sylvarresta. He worried at how many guards waited for him.

He sat at the edge of the wood for long hours, while the storm brewed and clouds engulfed the sky. Winds began to send dry leaves skittering from the woods. As evening neared, the clouds hurled bolts of lightning through the heavens. Rain fell thick, unrelenting.

Borenson drew a blanket over his head and wondered about Myrrima, back in Bannisferre. She had three Dedicates – her witless mother and two ugly sisters. They'd given up much to unite the family, to win their fight against poverty. Myrrima had told Borenson, on the trip to her house, how her father had died.

"My mother was raised in a manor, and had endowments of her own," she said. "And my father was a man of wealth, at one time. He sold fine clothes in the market, made winter coats for ladies. But a fire burned his shop, and his coats burned with him. All the family gold must have burned in that fire, too, for we never found any of it."

It was a proud way to say that her father had been murdered, killed in a robbery.

"My grandfather is still alive, but he has taken a young wife who spends more than he brings in."

Borenson had wondered what she was getting at, until she whispered part of an old adage. "Fortune is a boat . . ." *on a stormy sea, which rises and falls with each mountainous wave.*

Myrrima, he'd realized, had been telling him that she did not trust fortune. Though their arranged marriage might seem fortunate at the moment, it was only because, for the moment, they crested the wave, and she feared that at any second her little boat would crash down deep in some trough, perhaps be submerged forever.

That was how Borenson felt now, submerged, drowning, hoping to keep afloat. The whole notion of sending one man to storm a Dedicates' Keep was a long shot. In all probability, Borenson would arrive at the keep, find it well guarded, and have to retreat.

But he knew, he knew, that even if he had only a slim chance of breaking into the keep, he'd have to take it.

When the storm passed that evening, he still sat unmoving, listening to the stealthy water dripping from trees, the creaking of branches in the wind. He smelled the leaf mold, the rich soil of the forest, the clean scent of the land. And ashes.

Murdering Dedicates did not sit well with him. Borenson tried to harden his resolve for long hours, imagining how it might be – climbing the walls in the escalade, battling guards.

Borenson imagined riding into the castle, going to the gates of the Dedicates' Keep, and riding down any defenders, then discharging his duty.

Such an attack would seem heroic, would likely get him killed. He wanted to do it, to finish this horrible task. He would have gladly made a suicide charge, if not for Myrrima.

If he tried to enter the keep during daylight, he'd jeopardize his mission. What's more, even if he gained entry into the keep and managed to slaughter the Dedicates, he'd then be forced to return to his king and report . . . what took place between him and Gaborn, and tell why he'd let Sylvarresta live.

Borenson could not stomach the thought. He couldn't lie to King Orden, pretend he hadn't seen Gaborn.

So he watched the sun drop in the west, spreading gold all through the clouds, even as another storm blew in.

He fetched his horse and rode to the hill south of Castle Sylvarresta.

I am not death, he told himself, though he had long trained to be a good soldier. He'd become a fine warrior, in every detail. Now he would play the assassin.

An image flashed in his mind, five years past, when Queen Orden was murdered in bed with her newborn babe. Borenson had tried to impale the fellow – a huge man who moved like a serpent, a man in black robes, face covered. But the assassin had escaped.

It hurt terribly to remember such things. It hurt worse to know that he would now go the nameless assassin one better.

As he neared, Borenson saw that few guards walked the walls of Castle Sylvarresta tonight. Sylvarresta's loyal soldiers had been decimated; Raj Ahten had left no one to guard the empty shell of a city. Borenson could not spot a single man on the walls of the Dedicates' Keep.

It saddened him. Old friends – Captain Ault, Sir Vonheis, Sir Cheatham – should have been on those walls. But if they lived, now they resided in the Dedicates' Keep. He remembered three years past, when he'd brought molasses to the hunt and had strewn it in a trail through the woods, leading to Derrow's feet, then smeared the captain's boots.

When he'd awakened to find a she-bear licking his feet, Derrow had roused the whole camp with his cry.

Borenson took out the white flask of mist, pulled the stopper, and let the fog begin to flow.

So it was that half an hour later, he laid aside his armor, and went to make a lone escalade. He climbed the Outer Wall on the west side of the city, protected by the fog that crept over with him.

Then he made his way to the inner wall, the King's Wall, and scampered over quickly. Only a single young man had walked that wall, and he'd turned his back for the moment.

Borenson reached the base of the Dedicates' Keep near midnight, warily watched it. He did not trust his eyes, worried that guards might be secreted in the King's towers. So he scaled its walls from the north, coming at it by way of the woods in the tombs, where few prying eyes might spot him.

Rain pelted the keep, making it difficult to find purchase between the stones. Borenson spent long minutes clinging to the wall before he reached the top.

There, he found that the wall-walks really were all unmanned, but as he scurried down the steps into the inner court, he spotted two city guards – young men with few endowments – huddled away from the drenching rain in the protection of the portcullis.

In a moment when lightning filled the sky, he rushed them, slaughtered them as thunder shook the keep, so that no one heard their cries.

Even as he killed the young men, Borenson wondered. Not one Invincible? Not one man to guard all these Dedicates?

It felt like a trap. Perhaps the guards hid among the Dedicates.

Borenson turned and looked at the rain-slicked stones in the keep. The lights were out in the great rooms, though a lantern still burned in the kitchens. A wild wind burst through the portcullis, swept through the bailey.

There was an art, a science to killing Dedicates. Some of the Dedicates in there, Borenson knew, would be guards themselves, men like him who had dozens of endowments of their own and long years of practice in weaponry. They might be crippled – deaf or blind, mute or without a sense of smell – but they could be dangerous still.

So, when slaughtering Dedicates, common sense dictated that you avoid such men, kill first those who served as their Dedicates, weakening the more dangerous foes.

Thus, you began by slaughtering the women, and the young. You always sought to kill the weakest first. If you killed a man who had twenty endowments, suddenly you would find that twenty Dedicates would waken, who could sound alarms or fight you themselves.

Though it might be tempting to spare one or two Dedicates, the truth was that if you did, they might call for guards. So you killed them all.

You murdered commoners who had only given endowments, never received. And you started at the bottom of the keep, blocking all exits, and worked your way to the upper stories.

Unless, of course, someone in the keep was awake.

I had best begin in the kitchen, Borenson told himself. He took the dead gatekeeper's key and locked the portcullis, so no one could enter the keep or escape, then went to the kitchen. The door stood locked, but he set the prong of a warhammer in its crack. With endowments of brawn from eight men, it was no great feat to pry the door free from its hinges.

When he rushed into the kitchens, he found a lowly girl who'd been left to sweep the floor, long into the night. A young thing, perhaps eight, with straw-blond hair. He recognized the child – the serving girl who'd catered to Princess Iome last Hostenfest. Too young to have given an endowment, he'd have thought. Certainly Sylvarresta would never have taken one from her.

But Raj Ahten has been here, Borenson realized. The girl had given an endowment to him.

When she saw Borenson in the doorway, she opened her mouth to scream. Nothing came out.

A mute who had endowed Voice on her lord.

Almost, Borenson did not have the strength to carry his plan through. He felt nauseated, sickened. But he was a good soldier. Had always been a good soldier. He couldn't let the little thing wriggle through the wet bars of the portcullis and summon help. Though this child would die, her sacrifice could save thousands of lives in Mystarria.

He rushed, grabbed the broom from the girl's hand. She tried to shriek, tried to yank free from his grasp. She clawed at a table, overturned a bench in her terror.

"I'm sorry!" Borenson said fiercely, then snapped her neck, not wanting to make the girl suffer.

He gently laid her corpse to the ground, heard a thumping sound in the buttery – back in the shadows thrown by the lamplight. Another young girl stood back there, black eyes shining in the darkness.

In all his heroic imaginings this day, he'd not envisioned this – an unguarded keep, where he would have to slaughter children.

Thus began the most gruesome night of Borenson's life.

THIRTY-ONE: A TIME FOR QUESTIONS

As the horses raced through the woods, beneath the black trees, Binnesman held his staff high, shining its dim light for all to see by. Yet the very act seemed tiring, and Binnesman looked drained, old.

The trees whipped past.

Gaborn had a thousand questions, felt as many uncertainties. He wished to speak to Binnesman. But for now he held back his questions. In Mystarria it was considered rude to interrogate a stranger in the way that Gaborn wanted to question Binnesman now. Gaborn had always thought this rule of civility a mere custom, formed without reason, but now he saw that it was more.

By asking questions, one intruded on another's Invisible Domain. At the very least, you took time from him. And information often had its own value, as much value as land or gold, so that in taking it, one robbed another.

To keep from musing about the obalin and the loss of Binnesman's wylde, Gaborn concentrated on this insight, wondering how often courtly manners were rooted in man's need to respect the Domains of others. Certainly, he could see how titles and gestures of respect fit into the larger scheme.

Yet Gaborn's thoughts quickly turned away from such matters, and instead he considered what he'd seen.

Gaborn suspected that Binnesman knew far more about the dark time to come than he would say in front of

Raj Ahten, perhaps far more than he *could* say. The study of wizards was long and arduous, and Gaborn had once heard that certain basic principles could only be understood after weeks or months of intent study.

After long minutes, Gaborn decided that there were some things one should not ask a wizard. What price had Binnesman paid to give life to the wylde? Gaborn wondered.

Now the Earth Warden turned from the road and picked his way among twisted paths here under the shadowed trees. No other scout could have made his way in such maddening darkness. Gaborn left the wizard to his work in silence, in the starlight, for an hour, until they came upon an old road. From there, Binnesman raced the horses north, until suddenly the road dropped down to a ridge overlooking the broad fields outside the village of Trott, twelve miles west of Castle Sylvarresta.

On the plain below lay hundreds of multicolored tents from the hordes of Southern traders who had journeyed north for Hostenfest but who had been forced to vacate the fields near Castle Sylvarresta when Raj Ahten's troops laid siege.

Binnesman called the horses to stop, gazed down over the dark fields. The grass had been burned white by the late-summer sun, so that even by starlight reflecting off the grass one could see.

"Look!" Iome whispered. Gaborn followed her pointing finger, saw something dark creeping across the fields, toward the pavilions with their horses and mules for the caravans.

Nomen were down there, eighty or a hundred, creeping toward the tents on their bellies to hunt for food. To the east, along the ridge, he saw several large boulders move, realized that a trio of frowth giants were also prowling the edge of the forest.

Hungry. They merely hungered for meat. Raj Ahten had marched the giants and the nomen all this way, and they'd survived the battle at dawn, but now they would be hungry.

"We'll have to take care," Gaborn said. "These horses need to graze and to rest. But until it's safe, maybe we should ride in the open fields, where we can't be surprised." Gaborn turned his horse east, to head back toward Castle Sylvarresta. From there he could take the Durkin Hills Road south.

"No, we should go west from here," Iome said.

"West?" Gaborn asked.

"The bridge at Hayworth is out. We can't run the horses through the forest, so we can't go near Boar's Ford. Besides, we don't want to run into Raj Ahten's army in the dark."

"She's right," Binnesman said. "Let Iome lead you." His voice sounded tired. Gaborn wondered how much his spell-casting had drained him.

"West is the only way – over the Trummock Hills Road," Iome said. "It's safe. The forest does not encroach on the road. My father's men cut it back."

Binnesman let the horses rest a few moments. As one, the group dismounted, stretched their legs, adjusted the girths on their mounts.

"Come," Binnesman said all too soon. "We have a few hours until Raj Ahten awakens. Let us make good use of them." He urged them downhill, into the plains. Though the horses were hungry and the grass here grew high, it was also dry and without seed, worthless fodder.

They rode slowly along a dirt road for half an hour, and here at last they felt at ease enough to talk, to make plans.

"My horse will be the fastest over these road," Binnesman said. "If you do not mind, I will ride ahead. I will be needed at Longmot, and I hope to find my wylde there."

"Do you think it is there?" Iome asked.

"I really can't be sure," Binnesman answered, and seemed to want to say no more.

The company soon reached a weathered farmhouse beside a winding stream. The farm had a small orchard behind it, and a sloping barn for a few pigs. It looked as if the peasant who lived here feared attack, for a lantern had been set in a plum tree out front, another out by the door to the pig shed.

The farmer should be afraid, Gaborn realized. This hut was isolated, without benefit of neighbors for a mile. And giants and nomen were prowling the fields tonight.

Iome's father rode his steed up to the lantern, sat staring at it, mesmerized, as if he'd never seen one before.

Then Gaborn realized that the King probably never had seen one, at least not that he remembered. The whole world would seem new to him, like a vivid and fascinating dream, something he lived through but never comprehended.

Gaborn also rode up beneath the lantern, so his face could easily be seen, then called to the door. In a moment, an old turnip of a woman cracked the door enough to frown at him. She seemed frightened by so many riders.

"May we have some water and feed for the horses?" Gaborn asked. "And some food for ourselves?"

"At this time of night?" the old woman grumbled. "Not if you was the King!" She slammed the door.

Gaborn felt surprised at this, looked at Iome for a reaction. Binnesman smiled. Iome laughed softly, went up to the plum tree, then picked half a dozen of the large violet fruits. Gaborn saw movement inside the house as the woman tried to peer out the window, but she had no fine window of glass, only a piece of scraped hide, which let her see nothing but shadows.

"Leave them plums!" she shouted from inside.

"How about if we take all the plums we can carry, and leave a gold coin instead?" Gaborn called out.

Quick as a flash, the old woman was at the door again. "You have money?"

Gaborn reached into the pouch at his waist, pulled out a coin, tossed it to the woman. Her hand darted from the doorpost to catch the coin. She closed the door while she bit the coin, then cracked the door again to shout, more cordially, "There's grain in the pig shed. Good oats. Take as much as you want. And the plums."

"A blessing on you and your tree," Binnesman called out, "three years' good harvest."

"Thank you," Gaborn shouted, bowing low. He and Binnesman led the horses round back while Iome fed her father plums from the tree.

Gaborn opened the shed, found a burlap bag of oats, and began to dump them in a worn wooden trough to feed the horses. As he did, he was painfully aware that the wizard sat quietly on his horse, watching Gaborn.

"You have questions for me," Binnesman said.

Gaborn dared not ask the most pressing questions first. So he said easily, "Your robes have gone red."

"As I told you they would," Binnesman answered. "In the spring of his youth, an Earth Warden must grow in his power, tend it and nurture it. In the green summer of his life, he matures and ripens. But I am in the autumn of my life, and now must bring forth my harvest."

Gaborn asked, "And what happens in the winter?"

Binnesman smiled up at him discreetly. "We will not speak of that now."

Gaborn picked a question that had troubled him more. "Why could Raj Ahten not see me? He thought there was a spell upon me."

Binnesman chuckled. "In my garden, when Earth drew a rune on your forehead, it was a symbol of power that I, in my weakness, dared not try. You are invisible now, Gaborn – at least, you're invisible to your enemies. Those who serve Fire cannot see you, but see instead your love for the land. The closer they come to you, the more powerfully the spell affects them. I am amazed that Raj Ahten even knew that you were there in the glade. Fire could have given him such power. I did not realize that then, but I realize it now."

Gaborn thought about this.

"You cannot take great security in this gift of invisibility," Binnesman said. "Many evil men would do you harm, men who do not serve Fire. And flameweavers of great power can pierce your disguise if they get close."

Gaborn remembered the flameweaver in Castle Sylvarresta, the way she'd looked at him in recognition, as if he were a sworn enemy.

"I see . . ." he whispered. "I understand why Raj Ahten could not see me. But why could I not see him?"

"What?" Binnesman said, his brows arching in surprise.

"I had seen his face before, at the castle. I know his helm, his armor. Yet tonight his face was hidden from me, as mine was from him. I looked at him and saw . . . multitudes of people, all bowing to worship. People in flames."

Binnesman laughed long and hard. "Perhaps you were looking too deeply. Tell me, what were you thinking when this vision appeared?"

"I simply wanted to see him as he was, beneath all those endowments of glamour."

"Let me tell you a tale," Binnesman said. "Many years ago, my master was an Earth Warden who served the animals of the forest – the harts and the birds and such. They would come to him, and he would feed them or heal them as needed.

"When I asked how he knew their needs, he seemed surprised. 'You can see it in their eyes,' he said. As if that were all the answer. Then he sent me away, out of his service, for he thought me unfit to be an Earth Warden.

"You see, Gaborn, he had the gift of Earth Sight, of looking into the hearts of creatures and divining what they wanted, or needed, or loved.

"I've never had that gift. I cannot tell you how to use it, how it works. Believe me, I wish I had your gift."

"But I don't have such a gift–" Gaborn objected. "I

don't see into your heart, or Iome's."

"Ah, but you were in a place of great earth power," Binnesman said. "You *do* have the gift, though you do not know how to use it. Study it out in your mind. Practice it. It will come to you, in time."

Gaborn wondered. Wizards often said that they needed to "study things out."

"Yet you have a greater duty now," Binnesman said. "As Erden Geboren chose his loyal men to fight at his side, you must also begin to choose your followers. It is an awesome responsibility. Those you chose will be bound to you."

"I know," Gaborn said. He had heard the legends, how Erden Geboren would choose those to fight at his side, and always he knew their hearts, knew when they faced danger, so that forever after, they never fought alone.

"You must begin to choose . . ." Binnesman mused, looking off over the dark fields.

Gaborn studied the old man, wondering. "You never needed the gift of Earth Sight, did you? Other Earth Wardens may serve the field mice and the snakes – but the earth commanded you to serve *man* . . . in the dark time to come."

Binnesman stiffened, glanced at Gaborn. "I beg you never speak that thought aloud. Raj Ahten is not the only lord who would seek my life if he guessed at what you know."

"Never," Gaborn said. "I will never tell."

"Perhaps my old master was right," Binnesman said. "Perhaps I do not serve the earth well. . . ."

Gaborn knew that he thought of the loss of his wylde. "Is it lost to us, destroyed?"

"It is of the earth. A mere fall will not kill it. Yet, I . . . I worry for this creature. It will have come naked from the earth. It knows nothing, will be lost without me to teach and nourish it. . . . And it is more powerful than anyone knows. The blood of the earth flows in its veins."

Gaborn asked. "Dangerous? What can it do?"

"It is a focus for my power," Binnesman said. "Just as water wizards draw power from the sea, or as flameweavers draw it from fire, I draw strength from the earth. But some earth contains more elemental force than others. For decades I have scoured the ground for just the right soils, just the right stones. Then I called my wylde from them."

"So . . . it is nothing more than dirt and stones?" Gaborn asked.

"No," Borenson said, "it is more than that. I cannot control it; it is as alive as you or I. The wylde chose its shape from my mind. I tried to envision a warrior to fight the reavers, a green knight like the one who served your forefathers. Yet even in that, I could not control it."

"We will have to send word," Gaborn said, "ask people to help us search for it."

Binnesman smiled weakly, pulled a blade of wheat from the ground and chewed at its succulent end.

"So Raj Ahten is lost to us," Binnesman mused. "I'd hoped for better."

Leading her own mount out back, Iome found Gaborn and the wizard beside a trough, feeding the horses, which ate as only force horses can, chewing so rapidly she feared for them.

Iome left Gaborn and Binnesman to tend the beasts while she took her father to the creek and washed him in the clear water. He had soiled himself near the Seven Stones, and she'd never had time to care for him.

When at last Gaborn came to her, leaving the horses in Binnesman's able care, Iome had her father dried and in fresh clothes, and he lay at the edge of the orchard, using a tree root for a pillow, snoring contentedly.

It seemed an uncommon, yet peaceful sight. Iome's father was a Runelord, with several endowments of stamina, and others of brawn. Only once in her life had she known him to sleep, and then only for half an hour. Yet she wondered if from time to time he might have slept beside her mother. Certainly, Iome knew, at times he'd lain beside her mother as he pondered the kingdom's problems, long into the night.

But sleep? Almost never.

The long day must have worn her father out.

Gaborn took a seat beside Iome, both of them leaning their backs against the same tree. He took a plum from the pile near her hand, and ate.

Clouds were beginning to scud in again, darkening the sky, and the wind gusted from the south. It was like that in Heredon in the fall. Weak fronts of cloud passed overhead in bursts, with storms that rarely lasted more than an hour or three.

Binnesman brought the mounts down to the stream. The horses all quenched their thirst, then stopped drinking at Binnesman's command. Afterward, some grazed in the short grass at the edge of the stream; most just slept on their feet.

Yet Raj Ahten's great mount stood by the water, restless, matching Binnesman's mood. After a few moments, Binnesman said, "I must leave you now, but I will meet you at Longmot. Ride fast, and there is little on this earth that you need fear."

"I am not worried," Gaborn answered. Binnesman's uncertain look suggested that he disagreed, that he felt Gaborn should be concerned. Yet Gaborn had spoken courageously only to ease the wizard's mind.

Binnesman mounted the big warhorse that had belonged to Raj Ahten. "Try to get some rest. You can only let the animals sleep for an hour or two. By midnight, Raj Ahten will be free to come after you again – though I shall lay a spell to protect you."

Whispering some words, Binnesman pulled a sprig of some herb from the pocket of his robe. He rode forward, dropped it on Gaborn's lap. Parsley.

He said, "Keep it. It will absorb your scent, hide it from Raj Ahten and his soldiers. And before you leave here, Gaborn, pluck a single hair from your head and tie it in seven knots. Should Raj Ahten chase you then, he'll find himself wandering in circles."

"Thank you," Iome and Gaborn said. Binnesman turned his great steed and galloped off in the dark, heading south.

Iome felt tired, dreadfully tired. She glanced around for a soft spot of ground to lay her head on. Gaborn reached out, took her shoulder, guided her toward him, so she could rest her head in his lap. It was a surprising gesture. Intimate.

She lay there, closed her eyes, and listened to him eat a plum. His stomach made surprising noises, and she couldn't quite feel comfortable.

Gaborn reached down, gently stroked her chin, her hair. She'd have thought his touch would feel . . . reassuring, right. But it didn't.

Instead it made her nervous. Partly, she feared rejection. Though he'd said he loved her, she did not believe he could love her deeply.

She was too ugly. Of all who are ugly on the earth, she thought, I am among the worst. A frightened corner of her mind whispered to her, And you deserve to be ugly.

It was the endowment, of course. Iome could never remember having felt this way before. So devoid of worth. Raj Ahten's rune of power pulled at her.

Yet when Gaborn looked at her or touched her, it seemed that some part of the spell was broken for a moment. She felt worthy. She felt that he, alone of all men, might actually love her. And she feared to lose him. It was a terrible fear. For it seemed so reasonable.

Another thing made her uneasy. She'd never been alone with a man. Now she was alone with Gaborn. She'd always had Chemoise by her side, and a Days watching her. But now here she sat with a prince, and her father slept, and it made her feel profoundly uncomfortable. Aroused.

It was not Gaborn's touch, she knew, that made her feel this way. It was the draw of his magic. She could feel the creative desires in her stirring, like an animal burrowing into her skull. She'd felt this when she was near Binnesman, but never so powerfully. Besides, Binnesman was an older man, and none too pleasing to look at.

Gaborn was different, someone who dared say he loved her.

She wanted to sleep. She had no endowments of brawn or metabolism, only a single endowment of stamina she'd gotten shortly after birth. So though she had fair endurance, she needed rest almost as much as any other person.

But now she had Gaborn's electrifying touch to contend with.

This is innocent, she told herself as he stroked her cheek. Merely the touch of a friend.

Yet she craved his touch so, wanted him to move his hand down farther, along her throat. She dared not admit even to herself that she wanted him to touch her deeper.

She took hold of Gaborn's hand, so that he'd stop stroking her chin.

He responded by taking her hand, kissing it softly, letting it rest between his lips. Gently, so gently it took her breath away.

Iome opened her eyes to mere slits, looked up. The darkness had fallen so completely, it was as if the two of them lay hidden beneath a blanket. There are trees between us and the house, Iome thought. The woman there can't see us, doesn't know who we are.

The thought made her heart pound fiercely. Certainly, Gaborn must have felt her heart pound, must have seen how she fought to keep from drawing a ragged breath.

He placed his hand beside her face, began stroking her cheek again. Iome's back arched slightly at his touch.

You can't want me, she thought. You can't want me. My face is a horror. The veins in my hand stand out like blue worms. "I wish I were still beautiful," she whispered breathlessly.

Gaborn smiled. "You are."

He leaned down and kissed her, full on the lips. His moist kiss smelled of plums. The touch of his lips made her dizzy; he took the back of her hand, pulled her up and kissed her fervently.

Iome grabbed him round the shoulders, scooted up until she sat in his lap, and felt him trembling softly with desire. In that moment, she knew he believed it: he believed she was beautiful despite the fact that Raj Ahten had taken her glamour, felt she was beautiful though her father's kingdom lay in ruins, felt she was beautiful and wanted her as much as she wanted him.

Gaborn held some strange power over her. She wished he would kiss her roughly. He nuzzled her cheek and chin. Iome raised her neck for him, so he might kiss the hollow of her neck. He did.

Wanton. I feel wanton, Iome realized. All her life, she'd been watched, had been handled so that she would remain proper and free of desire.

Now, for the first time, she found herself alone with a man, a man whom she suddenly realized she loved fiercely.

She's always kept such a tight rein on her emotions, she'd never have believed she could have felt so wanton. It's only his magic, she told herself, that makes me feel so.

Gaborn's lips strayed over the hollow of her throat, up to her ear.

She took his right hand in her own, brought it toward her breast. But he pulled away and would not touch it.

"Please!" she whispered. "Please. Don't be a gentleman now. Make me feel beautiful!"

Gaborn pulled his lips away from her ear, stared hard into her face.

If what he saw in the dim light displeased or repelled him, he gave no sign of it.

"I – uh," Gaborn said weakly. "I'm afraid I can be nothing but a gentleman." He tried to smile reassuringly. "Too many years of practice."

He pulled away a bit, but not entirely.

Unaccountably, Iome found her eyes full of tears. He must think me brazen. He must think me wicked, a voice inside her whispered. He sees me truly now, a craven animal. She felt sickened by her own lust. "I . . . I'm sorry!" Iome said. "I've never done anything like that!"

"I know," Gaborn said.

"Truly – never!" Iome said.

"Truly, I know."

"You must think me a fool or a whore!" Or ugly.

Gaborn laughed easily. "Hardly. I'm . . . flattered that you could feel that way about me. I'm flattered you could want me."

"I've never been alone with a man," Iome said. "I've always had my maid with me, and a Days."

"And I've never been alone with a woman," Gaborn said. "You and I have always been watched. I've often wondered if the Days watch us only so that we will be good. No one would want to have their secret deeds recorded for all the world to see. I know some lords who are generous and decent, I believe, only because they would not want the world to know their hearts.

"But how good are we, Iome, if we are only good in public?"

Gaborn hugged her, pulled her back against his chest, but did not kiss her. Instead, it seemed an invitation to rest again, to try to sleep. But Iome could not rest now. She tried to relax.

She wondered if he meant it. Was he trying to be good, or did he secretly find her repulsive? Perhaps even in his own heart, he dared not admit the truth.

"Iome Sylvarresta," Gaborn said, his voice distant,

highly formal. "I have ridden far from my home in Mystarria to ask you a question. You told me two days ago that your answer would be no. But I wonder if you would reconsider?"

Iome's heart pounded, and she thought furiously. She had nothing to offer him. Raj Ahten was still within the borders of her country, had taken her beauty, destroyed the heart of her army. Though Gaborn claimed to love her, she feared that if Raj Ahten lived, Gaborn would never see her natural face again, but would instead be forced to gaze upon this ugly mask for as long as she lived.

She had nothing to give him, except her own devotion. How could that hold him? As a princess of the Runelords, she'd never have imagined herself in this position, where she would love a man and be loved, though she had nothing but herself to offer.

"Do not ask me that," Iome said, lips trembling, heart racing. "I . . . cannot consider my own desires in this matter. But, if I were your wife, I'd try to live in such a way that you would never rue the bargain. I'd never kiss another the way I just kissed you now."

Gaborn held her, comfortably, easily, so her back was cupped against his chest. "You are my lost half, you know," Gaborn whispered.

Iome leaned back against him, luxuriating at his touch, while his sweet breath tickled her neck. She'd never believed in the old tales which said that each person was made of but half a soul, doomed to constantly seek its companion. She felt it now, felt truth in his words.

Playfully, Gaborn whispered into her ear. "And if you will someday have me as your husband, I'll try to live in such a way that you will never think me too much a gentleman." He wrapped his arms around her shoulders, hugged her tightly and let her lean her head back against his chest. The inside of his left wrist rested on her breast, and though she felt aroused by his touch, she no longer felt wanton or embarrassed.

This is how it should be, she thought – him owning me, me owning him. This is how we would become one.

She felt tired, dreamy. She tried to imagine what it would be like in Mystarria, in the King's Palace. She dared to dream. She'd heard tales of it, the white boats on the great gray river, floating through the canals in the city. The green hills, and smell of sea salt. The fog rolling in each dawn. The cries of gulls and endless crashing of waves.

Almost she could imagine the King's Palace, a great bed with silk sheets, the violet-colored curtain flying through the open windows, and herself naked beside Gaborn.

"Tell me of Mystarria," Iome whispered. "'In Mystarria lagoons lay like obsidian, among the roots of the cypress trees . . .'" she quoted an old song. "Is it like that?"

Gaborn sang the tune, and though he had no lute, his voice was lovely:

> "In Mystarria lagoons lay like obsidian,
> among the roots of the cypress trees.
> And pools are so black they reflect no sun,
> as they silently buoy the water lilies."

Those lagoons were said to be the homes of water wizards and their daughters, the nymphs. Iome said, "Your father's wizards, I've never met them."

"They are weak wizards. Most of them have not even grown their gills. The most powerful water wizards live out in the deep ocean, not near land."

"But they influence your people, all the same. It's a stable country."

"Oh yes," Gaborn said, "we in Mystarria are always seeking equanimity. Very stable. Some might say boring."

"Don't speak ill of it," Iome said. "Your father is tied to the water. I can tell. He has a way of . . . counteracting instabilities. Did he bring one of his wizards? I'd like to meet one."

Iome imagined that he would, that if he'd brought soldiers to parade about and display his power, he might have brought one of the water wizards. She hoped such a wizard might help fight Raj Ahten at Longmot.

"First of all, they aren't 'his' wizards, any more than Binnesman could be *your* wizard–"

"But did he bring one in his retinue?"

"Almost," Gaborn said, and she could tell he wanted the wizards' help, too. Water wizards, unlike Earth Wardens, could be counted on to meddle in the affairs of mankind on a regular basis. "But it's a long journey, and there isn't much water on the plains of Fleeds. . . ."

Gaborn began to talk to her then about his life in Mystarria, the great campus of the House of Understanding with its many Rooms spread out all over the city of Aneuve. Some Rooms were great halls, where thousands came to hear lectures and participate in discussions. Others were cozy, more like the common room in a fine inn, where scholars sat beside roaring fires in winter, like the hearthmasters of old, and taught lessons while sipping hot rum. . . .

Iome woke with a start as Gaborn shifted his weight beneath her, shook her shoulder gently.

"Come, my love," he whispered. "We must go. It's been nearly two hours."

Rain drifted from the cloudy skies. Iome looked around. The tree above them provided surprisingly good shelter, but Iome marveled that no rain had spattered her or wakened her earlier. She wondered how she'd slept at all, but recognized now that Gaborn had used the power of his Voice to lull her to sleep, speaking softer and softer, in a singsong cadence.

Her father sat beside her, wide awake, reaching out to grasp at some imaginary thing. He chuckled softly.

Catching butterflies.

Iome's face, hands, body all felt numb. Her mind was

waking, but not her limbs. Gaborn helped her rise, unsteadily. She wondered at how to best care for her father. Raj Ahten has turned me into an old woman, filled with worries, and my father into a child, Iome thought.

Fiercely, she suddenly wished that her father could stay this way, could hold on to the innocence and wonder that he had now. He'd always been a good man, but a worried one. In a way, Raj Ahten had given her father a freedom he'd never known.

"The horses have rested," Gaborn said. "The roads are getting muddy, but we should make good time."

Iome nodded, recalled how she had kissed Gaborn a few hours ago, and suddenly her mind was awake, swimming once again, and all that had happened yesterday now seemed a dream.

Gaborn stood before her a moment, then grabbed her roughly, briefly kissed her lips, convincing her she recalled everything from this evening only too well.

She felt weak and weary, but they rode through the night, let the horses run. Binnesman had left them a spare mount from Raj Ahten's men, so they stopped to change horses each hour, letting each beast take a turn at rest.

They blew through villages like the wind, and as they rode, Iome had the most vivid memory of a dream she'd dreamt as she lay in Gaborn's arms:

She'd dreamed she stood on the aerie tower, north of the Dedicates' Keep in her father's castle, where the graaks would land when skyriders sometimes came in summer, bearing messages from the South.

In her dream, Raj Ahten's armies moved through the Dunnwood, shaking the trees, flameweavers clothed only in robes of living fire. She could glimpse the armies only in flashes – nomen with black hides creeping in the shadows under the trees, knights in saffron and crimson surcoats riding armored chargers through the wood. And Raj Ahten stood, so proud and beautiful at the edge of the trees, gazing at her.

She'd been terrified in her dream, had watched her people, the peasants of Heredon, racing to the safety of the castle. The hills to the north, east, and west were full of them – peasants in brown tunics and thick boots, hunched and running for cover. Hefty women with babes in tow, men pushing wheelbarrows full of turnips. Boys driving calves with sticks. An old woman with sheaves of wheat tied to her back. Young lovers with dreams of immortality in their eyes.

All of them raced, seeking cover.

But Iome knew the castle could not protect her people. Its walls would never hold back Raj Ahten.

So she pursed her lips and blew with all her might, blew to the west, then to the east, then to the south. Her breath came out smelling of lavender, and it purpled the air. Every person it touched, everyone she breathed upon in all the kingdom, turned to white thistledown, white thistledown that bobbed and swirled in every small eddy of wind, then suddenly caught in a great gust and went floating high and away over the oaks and birches and alders of the Dunnwood.

Last of all, Iome breathed on herself and upon Gaborn, who stood beside her, so they too turned to thistledown and went flying high over the Dunnwood, gazing down at the autumn leaves, all golden and flame and earthy brown.

She watched as Raj Ahten's armies burst from under the trees with a shout, soldiers waving battle-axes and spears toward her castle. No one stood to oppose them.

Desolation. Raj Ahten might have hoped to win something, but all he would inherit would be desolation.

As her horse carried Iome south through the night, she felt as if she flew, leaving the world behind. Until just after midnight, when a sudden dizziness swept over her, and she looked up to see her father, too, weaving in his saddle. Grief struck her as she recognized what was happening.

At Castle Sylvarresta, someone – Borenson, she suspected – had begun to slaughter her Dedicates.

THIRTY-TWO: A HIGH PRICE
FOR HOSPITALITY

The army of Raj Ahten came to Hayworth after midnight, as King Orden had said it would.

The innkeeper Stevedore Hark woke in his cot beside his wife to the sound of hoofbeats on the far side of the river. It was an odd trick of sound that let one hear them so clearly here on the promontory above the water. The stone cliffs on the hillside above the road caught all sounds, sent them echoing down over the flood.

Stevedore Hark had taught himself years ago to wake at the sound of such hoofbeats, for more often than not, if a man was riding abroad at night, it meant Hark would have to find the traveler a bed.

His inn was small, with but two rooms, so often his guests were obliged to sleep four or five on a straw mat. A stranger coming in the middle of the night meant that Hark might have guests to waken and placate, as he stuffed a new customer in their bed – all kinds of such worries.

So when he heard hoofbeats, Stevedore Hark lay abed trying to count the number of riders. A thousand, two? his sleepy mind wondered. Which bed shall I put them in?

Then he recalled that the bridge was out, and that he'd promised King Orden to send these men south to Boar's Ford.

He jumped up, still in his bedclothes, and struggled quickly to pull on some socks, for it grew cold here at night, so near the mountains. Then he rushed from his inn, looked out over the river. He'd left a lantern posted under the eaves of his roof, just for this moment, but he did not need his own light.

The soldiers stood there, across the river. Knights in full armor, the four lead men carrying guttering torches to light their road. Torchlight reflected off brass shields, and off water. The sight of the warriors frightened him – the white wings engraved on the helms of the Invincibles, the crimson wolves on their surcoats. Mastiffs and giants and darker things could be seen, too.

"Hail, friends, what do you want?" Hark called. "The bridge is out. You cannot pass. The closest place is upstream, at the Boar's Ford. Twenty miles! Follow the trail."

He nodded encouragingly, pointing the way. A little-used trail let upriver to the ford. The night air smelled heavy-laden of rain, and the wind swirled about Hark's head, carrying the scent of pine. The dark waters of the river lapped softly at their banks.

The soldiers studied him quietly. Tired, it seemed. Or perhaps they did not speak his tongue. Stevedore Hark knew a few words of Muyyatinish.

"*Chota! Chota!*" he shouted, pointing toward the ford.

Among the horsemen, a shadowy figure suddenly pushed its way forward. A small dark man with glittering eyes, and no hair. He gazed across the river toward Hark and smiled broadly, as if sharing a private joke.

He shrugged off his robe and stood naked. For one brief moment, his eyes seemed to glow; then a blue flame licked the side of his face, rising into the night.

"The darkness of deception – I can see it in you!" the small man cried.

He raised a fist, and the blue flame shot along his arm, came skipping across the surface of the river like a stone, and bounced toward Stevedore Hark.

Hark shouted in terror as the thing touched the side of

his inn. The ancient timbers screamed as if in pain, then burst into flames. The oil in the lamp posted under the eaves exploded all along the wall.

The small blue light then went racing back across the river, to rest in the small man's eyes.

Stevedore Hark shouted and rushed into his inn to fetch his wife and guests before the whole building burst into a conflagration.

By the time he'd dragged his wife and guests from their beds, the roof of the inn was afire, orange flames writhing up in great sheets.

Stevedore Hark raced from the inn, gasping from smoke, and looked out across the river. The dark man stood watching, smiling broadly.

He waved toward Hark with a little flourish, then turned and headed along the road – downstream, toward Power's Bridge, some thirty miles to the east. It would take Raj Ahten's army far out of their way, but the Wolf Lord's soldiers would circumvent Orden's ambush.

Stevedore Hark found his heart pounding. It was a long way for a fat old innkeeper to ride to get to Longmot, and there were no force horses in town. He couldn't warn Orden that his ambush would fail. He'd never make it riding through the woods at night.

Silently, he wished Orden well.

THIRTY-THREE:
TREACHERY

King Mendellas Draken Orden toured the defenses of Longmot in the failing light, considering how best to defend the rock. It was an odd castle, with outer walls exceptionally tall, carved of granite from the hill Longmot squatted upon. The fortress had no secondary or tertiary walls, as one found in a larger castle, such as at Sylvarresta. It had no fine merchants' quarter, held only two defensible manors for minor barons, along with the keeps for the Duke, his soldiers, and his Dedicates.

But the walls were solid, protected by earth runes of bonding.

The tallest building in the keep was the graaks' aerie – a merely functional building on a rock pinnacle that could nest up to six of the large reptiles. One reached the aerie by means of narrow stone stairs that zigzagged along the east wall of the pinnacle. The aerie was not meant to be defended. It had no merlons archers could hide behind, no landings on the stairs where swordsmen had room to swing. It held only a wide landing field atop the pinnacle for graaks, then six circular openings in nests above the field.

The dukes of Longmot had not raised graaks here in generations. A hundred and twenty years past, several harsh winters came, and here in the north the graaks had frozen from cold. During those same winters the frowth giants had traveled north over the snow. But when the winters warmed and the wild graaks flew up again from the south, the kings of Heredon hadn't tamed them, as their forefathers had. When they sent messages, they trusted riders on force horses.

It seemed a shame to Orden. A rich tradition had been lost. In some small way, the nation became poorer for it.

The aeries were badly kept. Stone watering troughs lay empty. Gnawed bones lay about, leftovers from past feedings.

Over the years, Orden had sent messages north by graak, and some graaks had stopped here. No one had ever cleaned the dung from the floors; now lime liberally covered the stone. The stairs leading to the aerie were age-worn. Vines of morning glory climbed from cracks in the rock, their blue flower petals open now to the evening sun.

But Orden found that one could see well from the landing field on the aerie – even down to the roofs of the Dedicates' Keep and Duke's Keep. So he secreted six archers with steel bows there, ordering them to hide and watch, shooting only if Raj Ahten's forces made it through the gates. He added a single swordsman to guard the steps.

In the semidarkness, he waited for his body servant to light a lantern; then by its light he toured the Dedicates' Keep. From the outside, it looked to be an austere, grim keep – a round tower that could hold a thousand Dedicates. For windows, it had a handful of small slits in the stone. Orden imagined few Dedicates ever stood in the full sunlight once they gave endowments. To become a Dedicate for the Duke, one virtually had to consign one's self to a prison.

But the interior of the Dedicates' Keep was surprisingly plush. The walls were painted white, with images of blue roses or daisies stenciled along the small window-sills. Each level in the tower had its own common room, with beds arranged around the outer walls, and a fine hearth in the center. Such rooms were devised so that at night a pair of caretakers might watch over a hundred or more Dedicates at once. The rooms each had chessboards, comfortable chairs to sit in, fresh rushes mingled with lavender on the floors.

King Orden worried for his son. He still had no word of Gaborn's whereabouts. Had the boy been killed? Did he sit in Sylvarresta's keep, a Dedicate to Raj Ahten? Perhaps he rested beside a warm fire, weak as a kitten, playing chess. One could only hope. One had to hope. But Orden's hope was waning.

The Duke's Keep now cloistered less than a hundred Dedicates, all in a single room. Orden calculated that it should have held at least five hundred Dedicates to serve the fortress defenders. But over four hundred Dedicates had died in the fight to win back the castle.

The battle for freedom claimed that many victims.

Fortifications for the tower concentrated at its lowest level. With great thoroughness, Orden inspected these defenses, for he hoped to fight Raj Ahten here, where he might have some advantage.

A portcullis opened to a guardroom where a dozen pikemen might keep watch. The gears to the portcullis were kept some eighty feet back, in a separate room. A pair of guards could be houses in the gear room.

Off from the gear room lay an armory and the Duke's treasury. The armory was well stocked with arrows and ballista bolts – more than Orden would have imagined. The arrows were bound into bundles of a hundred. A quick guess told Orden that at least two hundred thousand arrows lay there, most newly fletched with gray goose feathers – as if the Duke had been vigorously preparing for the end of the world.

The Duke's armor and that of his horse were gone, taken by one of Raj Ahten's Invincibles, no doubt. Still, Raj Ahten's men had left a princely long sword – fine Heredon spring steel, honed to a razor's edge.

Orden studied its hilt. The name of Stroehorn was branded into it, an artificer of exceptional skill some fifty years past – a veritable Maker.

The Indhopalese, who'd never worn anything but leather mail in battle till fifty years ago, didn't value Northern armor or swords. In the desert, heavy ring mail or plate was too hot to fight in. So men there had worn lacquered leather armor, and instead of the heavy blades of the North fought with curved scimitars. The curved blades maximized the cutting edge of the sword, so that a single strike could slice through a man's body. Against lightly armored opponents, curved scimitars proved to be elegant, graceful weapons. But when a scimitar's edge met ring mail, the blade quickly dulled or bent.

For fighting a man in ring, one needed a thick Northern blade, with its straight edge and hard steel. These could pierce armor with a lunge, or could chop through small rings.

Seeing this fine sword abandoned here in the armory gave Orden hope. Raj Ahten marshaled a great number of troops. He might terrify, but he fought in an unfamiliar clime, with inferior Southern steel. How would his desert troops fare come winter?

Eight hundred years ago, the kings of Indhopal had sent gifts of spice, ointments, and silk, along with pet peacocks and tigers, to Orden's ancestors, in hopes of opening trade. In return, Orden's forefathers sent back a gift of horses, gold, fine furs, and wool, along with Northern spices.

The kings of Indhopal spurned the gifts. The furs and wool seemed overburdensome in warm lands, the spices unsatisfactory. The horses – which they thought of inferior quality – were fit only for use as draft animals.

But they loved the gold, enough to send the caravans.

So Orden had to wonder how the Indhopalese would acclimate. Perhaps they'd not learn the value of wool or fur until half of them froze. Perhaps they'd spurn mounts bred for Northern mountains, just as they spurned Northern steel.

Last of all, Orden inspected the treasury. The Duke had stocked it with a surprising amount of gold blanks, used for striking coins. King Orden studied the stamps – which bore Sylvarresta's image on the front and the Seven Stones on the back.

It seemed odd that the Duke should be striking coins. A balancing scale sat on the floor, and Orden took a golden coin from his pocket, placed it on one pan of the scale, then placed the Duke's blank on the other pan of the scale.

The blank was light. Whether it had been shaved too small, or whether it was light because the gold had been mixed with zinc or tin, King Orden could not tell.

But it was clear that the Duke of Longmot had been a counterfeiter before he'd turned traitor. "Scurvy-infested dog!" Orden muttered.

"Milord?" one of his captains asked.

"Go cut down the carcass of the Duke of Longmot. Cut through the intestines that keep him hanging from the keep, then fling the corpse into the moat."

"Milord?" the captain asked. It seemed a singularly disrespectful way to treat the dead.

"Do it!" Orden said. "The man doesn't deserve another night of royal hospitality."

"Yes, milord," the captain answered, rushing off.

After touring the Dedicates' Keep, Orden decided not to tour the others in the castle. The manors for the Duke and his lords seemed paltry. Orden saw no sense in guarding them.

Besides, it would be better to concentrate his men on the outer walls. Longmot was so narrow that an archer on the east wall could shoot the hundred yards to the west wall, which meant that if enemy soldiers managed to breach one wall, numerous defenders could still fire on them.

Fifteen hundred men, maybe sixteen hundred. That was all King Orden had at the moment. He'd sent messengers to Groverman and Dreis, hoped for reinforcements. Perhaps Borenson would return with most of his army intact.

But they would have to get here soon. Reinforcements that did not arrive before dawn would not get in.

King Orden had finished inspecting the Dedicates' Keep when Captain Cedrick Tempest, the Duchess's aide-de-camp, came to meet him, followed by a Days, a plump woman of middle age. Captain Tempest was a stout man, with thick curly brown hair cropped close. He carried his helm in hand, a sign of respect, but did not bow on meeting King Orden. For a flicker of a second, Orden felt slighted, then realized this man was acting lord of the castle. As such, by right, he did not need to bow.

Instead, Tempest reached out to shake hands at the wrist, as an equal. "Your Highness, we are happy to receive you, and offer you and your men such comforts as we can. But I fear there may be a battle soon. Raj Ahten has an army advancing from the south."

"I know," Orden said. "We'd like to fight beside you. I've sent to Groverman and Dreis, begging reinforcements, but I suspect they'll hesitate to honor a request from a foreign king."

"The Duchess also sent for reinforcements," Tempest said. "We should soon see what it gains us."

"Thank you," Orden said, watching the man's eyes.

This was the worst news. If no help had come yet, it meant Dreis and Groverman, on hearing of the invasion, had chosen to fortify their own positions rather than send aid. One could hardly blame them.

After a moment Orden asked, "May we speak privately?"

Tempest nodded discreetly; together they walked into the Duke's Keep, climbed a flight of stairs. Orden's men waited outside. Only Orden's and his son's Days followed him into the room, with the matronly Days who followed Tempest at their heels.

In the great room, blood still smeared the floors from a fierce battle. Wood chairs lay in splinters; a gore-covered axe lay on the floor, along with a pair of long daggers.

The Duchess's battle had come down to knife work in here.

A pair of red hounds looked up curiously as Orden entered, thumped their tails in greeting. They'd been sleeping before the cold fireplace.

King Orden got a torch, lit it, placed it under the kindling in the fireplace. Then he took a seat by the fire, ten feet from Tempest's own chair.

Tempest looked to be in his early fifties, though it was impossible to tell. A man with endowments of metabolism would age fast. But Mendellas could often guess a warrior's age by looking in his eyes. Even with endowments of metabolism, some men maintained a look of innocence, a look of inexperience. A man's eyes stayed young – like his teeth and his mind and his heart – though his skin might become spotted and wrinkled.

But Tempest's brown eyes looked full of pain, battle, and fatigue. Orden could tell nothing by gazing into them. Tempest's eyes looked a thousand years old.

The King decided to lead to his subject tactfully. "I'm curious to know what happened here. Raj Ahten obviously garrisoned soldiers here – good force soldiers. How is it that the Duchess defeated them?"

Captain Tempest said, "I – must base my report on hearsay. I myself was forced to give an endowment, and so was housed in the Dedicates' Keep when the revolt took place."

"You say Raj Ahten 'forced' you to give an endowment?"

A strange look came over Captain Tempest, one of revulsion mingled with worship. "You must understand, I gave myself willingly. When Raj Ahten asked for my endowment, his words seemed to be daggers that pierced me. When I looked at his face, it seemed more beautiful than a rose or the sun rising over a mountain lake. He seemed beauty itself; everything else I've ever thought noble or beautiful seemed a dim forgery.

"But after I gave the endowment, after his men dragged my body down to the Dedicates' Keep, I felt as if I awoke from a dream. I realized what I'd lost, how I'd been used."

"I see," King Orden said, wondering idly how many endowments of glamour and Voice Raj Ahten had, that he could gain such power over men. "So, what happened here? How did the Duchess manage this coup?"

"I am not certain, for I was weak as a pup in the Dedicates' Keep, and could not stay awake. I heard only snatches of reports.

"As I understand, the Duke apparently got paid to let Raj Ahten pass through the Dunnwood. But he dared not let his wife know of the payment, and so kept it hidden in his private apartments, not daring to show it.

"After his death, when the Duchess realized that he must have been paid for his treason, she searched his private apartments and found some hundred forcibles."

"I see," King Orden said. "So she used the forcibles to furnish some assassins?"

"Yes," Tempest answered. "When Raj Ahten entered the city, not all our guard was in the keep. Four young soldiers were in the wilds, investigating a report that a woodcutter in Greenton had spotted a reaver–"

"Have you had many reports of reavers hereabouts?" Orden asked, for this was important news.

"No, but last spring we tracked a trio in the Dunnwood."

Orden thought. "How large were the tracks?"

"Twenty to thirty inches long."

"Four-toed, or three-toed tracks?"

"Two were three-toed. The largest was four-toed."

Orden licked his lips, found his mouth suddenly dry. "You knew what that meant, didn't you?"

"Yes, Your Highness," Captain Tempest said. "We had a mating triad."

"And you did not kill them? You didn't find them?"

"Sylvarresta knew of it. He sent hunters after them."

No doubt Sylvarresta would have told Orden of the reavers. We might have hunted more than boars this year, Orden thought. Yet this news bothered him, for he'd heard other troubling reports of reavers moving through the mountains along the borders of Mystarria – war bands of nines and eighty-ones. Not since his great-grand-father's day had he heard so many reports. And on his journey north, while traveling through Fleeds, Queen Herin the Red mentioned problems with reavers killing her horses. But Orden had not expected the depredations to extend so far north.

"So," Orden said, "you had soldiers on patrol when Raj Ahten took possession. . . ."

"Right. They stayed out of the city, until Raj Ahten left. They saw the Duke hanged, so they sent a note to the Duchess, asking her orders. She sent her facilitator into town with the forcibles, and the soldiers took endowments from whomever would grant them, until they had enough to attack."

"So they performed an escalade?" Orden asked.

"Hardly. They entered casually enough, after Raj Ahten left. They played at being candlemakers and weavers, bringing in goods to display to the Duchess. But they hid daggers beneath the candles, and chain mail beneath folds of cloth.

"Raj Ahten had only two hundred loyal soldiers here, and those young lads – well, they handled the situation."

"Where are they now?"

"Dead," Captain Tempest said, "all dead. They broke into the Dedicates' Keep and killed half a dozen vectors. That's when the rest of us joined the fray. It wasn't easy."

Orden nodded thoughtfully.

"Captain Tempest, I suppose you know why my men and I have come?" It was a delicate subject, but Orden needed to know if Tempest had captured the forcibles, moved them from Bredsfor Manor. Though he'd sent a man to find them, Orden didn't want to be kept waiting, especially if he waited only for bad news.

The captain stared up at him, incurious. "You heard we were under attack?"

"Yes," Orden said, "but that is not why I came. All of Heredon is under attack, and I'd have preferred to bend my efforts to freeing Castle Sylvarresta. I came for the treasure."

"Treasure?" Captain Tempest asked. His eyes widened. Almost, Orden believed the man knew nothing about it. But he didn't quite trust that response. Tempest was working too hard to control his emotions, to show no reaction.

"You know what I'm talking about?"

"What treasure?" Tempest asked, with no hint of deception in his eyes.

Had the Duchess kept the existence of the forcibles hidden even from her own aide-de-camp? Orden had expected so, had hoped so.

"You knew the Duke was a forger, didn't you?" Orden asked. He let just a little of the power of his Voice slide into the question, in a tone that would elicit guilt.

"No!" Tempest protested, but his eyes flickered, and his pupils contracted.

The dishonest, miserable cur, Orden thought. The man lies to me now. When I asked about treasure, he thought I spoke of the gold blanks in the treasury. Truly, he had not heard of Raj Ahten's forcibles. That interested Orden.

So the Duchess had not trusted Tempest. Which meant Orden could not trust him, either.

King Orden forged ahead with a half-truth. "King Sylvarresta sent a message, saying the Duchess had over-

thrown Raj Ahten's forces here, and she had hidden or
buried a treasure here in the castle. Have you seen signs of
digging hereabout? Has anyone recovered the treasure?"

Tempest shook his head, eyes wide. Orden felt sure
Tempest's men would be digging within the hour.

"Who did the Duchess trust most? Who would she
have had bury the treasure?"

"The chamberlain," Tempest said quickly.

"Where is he now?"

"Gone! He left the castle shortly after the uprising. He
– I haven't seen him since!" From the tone of Tempest's
voice, he seemed worried that the chamberlain had made
off with the treasure.

"What did he look like?"

"A thin fellow, like a willow switch, with blond hair and
no beard."

The very messenger Orden had found slain. So the
Duchess had sent the message to Sylvarresta using the
man who'd hidden the forcibles, then told no one else
about them. Captain Tempest might be a fine soldier,
capable of defending the castle, but he was obviously dishonest. Knowledge of the treasure would have tempted
him, and the Duchess had not wanted to let her king get
betrayed again.

This news filled King Orden with sadness, a heaviness.
Such a waste, that a fine king like Sylvarresta could suffer
from such disloyalty. A whole nation compromised.

If a man like Sylvarresta was so little loved by his lords,
Orden wondered, how can I trust my own vassals?

"Thank you, Captain Tempest," King Orden said, in a
tone of dismissal.

"Oh, and Captain," Orden added, as Tempest hesitated
in the doorway, strapping on his helm, "relief will come
from Groverman and Dreis, as soon as they make
arrangements. I sent a message asking for aid, and I told
them of the treasure. The armies of the North will gather
here!"

Tempest nodded, breathed a sigh of relief, departed. The matronly Days followed him out.

Orden sat for a long hour in the darkness, in a chair carved of dark walnut, finely wrought – too finely. The chiseled emblems of feasting men on its backboard dug into his flesh. One could not rest in these chairs.

So Orden stoked the fire in the fireplace, threw in a couple of shattered chairs for fuel, then lay on a bearskin, petting the Duke's hunting hounds, who batted the floor with their tails, reveling in his affection.

His Days had been standing in a corner, forgotten. Now the man came and sat in one of the uncomfortable chairs. Gaborn's Days remained in the corner.

Orden had not lain on the floor with a dog since he was a boy. He remembered the first time he'd come to Longmot with his father. He'd been nine years old, on his way home from his first big hunt, a hundred men in his retinue. It was in the fall, at Hostenfest, of course, where he'd met a young prince with long amber hair and narrow shoulders.

Sylvarresta. Prince Mendellas Orden's first friend. His only true friend. Orden had had soldiers who schooled him in the arts of war, and he'd made alliances with fawning sons of minor nobles who might have liked him but who always seemed too much aware how their inherited stations forever separated them from a prince.

Even the other princes had treated Orden with too much deference – always aware that his realm was richer and larger than any other.

It was only Sylvarresta whom Mendellas could trust. Sylvarresta would tell him if some hat made him look stupid instead of stylish, or would laugh at him when he missed a quintain with his lance. Only Sylvarresta ever dared tell him when he was wrong.

King Orden found himself breathing hard. I am wrong now, he realized. Wrong to have sent Borenson to kill Raj Ahten's Dedicates.

What if Borenson kills Sylvarresta? Could I ever forgive myself? Or will I have to bear the scar of it for the
rest of my life, as a badge of this war?

Other kings had borne such scars, Orden told himself.
Others had been forced to slaughter friends. As a child,
Orden had begrudged the men who killed his own grandfather. Now he knew that too often, guilt became the
price of leadership.

"Days?" King Orden whispered to the man who sat at
his back.

"Yes, Your Lordship," his Days answered.

"What news have you of my son?" He had known the
man all his life, had never considered the Days a friend or
confidant. Yet he also admired the man as a scholar.

"To speak of it would violate my most sacred oaths,
milord. We do not meddle in the affairs of state," the
Days whispered.

Of course he knew the answer. The Days were never to
hinder or help. If the King were drowning two feet from
shore, the Days could not grasp his hand. "Yet you could
tell me," Mendellas asked. "You know the answer."

"Yes," the Days whispered.

"Do you not care for me? Are my feelings unimportant?" Orden asked. "Is my fate unimportant, or
the fates of my people? You could help me beat Raj
Ahten."

The Days did not speak for a long moment, and Orden
knew he was considering. Other Days had broken their
vows, spoken to kings of great secrets. Of that, Orden felt
sure. So why not this man? Why not now?

From the corner Gaborn's Days said, "If he answers
your questions, he would violate a most sacred vow. His
twin would know." A threat sounded in those words.
Watchers watching the watchers. "Surely you understand, Your Lordship."

Orden didn't really understand, could hardly comprehend such callousness. Often he'd thought the Days and

their religion quaint and strange. Now he thought them hard of heart.

Yet he sought to understand them. Gaborn's Days remained here, instead of going to Gaborn. Why? Had his son died, so the Days could not follow? Or did the Days merely wait for Gaborn to come back here? Or . . . had his son disappeared even from the sight of the Days?

Orden pondered. His Days had called him "milord," a title he'd never used before. The man wanted to speak, found it hard to remain a bystander. He restrained himself, but wanted to ameliorate any hard feelings in the nasty affair.

Might a Days not counsel him, even if his own life became forfeit in the process? Orden had studied history, knew that in some wars a Days had revealed secrets. But Orden had never learned the fate of such Days.

The chronicles told the deeds of kings and nations. If a Days had ever gone rogue, had become a counselor, the fate of such a Days was never mentioned.

Instead, the chronicles flowed as if a single dispassionate watcher had observed the king, studying his affairs. For a long hour, Orden wondered at this.

When Captain Stroecker returned from Bredsfor Manor, he found Orden lying before a dying fire, petting the hounds.

"Excuse me, milord," Captain Stroecker said from the doorway.

King Orden turned over, sat up. "What did you find?"

Stroecker smiled grimly. He held a bunch of fresh turnips in his right hand; his eyes shone with what might have been anger. "These, milord. Enough turnips to feed an army."

Intense terror struck King Orden as he realized the forcibles were gone, had been taken.

Stroecker smiled wickedly. "And these," he said, reaching behind his back. He pulled a small bundle of forcibles from his belt.

King Orden's heart leapt in relief, so much so that he forgave the captain's jest immediately.

He jumped up, grabbed the forcibles, inspected them. The runes in each looked perfect, without dents or abrasions in the blood metal, all in the Kantish style. Orden had no facilitator here to perform the rites, but he needed none. With the wits of twenty men, and gifts of voice from fifteen, Orden could chant the spells as well as the best of them.

A weapon. He had his weapon.

"Captain Stroecker," Orden said softly. "You and I and Borenson are the only three men who know where this treasure lies. We must keep it that way. I can't risk that the enemy find these. I can't risk that you get captured."

"Agreed," Stroecker said in such a tone that Orden realized the man thought Orden wanted him to make the ultimate sacrifice. In a moment, Stroecker would disembowel himself.

"Therefore, Captain," Orden said, "I want you to tell the men that we need guards to take a great treasure back to Mystarria. Choose three men – young family men with children – to accompany you as guards. Choose them carefully, for you may be saving their lives. Then take the men and four fast horses, and fill your saddlebags with stones, and leave here, taking every effort not to get caught."

"Milord?" Stroecker asked.

"You heard me right. A war will be fought here near dawn. I expect Raj Ahten to throw his full force against us. He anticipates the help of an army of a hundred thousand, and I – do not know what allies I might have. If this castle falls, if we all die, it will be your duty to return here and retrieve the treasure, then deliver it to Mystarria."

"Milord, have you considered retreat?" Stroecker asked. One of the dogs stood, pushed its muzzle against the King's thigh. The dog seemed hungry, but would settle for affection.

"I think about it every moment," Orden said, "but my son is missing in the wilderness, and, so far, I have no word of him. Until I hear word, I must consider that Raj Ahten holds him prisoner and has taken an endowment – or that he is dead." Orden took a deep breath. For all his life, he'd sought to protect and nurture his son. His wife had borne him four children. Only Gaborn had survived. Yet his worry for Gaborn was but one of a multitude of pains. His voice faltered as he admitted, "And I have sent my most fearsome warrior to kill my best friend. If my fears prove true, Captain Stroecker – if the worst comes to pass – I won't want to live through this battle. I'm going to raise my sword against Raj Ahten. I'm going to attack him, personally. Either he will die or I will die. At dawn we will be forming a serpent ring."

King Orden held up the forcibles.

Captain Stroecker's face paled. Creating a serpent ring was a dangerous gambit. With these forcibles, Orden could take an endowment of metabolism from a man, who would then take an endowment from another, who would take an endowment from another, so that each man became one in a long line of vectors. In the parlance of facilitators, this line of men was called a "serpent," for the man at the head of the chain became very powerful, deadly as a poisoned serpent, and should he be destroyed, should the serpent be beheaded, the next man in line would arise, hardly diminished in power from the first.

But if a man took too many endowments of metabolism, it was sure death. He might become a great warrior for a few hours or days, but he would burn himself out like a shooting star. Desperate men had done it in the past, at times. But it would be hard to find twenty able fighters willing to form a serpent, to throw away their lives.

So Orden offered them some hope. In this case, last of all, the King would give his own endowment of metabolism to the last man in the serpent, so that every man in the serpent became vectored to another. Thus, with twenty forcibles, twenty men could all share their metabolism, forming a pool from which any one warrior could draw. Since Orden had the most endowments and the greatest skill in battle, that task of fighting Raj Ahten would fall to him. He would volunteer to act as "the serpent's head," and so long as the other men in the ring remained inert, Orden would be able to draw upon their surplus metabolism. Many of Orden's soldiers had metabolism from one or two men. So, as the serpent's head, Orden would be able to move with the speed of thirty or forty men.

And the hope that Orden offered his men was this: that if he himself managed to survive the battle, the serpent ring would remain unbroken, and each man in the ring would thus be able to continue his life with some degree of normalcy.

But still it was a dangerous gambit. If any other man in the ring were forced into battle, that man might well draw away metabolism that Orden needed at a critical moment, sabotaging Orden's chances in the fight. Even worse, if a member of the serpent ring were slain, Orden himself might find himself a mere vector to another man, might suddenly fall in battle, unable to move.

No, if anyone died in this battle, it would best be the serpent's head – Orden himself. For if Orden died, if the ring broke, then the burden of metabolism would fall to the person who had granted Orden his endowment.

This next man in line would become the new serpent's head. And he could continue to fight Raj Ahten's forces, spreading destruction.

Should he be defeated, the serpent would form another head, and another. On and on, the members of the circle would fight and sacrifice their lives.

Yet even if Orden won his battle with Raj Ahten, even if the serpent ring remained intact today, Orden was still calling upon all his men to make a terrible sacrifice. For at some time, hopefully on some distant morning, the circle *would* break. A man from the circle would die in some battle, or would fall prey to illness. When that happened, all other vectors would fall into the deep slumber of those who'd given metabolism, with the exception of one man, the new serpent's head, doomed to age and die in a matter of months.

Regardless of how the battle played out today, every man in the ring would be called upon to sacrifice some portion of his life.

Knowing all this, Orden felt gratified when his captain bent low at the waist, smiling, and said, "I would be pleased to serve with you, if you would have me in this ring."

"Thank you," Orden said, "but you'll have to miss this opportunity to waste your life. Duty calls you elsewhere."

Captain Stroecker turned smartly and left the great hall. Orden followed him out to gather his troops for battle.

Already his captains had set men on the walls. Artillerymen had pushed the catapults out from beneath the protective enclosures in the towers above the gates, had begun firing, testing their ranges in the dark. It was a poor time for such tests, but Orden did not know if they'd ever get a chance to test the catapults in daylight.

At that moment, a horn sounded in the western hills, off toward the road from Castle Dreis.

Orden smiled grimly. So, he thought, the Earl comes at last, hoping for a share of the treasure.

THIRTY-FOUR: THE RUNNING MAN

In Kuhram it is said that a running man with a knife can kill two thousand men in a single night. Borenson worked faster than that, but then he was a force soldier, and he carried a knife in each hand.

He did not think about what he did, did not watch the quivering of his victims or listen to the thrash of limbs or gurgle of blood. For most of the night, he hurried through the job, in a mindless horror.

Three hours after he entered the Dedicates' Keep, he finished the deed. It was inevitable that some of the Dedicates woke and fought him. It was inevitable that some women he killed were beautiful, and some men were young and should have had full lives before them. It was inevitable that no matter how hard he tried to block the memories of their faces from his mind, moments would come that he knew he'd never forget: an old blind woman clutching at his surcoat, begging him to wait; the smile of an old drinking companion from the hunts, Captain Derrow, who bid him a final goodbye with a knowing wink.

Halfway through the deed, Borenson recognized that this was wanted of him, that Raj Ahten had left the Dedicates unguarded, knowing they would be killed. He had no compassion for these people, valued them not at all.

Let friend dispose of friend, brother raise knife against

brother. Let the nations of the North be torn asunder. That was what Raj Ahten wanted, and Borenson knew that even as he slaughtered these innocents, he had become a tool in Raj Ahten's hand.

Leaving the Dedicates totally unguarded was not necessary. Four or five good men could have provided some protection. Could the monster take such delight in this?

Borenson felt his mind tear open like a seeping wound, every moment became a pain. Yet it was his duty to obey his lord without question. His duty to kill these people, and even as he revolted at the slaughter, he found himself wondering time and time again, Have I killed them all? Have I fulfilled my duty? Is this all, or has Raj Ahten hidden some of them?

For if he could not reach the vectors that Raj Ahten had taken, Borenson needed to kill every Dedicate who fed Raj Ahten's power.

Thus, when he finally unlocked the portcullis to the keep, blood covered Borenson from helm to boot.

He walked into Market Street, dropped his knives to the pavement, then stood for a long time, letting rain wash over his face, letting it wash over his hands. The coldness of it felt good, but during the past hours the blood had clotted in gobbets. A little rainwater would not wash it free.

A fey mood took Borenson. He no longer wanted to be a soldier for Orden, or for any king. His helm felt too constraining, as if it would crush his head, it hurt so. He threw it to the ground so that it rattled and clattered as it rolled along the paving stones, down the street.

Then he walked out of Castle Sylvarresta.

No one stopped him. Only a pitiful guard had been set.

When he reached the city gate, the young fellow took one look at his blood-covered face and fell back, crying, raising his index finger and the thumb as a ward against ghosts.

Borenson shouted a cry that rang from the walls, then

ran out into the rain, across the burned fields toward the distant copse where he'd hidden his horse.

In the darkness and rain, a half-dozen nomen with long spears made the mistake of jumping him. They came rushing toward him in a little vale, leaping from the blackened earth like wild things, running forward with their longspears.

Their red eyes nearly glowed in the darkness, and their thick manes made them look somehow wolfish. They snarled and loped forward on short legs, sometimes putting a knuckle to the ground.

For a moment, Borenson considered letting them kill him.

But instantly an image of Myrrima formed in his mind: her silk dress the color of clouds, the mother-of-pearl combs in her dark hair. He recalled the smell of her, the sound of her laugh when he'd kissed her roughly outside her little cottage.

He needed her now, and saw the nomen as mere extensions of Raj Ahten. They were his agents. He'd brought them here to kill, and though Borenson's men had driven and scattered the nomen through the hills, they would become a scourge on this land for months.

It did not matter to Raj Ahten. The nomen would do his will as they sought to feed on human flesh. They would do all the killing he'd asked, but they'd take the weak first – the children from cradles, the women at their wash.

The first noman rushed Borenson, hurled its spear at close range, so that the stone blade shattered against Borenson's mail.

Quick as a snake, Borenson drew the battle-axe at his hip, began swinging.

He was a force warrior to be reckoned with. He cleaved the arm off one noman, spun and hit another full in the chest.

He began smiling as he did so, considered each move

in the battle. It was not enough to kill the nomen; he wanted to do it well, to turn the battle into a dance, a work of art. When one noman rushed him, Borenson slammed his left mailed fist into its fangs, then grabbed its tongue and pulled.

Another tried to run. Borenson gauged its pace, watched the bobbing of its upright ears, and threw his axe with all his might. It was not enough to split the beast's skull; he wanted to do it perfectly, to hit the target just so, so the bone would make that splitting noise and part like a melon.

The noman went down. Only two stood, rushing him as a pair, spears ready. Without his endowments of sight, Borenson would never have been able to evade those black spears.

As the nomen lunged, Borenson simply slapped the speartips away, so the jabs went wide, then he grabbed a spear, launched himself forward and spun, impaling both beasts through the naval.

Both nomen stood in shock, pinned together.

When he finished, Borenson stepped back and observed the nomen. They knew they would die. They couldn't heal from such a wound. The creature in back fainted, dragging its companion to its knees.

Borenson walked on, considering the way he'd fought, the precise movements. His deed had been as close to poetry or dance as he could achieve.

He began laughing, chuckling a throaty rumble, for this was the way war should have been – men fighting for their lives. A good man struggling to protect home and family.

The skirmish itself somehow seemed more a balm for his troubles than the rain. Borenson retrieved his axe and hurried to his horse, running through the downpour.

I will not wash these hands, he told himself. I will not wash my face, until I stand before my prince and my king again, so they can see what they have done.

Thus Borenson took horse and began racing through

the darkness. Four miles down the road east of town, he found a dead knight of Orden, took the man's lance.

His mount could not equal Gaborn's fine hunter. But the road was clear, if somewhat muddy, and on a night like this, with rain to cool them, Borenson's horse could run forever.

So Borenson raced over the hills until the rain stopped and the clouds dispelled and stars shone bright and clean.

He'd planned to head to Longmot. But when the road branched both east and south, the fey mood was still on him, and he suddenly turned east, toward Bannisferre.

Dawn found him riding over green fields that held no sign of war, through vineyards twenty miles north of Bannisferre where young women stooped to fill baskets of ripe grapes.

He stopped in such a field and ate, found the grapes dripping with water from the night's rain; they tasted as succulent as the first grape must have tasted to the first man who ate it.

The river here was wide, a broad silver ribbon gleaming beneath the green fields. Borenson had thought last night to leave himself bloody, but now he did not want Myrrima to see him this way, to ever guess what he'd done.

He went down to the river and swam, naked, unmindful of the pig farmers who herded animals past on the road.

When the sun dried him, Borenson put on his armor, but threw his bloodied surcoat into the water, letting the river carry away the image of the green knight on the blue field.

Surely, he thought, Raj Ahten's troops have reached Longmot. I'm so far behind them, I'm too late to join the battle. In truth, he no longer cared. No matter what the outcome at Longmot, he planned to renounce his lord.

In assassinating innocent Dedicates, men and women who had committed no crime but that of loving a good and decent king, Borenson had done more than any master had a right to ask. So now he'd renounce his vows to Orden, become a Knight Equitable. Of his own free will he'd fight as he deemed best.

Borenson went on to a pear tree beside an abandoned farm, and climbed, taking the fattest pears from the top – some for himself, some for Myrrima and her family.

From the treetop he saw something interesting: over a rise lay deep pools with steep sides beneath a grove of willow trees, pools as blue as the sky. Yellow willow leaves had fallen into water in great drifts, floating over the surface. But also on the pools were roses bobbing, red and white.

A wizard lives there, Borenson realized, dully. A water wizard, and people have thrown roses into the water, seeking its blessings.

He climbed quickly down from the tree, ran over the rise to the still waters, and approached solemnly, hopefully. He had no roses or flowers to sweeten the wizard's water, but he had pears that it might eat.

So he went to the edge of the pool, where the willow roots twisted down a gravel bank, and there he sat on a broad black root. The crisp leaves of the trees above him blew in a small breeze, rustling, and Borenson called for long minutes, "O wizard of the water, lover of the sea, O wizard of the water, hear my plea."

But the surface of the pool remained unperturbed, and he saw nothing in the shining pool but water striders that skated over its flat surface and a few brown newts that floated beneath, watching him from golden eyes.

In despair, he began to wonder if the wizard had died long ago, and people still sweetened the pools in hopes that someday another might come. Or if this was a haunted place, and the local girls threw roses in the water to placate someone who had drowned.

After long minutes of sitting on the willow root, and calling with no results, Borenson closed his eyes, just smelling the sweet water, thinking of home, of Mystarria, of the peaceful healing waters of the pools of Derra where madmen might go to bathe, and have their troubling thoughts and memories washed from them.

As he lay thinking of that place, he realized that a cold root was brushing his ankle, and thought to move his foot, when suddenly the root wrapped around his foot, squeezed tenderly.

He looked down. At the water's edge, just beneath the waves, was a girl of ten, skin as pale blue and flawless as ceramics, hair of silver. She stared up at him from beneath the water with eyes as wide and green as all the seas, and her eyes were unblinking, completely motionless. Only the crimson gill slits at her throat pulsed slightly as she breathed.

She withdrew her hand from his foot, instead reached underwater and grasped at the willow roots.

An undine. Too young to be of great power.

"I brought you a pear, sweet one, if you will have it," Borenson said.

The undine did not answer, only stared up at him and through him with soulless eyes.

I killed girls your age last night, Borenson wanted to tell her, wanted to cry.

I know, her eyes said.

I will never have peace, Borenson whispered wordlessly.

I could give you peace, the undine's eyes said.

But Borenson knew she lied, that she'd pull him down into the waves, give him love, and that while she loved him, he could survive beneath the pools. But in time she'd forget about him, and he would drown. She could give him only a brief few days of pleasure before death.

I wish that, like you, I could be one with the water, and know peace, Borenson thought. He remembered the great seas of home, the white breakers rolling over a green as deep as aged copper.

The undine's eyes went wide at his memories of the sea, and a smile formed on her lips, as if grateful for the vision.

Then he took one of his golden pears, reached down to the water, gave it to the undine.

She reached for it with a wet, slender blue hand, with long nails of silver, but then grasped his wrist and pulled herself up enough so that she could kiss his lips.

The move was unexpected, quick as a fish jumping for a fly, and Borenson felt her lips brush his for only a moment.

He placed the pear in her hand and left, and for a long hour afterward he could not quite remember what pain had brought him to that pool, with roses of red and white bobbing among the golden leaves.

He managed to find his mount, then rode at leisure, letting the horse graze as it walked; soon enough he reached the little meadow outside Bannisferre where Myrrima's cottage lay among the wild daisies.

Blue smoke curled up from a cooking fire, and one of Myrrima's ugly sisters – Inette, he recalled her name – stood feeding grain to the scrawny black chickens at the front door.

As he rode up, Inette looked up at him, a smile on her ruined face. The smile quickly faded. "You all right?"

"No," Borenson said. "Where's Myrrima?"

"A messenger came through town," Inette said. "Troops are gathering. Lord Orden is at Longmot. She – Myrrima left last night. Many of the boys from town have gone to fight."

All the ease of heart he'd felt for the past hour now drained from him. "To Longmot!" Borenson shouted. "Why?"

"She wants to be with you!" Inette answered.

"This – this won't be a picnic or a day at the fair!" Borenson shouted.

"She knows," Inette whispered. "But you're betrothed.

If you live through it, she wants to live with you. And if you don't . . ."

Borenson hung his head, thinking furiously. Sixty miles. Nearly sixty miles to Longmot. She could not have walked there in a night, even in a pair of nights.

"Did she travel afoot?"

Inette shook her head numbly. "Some boys from town went. In a wagon. . . ."

Too late. Too late. Borenson spun his horse, raced to catch her.

THIRTY-FIVE: BETWEEN STRONG ARMS

Gaborn heard Iome cry out as he rode toward Longmot. Her cry was so startling that at first he feared that she'd been shot with an arrow. For hours now they had been traveling, stopping every few minutes to switch horses, and Iome had not made a single complaint. He slowed and turned in his saddle to look back.

He saw at first that King Sylvarresta sat in his saddle, head nodding. The King clutched the pommel of his saddle with both hands. He wept softly, breathing in gasps. Tears streamed from his eyes.

Iome, too, was hunched. "Gaborn, stop. We've got to stop!" she cried, taking the reins of her father's horse.

"What's wrong?" Gaborn asked.

"Gaagh," King Sylvarresta said.

"Our Dedicates are dying," Iome said. He . . . I don't know if my father has the strength to go on."

Gaborn felt an overwhelming sadness envelop him. "Borenson. I should have guessed." He felt dazed. "I am so sorry, Iome."

He rode up next to the King, took the King's jaw in his hand. "Can you ride? Can you stay on the horse? You have to ride! Hold on!"

Gaborn pushed the King's hands firmly to the pommel of the saddle. "Hold! Like this!"

King Sylvarresta looked into Gaborn's face, clutched tightly.

"Do you have the strength to ride?" Gaborn asked Iome.

She nodded grimly in the dark.

Gaborn let the horses canter lightly, kept a close watch on his charges. King Sylvarresta was gazing up at the stars as they rode, or watching the lights of a town as they passed.

Five miles later, they rounded a corner, and King Sylvarresta went flying off his horse. He landed on his hip, slid in the mud and grass at the side of the road. Then just lay, sobbing.

Gaborn went and whispered soft words to him, helped King Sylvarresta back on his horse; then Gaborn rode behind, cradling King Sylvarresta between strong arms.

THIRTY-SIX: THE SERPENT RING

Through the long night, King Orden waited impatiently for sign of his son. It was hard, this waiting, the hardest thing he'd ever done.

Orden's men carried all two hundred thousand arrows from the armory to their perches along the castle's battlements. On the wall-walk beneath the west tower, they set a great bonfire, a message of distress, in an effort to call aid from any who might see its light or smoke. Near that fire, his men set great cauldrons of oil to boil, so that the putrid scent of them filled the castle.

Orden commanded five men to go north three miles, to set a similar fire on the peak of Tor Loman, so everyone within twenty leagues might see it. Duke Groverman had not heeded Orden's petitions. Perhaps sight of the battle pyres would shame him into it.

Just before dawn, two thousand knights arrived from Groverman, explaining their delay. Groverman had heard of the fall of Longmot, and thought to retake it, but had sent word to Sylvarresta. Apparently his messengers never made it to the King alive. After a day of waiting, he'd sent a hundred scouts on force horses to Sylvarresta and learned that the castle had fallen.

Orden wondered which road the scouts had taken, thought it odd that his men hadn't spotted them. Which meant that the knights had taken trails through the forest.

Then the scouts had returned with the ill news of

Sylvarresta's defeat, and Groverman waited still for re-inforcements from distant castles.

The knights Groverman sent were good men, solid warriors. But despite his best efforts, Orden did not feel prepared. He suspected this battle would bring trials he couldn't prepare for.

The Earl of Dreis gave King Orden no comfort. The man was incompetent. He had been in the castle for less than an hour before he tried to assume command. One of his first tasks had been to order the artillerymen to push the catapults back into the shelter of the towers, foiling all the work the artillerymen had done setting the ranges.

Orden found the Earl lounging in the Duke's old quarters, letting a body servant massage his feet while he sipped warm tea.

"Why have you ordered the artillery stored?" Orden asked.

The Duke seemed to struggle to decide whether to affect an imperious tone or become defensive. "A strata-gem, my dear fellow, a stratagem. You see, I realized that if we keep them hidden until the heat of battle, we can whisk them out suddenly, and the sight of them will dis-may Raj Ahten's forces!"

King Orden did not know whether to laugh or weep at such stupidity. "Raj Ahten has seen many catapults," he said simply. "He has taken a hundred castles by force. His men will not be dismayed at the sight of these."

"Yes, but—"

"Indeed, Raj Ahten has seen these catapults, for he came here not a fortnight ago. He *knows* they are here."

"Ah, of course! Point well taken!" the Earl said, shoving his masseuse away as he struggled from his chair.

"We need to put the catapults back, then let our men test the settings once again, and their ranges."

"Well . . . all right," the Earl grumbled, as if consider-ing some other plan.

"Also," King Orden said, "you've ordered your men to

defend the castle gates, and my men to man the walls. Is there some reason for this?"

"Ah, of course!" Dreis said. "You must realize that my men are fighting for home and country. It is a matter of honor for them to defend the gates."

"Your Lordship," Orden tried to explain patiently, "you must understand that in the thick of this battle, all our men will be fighting for their lives. My men fight for their homes and their countries, as well as yours do. And I've brought my best force warriors, men with ten and twenty endowments each. They will fight better than commoners."

Dreis rebutted, "Ah, your men may fight with swords and hammers, but our men will fight with heart, and with a will!"

"Your Lordship—"

Dreis raised a hand to stop him. "You forget your place, Orden," he said fiercely. "This is Heredon, not Mystarria. I command this castle, until some greater lord takes my place."

"Assuredly," Orden said with a slight bow, though a bending of his back had never come harder. "I did not mean to seem presumptuous. I merely hoped that some of my better guards might fight beside yours. It would show Raj Ahten . . . our unity."

"Ah, unity!" Dreis said, taking the bait. "A noble concept. A fine ideal. Yes, yes, I'll order it immediately."

"Thank you, Your Lordship," King Orden said with another bow, then turned to leave. He felt he had just got a handle on how Dreis' counselors must have had to work him.

"Ah," Dreis said, "do not leave. If I might ask: I understand you are recruiting men for a serpent ring?"

"Yes, Your Lordship," Orden answered, dreading the next question.

"I will be in it, of course. I should be the head."

"And expose yourself to such risk?" Orden asked. "'Tis

a brave and noble sentiment, but surely we will need you to direct the battle." He could not help but put a little whine in his tone, as Dreis' counselors must have done.

"Ah, well, I believe in teaching men correct principles, then letting them direct themselves," Dreis countered. "I will not need to direct the battle."

"Then, please, milord, at least consider the safety of your lands after the battle. Heredon has suffered losses enough. Should you get killed, it would be a terrible burden. Let us not have you serve as the serpent's head, but only somewhere near the head, in a place of honor."

"Oh, no, I insist—"

"Have you ever killed a man, milord?" Orden asked.

"Why, yes, yes I have. I hanged a robber not three years back."

Of course the Earl had not hanged the man, Orden knew. He'd have let the captain of his guard perform the feat.

"Then you know how difficult it is," Orden said, "to sleep at nights afterward. You know how it is to look another man in the eye as you seize his very existence. Guilt. Guilt is the price we pay for leading our people.

"I killed my first man when I was twelve," Orden added. "Some mad farmer who tried to cudgel me. I've killed some twenty men in battle since.

"My wife . . . grew distant over the affair, cold and unresponsive. You would think they'd love you better for it, but the women imagine that a little blood on your hands makes you grow more callous and cruel. It stains the soul, so. Of course, I am no Raj Ahten. . . . Who knows how many men he has personally killed. Two thousand, ten?"

"Yes, the guilt . . ." the Earl mused. "Nasty business, that."

Orden could see the slow wheels of the Earl's mind begin to creep, as he wakened the man's fears. Orden was not at all concerned with guilt. He needed only to remind this fool how many men had died at Raj Ahten's hands. "It does stain a man's soul." Now the Earl had a way out of battle. He could flee it in the name of righteousness, rather than fear.

"Very well, they are your forcibles," the Earl said. "Perhaps you should be the serpent's head."

"Thank you, milord," King Orden said. "I will try to serve with honor."

"But I will be next in line."

"Actually," King Orden said, "I hoped to reserve that spot for another, the captain of my guard. A very formidable fighter."

"Ah, aha!" Dreis said. Now that he was considering it, he did not seem at all certain he wanted to fight this battle. "Well, perhaps that would be best."

"But we can reserve the spot after him for you, milord," Orden said. He knew that he did not have to reserve a place of honor for this nincompoop. Once Dreis gave his endowment to the captain, Orden would be free to put the Duke anywhere in the serpent. Someplace close to the middle would be nice.

"Very well, then," Dreis said in a tone of dismissal. Then he made it clear to his servants that he was not to be disturbed before dawn, for he would need his sleep.

So King Orden went back to the battlements and fretted and watched for signs of aid, signs of trouble. He put his far-seers, men with many endowments of sight, on the highest pinnacle of the graak's aerie, then sent scouts out to keep watch on the hills and roads both east and west for sign of Raj Ahten's occupying army.

But they caught no wind of it.

Instead, hour by hour, all through the night, men came riding in to give aid – three hundred more farmers from the area around Castle Dreis, all with longbows; they had no armor, but wore woolen vests that might keep out a poorly sent shaft. Borenson's regiment came racing in near dawn – eighty warriors who bore many wounds from yesterday's battle.

They told how Raj Ahten's troops never showed for the ambush at Boar's Ford. Said they'd heard no word of Gaborn.

From the west came a regiment of two hundred lancers on force horses from out of Castle Jonnick, men who'd ridden when they heard Castle Sylvarresta had fallen, then had neared it only to hear that a battle would be fought at Longmot.

From the east, Knights Equitable trickled in from freeholds, a dozen here, fifty there. Mostly, they were older men who had nothing to lose, or young men still naive enough to believe that war was glorious. All of these added to the fifteen hundred knights and archers that the Earl of Dreis had brought in, and the two thousand from Groverman.

Then there were the farmers' sons and the merchants out of towns that bordered the woods. Boys with grim faces, some armed with nothing but an axe or a scythe. Young men from the cities who were dressed in finery, who bore light swords that had too much gold in the baskets of their ornate hilts.

Orden did not relish the arrival of such commoners, hardly counted them as defenders. Yet he dared not deny them the right to fight. This was their land to protect, not his.

As each little troop rode between the twin fires burning along the road before the castle gates, men on the walls would shout in triumph and blow their horns, calling "Hail Sir Freeman!" or "Hail Brave Barrows!"

Orden knew men's devices, could name most knights by glancing at their shields. But one rider who came in near dawn both mystified and excited him.

Almost last to ride in that night was a huge fellow, big as a bear, riding a black, swaybacked donkey as fast as it would trot. He bore no coat of arms, only a round shield with a huge spike in it, and he wore a squat helm from which a single cow's horn curled. He had no mail but a thick coat of pig's hide, and his only weapon, beside the dagger on his belt, was a huge axe with an iron handle some six feet long, which rested across the pommel of his saddle. With him rode fifty men as grungy as himself – men with longbows and axes. Outlaws.

The knights on Longmot's walls hesitated to name this warrior and his band, though they could not help but recognize him. Shostag the Axeman. For twenty years, Shostag and his outlaws had been a scourge to every Runelord along the Solace Mountains.

It was said that he was a Wolf Lord of the old school, that he'd taken many endowments from dogs. As Shostag neared the castle gates, King Orden watched the downs behind him, saw the fleeting gray shadows of wolves race nervously through the starlight along the hedgerows, leaping stone fences.

Shostag stopped a hundred yards from the gates with his henchmen, among the last ruins of the burned city. Even in the near-total darkness, the firelight showed his face to be dirty and unshaven, his every manner vile. He spat in the ashes, looked up to the battlements, stared Orden in the eye.

Shostag asked, "I saw your signal fires. I hear you want a Runelord dead. Are we invited to this festivity?"

Orden was not certain he trusted the man. The Axeman might well turn on him, wreaking havoc within the castle's walls at the battle's climax.

"I'd be honored to fight beside men of your . . . reputed skill," King Orden answered. He could not afford to turn down any aid, even from the Axeman.

Shostag cleared his throat, hawked on the ground. "If me and my boys kill this fellow for you, I'll want a pardon."

Orden nodded.

"I'll want a title and lands, same as any other lord."

Orden considered. He had an estate in the dark forests on the borders of Lonnock. It was a gloomy swamp, infested with bandits and mosquitoes. The estate had laid idle now for three years, waiting for the right man. Shostag would either clear the bandits from the woods, or he'd let them join him.

"I can promise an estate in Mystarria, if King Sylvarresta cannot do better."

"I'll take it," Shostag grunted, waved his men in.

Two hours before dawn, Orden still had seen no sign of Gaborn or Borenson, had heard no word. Another messenger brought news that the Duke of Groverman would offer aid from neighboring castles, but couldn't reach Longmot before dusk.

Of course, Raj Ahten will get here first, Orden realized.

Groverman did right by maintaining his own hold until he was sure it could be defended, regardless of the promise of treasure.

So it seemed that no more aid would come. Though his scouts had not yet warned him of Raj Ahten's approach, Orden expected it within an hour or two.

The very fact that he hadn't yet received word of Gaborn worried King Orden. Hour by hour, his hopes for his son's well-being dwindled, until he felt it vain to hope. Surely Raj Ahten had captured him.

And the Wolf Lord would have either killed him or taken the boy's endowments.

So Orden took his forcibles, lined up his volunteers, and let the facilitator for the Earl of Dreis sing the ancient spells that made the forcibles glow, creating ribbons of light as man after man gave up metabolism.

Last of all, Orden gave his own endowment, completing the serpent ring. It was a desperate act.

With a heavy heart and fewer than six thousand men, Orden closed his gates at dawn and waited for the gathering conflict. He'd left a few scouts outside the walls to bring advance word of any sighting of Raj Ahten's troops, but had no more hopes of reinforcements.

He gave one last speech, calling on the full powers of his Voice to cut across distance, penetrate every stone of the castle. The knights and commoners and felons on the walls all looked up at him expectantly, every man bundled in his armor.

"Men," he said, "you've heard that Raj Ahten took Castle Sylvarresta without benefit of arms. He used nothing but glamour and Voice to disarm Sylvarresta's troops. And you know what happened to the knights in that castle afterward.

"Well, we'll allow none of that here. If Raj Ahten seeks to use his Voice, I'll expect every man within range to fire on him the same as if he were a charging army.

"When he leaves this field, either he'll be dead, or we'll be dead. If any of you young men succumb to the power of his Voice, my knights will throw you over the castle walls.

"We'll not suffer children to spoil a man's fight.

"May the Powers be with us!"

When he finished speaking, six thousand men raised their arms, chanting "Orden! Orden! Orden!"

King Orden gazed out over the walls. He knew that this warning, given with the full power of his Voice, would have great influence over his men. He only hoped Raj Ahten would not be able to unravel the spell his words had woven.

On the horizon, over the Dunnwood, he felt cool air blowing in. It felt like snow.

But where was Gaborn?

THIRTY-SEVEN: BOYS ON
THE ROAD

Myrrima sat in the bed of a rickety wagon as the team of horses hurried down the road early that morning. The wagon swayed and creaked as it followed its rut. Once they'd moved up from the fields near Bannisferre and crossed into the Dunnwood, the wagon had become especially uncomfortable, for large tree roots that crossed the road underground provided ample bumps.

She was but one of ten passengers from Bannisferre. The others were all young farm boys armed with nothing but their bows and spears and dreams of retribution for the murders committed against their kin during the past week.

Even the wagon did not belong to any one of them, but had only been lent by farmer Fox up the road toward town. These boys had no horses of their own to ride into war.

But they talked like the brave sons of noblemen. Ah, they could talk. "I'll kill me an Invincible, sure as I'm ugly," said one young lad, Hobie Hollowell. He was slender and strong, with wheat-straw hair and blue eyes that shone each time he looked at Myrrima. There was a time not many weeks past when she'd have hoped for a match with him.

"Ah, you can't hit anything with that bow of yours." Wyeth Able chortled. "All your arrows are as crooked as your aim."

"It's not arrows I plan to kill him with." Hobie laughed. "I plan to wait till one is scaling the castle walls, then throw your fat carcass over on him! It would flatten him sure, without any harm to your wide buttocks."

"Hah, as if you could wrestle me over the wall," Wyeth said, pulling off his hat and slapping Hobie. Wyeth was a stout boy, destined to be almost as wide as he was tall, and then the boys were at it, tussling and laughing in the wagon.

Myrrima smiled faintly. She knew their antics were for her, that they all competed for her attention. She'd known most of these young men all her life, yet since she'd received her endowments of glamour, their relationships had shifted dramatically. Boys who had once thought her just another waif now smiled shyly and forgot their manners, if not their own names, in her presence.

It seemed a great shame that her beauty had become a barrier to common relationships. She'd not have wished it.

Wyeth wrestled Hobie to the bottom of the wagon with little effort, then grinned up at Myrrima for approval.

She nodded kindly, smiled.

So the team of horses raced the last few miles to Longmot, over grassy hills where oaks spread their branches wide. She felt very tired after the long ride. The horses that drew the wagon were no force horses, but they were a strong team, used to working together, much like the boys in the wagon.

When they reached Longmot, saw its long, high walls and foreboding towers, Myrrima almost wished she had not come. It hurt to see the blight on the land, the charred ruins of the city before the castle, the burned farmhouses dotting the downs.

The hills and mountains to the north and northwest of Longmot were still part of the Dunnwood, covered in oak and aspen and pine. But the hills south of the castle undulated like huge, gentle waves. Grasslands, orchards, vineyards, and gardens covered these hills.

Fences made of piled stones or hedgerows of sturdy thorns divided the land into squares and rectangles, each of different colors, like the rags in a quilt.

But the land lay empty now. Wherever a farmhouse or a barn or a dovecote had stood, now there squatted only a blackened ruin, like an open sore upon the land. All the gardens and orchards had been harvested. Not a cow or horse or pig or duck could be seen in the fields.

Myrrima understood why the people of Longmot had done it, why the soldiers had burned the town, salted their own wells. They would not give succor to Heredon's enemies. So they had destroyed everything of value near the castle.

This land . . . looked too much like the fertile fields of Bannisferre. That was why Myrrima mourned it. Seeing the houses black, the fields empty, gave her a chill, for it seemed a portent of the future.

When the wagon reached the castle gates, the gates stood closed. The guards nervously watched the fields and hills to the west.

Seeing the men who stood on those walls, Myrrima became even more nervous. If most of the defenders were common boys like those she rode with, how could Orden hope to defend himself against Raj Ahten's Invincibles?

"Who are you? Where do you hail from?" a guard at the gate asked gruffly.

"Bannisferre," Wyeth Able shouted, raising his bow. "We've come to avenge the deaths of our people."

Above the gates, on the castle wall, stepped a man with a broad face, wide-set smoldering eyes. He was dressed in full armor. His fine breastplate was enameled with the image of the green knight, and he wore a cape of shimmering green samite, embroidered with gold.

King Orden.

"Can you gentlemen hit anything with those bows?"

Orden asked. "Raj Ahten's soldiers move quickly."

"I've dropped my share of pigeons," Wyeth answered.

Orden jutted a chin at Wyeth's portly figure. "I'd say you'd dropped more than your share of pigeons. Welcome."

Then his eyes lighted on Myrrima, and there was such admiration in them that his glance took her breath away.

"And what have we here, a swordswoman? A noble?"

Myrrima looked down at her hands folded in her lap, more from shyness than from respect.

"A friend . . . of your son's. I'm betrothed to one of your guard – Borenson. I came to be with him. I'm no swordswoman, but I can cook a good stew, and I can wrap bandages."

"I see," Orden said softly. "Borenson is a worthy man. I had not known he was betrothed."

"Only recently," Myrrima said.

"Milady, he has not reached the castle yet. I'd hoped he would have come by now, but I left him with an assignment at Castle Sylvarresta. I hope to see him shortly, but to tell the truth, Raj Ahten's troops will also reach us soon. I cannot say who will arrive first."

"Oh," Myrrima said, thinking furiously. Borenson did not expect her, and she had not imagined he would be occupied elsewhere. She had no illusions about how well this battle might go. But in the short time she'd had with Borenson, she'd grown to see how important devotion was to him. It did not occur to her to think that he might have failed his mission, that Borenson might already have died.

She wanted to be with him now, in his hour of need. For in her family, devotion to loved ones was all that had ever allowed them to survive.

Myrrima licked her lips. "I'll wait for him here, if you don't mind."

THIRTY-EIGHT:
THE HOPE

Just after dawn, Iome and Gaborn rode to the tiny village of Hobtown, twenty-two miles northwest of Longmot. Hobtown was a collection of fifteen cottages with a smithy. But on Saturdays, like today, a few farmers brought merchandise to town to exchange.

So when Gaborn, Iome, and King Sylvarresta rode into the village, a couple of people had already wakened. The horses needed food and rest.

Iome spotted a young woman, perhaps twelve, digging onions and leeks from her garden. Clover grew high next to the garden fence. Iome called out, "Excuse me, good lady. May we let our horses graze on your clover?"

The girl said, "Of course, you're welcome to . . . it." She'd turned at the last moment, and froze at the sight of Iome.

"Thank you," Gaborn said. "We'd gladly pay, if we may purchase something for breakfast."

The girl turned, stared at Gaborn, pointedly avoiding the sight of Iome, trying to regain her composure. "I have bread from last night, and some meat," she offered, delighted at the prospect of money. In a farming community such as this, barter was the norm, and a man could live from one season to the next without feeling the weight of a worn coin in his palm.

"Please, that would be good," Gaborn said.

The girl dropped her onion basket, ran into the house.

Iome tried to calm herself, to forget how the girl's slight had affected her, made her feel worthless and wretched.

Iome's father had finally drifted to sleep in the saddle last night after sobbing for hours. Iome felt glad of it. Gaborn now held the King in the saddle in front of him, the way one might hold a child.

The mounts began to tear at the clover, ravenous.

Iome looked about. The cottages here were of stone and wood, with thatch roofs. Flowers and herbs grew from pots beneath windows made of real glass. The few people in Hobtown seemed wealthy enough.

The town occupied a lovely meadow between the oak-covered hills. Bachelor's buttons and pinks grew wild in the grass, alongside daisies. Fat cattle grazed just outside town. Rich. This town is rich in contentment, Iome thought.

If Gaborn's fears proved true, Raj Ahten's army of re-inforcements would march through this town today. Something of great value would be lost, a sort of innocence.

Iome looked up, caught Gaborn smiling at her. Yet only a moment before, the girl had put her hand to her mouth in horror at the sight of Iome.

Iome feared she'd never be beautiful again. But when Gaborn turned his gaze on her, he made her feel that she'd never lost her glamour.

"How do you do that?" Iome said, grateful for his attention.

"Do what?"

"How do you look at me like that and make me feel beautiful?"

"Let me ask you another question," Gaborn said. "In Internook, a woman must have flaxen hair to be beautiful, but in Fleeds she must have red hair and freckles. In Mystarria, our people have long admired women with wide hips and pendulous breasts. But here in Heredon, beautiful women must have small, pert breasts and boyish figures.

"All over Rofehavan, women must be pale to be beautiful. But in Deyazz they must be dark and brown. Also in Deyazz, the women wear heavy golden earrings that pull down the ears. But here, such enlarged ears would seem grotesque.

"So I ask you, who is right? Are all these women really beautiful, or are they all ugly, or are they all the same?"

Iome considered. "Perhaps physical beauty is only an illusion," she said. "And you look beyond the illusion?"

"I do not think beauty is an illusion," Gaborn said. "It's just so common, we often don't see it. It is like these meadows: We as travelers see the flowers, but the townsfolk probably seldom notice how handsome their lands are."

Iome countered, "But what if our beauty is taken from us, and there is nothing left to see?"

Gaborn's horse stood next to hers, and it shifted its feet, so Gaborn's knee suddenly touched Iome's. "Then you should rejoice," Gaborn said. "People can be beautiful on the inside, too. And when they feel most bereft of outer beauty, then they so long to be beautiful that they rearrange their hearts. And beauty springs from them, like these flowers spring from this field.

"When I look inside you," Gaborn said, staring at her, staring into her, "I see your people smiling. You love their smiles, above all. How can I not love what is in your heart?"

"Where did you get such strange ideas?" Iome said, wondering at his last words, wondering how he had managed to capture her love and hope for her people in so few words.

"From Hearthmaster Ibirmarle, who taught me in the Room of the Heart."

Iome smiled. "I should like to meet him someday, and thank him. But I begin to wonder about you, Gaborn. In the House of Understanding you studied in the Room of the Heart – a strange place for a Runelord to spend his time. Why spend your time among troubadours and philosophers?"

"I studied in many places – the Room of Faces, the Room of Feet."

"To learn the ways of actors and travelers? Why not the Room of Arms, and the Room of Gold?"

Gaborn said, "I received training in arms from my father and from the palace guards, and I found the Room of Gold . . . boring, with all those little merchant princes watching one another with such envy."

Iome smiled at Gaborn, bemused.

Presently the girl issued from her cottage with some scones and meat, and three fresh figs. Gaborn paid her, warned her that Raj Ahten's army might pass this way in a matter of hours, then let the horses walk for a while.

They stopped outside town, beneath a tree, and let the horses drink from a pool beside the highway. Gaborn watched Iome eat in silence. He tried to rouse the King, so he might eat too, but Iome's father remained asleep.

So Gaborn saved some bread, meat and a fig in his pocket. Ahead of them, the mountains rose dark blue and threatening. Iome had never been so far south. She knew of Harm's Gorge, of the deep canyon just beyond the mountains, which divided much of the realm.

She'd always wanted to see it. The road, she'd been told, was very dangerous. For miles it consisted of a narrow track beside a precipice. The duskins had carved that road centuries ago, made the great bridge across Harm's River.

"I still think it odd," Iome said, "that you spent your time schooling in the Room of the Heart. Most lords study little else but arms, or perhaps Voice."

"I suppose," Gaborn said, "if we Runelords only want to win battles and hold our fortresses, we need only study in the Room of Arms.

"But . . . I guess I don't believe in it. We seek ways to use one another all too much. It seems deplorable that the strong should dominate the weak. Why should I study that which I deplore?"

"Because it's necessary," Iome said. "Someone must enforce the laws, protect the people."

"Perhaps," Gaborn said. "But Hearthmaster Ibirmarle always found it deplorable, too. He taught that not only is it wrong for the strong to bully the weak, but that it is just as vile for the wise to rob the stupid, or the patient to take advantage of another's impatience.

"These are all just ways that we harness other men to our plows. Why should I treat men as tools – or worse, as mere obstacles to my enjoyment?" Gaborn fell silent a moment, and his glance strayed northward, to Castle Sylvarresta, where Borenson had slain the Dedicates last night. Iome could see how Gaborn regretted it, how he perhaps even thought it a personal failure that he had been so naive.

He said, "Once, ages ago, an old shepherd, who was the highman of his town, sent word to my grandfather, asking him to buy his wool. The shepherd's town had long had a contract with a certain merchant from Ammendau, who carried their wool to market, but the merchant died unexpectedly. So the highman sent to the King, asking him to purchase the wool for his troops at a bargain price.

"But the highman did not know that rain in the west hills had caused a blight of wool rot on the sheep there. In all likelihood, the highman's wool would fetch triple its price, if the townsmen could get it to market.

"My grandfather, on seeing the situation, could have leapt at the chance to buy the wool cheap. If he'd listened to the merchants who schooled in the Room of Gold, he'd have done so. For they think it a virtue to buy cheap and sell high.

"Instead, Grandfather sent to the hearthmaster at the Room of Feet and arranged for a caravan to transport the wool at a fair price, cheaper than the villagers had paid before.

"He then sent to the highman and told him all that he had done. He begged the highman to sell his wool to the poor at its normal price, so that they would not go cold through the winter."

Iome listened to the tale somewhat in awe, for she'd often thought Orden's line to be hard, cold men. Perhaps it was only Gaborn's father. Perhaps he'd grown cold, after his own father's bad end.

"I see," Iome said. "So your grandfather won the love of the poor."

"And the respect of the highman and his village," Gaborn said. "That is the kind of Runelord I would want to be, one who can win a man's heart and his love. That is my hope. It is harder to storm a heart than to storm a castle. It is harder to hold a man's trust than to hold any land. That is why I studied in the Room of the Heart."

"I see," Iome said. "And I am sorry."

"For what?" Gaborn asked.

"That I ever said I would turn you down, if you asked me to marry you." She smiled at him, and spoke teasingly, but realized it was true. Gaborn was a strange and wondrous young man, and in the past day she had begun to recognize that he was much more than he seemed. She feared that at this rate, she'd fall in love with him so fiercely by the end of another day that she'd never want to separate from him again.

When the horses finished watering, Gaborn cantered them for a while.

The magnificent crevasse at Harm's Gorge opened suddenly – a deep rent where a river rushed, and the trail they took snaked around its edge. According to legend, the duskins had created this place, had broken the pillars that held the Overworld.

They let their animals creep along a narrow trail beside the ledge, and Iome looked at the pillars of gray and white stone that rose up from the canyon, a marvel to see. She wondered if these were the pillars of legend or merely the roots of mountains long since eroded away.

Beside the steep sides of the canyon, huge trees clung, looking like bristles on a horse brush. A mile to the north, Harm's River churned in a waterfall and fell far into the chasm, but Iome could not see where the waters landed, for the canyon was so deep that its heart was lost in darkness, and no sound escaped from its silent depths. Enormous bats wheeled in the canyon, down where the shadows filled the endless chasm.

If a person fell from the road, it was said that you could hear his scream for a month until the sound was lost.

They took the narrow pass slowly, the idiot King Sylvarresta walking along the treacherous edge of the road, often stopping to peer into the mists so far below.

THIRTY-NINE: THE GREEN MAN

King Sylvarresta woke, and moved through a world of dream. The doors of his mind were closed. He did not remember much. No words, no names – not even his own. Yet much in the world had a vague familiarity. The horses, trees.

He woke to see a great light in the sky, the color of gold and roses. He felt certain that he had seen it somewhere before.

They rode slowly on a narrow road, with a gray earth wall to his left, a tremendous precipice to his right. He had no words for names, nor for left and right. Everything carried with it a sense of discovery. Far, far down, he could see only misty grayness. Pine trees stood far below, prickling along the edges of rock.

They reached a narrow bridge carved from a single stone, spanning the gorge. The bridge curved up into the sky, and Sylvarresta looked down into the gorge, and felt as if he hung in the air, just so.

He did not recall ever having been here before, nor having felt thus.

A few dozen soldiers were on the bridge, guardsmen in dark-blue surcoats, wearing the face of the green man on their shields – a knight whose face was surrounded by green leaves. The young man and woman that King Sylvarresta rode with greeted these soldiers joyfully. For a while, the soldiers talked to the young man of their plans for guarding the bridge; then the young man bid the soldiers farewell, leaving them behind.

King Sylvarresta, the young man, and the young woman crossed the bridge, rode high up in the pine woods toward a mountain's summit. Then the horses raced under the trees.

Huge birds, the color of sky, flitted overhead, calling among the trees, and the wind came fresh and cold. Then they reached a mountaintop and rode down from the wooded hills, to a land where fields of crops checkered the downs.

A castle loomed up from the fields, a tall edifice of gray stone. Horns began blowing on its battlements at Sylvarresta's approach, and a dimly remembered pennant flew – the midnight black with the silver boar.

Men stood on the walls of the castle by the hundreds – men with bows and helms with wide brims, men with spears and hammers. Other men wore surcoats with the image of the green man, and they bore bright shields that shone silver like water.

The men all cheered and waved as they saw him, and King Sylvarresta waved back and cheered himself, until the huge drawbridge on the castle opened, and they entered.

The horses walked up a short, steep hill, hooves clanking over cobblestones. Men shouted joyfully at him and clapped, until an odd look came over their faces.

Some pointed at him, faces pale with emotions he did not recognize – horror, shock, dismay. They shouted, "Dedicate! He's a Dedicate!"

Then his horse stopped in front of a gray building, a small keep. King Sylvarresta sat for a moment watching a reddish-brown lizard, as long as Sylvarresta's finger, sun itself on the stones in the rock garden beside the door. He could not recall having ever seen such a thing, and wondered.

Then, in all the commotion, the lizard raced up the side

of the building and over its gray roof. The King knew it was alive and he began shouting and pointing.

The young man behind King Sylvarresta had dismounted, and now he helped Sylvarresta down from his horse.

Together with the young man and the ugly woman, Sylvarresta walked under the eaves of the building, up some stairs. He felt so tired. Walking the stairs hurt his legs, made them stretch uncomfortably. He wanted to rest, but the young man urged him forward, into a room thick with good smells of cooked food, where a warm fire burned.

A pair of dogs thumped their tails as King Sylvarresta approached, so that at first he did not really notice the two dozen men sitting at a table, eating things that smelled good.

Then he looked across the table and gasped. There sat a tall man, dark-haired and beautiful, with wide-set blue eyes and a square jaw beneath his beard.

Sylvarresta knew the man, knew him better than he knew anything else. A green man. In a green tunic, with a shimmering cape of green samite.

A warm sensation filled King Sylvarresta's heart, an overwhelming joy. He recalled the man's name. "Orden!"

At King Sylvarresta's side, the young man shouted, "Father, if you want this poor man dead, at least have the decency to kill him yourself!"

King Orden half rose from the table, stepped hesitantly forward. He glanced back and forth between Sylvarresta and the young man. His eyes looked pained and angry, and his hand went to the hilt of his short sword. He struggled with it, as if he could not draw it, brought it halfway out.

Then in a rage he slammed the sword back into its sheath and staggered forward, threw his arms around Sylvarresta's shoulders, and began to weep.

King Orden sobbed, "My friend, my friend, what have

we done? Forgive me. Forgive me!"

Sylvarresta let King Orden hold him for a long time, wondering what was wrong, until his friend's sobbing lessened.

FORTY: AN ORDER RESCINDED

Gaborn had never seen his father cry. No tears of sadness escaped him when Gaborn's mother and infant brother were murdered. No tears of joy had ever glistened in King Orden's eye when proposing a toast.

Now, as Gaborn's father hugged King Sylvarresta, he wept tears of joy and relief.

King Mendellas Draken Orden cried in great racking sobs. Orden's sorrow was such an embarrassing sight that the two dozen lords and dignitaries who had been breakfasting in the room now all took their leave, so that only Iome, King Sylvarresta, three Days, and Gaborn stood in the room.

For the barest moment, Gaborn glanced across the room, saw his Days and felt uncomfortable. He had been without a Days for nearly half a week, and had found it pleasant.

Now he felt like an ox waiting to be yoked. The small fellow nodded politely, and Gaborn knew he would not be left alone again for a while. Another Days in the room was a matronly woman in her forties, a woman with reddish hair going silver. She'd have been Emmadine Ot Laren's Days when the Duchess still lived. Now she nodded a greeting at Iome, perhaps all the formal introduction the woman would ever give, yet with that introduction she spoke volumes: *I am assigned to you.*

So the Days watched, and recorded.

Gaborn felt grateful that the Days had not had to record how King Orden murdered his best friend in his hour of greatest need. Instead, in some far day when his father died and his chronicles were penned, it would be told how Orden hugged Sylvarresta and sobbed like a child.

How odd, Gaborn thought, that he cries no tears of relief at seeing me.

Sylvarresta let King Orden hug him until he could no longer withstand the power in the King's arms, then tried to pull away. Only then did King Orden grasp Sylvarresta's biceps, feel the lack of muscle there.

"He's lost his own endowments?" Gaborn's father asked.

Iome nodded.

Gaborn added angrily, "They both have. Borenson was at Castle Sylvarresta yesterday. He stayed behind when we left. You sent him to kill them, didn't you?"

Gaborn watched his father's eyes as he considered the accusation. Gaborn had foolishly believed – when Borenson had said that he was under orders to kill Raj Ahten's Dedicates – that he spoke only in general terms. He hadn't imagined that one man alone would be sent to kill those in the Dedicates' Keep at Castle Sylvarresta.

Now his father's expression confirmed it. His father glanced down, but recovered quickly, looking sorrowful instead of guilt-ridden. Gaborn gave his father time to consider the implications. All the Dedicates in Sylvarresta's keep had died. Even if Iome and the King had become vectors for Raj Ahten, now they gave him almost nothing, only their own endowments.

"So," Gaborn's father asked, "did Raj Ahten leave all his Dedicates behind when he fled Castle Sylvarresta?"

"Almost. He took his vectors–" Gaborn answered. His father raised a brow. "But I managed to get Iome and King Sylvarresta out."

King Orden tilted his head, considering. He must have

recognized the struggle Gaborn had gone through. "I – wonder . . ." He cleared his throat. ". . . why Borenson would let these two go. I ordered him to do otherwise."

"I countermanded your order," Gaborn said.

His father's reaction was so swift, Gaborn had no time to react. His father lashed out and slapped Gaborn's face so hard that when spittle and blood flew from his mouth, Gaborn thought it was a tooth.

"How dare you!" King Orden said. "You may disagree with me, and belittle me, and even second-guess me. But how dare you fight me!"

Rage burned in Orden's eyes.

Then his mouth opened in a little O of grief at what he'd done. He turned away and walked to an archery slot, stood with both hands on the stones of the casement, gazing outside.

"Iome and her father were under my protection, bound by oath," Gaborn said hastily, realizing that he'd just broken his promise to Borenson. He'd told Borenson that he'd not let his father know that they'd met. Yet, at the moment, Gaborn felt so betrayed he did not much care if he broke his word. "I'd have fought him for them. I told him that I would take the matter up with you." He hoped these final words might appease his father.

Through a window, Gaborn could hear men cheer. More troops were coming into the castle, gathering for battle.

"Your actions are akin to treason," King Orden muttered, back still turned. "They run against everything I've ever taught you."

"Yet they followed precisely the desires of your own heart," Gaborn said. "You ordered your friends' deaths with your lips, but could not consent to it in your heart."

"How can you think to know my heart?" Orden said distantly.

"I . . . just do," Gaborn said.

King Orden nodded thoughtfully, then turned and

gazed at Gaborn a long moment, at war with himself. He took a deep breath, tried to sound casual. "Then I, too, rescind the order. Thank you, Gaborn, for bringing my friend back. . . ."

Gaborn sighed in relief.

King Sylvarresta had wandered over to the breakfast table. He began eating from plates, pulling off huge chunks of ham with both fists. Gaborn's father whispered, "But I fear he is lost to me still."

"Until Raj Ahten is dead," Gaborn said. "Then you will win back your friend, and I will win my wife."

Gaborn did not want to bear this news now, but he felt it was important, and he wanted his father to hear it from him, rather than discover it later from a stranger. He fully expected another blow. "Father, I told you that I took an oath to protect Iome. I am bound to her, as one Oath-Bound Lord to another."

Gaborn's father looked off toward the hearth. His jaw clenched. He seemed dismayed by the news, but his voice cracked only the tiniest bit as he said, "Ah, I see. It was only a matter of time, I suppose."

"You are not disappointed?" Gaborn asked.

"Disappointed, yes," Orden said, "but not surprised. Though I cannot help but say that you picked the worst possible time to have this attack of conscience."

"But you are not angry?"

His father suppressed a chuckle. "Angry? Hardly. Dismayed, perhaps. Saddened. But how can I be angry? My only friend is an Oath-Bound Lord." He stood a moment in thought, nodding his head. "But still . . . I feel that I've lost you."

"Once we've beaten Raj Ahten, you will see that we've lost nothing," Gaborn said.

"You make it sound easy."

"With forty thousand forcibles, it should be."

"Ah, so Borenson told you about those? Well, we have the forcibles, now we're only forty thousand people shy of the Dedicates necessary to make them worthwhile."

"You mean you haven't begun putting them to use?" Gaborn asked.

"I have them hidden still, in the place where the Duchess hid them," Orden said. "I've used only a handful."

Gaborn gasped, felt his chest constricting. Without Dedicates there was only one way his father could hope to beat Raj Ahten. "A serpent? You've created a serpent? How large?"

"A serpent ring," he answered easily, trying to soothe Gaborn. "Twenty-two men, most with at least two endowments of metabolism. Most of the same men you just saw here, leaving this room."

A moment before, King Orden had said he felt he'd lost his son. It seemed an overreaction to Gaborn's announcement. Now Gaborn saw that in all likelihood his father was right. One way or another, they were lost to each other. In time, the serpent ring would be broken, and only then would Gaborn learn how great a sacrifice his father had made this day.

Yet his father's announcement explained why he did not grow angry when Gaborn told him of his oath. His father was withdrawing, pulling away from Gaborn.

King Orden licked his lips. "I plan to kill Raj Ahten for you, today, myself. A wedding present, let's call it. I'll make his head a wedding present for you, Gaborn. And my friend will have his wits back."

"How? How many troops do you have?" Gaborn asked.

"Six thousand, more or less," Orden answered. He went to the window, looked out, spoke thoughtfully. "We had riders from Groverman this morning. He refused us aid. Instead he's fortifying his own keep. Only a few men have come from him, some Knights Equitable who couldn't support him in his cowardice.

"It's too bad – we'd had high hopes. Groverman is a fine man, a sensible man, really. He's doing what I'd do, fortify my keep."

Gaborn smiled. "Your keep is in Mystarria, twelve hundred miles from here. You would not turn your back on a friend."

King Orden gave Gaborn a sidelong look. "I want you to take Iome and King Sylvarresta, now, and get away from here. Go to Castle Groverman. It should be well defended."

"I think not," Gaborn said. "I'm tired of running."

"And if I order you to do it?" his father asked. "I'm not divided on this matter. My heart and my mind both agree."

"No," Gaborn said more firmly. His father had always tried to protect him. Now he saw that his father would continue to do so, even if it cost his own life. But Gaborn was a Runelord, and though his endowments were few, they were over a broad spectrum. With wit and grace and stamina, he could fight in a battle like this better than any common soldier. Besides, he'd trained a good deal in tactics and swordplay.

As the son of a king, he'd learned to defend himself, though he doubted he'd be much of a match for one of Raj Ahten's Invincibles.

Iome grabbed the sleeve of Gaborn's tunic, whispered fiercely. "Do as your father says! Take me to Groverman. When we reach him, I will order him to fight!"

With a sinking feeling, Gaborn realized she was right. Groverman's castle stood little more than thirty miles away. If he ran the horses, he could be there within a couple of hours.

"Do as she asks," Orden said. "Perhaps it would help. Groverman has been gathering his forces. He may have ten thousand defenders on his walls by now."

Gaborn knew he would have to do it, would have to take Iome to Groverman. Yet he'd be five hours or more at the task. He wouldn't be able to return here before noon. By then Raj Ahten's troops would have reached

Longmot; their siege would be set.

If Raj Ahten's hundred thousand reinforcements arrived, Gaborn wouldn't be able to dislodge the Wolf Lord.

"Iome," Gaborn asked, "may my father and I speak alone for a moment?"

"Of course," Iome said, and she left. King Sylvarresta remained in the room, eating at the tables. Gaborn's and his father's Days also stayed.

Gaborn felt . . . strangely cognizant of their presence, embarrassed by it. Still, when Iome left, he went to his father, put his arms around the man's shoulders, and cried.

"Here now," his father whispered, "why should a prince weep?"

"You're sending me on a fruitless mission," Gaborn said. "I can feel it. Something . . . is terribly wrong." He did not know how to speak of it, but he felt that they needed to discuss things – what should happen if one of them died. They'd spoken of this possibility many times over the years, after Gaborn's mother was murdered, other times since. Yet this time, Gaborn felt a sense of inevitability.

What he really wanted, what he needed, was to say goodbye.

"How can we know our fight is fruitless?" his father asked. "I can detain Raj Ahten until you return.

"I'll put mounted knights in the bailey, ready to issue from the castle gate. When Groverman's men come in, I want you to have them sweep in from the north side of the hill. It's a gentle slope down. It should give your lancers a great deal of benefit. Then my knights will ride out to your side, and we'll have the old monster in a vise–

"But you must promise me one thing, Gaborn. You will let me fight Raj Ahten personally. I will be the serpent's head. I alone am prepared for this fight."

"Raj Ahten may be more dangerous than you know,"

Gaborn said. "He seeks to become the Sum of All Men. He has so many endowments of stamina, you cannot kill him easily. You will need to strike for the head, take off his head."

"I surmised as much," King Orden said, smiling down at his son.

Gaborn looked into his father's eyes, felt his heart lightened a bit. The castle walls were growing thick with men, and this was a small castle, easily defensible. With six thousand men on those walls, his father should be able to hold this castle even against Raj Ahten's Invincibles.

His father wasn't rushing headlong to his death. He'd fight a measured battle. Already the die had been cast. As head of the serpent ring, his father would have to battle Raj Ahten. In his heart, Gaborn knew that of all the men in the castle, his father was most qualified for this task.

Yet it hurt, it hurt terribly to know what might come, to let it come without saying goodbye.

"Where is Binnesman?" Gaborn asked. "He can help protect you."

"Sylvarresta's wizard?" Orden asked. "I haven't the slightest idea."

"He said . . . he'd meet me here. He called a wylde from the earth last night, and hopes to bring it into battle. He is coming to Longmot." Gaborn felt certain that Binnesman *would* come.

Gaborn hugged his father, leaned his forehead against the older man's cheek. I've been anointed to become king of this earth, Gaborn thought. It was said that Erden Geboren had been so sensitive to the earth powers, to life, that when one of his chosen friends was in danger, he could sense that man's fear. When one of them died, he sensed the loss of that life.

Right now, Gaborn could smell danger around his father, and as he leaned against his father's face, he probed with his mind, sensed life there, like a lamp struggling to stay lit. It was an odd sensation, one he'd never imagined before, and Gaborn wondered if he only imagined it now.

Yet Gaborn had ridden all last night. In that time, he'd seen the world more clearly than ever before. The eye-bright still affected him, long after he thought its effects would diminish. Perhaps it always would affect him.

It was but one change in him. Something more wondrous was happening. He suspected that if he only tried, he could see much farther, much deeper now. He could use the Earth Sight. He hugged his father tight, and closed his eyes, and with his heart, he sought to peer into King Orden.

For a long moment, he saw nothing, and he wondered if he really had seen into Raj Ahten's heart last night.

Then, as if at a great distance, a strange collage of sights and smells and sounds assaulted Gaborn. First he saw the sea, the blue waves of the ocean rolling proud and strong under clear skies, the whitecaps rolling toward shore. Gaborn's own mother and sisters and even himself rode in those waves, bobbing like seals in the water, and King Sylvarresta rode those waves, too. Yet Gaborn's mother was larger than all the rest, as if she were a great walrus, while the others were mere harbor seals. Gaborn tasted fresh pumpkin bread in his mouth, all covered with sunflower seeds, then washed it down with apple wine. Distantly he heard the horns of the hunt. As he listened, he sensed the motion of a horse running beneath him, then his chest seemed to swell wide in exultation as he looked out over the rooftops of the castle in Mystarria and heard the swell of people chanting "Orden, Orden, Orden."

A tremendous swelling sensation rose in Gaborn's chest, a sense of love and warmth, as if all the tender feelings he'd ever felt rolled into one great burst.

Gaborn could see more clearly today than ever before. He could see into his father's heart, and these were the things his father loved: the sea, his family, pumpkin bread and apple wine, the hunt, and to please his people.

At this insight, Gaborn pulled back, suddenly feeling guilty. Why am I doing this? he wondered. Looking into his father's soul was somehow embarrassing, an act of voyeurism.

Clearly, Gaborn recalled his duty, remembered the tales of what Erden Geboren had done when choosing warriors. Gaborn feared for his father, wished to do all that he could to protect him in this, his darkest hour.

You will fight today, Gaborn whispered within himself, but I will fight beside you.

FORTY-ONE: SELECTING A SACRIFICE

The race from the Seven Stones to meet up with his army was long and hard, even for Raj Ahten. A Runelord with endowments of stamina and metabolism can run faster than other men, and far longer, but it requires energy. Even a Runelord cannot run forever.

So it was that Raj Ahten reached his army well before dawn, but the toll was heavy. In jogging well over a hundred miles in armor, with no food, he lost some twenty pounds of fat. The sweat stormed off him in waves, so that even though he stopped frequently to drink from streams and puddles, he'd lost another ten pounds in water. The pounding to his kidneys and bones left him weakened. It was not the condition he would have chosen to fight in.

As Raj Ahten traveled, he found signs that his army, which had traveled ahead, was faltering. Dozens of horses had fallen by the roadside, still in their armor. Another dozen foot soldiers had succumbed during the march. He found frowth giants and mastiffs lying senseless by pools, wheezing, overheated from their run.

When he reached his troops, he did not mind that his men had been delayed by the ruined bridge at Hayworth, for the delay had cost them but four hours. Four hours he spent resting and eating as he rode the remainder of the way to Longmot.

All the way, he worried. Jureem's betrayal and running off into the night, the portents at the Seven Stones – both weighed on him. Yet Raj Ahten discounted them. He wanted but one thing from Longmot: his forcibles. Once he had them, he would have time to consider other matters.

His men made such good time that he called a halt for an hour, in the city of Martin Cross, so his men could rummage through the houses and barns for food.

Shortly after dawn, thirty miles from Longmot, his out-riders reported that a contingent of several hundred knights was fleeing before their army, men riding under a dozen banners. Knights Equitable from Castle Dreis and estates thereabouts.

Raj Ahten felt tempted to give chase in earnest, but knew that his men were now ill-equipped for a race.

So he took his time riding to Longmot, resting on the way. At ten in the morning, he rounded the big bend in the hills and spotted Castle Longmot on its promontory, some two miles distant.

His outriders climbed a hill to get a clearer view, then called down a report. "General Vishtimnu hasn't arrived yet, O Great Light."

Raj Ahten did not worry. With over six thousand men and giants, he could hold Longmot until reinforcements arrived. In fact, he could set up the siege engines and begin pounding the castle within hours, while waiting for Vishtimnu's advent.

Orden had not bothered to raise Longmot's hoardings – timber frames that could protect the castle's roofs from missiles. With Raj Ahten's flameweavers, the hoardings would have simply become fuel for a grand blaze.

So the bombardment would begin soon. If Raj Ahten had to wait a day for reinforcement, his men could begin working on mantelets and shelters, siege towers and bel-fries. There were plenty of stone fences around that could be dismantled, either to help fortify entrenchments or to hurl as missiles. But Raj Ahten did not want to try to build a city here at the foot of Longmot while waiting out some elaborate siege. The longer he camped here, regardless of what fortifications he managed to erect, the longer the kings of Rofehavan would have to mount a counterattack. No, he'd not set a great siege.

Not when he had so many Invincibles, so many weapons magical and mundane that he could employ.

Damn your meddling ways, King Orden, Raj Ahten thought. I will roust you from your burrow by tomorrow dawn!

So his men overturned some wagons as temporary shelters and erected pavilions on the hill south of Longmot, began setting the siege. Watchmen were posted on every road to the castle. Three thousand archers and knights took positions in the field. Another five hundred men and giants went under the trees on the western hills to cut tall pines for use in building siege ladders and battering rams.

Raj Ahten brought his spy balloon out, tied its basket to a stout tree, and set a flameweaver to heating the air for it.

Then the Wolf Lord let the remainder of his men eat and relax. Raj Ahten himself rested in the shade of the single huge oak tree on the hill, thirty feet from his Dedicates' wagon. He sat on pillows covered in purple silk, and ate dates and rice while he studied Longmot's defenses.

He counted only some four thousand men on the walls – a haphazard collection of nobles, young boys, and ruffians. The wizard Binnesman was not with them. Nor did Raj Ahten see Jureem.

"A king is coming, a king who can destroy you!" The words rang through Raj Ahten's memory. King Orden was all shimmering in green samite, with his gold shield.

The king of one of the world's most powerful nations. It gave him pause. The men here on the walls would fight like berserkers for such a king. This was the kind of battle songs were made of. And if Raj Ahten was right, Orden was the Earth King.

Raj Ahten's Invincibles would normally take such a castle with relative ease. Yet, today, he felt uncertain.

Though he did not tremble at the sight of the warriors on the wall, something about their positioning bothered him – a wrongness that left him unbalanced. He studied the men, checking their spacing, armaments, armor, and expressions. He could see worry in their faces, saw that those who had no armor were evenly spaced between those who did. The men were clustered in fighting groups – pikemen and swordsmen together, archers at their backs.

Nothing he saw explained the worry that gnawed him.

The moat around the castle was brackish and foul this time of year, a breeding ground for mosquitoes and disease. A corpse floated in the moat. Despite the fact that the water was stagnant, Raj Ahten knew from his own measurements that it was quite deep – some forty feet. Too deep to let sappers easily dig at the castle's founding stones.

There had been a city here last week, a small city of five thousand souls. Over generations, the walls of the city had crept within bowshot of the castle. One could have moved siege engines up behind those homes, tossed rocks over the battlements. But Orden's soldiers had wisely burned the city, cleared the ground of cover in preparation for battle.

No, this castle could not easily be taken, not with four or five thousand men on the walls, others waiting in the baileys and towers. The castle's armaments were well stocked. He'd seen the arrows piled in the armory not a week ago.

Raj Ahten sighed. If he laid siege to the castle through the winter, Orden's men might be forced to burn some of those arrows just to stay warm. But, of course, this siege would not last so long.

An hour before noon, General Vishtimnu still had not arrived, and the first six catapults were built. Raj Ahten's men fashioned a hundred crude siege ladders and brought them to the hill, laid them out, ready for battle.

The far-seers in the balloon could spot few men inside the castle – most held the walls, though several hundred knights waited on their mounts in the inner bailey. None of the inhabitants from the city were inside the gates. The only exception was possibly the Dedicates' Keep, where two hundred of Orden's elite guard watched the keep. Perhaps Orden had drained some of the people of this city for endowments, had hundreds of Dedicates secreted in the keep. Yet the keep could not hold many.

This was good news. Though Orden had captured the forcibles, he did not have forty thousand or even four thousand people here who could have granted endowments.

It meant that the vast majority of the forcibles might still be within the castle, unused.

Raj Ahten had four hundred forcibles remaining in his possession from the hoard he'd taken to Castle Sylvarresta.

He called his facilitators and studied his assets. Most of the forcibles were worthless to him. The irons bore only runes of the senses. He had no use for more endowments of hearing or smell or touch.

He'd used most of the forcibles for taking major endowments in subduing Sylvarresta. None in his hoard bore the runes of metabolism.

He wished now that he'd brought more. A cold uncertainty took him as he pondered. His pyromancer had gazed into the future, warned him that a king in Heredon could slay him. He'd already humbled Sylvarresta. So it was Orden.

And Orden had surely taken endowments of metabolism. A Runelord of his stature would not need more grace or brawn in battle. He would not need more wit. Stamina would be of some help. But the only attribute that would let him defeat Raj Ahten would be metabolism.

But how much had Orden taken? Twenty endowments? Orden was chronologically in his mid-thirties, but if he had taken the customary endowment of metabolism after rearing his family, he'd have a physiological age close to forty-five. Even a dozen endowments of stamina could not completely ameliorate the effects of his advancing age. So he'd have endowments of brawn, grace, stamina, and wit to counteract his aging.

Raj Ahten's spies had told him that as of a year ago, Orden had had over a hundred endowments to his reckoning. How many over a hundred, Raj Ahten could not guess.

At any event, Orden would be a worthy adversary.

So how many endowments of metabolism had he taken? Five? No, that would be too few. Fifty? If so, he'd have taken his death. He would age and wither within a year. Raj Ahten would not even need to fight today. He could simply withdraw his troops for the winter, and Orden would age. By spring he'd be a dotard.

It was said that in the days of Harridan the Great, the messenger Marcoriaus had so needed speed to deliver news of the impending battle at Polypolus that he'd taken a hundred endowments of metabolism – enough so that he ran barefoot across the Caroll Sea, relying only on the surface tension of the water to keep him aloft. Marcoriaus had died within three months, of course.

But the idea of such phenomenal speed attracted some men. Yet, such speed could be a great danger. A Runelord who moved too suddenly, too sharply, could snap a leg. The force of an object seeking to remain at rest was too great. It took a great deal of wit and grace to learn how to move with control.

Orden had that wit and grace, and now he might have the metabolism to go with it.

So King Orden would have taken between ten and twenty endowments of metabolism, Raj Ahten decided.

He would need to match him.

Or, I could take endowments of metabolism, then kill my own Dedicates afterwards. He had used the tactics before. However, in order to maintain the proper fighting spirit among his men, he'd made certain that he left no witnesses.

"Call to me the twelve Invincibles who have great endowments of metabolism," Raj Ahten told Hepolus, his chief facilitator. "I need them."

The facilitators left the tent, hurried back a few minutes later, bringing the desired Invincibles – elite guards and assassins who each had at least three endowments of metabolism. They were all big men, strong of bone, so that they could handle the stress of great brawn and metabolism. And they were strong in wit and grace. He would sorely miss any one of them.

Raj Ahten knew his men well. The man he least valued was Salim al Daub, an old household guard who had been elevated in status several times, despite the fact that Salim had failed him as an assassin. Twice he'd gone to kill Prince Orden, and twice he'd returned a failure, with only the ears of women and children.

"Thank you for coming, my friends," Raj Ahten said when he'd decided. "You have all served me valiantly for many years. I ask now that you serve me once again, for I need your metabolism. You, my friend Salim, will have the honor to serve as vector."

The words slid from Raj Ahten's tongue as sweetly as candied dates. The men could not resist the power of his Voice. The facilitators drew out the forcibles.

A cold wind blew from the south, rippling the silk walls of Raj Ahten's pavilion.

FORTY-TWO: A COLD WIND

Faintly, across the battlefield, from the huge purple royal tent that Raj Ahten had entered, Orden heard the chants of facilitators borne on the cold wind. The sound came dimly, so dimly that few men on the walls could have discerned it. Orden could hear it only because he focused, detected it beneath the song of the wind rushing through the leaves of grass along the hills, a sound so much like the waves of the ocean back home.

"What's taking them?" an "archer" on the castle walls asked, a farm boy who knew nothing of war. They'd been waiting an hour. In that time, Raj Ahten's men had not sought to parley. They did not seem to want to attack.

King Orden began to pace the walls, past men who stood shoulder to shoulder, four deep. He watched them with mounting nervousness as Raj Ahten set his forces, laid his siege.

"I do not like that chanting," Captain Holmon said softly in Orden's ear. "Raj Ahten has endowments enough without it. We would be better off if we got this battle under way, before their reinforcements arrive."

"How?" Orden asked. "Mount a charge?"

"We can goad the old dog into battle."

Orden nodded to Captain Holmon. "Sound your horn, then. Call Raj Ahten to a parley. I want him out here, within bowshot."

FORTY-THREE:
THE SPARK

The facilitators had just finished granting endowments of metabolism from nine of Raj Ahten's men to Salim when the horns sounded, calling for a parlay.

The facilitators looked at Raj Ahten, curiously.

"Finish it," Raj Ahten said to his chief facilitator. He'd stripped from his armor, and sat on a cushion, awaiting the endowment.

He listened with rising excitement as the facilitator sang the familiar words to the chants. Salim shrieked in pain while the forcible burned his flesh, adding to the scent of charred fat and burning hair that filled the pavilion.

To take an endowment, to feel the kiss of the forcibles, gave profound delight. It was like making love to a beautiful woman. But to take an endowment from someone who already had received many endowments, to combine that euphoria over and over again – that gave unspeakable ecstasy. By the time Salim had taken his endowments from eleven men – men who had all received endowments of their own – he had combined nearly forty endowments of metabolism, all waiting to burst free into Raj Ahten at once.

Seldom did Raj Ahten receive such great pleasure.

He was sweating with anticipation by the time the facilitator drew the forcible away from Salim, held its glowing tip high, and danced across the room, painting the air inside the tent with ribbons of sulfurous light.

When the tip of the forcible touched the skin beneath Raj Ahten's nipple, the Wolf Lord shuddered with such unspeakable ecstasy that he could barely contain it. He fell to the floor, his body racked by waves of pure pleasure, and he cried out as if in orgasm. Only his many endowments of stamina allowed him to survive the pleasure. For several moments, he blacked out.

When he woke, the facilitators knelt over him nervously. Raj Ahten's sweaty skin shivered. He looked up at his men.

"My lord, are you well?" Facilitator Hepolus asked. The words slurred, as if he spoke very slowly. The whole world seemed strange and exotic, as if in some liquid dream. The men around him moved slowly, and the air felt heavy, thick.

Raj Ahten wiped the sweat from his body, took care not to leap up too quickly.

Long ago, he'd learned that when one takes an endowment of metabolism, it affects the hearing. Not only do people around you speak and move very slowly, but the entire way that sound is perceived is affected. High pitches become lower, while low pitches become almost inaudible. To reply to a question in a manner that others could understand required both patience and great control of Voice.

"I am well," Raj Ahten answered with care.

The facilitators glanced around meaningfully, moving with such seeming deliberation they looked like old, old men.

Raj Ahten waved at Salim, lying on the carpets within the tent. "Move my vector to the Dedicates' wagon. Place guards to watch these others."

Raj Ahten currently had forty-two endowments of metabolism. With so many, if he tried to walk at an average pace, he'd travel at over a hundred and forty miles per hour. If the air stood still, his movement alone would make it feel as if he pressed through a hurricane.

With forced slowness he pulled on his scale mail, donned his helm. He accidentally moved too fast while fastening his helm, so that his left pinky finger snapped under unexpected pressure. It healed instantly in a crooked position.

Raj Ahten broke it again, pulled it straight, let it heal.

He ambled slowly outside the tent, tried to appear as natural as ever.

On the battlements of Castle Longmot, above the gate, King Orden's men waved the green flag of parlay.

Between a pair of giants who stood like a wall, eleven Invincibles had already mounted imperial horses, prepared to act as Raj Ahten's honor guard. A footman held the twelfth horse for him.

Raj Ahten ambled to his horse, nodded toward his flameweavers, giving them their signal.

Then he forced himself to sit very still as the horse galloped toward Longmot's gates.

It was an odd situation. As the horse ran, Raj Ahten often found himself momentarily thrust into the air, but those moments stretched out interminably, so that for half of the short ride, it seemed he was airborne, just floating above the ground.

He had not gone far when a shimmering nimbus took shape above his head, courtesy of the flameweavers, a scintillating golden light that emitted brief sparks of titanium white.

In the glimmering light he gazed steadfastly at the wide eyes of the defenders on the castle walls.

The knights were grim men, skeptical. Not the soft city folk he'd seen at Castle Sylvarresta. Many of them clutched their weapons fiercely, and it seemed a thousand bowmen on the walls nocked their bows, drew arrows full. Their eyes shone with calculation.

"People of Longmot," Raj Ahten called, modulating so that he spoke slowly, sliding all the power of his Voice into the words, so that he'd seem like a man of peace and reason.

On the castle walls, Orden clenched his fists, calling, "Fire!"

In slow motion, the hail of arrows descended, a black wall of arrows and bolts from steel longbows and ballistas.

Raj Ahten tried to sit still in his saddle, tried not to overreact as bolts sped toward him. He could dodge them or push them aside, as needed.

The arrows hurtled toward him in a deadly rain, and Raj Ahten glanced to each side. The knights in his honor guard were raising their shields, dismayed by this act of premeditated butchery.

He did not have time to save them.

As the first arrows sped to him, he grabbed for it, thinking to knock it from the air. But when his mailed fist slapped the arrow, such was the velocity and momentum at which both his hand and the arrow traveled, that the wooden shaft snapped in two. The head of the arrow veered toward his chest, and Raj Ahten had to grab for it again quickly, catch it in his hand.

At that moment, the deadly rain of arrows slammed into his knights, their mounts.

A huge iron ballista bolt unseated the knight next to him, and the Wolf Lord was forced to raise his small shield, knock away more arrows that sang through the air toward him.

A shaft struck between the plates of his horse's armor, sliding into its ribs, and the mount began to stagger. It stepped on a caltrop and let its feet give way.

Suddenly Raj Ahten found himself flying through the air, seemingly in slow motion, unhorsed, grabbing and kicking arrows from his path, twisting so that a shaft broke against his vambrace rather than pierced his scale mail.

He was a strong man, but even Raj Ahten could not break the fundamental laws of motion.

The momentum of the horse's fall threw him somersaulting headfirst over the beast's shoulder.

He knew that if the force of his landing did not crack his skull, the weight of the armored horse rolling over him afterward might crush him.

Raj Ahten managed to reach out, push himself slowly off the ground as he moved toward it, then tuck, so that he rolled cleanly over the grass, away from the charger.

But that maneuver cost him, for as he came around, a vividly painted red arrow lodged in his collarbone just above the line of his mail, and another bit into his thigh.

Raj Ahten crawled away from his falling horse, looked up at the grim soldiers on the castle walls.

He grabbed the arrow in his thigh, pulled it free, and hurled it back at his attackers.

But when he grasped the red shaft in his collarbone, it snapped in two.

He held it up, astonished, for he'd taken it gingerly. It should not have broken under so slight a pressure.

The shaft broke, he now saw, because the arrow had been hollowed and notched. The shaft was meant to break away. Raj Ahten guessed the reason behind this even before he felt the fiery poison creeping toward his heart.

He stared hard at the castle wall, saw one soldier a hundred feet above him – a tall fellow with a thin face and yellow teeth, a tunic made of pig hide. The fellow threw his longbow in the air, shouting in triumph at having killed the Wolf Lord of Indhopal.

As this first volley of arrows finished landing, a quiet moment followed where the skies remained free of missiles.

Raj Ahten pulled his dagger from its sheath. The wound in his collar hurt fiercely. The poison rushed through his bloodstream so fast, Raj Ahten did not know if even his thousands of endowments of stamina could save him.

The skin on his collarbone had already healed over the

wound, sealing the arrowhead beneath. With a quick shove, Raj Ahten slammed his dagger into his collar, cutting it open, and pulled out the arrowhead.

With deadly accuracy, he then hurled the dagger at the jubilant archer.

He turned and began slowly running before more arrows fell, not even bothering to watch the archer on the castle wall take the dagger through the forehead, fall back under the force of the blow.

It was enough to hear the man's death scream.

Raj Ahten ran a hundred yards over the grass. The poison made him weary, made it hard to raise one foot, then the next. His breath came slow and labored. He feared that the poison would asphyxiate him. The arrow had fallen close to his lungs, deep in his chest, and the poison had not been able to bleed out before the skin healed over the wound.

He struggled for each step, collapsed from fatigue. The wound in his shoulder hurt like death, and he could feel the poison clutching at his heart, holding it like a mighty fist.

He reached toward his men, begging aid, begging for healers. He had physics to care for him, herbalists and surgeons. Yet he was living so quickly, a minute to him now seemed like the better part of an hour. He feared he'd succumb long before an herbalist could arrive.

His heart beat sporadically, pumping hard. Raj Ahten gasped for each breath. With his endowments of hearing, Raj Ahten could hear every surge and gurgle of his failing heart. With his head pressed against the ground, he could hear worms stirring in the ground beneath him.

Then his heart stopped.

In the sudden silence, the sound of worms beneath the ground came louder, as if it were all the sound in the world.

Raj Ahten willed his heart to beat again, willed it to start. Beat, damn you. Beat. . . .

He struggled for air, gasped. He slapped his own mailed chest in frustration.

His heart beat, weakly, once. Then it began to stutter, jerking spastically.

Raj Ahten concentrated. Felt his heart beat once, strongly. A second later, it came again. He gasped air that felt black in his lungs.

Silently, he cried out, willed his facilitators in far lands to give him more stamina, so that he might withstand this. "A king is coming," he heard the words echoing through his memory. "A king who can kill you!"

Not like this, he begged the powers. Not so ignoble a death.

Suddenly the clutching in his heart eased. It began pumping furiously, and Raj Ahten peed in his armor like an old man with no control over his bladder. He felt some relief as his body rid itself of poison.

As he lay on the grass, the pain receded. He'd been lying on the ground for what seemed to him minutes, though the archers on the wall must have felt only seconds fly by.

He fought to his feet once again, staggered to his line of troops, fell to his knees behind a frowth giant that he used as a shield.

He glanced back, saw some of his honor guard still struggling to rise under the onslaught of arrows, shields high. But bowmen on the walls were riddling them with shafts.

Rage threatened to take him, a blind and burning rage. Raj Ahten fought it down. Destroying these men would gain him nothing.

Out of bowshot, Raj Ahten stood, panting, and shouted at the castle, "Brave knights, dishonorable lords: I come as a friend and ally in these harsh times. Not as your enemy!"

He let the full power of his Voice flavor the words. Surely these men could see he was the injured party here.

Eleven of his finest warriors lay dying on the battlefield.

Though he was far away, too far for his glamour to take full effect, his Voice alone might sway the men.

"Come, King Orden," he shouted reasonably. "Let us counsel together. Surely you know I have a great army in the wings. Perhaps you can see them now from your vantage point?"

He hoped Vishtimnu was coming. Perhaps such a sighting had prodded Orden to this dastardly deed. With all the sweetness he could muster, he said soothingly, "You cannot defeat me, and I bear you no malice. Throw down your weapons.

"Throw open your gates. Serve me. I will be your king, and you will be my people!" He waited expectantly, as he had at Castle Sylvarresta.

It seemed he waited for a full minute for any reaction at all. When it came, it was not what he had hoped.

Only a couple dozen of the younger men tossed weapons over the walls, so that spears and bows clattered against the battlements, splashed into the moat.

But as quickly as the weapons fell, so did their bearers – for the hardened warriors on the wall tossed their weak-willed companions to their deaths. The bodies bounced down along the sloped walls of the castle.

A great, greasy-looking bear of a man stood directly above the gates, and he spat as far as he could, so that a wad of spittle hit Raj Ahten's dying knights. Orden's men burst into laughter and shook their weapons.

Raj Ahten sat in the cool wind, gritted his teeth. He had not spoken any better at Castle Sylvarresta, but the effect had been profoundly different.

It might have been that with his increased metabolism, he had not spoken the words as slowly as he'd hoped, enunciated them with the proper intonation. Each time one took endowments of metabolism, one had to learn the arts of speaking and hearing all over again.

Or perhaps it was the endowments of glamour, he told

himself. I've lost glamour since Castle Sylvarresta. He'd felt it when the Duchess of Longmot had died, taking her endowments of glamour with her.

"Very well!" Raj Ahten shouted. "We shall do this the hard way!" If Orden had been seeking for some goad to spark Raj Ahten's anger, he'd found it.

Raj Ahten struggled for control, found himself seething. He knew it would be hard for these men in the castle. It would have been quicker for all concerned if they had surrendered. Raj Ahten had taken a hundred castles, many better than this, until it was a practiced art.

I'll make an example of haughty King Orden, he vowed.

He stood before his battle lines, raised his warhammer high, then dropped it with a cutting motion.

The first volley of stones lofted from his catapults. Some smaller stones disappeared over the walls, while heavier loads slammed lower on the battlements. Two of Orden's cutthroats dropped under the weight of the stones.

Orden countered with artillery from the city walls – six catapults, and four ballistas. The catapults hurled small iron shot that fell like a deadly hail – five yards short of his men. Orden would have done better with some lighter shot.

The ballistas were another matter. In all the South, Raj Ahten had never seen a ballista made with Heredon's spring steel. In cities like Bannisferre and Ironton, artificers – earth wizards who had mastered secret arts of metallurgy and artifice – had labored long to make such steel. Raj Ahten was unprepared when bolts flashed from the walls in a dark blur, striking through the ranks of his men.

One ballista bolt, like a huge arrow cast of iron, flashed toward him. He leaned away from it, only to hear the bolt plummet into someone behind with a sickly thud.

He turned to see a flameweaver slump roughly to the ground, a hole the size of a grapefruit through his navel.

The young man's saffron robes suddenly burst into white flame, as his power raged out of control.

"Retreat!" Raj Ahten called for his men to take cover. They needed little urging.

Raj Ahten raced over the hill as the flameweaver erupted – the massive form of the elemental that had coiled like a worm at the center of his soul suddenly escaping.

A lean, bald man took form, a hundred feet tall, sitting on the ground. Flames licked at his skull and swirled at his fingertips. He gazed at Longmot with a troubled expression.

Raj Ahten watched. Such an elemental could wreak havoc, blast the stone walls to oblivion, burn the gate, fry the inhabitants of the castle like maggots on a griddle. Just as the elemental had done at Castle Sylvarresta.

Yet Raj Ahten felt disappointed. For years he'd nurtured these flameweavers. Now two had already been slaughtered in this campaign. It was a damnable waste of resources.

There was nothing to do for it but wait, watch the elemental do its work, then clean up after.

The elemental became a raging inferno that set the grass at his feet burning. The air roared like a furnace, and heat smote Raj Ahten, searing his lungs with each breath.

The hot-air balloon still hovered five hundred feet over the battlefield. Raj Ahten's men pulled it away before the elemental's heat made its silk burst into a ball of fire.

The elemental pointed itself toward the city, began striding across the battlefield.

Men on the walls of Longmot fired bows in terror. The tiny arrows flew toward the monster like stars that burst into flame in the night sky before they were consumed. The arrows could not defeat the elemental, only feed it.

The elemental reached for the nearest wood, its fingers extending in a twisting green flame that caressed the drawbridge of Longmot. The sounds of crackling wood and splintering beams filled the air. The soldiers atop the walls rushed to escape as a fiery blast slammed against the castle.

A cheer now rose from the throats of Raj Ahten's men, though Raj Ahten only smiled grimly.

Suddenly, water began gushing from the walls over the arch, flowing in runnels from the mouths of the gargoyles above the gate, wept from the castle's stone everywhere in great waves, so that the gray walls glistened.

Everywhere, water was rushing up the stone battlements from the moat, forming a wall. The great elemental turned to steam at its touch, began to shrink and dissipate.

Raj Ahten seethed, wondering.

One of his flameweavers shouted, "A water wizard's ward!" It seemed the castle had some unanticipated magical protection. Yet there were no water wizards here in Heredon that Raj Ahten had ever heard of.

Raj Ahten wondered. Such wards could not last out a year and required a magical emblem to be placed on the castle gate. He'd seen no such emblem or rune four days past.

Then he looked above the gate: Orden stood on the arch, holding his golden shield against the castle wall. The ward had been built into his shield, and by laying the shield against the castle wall, the entire castle, by extension, became shielded.

Raj Ahten's face twisted in rage as he watched his elemental shrivel amid the water's onslaught. It cringed and huddled like a lonely child, then became a common fire burning in the grass. In half a moment, even that was smothered.

Raj Ahten felt impotent, maddened.

Then the wizard Binnesman appeared on Raj Ahten's own horse, racing down from the wooded hills to the west, to put himself between the Wolf Lord's army and the castle.

FORTY-FOUR: THE WIZARD BINNESMAN

King Orden pulled his golden shield up to his chest. He'd brought it as a gift to Sylvarresta, to celebrate their children's betrothal. The ward on the shield was to have protected Castle Sylvarresta. Now it had saved Longmot.

But the shield had become worthless, save as a target for arrows, drained of all its water spells.

Silently, Orden cursed himself. When he'd seen Raj Ahten fall from the arrow, he'd hesitated. He could have gone then, rushed down to attack the Wolf Lord and lopped off his head. Instead, he'd let his hopes soar, had thought for one breathtaking moment that the Wolf Lord would succumb to the poison. Then the opportunity to strike was gone.

Now this.

Orden studied the herbalist as he rode across the green grass on a great force horse, felt bemused. Earth Wardens seldom meddled in the affairs of men. But this one, it appeared, was fool enough to try to stop a war.

Though Orden had not seen Binnesman in a year, the old wizard had changed much. He wore robes in the colors of autumn forest – scarlets with bits of tan and gold. His brown hair had turned the color of ice. But his back was unbowed. He looked older, yet vigorous.

On the battlefield before him stood Raj Ahten's Invincibles, archers by the thousands, giants in armor, and mastiffs with leather helms and fierce collars.

Binnesman rode his mount before the castle gates.

Orden felt strange, expectant, filled with vast reserves of energy. Twenty-two warriors hid in various cellars, closets, and rooms throughout Castle Longmot. Each man, bearing arms and armor, was curled in a ball, waiting for the moment when Orden would draw upon their metabolism. Orden could feel their energy course through him. His blood seemed to burn, as if he were a pot ready to boil.

Across the battlefield, Raj Ahten's men stood under the trees, bristling at the way the battle had gone. Raj Ahten strode toward Binnesman, his motions almost a blur.

"Raj Ahten," the old wizard grumbled, straightening his back to gaze at the Wolf Lord from beneath bushy brows, "why do you insist on attacking these people?"

Raj Ahten answered calmly, "It is no concern to you, Earth Warden."

Binnesman said, "Oh, but it is my concern. I've spent the night riding through the Dunnwood, listening to the talk of trees and birds. Do you know what I've learned? I have news that pertains to you."

Raj Ahten had moved forward a hundred yards – still out of easy bowshot, yet once again he stood before his army.

"Orden has my forcibles," Raj Ahten said in answer to Binnesman's earlier query. "I want them back!" The sound carried well over the fields. Orden could hardly believe Raj Ahten spoke from so far away.

The old wizard smiled, leaned back in his saddle, as if to rest. On the green across the field, Raj Ahten's three remaining flameweavers stood. Each began giving their bodies to fire, so that their clothes burst into flame and tendrils flared out from them, yellow, red, and blue.

"Why is it," Binnesman asked, "that every forcible on earth must be yours?"

"They came from my mines," Raj Ahten said, striding forward, his face alight with seductive beauty. "My slaves dug the ore."

"As I recall, the Sultan of Hadwar owned those mines – until you slit his throat. As for the slaves, they were someone's sons and daughters before you took them. Even the blood metal you cannot claim – for it is only the crusty remains of your ancestors who died long ago in a great slaughter."

"Yet I can claim it as mine," Raj Ahten said softly, "and no man can stop me."

"By what right?" Binnesman called. "You claim the whole earth as your own, but you are a mere mortal. Must death force you to release all that you claim before you recognize that you own nothing? You *own* nothing. The earth nourishes you from day to day, from breath to breath! You are chained to it, as surely as your slaves are chained to the walls of your mines. Acknowledge its power over you!"

Binnesman sighed, glanced up to Orden on the castle wall. "What of it, King Orden? You strike me as a fair-minded man. Will you give these forcibles to Raj Ahten, so that you two may finish with this squabbling?" Binnesman's eyes smiled, as if he expected Orden to laugh.

"No," Orden said. "I'll not give them. If he wants them, he must come against me!"

Binnesman clucked his tongue as if he were an old woman, scolding a child. "You hear, Raj Ahten? Here is a man who dares defy you. And I suspect he will win. . . ."

"He has no chance against me," Raj Ahten said with dignity, though his face seemed livid with rage. "You lie."

"Do I?" Binnesman asked. "For what purpose do I lie?"

"You seek to twist us all, to do your own bidding."

"Is that how you see it? Life is precious – yours, mine, your enemy's. I cherish life. Am I 'twisting' you to save your miserable life?"

Raj Ahten did not answer, but only studied Binnesman with subdued rage.

Binnesman said, "I've come before you twice now. I warn you one last time, Raj Ahten: Give up this foolhardy war!"

"You had best move from my way," Raj Ahten said. "You can't stop me."

Binnesman smiled. "No, I can't stop you. But others *can* stop you. The new King of the Earth has been ordained. You cannot prevail against him.

"I see hope for House Orden, but none for you.

"I did not come here to beg you yet again to join my cause," Binnesman said. "I know you will not join me.

"But hear me well: I speak now in the name of the Power I serve: Raj Ahten, the earth that gave you birth, the earth that nurtured you as a mother and father, now rejects you! No longer will it nourish or protect you.

"I curse the ground you walk upon, that it will no longer give you sustenance! The stones of the earth shall trouble you. Accursed be your flesh, your bone, your sinew. Let your arms be weakened. Cursed be the fruit of your loins, that you leave no issue. Cursed be those who band themselves with you, that they too shall suffer your lot!

"I warn you: Leave this land!"

The Earth Warden spoke with such force that Orden expected some sign – the ground to sway and tremble or swallow Raj Ahten, or for stones to drop from the sky.

But the downs looked the same as ever, the sun still shone bright.

Earth does not kill, Orden knew. It does not destroy. And Orden could see that Binnesman had no wylde to back him, no power to effect some astonishing curse.

Or perhaps, in time, the effects of the wizard's curse would be seen. Such curses were never given lightly, and old wives' tales warned that they were the most potent form of magic. If that were true Orden almost pitied Raj Ahten.

Yet, for the moment, nothing happened. Orden

shouted a warning. "Binnesman, leave this battle. You can do nothing more."

Binnesman turned up and looked at Orden, and there was such a look of anger there in the wizard's eyes that Orden stepped back a pace.

As if Binnesman, too, suddenly recognized the danger, he turned his mount west, toward the Dunnwood, and fled.

FORTY-FIVE: THE CAVILING CAVALIER

Castle Groverman lay on a shallow sandy mound on Mangon's Heath, just where Wind River made a slow turn. It was not the stoutest castle in Heredon, nor the largest, but as Iome rode across the plains that morning, it seemed the most beautiful, with its sprawling grounds, its palatial towers, and its vast gates. The morning sun shone golden on the heather and on the yellow sandstone of the castle, so it gleamed like something molten.

Iome, her father, Gaborn, and the three Days swept over the heather, racing past herds of half-wild horses and cattle that startled away each time they crossed a line of hills.

Iome knew this place only from maps and tomes and conversations. Groverman came to her father's castle for the Council of Lords each fall and winter, but she'd never seen his home. For centuries the lords of Groverman had governed this land, supplying Heredon with force horses and beef. Iome's father did not keep large stables in his own castle – not like the extensive stables at Groverman. Here, on the banks of Wind River, the horses grew fat and frolicked, until the lord's horsemen brought them to the King's stables and introduced the foals to the herd leaders.

The herd leaders were spirited. A herd leader, once given endowments of strength and metabolism, would dominate any wild horse. The wild foals were used as

Dedicates, for these horses stood most in awe of the herd stallions, and could therefore best be counted on to provide attributes.

Thus Castle Groverman had grown to be an important fortress, for this was the Dedicates' Keep for the horses that supplied Sylvarresta's messengers and soldiers.

But this late in the fall, it was also a busy center for commerce. The local vassals and villeins herded cattle in for the fall slaughter. Tomorrow was the first day of Hostenfest, a time of celebration before the last of the fall labors. A week from today, when the feasting ended, the fatted beeves would be driven all across Heredon for slaughter on Tolfest, in the twenty-fifth day of the Month of Leaves, before the winter snows set in.

With the beef came horsemen, driving in the summer's foals. The fields around Castle Groverman had thus become a maze of stockyards and tents.

On seeing it, Iome's heart sank.

She'd been outraged to learn that Duke Groverman refused aid to Longmot. It had seemed a small and evil gesture, not in keeping with the graciousness and courage expected from the lords of Heredon.

But now Iome saw that Groverman might not go to Longmot, with good reason. Outside the castle, people and animals crowded the grounds – the horsemen and cattlemen, merchants for the festival, refugees from Longmot, plus some refugees who'd left their own unprotected villages.

The refugees from Longmot broke Iome's heart. They huddled on the banks of Wind River – women, babes, men. For most of them, only blankets slung over poles would shelter them from the snows this winter. Groverman had generously allowed the refugees to camp near the castle walls, protected from the winds that swept these plains.

Still, it looked as if a town of rags had sprung up by the river, a town inhabited by ragged people. Silver-haired men puttered aimlessly, as if only waiting for winter so they could freeze. Women wrapped their babes in thick woolen blankets and kept them tucked under their arms, having nothing better than their bodies and cloth to warm the children.

From the sounds of coughing as she passed through this crowd, it appeared that plagues would soon sweep the camp.

Iome estimated that between refugees, the inhabitants of Castle Groverman, and those who had come for the fair, some thirty thousand people had gathered. A vast throng, not easily protected.

And Groverman's walls, for some reason, were not as thick with knights as Iome would have expected.

So Groverman must be exerting all his influence to care for his people.

All this Iome saw as she rode past corrals filled with red cattle, through the broad streets. Everyone stared at Gaborn as he entered the city. Groverman was not used to entertaining soldiers who wore the livery of the green knight. The trio of Days who rode behind signaled that this was an important procession, regardless of how ragged Iome and her father looked.

At the castle gate, four guards stopped them. "You have another message for milord?" one guard asked Gaborn, ignoring Iome and her father.

"Yes," Gaborn said softly, "please tell His Lordship that Prince Gaborn Val Orden begs his audience, and that he has come in company with King Jas Laran Sylvarresta, and the Princess Iome."

The guards gaped at the news, stood staring at Iome's mud-stained robes. King Sylvarresta did not look kingly, not with his endowments stripped. In fact, Iome imagined she and her father were the saddest-looking pair on the road.

So Iome tried to sit all the more proudly, high in the saddle. It cost her dearly, for she could ill bear the stares of the guards.

Behold the horror of your princess, a sad voice whispered in her mind. She desired to cringe and hide her face, as some Dedicates did after giving glamour. Yet Iome steeled herself for the guards' inspection, still fighting the power of the rune Raj Ahten's men had branded into her flesh.

The guards studied the three Days who rode, as if to verify his claim. Two men bumped into each other in their rush to fetch Duke Groverman.

The Duke hurried into the broad courtyard of his estate, his richly embroidered robes flapping in the wind. Azurite and pearls were bound into the leather trim of his ocher cloak. His Days hurried behind.

"Here now! What's this? What's going on?" Groverman cried, pulling his cloak tighter about his neck. The morning was growing cold; gray clouds raced in from the south.

He stopped a dozen yards off, gawking back and forth between Gaborn, Iome, and the King.

"Good morning, sir," Iome said softly, without dismounting, proffering her hand so that he could kiss her ring. "Though it has been but four months since last you visited Castle Sylvarresta, I fear much about my appearance has changed."

It was understatement, of course. As for her father, he looked but a shadow of his former self. Stripped of glamour, his face seemed a worn mockery of the handsome figure he had cut. Shorn of his brawn, he slumped wearily in his saddle. Without wit, King Sylvarresta gaped about stupidly, enamored of the cattle.

"Princess Iome?" Groverman asked, as if unconvinced.

"Yes."

Groverman stepped forward, took her hand, and unashamedly sniffed it.

Groverman was an odd man. Some might have called him a Wolf Lord, for he'd taken endowments from dogs, but unlike men who took such endowments only to satisfy a rapacious hunger for power, Groverman had once argued with Iome's father long into the night, suggesting that it was more morally correct to take endowments from animals than from men. "Which is more benevolent, to garner fifty endowments of scent from a man, or to take one endowment of scent from a tracking dog?"

So Duke Groverman had several endowments from dogs, yet he was a kind leader, well-liked by his people.

He had a narrow face, and dark-blue, close-set eyes. He looked nothing like King Sylvarresta. No one who saw them together would have ventured that the Duke hailed from the same family.

Satisfied with her scent, the Duke kissed her ring. "Welcome, welcome to my home." With a wave of his hand, Duke Groverman bid Iome to dismount, come into the courtyard.

"We have urgent matters to discuss," Gaborn said, as if to get to the point. He was in such a hurry to get back to his father, he did not even want to dismount.

"Assuredly," Groverman said, still waving Iome toward his palace.

"We are in a hurry," Iome said. Almost, she wanted to shout at Groverman that she had no time for formalities, that he needed to call his warriors, send them to battle.

Iome suspected Groverman would resist her will, would try to dissuade her or placate her with lesser offers of aid. She did not want to listen to his caviling and his dodges.

"We must speak immediately," Gaborn said.

The Duke caught Gaborn's tone, glanced up with a hurt look. "Milady, does Prince Orden speak for you and the King?"

"Yes, he does," Iome said. "He's my friend, and our ally."

"What would you have of me?" Groverman asked. "You have only to name it." His tone was so submissive, his manner so meek, that, almost, Iome thought he feigned it. Yet when she looked into the Duke's eyes, she saw only submission.

Iome came to the point, "Longmot will soon be under attack. King Orden is there, with Dreis and others. How dare you refuse him aid!"

Groverman opened his hands wide, as if stunned. "Refuse him aid? Refuse aid? What more can I do? I've sent the best knights I could, having them ride as soon as they were able – over two thousand men. I've sent word to Cowforth and Emmit and Donyeis and Jonnick – and they'll converge here before noon. As I wrote in my message, I can promise another five thousand men by night-fall!"

"But . . ." Iome said, "Orden told us you refused aid."

"On my honor, he is mistaken! I never!" Groverman shouted. "If women were squires and beeves were mounted knights, I'd march within the hour with an army of a quarter million. But I never denied him aid!"

Then she wondered. There had been too many knights on Longmot's walls. She'd thought they'd come from Dreis, or that Orden had gathered them in his travels.

Gaborn touched Iome's elbow. "My father has played us for fools. I see it now. I should have recognized what I felt. My father has always said that even the wisest man's plots are only as good as his information. He's fooled us, just as he seeks to fool Raj Ahten. He knew we wouldn't leave Longmot, so long as we trusted in reinforcements. For our own protection, he schemed a way to get us out of danger."

Iome's head spun. Orden had lied with such seeming sincerity, had made her so furious with Groverman, it took her a moment to reassess the situation.

By now, if her estimates were right, Raj Ahten's troops should be reaching Longmot. Even if she and Gaborn turned now, they'd never make it back inside Longmot's gates. And a hundred thousand men should join Raj Ahten this day.

If Groverman waited until tonight to ride, he'd ride too late. Yet Iome could not bear to sit here while her allies fought in Longmot. There had to be something she could do. Iome tensed in her saddle as a plan took shape.

"Duke Groverman," she asked, "how many shields do you have, at this very moment?"

"Ten thousand fighting men," Groverman said. "But they are only commoners. My finest knights are in Longmot."

"Not men – shields. How many shields do you have?"

"I – maybe I could scrounge twelve thousand, if we raided the armories of nearby estates."

"Do so," Iome said, "and get all the lances and armor and mounts you can – and all the women and men and children above the age of nine who can ride – and all the cattle and horses from their corrals. We'll make every blanket from your refugees into a pennant, and they shall fly hoisted on rails from your corrals. Bring all the war horns you can find. And do so quickly. We must depart no later than two hours from now.

"A great army is about to march on Longmot, so huge an army that even Raj Ahten must tremble!"

FORTY-SIX: THE CURSE

In the cold, graying skies above Longmot, darkness flashed among the clouds like inverse lighting. Raj Ahten's three remaining flameweavers were in their battle-splendor now, clothed only in brilliant crimson flames. They hunched behind a battle wall of piled stones – a stone fence left by a farmer, really – and hurled flames at Castle Longmot. Each of the flameweavers would reach up to the sky and grasp the sunlight, so that for a moment the whole sky would darken, and then strands of twisted light and heat would plummet into their hands and sit glowing like small suns, just before the flameweavers hurled.

It did little good. Castle Longmot was made of ancient stone. Spells had been woven into it by Earth Wardens over the ages. The balls of light and heat would sail from the flameweavers' hands, expanding in size as they moved toward the castle – for the flameweavers could not concentrate their power at this distance – until the giant glowing balls harmlessly splashed against the battlements.

Yet the efforts had some effect. King Orden's warriors had been forced to hide behind the battlements, seeking cover, and one flameweaver had hit a ballista on his first toss, forcing Orden's artillerymen to withdraw the ballistas and catapults into the towers.

So, for the moment, the battle was a quiet struggle –

flameweavers hurling fireballs with little effect, tiring themselves, giants loading the catapults to send stones over the walls.

Sometimes, when a ball of flame smashed the high walls just below the machicolations, the inferno would send a blast of heat upward through the kill holes, where archers hid. Then Raj Ahten would hear a gratifying scream as a soldier felt the sharpness of his teeth. In places, bundles of arrows had burst into flame like kindling.

Even now, Raj Ahten had men and giants gathering fuel to build a huge inferno. Sunlight often served adequately as a source of energy for his flameweavers, but the afternoon skies were going gray, and the weavers' work was of poorer quality. If they could depend on a more immediate source of energy, their balls of flame would be tighter – perhaps small enough, even, to penetrate the archer's slots along the twin towers.

So the giants hacked down great oak trees and pulled fallen logs from the hills, where they stacked them before the castle like a great dark crown made of writhing limbs. When the flameweavers tapped this crown for fuel, they would increase their powers greatly.

Half an hour after Binnesman left the castle, an outrider came thundering from the west with urgent news. He raced his horse through camp and leapt to the ground at Raj Ahten's feet.

Ah, Raj Ahten thought, Vishtimnu's army has finally been sighted. In Raj Ahten's state, with his high metabolism, it seemed the man took forever to speak. Fortunately, he did not wait for permission.

"I beg pardon, Great King," he said, head bowed. The man's eyes were wide with fear. "But I have urgent news. I was placed to watch at Harm's Gorge. I must report that a horseman came to the gorge and destroyed the bridge. He pointed a finger, uttered a curse, and the bridge collapsed."

"What?" Raj Ahten asked. Could the Earth Warden be seeking to cut off Raj Ahten from his reinforcements? The wizard had claimed that he would not take sides in this battle, and Raj Ahten had believed him. But the wizard was obviously up to something.

"The bridge is destroyed. The gorge is impassable," the scout repeated. Raj Ahten's scouts were trained to treat every question, even rhetorical questions, as queries. They reported only what they saw, without embellishment.

"Have you spotted signs of Vishtimnu?"

"No, O Great Light. I saw no signs – no scouts, no clouds of dust on the road. The forest lies quiet."

Raj Ahten considered. Just because his scout did not see signs of reinforcements, it did not mean that Vishtimnu was not coming. It could well be that the wizard had his own means of detecting them. And in an effort to delay the army from reaching Longmot, the wizard had destroyed the bridge. But this would only slow Vishtimnu, not stop him. Vishtimnu's armies brought great wains filled with food, clothing, and weapons, supplies enough to last the whole winter, to last for a long campaign. The wagons would not be able to pass the gorge, would have to go around, some hundred and twenty miles.

This would slow the caravan at least four days, probably five or six. It would slow even those knights mounted on force horses, so that they wouldn't reach Longmot today.

Destroying the bridge would do Raj Ahten little harm. Unless . . . the wizard knew that more than one army marched through these woods, and therefore sought to cut off Raj Ahten's escape.

Raj Ahten suddenly realized that Jureem had run off only hours ago. Perhaps he had feared to come to Longmot. Perhaps Jureem himself had conspired to create a trap!

Raj Ahten didn't hesitate. Two and a half miles north-east of Longmot, on a lonely mountain, an ancient observatory stood on a promontory that rose above the woods higher than any other hill for many miles. Raj Ahten could see the observatory from here – a round tower with a flat top, made of bloodred stone. It was called the Eyes of Tor Loman.

From its lonely seat, the Duke's far-seers could watch the land for many leagues. Raj Ahten did not have a man there now. His scouts and far-seers had spread out along the roads north, south, east, and west, increasing their view. Yet it was possible that at this moment, his far-seers could be racing this way with some evil report.

Raj Ahten called to his men, "Maintain the attack! Get the pyre burning!"

He spun and raced over the green fields of Longmot with all the speed he could safely muster.

FORTY-SEVEN: THE EYES OF TOR LOMAN

On the castle wall, Orden watched in fascination as the messenger rode to Raj Ahten, gesticulating. Several giants ambled between Orden and the Wolf Lord, blocking Orden's view.

Orden had studied the Wolf Lord, hoped the man would try to rush the castle. He had his men and dogs and giants and ladders all prepared. The mages were ready. But Raj Ahten remained patient.

Yet when the messenger came, Orden took heart. Bad news for Raj Ahten, Orden guessed by the demeanor of the messenger. Desperation might only be a moment away.

Then Raj Ahten fled. He leaped a stone fence, raced over the downs.

Orden counted off seconds, trying to guess Raj Ahten's speed. A hundred and ten, perhaps a hundred and twenty miles per hour the Runelord raced over the flats, slowing as he careered round the castle, taking to the air as he raced over a hill up the north road – toward the old observatory.

If that is the fastest you can run, I can beat you, Orden exulted. He glanced at his men along the wall-walk.

He had a hundred young men lying beneath the merlons, waiting for flameweavers to send their infernal missiles to smash against the castle. Spurts of fire would rise up through the grillwork of the machicolations. Each four or five times such a missile hit, the young men were to cry out as if wounded. Some young men were very dramatic, and at that moment, one of them leapt up, holding a leather vest against himself and batting at it furiously before pretending to fall as one slain. The boy had set the vest there ten minutes earlier, waiting for it to catch fire.

Many boys nearby tried to stifle chuckles at these antics. But those antics served a purpose. So long as Raj Ahten believed his tactics wore the castle down, he'd keep at them.

Orden took quick stock. If he could follow Raj Ahten, catch him, he'd be able to battle him alone, man to man.

"I'd better go," Orden said.

Beside him, one of his captains gazed longingly toward Raj Ahten. "May the Powers be with you!" The captain clapped Orden on the back.

"You and I and Sylvarresta shall be hunting in the Dunnwood by nightfall," Orden said. "Have no fear."

Orden blew a deep, bass hunting horn in signal. Immediately his men at the gates let the drawbridge drop. His energies swelled as all through the castle the men in his serpent ring held perfectly still.

Suddenly the air seemed to thicken to the consistency of syrup. Orden had the strength of twelve men, but with the metabolism of sixty, it required considerable effort to breathe.

He leapt forward, bearing a single weapon – a thin half-sword, sharp enough to strike off Raj Ahten's head. He planned to take Gaborn's warning to heart, decapitate the Wolf Lord. And he carried his shield.

He began running, leaping down the stairs from the castle wall, surprised at the initial push it took to combat inertia. Running required constant, steady pressure. As he spun round a corner, his momentum was such that he accidentally veered from his course.

He raced down to the gate, and already his men had begun raising the drawbridge, as he had ordered. He bounded up the slight incline, gingerly leapt forty feet to clear the moat, running as he landed, and hurried after Raj Ahten.

The resistance of the wind against his shield felt tremendous. After a few yards he dropped it, hurried through the charred streets of the city, then veered on to a footpath that led over the downs.

The grass seemed marvelously green this morning, having been cleansed by last night's rains, and everywhere the little white winterstar flowers lay among the fields.

Orden raced over the downs, found that like Raj Ahten, when he reached the top of a mound, he was traveling so fast that he became airborne.

Orden had read of men who had taken great endowments of metabolism. He knew that going airborne was of little danger, so long as when he landed he made certain that he sped a little, kept his feet moving to absorb the impact of his fall.

He turned a corner. Learning to lean into a turn, he knew, was perhaps the most difficult aspect of running with high metabolism.

Many people found it difficult to adopt the easy rolling gait necessary to run. They wanted to move fast by pressing hard with their feet, as a normal man would when seeking a quick start, but those who tried it would snap their legs. The resting body had too much inertia to overcome.

Orden understood this principle well.

But remembering to lean into curves at the proper angle, that just felt unnatural. As Orden gained speed, he found he'd be running, trying to make a turn in the trail, and it seemed that strange forces grasped him. Gravity did not pull down so much as momentum kept him running in whatever direction he'd taken, and as he hit a muddy spot on one turn, only a great deal of dancing let him stay afoot and keep from smashing into a tree beside the trail.

Now he saw that Raj Ahten had kept his running speed down to a hundred miles per hour for good reason. It didn't feel safe to run faster.

Yet Orden sped up, for his life and the lives of all his people depended on it. He raced higher up Tor Loman, through the white-trunked aspens, under their golden leaves.

As he climbed one hill, looked down into the sun-dappled glen below, he saw a huge hart, its antlers wider than a man's arm span. Startled, it leapt gracefully in the air, seemingly to hang just a few feet above the ground.

I could run that deer down in a heartbeat, Orden realized, as he raced toward it, passing a span behind as it dropped toward a creek.

Orden climbed toward the pines, running up a rocky, narrow crag. Ahead, he saw the glint of dark metal as Raj Ahten entered the woods.

The sound of the steel rings in mail warned Raj Ahten of a pursuer. He glanced back. Orden rushed up the trail.

Raj Ahten could not imagine someone running fast enough to catch him. He redoubled his speed. The trail now led straight between the dark pines. A shaft of sunlight shone at the trail's end. Beyond it stood the red sandstone of the Eyes of Tor Loman.

Raj Ahten knew that fleeing was useless. Orden was gaining on him, and had the greater speed.

"I have you!" Orden shouted in triumph, a hundred yards behind.

Raj Ahten decided to use Orden's speed against him. He crested a small rise, leapt. He felt a sharp pain in his right leg, for his fibula snapped on takeoff.

He knew he could heal in seconds.

As Raj Ahten rose, he twisted, drew the hatchet from his belt, and hurled it just where Orden should be.

To his surprise, Orden had begun to stutter-step, slowing. The hatchet should have cleaved him at something close to two hundred miles per hour, but the aim was high.

Deftly, Orden dodged under the projectile.

Raj Ahten's trajectory carried him high. Though the break in his leg seemed minor, it did not have time to do more than begin healing before he hit the ground.

His tibia snapped, along with the first break, and he tried to let himself roll forward, take the weight from his fall on his good leg and shoulders.

As Raj Ahten came up, Orden fell on him, hacking viciously with his short sword. With Orden having so many endowments of metabolism, Raj Ahten could not prepare for the assault.

Raj Ahten leaned back from the attack. Orden's first swing hit him full in the throat. Crimson droplets sprayed from Raj Ahten's neck, and he felt the chink of metal as the blade struck bone.

King Orden exulted as he saw the horrible wound, watched flesh peel from Raj Ahten's throat, saw the Wolf Lord's handsome eyes widen in terror.

Yet the blade had hardly cleared Raj Ahten's flesh when the wound began to close over, seamlessly. The man had so many endowments of stamina, he seemed no longer human.

The Sum of All Men, Orden feared, that creature which drew life from so many people that it could no longer be classified as mortal, could no longer die. Raj Ahten was becoming a Power, one to vie the elements or the Time Lords.

The chronicles spoke of it. The chronicles said Daylan Hammer had lived in Mystarria for a time, sixteen centuries past, before he went south, seeking to suffer in silence. For immortality had become a burden. Daylan's Dedicates passed away, yet he could not die, for in some fashion he had been transformed. The gifts transmitted through the forcibles remained with him eternally – unwanted, a curse.

Orden had perfect recall, and he saw the words now before him, as he'd read them while young, studying the fragment of an ancient chronicle written by a distant forefather:

"Having loved his fellow men too deeply, Daylan found that life became a burden. For men he befriended, women he loved, blossomed and died like the roses of a single season, while he alone remained perennial. So he sought solitude beyond Inkarra, in the Isles of Illienne, and I suppose he lives there still."

All this flashed through Orden's mind as his sword cleared Raj Ahten's throat; then he realized he had swung so hard that the blade was getting away from him. Pain filled his arm as he strained muscles and pulled tendons, trying to hold it.

The sword flashed away into a bed of ferns upon the knoll.

He had no other weapon. But Raj Ahten still sat, frozen in horror at the power of his attack. Orden leapt, kicking at Raj Ahten's head with all his might.

He wore the steel-toed boots of war, each with a heavy bar across the toe. The blow, he knew, would shatter his own leg. But it could also crush Raj Ahten's skull.

As Orden kicked, Raj Ahten twisted away. Orden's heel struck beneath Raj Ahten's epaulets.

A ripping pain tore through Orden's leg as every bone in it shattered, a pain so profound it wrung a cry from his throat.

Yet if I ruin myself, Orden thought, then I ruin Raj Ahten. Raj Ahten's shoulder crumpled. Orden felt the bones of the Wolf Lord's arm snap, followed by his collarbones, then the ribs caving in, one by one, snapping like twigs beneath his heel.

Raj Ahten screamed like one dying.

Orden landed on Raj Ahten's shoulder, and sat for what seemed a few seconds, gasping, wondering what to do next. He rolled off the Wolf Lord, to see if the man had died.

To his astonishment, Raj Ahten groaned in pain, rolled in the grass. The impression of Orden's boot lay stamped on the Wolf Lord's shoulder.

The scapula had caved in. Raj Ahten's right arm twisted at an unnatural angle. The flesh of his shoulder was pushed down six inches.

Raj Ahten lay in the grass, eyes glazed with pain. Blood frothed from his mouth. The Wolf Lord's dark eyes and chiseled face were so beautiful in that moment, Orden marveled. He'd never seen the Wolf Lord so close, in all his glamour. It took Orden's breath away.

"Serve me," Raj Ahten whispered fervently.

In that second, Mendellas Draken Orden was swept away by the force of Raj Ahten's glamour, and wished to serve him with his whole heart.

Then the second passed, and he grew frightened: for something moved beneath Raj Ahten's armor; the shoulder settled and swelled, settled once again, as if years of inflammation and healing and pain all rolled into one infinite, heart-stopping moment. The shoulder finally grew to a bulbous hump.

Orden tried to roll to his feet, knowing the fight was not over.

Raj Ahten crawled after him, grasped Orden's right arm by the wrist, and smashed his helm into Orden's own shoulder, so hard that the helm was jarred loose from Raj Ahten's head.

Bones shattered all along Orden's arm, and he cried out. He writhed on the ground, his right leg a ruin, his arm and shoulder useless.

Raj Ahten backed away, stood gasping for breath. "It is a shame, King Orden. You should have taken more stamina. My bones are already fully healed. How many days will it be until you can say the same?" He kicked hard, snapping Orden's good leg. Orden collapsed to the ground, on his back.

"Where are my forcibles?" Raj Ahten said calmly.

Orden gave no answer.

Raj Ahten kicked King Orden in the face.

Blood spurted from Orden's right eye, and he felt it hanging against his cheek. Orden fell to the ground in a near faint, and covered his face with his good hand. Raj Ahten kicked his unprotected ribs. Something tore loose inside, and Orden began coughing, spewing flecks of blood.

"I'll kill you!" King Orden spat. "I swear it!"

It was a vain threat. Orden couldn't fight back. He needed to die. Needed Raj Ahten to kill him so the serpent ring would break and another warrior could fight in his stead.

King Orden began to cough; he could hardly breathe in air so thick, so liquid. Raj Ahten kicked his ribs again, so that Orden lay gasping.

Raj Ahten turned and scrambled up the trail fifty yards, through dry grass filled with yellow tansy, to the base of the Eyes of Tor Loman. A stone stair spiraled three times outside the circumference of the tower. Raj Ahten scrambled up it, limping painfully, one shoulder five inches lower than the other. Though his face looked beautiful, he seemed from the back to be little more than just another twisted hunchback. His right arm hung askew, and his right leg might have healed, but it looked shorter than the left.

Orden panted, sweated with exertion, tried to breathe in air that felt thick as honey. The grass near his head smelled so rich, he wanted to lie in it a moment, to rest.

On the heath, Iome and Gaborn rode side by side through the great throng. Gaborn held a shield high, and carried one of the Duke's lances. Tied atop it was a bit of a red curtain from the windows of the Duke's Keep. A white circle of cloth pinned in its middle would make it look, at a great distance, much like the Orb of Internook. That is, it would appear like Internook's colors to anyone watching twenty miles away. Gaborn suspected Raj Ahten's far-seers would be watching. It was standard tactics during any siege to place scouts all around the battle.

For the past half-hour, Gaborn had been busy worrying about the logistics of what he did: trying to drive a couple of hundred thousand head of cattle and horses across the plain was hard work. Even the experienced drovers and horsemen in the retinue could not manage the task easily.

The work was made harder by inexperienced boys who tried desperately to help but who tended to startle the cattle at every turn. Gaborn feared that at any moment, the huge herd might stampede right or left, tramping the women and children who bore shields in a great line before the herd, as if they were warriors.

Yet as he watched the skies above Longmot, fear seized Gaborn even more. The skies looked gray overhead, but far on the horizon darkness flashed as Raj Ahten's flameweavers pulled fire from the heavens.

Gaborn feared he had caused it, that his ruse had led Raj Ahten to hurry his attack on Longmot rather than to simply drive the Wolf Lord off in terror, as Gaborn had hoped to do.

As he rode, words began to from in his mind, a half-remembered spell from an ancient tome. Though he'd never fancied himself as one with earth powers, now he found himself chanting,

> "Earth that betrays us, on the wind,
> become a cloak to hide us, wrapped within.
> Dust that reveals us, in the sky,
> Hide our numbers from the predator's eye."

Gaborn felt shocked that such a spell had come unbidden to his mind. Yet at that moment, he recalled the spell, and it felt right to speak it, as if he had stumbled upon the key to a nearly forgotten door.

The earth powers are growing in me, he realized. He

did not yet know what he would become.

He worried for his father, and as he did so, he felt the man's imminent danger, felt danger wrapped around him like grave clothes.

Gaborn hoped his father could hold out through the attack. He raised his war horn to his lips, blew once, and all around him, others did the same. Before his army, the marchers began singing songs of war.

Raj Ahten had dozens of far-seers in his retinue, but none were like him, none had so many endowments of sight. Raj Ahten did not know how many endowments he had, but he knew it numbered in the thousands. He could discern the veins in a fly's wings at a hundred yards, could see as clearly by starlight as the average man did by sunlight. While most men with so many endowments of sight would have gone day-blind, Raj Ahten's stamina let him withstand the full sun.

It took nothing to spot the towering cloud to the east, an army marching on him.

As he made his way up the tower, Raj Ahten kept searching to the south and west for signs of Vishtimnu's army, signs of help. With his heightened metabolism, it seemed he scanned the horizon for many long minutes for sign of a yellow pennant rising through the forest canopy, or the glint of sunlight on metal, the dust rising from the march of many feet, or the color that mankind had no name for – the hue of warm bodies.

But there are limits even to a far-seer's vision. He could not see through walls, and the forest canopy off to the west was wall enough that it could have hidden many armies. Moreover, a moist wind from the south blew in off the heath, from the vast fields of Fleeds, which were thick with dust and pollen, limiting his vision to thirty or forty miles.

He stood breathlessly, for a long moment. He did not worry about time. With so many endowments of metabolism, he could not have been six seconds searching the horizon in the southwest before he realized he'd see nothing. Vishtimnu's army was too far away.

He turned east, felt his heart freeze. In the distance, Binnesman's horse hurtled across the plains. Raj Ahten could see his destination: at the limit of vision, the golden towers of Castle Groverman rose from the plains beside a river of silver. And before the castle marched an army the likes of which he had seldom seen: hundreds of thousands of men.

A line of spearmen marched in front, five thousand across, and sunlight gleamed on their shields and helms. Behind them marched bowmen by the thousands, and knights mounted on chargers.

They had already crossed the heath a distance of some five to seven miles from Castle Groverman. At such a great distance, in such dirty air, he could not see them clearly. The dry dust of their passage obscured their numbers, rose from their feet in a cloud hundreds of feet high. It looked almost like the smoke of a range fire.

But it was not the heat of a fire he saw beneath that dust. He saw the heat of life, of hundreds of thousands of living bodies.

Among the horde, pennants waved in dozens of colors – the green banners of Lysle, the gray of North Crowthen, the red of Internook. He saw horns among the crowd, the horned helms of hundreds of thousands of warriors – the fierce axemen of Internook.

It can't be, he reasoned. His pyromancer had said that the King of Internook was dead.

Perhaps, Raj Ahten's troubled mind told him, *but Internook's armies are marching*.

Raj Ahten stilled his breathing, closed his eyes. In the field below, rising winds hissed through the trees, but distantly, distantly, beneath the sound of the blood rushing through his veins, war horns pealed. The cries of thousands of voices raised in war song.

All the armies of the North, he realized, gathering against him.

At the gates of Castle Sylvarresta, Orden's messenger had said King Orden planned this assault for weeks. And he'd hinted that traitors in Raj Ahten's own ranks had revealed the presence of the forcibles to King Orden.

Raj Ahten had rejected the tale, never considered the possibility it might be true – for if it was true, it portended such dire consequences for this invasion that Raj Ahten could hardly dare ponder them.

If it was true, if Orden had planned this raid weeks ago, then he could have sent for aid, he could have summoned the kings of the North to battle.

Four weeks ago Orden had set march. Four weeks. It was possible. The fierce Warlord of Internook could have marshaled his hordes, sent them in longboats to land on the rocky beaches of Lysle, then marched them here, joining with Knights Equitable of various kingdoms.

These would not be common soldiers. These would not be men who trembled at the sight of Raj Ahten's Invincibles.

Raj Ahten opened his eyes again, just as Binnesman's horse wheeled to join the procession, taking its lead.

"The new King of the Earth is coming," the old wizard had said. Now Raj Ahten saw the truth. This Earth Warden would join his enemies. This Earth Warden would indeed serve a king. "The Earth rejects you. . . ."

Raj Ahten felt a strange terror beginning to swell up inside him. A great king marched at the head of that army, he felt sure. The wizard's king. The king his pyromancer had warned him of.

And he brought an army Raj Ahten could not match.

Even as he watched, a marvelous thing happened: at that very moment, the great cloud of dust over the army began to form – tall spires of dust rose hundreds of yards into the air like the points of a crown, and a face took form in the roiling dust, a stern visage of a cruel man with death in his eyes.

The Earth King.

I came here to hunt him, and now he hunts me, Raj Ahten realized.

Raj Ahten had little time remaining. He needed to return to the castle, take it quickly, win back his forcibles before he retreated.

He raced down the stairs of Tor Loman, heart pounding in terror.

FORTY-EIGHT: FIRE

Raj Ahten raced back down the forest trail, leaping rocks, speeding through glens. He suspected now that Longmot held no treasure, that the forcibles had moved.

Everything pointed to it – Orden practically begging for execution. The man was obviously joined in a serpent. To kill him would behead the serpent, freeing another soldier to fight with almost as much metabolism as Orden now carried.

But leaving Orden alive and incapacitated kept the serpent intact. Raj Ahten had only to find warriors dedicated to the serpent, slaughter them quickly, and cut the serpent into pieces.

The existence of a serpent seemed evidence that the forcibles had left Longmot, for if Orden had really taken hundreds of endowments, he'd not have relied on a serpent for power. He'd have garnered greater stamina. But the man was too easily wounded, too slow to heal.

No, he couldn't have taken hundreds of endowments, or even dozens. He didn't have the people here to serve as Dedicates. So he'd moved the forcibles. Probably not far. People who hide valuables seldom want to hide them far. They want to be able to check on them frequently.

Yet it was possible Orden had given them to another.

All morning, Raj Ahten had hesitated to attack the castle for some reason he could not name. Something about the soldiers on the walls had disturbed him. Now

546

he realized what it was: Prince Orden wasn't on those walls. He'd expected father and son to fight together, as in the old songs.

But the son was not here.

The new King of the Earth is coming, the old wizard had told him. But the wizard had not emphasized the word *new*. "I see hope for House Orden," the wizard had said.

Prince Orden. It made sense. The boy had earth spells protecting him, a wizard in his employ. Gaborn was a fighter. Raj Ahten knew. He'd sent Salim to kill Gaborn on two occasions, in an effort to keep Mystarria from uniting with a more defensible realm. Yet the assassin had failed.

He has bested me at every turn, slain my pyromancer, evaded me.

So Gaborn now has the forcibles, Raj Ahten realized, and has taken endowments, and rides at the head of the advancing army. True, Gaborn hadn't had much time to garner endowments, but the matter could be easily handled. Orden had recaptured Longmot three days ago. In that time, a dozen faithful soldiers could have taken endowments on Gaborn's behalf, preparing themselves to act as vectors, waiting for Gaborn to return to Castle Groverman to collect his due. The new Dedicates might be secreted in Longmot or Groverman or any of half a dozen castles nearby.

Raj Ahten had used the same tactics on occasions.

As Raj Ahten raced back to Longmot, he considered all these things. He calculated how much time it would take to seize Longmot, destroy the forces within, and search for his treasure, to verify his guess.

He had tricks up his sleeves, weapons he'd not planned to employ this day. He'd not wanted to reveal his full strength in battle, but perhaps it would be necessary.

He considered how much time it would take afterward to flee. Groverman's army stood twenty-five miles off.

Many of those men were afoot. If every soldier had an endowment of metabolism and one of strength, they might make it here in three hours.

Raj Ahten planned to be gone in one.

In Castle Longmot, Captain Cedrick Tempest worried for his people, worried for Orden, worried for himself. After Orden and Raj Ahten had raced north, both armies waited expectantly while Raj Ahten's men prepared for battle.

The giants had carried whole trees of oak and ash to the slope of the hillside, as if to make a bonfire, and there the flameweavers had stepped inside, turning the dead trees into a conflagration.

For long minutes, the three danced within the fire, letting it caress their naked flesh, each of them walking around the edge of the bonfire, drawing magical signs in the air, emblems of blue-glowing fire that clung in the smoke as if they hung on a castle wall.

It was an eerie, mesmerizing sight.

Then they began to whirl and chant in an odd dance, as if each man himself were synchronizing with the flames, dancing with the flickering lights of the fire, becoming one with it.

Thus each flameweaver weaved and bobbed and cavorted, and began to sing a song of desire, calling, calling.

It was one of the flameweaver's greatest powers – that of summoning fell creatures from the netherworld. Tempest had heard of such things, but few men ever witnessed a Summoning.

Here and there, men on the walls began drawing symbols of protection, vainly muttering half-remembered spells. Some hedge wizard from out of the wild began to draw runes in the air, and the men around him clustered near for protection.

Tempest chewed his lip nervously as the wizards

gathered their powers. Now, in the bonfire, the walls of flame thickened, becoming green things like no earthly fire. A luminous portal was forming.

In another moment, Tempest saw shapes materialize within that light – white flaming salamanders from the netherworld, bobbing and leaping, not wholly formed.

At the sight of those creatures summoned into the flames, Cedrick Tempest was chilled to the bone. His men could not fight such monsters. It was folly to stay here, folly to fight.

A cry of consternation caught in Tempest's throat. Help. We need help, he thought.

He'd hardly thought this, when he spotted a blur to the east of the castle, someone rushing over the downs, returning from Tor Loman. He hoped it was King Orden, pleaded to the Powers that Orden had returned victorious.

But the man racing over the downs did not wear Orden's shimmering cape of green samite. Raj Ahten raced toward them, his helm gone.

Tempest wondered if Orden had even caught the Wolf Lord, then glanced down into the keep. Shostag the Axeman was Orden's second. If Orden had died, then Shostag should be up, should be the new head of the serpent. Tempest saw no sign of the burly outlaw down in the keep.

Perhaps Orden still lived, would come to fight in their behalf.

Raj Ahten shouted a command, ordering his troops to prepare for battle.

An old adage said, "When Runelords battle, it is the commoners who die." It was true. The Dedicates in their well-protected keeps, the common archers, the farm boys skirmishing for their lives – all would fall without notice before a Runelord's wrath.

All his life, Cedric Tempest had sought to be more than a commoner, to avoid such a fate. He'd become a force soldier at the age of twelve, made sergeant at sixteen, captain of the guard at twenty-two. In all those years, he'd grown accustomed to feeling the strength of others in his arms, to having the health of Dedicates flowing in his blood.

Until now. He stood in nominal command of Longmot, struggling to marshal his forces against Raj Ahten's troops. Yet he was little more than a commoner. In the battle for Longmot, most of his Dedicates had been slaughtered. He had an endowment of wit, one of stamina, one of grace. Nothing more.

His chain mail weighed on him heavily, and his warhammer felt clumsy in his hand.

The winds sweeping from the south chilled him, and he wondered what this day would bring. He cowered behind the battlements. Certainly, he felt death in the air.

Yet for the moment the preparation for battle stood at a standstill. The soldiers and giants and dogs of Raj Ahten all kept beyond bowshot. For several more long minutes, only the flameweavers worked, dancing, twisting, gyrating in the heart of their bonfire, one with the flames; and the glowing salamanders took clearer form, becoming worms of white light, adding their own magical powers to those of the flameweavers.

Now, in the center of the great fire, the flameweavers stopped their wild dance and raised their hands to the sky as one.

The sky went black as onyx as the flameweavers began drawing ropes of energy from the heavens. Time and again, the flameweavers reached into the sky and caught the light. Time and again, they gathered it into their hands and merely held it, so that their hands became green blazing lights of their own that glowed brighter and brighter.

The hedge wizard muttered and cursed.

The flameweavers' magics took more than the mere light from heaven. For minutes now, the air had been growing colder. Tempest saw that a rime of frost began to cover the castle walls, and the haft of the warhammer in his hand had gradually become stinging cold.

Frost formed along the ground – heaviest near the bonfire, and fanning out over the fields and all around the army, as if this otherworldly fire drew heat, rather than gave it off. The flameweavers were drawing the energy from the fire so efficiently now that Tempest imagined that even he could have stood in those emerald flames, walked through them unburned.

Tempest's teeth chattered. It seemed that the very heat of his body was beginning to be sucked from him. Indeed, he could see the salamanders more clearly in the flames now – ethereal beings with tails of flame, leaping and dancing about, staring at the men on the castle walls.

"Beware the salamander's eyes. Don't look into the flames!" the hedge wizard began to shout. Tempest recognized the danger. For when his eyes met those pinpricks of flame that formed the orbs of a salamander, though for only a flickering instant, the salamander grew more solid in form while Tempest's blood ran all the colder. Men averted their gaze, studied the frowth giants or the mastiffs or the Invincibles in Raj Ahten's army – anything but the salamanders.

In the foreboding gloom, the bonfire grew surreal – became a green flaming world of its own, its walls decorated in fierce runes, the creatures at its heart growing in power with each passing moment.

The clouds above had become so cold that a thunderous hail now began to fall lightly, bouncing like gravel from the battlements, pinging against the helms and armor of the castle's defenders.

Tempest felt frightened to the core of his soul. He did not know what the flameweavers might try. Would they simply suck the life heat from the men on the walls? Or would they send gouts of fire lancing into the ranks? Or did they have some scheme that was even more nefarious?

As if to answer his question, one flameweaver suddenly stopped his gyrations among the heart of the emerald flames. For a long moment, ropes of green energy coiled from the skies, falling into each of his hands. Now, the skies all around grew blacker than the darkest night. Distantly, thunder grumbled, yet if lightning flashed, Tempest never saw it.

In that moment, it seemed as if all time, all sound, suddenly stilled in expectation.

Then the flameweaver compacted the energy in his hand, as if he were forming a snowball, and hurled a green bolt of fire toward the castle walls. Immediately the flameweaver dropped back, as if spent.

The green bolt exploded into the drawbridge with a sound of thunder, as if answering the heavens. The castle rattled under the impact, and Tempest grasped a merlon for support. The ancient earth spells that bound the oak planks and stone of the bridge were supposed to resist fire. Even the touch of the elemental some fifteen minutes earlier had only barely charred the wood of the bridge.

But never was anything made to resist an accursed fire like this. The green flames smote the iron crossbars on the bridge, then raced up the metal, burning the iron with a fierce light, racing up the chains that held the drawbridge closed. Wondrously, the flames did not scorch the wooden planks of the bridge, did not burn the stone casements around it. Instead, they ate only the iron, burned only iron.

In horror, Cedrick Tempest imagined how the touch of that flame would have affected an armored warrior.

With a creaking sound, the bridge fell open.

Tempest shouted, ordering defenders down from the walls, to bolster the troops behind the ruined bridge. Three hundred knights were down in the bailey, mounted on warhorses, ready to issue out to attack if needed. But carts and barrels were also crowding the bailey, forming a barricade that would not be enough. In the hail and darkness, men struggled for better positions. Some knights were shouting, wanting to charge out now, attack while they might be of use. Other defenders on the ground sought to further barricade the gates. Warhorses were whinnying and kicking, and more than one knight fell from his charger and was trampled.

Overhead, the whole sky went black again while ropes of twisted energy began to feed a second flameweaver. A long minute later, the flameweaver hurled a great ball of green flames at the east tower, which overlooked the drawbridge.

Instantly the flames raced in a circle all about the base of the tower, so that for a moment it looked like a green ring upon a stone finger. But these flames were alive, seeking entry. They seemed to squirm through archery slots and up the kill holes. They flickered and licked the dull stone, limning the mortar that sealed the tower closed, then raced into windows. If anything, Tempest realized with mounting horror, this flameweaver's spell was more powerful than the first's.

What happened next, Cedrick Tempest did not want to know, yet he could not help but watch.

The stones of the tower seemed to wail in pain, and a rush of wind and light escaped all the holes in the tower from ground to rooftop as every piece of wooden planking or shield, as every wool tapestry, as every scrap of hide and hair and cloth on every man in that tower all simultaneously burst into flames.

Fierce lights raged from the windows, and Captain Tempest could see his warriors trapped inside, lurid dancers shrieking in horror among the inferno.

There could be no fighting such magic. In despair, Tempest wondered what to do. No charge had begun, yet already the castle gates were down, and half-undefended.

Before the castle gates, with a shout that seemed to echo from the sky, cutting through the blackness and the curtain of hail, came Raj Ahten's voice: "Prepare the charge!"

Somehow, in the past minutes, Tempest had lost sight of the enemy commander. Now he saw Raj Ahten on the hillside, standing among his men, staring toward the castle with – an expression of apathy.

The Wolf Lord's well-trained troops knew what to do. His artillerymen began to feed iron shot into the baskets of their engines, send it hurling high against the walls.

All along the walls, Tempest's men hunched behind the battlements, and now the hail that fell from the skies grew deadly to the castle's defenders. An archer next to Tempest took a ball to the head, was swept from the castle walls. Men raised their shields high for protection.

Tempest looked to the hedge wizard, but now the wizard was crouched behind the battlements, eyes filled with terror.

Wind buffeted from the south, and for a few seconds there was light as the flameweavers took their rest. Tempest saw Raj Ahten's spy balloon, which had been moored a moment earlier, suddenly lift like a graak, despite the battering hail. Four balloonists began emptying sacks of arcane powders into the air, powders which floated down toward the castle in dirty clouds of yellow, red, and gray.

Tempest gaped, wondering where King Orden might be, whispering under his breath for the King to come, to save them all. Longmot is a great castle, protected by earth runes, he told himself.

Now, seeking power once again, Raj Ahten's flameweavers began grasping ropes of fire from the skies. Green walls of flame shone like emerald around the great bonfire, bedazzling, their intricate runes gleaming. The blackening trees within the wall were a bizarre sight, like twisted fingers and arms in an enormous heap of burning body parts. Or like scraps of iron in the forge. Everything became luminous in the heart of the inferno – flameweavers, fiery salamanders, dancing among the logs at the fire's center.

As the flameweavers stole fire from heaven, darkness deepened, making the battlefield a garish, flickering, half-glimpsed sight. The hail fell heavier for a few seconds then, and the air froze in a cloudy fog before his face as Cedrick Tempest breathed.

In that flickering darkness, Tempest glimpsed giants gathering their ladders, men on the battlefield drawing weapons.

"Bowmen at the ready!" Tempest shouted. He watched the track to the north, hoping Orden would appear.

Yet he now feared it would not happen, feared that Orden still lived, and that the serpent ring had not broken. Perhaps Orden had never met up with Raj Ahten, and was even now racing off on some fruitless hunt. Or perhaps Orden was incapacitated.

Tempest's heart pounded. He needed a protector. There was only one thing to do – call upon the knights in the ring to form a new head. But *no*, he realized, that would not do. The Dedicates in the castle were widely dispersed. He did not have time to find them, speak to them all.

He needed to break the serpent ring, slay a Dedicate so that the serpent would form a head.

Across the hill, Raj Ahten made a pulling gesture with his hand, as if to yank clouds from the sky. Hundreds of mastiffs began racing for the castle in a black wave, their red masks and iron collars making the mastiffs a horrendous sight, their commander barking in short yaps.

Now the frowth giants hoisted the great siege ladders, two giants to a ladder, and loped for the castle at a seemingly slow pace, yet covering four yards to the stride. Black behemoths struggling in the night.

Tempest did not have time to explain to another what needed to be done. He turned from his post above the gate, and ran for the stairs.

"Captain?" one of his men cried, as if worried that Tempest had become a craven coward in that moment.

Tempest had no time to explain. A shout rose across the battlefield as three thousand of Raj Ahten's archers raced forward, hurrying to give cover fire against the castle walls.

Tempest glanced over his shoulder before descending the stone steps. Raj Ahten's Invincibles raised their shields and charged. At their head, fifty men raced with a battering ram, a giant iron wolf's head at the ram's end. Tempest knew little of siege magics, but he could see that the iron wolf's head was bound with powerful spells. Fire glowed in its dead eyes.

Though the drawbridge had fallen open, Tempest's men had hastily set a wooden mantelet – a frame of timbers – just inside the green. The ram would smash into the inner defenses. Behind those defenses, Longmot's mounted knights had become restive. They held their great lances at the ready, helm visors down. Their horses shifted their weight from foot to foot, eager to charge.

Raj Ahten's Invincibles raced forward, the earth thundering beneath their iron-shod feet, pounding under the hail that began to fall more earnestly. These Invincibles were men with great endowments of stamina and brawn and metabolism.

Giants loped ahead with ladders, Invincibles with their ram. Arcane powders strewn from the balloon hung over the castle gate now, like a gray hand of doom.

For a moment, Tempest hesitated behind the ramparts inside the gate, wondering if he should stand with his men or hurry forward to slay Shostag.

Across the fields, Raj Ahten's artillerymen let catapults fly. . . .

Raj Ahten watched approvingly as the catapults let fly shells bearing mineral powders of sulfur, potash, and magnesium that would mix with other salts in the cloud above the castle wall.

The firing of these shells was timed so that they would stream through the skies at the same moment his battering ram drew within a hundred yards of the drawbridge.

In the darkness and hail, the bowmen on Longmot's walls saw the catapults fly, and dropped for cover, losing the precious second they needed to choose a target from among Raj Ahten's Invincibles.

For long years Raj Ahten had nurtured his flameweavers, feeding them. On the mountains south of Aven, fires burned constantly so they might appease the Power the sorcerers served. His flameweavers were, Raj Ahten believed, the most fearsome of their kind on earth.

And these flameweavers had made great studies in the use of explosive fires. It had long been known that when wheat and rice were poured into their granaries, the flame of a small lantern could ignite the air with explosive force. Miners pounding out coal deep beneath the mountains of Muyyatin had long known that coal dust would spark at the touch of their lamps, sometimes exploding so ferociously that entire passages within the mine would cave in.

For generations, people had raised borage flowers to give them courage, and children had delighted in throwing the dried stalks into the fire to hear the popping sounds they exuded as they exploded.

But no one had considered how to benefit from the explosive force of such agents. So Raj Ahten's flameweavers studied the phenomenon, learned to prepare and grind and mix the powders.

Now Raj Ahten watched in awe and satisfaction as years of nurturing his sorcerers and financing their grim study paid off. The skies all around went blacker than the deepest night as the final ropes of fire twisted down from heaven. Hail plummeted from the air, and the sound of thunder raged overhead.

The huge bonfire where the flameweavers stood with the beings they summoned suddenly snuffed out like a candle, the green walls collapsing, the creatures within drawing all light and heat into themselves.

The skies remained black, and in that sudden total darkness, no archer could have seen his target to fire. For ten seconds, the skies gave no light.

Atop the castle walls, Orden's knights performed one last defiant act. They broke into a grim song.

Under the cover of that shadow, Raj Ahten's troops continued to race for the walls.

As the bowmen on the castle walls rose to shoot at unseen attackers, a blinding light shot from the center of the flameweavers' infernos.

The sorcerous blast roared like a living sun from flameweavers and salamanders, and a green flaming wave of fire swept from the hilltop, raced toward the castle.

In the sudden rush of light, one could see the terrified faces of Longmot's defenders. Brave boys unmanned, brave men trembling but still defiant.

As the wave of flame traveled inexorably toward Longmot, it touched the arcane powders in the sky.

Then the whole arch above the gate roared into an inferno. Raj Ahten's powders exploded in a cloud of fire that rose like a mushroom some hundred yards at the base, slowly ascending a mile into the air. The concussion threw defenders from the walls like rag dolls. Many fell, stunned. Others staggered back in abject terror.

But the great green wave of flame was not a mere spark to touch off the explosive powders. It was much more than that.

The wave of green fire smote the castle walls, washing over hundreds of defenders who still stood.

On the crowded walls, away from the initial explosion above the arch, warriors were crammed shoulder to shoulder in ranks six deep. The green flames rolled over them like the roaring waves of the sea.

Longmot had been the perfect castle for Raj Ahten to use his powders on. Its south face was but a hundred and twenty yards wide. Defenders had concentrated along the upper wall-walk in that hundred yards.

Raj Ahten's flameweavers incinerated perhaps some two thousand men. As the mushroom cloud rose, Raj Ahten's flameweavers now fell unconscious into the ruins of their own bonfire. No flames leapt in the remains of the fire. No smoke rose, for the flameweavers had drained the vast majority of the energies from it, and in an instant the great blackened logs had incinerated, become ash. So now the flameweavers lay dazed among the hot coals.

But the white-hot salamanders suddenly leapt, as if freed from a cage, rushing hungrily toward the castle.

The scene before the castle gate was a pandemonium. Under the cover of darkness, Raj Ahten's giants had made the wall. Raj Ahten's archers unleashed a hail of deadly arrows – a hail that proved almost unnecessary – while his Invincibles began to race up ladders to the tops of the battlements.

No defenders stood on that south wall now. The explosion and waves of fire had all but emptied the wall-walk.

The castle gate stood undefended. The east tower was a smoking ruin. But within the west tower, a few men tried one last trick. King Orden's men unleashed a rain of burning oil, pouring it down runnels within the tower. Stone gargoyles above the gate suddenly spewed the vile stuff as Raj Ahten's troops raced in with their battering ram.

Some of Raj Ahten's men faltered under the heat of that oil, but such was the speed of the men running that the head of the ram still struck the mantelet behind the castle gate.

All the energy of the spells bound within the wolf's head exploded against the mantelet, sending timbers of wood splintering in all directions. Defenders behind the mantelet shrieked and died under the onslaught.

And in Raj Ahten's mind, a peculiar flame began to dance.

He knew that he should restrain himself now, that it was wrong to destroy men so ruthlessly. It would have been better to use those he could, take their endowments. These men had virtues and strengths that should not have been wasted in such a brutish fashion. Their ugly, fleeting little lives could have been converted to a grander purpose.

Yet the smell of burning flesh suddenly enticed Raj Ahten, left him tingling in anticipation. Against all his better reason, he hungered for destruction.

Cedrick Tempest had been standing behind the mantelet, racing between two warhorses toward the Duke's kitchens, where Shostag lay hidden, when the green wave of flame touched the battlements and a great ball of fire filled the sky overhead.

Fortunately, he'd been staring down, running away from the blast. The heat and energy of it shoved him face-first into the paving stones, so that his helm bent close to his head. For one moment, he'd felt the searing heat of the blast crisp his clothing, burn his skin at a touch. Then he tried to draw a breath in the hot wind of the fireball's passage.

Horses kicked and fell under the impact of the blast. One of them landed half atop him, the body of a knight crushing him.

For a moment, Tempest fell unconscious. Found himself crawling among the stones, among the fallen horses. Men and parts of men rained from the castle walls, a gruesome storm of burned bodies, destroyed flesh.

In that moment, he gazed about in horror as a blackened boy plopped at his head, an arm fell near his hand. He knew then that he would not survive this day. Three days past, he'd sent his wife and children to Castle Groverman, hoping they'd be safe, hoping he'd live to see them again. He remembered how they'd looked as they left – his two toddlers riding the back of a goat, his wife carrying their babe in her arms, his oldest daughter trying to look mature, her lips trembling as she stifled tears of fear.

Tempest looked up to the castle walls, on the west. The walls were nearly empty. Those men still up looked dazed, confused.

Suddenly, a flaming white salamander leapt up on the merlon of the south tower, gazing about. Tempest hid his face, lest the pearly orbs of its eyes touch him.

A second, smaller explosion sounded fifty yards behind him. Tempest tried to scrabble to his knees, looked back. Raj Ahten's Invincibles had just hit the little mantelet barricade inside the gates with their ram. The barricade exploded, sending shards of woods flying, flaming out.

Any men who stood near that barricade blew back under the onslaught of fiery debris, yet painfully few men had been standing at all. A few knights were still up on their horses, but the fallen bodies of their comrades hemmed them in.

The battle was lost. All along the walls before him, defenders were down. Thousands of men screamed and writhed in pain. Arrows were hurtling over the castle walls now, a dark and deadly rain, dropping into wounded men.

Some few hundred men were rushing from the north side of the castle, trying to reach the gates, to put up some kind of defense. Yet Raj Ahten's Invincibles rushed to meet them by the thousands.

War dogs in grim leather masks raced through the streets, leaping over fallen knights and their horses, ripping apart any man or beast that lived, feeding as they slaughtered.

Tempest hoped still that he might find Shostag, slay him so that the serpent would form a head. Yet he felt stunned, confused. Blood dripped from his face.

He collapsed as Raj Ahten's war dogs raced over him, leaping through the fray.

FORTY-NINE: THE EARTH KING STRIKES

Binnesman rode over the heath toward Gaborn and Iome, beneath the cloud of dirt and pollen raised by the feet of hundreds of thousands of men and cattle.

Gaborn stared at the wizard. It was the first time he had seen him in full daylight. His hair had gone white, and the baggy robes he wore had turned from a forest green to shades of scarlet and orange, like leaves that had changed color.

Gaborn rode so close to Iome that at times her knee touched his. He dared not try to call a halt as the wizard neared, his mount speeding over the purple heather. Too many people and animals moved in the great throng. Yet Gaborn wanted to talk to Binnesman, wanted to hear his report.

Binnesman stared at Gaborn's troops for a long moment, wheeled his horse to a near halt, and at last asked in surprise, "Do you plan to feed Raj Ahten's army with all these cattle, or trample him with them?"

"Whatever he desires," Gaborn said.

Binnesman shook his head in wonder. "I heard the startled cries of birds here, felt the earth groan under the weight of feet. I thought that you had conjured an army. I thought it fortunate that I'd gone to the trouble of destroying the old Harm's Gorge Bridge, blocking Raj Ahten's hopes for reinforcements from the west."

"I appreciate the gesture," Gaborn said. "What can you

tell me? Have Raj Ahten's reinforcements been spotted?"

"No," Binnesman said, "nor do I think they are close."

"Perhaps luck is with us," Gaborn said.

"Perhaps so," Binnesman said.

On the horizon, just along the line of green hills covered with trees, the blackness flashed again, much more fiercely than ever before – a line of blackness that split the sky from horizon to horizon.

Then a great pillar of fire roared slowly into the air, an explosion so massive, Gaborn had never seen the like. Something terrible was happening.

"Gaborn," Binnesman said. "Close your eyes. Use your Earth Sight. Tell me what is happening."

Gaborn closed his eyes. For a moment, he felt nothing, and he wondered if Binnesman had erred in asking him to use the earth sight.

Then, faintly, he felt the connections, felt the invisible lines of power between him and his people. He had only consciously chosen his father. Now he realized that he'd been choosing people for days. He'd chosen Myrrima that morning in the market, and he'd claimed Borenson. He'd chosen Chemoise when he saw her helping her father in the wagon, and had chosen her father.

Now, he felt all those he had claimed – Borenson, his father, Myrrima, Chemoise and her father. He felt . . . danger. Terrible danger. He feared that if they did not fight now, they would all die.

Strike, Gaborn silently willed them. *Strike now, if you can!*

Twenty second later, the sound of an explosion roared across the plain, shaking the earth, like distant thunder.

FIFTY:
THE OPENING

At Castle Sylvarresta, Chemoise was getting dinner in the buttery when she felt the urge to strike. The desire came so quickly and so profoundly that she struck her hand against the table by reflex, smashing a round of cheese.

Myrrima tempered her response with reason. The thunders of war shook the manor house where she hid, and outside the sky was black. She couldn't strike against Raj Ahten's soldiers, knew she was no match. So she raced upstairs, hoping to hide beneath some lord's bed.

Six years past, Eremon Vottania Solette had chosen to live as a Dedicate to Salim al Daub because he had two dreams: The first was to see his daughter again. The second was to survive until his grace returned so he would waken among Raj Ahten's Dedicates, able to fight.

Yet over the years, Eremon's hopes faded. Raj Ahten's facilitators drained too much grace from him, left him near death. Robbed of flexibility, his arms and legs became useless, so that he lay as stiff as in rigor mortis.

Life became torment. The muscles in his chest contracted easily enough to let him inhale, but afterward for long moments he had to consciously relax in order to exhale. Sometimes, his heart would clench and not open, and he'd struggle silently, fearing death.

Unable to relax his lips, he spoke with difficulty,

through clenched teeth. He could not chew. If he swallowed anything but the weak broth Raj Ahten's servants fed, it sat like lead in his stomach; the muscles in his gut could not contract enough to digest it.

To empty his bladder or pass a stool was an embarrassment, a process requiring hours of work.

His five endowments of stamina had become a burden, for they kept him alive long after he wished for death. Often he'd wished that King Sylvarresta would slay the men who served Eremon as Dedicates. But the King had been too soft, and so Eremon languished. Until last night. Now, at last, it seemed that death was within reach.

His fingers curled into useless fists. He had lain for years in a ball, bent at the hips. Though endowments of brawn kept him strong, some muscles in his legs and arms had atrophied. So he'd lain imprisoned in weakening flesh, knowing he'd never get vengeance, a helpless tool of Raj Ahten.

Thus it seemed miraculous when his first dream came true, when Raj Ahten decided to take him to Heredon and throw his failing body in front of King Sylvarresta. The deed was supposed to shame the good king. Raj Ahten often went to great lengths to shame a man.

It had seemed miraculous when Eremon saw his daughter Chemoise. She'd grown beautiful, no longer the freckle-faced child of his memory.

Seeing her had been enough. Eremon now felt his life was complete; hereafter he'd take a long slide into oblivion.

Yet one deed more lay before him. As he languished in the Dedicates' wagon, it began to shake as men climbed on to the buckboard, opened the door. Slowly, Eremon opened his eyes. In the dark wain, flies rose in clouds from forlorn Dedicates around him. Men and women were crammed together like salted minnows in a keg, lying on beds of moldering hay.

Facilitators in gray robes stood huffing by the open

door. Shafts of sunlight stabbing into the room blinded him, but Eremon could see that they'd set a body against the wall. A new Dedicate. Another victim.

"What have we here?" the guard asked. "Metabolism?"

The facilitator nodded. Eremon could see the scars on the man – a dozen endowments of metabolism he'd taken, and now he served as a vector.

Raj Ahten's facilitators looked for a place to lay the newcomer. A blind Dedicate who slept next to Eremon rolled in his sleep, huddling for warmth next to a limp rag of a man.

Thus a slim spot opened beside Eremon, and now the facilitators muttered in their own tongue, "*Mazza, halab dao abo*" – "Here, move this brick of camel dung."

One man nudged Eremon's stiff legs aside, as if he were the brick in question. They lay the new Dedicate beside him.

Eremon stared into the fat face of the eunuch Salim al Daub, not five inches from his own. The fat man breathed oh so slowly, in the way of one who has given metabolism. The man who held Eremon's endowment lay next to him, defenseless. A vector for metabolism. A vector, Eremon suspected, for Raj Ahten.

Salim slept a deep slumber from which Eremon swore he'd never wake.

A guard sat in the wagon, an Invincible on a stool in the far corner, wearing a curved dagger and bored expression. Eremon could not risk moving quickly, could not attract attention, but, then, he'd not moved quickly in six years.

For long minutes Eremon slowly tried to unclench his right hand. This unclenching came hard. He felt too excited, too wrathful. A thrill took him, for if he could destroy this man, he would win a double boon – his own endowments back, while he robbed Raj Ahten of metabolism.

Yet outside, a battle raged. Darkness strobed the sky,

glimpsed as shadows and light breaking into the wagon. Men were screaming on the castle walls.

Eremon wished he still had his endowments of strength, wished he could throttle Salim with supernatural finesse. But those had been lost last night.

For many long minutes he worked to open his damned useless hand. Suddenly, as he struggled, Eremon felt a great burning desire. Strike. Strike now if you can!

And as the thought filled him, his hand suddenly unclenched as slowly as a flower opening.

FIFTY-ONE: ON A MOUNTAIN TRACK

Borenson felt more than half-crazed when he rode from Bannisferre. He was possessed, only partly conscious. He imagined the havoc he'd wreak upon Raj Ahten's troops.

Coming from the north, he saw no signs of battle. Too many hills and mountains sheltered Longmot from his view. He could see no darkening skies, for the low clouds sweeping over the mountains blackened everything. Once he thought he heard cries, but he heard them distantly and thought them voices from some waking dream, a remnant of the fantasies of destruction that played in his mind.

South of the mountain village of Kestrel, he turned aside on his trail, spurred his mount over the forest track, hoping to make better time. He had hunted these hills often with his king. He was a bit north of Groverman's hunting retreat, a lodge both large and comfortable.

He did not fear wights or beasts of the wood. He feared only that he'd reach Longmot too late.

As he climbed the mountains, the day turned cold. An icy drizzle soaked him, made the mountain trail slippery. Soon rain turned to sleet and snow, so that he lost more time by taking this trail than if he'd stayed to the road.

High in the hills where aspens bordered a glade, he saw sign of a reaver – tracks crossing the wooded trail. The reaver had dragged something heavy through here within the past few hours, just before dawn. Red blood clots lay on the ground, with bits of oily synovial fluid from a cracked joint. The scuff marks where the creature had been dragged still had tiny balls of clay rolled in them. Very recent marks.

The imprint of the reaver's track was nearly three feet long, two wide. Four toes. A female. A big female.

Borenson stayed on his horse as he studied the trail. Among a jumble of sharp stones lay some black hairs. It looked as if the reaver had dragged a carcass across the road, perhaps a boar. But the hair was too fine for a boar. Borenson sniffed. Bear, definitely. A big male. As musky as the scent of Dunnwood's boars, but not as dirty.

Borenson sniffed again, tried to catch the scent of the reaver, but smelled nothing. Reavers were uncanny in their ability to mimic the scent of their surroundings.

Borenson looked up the trail, wishing that he could track the reaver – if only for a moment.

Myrrima could be in danger. Most likely, Raj Ahten would lay siege for a bit, spend the day resting, preparing for battle. His occupying army should arrive soon.

Borenson feared he couldn't possibly reach the castle before the siege, couldn't help Myrrima.

Then he had to consider the challenge of hunting the reaver. She'd be up in the woods, near the mountaintop, feeding on the bear. The ground here was too cluttered for a man to negotiate easily: aspen limbs had blown from trees; underbrush grew thick and tall after a long summer.

Catching her would be hard. Reavers could sense movement, feel sound as a trembling. The only way to get close to one was to sneak, ever so slowly, letting footfalls come at uneven intervals.

For a moment, Borenson considered following the reaver.

Distantly, as if a voice called from far off, he felt a powerful compulsion. Strike. Strike now if you can!

His king needed him. Myrrima needed him.

He spurred his charger over the mountain trails as snow began to pile, the first of the season. The breath of Borenson's warhorse came in tiny swirls of cloud. His heart pounded.

Tomorrow is the first day of Hostenfest, the first day of the hunt, Borenson realized, and he started thinking about this in order to keep calm. It would have been a good hunt, with snow falling. The boars would have moved to the valleys, leaving tracks at the edges of the glades. He'd have bet with Derrow and Ault as to which of their lords would first put a spear into a pig.

He longed for the yapping of dogs, the deep call of horns. The nightly feasts beside the fires.

But I must strike now, he thought, spurring his mount faster. He wished to strike, wished he had a target.

Again he worried whether he'd killed all the Dedicates at Castle Sylvarresta. I've struck as I can, he told himself. He'd killed all he'd seen, but some might have been taken from the keep into the city, so that invisible lines of power still tied Raj Ahten to Dedicates there.

A battle between Runelords could be complex. The number of endowments played a great part in a battle, as did the skill and training of the warriors.

But a balance of traits was also important. Raj Ahten had so many endowments, it seemed almost futile to slay his Dedicates. But a strong Runelord stripped of wit and grace could become a mere lout, nothing in battle. Take away his metabolism, and though a Runelord had ten thousand endowments of brawn, he'd move so slowly compared to a balanced soldier that he might as well be a coatrack; he became a "warrior of unfortunate proportion."

By killing men in Castle Sylvarresta, Borenson had robbed Raj Ahten of many endowments of grace. The Runelord had been hoarding it, had drawn it from hundreds of men at the castle. Which meant he felt over-balanced in brawn. This would leave him muscle-bound, lacking agility. Perhaps, given such imbalance, King Orden might stand a chance against the Wolf Lord.

So Borenson hoped he'd accomplished his job. He couldn't bear to think his incompetence might cost Orden this battle. Couldn't bear – couldn't stomach the shame that coursed through him when he thought of King Sylvarresta and Iome, still alive.

Sparing those two had cost the lives of dozens of others. Sparing them lent power to Raj Ahten.

A small amount of power, true. But if Borenson and some other assassins struck Raj Ahten's Dedicates at the right time, the Wolf Lord might reach some unfortunate proportion.

Today I hunt Raj Ahten, Borenson told himself, and he let a killing mood seep through every muscle and bone, blanket him like a cloak.

Today I am death. Today I hunt him, and nothing else.

In his imagination, he practiced killing, preparing his every fiber, his every response for cold murder. He imagined how it would be when he met Raj Ahten's scouts here, miles north of Longmot, along the road. He'd ride them down, impale them on his lance so that their warm blood washed him in a wave, leaving no witnesses. Then he'd steal a uniform and ride pell-mell to the battle lines, bursting in on Raj Ahten, as if delivering a message. His message would be death.

The warriors of Inkarra claimed that War was a dark lady, and that those men who served her best gained her favor. They claimed she was a Power, like Earth or Air, Fire or Water.

Yet in the Kingdoms of Rofehavan, it was said that War was but one aspect of Fire, and that no one should serve it.

But the damned Inkarrans should know, Borenson thought. They were masters of war.

Borenson had never sought the Dark Lady's favor, had never addressed her before, but now a prayer formed on his lips, an ancient prayer he'd heard from others but never dared voice himself.

> "Take me in your arms, Dark Lady, take me.
> Wrap me in grave clothes, and let your sweet breath
> lie cold on my cheeks. Let darkness steal
> over me, and fill me with your power.
> Today, I call to you. Today, I am death."

As he rode, Borenson began to smile, then to laugh a deep, throaty chuckle that seemed to rumble from someplace outside him, to well up from the hills or from the trees.

FIFTY-TWO: A PERFECT DAY

Orden woke in pain, unable to tell how long ago he had passed out. The blood around his mouth was still wet, tasted coppery on his tongue. Any moment, Mendellas Orden thought, Raj Ahten will kick me again, begin pummeling me to death.

But nothing happened. Orden lay weak, at the edge of consciousness, waiting for a killing blow that never came.

With his many endowments of stamina, Orden could sustain tremendous damage. His wounds, as extensive as they were now, would not lead to his death. Weeks of convalescence, perhaps, but not death.

That is what he feared.

He opened his good eye, tried to see. The sun high above shone very dim through clouds; then the sky went black.

The glade nearby was empty.

He swallowed, struggled to think. He'd heard the faint *ching* of ring mail as he passed out. Realized numbly that it could have been the sound of Raj Ahten lunging away.

Orden looked around the field at the edge of the knoll. The wind faintly swayed the pines; the grass sat as if bent in a stiff gale. A flock of starlings hung in the air like thistledown, not five spans from him. But Orden was living so quickly, the wind seemed to blow slowly in comparison.

Raj Ahten had fled.

He's left me, Orden realized, because he suspects I'm part of a serpent. He's left me so he can attack the castle. Dimly, he heard a roar like the sound of the sea. Loud sounds, as if tides surged and churned. In his quickened state, the world of sound had vastly changed.

Now he recognized that these must be loud noises, must be cries of war. With one hand, he pushed himself up, gazed over the rolling slope of Tor Loman to Castle Longmot.

What he saw horrified him.

Beyond a curtain of rain or sleet, a huge fire raged on the hillside above Longmot. From that otherworldly fire, flameweavers and salamanders had drawn terrible energies, sending a green wave of flame screaming across the downs to the castle. Frowth giants lumbered over the fields carrying great scaling ladders. The mastiffs of war, with their iron collars and fierce masks, boiled like a dark tide toward the castle gates.

Everywhere in the blackness Raj Ahten's Invincibles raced like dark roaches for the castle, shields high to deflect arrows, weapons drawn.

Raj Ahten's forces were storming Longmot. The sky above the castle was black, ropes of twisted fire funneling from the sky.

King Orden watched from Tor Loman. With his endowments of metabolism, it seemed the skies had gone black for long minutes; one could only discern the dim ropes of flame winding down from heaven – coiled and churning like the winds within a tornado.

He could do nothing to help. He could not charge into battle, could barely crawl.

Quietly, he began to sob. Raj Ahten had taken everything from him – his past, his present. Now his future.

In the darkness, Mendellas turned and painfully struggled up the rough stone steps of the tower to the Eyes of Tor Loman.

To block the agony of his ruined limbs from his mind,

he tried to remember good times. The feasts in his palace in Mystarria during midwinter, on Alms Day.

Always the fogs washed over the green swales on those winter mornings, and from the pinnacles of the great tower one could look down over the marshes as if one were a Sky Lord in a ship of cloud – the gauzy fog so pure. In places, lesser towers of the Courts of Tide could be seen, or the greens of distant pine forests on the western hills, or to the south the shimmering waters of the Caroll Sea reflecting the sky.

On such mornings, he'd always loved to stand on his own observatory in the tower, and watch the geese in their winter migration come winging below him in dark Vs.

He conjured the memory of a perfect day long ago, when he'd descended from his tower, invigorated at dawn, gone to his wife in her bedchamber.

He'd planned to fetch her up to the observatory, to show her the sunrise. Weeks before, an early frost had killed the roses in her garden, and he'd planned to show her how the sun crept up the horizon in the color of the softest blushing rose, a rose that painted the fog for miles around.

But when he reached her bedchamber, she had only smiled at his request, then devised other entertainments.

They'd made love on the tiger-skin rug before the hearth.

By the time they finished, the sun had been up for hours. The poor of Mystarria had gathered in the streets before the castle to collect the winter's alms.

Thus the King and Queen had been required to go out in the afternoon, to spend the remainder of the day riding the huge wains through the street, where they passed out meat, turnips, dried fruit, and silver to those who stood in need.

Orden and his wife had labored hard, stopping often to exchange smiles, or to let a touch linger.

Orden hadn't thought of that day for years, though every sight, sound, and smell remained perfect in his memory. With twenty endowments of wit, Orden could relive such moments at will. It had been a magic day. It was the day, he discovered weeks later, he'd got his wife with her first child, Gaborn.

Ah, how he longed for her still.

As Orden reached the top of the Eyes of Tor Loman, the light reappeared in the heavens, and he stared in horror to see the monstrous wall of fire that Raj Ahten's beasts had hurled against the castle. The skies were painted with strange powders – gray and black, the yellow of sulfur, something red.

The vast, seething green wave of fire seemed to roll through the sky slowly from this distance, at the pace he lived. For what seemed agonizing minutes, Orden crawled across the stone steps.

As he crawled, Orden wondered why Raj Ahten had come here. Certainly not to see down into Longmot. The view here offered nothing.

No, something else had alarmed the Wolf Lord.

So King Orden gazed east, saw dust rising from the plains as if they were aflame, the light shining from shields. An army marching from Castle Groverman.

Despite the immense dust cloud, it could not have been a large army, Orden knew. Thirty thousand commoners come to his aid, marching across a dusty heath, nothing more. They'd be no match for Raj Ahten's Invincibles.

But Orden knew his son marched at the head of that army.

Certainly Gaborn would not be fool enough to attack Raj Ahten. No, this had to be a ruse. Orden smiled. Against a man of Raj Ahten's wit, misinformation could be a potent weapon. His son was fighting as best he could.

In almost every contest, victory came to those who refused to be subdued. The Prince was not cowed.

A good ruse, this, Orden told himself. Raj Ahten believes Longmot was taken days ago. Now he sees an army come to smash him. King Orden only hoped the ruse would work.

And a darker fear crept into his mind. Certainly Gaborn would not attack, would he? Would he?

Yes, he would, Orden realized. If he believed that by doing so he could save his father. Didn't I tell him to attack? Orden thought. Didn't I tell him to sweep down the hill with his knights?

Orden was filled with dread. This was a boy who risked himself to save enemy Dedicates. This was a boy who had become an Oath-Bound Lord.

Orden didn't doubt. Though he'd die in the attempt, Gaborn would certainly attack!

At that moment, the great wave smashed into the castle, sent pillars of fire racing into the sky. Orden could see the horrible damage it wrought, men flying over the walls like flaming birds, could see giants and war dogs, Invincibles and archers all rushing for the castle gates.

Yet he could not feel the stirring within that marked the death of a Dedicate. None of the Dedicates in his serpent ring burned in that flame. Surely the castle would fall.

Deep inside, he felt an overpowering urge. Strike. Strike now as best you can!

Orden recognized that he himself might hold the key to insuring that this great fiasco of a battle served some higher purpose. The men in the castle were joined in a serpent ring, and if the castle were overrun, the men in the ring would all be forced to fight, none drawing metabolism from the others. Eventually one of them would die, and a serpent would form. But who would be at its head?

Certainly not that idiot Dreis, Orden hoped.

No. It had to be Shostag. Formidable, venerable in his own crude way. A fierce warrior.

Orden crawled to the edge of the observatory, looked down.

The Eyes of Tor Loman perched on the edge of a promontory, and on the west edge, huge rocks thrust up from the ground. There, Orden thought. I will hit there.

He threw himself from the tower. It was time for the serpent ring to break. Now let Shostag the Axeman earn his lands and title. Let Gaborn live to inherit his birthright.

And let me return to the arms of the woman I love.

With so many endowments of metabolism, Orden seemed to fall slowly, almost as if he floated to his death.

FIFTY-THREE: THE FLUTTERING

A pillar of fire rose into the far-off skies like a mushroom, and the sound of thunder rumbled over the plain.

Yet Gaborn felt something far more disturbing – distantly, distantly he felt a single heartbeat flutter and fail.

It tore him, dismayed him, far more than that flash of light or the groaning of the earth.

He swayed in his saddle, whispered, "Father."

Somehow, somehow Gaborn feared that his wish to strike at Raj Ahten had caused his father's death.

It had not been the will of the earth to strike. Gaborn had felt no compulsion greater than his own anger. Yet he'd given the command.

No, Gaborn thought. I don't believe it. I don't believe I caused it. How can I know he's dead until I've seen it?

The wizard Binnesman turned to Gaborn, infinite sadness in his eye, and whispered, "You called for your father. Is he gone, then?"

"I . . . don't know," Gaborn said.

"Use the Earth Sight. Is he gone?"

Gaborn felt inside himself, tried to reach out to his father, but could feel nothing. He nodded.

Binnesman whispered so that only Gaborn could hear. "So the mantle passes. Until now you have been but a prince. Now you must become a king in deed."

Gaborn slumped forward in his saddle, sick to his heart. "What? What can I do? How can I stop this?"

Gaborn asked. "If I am Earth King, what good can I do?"

"Much good. You can call the earth to your aid," Binnesman said. "It can help protect you. Hide you. You only need to learn how to do so."

"I want Raj Ahten dead," Gaborn said blankly.

"The earth will not kill," Binnesman whispered. "Its strength lies in nurturing life, protecting. And Raj Ahten is backed by other Powers. You must think, Gaborn. How can you best protect your people? All mankind is in jeopardy, not just these few at Longmot. Your father is but one man, and I fear he chose to place himself in peril."

"I want Raj Ahten dead! Now!" Gaborn shouted, not at Binnesman, but to the earth that had promised to protect him. Yet he knew the earth was not at fault. Gaborn had felt a premonition that his father was in jeopardy. Yet he had not heeded that warning, had not pulled his father from Longmot.

Gaborn felt ill to his heart.

He was twenty miles from Longmot. His force horse could cover that distance in less than half an hour. But if he did, what would it gain him? He'd lose his life.

He considered spurring his horse on, anyway.

Beside him, Iome seemed to read his thoughts. She touched his knee with her hand. "Don't," she whispered. "Don't go."

Gaborn looked at the ground. At his horse's feet, gray-green grasshoppers flew up in fright, fat grasshoppers, sluggish at the end of the autumn.

"Can we help them at Longmot, do you think?" Gaborn asked Binnesman.

The wizard shrugged. Worry lined his face. "You help their cause even now, with this ruse. But do you mean, can you defeat Raj Ahten? Not with these troops. The battle goes ill for Longmot – as it would for you, should you attack too soon. Your strength lies not in slaughter, but as a defender. Let your men kick up more dust as they walk. Then we will see what happens. . . ."

They rode on in palpable silence for two long minutes. All that time, Gaborn felt torn, fey. He blamed himself for his father's death, for the death of Rowan, for the deaths of all the Dedicates at Castle Sylvarresta. Such a toll, such a heavy price the world was paying for his weakness. For he felt sure that if he were stronger, if he had just done something different, turned left when he'd turned right, he could have saved them all.

A strange noise began to rumble across the plains – a single note, a cry like none Gaborn had ever heard or thought to imagine. It rolled over the plains like a distant shout.

Raj Ahten's death cry! he thought.

But almost immediately, it was followed by another such cry, echoing over the heath.

Binnesman's mount kicked and raised its ears, just as heavy wet drops of sleet began to splash over the ground. With an ache in his heart, Gaborn watched the wizard spur his horse toward Longmot, and wished he could follow.

"Come, Gaborn, bring your army!" Binnesman shouted. "The earth is in pain!"

Then he saw – the sleet ahead had begun to fall in great sheets from the sky, watering the heath. No far-seer would be able to pierce the oncoming deluge. If Gaborn's ruse had not worked already, it could have no further effect.

With a shout, Gaborn raised his fist, called the charge.

FIFTY-FOUR: SHOSTAG

Shostag the Axeman hid in the Duke's cellars when he felt the quickening. A sense of profound energy tingled through every inch of his skin, and he leapt into action.

So Orden had died. Shostag wondered how it had happened.

Shostag had outwitted dozens of Runelords in his short life. He was not a man of deep understanding or broad study, but he kept his eyes open, reached decisions fast. Most people assumed that because fat covered his bear-like muscles, he was also dull-witted. Not so.

As he clutched his huge double-headed axe, he raced up the steps and burst through the cellar doors. He did so with calculated efficiency, hitting doors no more quickly than if he'd run full-tilt. He even slipped the bar from a door as he exited, so the door burst open from the impact of his blow.

Then he raced through the buttery of the Duke's kitchens, out the kitchen doors, and to the green before the great hall.

Hundreds of Raj Ahten's Invincibles were in the green, battling the defenders of Longmot. War dogs raced among them, huge mottled gray horrors in red leather masks. Along the west wall he saw a fiery salamander, and along all the walls were men, burning or fallen in battle.

A few of Orden's archers along the north castle walls were firing into the green, for his men were faring so poorly that any arrow would likely strike Raj Ahten's men without a chance of hitting a defender.

But even the fastest war dog or Invincible in the group could hardly move at an eighth of Shostag's speed. They seemed little more than statues. Here in the green, Shostag could see no sign of Raj Ahten.

Shostag took his great iron axe and began moving through the crowd, swinging in complex arcs, lopping the heads off of Raj Ahten's Invincibles in almost a casual manner, cleaving dogs in two, dodging arrows and whatnot.

He'd hardly murdered two hundred of the bastards when he spotted a swift movement at the gates. Raj Ahten himself, rushing toward him.

The Wolf Lord wore no helm, but bore a battle-axe in one hand and a scimitar in the other. Or at least Shostag imagined it was the Wolf Lord. His face shone like the sun, but he had a hideously deformed shoulder. All the easier to fight him, Shostag imagined.

Raj Ahten took one look at Shostag, smiled. "So, King Orden is dead, and you think you are next, do you?"

Shostag jutted his chin, and spun his huge axe with a flourish. "You know, that arm would look better if I hacked off the rest of it for you."

"Come give it a try," Raj Ahten urged. The Wolf Lord was studying the swath of corpses, some of them still in the process of falling, strewn in a path from the kitchens.

With a start, Raj Ahten dashed left, darted up the narrow road to some lord's manor, away from Shostag. As he sped along the street, he slashed the throat of any defender within reach, shoved his own men from his path.

Shostag leapt after him. He saw Raj Ahten's plan.

Shostag was at the pinnacle of twenty-one men, each vectoring metabolism to him. And several of those men had taken endowments of metabolism before, so that Shostag now ran with the speed of forty. If Raj Ahten could find a man in the serpent and slaughter him, he'd break the line of Shostag's power, "slice the serpent" in two.

By doing so, he'd give two separate warriors high metabolism, create two serpents' heads, neither able to strike as quickly as Shostag could now. Raj Ahten was hunting for Dedicates.

If Shostag was lucky, Raj Ahten would find a man near the tail of the serpent. Killing the tail would still leave Shostag with high metabolism, leave him with the speed of something close to forty.

But Shostag preferred not to rely on luck.

Raj Ahten had glanced at the corpses strewn across the yard, seen that Shostag came from the kitchens. Now Raj Ahten suspected that the Dedicates wouldn't be hiding in the Dedicates' Keep, but were secreted around the castle. Raj Ahten ran to the nearest unsecured building.

Shostag followed, rounded a corner too fast. His center of gravity kept him traveling so that he bowled into half a dozen of the castle's defenders. He scraped his leg on some man's pike. Regained his feet. Ran.

The air felt heavy, hard to breathe. Shostag did not have the endowments of brawn necessary to easily draw breath with such high metabolism. His head spun; he felt dizzy.

Raj Ahten turned at a doorway leading to the lord's apartments, raced into the manor. Shostag followed.

Shostag was a Wolf Lord, with endowments of scent from three dogs. He could smell better than most men ever dreamed, and men are such smelly brutes. Thus he wasn't surprised to enter the room and see Raj Ahten tearing at the door of a cedar wardrobe. Like Shostag, Raj Ahten didn't need to see a man to know that one was hiding in the room.

Shostag rushed Raj Ahten, axe whirling.

Raj Ahten spun, blocked Shostag's blow with his own battle-axe; sparks flew from the weapons. The iron handle of Raj Ahten's smaller axe bent. Shostag marveled that his blow didn't shatter Raj Ahten's arm. With deadly grace Raj Ahten swung his icy scimitar beneath Shostag's guard, pierced Shostag's belly with a blow of cold horror.

But Shostag was no commoner, dismayed at the sight of his own guts. He had more stamina than most lords, the stamina of wolves who hunted the winter woods for bear and boar.

The little prickling wound only angered him, so that Shostag whirled his mighty axe with both hands, spun and delivered a blow that should have cleaved the Wolf Lord in two.

But Raj Ahten threw himself back, dropping his bent axe, dodging Shostag's blow, smashing the finely wrought cedar door of the wardrobe, falling into it himself.

A Dedicate lay beneath Raj Ahten, half buried by splintered cedar, crouching among some maids' dresses, a warhammer in one hand, shield in another. Sir Owlsforth, a warrior five men down the line of defenders from Shostag in the serpent.

If Shostag didn't kill Raj Ahten now, he'd never get another chance. He drew back his great axe, preparing to cleave the Wolf Lord in two.

At that moment, Raj Ahten plunged two fingers through the eye slits of Owlsforth's helm, into the brain.

Shostag felt a piercing nausea, and watched in horror as Raj Ahten leaned away from the falling axe and suddenly became an indistinct blur, leaping toward him.

Shostag knew nothing more.

FIFTY-FIVE:
THE CRY

Raj Ahten did not trouble himself with finding the heads of the serpent. He followed his keen nose through buildings, and in a few moments found several more men hiding, slaughtered six more Dedicates. As he did so, he also murdered another sixty of Longmot's defenders. He half-hoped to find Jureem here.

The battle was winding down. King Orden was dead, most of the defenders. Seldom had Raj Ahten dealt a foe such a fell beating. Never had he personally spilled so much good blood.

Once, he came upon a man running from a building with uncommon speed – a nobleman. He recognized the Earl of Dreis by the gray horse and four arrows on his shield, more than by any finery. Another head to a serpent.

A fine-looking warrior, the Earl was. Spooky gray eyes, tall and noble in every mannerism.

Ahten slowed enough to hamstring the fellow, then slashed the Earl's throat as he fell.

By now, Raj Ahten had the battle well in hand. He stood on the rise below the Dedicates' Keep, perhaps fifty paces from the two hundred or so knights who kept guard there.

He stopped for a moment to survey the battlefield. Down below, his men had taken the courtyard. The walls were almost empty of defenders.

Now Raj Ahten's men raced along the wall-walks to the east, while a trio of salamanders cleared the walls to the west. Everywhere the cries of dying men arose, insubstantial to his ears. The scents of blood and smoke and sulfurous powders carried on the wind.

Little remained for him to do.

He raced for the Dedicates' Keep, thinking to slaughter the two hundred warriors who stood guard, when a great feeling of anxiousness swept over him, that familiar twist of the stomach that accompanies the death of a Dedicate.

Eremon Vottania Solette throttled Salim al Daub. It takes a long time to strangle a man, particularly if he has endowments of stamina. Eremon found the job immensely difficult. Sweat began to bead on his brow, and his fingers grew wet, making his fingers slip.

Salim didn't fight, remained unconscious. Yet he turned his head slowly, uncomfortably, tried even in his stupor to escape. His legs began to kick feebly, rhythmically. Salim's lips went blue, and his tongue bulged. His eyes opened in blind panic.

The guard didn't see, for the man stood gazing out the rough door of the wagon to watch the storming of the castle. Among the stinking, ill-kept Dedicates, the silent struggle attracted no notice. The rhythmic kick of Salim's feet seemed but a background noise, the shuffle of a sleepy Dedicate as he sought comfort among the moldy hay.

Nearby a deaf Dedicate watched Eremon, eyes wide in fear. This was no knight brought to embarrass a Northern lord. This was one of Raj Ahten's own Dedicates, a fellow who vectored hundreds of endowments of hearing to the Wolf Lord. For his service, he was treated worse than a dog. The Dedicate had reason to hate his lord, had reason to wish him dead. Eremon held the deaf man's eye as he strangled Salim, silently hoped the man would not raise a cry.

Salim kicked once, hard, made a pounding noise with his boot.

At the wagon door the guard spun, saw Salim's feet kicking. The guard lunged forward, sliced Eremon's arm with his curved knife, hacking it off.

Blood spurted from Eremon's arm, just below the elbow, and the severed stump burned like fire. But his hand, the hand that had been robbed of grace, that could hardly unclench over these many years, clung to Salim's throat like death itself, fingers locked on the big eunuch's esophagus.

The guard snatched at it, tried to pull the severed hand from Salim's throat. Eremon managed to kick the guard behind the knee, so that he fell back among the Dedicates.

In that moment, Eremon felt a great easing in his chest as grace flowed through him, felt his heart and muscles unclench completely for the first time in many years.

He gasped a deep breath, tasted in one last gasp the sweet air of freedom. Then the guard was on him.

In a moment of vertigo, the world slowed profoundly for Raj Ahten. The deep-toned clickings of the Earl of Dreis' dying shout now came as a call for aid to his ears, and Raj Ahten found himself sliding on his feet as he tried to stop before the crowd of soldiers who guarded the Dedicates' Keep.

He realized he had only his normal six endowments of metabolism. Some of these guards might nearly equal him.

He shouted a battle cry of such incredible volume that no human tongue had ever matched it. He had begun thinking only that he might dishearten a few warriors.

But as he shouted, the effect astonished even him.

The men began to drop to their knees, grasping in pain at their helmets. The walls of the keep behind them shuddered and vibrated, dust cascading from cracks in the stone as if the walls were a rug, and his Voice a stick that beat it.

The Wolf Lord had endowments of Voice from thousands, and brawn that let him expel air with incredible force. Yet even he had never guessed that his cry might carry such power.

So astonished was he that as Raj Ahten shouted, he shaped his call, lowering the tone several octaves until stone and gravel chipped away from the wall.

Then he shouted anew, increased his volume, chipping deeper at the stone, turning his voice into a fey weapon.

It was written in Taif that the Emir Moussat ibn Hafir once had his warriors raise such a cry. In the deserts of Dharmad, the brick walls of the city of Abanis had crumbled under such a sound, letting the Emir send his cavalry through the rubble.

But then the sound had come from the voices of a thousand trained warriors, crying as one, and the city walls had been made of weak adobe brick.

It was called the Death Cry of Abanis, a sound legend said could rend stone much as certain singers could train themselves to shatter crystal.

Now, Raj Ahten raised such a shout alone.

The effect felt gratifying. Before him, warriors dropped as if clubbed, many falling in shock, some dropping in death. Blood poured from men's ears and from their noses.

Behind them, as Raj Ahten reached his crescendo, the huge stone tower of the Dedicates' Keep suddenly cracked, rending nearly from top to bottom.

Yet the tower did not quite crumble or fall.

Raj Ahten raised the shout again, playing his voice back and forth over the stone, experimenting with various harmonic frequencies, until he struck just the right chord.

This time the tower crumbled like magic, falling in a mighty crash that pummeled the earth, raising a cloud of dust. Great stones dropped, slamming into prostrate defenders who had guarded the tower's steps.

Raj Ahten turned, looked on the walls of Castle Longmot. In places, the walls of the castle had cracked. The Duke's Keep looked as if artillery had struck it, blasting off huge chunks of stone, crumbling a windowsill, toppling gargoyles.

Those men who still could gazed at Raj Ahten in horror.

Defeated. Longmot lay defeated.

Raj Ahten stood, gloating in his power. The King of the Earth may come, he thought, but I am mightier than the earth.

Everyone, even Raj Ahten's own men, watched him in terror. Among his Invincibles, few had been damaged by the Death Cry. Raj Ahten's Invincibles each had a minimum of five endowments of stamina – and, apparently, that was enough for them to withstand the destructive power of his Voice.

But many commoners who had defended the walls had punctured eardrums or had lost consciousness.

In the moment that followed, Raj Ahten's Invincibles finished their swordplay, slaughtering those who resisted, dragging those who surrendered down into the courtyard.

When the defenders of Longmot were disarmed, their armor taken, less than four hundred men remained. To Raj Ahten's pleasure, the others had all died, either in battle or from his shout.

On the castle walls, the salamanders stood a moment, gazing longingly at the prisoners. But with the battle won and no more prey to be had, they began to waver, until their fiery forms became a mere shimmering heat, and were gone back to the netherworld from whence they had been drawn.

For a long moment, Raj Ahten merely stood, surveying the scene, tasting his victory.

He addressed the survivors simply. "I need information. To the man who supplies an answer first, I'll grant life. The rest of you shall die. Here is my question: Where are my forcibles?"

To their credit, most of the knights refused to answer. Some shouted curses, but half a dozen shouted variations of "Gone! Orden sent them away!"

Six men tried to purchase their lives. Some had blood trickling from ears. Some wept. Some were young men who had never faced danger. Others were family men, perhaps, who worried for the welfare of wives and children. Raj Ahten recognized a captain who had been made a Dedicate just days before. He did not know the captain's name. One silver-haired old fellow, Raj Ahten imagined, was just a coward.

Raj Ahten called them forward, led them to the drawbridge while his Invincibles moved in for the slaughter.

"You six men," Raj Ahten said. "One of you has saved your life, but I do not know yet who among you shall live. Perhaps one shall live, perhaps all. . . ." He knew full well who had spoken first – the old coward. But he dared not admit it. He needed them all to answer, needed to learn if his source spoke truthfully. "So, I must ask you another question. Where did he send my forcibles?"

"We don't know." "His guards rode off without telling," the men answered in unison.

Two men had been slow to answer. Raj Ahten lunged forward with his saber, cut them down, perhaps with too much enthusiasm. He'd feared that the forcibles would be gone, that this attack had been a waste of his time.

"The odds narrow," he whispered viciously. The four remaining men watched in terror. Beads of sweat formed on their brows. "Tell me, when did the forcibles leave?"

Two more men hesitated. The captain said, "Just after Orden's men arrived."

A fourth man nodded silent agreement, eyes blazing, becoming suddenly disheartened. The older fellow, the coward. He'd been too late to speak, he knew.

Raj Ahten slaughtered two more men, left only the last two soldiers. The captain still wore the colors of Longmot. Perhaps the man would make a valuable spy. The older coward was dressed in pigskins, a gamy fellow of the woods. Raj Ahten suspected that he did not really know his answers firsthand, and so was forced to merely concur.

"Where is Gaborn Orden?" Raj Ahten asked. The man in pigskins had no answer. Raj Ahten could see it in his face.

"He rode into the castle at dawn, then rode out again just after dawn," the captain of Longmot answered.

From the castle, the last agonized cries of dying prisoners sounded, the grunting and screams. The old man in pigskins cringed, knowing he would be next, while the captain sweated heavily, panting.

The captain had that inward gaze that men of conscience get when doing evil. Raj Ahten did not trust him to answer another question honestly. You could only push a man so far.

Raj Ahten stepped forward, slashed the old fellow who wore pigskins in half.

He considered killing the captain of Longmot. He had not wanted to leave any witness to tell the secret of his magic powders, or to reveal his battle tactics. It would be a small matter to gut the fellow.

Yet the captain might serve a greater purpose. By telling how Raj Ahten had destroyed the walls of Longmot with a mere battle cry, this lone survivor would spread fear across the kingdoms of the North.

All the Northern castles, all the proud fortresses that had stood for thousands of years as men battled the Toth and the nomen and each other – all were useless now. Death traps.

The men of the North should know. They should be prepared to surrender.

"I'm most grateful," Raj Ahten told the captain. "You've

won your life. You served as my Dedicate once. Now you shall serve me again. I want you to tell others what happened here. When men ask how you survived the battle, tell them: Raj Ahten left me to testify of his power."

The soldier nodded weakly. His legs shook. The captain wouldn't be able to stand much longer. Raj Ahten put a hand on his shoulder, and asked casually, "Do you have a family, children?"

The man nodded, burst into teras, and turned away.

"What is your name?"

"Cedrick Tempest," the young man cried.

Raj Ahten smiled. "How many children, Cedrick?"

"Three . . . girls and a boy."

Raj Ahten nodded appreciatively. "You think yourself a coward, Cedrick Tempest. You think yourself disloyal. But today, you were loyal to your children, yes? 'Children are gems, and he who has many is rich indeed.' You will live for them?"

Cedrick nodded vigorously.

"There are many kinds of heroes, many forms of loyalty," Raj Ahten said. "Do not regret your decision."

He turned to walk back to his pavilion on the hill, stopped to clean the gore from the blade of his scimitar on a dead man's cape. He considered his next move. His forcibles were gone – to Mystarria, perhaps, or any of a hundred keeps. His reinforcements were late. An army was marching on him.

Yet he had a new weapon, one that might yet win the day, beyond all hope or expectation.

The men closest to Raj Ahten had taken great damage from his cry, as did men with but a few endowments of stamina. Raj Ahten dared not use his weapon too near his own men. Which meant that if he sought to kill Gaborn by the power of his Voice, he'd have to stand alone.

A few small flakes of snow began to fall from the leaden skies, swirling at his feet. He had not noticed how cold it had become.

He studied the damage to Castle Longmot from outside. Cracks had broken the walls, splitting the stone in numerous places. Massive walls of black stone nearly a hundred feet tall loomed above him. The foundation stones were thirty feet thick, fourteen feet wide, twelve feet tall. Each stone weighed thousands of tons. This fortress had stood for centuries, indomitable. He'd seen the wards of earth-binding on its gates.

His flameweavers' most powerful spells could hardly pierce the walls. His catapults hadn't chipped them. Yet his voice had rent some of the massive foundation stones.

Even Raj Ahten marveled. It was not clear yet what he was becoming. He'd taken Castle Sylvarresta with nothing more than the power of his glamour. Now he found that his Voice was becoming a potent, dazzling weapon.

In his realms to the south, Dedicates died from moment to moment, while new ones were recruited. The configuration of his attributes was always in flux. But of one thing he felt certain: More endowments were being added than were lost. He was being added upon. Becoming the Sum of All Men.

Perhaps now was the time to face this young fool – the Earth King and his armies. Raj Ahten glowered.

He turned and gave a great roar, threw his voice against the near wall. "I am mightier than the earth!"

Longmot cracked – the whole southern wall shuddered.

Cedrick Tempest fell, too, running from the gate, clutching his helm, curling in on himself when he could run no more.

To Raj Ahten's dismay, the upper half of the Duke's Keep crumbled to the left. Some of his men screamed within the castle as the building collapsed on them. It was as if the wards of earth power that bound the castle crumbled, leaving the keep in ruin.

At the same time, on the hill behind him, Raj Ahten

heard a branch crack.

He turned, glimpsed the great oak by his pavilion. The trunk of the great oak snapped . . . and half of the tree crashed through the roof of his Dedicates' wagon.

In that moment, Raj Ahten felt a dozen small deaths, the dizzying breathlessness that accompanied the loss of virtue.

The world slowed terrifyingly. For long years, Raj Ahten had brought his wagon with him. In it he bore Dervin Feyl, a man who had bequeathed Raj Ahten an endowment of metabolism many years back, had become a vector.

Dervin had just died, along with the Dedicate who vectored glamour to Raj Ahten, and several other minor men.

Raj Ahten marveled at his sudden sluggishness. Did my Voice smite the tree, or does Earth seek to punish me? he wondered.

Did the earth strike at me? He had no way to answer the question. Yet it mattered a great deal. The wizard Binnesman had cursed him, seemingly with no effect. Had the wizard's curse weakened that tree?

Or had his own Voice been his downfall?

Such a small blow. Yet so profoundly effective.

Raj Ahten wondered, but at that moment, it no longer mattered. Raj Ahten, despite his victory at Longmot, stood defeated. Though he had the wit and grace and brawn of thousands, without his speed he'd become a "warrior of unfortunate proportions." Even a common soldier, some boy without endowments, might be able to slaughter him.

If Gaborn came against him with the speed of even five men and endowments of stamina from another five, Raj Ahten could not prevail against him.

Raj Ahten cast his eyes about in desperation. His flameweavers had burned themselves out. His forcibles were gone. The salamanders had returned to the netherworld, and would not be summoned easily for a long while. His arcane explosive powders were all used up.

I came to destroy Orden and Sylvarresta, he thought, and that much I've accomplished. But in doing this, I've created a greater enemy.

It was time to flee Longmot, flee Heredon and all the Kingdoms of Rofehavan while he reconsidered his tactics. At this moment, despite whatever other victories his men might win here in the North, he could feel the Kingdoms of Rofehavan all slipping from his grasp.

Raj Ahten had his endowments, thousands upon thousands of them. But his mines were petering out, and his forcibles were in the hands of his enemy. Whatever gifts he had now, the young king might soon match.

Raj Ahten felt utterly dismayed.

The snow was blowing. The first snow Raj Ahten would see this winter. In a few weeks, the passes in the mountains would be blocked.

He could continue this contest later, he reasoned. Shocked. He dreaded the thought of waiting until spring.

He shouted orders for his men to begin the retreat, leaving no time to loot the castle.

He stood for several long minutes as his soldiers scrambled to obey, pulling down pavilions, harnessing the horses, loading wagons.

The frowth giants emerged from the castle, bearing corpses of defenders in their paws to eat on the way home. Along the western hills, wolves howled mournfully, as if in loss, at the sight of Longmot in ruins.

Raj Ahten's counselor, Feykaald, shouted in a high voice, "Move, you sluggards! Leave the dead! You, there – help load those wagons!"

The snow thickened. In moments it piled two inches deep at Raj Ahten's feet. He only stood, gazing at Castle Longmot. He wondered how he had failed here, considered how Jureem had betrayed him to King Orden.

When he finished musing, Castle Longmot lay dead.

No fires burned in it, no men cried out in pain.

Cedrick Tempest wandered before the gates, the lone soldier holding his bleeding ear, cursing and muttering under his breath. Perhaps his mind had gone.

Raj Ahten took a horse, considered again how the wizard Binnesman had stolen his, and rode over the hills.

FIFTY-SIX: THE GREETING

By the time Gaborn reached Longmot, the land lay empty of troops, the ruins of the castle covered beneath a layer of new-fallen snow.

Most of Gaborn's army was still far behind. Only some fifty knights rode mounts swift enough to keep up. In the woods to the west, wolves howled forlornly, their voices rising and falling in eerie cadences.

Binnesman had ridden ahead, rummaged near the ruins of the Dedicates' Keep, searching among the rubble.

Everywhere lay carnage and destruction – walls and towers of Longmot in ruin, the soldiers of Orden crumpled under stone. Only a dozen or so of Raj Ahten's troops lay dead outside the castle, riddled with arrows.

Raj Ahten had carried off a great victory here, a mind-numbing victory, almost unparalleled in any chronicle Gaborn had ever read. For the past hour, Gaborn had tried to deny his feelings, his suspicion that his father had died. Now he feared the worst.

Only one warrior stood alive on the battleground, a captain who wore the colors of Longmot.

Gaborn rode up to him. The soldier's face was pale, his eyes full of horror. Blood dribbled under his helmet from his right ear and had crusted in the dark hair of his sideburns.

"Captain Tempest," Gaborn asked, recalling the man's

name from earlier in the day, "where is my father, King Orden?"

"Dead, mi – milord," the captain said, then sat down in the snow, his head hanging. "They're all dead."

Gaborn had expected it. Yet the news punched him. He put one hand over his belly, found himself breathing hard. I was no help, he thought. Everything I've done has been in vain.

He surveyed the damage, his shock and horror growing more profound. He'd never seen a castle so destroyed – not in a matter of hours.

"How is it that you survived?" Gaborn asked weakly.

The captain shook his head, as if searching for an answer. "Raj Ahten took some of us prisoners. He – killed the others. He left me alive, to bear witness."

"To what?" Gaborn asked.

Tempest pointed numbly at the towers. "His flameweavers struck first. They summoned creatures from the netherworld and hit the castle with spells that burned iron – and a fireball that burst in the air above the gates, tossing men about like sticks.

"But that was not the worst of it, for then Raj Ahten himself came and shattered the castle's foundations with the cry of his Voice. He killed hundreds more of us!

"I . . . my helm has thick leather pads, but I can't hear from my right ear, and my left is still ringing."

Gaborn stared at the castle, numb.

He'd imagined that Raj Ahten had brought some terrible engines to bear on those walls, or had his flameweavers conjure some unspeakable spell.

He'd seen that great mushroom of fire rise in the air. But he'd never imagined that the walls could crumble from a mere shout.

The soldiers behind him had spread out, were slowly riding over the battleground, to seek for signs of life among the ruins.

"Where is – where can I find my father?"

Tempest pointed up a trail. "He ran that way, toward Tor Loman, chasing Raj Ahten, just before the battle commenced."

Gaborn turned his horse, but Captain Tempest rushed forward, dropped to his knees. "Forgive me!" he cried.

"For what, surviving?" Gaborn asked. Gaborn himself felt the guilt of those who live, unaccountably, while all around them die. It was heavy on him now. "I not only forgive you, I commend you."

He let his horse trot over the snowfield to the sound of Tempest's sobbing and the howls of wolves.

The rings in his mail rang as the horse broke into a gallop, and Gaborn rode up a muddy trail. At first he could not be certain he headed the right direction. Snow covered the trail, and he could discern no tracks.

But after half a mile, as the trail moved under the aspens, he saw signs in the mud and fallen leaves – the huge strides of men with enormous metabolism racing through the woods. Tracks ten steps across.

After that the trail was easy to follow. The path to Tor Loman had been well maintained, the brush cut away. It made for an easy, almost pleasant ride.

Along the path, Gaborn watched for sign of his father, but found none.

At last he reached the bare peak of Tor Loman, found the meadow with the Duke's old observatory at its top. The snow had fallen heavy here, stood three inches deep, and Gaborn found Raj Ahten's fine helm lying at the base of the observatory.

The helm itself was deeply embossed, with intricate silver designs like braided ropes or the braided fires a flameweaver pulled from heaven. These ran down the noseguard and over the eye slots. A single huge diamond fit between the eyes. Gaborn took it as a prize of war, tied its broken strap to his saddle, careful not to crush the white owl's wings on the helm.

As he tied it, he sniffed the cold air. The snow had

cleansed the sky, carried away most of the scent, yet Gaborn could still discern the odor of his father's heavy samite cape, the oil he used to protect his armor. His father had been here. Might be nearby – alive and wounded, perhaps.

Gaborn climbed the observatory, gazed off into the distance. The snow had stopped falling ten minutes ago, so he could see fairly well, though with but two endowments of sight, he could not be called a far-seer. To the east, Iome and her people pushed across the heath, ten miles back. They had neared the Durkin Hills Road.

In the distance to the southwest, at Gaborn's limit of vision, Raj Ahten's troops retreated over the hills, the red and gold of their colors muted by distance.

He saw men stopping on their horses, gazing back toward him. Gaborn imagined that some far-seers watched him, wondering who now stood on the Eyes of Tor Loman. Perhaps even Raj Ahten himself watched.

Gaborn whispered, "I reject you, Raj Ahten. I will destroy you." Gaborn raised a fist in the sign of challenge. But if the men on the far hill made any gestures of their own, he could not see. They merely turned their mounts and galloped over the crest of the hill.

Even with an army, Gaborn realized, I couldn't catch Raj Ahten now.

Yet in his heart, Gaborn felt some relief. He loved this land, as his father had. They had wanted nothing more than to drive Raj Ahten from it, keep it beautiful and free. For a time, perhaps, they had succeeded.

But at what price?

Gaborn glanced down at his feet. The snow had fallen after Raj Ahten's descent. Yet the scent of both Gaborn's father and the Wolf Lord lingered here. The metallic tang of blood.

So, Gaborn surmised, Raj Ahten had come here, had seen the clouds of Gaborn's passage, the distant herds of cattle and soldiers mingled together, had fallen for the ruse.

That gave Gaborn some comfort. Raj Ahten could be fooled, could be beaten.

Gaborn circled the tower, tried to see down into the woods. He imagined his father and Raj Ahten struggling on the tower, until at last, perhaps, his father was thrown over.

He looked down, saw what he dreaded: at the base of the observatory, among the rocks, a hand thrust up, dead fingers clutching a palm full of snow.

Gaborn raced down the winding stairs, found his father, and pulled at the corpse, shaking it to clear the snow off.

What he saw broke his heart. For on his father's frozen face was a broad smile. Perhaps in death, some fleeting memory had made him smile. Or perhaps it was but a grimace of pain. Yet Gaborn imagined that his father smiled at him, as if to congratulate him for his victory.

FIFTY-SEVEN: TODAY I AM DEATH

Gaborn had already ridden ahead when Iome's glamour returned. Iome had no idea how Raj Ahten's vector had died, felt little relief at the woman's passing. Like Iome, the woman had been a mere tool in Raj Ahten's hand, one that was poorly used.

Yet Iome's beauty returned. She felt it as an easing of her heart, a return of her confidence. Like a flower blossoming.

Yet it was not the unnatural beauty she'd had since birth, not the borrowed glamour. The skin on her hands softened and lost their wrinkles. The blush of youth returned to her cheeks. For once in her life, for the first time, Iome was simply herself, without benefit of endowments.

It was enough. She wished that Gaborn could have been there to see, but he had ridden ahead.

Though messengers from Longmot had told Iome what to expect when she reached the castle, had said that Raj Ahten had destroyed it with a shout, nothing they said could have prepared her for the ruin.

She rode at the head of ten thousand people from out of Groverman and the villages round about. Many of the women had already turned back, heading for their own hearths, their own homes. Their work here was done.

But others followed Iome, particularly people who'd lived in Longmot, who had come to see what was left of their homes.

As they neared the ruined castle, saw the empty fields with wolves slinking about the hedgerows, many women and children began crying for what they'd lost.

They'd deserted their homes three days ago, but a few days of huddling under ragged shelters at Groverman had shown them just how difficult it would be to make do once the snows fell.

Certainly, most of them hoped to come home, to rebuild. But in hard times, with war approaching, Iome's people could not rebuild without some nearby fortification.

The castle was nearly ruined. Huge blocks of stone that had lain in place for twelve centuries now lay cracked and shattered.

Almost subconsciously, Iome began calculating what it would take to repair the fortress: five hundred stonemasons out of Eyremoth, for they were the best. Carters to drag the stones, frowth giants hired out of Longnock to place them. Men to dig moats. Lumberjacks to cut trees. Cooks and ironsmiths, with mortar, chisels, saws, awls, axes, and . . . the list went on and on.

But to what purpose? If Raj Ahten could simply shatter the castle with a shout?

She looked up on the hill, saw Gaborn kneeling in a patch of snow, in the field. Gaborn had laid his father's body out on the hill above the castle, beneath a great oak tree. A huge limb lay near them.

Gaborn had collected dozens of spears, and he ringed these about his father's corpse, creating a fence of sorts, to keep out the wolves.

In the tree above his father's corpse, he had hung his father's golden shield. He took his father's helm, laid it in the snow at his father's feet – a sign that his father had fallen in battle.

She turned her horse, went to him, leading her father's stallion. Behind King Sylvarresta followed the three Days: hers, her father's, and Gaborn's. King Sylvarresta had verged on falling dead asleep in his saddle a few minutes before, but now stared about, grinning broadly at the snow through bleary eyes, a child filled with delight.

Gaborn looked up at Iome as she approached; his face looked bleak, desolate. Iome knew then that she would find no words to comfort him. She had nothing to offer him. In the past few days, she'd lost nearly everything – her home, her parents, her beauty . . . and things less tangible.

How will I ever sleep again? she wondered. In her mind, the castle had always been the supreme icon of security. In a world fraught with danger, it had always been a safe haven.

No more.

She felt now that she'd lost her childhood, her innocence. Her peace of mind was torn from her.

Not just because her mother lay dead and one of her castles lay in ruins. As she rode that morning, she considered what had happened. Yesterday, she'd feared that Borenson would sneak into Castle Sylvarresta, kill her Dedicates. She imagined that secretly she'd known what he would do, though she hated it.

By not challenging him, not confronting him, Iome had agreed to it. The horror of it had all been creeping up on her since noon yesterday. Now she found herself defenseless. She hadn't slept for two nights. She'd felt dizzy for hours, had feared she would topple from her horse.

Now it seemed as if a great invisible beast, lurking beneath her consciousness, suddenly sprang and seized her.

Iome had meant to say some words of comfort to Gaborn, but suddenly found icy tears coursing down her cold cheeks. She tried to wipe them, began shuddering quietly.

Gaborn had prepared his father's body well. The King's hair was combed, his face was pale in death. The glamour he'd worn had died with him, so that the man she saw was not the King Orden who had seemed so regal, so power-ful, during life.

He looked like some aging statesman, with a broad face, skin somewhat weather-beaten. He smiled enig-matically. He was dressed in his armor, and lay on a plank. His richly embroidered cape of shimmering samite covered him like a robe.

In his hands, he clasped the bud of a single blue rose, perhaps taken from the Duke's garden.

Gaborn turned to look up at Iome, saw the expression on her face, then stood slowly, as if the effort pained him. He walked to her, grabbed her shoulders as she slid from her horse, and held her close.

She thought he would kiss her, tell her not to weep.

Instead his voice sounded hollow and dead as he whis-pered fiercely, "Grieve for us. Grieve."

Borenson thundered into Longmot in a red fury. From the moment he had crested a ridge five miles back and seen the ruined towers, the crowd milling on the downs outside the castle, he'd known the news would be bad. Among the crowd, many colors flew, but none for Raj Ahten.

He wished Raj Ahten were dead, wanted to strike against him with a rage so burning that Borenson had never felt its like.

So he was still in a frustrated rage when he galloped down the north road into Longmot and met the ragged commoners milling about by the thousands. He looked among the crowd for the colors of Orden, saw them nowhere.

He rode up to a pair of teens who scrambled among the snow outside the castle, robbing the corpse of one of Raj Ahten's soldiers. One young man was perhaps fourteen, another eighteen. At first he thought the vermin were stealing money pouches or rings, and he'd have belittled them for doing so. Then he recognized that one lad was wrestling the armor from the corpse, while the other helped lift the dead weight.

Good. They sought armor and weapons that they could never otherwise purchase.

"Where is King Orden?" Borenson asked, trying to keep the emotion from his voice.

"Dead, like all them buggers in the castle," the youngest lad answered. He had his back to Borenson, hadn't seen to whom he was speaking.

A sound escaped Borenson's throat, something like a growl or a snort. "Everyone?"

Pain must have sounded in his voice, for the lad turned and looked up, eyes widening in fear. He dropped the body and backed away, raising a hand in salute. "Yes – yes, sir," his older friend said formally. "Only one man lived to tell the tale. Everyone else is dead."

"A *man* survived?" Borenson asked distantly, though he wanted to cry out, call Myrrima's name and see if she would answer. Myrrima had been in this castle.

"Yes, sir," the older lad said. He staggered backward, afraid Borenson would strike. "You – your men fought bravely. King Orden made a serpent, and fought the Wolf Lord man-to-man. They – we won't forget such sacrifice."

"Whose sacrifice?" Borenson asked. "My king's, or the buggers'?"

The young men turned and ran as if Borenson would strike them both down, and he very nearly did, but he felt little anger toward them.

Borenson scanned the downs wildly, as if Myrrima might stand on the brow of a hill waving to him, or as if he might see one of Raj Ahten's scouts crest a ridge. Instead, as he looked up, he spotted Gaborn beneath an oak.

The prince had laid out King Orden's body, ringed it with spears from his fallen guards, as was the custom in Mystarria. He just stood there, over his dead father, hugging Iome. The Princess had her back to Borenson, and wore a hood, but there could be no mistaking the curves of her body. A knot of three Days all huddled a few yards off to the side, watching the scene with studied patience.

The idiot King Sylvarresta had come off his horse, was in the circle of spears, fawning over King Orden, gazing about dumbly, as if to beg for help.

A sense of horror and desolation swept Borenson, so that he cried out in astonishment and despair.

The fallen castle, the fallen king.

I may have killed him, Borenson thought wildly – my own king. Orden had fought Raj Ahten hand-to-hand, and lost. I could have followed my king's orders, slain all the Dedicates. Had I obeyed in every detail, perhaps it would have changed something. Perhaps Raj Ahten would have died in that battle.

I let my king die.

The guilt that welled up in Borenson was a wild thing, a storm that came from everywhere and seemed to uproot every fiber of his sanity.

An ancient law in Mystarria said the last command of a king must be obeyed, even if the king falls in battle. The command must be obeyed.

The air seemed to grow thick around Borenson. From deep in his throat, the battle chuckle issued as he lowered his lance, flipped down the visor of his helm with a rapid nod of his chin, then spurred his horse into a gallop.

His white lips clenched tight against his teeth.

White had fallen from gray clouds earlier. Soft cold. Frozen beauty, covering everything, sparkling when a patch of sunlight struck it.

King Sylvarresta gaped in wonder, sometimes moaning in delight when he saw a new beauty – the mounds of snow crusting a pool in the road, or clumps of melting snow dropping from a tree. He had no word for "snow," could not recall it.

Everything seemed new, brimming with wonder. He felt very tired, but could not sleep once he came to the castle.

There were too many oddities here, people behind him crying out in pain. He looked at the castle, saw fallen towers. He could only marvel at how they had fallen.

A woman led his horse up a hill, to a great tree where spears stood about in a circle.

Sylvarresta listened to the young man talk to the woman, then gazed up in the tree. An orange cat, the kind of half-wild mouser common to farms, sat on a branch, staring down at him. It stood, arched its back, then walked out on a huge limb above King Sylvarresta, its tail twisting in the air. It meowed hungrily and gazed at something on the ground.

King Sylvarresta followed its gaze, noticed a man lying on the ground, under a shimmering green cape. He recognized that royal cape, the one that had mesmerized him just this morning. He recognized the man beneath it.

King Orden. His friend.

At the same moment, he knew something was profoundly wrong. Orden did not move. His chest did not fall and rise. He only clasped his hands over a blue flower.

In an instant Sylvarresta's world shattered. He remembered what this was, dredged it up from some deep place where all horrors lay hidden.

He shouted wordlessly, not knowing the name for this thing, and leapt from his horse. He hit the ground, scrambled over the snow, sliding in the muck, till he broke through the fence of spears that stuck in the ground, reached Orden's hand.

Orden's cold fingers held a single flower, blue as sky. Sylvarresta grasped the cold fingers, picked them up and tried to get them to move. Reached for Orden's cheek, stroked it, to find it as cold as the rest of him.

Sylvarresta cried, and turned back, to discover whether the others knew this great dark secret, knew of this beast that stalked them all.

As he caught the eyes of the young man and the

woman, he saw horror there.

"Yes," the young man said softly. "Death. He is dead."

Yes, they knew the secret.

The woman said in a sad if scolding tone, "Father – oh please, come away from there!"

In the fields below, a knight rode a great warhorse, speeding toward them like an arrow, his visor and his lance lowered. So swift he came. So swift.

Sylvarresta shouted the great secret. "Death!"

FIFTY-EIGHT: BROKEN MEN

Gaborn heard the thud of hoofbeats, the ringing of mail as links clanged against one another. He had thought it only a local knight riding across the downs – until he recognized the throaty battle chuckle, a sound that filled him with dread.

Gaborn had been watching King Sylvarresta, shocked and saddened that the poor fool, though he knew almost nothing at all, had been forced to confront mortality. It felt like watching a child get torn apart by dogs.

Gaborn only had time to push Iome behind him, spin and raise a hand to shout "No!"

Then Borenson's gray steed thundered past, its armor rattling. Huge. Unstoppable.

Borenson's lance was lowered on the far side of the horse, twenty feet of polished white ash with its blackened steel tip at the end. Gaborn thought of throwing himself forward, pushing that lance tip away.

But Borenson raced past before Gaborn could act.

Gaborn stood but thirty feet from King Sylvarresta, yet time seemed to slow in that second.

Gaborn had seen Borenson joust a hundred times. The man had a steady hand, a deft touch. He could skewer a plum off a fence post with a lance, even on a force horse galloping sixty miles an hour.

Borenson approached with his lance low, as if he'd go for a stomach wound, and Gaborn saw him raise it just a bit, holding steady, aiming at Sylvarresta's heart.

For his part, Sylvarresta seemed not to recognize what was happening. The King's face had twisted in a grimace, for he'd just remembered the one thing Gaborn had hoped he'd never come to learn, and he had been shouting the word "death," though he could not have foreseen his own.

Then the steed bore down on Sylvarresta. Borenson pulled his lance to the right a fraction of an inch, so it would not graze one of the spears in Gaborn's spear wall.

Then the horse charged through the spear wall, sent some shafts flying, shattered others. Almost at that same moment, the tip of Borenson's lance took King Sylvarresta just below the sternum.

The spear entered deftly, pushing the King backward and lifting him from his feet.

Borenson let the lance slide ten feet through the King's chest, so the tapering wood spread his ribs open wide, then suddenly released the haft and leaned clear of the dying man.

The horse thundered two steps, leapt the corpse of Gaborn's father, crashed through the far wall of spears, and charged on past the trunk of the huge oak tree.

King Sylvarresta stood a moment, blinking stupidly at the huge lance that skewered him, staring in wonder at his own blood as it spurted over the polished white ash. Then his knees buckled. His head sagged, and he pitched to his left.

As he died, he looked at his daughter and moaned weakly.

Gaborn had no weapons at hand. He'd left his horseman's warhammer sheathed in his saddle.

He rushed forward, grabbed a spear from the ground, and called to Iome. She did not need prodding. Her horse had startled away at Gaborn's shout.

Iome ran behind Gaborn. He thought that she would let him shield her. But in a moment it became clear that she did not plan to hide behind him at all. She merely sought her way past him, to get to her father, who lay crumpled and bleeding.

Borenson spun his horse, pulled the horseman's battle-axe from its sheath on the back of the saddle, and flipped up the visor of his helm. For half a second, he merely glared.

There was pain in his blue eyes, the pain of madness. His face was red from rage, his teeth gritted. He smiled no longer.

Running forward, Gaborn grabbed his father's shield from the spot where it hung to the oak, raised it to protect Iome and Sylvarresta, then backed away, standing five feet behind the cold corpse of King Orden.

Gaborn knew Borenson would not risk letting his mount trample King Orden's corpse, defiling it. He'd not spur his horse into battle.

But Gaborn did not feel so certain Borenson would refrain from striking him: Borenson had been compelled to commit bloody murder in assassinating the Dedicates at Castle Sylvarresta. He'd been forced to choose between slaughtering King Sylvarresta and the King's men – his own friends – or letting the Dedicates live to serve Raj Ahten.

It was an evil choice, with no fair answer, no answer that any man could hope to live with.

"Give her to me!" Borenson shouted.

"No!" Gaborn said. "She is a Dedicate no longer!"

In that moment, Borenson looked down beneath Iome's hood, saw her fair face, no longer wrinkled. Saw her eyes clear. A look of astonishment came over him.

A dark blur rushed past Gaborn, some knight of Sylvarresta with great metabolism, running with his might at Borenson. The fellow leapt, and Borenson leaned back from the attack, swung his warhammer, caught the warrior full in the face. Blood sprayed the air as the dying warrior hurtled over Borenson's horse.

Hundreds of people had witnessed Sylvarresta's murder. Gaborn had been totally focused on Borenson, but now he became aware of the others.

Duke Groverman and a full hundred knights were rushing up the hill with weapons drawn. Behind them ran commoners. Some looked furious, others dismayed. Some could not believe what had happened. Gaborn heard shouts, the hue and cry of "Murder, murder most foul!" and "Kill him!" and others were shouting in wordless grief at the death of their king.

Young boys with scythes and sticks were running up the hill, their bloodless faces twisted in dismay.

Iome dropped to her knees, took her father's head in her lap. She rocked back and forth, weeping. Her father's blood was pumping out quickly through the huge wound, as if he were a steer being bled by a butcher. The blood pooled and mingled with the melting snow.

Things had happened so quickly, Gaborn just stood, dazed. His guard had killed the father of the woman he loved. Gaborn's own life might well be in jeopardy.

Some here would see it as their duty to avenge House Sylvarresta. A tide of people swept toward Borenson. Some young men were stringing longbows.

Gaborn shouted, using all the power he could muster in his Voice, "Stop! Leave him to me!"

Borenson's horse danced backward at the shout, and he fought to control the mount. Those nearest Gaborn all stopped expectantly. Others still rushed up the hill, unsure.

Iome looked down at her people, raised a hand for them to halt. Gaborn suspected that her command alone would not have stopped the mob, if Borenson were not such a deadly foe. But partly from fear, partly from respect for their princess, the crowd advanced only falteringly, and some older and wiser lords near the front spread their arms, to hold the more hot-tempered men back.

Borenson glared at the mob in contempt, then flourished his hammer, pointing at Iome, and gazed into Gaborn's eyes: "She should have died with the rest of them! By your father's own orders!"

"He rescinded that order," Gaborn said calmly, using all his training in the control of Voice, precisely repeating every studied inflection, so he could convey to Borenson that he spoke the truth.

Borenson's mouth fell open in horror, for he was full of guilt, and Gaborn now laid it on him thicker. Almost, Gaborn imagined that he could hear the sneers that would be cast at Borenson's back for years: "Butcher. Assassin. Kingslayer!"

Yet Gaborn could not speak anything but the truth, no matter horrible it might be, no matter how it might destroy his friend. "My father rescinded that order, when I presented King Sylvarresta before him. He hugged the man as a friend dearer than a brother, and begged forgiveness!"

Gaborn pointed down with his spear at King Sylvarresta for effect.

If he had thought Borenson gone in madness before, now he became certain of it.

"Noooo!" Borenson howled, and tears filled eyes, eyes that now gazed past Gaborn's head, at some private torment. "Noooo!"

He shook his head violently. He could not bear for it to be true, could not live with it being true.

Borenson half-dropped and half-threw his warhammer to the ground, then turned in his saddle, pulled his right leg over and stepped off his horse awkwardly, as if he were walking down a great stair.

"No, please, no!" he said, shaking his head from side to side. He grabbed his helm, pulled it off, so that his head lay bare. He bowed to the ground, neck stretched, and as he walked forward, he stammered under his breath, staring at the ground.

He walked in a strange gait – back bent, head low, knees almost touching the ground at every step.

Gaborn realized that Borenson was torn, did not know whether to approach him or drop to his knees. He was trying to keep his head bowed.

"My lord, my lord, ah, ah, take me, milord. Take me!" Borenson said as he crept forward.

A young man dashed up with a hammer, as if to deal the death blow himself, but Gaborn shouted at the lad to stay back. The mood of the crowd was growing uglier. People were bloodthirsty.

"Take you?" Gaborn asked Borenson.

"Take me," Borenson begged. "Take my wit. Take it. Please! I don't want to know anymore. I don't want to see anymore. Take my wit!"

Gaborn did not want Borenson to become as Sylvarresta had been, did not want to see those eyes that had laughed so often grow vacant. Yet, at that moment, he wondered if he'd be doing the man a kindness.

My father and I are the ones who took him to the brink of madness, Gaborn realized. To take his endowment would be vile – like a king who taxes the poor till they can pay no more, then tells himself that by relieving them of endowments he shows generosity.

I have violated him, Gaborn realized. I have violated his Domain Invisible, taken his free will. Borenson had always tried to be a good soldier. Now he will never see himself as good again.

"No," Gaborn said softly. "I will not take your wit." Yet even as he said the words, he wondered at his own reasons. Borenson was a great warrior, the best fighter in Mystarria. To take wit from him would have been wasteful, like a farmer killing a fine horse in order to fill his belly when a chicken would have served as well. Do I deny him this because it is merely pragmatic? Gaborn wondered.

"Please," Borenson shouted again. He hobbled next to

Gaborn now, not more than an arm's length away. His whole head shook, and his hands trembled as he pulled at his own hair. He dared not look up, but kept his eyes at Gaborn's feet. "Please – you, ah, you don't understand! Myrrima was in that castle!" He pointed to Longmot and wailed, "Myrrima came. Take my – my metabolism then. Let me know nothing until this war is over!"

Gaborn shrank back a step in horror, wondering. "Are you certain?" he asked trying to sound calm, trying to sound reasonable when all reason left him. Gaborn had felt other deaths – his father's, Chemoise's father's, even King Sylvarresta's. But he had not felt Myrrima's. "Have you seen her? Have you seen her body?"

"She rode from Bannisferre yesterday, to be here in the battle, with me. She was in the castle." Borenson's voice broke, and he fell to his knees and sobbed.

Gaborn had felt so right when he matched Borenson and Myrrima. He'd thought he felt another Power guide him, the powers of the earth coursing through him. Surely he had not felt impressed to match them so that they could meet so tragic an end?

"No," Gaborn said more firmly, deciding. He would not take Borenson's endowment, even if the guilt did promise to destroy him. Kingdoms were at stake. He could not afford such mercy, no matter how it rankled him.

Borenson dropped to his knees, put both hands palm-forward on the ground. It was the traditional stance of prisoners in war who offered themselves for beheading. He cried, "If you will not take my endowment, then take my head!"

"I will not kill you," Gaborn answered. "If you give your life to me, I will take it – glad for the bargain. I choose you. Serve me. Help me defeat Raj Ahten!"

Borenson shook his head and began to sob, great wracking sobs that left him breathless. Gaborn had never seen anything like that from the warrior, felt stunned to learn the man was capable of experiencing such pain.

Gaborn put his hands on Borenson's shoulders, signaling for him to rise, but Borenson only knelt, weeping.

"Milady?" someone called.

Down in the fields below Gaborn, utter silence reigned. Groverman and a hundred other knights now drew near, aghast. Staring at Borenson in horror. Wondering what they should do. Some knight had called Iome, but she only held her father's head, rocking it, almost oblivious of her surroundings.

After a long moment, Iome looked up. Her eyes filled with tears. She bent to kiss her father goodbye, on the forehead.

Her father had not even known her at the last, Gaborn realized. He'd forgotten her existence, or did not recognize her, robbed of glamour. That seemed perhaps the worst blow of all.

Iome straightened, looked downhill at her knights. "Leave us," she said in the firmest voice she could muster.

There was a long, uncomfortable silence. Someone coughed. Duke Groverman watched her with unblinking eyes. "My Queen . . ."

"There's nothing you can do. There's nothing anyone can do!" Iome said. Gaborn knew she spoke not of the murder, not of the demands of justice, but of everything – Raj Ahten, this whole senseless war. Most of all, she spoke of death.

"These men . . . this is murder." Groverman insisted. "House Orden should pay for this insult!" By ancient law, a lord was responsible for the behavior of his vassals, just as a farmer was responsible for damage done by his cow. By law, Gaborn was as guilty of murder as Borenson.

"Gaborn's father lies dead with two thousand of his best knights," Iome answered. "What more do you want of House Orden?"

"He's not the killer – it's the knight at his feet we want! This is a matter of honor!" some knight shouted, after having decided all on his own that Gaborn was innocent.

Gaborn did not recognize the fellow's device, two crows and an oak tree over the Sylvarresta boar.

Iome said, "You say honor is at stake? The knight at Gaborn's feet, Sir Borenson, saved my life yesterday, and the life of my father. He slew an Invincible outside Longmot for us. And he matched wits with Raj Ahten and helped drive the knave from our kingdom–"

"It's murder!" the knight shouted, shaking his axe. But Groverman reached out a hand, silencing the fellow.

"You say," Iome stammered, "it's a matter of honor, and perhaps it is. King Orden, my father's best friend, first ordered our deaths.

"And who among you is to say he was not right in this? My father and I were Dedicates to our sworn enemy. Who of you would have disobeyed such an order, were our roles reversed?

"My father gave endowments to Raj Ahten, thinking it a small thing, just as I did. But many small wrongs can make a very great evil.

"Is it murder for this knight to slay his enemies, to follow orders? Or is it honorable?"

Iome arose now, hands covered in blood; tears streamed down her face. She argued for Borenson's acquittal with her whole heart, and Gaborn wondered if he'd have had the presence of mind to do the same under such circumstances.

For his part, Borenson just glared at the knights blankly, as if he did not care how they judged him. Kill me, his eyes said, or let me live. Just be done with it.

Groverman and his men neither advanced nor retreated. They held their ground, as yet undecided.

Iome bit her lip, and her jaw trembled so that she pierced the lip, unnoticed. Such rage and hurt shone in her eyes. She couldn't deal with this any longer, couldn't argue. Her people were angry; she felt hurt and betrayed to the core of her soul – to lose all her family in the space of two days.

Gaborn had seen the aftermath when his own mother was slain, and now his father. He knew how desolate Iome must feel, knew how her pain must outmatch his own.

Iome said to Gaborn facetiously, "Milord King Orden, Sir Borenson – after all your great kindness these past two days, I bid you get away from here, lest my people slay you. Ours is a poor land, and our hospitality suffers for it. Get out of here. For your service, I grant you your lives, though my vassals wish me to be more penurious."

She spoke in a tone that mocked her own people, but Gaborn knew that she was serious, that she could not cope any longer.

"Go on," Gaborn whispered to Borenson. "I'll see you at Bredsfor Manor." To his relief, Borenson stood and marched to his horse, executing the order without complaint.

Gaborn went to Iome, pulled off his right gauntlet, and let his hand rest on her shoulder. She seemed so slight, so frail beneath the thin cotton of her dress. He could not imagine that she'd hold up under the pressure she now felt.

She no longer looked as beautiful as the first star of evening. She no longer looked wretched. Her only glamour now was her own, and Gaborn could not have loved her any more than he did at this moment, could not have longed to hold her any more than he did right now.

"I love you, you know," he said. Iome nodded once, only slightly. "I came to Heredon to ask for your hand, milady. I want you still. I'd have you for my wife." He did not say it to confirm his feelings to Iome. He said it only for the benefit of her people, so that they would know.

In the crowd, several people hissed at the proposal. Some cried aloud, "No!"

Gaborn could see he wasn't in favor at this moment. These people didn't know how he had schemed and fought for their freedom. They'd witnessed only this last craven deed. He would not win their hearts this day, though he hoped to, in time.

Iome reached up and stroked his hand, but offered no words of comfort.

Gaborn walked to the top of the hill, where his horse pawed the snow in an effort to graze on the sweet grass beneath, then followed Borenson south.

At his back, Gaborn's Days broke from the crowd, following in his shadow.

FIFTY-NINE: THE HEALER

As Iome sat over the body of her father, she wondered if she could even live another day. It seemed that her energy, her will to struggle, had been drawn out from her as completely as her beauty had been drawn out two days before.

She stood over her father's body, wanting desperately to sleep or to scream. The cold snow melted, penetrating her thin boots, just as the stout wind penetrated her thin dress.

Her people were a cold comfort. They knew they needed a lord to protect them, but Iome had no wit with which to guide them, no glamour to inspire them to follow, no brawn or skill in battle.

Without my glamour, they see through me, Iome thought. They see that I am sham, a nothing. All Runelords are nothing, without their Dedicates to fill them with power, make them substantial.

As she shivered on the hill, Iome found that her people offered her nothing now. No one brought her a shawl or offered a shoulder to lean on. None dared approach her. Perhaps they believed she needed time to suffer alone.

But Iome was no good at suffering alone.

She felt confused. Gaborn had not ordered her father's death. He'd struggled mightily to keep her father alive. Yet, somehow, she felt betrayed. Perhaps it was because he did not grow irate at Borenson.

Had Gaborn taken the man's wit, or his head, Iome would have thought Gaborn cruel and hard. Yet part of her felt Borenson deserved some unnamable punishment.

To her surprise, it was the wizard Binnesman who first came to her, after an hour, and wrapped a blanket over her. The wizard huddled beside her, handed her some warm tea.

"I – don't want anything," Iome said. It was true. Her throat felt tight, her stomach in knots. "I just need sleep." She was too weary to even look up at him.

"Sometimes rest is as good as sleep," Binnesman said, and he stood watching her. "I put lemon balm and linden blossoms in the tea, along with a bit of chamomile and honey."

He pressed the hot mug into her hands, and Iome drank. She'd learned long ago that Binnesman knew her needs better than she did, that he could soothe a heart as easily as he could soothe wounds.

The tea seemed to loosen her tight muscles, unknot her. She closed her eyes, leaned her head back, marveling at its effect. The tea made her feel almost as if she'd just been wakened from bed a few moments ago. Yet she felt a deep-seated weariness even the tea could not touch, a tiredness and ache close to the bones.

"Oh, Binnesman, what should I do?" Iome asked.

"You must be strong," Binnesman said. "Your people need you to be strong for them."

"I don't feel strong."

Binnesman said nothing in answer, only put his gnarled arms around her shoulders and held her, as her father had when she was a child and she'd awakened from an evil dream.

"Gaborn would help you be strong, if you would let him," Binnesman offered.

"I know," Iome said.

Down below her, most of the knights had begun to set

a camp in the fields. The thin snow had melted now, and the night would not be cold. But only part of the castle looked serviceable. The Duke's barracks and one of the manor houses still stood, though they had cracks in them. By no means could the castle house the thousands here, but some knights had brought squires and tents – enough so everyone would have shelter for the night.

Yet as the people put up tents, Iome caught many distrustful glances, heard grumbled comments. "What are the people down there saying about Gaborn?"

"The usual things . . ." Binnesman said. "Rumor-mongering."

"What kinds of things?" Iome demanded.

"They feel you should have reacted more strongly to your father's death."

"He died when Raj Ahten took his wit. There was nothing left of my father."

"You are made of stern stuff," Binnesman said. "But had you cried and demanded Borenson's death, perhaps your people would feel more . . . relieved."

"Relieved?"

"Some people suspect that Gaborn ordered your father's death."

"Gaborn? How could they suspect that?" Iome asked, astonished. She looked downhill. An old woman bearing a load of sticks from the woods glanced at Iome, suspicion deep in her eyes.

"So he could marry you, take over your kingdom. Some people think that the fact that you let him live is ample proof that he has you fooled, and that now you are about to swoon into his foul clutches."

"Who would say such things? Who would even think such things?" Iome asked.

"Do not blame them," Binnesman smiled at her. "It is only natural. They have been deeply hurt these past few days, and suspicion comes easily. Trust comes much harder, and it takes time."

Iome shook her head, dumbfounded. "Is it safe for Gaborn here? He's not in danger?"

"As it stands," Binnesman said, "I think some people in this valley pose a threat, yes."

"You must go warn him to stay away!" Iome said. She realized that she'd been hoping for Gaborn to come back tonight, that she could not stand the thought of being away from him. "Tell him . . . tell him we cannot see each other, that it's dangerous. Maybe in time . . . a few months." Iome found herself shaking at the thought, tormented.

A few months seemed an eternity. Yet in another month or two the snows would begin to fly in earnest. Travel between their kingdoms would become difficult.

She wouldn't see Gaborn again before spring. Five months or six at the soonest.

Iome nearly collapsed in on herself at the thought. Yet it would be best for both of them to take this slowly, to give her people time to see. No other princes would want her, no one would take a wife who had been an enemy's Dedicate.

Now that her father and King Orden were dead, within a few weeks the chronicles of their deeds would begin to be slowly distributed by the Days, a volume here, a volume there. Perhaps when the truth came out, Iome's people would think better of Gaborn.

Yet another problem presented itself. Iome's Maid of Honor, Chemoise, would be heavy with child by the time Iome saw Gaborn again. If Iome's people disapproved of her match with Orden, how would *Gaborn's* people feel about her?

Ostensibly, Gaborn had come here seeking a union because the wealth and security of Heredon were to have been a boon to Mystarria. But Raj Ahten had taken the wealth, made a mockery of Heredon's castles, stolen away the Princess' beauty.

Iome had nothing to offer but her affection. And she

knew that affection comes cheaply.

She still hoped that Gaborn might love her. She feared that she deluded herself in even hoping for a union with him. It seemed foolish, like the child's fable of the lazy man who planned to get rich someday by discovering that rain had washed dirt off a pot of gold that lay hidden in his fields.

Surely, in the months to come, Gaborn would come to see that she had nothing to offer, would reconsider. Though he spoke of loving her, surely he'd see that love was not reason enough to unite their kingdoms.

As Iome considered these things, Binnesman nodded kindly, worry on his face, lost in his own private musings. He studied her from under bushy brows. "So you want me to warn Gaborn away. Do you have any more messages for him?"

"None," Iome said. "Except . . . there is the matter of Borenson."

"What of him?" Binnesman asked.

"I . . . don't know what to do about him. He killed my father, a king. Such a deed cannot go unpunished. Yet his guilt is almost more than he can bear. To lay further punishment upon him would be cruel."

Binnesman said, "There was a time when knights who inadvertently erred were given a second chance. . . ."

SIXTY: A TREASURE FOUND

In the House of Understanding, in the Room of the Heart, Gaborn had learned that there are dreams and memories so disturbing the mind cannot hold them.

As Gaborn rode in silence on the road south to Bredsfor Manor, he caught up to Borenson, watched his knight's face, and wondered if the man would break.

Time and time again, Borenson's head would nod, his lips quivering as if he were about to say something unspeakable. Yet each time he raised his head, his eyes would be a little clearer, a little brighter, his gaze a little steadier.

Gaborn suspected Borenson would forget his deeds, given a week or a month. He might claim that some other knight had slaughtered Sylvarresta, or that the good king had died in battle or fallen from a horse.

Gaborn hoped Borenson would forget. They rode in silence. Gaborn's Days coughed from time to time, as if he were developing a cold.

After twenty long minutes of this, Borenson turned, and on the surface his manners seemed almost carefree, the pain had retreated so deeply. But it was there, lying far within. "Milord, I was up above the Duke's lodge a bit ago, and I saw the tracks of a reaver. A big female. May I have your leave to hunt her tonight?"

It was an obvious jest. "Not without me," Gaborn said, musing. "Last autumn, I came to the Dunnwood to hunt boars. This year we shall hunt reavers. Perhaps Groverman will ride with us. What think you?"

"Hah, not bloody likely," Borenson spat. "Not after what I've done!"

Immediately, Borenson's eyes looked troubled again, and Gaborn sought to turn his thoughts. "Tell you what, if we kill a reaver, you get to eat the ears," Gaborn jested. To eat the ears of the first boar of the hunt was a great honor. But reavers had no ears, and no part of a reaver was edible. "Or at least I'll cut off a patch of hide shaped like an ear."

"Oh, you are too generous, milord," Borenson chortled like some peasant woman in the marketplace, heaping unearned praise on a noble. "Oh, you're so gracious. All you lords are so . . . er, well, lordly, if you catch my meaning."

"Well, uh, thank you, dear lady," Gaborn said, affecting a stodgy accent much like that of the Marquis of Ferecia, a noted poser. He raised his nose in the air, just as the Marquis would, then used the full powers of his Voice to imitate the Marquis' accent. "A blessing on you and your hovel and all your snot-nosed prodigy, dear lady. And please don't come any nearer, or I think I might sneeze."

Borenson laughed deeply at the jest, for the Marquis often sneezed when dirty peasants got too near his person. His threats of illness kept peasants away, so that the Marquis would not have to tolerate the scent of their poverty.

It was a grim sort of humor, but it was the best Gaborn could manage at the moment, and it eased Borenson's spirits somewhat. Gaborn almost hoped that someday things between them would be as they had been before.

A week ago, Gaborn had ridden into Heredon with hardly a care. Now he felt the weight of the whole world landing squarely on his shoulders. Deep in his heart, he knew nothing could ever be the same.

They crossed the downs for several minutes, riding

over the rolling hills.

The clouds began to break, and the afternoon sun began melting the snow. A mile from Longmot, farm-houses still stood along the road, stone cottages whose thatch roofs had not been torched. All the animals were gone from their pens and the fruit had been harvested, giving the place an eerie sense of emptiness, but the shel-ters still stood.

Then they crossed a hill and saw Bredsfor Manor nes-tled in a cozy vale, a long building of gray stone with two wings fanning out. Behind it lay barns and dovecotes, car-riage houses, servants' quarters, and walled gardens. A circular drive curved among the flower beds and topiaries before the manor. A deep brook cut through the vale, and a white bridge spanned the brook farther down the road.

On the steps of the manor sat a woman in cloud-colored silk, her dark hair cascading over her left shoulder.

Myrrima gazed up at them, stood nervously. Her beauty had not diminished in the past few days. Gaborn had almost forgotten how lovely she looked, how inviting.

Borenson spurred his horse and charged downhill, shouting, "How – what are you doing here?"

In a moment Borenson leapt from his horse, and Myrrima melted into his arms.

Gaborn halted a hundred yards off.

Myrrima laughed and hugged Borenson, weeping. "You didn't make it to Longmot in time. King Orden told me to wait here for you. Oh, I was so afraid. The skies went black, and frightful screams shook the ground. Raj Ahten's army passed here – right down this road, so I hid, but they were in such a hurry – they never slowed. . . ."

Gaborn turned his horse around, rode back over the hill, followed by his Days, so that the two could have a few moments of privacy. There he rested beneath an elm tree, where the ground was free of the slushy melting snow. Part of him felt relieved. He'd believed, somehow, that

Myrrima was important to his future, that she would play a major role in the wars to come, and he felt grateful to find that his father had chosen to save her, to send her out of harm's way.

Yet at the same time, he could not help but feel somewhat jealous of whatever happiness she and Borenson might have.

Iome had been so horribly scarred by her encounter with Raj Ahten, so shattered. The manner of her father's death was sure to divide them. Gaborn did not know if she would ever want to speak to him again.

Perhaps it would be better to forget her, he mused. Yet her happiness mattered to him. Gaborn still felt numb; his breathing came ragged, and he trembled.

Both of them bore wounds form this war, and these deep cuts were just the beginning.

But we cannot give in to pain, Gaborn thought. It is a Runelord's duty to place himself between his vassals and danger, to take the enemy's blows, so that fragile people do not have to suffer.

Though Gaborn felt hurt beyond telling, he did not weep, and he did not let himself mourn his loss. Just as, he vowed, he'd never let himself flinch in the face of danger.

Yet he feared that this day, these deeds, would haunt his dreams.

Gaborn's Days stood behind him, under the elm. Gaborn said, "I missed you, Days. I'd not have thought it, but I missed your presence."

"As I missed you, Your Lordship. I see you have had a little adventure."

It was the Days' way of asking Gaborn to fill in the blanks in his knowledge. It occurred to Gaborn that the Days did not really know how many things had happened to him, how he'd given himself to the earth, or how he'd read the Emir of Tuulistan's book, or how he'd fallen in love.

"Days, tell me," Gaborn said, "in ancient times, the men and women of your order were called the 'Guardians of Dream.' Is that not right?"

"Long ago, in the South, yes," the Days answered.

"Why is that so?"

"Let me ask you another question, Your Lordship. When you dream, do you sometimes find yourself wandering through familiar lands, to places unconnected?"

"Yes," Gaborn said. "There is a path behind my father's palace in Mystarria, and in my dreams, when I ride my horse behind it, I sometimes find myself in the fields behind the Room of the Heart, which is at least forty miles from the palace, or I ride through those fields and find myself by a pond in the Dunnwood. Is this significant?"

"It is only the sign of an organized mind, trying to make sense out of the world," his Days answered.

"Then how does this answer my question?" Gaborn asked.

"In your dreams, there are paths you fear to tread," the Days answered. "Your mind shies from the memory, but they too are part of the landscape of dreams. Do you remember them, also?"

Gaborn did. As the Days spoke, he remembered a time many years ago, when he'd been traveling with his father in the mountains, and his father had wanted him to ride up a trail through a steep, narrow ravine of black stone, where cobwebs hung between the rock. "I remember."

His Days looked at Gaborn with slitted eyes, nodded slightly. "Good, then you are a man of courage, for only men of courage remember that place. Someday soon, you will find yourself riding through your dreams. When you do, take that trail, and see where it leads you. Perhaps then you will have the answer to your question."

Gaborn gazed at the Days, wondering. It was a trick, he knew, to tell someone what to do in their dreams. The mind would do as instructed, fulfill the command.

"You want to know what happened to me over the past three days," Gaborn said. "Would it be selfish, if I kept that knowledge to myself?"

"A man who fancies himself to be the servant of all, should never give in to a selfish desire," the Days answered.

Gaborn smiled. "After I left you," he said, and he told the tale in full, though he never mentioned the Emir's book.

For a long hour Gaborn related his tale, and as he did so, he considered his new responsibilities. By now, his father's Dedicates had regained their endowments, and so the people of Mystarria would know that their king was dead. People would be frantic for news. Already, little boys riding their graaks would be on their way to Castle Sylvarresta. Gaborn would need to go there, send letters home. Plan his war.

Myrrima herself walked over the hill to disturb his worrying, her hips moving like boiling waves beneath her gray silk.

She did something no woman had ever done to him.

She came to him, put a hand over his in sympathy, and just stroked it, staring deep into his face. Few women had ever dared touch him so familiarly.

"Milord," she whispered, "I . . . Your father was a good man. As deeply as he loved, so shall he be missed. I will always . . . revere his memory."

"Thank you," Gaborn said. "He deserved that."

Myrrima pulled at Gaborn's hand, and said, "Come down to the manor, into the garden. It is a beautiful garden. It will ease your spirits while Borenson and I fix dinner. Grapes hang on the vines, and vegetables are in the field. I found hams in the smokehouse."

Gaborn had not eaten since last night. He nodded wearily, took her hand, led his horse down to the manor. Behind them, his Days rode in silence.

The garden behind the manor was everything Myrrima

had promised. The snow had nearly all melted, leaving the garden wet, fresh. Rock walls covered with rose and wisteria enclosed the garden; herbs and pleasant flowers grew all about.

A wide brook meandered through the lawn. In its deep, rocky pools, fat trout sunned themselves and snapped at bees that buzzed through the flowers beside the water.

Gaborn walked among the herbs for a long hour, examining plants. It was not as marvelous as Binnesman's garden had been, nowhere near as sprawling and wild and diverse. Gaborn had a little knowledge of herb lore, as much as most princes learned. So as Gaborn wandered about, he could not help but find things he'd need: dogbane growing on a trellis on the south wall of the manor, a bit of shepherd's purse for stanching wounds, nightcap poppy to help him sleep. There were so many herbs, and Gaborn did not know what to do with them.

He was so involved in harvesting the root of mallow to treat burns, that at first he did not notice when Binnesman arrived just before dinner.

"Hello," Binnesman said at Gaborn's back, startling him. "So, you gather herbs now?"

Gaborn nodded, afraid that to a master herbalist such as Binnesman, his efforts would seem feeble. Gaborn knelt near the aromatic, serrated leaves by the ground, and suddenly felt unsure, wondered if these rose-pink petals really were mallow, or if he'd been mistaken.

Binnesman only nodded kindly, and smiled, then knelt beside Gaborn and helped him dig. "The root of mallow is best for burns when it is still fresh," he said, "though vendors hawk it dried. It is the cooling sap that you need, not some desiccated twig. But a dried mallow root, once soaked in water, can still give some relief."

Gaborn stopped digging, but Binnesman urged him to keep on. "Look to the tops of the roots, the thickest parts. It's good that you do this, learn which parts to use."

He pulled at the mallow, then broke off its purplish-brown root for Gaborn to see. The sap oozed on to Binnesman's fingers, and the old wizard touched the cool stuff to Gaborn's forehead. "See?"

"Yes, I see," Gaborn answered.

There was an uncomfortable silence between them, and the wizard stared into Gaborn's eyes. Gaborn could see flecks of green in the old man's skin, but his robes had gone a ruddy flame, the color of maple leaves in autumn.

"You think I have some great powers," Binnesman said, "but it is only the power that comes from serving the earth."

"No, your herbs are far more potent than any I've seen in Mystarria," Gaborn said.

"Would you like to know the secret of it?" the wizard asked.

Gaborn nodded dumbly, hardly daring believe the wizard would tell him.

"Plant the seeds yourself, My King," Binnesman said, "in soil fertilized and turned by your own hands. Water them with your own sweat. Serve them – fulfill their every need – and they'll serve you fully in return. Few men, even among the wise, understand the great power one can gain from service."

"There is nothing more?" Gaborn asked.

"My plants grew to serve the people of this land. You saw how I dunged them with human waste. I used dung from many people, over many generations. So the plants serve these people.

"We are all . . . intertwined. Man, plant, earth, sky, fire, water. We are not many things, but one thing. And when we recognize that we are all but one thing, then we begin to tap into that One Greater Power – the communion."

Binnesman fell silent and watched Gaborn intently. "Do you understand?"

As he considered, Gaborn thought he began to apprehend what Binnesman tried to say, but he did not know if he could comprehend it yet.

"There are gardens in Mystarria," Gaborn said, for lack of any other response. "I'll speak to my gardeners, learn what seeds I have to plant. I should be able to get many kinds of seeds, at the House of Understanding."

"May I see your gardens?" Binnesman asked. "Perhaps I could advise you on matters of their cultivation."

"I'd like that," Gaborn said. "But you've spent your life here. Won't you stay in the Dunnwood?"

"To what purpose?" Binnesman asked. "The Seventh Stone has fallen. The last of the obalin is dead. I've nothing more to learn from it, and can no longer serve it. My garden is destroyed."

"Your wylde. What of it?"

"I searched for it all this afternoon, listened to the trees and grass. If it walks the earth, it does so far from here. I will search for it in Fleeds and farther south, until I find it. Perhaps in Mystarria."

"But the woods?"

"Are beautiful indeed," Binnesman said. "I will miss them. Now you are my king. I will follow you."

It had such an odd sound, this exclamation of devotion. To Gaborn's knowledge, no Earth Wardens had ever claimed fealty to a king. Wizards were solitary beings, living outside the bounds of common men.

"It will be terrible, won't it?" Gaborn asked. "The war. I feel it coming. I feel . . . a shifting under the earth. Energies stirring."

Binnesman merely nodded. Gaborn looked down, noticed that the old wizard stood barefoot, though a few dollops of snow still hid among the leaves in the garden.

Gaborn said now the thing that had been haunting him all afternoon. "I claimed him with my whole heart. I claimed my father. I tried to protect him, and I tried to serve him – just as I claimed Sylvarresta and Chemoise's father and Rowan. Yet I failed them. They're all dead – seeds of mankind that I chose to save. Tell me, Binnesman, what more must I do?"

The wizard studied Gaborn frankly. "Don't you understand, milord? It is not enough simply to want them. You must serve them with your whole mind, your whole will."

Gaborn wondered deep in his heart what he needed to do, and in answer he felt a terrifying sense of distress, a sense that the whole world was rocking, shifting under his feet, and he had nothing to cling to. Certainly he'd loved his father and Sylvarresta, had struggled to keep both kings alive.

"It is my fault that Raj Ahten still lives," Gaborn mused. "I spun too thin a web to catch such a large fly." Gaborn smiled at the image.

Yet there was something more he needed to do, something he could not quite grasp or voice. Gaborn was so new in his powers. He didn't know his own measure, his own responsibilities.

Binnesman said something then, words that would haunt Gaborn forever. And as Binnesman spoke the secret, Gaborn felt his mind begin to unhinge: "Milord, have you not understood? Choosing a man for the earth is not enough. The powers of Earth are weakening, while Fire grows strong. *Each person you seek to save, Fire will only seek more fully to destroy. And it will seek to destroy you above all.*"

Gaborn gasped and his heart froze at the recognition, for surely he'd felt this all along – this secret nagging suspicion. The new powers he'd felt stirring within him bore a tremendous price. By choosing to love someone, by seeking to save a person, he marked the person, made him a target.

"How then? How can I do anything?" Gaborn asked. "What does it benefit a man to be chosen?"

"In time, we will learn to use your powers," Binnesman said. "You think that benefit is slight, and perhaps that is so. But is the benefit slight to a man, if it means the difference between life and death?"

As Gaborn considered, he recognized that he'd done

some things right. He'd saved Iome when Raj Ahten hunted them. He'd managed to save Borenson at Longmot. He'd drawn Myrrima here for reasons he did not yet understand, and he suddenly felt sure to the marrow of his bones that if he'd not sent Borenson back to warn Myrrima of the invaders in the woods, the whole family would have been slaughtered.

Without the aid of Gaborn's fledgling powers, many more would be dead now.

Yes, I've done something. But I must do far, far more.

"What will you now, milord?" Binnesman asked, almost as if divining his thoughts.

"What would you advise?" Gaborn said.

"You are the king; I am merely a servant, and no counselor," Binnesman said. "The earth will serve you in ways it would never serve me. I have no idea what you should do."

Gaborn considered. "There are forcibles hidden here in the garden," Gaborn said with a sigh. "I'll dig them up. Raj Ahten believes I already have them, that I've already used them. By the time he returns, I shall have done it. He may become the Sum of All Men, but I shall be the sum of all his nightmares.

"You know much about ancient lore," Gaborn said. "Can he do it? Can he become the Sum of All Men?"

"Not of *all* men," Binnesman said. "He craves power, the guarantee of a continued existence. I do not know much of the Runelords' arts, but I know this: If he seeks to become the Sum of All Men, perhaps he should go to the source, learn how it is done."

"What do you mean?" Gaborn asked.

"We Earth Wardens live a long time. Lives given in service are usually long, and lives given in service to the land can be longest of all. Yet when I was young, four hundred years ago, I once met a man of the South. I met him at an old inn near Danvers Landing. He seemed only a young Runelord, some traveling noble. But a hundred

and eighty years ago, he came north and visited Castle
Sylvarresta for the summer. At least I believe it was him.
There had been trouble that year to the north with
reavers and with robbers. He put an end to them both.
Then he went south again."

"Daylan Hammer? You are telling me that Daylan
Hammer still lives? The Sum of All Men? After sixteen
hundred years?"

"I am telling you that he may live," Binnesman said. He
shook his head thoughtfully. "I could be mistaken. I've
never told this tale to anyone. Perhaps it is unwise to tell
you now?"

"Why?"

"He did not seem to be a happy man. If he has secrets,
they should remain with him."

"Is happiness everything?" Gaborn asked.

"Yes, ultimately I believe it is," Binnesman said. "It
should be the goal of your existence, to live life in peace
and joy."

Gaborn considered. "Am I wrong to fight Raj Ahten
using his own tactics? To fight him at all."

"To fight him is dangerous," Binnesman said. "Not just
dangerous for you, dangerous for the whole world. If he
would join your cause, I would rejoice. But he will oppose
you, and it is not for me to say whether you should fight
him. It shall be your task to gather the seeds of humanity.
You must decide which to save, which to toss aside.

"You have already begun your task." He waved to the
manor house, where Borenson and Myrrima cooked in
the dining hall.

Gaborn shuddered at the thought of his task, that he
was supposed to somehow gauge the worth of men, save
some, discard others. This would have to become the
work of his whole soul, his every waking thought. Yet even
then, he had no guarantee that he could succeed. "What
of Iome?"

"A good woman, I think," Binnesman said. "She is very

much in touch with the powers, can feel their most subtle influence, better than you – or I. She would be an asset."

"I love her," Gaborn said.

"Then what are you doing here?" Binnesman asked.

"Giving her time alone, to grieve. I fear that if she accepts me, her people might revolt. They will not want me."

"I would not worry about her people, only about her. Do you think she wants you to leave her alone? Do you think she doesn't love you?"

"She loves me," Gaborn said.

"Then go to her, soon. If she grieves, then grieve with her. Sharing our pain makes our wounds heal faster."

"I . . . it wouldn't be a good idea. Not now. Not so soon – after."

"I spoke with her not an hour ago," Binnesman said. "She asked for you. She wants to see you on some urgent matter, tonight – soon."

Gaborn studied the wizard's face, wondering. It seemed madness to go to her now, considering how her people felt about him. Yet if Iome had asked for him, perhaps she had good reason. Perhaps, he thought, they had treaties to discuss. She would need money to repair her castle. House Sylvarresta might need loans, armies. . . .

He would give whatever she asked, of course.

"All right," Gaborn said. "I'll see her."

"At sunset," Binnesman said. "Don't let her be alone after sunset."

Binnesman's words encouraged Gaborn. What good was it to have a wizard as your counselor, he reasoned, if you did not listen to his wisdom?

SIXTY-ONE: PEACE

Gaborn did not leave the manor before sunset. He took time to warm some water in the kitchens, to bathe and rub his hair with lavender; to scrub his armor with the soft leaves of lamb's ear, so that he'd present himself well.

By evening the clouds blew out of the region altogether, and warmer air now suffused the night, almost as if it were any other afternoon in late summer. The scents of grass and oak grew strong in the air.

Borenson and Myrrima stayed behind at the manor.

Only the wizard Binnesman and Gaborn's Days rode with him to Longmot. There, thousands of people worked in the twilight, salvaging supplies from the castle, cleaning the dead. More warriors arrived from farther north – eight thousand knights and men-at-arms from Castle Derry, headed by Duke Mardon, arriving unexpectedly at the summons of Groverman.

Gaborn reached camp, and was escorted to Iome by a guard who seemed friendly enough.

Custom in Heredon dictated that the dead be interred before sunset on the day of their death, but so many lords and knights were swelling in from the hills around Longmot, setting up tents, that King Sylvarresta could not be buried. King Orden, too, had not been interred, and whether this was done as an honor, so that the kings might be buried together, or because the people did not want to bury a foreign king on their soil, Gaborn did not know.

But too many people wanted to view the bodies, to pay their last respects.

Gaborn found Iome still mourning her father. The bodies had been cleaned and laid out on fine blankets over beds of paving stones. The Earl of Dreis lay near their feet, in a place of honor.

Upon seeing the dead, the wounds on Gaborn's heart felt all fresh and new. He went to Iome, sat beside her, and took her hand. She clenched his fingers tightly, as if her very life depended on his touch.

She sat with her head lowered, eyes forward. Gaborn did not know if she was only deep within herself, fighting her pain, or if she kept her face down simply to hide it, for now she was no more lovely than any other maid.

For a long half-hour they sat while the soldiers of Sylvarresta came to pay their last respects, talking to one another in hushed whispers. Many a proud soldier shot Gaborn a disapproving scowl on seeing how he touched Iome so familiarly, but Gaborn defied them.

He feared Raj Ahten had won a small victory here, had succeeded in driving a wedge between two nations that had long been friends.

Vainly, he wondered how he could ever heal that wound.

All along the downs, for a mile around, campfires began to spring up for the night. A soldier came with two large torches, and planned to set one at the heads, the other at the feet of the two kings, but Binnesman warned the man away.

"They died fighting flameweavers," he said. "It would be inappropriate to put flames so close to them now. There is starlight enough tonight to see by."

Indeed, the sky was alive with stars, just as campfires lit the valley.

Gaborn had thought it an odd sentiment on Binnesman's part. Perhaps he feared the flames as much as he loved the earth. Even now, on the cool of the evening, he walked barefoot, keeping himself in contact with the source of his power.

Yet almost as soon as the torches were withdrawn, Iome tensed, as if every muscle in her body spasmed.

She leapt to her feet and raised her hands high over her eyes, gazing up to the surrounding hills, and shouted, "They come! They come! Beware!"

Gaborn wondered if Iome had lost too much sleep over the past few days, wondered if she dreamed now with her eyes open. For she was gazing all about, at the line of trees on the western hills, her eyes shining with a fierce wonder.

Gaborn could see nothing. Yet Iome began shouting and grabbing at Gaborn as if something horrible and wonderful were happening.

Then the wizard Binnesman leapt away from the bodies of the dead kings, shouting, "Hold! Hold! Everyone get back! No one move, on your peril!"

All over the camp, for hundreds of yards, people looked up toward the campfire at their mad princess, at the shouting of the wizard, worry etched into their brows.

Binnesman took Iome by one shoulder, holding her close, and whispered in satisfaction, "Indeed, they do come."

Then, distantly, distantly, Gaborn heard something: the sound of a wind moving through the trees, sweeping toward them from the forest northwest of the castle. It was an odd sound, an eerie sound that rose and fell, like the baying of wolves, or like the song of the night wind playing through the chimneys of his father's winter palace. But there was a fierceness, an immediacy to the windsong he had heard only once before.

Gaborn gazed to the west, and it seemed that a chill breeze touched him. But it was an invisible wind, one that moved without swaying branches or bending grass in its wake.

Not a wind, Gaborn decided, but the sounds of many dainty feet, rustling the leaves and grass. And from the woods, mingled with that odd windsong, came the faint sounds of hunting horns, and the yapping of dogs, and the shouts of men.

On the far hills, pale gray lights began playing under the trees as mounted riders appeared by the thousands. The gray lights shone dimly. The colors of the riders' livery was muted – as if Gaborn watched them through a smoked glass.

Yet he could make out the detail of their livery and devices: ancient lords of Heredon rode those horses, with their ladies and their dogs and their retainers and squires, all dressed for a great hunt, carrying pig spears. And more than lords rode with them, for Gaborn could see commoners and children in that retinue, madmen and fools, scholars and dotards and dreamers, maids and ladies, farmers by the drab score, pages and smiths and weavers and horsemen and wizards – a whole rollicking nation.

The strange howling in the woods was that of ghostly laughter, for all were laughing gaily, as if in celebration.

The spirits of the Dunnwood rode their mounts to a halt, just under the trees on the western hills, and stood, staring expectantly toward Gaborn and Iome.

Gaborn recognized some of the men there – Captain Derrow and Captain Ault, Rowan and other men and women from Castle Sylvarresta, most of whom remained nameless to him.

At their head rode a great king Gaborn recognized only from his device, for on his golden shield he bore the ancient emblem of the green knight.

It was Erden Geboren.

Tens and tens of thousands of other lords and ladies and peasants rode with him or followed after, a great horde that covered the hills and downs.

The ghost king raised a great hunting horn to his lips with both hands, and blew.

Its deep call echoed over the hills, silencing everyone who still spoke throughout all the mortal camp. He blew it plaintively twice more, in short riffs.

It was the call that King Sylvarresta had blown last year at the beginning of his hunt, an invitation for all riders to mount their horses.

At Gaborn's side, a cold wind stirred, a chill that smote him to the bone, so powerful and frightening was it. Fear gripped him, made him terrified to blink or twitch. To do so would surely kill him, Gaborn felt. So he stood, frozen, until he recalled his father's words. "No prince of Mystarria needs fear the spirits of the Dunnwood."

He looked from the corner of his eye to see the ghost of King Sylvarresta rise from the corpse there on its pallet. Sylvarresta bent at the waist, sitting up, and gazed longingly across the field, to the men of the great hunt.

Then he reached over and shook King Orden's shoulders, rousing him as if from a deep slumber, so that he, too awoke.

The kings rose together and seemed to call across the valley. Though their lips moved, they spoke no words that Gaborn could hear, yet a strange moaning issued over the downs.

Across the far valley came a quick response. Two ladies rode out of that distant crowd, emerging fifty yards from the edge of the wood, each of them leading a saddled horse.

Gaborn recognized them. One woman was the Queen Venetta Sylvarresta, and the other was Gaborn's own mother.

They smiled radiantly, and seemed to be talking as if neither had a care in the world. Grand. Happy.

King Sylvarresta and King Orden took each other's hands and walked casually down the field as they used to when they were but young men. Sylvarresta seemed to be telling a long joke, and Orden laughed at him heartily, shaking his head. Their voices carried on the wind as an odd twitter, the words escaping Gaborn.

They moved with deceptive swiftness, these ghosts, like deer leaping through the grass. In but a handful of steps, King Orden and King Sylvarresta both met their wives, and kissed them in greeting, then mounted their own steeds.

All across the fields, other knights rose to join the hunt. Men from the fallen castle. Chemoise's father appeared at the base of the oak, hurried across the fields to the great throng.

As the knights and kings joined the great hunt, the wraiths behind them all turned away, began riding back into the Dunnwood, the hounds baying distantly, faint sounds of laughter and cries of the hunt issuing from the lips of various lords, and Erden Geboren's horn sounding above all.

From his horse's back, Gaborn's father stared across the valley, as if glimpsing the living knights camped in their fields for the first time. For half a heartbeat, his mouth opened in dismay, as if he recalled the things of his mortal life, or as if he'd just remembered a troubling dream. Then his eyes cleared, and he smiled broadly. The mortal world concerned him no longer.

He turned his horse, galloped into the woods. Then he was gone.

Gone forever, Gaborn realized, until I can join him.

Gaborn found himself weeping, not in pain or joy, but in wonder. Last year as his father had camped with him during his hunt in the Dunnwood, his father had said that the kings of Mystarria and Heredon did not need to fear the ghosts of the Dunnwood. Now Gaborn understood why.

We are the ghosts of the Dunnwood, he realized.

Yet as the great horde turned and began disappearing into the wood, one rider remained. Erden Geboren stared off toward Gaborn for a long minute, his eyes piercing, then spurred his horse forward.

He sees me. He sees me, Gaborn realized, and his heart pounded in terror, for everyone knew that to attract the gaze of a wight brought death.

The great king moved as if in a dream, crossing the downs in a seeming heartbeat, so that only seconds later, Erden Geboren himself sat in his saddle above Gaborn's head, staring down.

Gaborn gazed up into the face of the wight. He bore his shield, and wore armor of green leather. His helm was a simple round thing of ancient design.

He stared deep into Gaborn's eyes, in recognition.

Gaborn had imagined that Erden Geboren would be young, as in the songs of old, that he would look noble and brave. But he was an aging man, well past his prime.

Erden Geboren pointed to the ground at Gaborn's feet, and Gaborn looked down, to see where he pointed.

As Gaborn did, dry oak leaves in the grass began to rustle and stir in a slight breeze, drawing upward as if in a whirlwind, then suddenly rose high and twined their stems together, then lodged in his fresh-combed hair.

All around the downs, the men and women of Heredon gasped in wonder.

Erden Geboren had crowned Gaborn with the circlet of leaves. It was the ancient symbol of Mystarria, the sign of the Earth King. Tonight was the eve of Hostenfest.

Yet among all the vast throng of people gathered there, only one man dared call out from the fields below, "All hail the new King of the Earth!"

Gaborn looked up into the eyes of the ghost king, Erden Geboren, and suddenly understood something. He could command these spirits. He could have commanded them all along. In rage Gaborn said, "If you make me your king, then I order you and your legions to do what you can to protect these woods. Raj Ahten has taken many lives here. See that he takes no more."

Erden Geboren nodded solemnly, then turned his pale horse and rode over the fields, his great charger leaping the fences and hedgerows as he retreated into the Dunnwood.

In moments, the sounds of hunting horns rang suddenly loud, and then faded again into the distance as the wights departed.

Everyone stared at Gaborn, utterly silent. Many looked troubled, as if uncertain what had happened, or unwilling to believe. Others merely gaped in astonishment. It was said that the ancient kings commanded the Dunnwood, that the wood served them. Gaborn understood now that it was the ghosts of the wood that had served his forefathers – and now Gaborn had dared command them.

Gaborn almost feared to breathe, for he knew that whatever he said this day, it would be remembered by all.

Iome looked up at Gaborn, tears glistening in her eyes. He was already holding her hand, but now she squeezed his fingers tightly, her right hand to his left. And she raised her hand high.

Among poor people in both their kingdoms, a marriage was made in a manner similar to this: the man and woman who wanted to wed would stand before witnesses, holding hands together, while a friend bound them at the wrist with a white ribbon. Then the newlyweds would raise their hands as one, for all to see.

So everyone understood the significance of her gesture. I am a poor woman, who wants to make a marriage.

Gaborn raised her hand in his higher, and shouted to all those in the camp, "You yourselves saw Sylvarresta and Orden ride together now as they did in life, united as true friends. Seeing as death cannot divide them, let our people not be divided!"

Everyone in the camp stood quiet, none yet daring to move.

Duke Mardon stood two hundred yards downfield from them. A campfire glowed at his feet, showing his face. His golden goblet had recently been filled. He was a huge man, more of a leader than any other in Heredon.

A lord that men loved and looked to.

Now, it seemed that hundreds of eyes turned to the Duke, seeking sign of his approval.

Mardon was no fool. Perhaps he recognized that Heredon needed this union. Perhaps he had time to consider the wealth and power Mystarria commanded. Perhaps he recognized the necessity of allying himself with the Earth King.

Yet if such mercenary thoughts crossed the Duke's mind, they did not show. For almost immediately he raised his golden goblet in salute to Gaborn, and a broad smile creased his face. He called, "And, milady, what say you?"

Iome clenched Gaborn's hand tightly, raised it higher. She turned to Gaborn now, and looked up at him, the starlight shining in her eyes. "For Sylvarresta's part, I accept . . . gladly."

Duke Mardon shouted and raised his goblet high. "It seems our King Sylvarresta celebrates Hostenfest this year with a hunt after all! Let us rejoice for him . . . and for his daughter. We double our cause for celebration!" He drained the cup quickly, and tossed it far into the night, into the camps of his troops, to be the prize of some poor soldier.

That action more than any other finally brought a cheer from the camp, and endeared Mardon to Gaborn forever after.

Book 5:
Day 23 in the Month of Harvest, Advent of the Earth King

AFTERWARD

The earth powers racked Iome on the evening she became engaged to Gaborn, making her desire him more than ever before. Perhaps it was because Gaborn and Binnesman both had come together, flanking her, so that she felt herself sandwiched between the two, buffeted by their creative energies. Or maybe her fatigue left her more open to his magic than normal.

Or perhaps it was because she could feel the earth power growing in Gaborn, quietly transforming him.

In any event, she felt grateful that her people accepted their betrothal. For when he touched her that evening and raised her hand, she felt more than a human touch. His fingers twined together with hers, like two vines espaliered together. She did not believe any longer that she could remain separated from him. She did not believe she could have separated again, not and lived, not and have been truly alive. If anyone had tried to tear her from him, Iome believed wholeheartedly that she'd simply have withered and died.

That night, she called Sir Borenson to her to bestow her judgment.

To his credit, Borenson came the three miles without complaint, knelt at her feet on hands and knees, ready once again to offer his neck, should she desire it. All around them had gathered thousands of knights and warriors. Feelings among them were mixed, Iome could tell

from their faces. Some would have rent the man alive.
Others frowned thoughtfully, fearing that someday,
under similar circumstances, they might find themselves
in his position.

She could have outlawed him, stripped him of rank and
protection. She could have executed him on the spot.

"Sir Borenson," Iome said, "you have grievously
injured House Sylvarresta. Do you have anything to say in
your own behalf?"

Borenson just shook his head, the great red beard
swaying above the dirt. No.

"Then I will speak in your behalf," Iome said. "You may
have injured House Sylvarresta, but you also have loved
it, and you have served the people of Heredon."

Iome sighed, "Yet justice demands a penalty. In ancient
times, I am told, an act such as yours could be forgiven,
should the offending knight complete an "Act Penitent.""

Iome found it hard to breathe, found it hard to speak
these next words, though the idea had been given her by
Binnesman, and it had seemed adequate at the time. Now
she wondered if it was too much. An act of penitence
should be something a man could hope to accomplish, a
great deed that would try his soul and let him grow. Not a
deed that would destroy a man.

She feared her sentence would break Borenson. "I sentence you to go south, beyond the lands of Inkarra. I bid
you find Daylan Hammer, the Sum of All Men, so that we
can learn how best to defeat Raj Ahten." An astonished
gasp issued from the crowd of bystanders, followed
quickly by whispers.

Borenson gave a little cough in surprise, looked up to
Iome, then to Gaborn, who stood at her side.

"How? When? I mean – I am under oath to House
Orden."

"Then I release you from all oaths, Sir Borenson,"
Gaborn said, "until your Act Penitent is complete. You
shall become a Knight Equitable, answerable only to

yourself, if you wish."

"If I wish?" He seemed to consider. He would have to travel through enemy countries, facing countless dangers, in some vain hope of finding a legend. It was a deed that might take a man a lifetime. Or more. Time, for a man with endowments of metabolism, could pass so swiftly.

Borenson glanced over his shoulder at Myrrima. If he accepted Iome's punishment, he'd have to leave her behind. He might never see her again. Myrrima's face was pale, etched with fear. As a signal to him, she nodded, barely.

"I accept your judgment," Borenson answered uncertainly. He got off his knees.

He no longer wore the livery of House Orden, and therefore had no need to strip himself of it. But he took his shield, cut the bindings behind the wood, so that the leather covering came away, with its painted image of the green knight. Beneath the leather covering, the shield was only blank steel riveted to a frame of wood.

"When will you leave?" Gaborn asked, clapping Borenson on the back.

Borenson shrugged, glanced at Myrrima. "Two weeks, four at the most. Before the mountains fill with snow."

After he has had time to wed, Iome realized.

She saw the calculating gaze that Gaborn gave, knew he wanted to go with Borenson.

But Gaborn's duties would hold him here in the North.

The next morning at dawn, Gaborn prepared a wagon to carry the bodies of the kings back to Castle Sylvarresta. There, Sylvarresta would be buried, while Gaborn's father would be embalmed and shipped back home to Mystarria.

With the bodies, Gaborn secreted ten large boxes of forcibles, covered in soil from the gardens of Bredsfor Manor.

Gaborn oversaw the whole affair. The camp had

become busy since dawn, with thousands of warriors striking their tents in preparation to leave, others still coming in from around Heredon.

When Gaborn had finished loading the bodies and checked the wagon's wheel and undercarriage to see if they could hold the heavy load, he got up to find that a small crowd had gathered. Locals who had lived here at Longmot.

"We come to ask you," a sturdy farmer said, "if you'll be willing to take our endowments."

"Why do you come to me?" Gaborn asked.

"You'll be our king," a young man in the crowd spoke up.

"You've got gold," the farmer said. "You can pay. We don't ask much, only that you care for our families, keep them through the winter. I'm a strong man. Been working all my life. I could sell you my brawn. And my son over there – never has been sick a day. You could use him."

Gaborn shook his head sadly. "There will be gold enough for you without selling your endowments." Gaborn spoke loudly, so that all the crowd could hear. "I'll need men to rebuild this fortress. I'll pay you well for your labor. Bring your families for the winter, and stay in the buildings that still stand. Every man of you will have beef for your children, and bread in your bellies." He thought to promise them more – acorns and mushrooms, deer and boar, all the fruits of the forest and of the fields. "You can work some days for me, others for yourselves, so you may build your own homes. I won't buy endowments from a man in need."

"And what about the rest of us who want you to fight for us?" an older man asked. "I've got no family. I'm too old to swing a warhammer. But you can have my wits. They're sharp as ever. I'll fight with you as I can."

Gaborn looked out over the crowd. This was the only kind of man he'd be willing to take endowments from, a man who knew that this was an act of war, that giving themselves was a commitment to be made in deadly earnest. Yet Gaborn did not want any endowments, thought to wait before taking them until spring or some far future day. But he knew that Raj Ahten was not far away, and might still send assassins. These people needed a lord, and Gaborn needed their aid.

"How many of the rest of you feel as this man does?" Gaborn asked.

As one, some fifty men and women shouted, "I!"

That day, Gaborn and Iome rode with five hundred lords and knights back to Castle Sylvarresta on force horses.

At each village and town, they slowed their movements and let the heralds announce their presence: the Earth King, Gaborn Val Orden, and his bride-to-be, Iome Sylvarresta. By now, the word of the rise of an Earth King had been shouted along almost every road in Heredon, and was making its way through the neighboring countries of Fleeds and South Crowthen, besides.

And before the King and Queen rode the wizard Binnesman, with an oak branch in his hand.

At every village, the children stared in awe and grinned at Gaborn, the young king. The wooden effigies of the Earth King all adorned the doors and windows of every house, and the faces of the children were all filled with joy, for this day marked more than the defeat of Raj Ahten. This was the first day of Hostenfest, and finally, after 1629 years, a new Earth King walked the land, one who could bless his people as did the great king of old.

And though children greeted Gaborn in awe and joy, the elders more often waved with tearstained faces. For some of them understood what a dire portent it was that an Earth King once again walked in the land. Hard times were upon them, harder than any known before.

As Gaborn passed one inn, the innkeeper went to the effigy by his door, tore off its fine crown of braided oak branches, and brought it to Gaborn to wear. After that, as a token of submission, at every home the people tore the crowns of oak leaves from the effigies by their doors, tossed them at Gaborn's feet, along with flowers.

And though the people could not understand the significance of what he did, as Gaborn passed each such humble home, time and again he would gaze into the face of some stout farmer or his wife and children, staring far away, as if looking deep into them or through them. Then he would smile secretively and raise his left hand in blessing, calling out gently, "I choose you. I choose each of you – for the earth. May the earth hide you. May the earth heal you. May the earth make you its own!"

As he spoke, he groaned within himself, for he could not bear the thought that any might be lost. Thus he began to gather the seeds of mankind, choosing for himself an entire nation.

The troop had not gone twenty miles when the soldiers began to notice that every oak tree in the forest seemed to have dropped its leaves during the night, for surely the leaves had still been on the trees when they'd passed the evening before.

When they remarked about it to the wizard, Binnesman told them, "This the oaks do in respect for their new king." And they found it was true. Every oak in all the Dunnwood had dropped its leaves in a single night.

Yet on that track, Gaborn found what seemed to him to be an even greater wonder. For as he rode, a man came out of the woods, riding a great imperial warhorse and wearing a robe of gold silk. A fat man, old and dark of skin. He tossed a jeweled dagger to the ground, and Gaborn recognized Raj Ahten's counselor from the Seven Standing Stones.

"All hail the King of Earth," the man said in a thick accent, folding his hands beneath his chin and bowing his head.

"I know your face," Gaborn said.

"My life is forfeit, if you wish to take it," the counselor said. "Or, if you wish, I will serve you. My name is Jureem."

Gaborn stared into the man's face a moment. "For long, the servants of Fire have bedazzled you. How can I trust you?"

"I was a slave, the son of a slave," Jureem said. "My father believed that a good servant was the best of men, and a good servant would anticipate his lord's needs. If you have not done so already, I bid you send messengers to Indhopal, bearing the news that an Earth King has risen in Heredon, and that Raj Ahten flees before him. Tell the people also that Raj Ahten fights the earth powers in his attempt to bring down the Kingdoms of Rofehavan.

"In Orwynne, two hundred thousand troops have laid siege to the capital. They have orders to simply hold the capital, draw off defenders, so that no aid may come here to Heredon.

"In your own homeland of Mystarria, three of your southern castles will have fallen by now. I will tell you the names of the lords who hold those keeps. I believe Raj Ahten will not return home, but will instead flee to one of those strongholds to advance his conflict.

"I will tell you also the castles where Raj Ahten has hidden his Dedicates, and give you the names and descriptions of his most important vectors.

"Whatever my lord desires, that will I give. For I, too, will now serve the earth.

"Great is the battle you have won, milord, but I promise you, it is only the beginning."

Gaborn wondered at all of this. "So you think that if I spread dissent in his homelands, Raj Ahten will be forced to retreat?"

Jureem shook his head. "I am thinking very much that he will not retreat, but such news will distract him. I am thinking, O Great Light, that I can be of some small help to win this war, if you let me. I offer myself as your good servant."

"Your life is your own," Gaborn said. "I keep no slaves, though I accept your service."

For long the two men rode together that day, plotting war.

As for Gaborn, there was great celebration when he reached Castle Sylvarresta that night. Riders had gone ahead to announce the King and Queen, and after King Sylvarresta was laid in a tomb beside his wife, a great feast took place.

Late in the night, some ten thousand knights rode hard to the castle, soldiers out of Orwynne. Old fat King Orwynne himself rode at their head.

Orwynne broke into tears at the sight of Gaborn, and bowed at Gaborn's knee. "Thank you," he said, sobbing.

"What have I done to merit such thanks?" Gaborn asked.

"Yesterday evening, my castles were besieged by two hundred thousand of Raj Ahten's troops, and I thought all was lost. But at your command, aid came to us."

Gaborn did not want to hear the rest, how the spirits had issued from the Dunnwood, what they had done. But he had to know.

"All of Raj Ahten's men, lost?"

"Every man within sight of the woods," Orwynne said triumphantly.

At this news, many in the Great Hall cheered, but Gaborn bid them to silence. "There is no triumph in the deaths of these men," Gaborn murmured. "By their deaths we are all diminished. We will need such men, in the dark time to come."

That night, Gaborn could not sleep. He went out into Binnesman's garden. The trees and grasses were but gnarled ash. Yet beneath him he could feel life – seeds and roots already beginning to stir. Though fire had burned this place, come spring it would once again become a riot of life.

On the plains of Fleeds, far from the borders of the Dunnwood, Raj Ahten's troops raced south for a day before they met the remains of Vishtimnu's army, bivouacked near a pinnacle of rock.

The Clan Lords of Fleeds had discovered the army moving through the wilderness, had feared that it had come to attack the stronghold at Tor Billius, so they had surrounded the army, then slain some eighty thousand men.

Raj Ahten broke the enemy lines. As he appeared before the clans, he admonished them to serve him. Thirty thousand men joined his army that day, though many others continued to fight against Raj Ahten.

Chief among those who fought were the great High King Connel and his valiant warriors, who led charge after charge against the Wolf Lord, until the knights' lances were all broken and their shields shattered.

Still, Connel fought on with hatchet and dagger.

At sunset, Raj Ahten fed Connel, alive, to his frowth giants.

Then for a long time Raj Ahten stood, gazing at the remnants of his army, considering, then he looked back to the north, as if torn in indecision.

Some say that he muttered curses under his breath, and that he trembled, alternately gripped by rage and fear. Others say that he merely stood, thoughtfully. With so many more men at his back, he felt sorely tempted to return to Heredon, strike at the Earth King now, and finish it.

At last, Raj Ahten turned his back on Heredon and raced for the mountains.

Three nights after the fall of Longmot, Gaborn and Iome married in Castle Sylvarresta.

The ceremony was a large one, for thousands of lords were gathering from nearby nations. Iome wore no veil, and if Gaborn was pleased that Iome's beauty had returned, he did not show it. His devotion had not faltered when she grew ugly; it did not suddenly sprout greater wings now.

On her wedding night, Gaborn kept his promise. He proved to be no gentleman in bed, at least no more a gentleman than she wanted him to be.

That night, after making love, Iome lay in bed for a long time with her hand gently placed over her womb, wondering what manner of child she carried.

For she knew she carried a child. The earth power in Gaborn was growing so strong, it was no longer possible that he could plant a seed and not have it take root.

Borenson and Myrrima married that same day with little fanfare, choosing a poor couple's wedding.

The next night, a quarter moon rose over the eastern hills outside Castle Sylvarresta. By its faint light, Gaborn, Borenson, and fifty Knights Equitable mounted their chargers and rode pell-mell into the Dunnwood, lances at the ready, to hunt for reavers.

The men were ferocious, longing for the hunt, and all promised that this would be one to remember.

Binnesman went with them, for he said that there were soils deep beneath the Dunnwood, soils once mined by the duskins, soils that carried magics of the deep earth, which could grant magical properties to the weapons that the Earth King's smiths would forge this winter.

Of what transpired on that great hunt, little was ever said thereafter. But the Earth King and his wizard and some of his knights returned shortly after dawn, three days later, on the last and greatest day of the Hostenfest, the day of the great feast.

By great misfortune, in the duskin mines they had found more than they could easily handle – twenty-seven juvenile reavers, along with their reaver mage.

Forty-one brave knights died in that battle.

Borenson himself slew the reaver mage in her lair, and brought back with him a trophy, dragging the creature's massive head behind his steed.

He laid the head of lumpy gray leather out on the green before Castle Sylvarresta for all to see. It was almost six feet in length, four feet high, and somewhat ovoid in shape. It looked much like the head of an ant or some insect, except that it had no eyes, ears, or nose. Its only sensory apparatus were the patches of feelers that hung like gray worms from the back of its head, in mockery of hair, and down near its mouth.

The rows of crystalline teeth in its great maw made a huge impression on the peasants and children, many of whom were afraid to touch the rigid lips. The thousands of teeth inside those maw sat in seven rows, like those of a shark, but each ragged tooth was as clear and tough as quartz. Like the bones of the skull behind it.

Peasants by the tens of thousands came to view the monster's head. The children shrieked in delight to touch it, and many a maid gaped at it and tittered, while the old folks just stared long and thoughtfully.

It was the first reaver mage found within the Dunnwood in nearly seventeen hundred years, and many of those present believed it would be the last one they'd see in their lifetimes.

But they were wrong. For it was not the last.

It was only the first.